Their eyes met and held

Cara held her breath, not sure she wanted to hear what made Jonah eager to never see her again.

"You know." His voice was low, his tone thick. Electricity arced between them, their attraction almost making the air crackle. "You throw me off. It's all I can do not to…" The words seemed pulled from him and he tilted his head, shifting slightly forward. She knew he wanted to kiss her. He could hardly keep from kissing her.

She opened her mouth, but couldn't say the words that formed in her head: *I want you to.* Some part of her did, anyway. The silence grew heavy.

Finally, Jonah pulled away. "But that can't happen."

As soon as he said it, she knew he was right.

Because one kiss would never be enough.

Dear Reader,

In this story, Cara is fleeing a man who claims to love her, but will kill her if he can't have her. Her situation is one that strikes fear in every woman's heart. Cara was young when she married and didn't recognize the danger signs until it was too late. The newspapers are filled with stories of the tragic outcomes of the dark side of love.

Cara's journey is to find safety for herself and her daughter, to heal them both, and to find her own purpose. Beth Ann's voice is here—her confusion about her troubled father, her yearning for friendship and love, her courage as she learns to forgive herself and accept the comfort of her mother's love.

When Cara and Beth Ann stumble into the Comfort Café, looking for a meal and a mechanic, they find a safe place where they can recover and people who love and support them. Jonah has suffered his own losses and betrayal. He must deal with his own guilt and regret, his belief that he is too broken to help those he loves.

Working together in the café, Jonah and Cara find new strengths and rebuild old ones, serving as mirrors to each other's growth and recovery. Cara conquers her fear and guilt, and finds her place in the world. Risking his life for Cara and Beth Ann, Jonah finally accepts that he is whole and worthy of the love he freely gives.

If your heart is heavy, my hope is that you find your own safe place to heal and loved ones to help you get there. And if you can cook, there's always room for more at the New Hope Café.

All my best,

Dawn Atkins

PS—Please visit me at my website, www.dawnatkins.com.

The New Hope Café

DAWN ATKINS

HARLEQUIN®
entertain, enrich, inspire™

Recycling programs
for this product may
not exist in your area.

ISBN-13: 978-0-373-60733-4

THE NEW HOPE CAFÉ

Copyright © 2012 by Daphne Atkeson

www.Harlequin.com

Printed in U.S.A.

ABOUT THE AUTHOR

Award-winning author Dawn Atkins has written twenty-five novels for Harlequin Books. Known for her funny, poignant romance stories, she's won a Golden Quill Award and has been a several-times *RT Book Reviews* Reviewers' Choice Award finalist. Dawn lives in Arizona with her husband and son.

Books by Dawn Atkins

HARLEQUIN SUPERROMANCE

HARLEQUIN BLAZE

Other titles by this author available in ebook format.

Don't miss any of our special offers. Write to us at the following address for information on our newest releases.

Harlequin Reader Service
U.S.: 3010 Walden Ave., P.O. Box 1325, Buffalo, NY 14269
Canadian: P.O. Box 609, Fort Erie, Ont. L2A 5X3

To my sister Diana and her husband, Joey,
who day by day build their own happily ever after

CHAPTER ONE

DRIVE FASTER. *Move. Go. Fly.*

No. Slow down. If you get a ticket, he can track you.

Choosing the wiser impulse, Cara Price eased her foot off the accelerator. She glanced at her daughter, hoping she hadn't picked up on Cara's panic. Beth Ann stared ahead, clutching her stuffed rabbit close to her chest. At nine, she was too old to cling to a comfort object, but the therapist had warned Cara that abrupt changes might set Beth Ann back.

Cara had been as upbeat about the move as possible, calling it an adventure, a chance to meet new people, see new places, take new names.

They'd had to run. Her ex-husband would come for them the moment he was released from prison and he wouldn't stop until he had them.

Cara would not allow that.

She'd counted on Barrett's six-year sentence for the time she needed to get her teaching degree, buy new identities and safely start new lives.

But prison overcrowding and legal maneuvers had gotten Barrett released three years early.

Three years.

He would be out any day now.

Any. Day. Now. The thought made her catch her breath.

"What's wrong?" Beth Ann jerked her gaze to Cara.

"Nothing. I'm just thinking." She forced a smile. "You sure you want to go by *Bunny?* Won't that be confusing?" *Bunny* was her rabbit's name.

"Not to me," Beth Ann said.

"Then *Bunny* it is. I'm CJ, remember? It's my initials—Cara Juliette—so it's easy. And our new last name starts with the same letter as *Price—Peyton*."

"CJ sounds like a man's name. I hate it. I hate new names. I hate moving. I don't want a new home or new people. I want Grandma Price and Serena and my teacher and my school. You made me miss Water Day and the class play and the awards. I was going to get the reading prize." Her voice broke, but instead of crying, she stiffened, lifted her head and locked her jaw. Beth Ann refused to cry, refused to let Cara comfort her and it broke Cara's heart every time.

Beth Ann didn't trust her. Not since Barrett had put Cara in the hospital.

"I know it's hard. I had to leave my teachers in the lurch," Cara said.

It was mid-May, two weeks shy of summer break, so Beth Ann wouldn't lose any academic ground, but the end of the school year was hectic for the teachers at the middle school where Cara was an aide.

She'd left a family-emergency note and fled. Her cheeks burned with shame. She'd always been a go-to person, someone people could count on. She was the one-woman sunshine committee—planning baby showers, potlucks and birthday celebrations. She'd let them all down. Her fingers tightened on the steering wheel.

Cara had come so far these past three years, become more self-confident, more sure of what she wanted, of who she could become.

But the moment she'd heard about Barrett, she felt lost again, timid and uncertain, the way she'd been when she'd married the man at eighteen.

His words played in her head. *The world will eat you up, Cara. You'll never make it on your own. You need help.*

"What about Serena?" Beth Ann asked. "Can't I at least call her to say goodbye?"

"The lady said no calls, no email, not even a postcard." The domestic violence counselor had been firm. The smallest slip could cost them their safety. The woman had seen it happen. "There will be girls at the center who've had troubles, too. Maybe the family we'll share the apartment with will be like us."

Their counselor had made the arrangements through a network that found housing and no-questions-asked jobs for women escaping abusive men.

"You'll make new friends."

"I don't want new friends. I want Serena."

Serena had been Beth Ann's first real friend since they'd moved in with Cara's mother three years before, so Cara felt sick about putting Beth Ann through this loss.

"You're sad now, but we'll be okay, I promise." Cara would keep her daughter safe, give her a good life, and heal her sad heart, no matter what it took. "Just a few hours and we'll be in Phoenix."

Except they'd barely crossed the Arizona border when the car's engine hesitated, gave an ominous clunk, then dropped into Neutral.

Fighting panic, Cara tapped the accelerator, but the engine only roared.

"What's wrong?" Beth Ann cried.

"I'm not sure." Cara jiggled the gearshift. The thud told her the engine had dropped into Drive. Whew. She held her breath, watching the lane stripes fly by. So far, so good.

Then there was a grinding sound, a high whine

and the engine light flashed on. *Damn.* She didn't dare drive farther without getting the car checked, so she aimed for the next exit.

"Maybe it just needs oil," Cara said. She'd taken her mother's car instead of the BMW registered to Barrett to keep from being traced. To be doubly sure, she'd traded plates with a car on blocks in a farmer's field a few miles out of town.

Please let it be minor. Please, please. Her mother tended to neglect belongings. People, too, but that was another matter.

Cara couldn't afford a big repair. All she had was $500 after paying summer school tuition and her mother's rent.

Off the highway, the sign pointed to a town called New Hope. To her immediate right was a Quonset hut that might be an auto repair shop. On the same lot was a diner. *The Comfort Café.*

Cara turned to her daughter. "I'm hungry. How about you?"

Beth Ann shook her head. Since the attack she had no appetite. Not even for ice cream, her favorite treat, which she now hated.

"Let's give it a try anyway," Cara said, forcing cheer into her voice.

New Hope and *Comfort.* They could use a little of both, though Cara would settle for a bite to eat and a decent mechanic.

THE SECOND SIDE of the patty had barely sizzled when Jonah Gold scooped it off the grill and slapped it onto the bun he'd laid open on the plate. Carver Johnson was a cattleman and he liked his beef fresh off the hoof, just this side of raw. He was one of the locals who still ate at the café despite the two new fast-food places and the fancy bistro that had opened up in the past year.

Jonah's aunt Rosie, who owned the café, had seemed oddly resigned to the dwindling number of diners. He'd expected her to throw pans and bitch out the traitors, but she'd only sighed and shrugged.

Not like her at all.

She hadn't been herself lately.

The bell jangled. Damn. Jonah had hoped to close early, since the new waitress Rosie had promised him hadn't showed.

Behind him, Ernesto, his ever-steady busboy, was slamming dishes into the dishwasher, singing in off-key Spanish along with whatever came through his iPod buds. The kid was nineteen and smart as a whip, but too shy to wait tables.

Jonah peered out the kitchen pass-through to see who'd decided to push his patience past its limit.

A pretty blonde, midtwenties, with a little girl, took a back booth. She looked too harried to be one of the day-trippers headed for the galleries and antique shops of New Hope, which was something of an artist colony. So probably a highway traveler.

"Menu's on the table," he called. "Yell out your order."

When he carried out the burger, he saw the woman and her daughter had moved to sit a few stools south of Carver.

"We thought it would be easier here," the woman said with a candle flicker of a smile. "Looks like you've got no waitress."

"You scare off Darlene?" Carver asked. He loved to needle people.

"She quit all on her own."

Darlene had moved in with her boyfriend to play house. Bad idea, not that she'd asked Jonah. He wasn't much for chitchat anyway, and he was no Dr. Phil.

Meanwhile, the little girl stared right at him. He respected that about kids—how direct they were in looks, words and deeds. Adults hid too much and faked the rest. They made him tired.

"Where's my damn steak sauce?" Carver yelled.

"Hold your water." Jonah bent to check beneath the counter. Napkins, flatware, salt and pepper, menus… Where the hell was the—

"Top shelf behind you."

He stood. The woman was pointing over his

shoulder. He grabbed the bottle and slid it down the counter like a bartender in an Old West saloon.

"Might not need it, after all," Carver drawled. "You've got more respect for beef than your brother. He charred the life out of every bite."

Only when he was drunk. Eight months ago, Jonah had come to New Hope to get Evan clean and sober. He'd been straight for three months this time and swore he was set. Jonah was not so sure. He'd learned the hard way not to take what people said at face value.

"How does a fish sandwich sound?" the woman asked her daughter in that bright voice nurses used when they were about to rip out a catheter.

The girl shrugged. She clutched a grimy, one-eyed stuffed animal, which reminded him of Louis, the feral cat who pretended not to care about the nightly head rub Jonah gave him.

"She'll try that." The woman shot him a fake smile. He got the feeling she faked a lot of smiles. "I'll have the Caesar salad with chicken. Is the chicken fried or boiled?"

"At the moment, frozen."

"Boiled then and two lemonades, please." She slid the menu back in its slot. "Also, is there a good mechanic nearby? My car's making a funny noise."

So that's what had her frazzled. Sunlight through the window made her blue eyes look almost silver.

"Duvall Auto Works. On the right just as you hit the town. Rusty'll talk your ear off, but he's good and he's honest."

"Thanks." She had blond, flyaway hair, a pointed nose, sharp cheekbones and a heart-shaped mouth, reminding him of...who?

After a second it came to him. The pixie in the fantasy video game Evan had loved as a kid. *Esmeralda*. All this woman needed were whirring wings and a sparkly wand and she'd be a dead ringer for the fairy warrior.

She looked at him strangely and he realized he'd been staring a hair too long. "Got it. Right."

Jonah ducked into the kitchen, slapped the fish patty on the grill and started on her salad. At least she hadn't ordered one of those everything-but-the-kitchen-sink numbers with crap like dried loganberries and coconut curls. Jesus, what a lot of fuss over a pile of roughage.

When that attorney from Tucson asked about arugula, he'd suggested she try the bistro in town, only to find out Rosie had dragged her in to meet him. Rosie thought he was lonely.

He was still raw from Suzanne—the ink on the divorce papers barely six months dry—though he wasn't sure he would ever get over that.

Jonah was looking for a carrot to shred—might as well make an effort—when the door clanged, followed by voices.

Lots of 'em.

He leaned down and looked out at the pack of senior citizens swarming the booths. Of all the days for a tour bus. Damn.

The woman at the counter met his gaze through the pass-through. "I used to waitress," she said. "I could pitch in if you'd like."

She looked too well-off for that kind of work. Her tailored blouse looked pricey and she wore a heavy filigreed locket and carried a hand-tooled bag.

"You sure?" he asked.

"I'm happy to help."

She seemed to mean it, so he grabbed an apron off the shelf and held it out. "Order pad's by the register."

She sent her daughter out to the car for a book to read, tied on the apron and got to work, acting like she'd been here months, not minutes. Maybe his luck had changed after all.

She was clipping slips to his wheel, rattling off the orders when he finished her food and set the plates on the ledge. "You should eat." He'd put her to work hungry. What a jerk.

"When there's time." She set up her daughter with lemonade, then came into the kitchen to prep the sides. The perfume she wore hung in the air. She smelled...pink.

How the hell did pink smell?

When she breezed past him going after the bagged slaw, he got a nice blast and figured it out. *Cotton candy.*

A few minutes later, he heard her speak to the little girl. "Please try. You didn't eat breakfast."

The kid *was* rail-thin. She buried her nose in the matted fur of that stuffed animal. What the hell was it? The ragged ears were long, so a rabbit maybe.

The woman huffed in frustration. Noticing Jonah watching, she shot him another fake smile. He'd bet a real one would be a sight to see.

Once she'd walked away, he leaned out the window. "Hey," he called to the girl. When she looked up, he said, "Try the ketchup cure." He nodded at the squeeze bottle by the napkin dispenser. "Squirt on a good dose. It works."

He turned to his grill so he wouldn't make her nervous. No one liked being watched when they ate, least of all a picky eater. Evan had gone through a phase.

After a bit, the mom came back to check on her daughter. "You ate a lot." She made it sound like a miracle. "What's on your cheek?" She wiped off the red smear.

"It's ketchup. He said it's a cure." The girl pointed at Jonah.

The woman looked at him. "I didn't realize condiments had healing powers."

He shrugged. "Depends on what ails you, I guess."

"Evidently." She held his gaze, her blue eyes full of relief and gratitude and…something else.

That certain spark.

He felt it, too—like an oil pop in the center of his chest, sharp and hot and surprising. He hadn't felt that in so long he'd forgotten its power.

The woman seemed startled as well, and when she called out the new orders, her voice had a rasp to it.

When the tour group finally cleared out, he took a twenty from the register and went to where she was paying Ernesto out of her tips.

He held out the cash. "You saved my ass. Your food's on the house, too."

"It was fun," she said, taking the twenty. "It brought back good memories." She reached behind her to untie her apron, arching her back and drawing his eye to her chest. *Great rack,* Evan would say. That made Jonah think of playing pool, but that made no sense because breasts weren't triangular or—

Why the hell was he analyzing her tits?

"Huh?" he said, realizing she'd said something.

"The tie's knotted. Would you mind?" She turned her back to him.

He was picking at the string when Rosie came through the door, saw them and stopped dead.

"You came in after all?" she said to the woman. "You're Dell Morgan's niece, right? Monica?"

"No. My name's, uh, CJ." She seemed to have to think about that. Rosie's gruffness threw people.

"She's a customer," Jonah said. "She used to waitress so she helped with a busload of tourists."

"Good deal. I'm Rosie Underhill. I own this place." She gave the woman's hand a hard shake. "You met my nephew."

"Not formally." She turned to him.

He would have sent her on her way without asking her name or giving her his. Typical. He did better alone in his shop, at the grill or in his cave of a trailer. "Jonah Gold." He held out his hand.

"Nice to meet you." Her hand was small, her fingers delicate as balsa, so he gentled his grip.

"You want the job, it's yours," Rosie said. "Hours are six to three. You'll probably clear one-fifty a shift, more on the weekends when the tourists hit."

"We're just passing through," CJ said. "We had car trouble. Jonah recommended Duvall Auto Works."

"Yeah?" Rosie thought about that. "Rusty's good. Just don't let him charge you for the chit-chat. So, you on vacation?"

"Uh, no. We're moving." She clearly didn't want more questions. "And I have a job there."

"Where's there?"

"Back off, Rosie," Jonah said. "She said no."

"It'll likely take Rusty a day or two to get parts. How about you cover a few shifts while you wait?"

"I hope it's minor," CJ said, biting her full bottom lip. Top and bottom made a puffy heart shape. A better look for the hearts he'd sketched for the mahogany bench he'd been working on, now that he thought about it. Very soft. Pillowy, even.

"You know how it is with engines," Rosie said. "Once they start messing around, all hell breaks loose." She was pushing hard, which meant there weren't any other waitress candidates. He'd be stuck with Rosie and she was too damn cranky to serve customers.

The door clanged. All three turned to see Larry Claymore and his poker buddies walk in. They'd had their monthly all-nighter, which they wrapped up with burgers, fries and trash talk.

Right behind them came a dozen high school girls in skimpy athletic gear. Cheerleader camp had let out for the day.

"Damn," he and Rosie said at the same time.

"If I get Rusty to come out here to look at your car will you finish out the day?" Rosie asked CJ.

"Rosie…" Jonah started.

"Fifty bucks on top of your tips. How's that?"

That caught the woman's attention. "And you'll get the mechanic out here?" When Rosie nodded,

CJ said, "Okay. Let me tell my daughter." She walked away, retying the strings Jonah had freed.

A minute later, she had the weary poker players cheerfully putting together their tables and gathering up flatware, while she took the cheerleaders' orders, acting relaxed, but moving quickly, not wasting a second.

"She's good," Rosie noted. "What's the big secret about where she's going?"

"Not everybody wants to blurt their life story to a nosy stranger."

"Like you're a shining example, Mr. People Person. You didn't even ask her name. You know the little girl's?"

He shrugged.

"Figures. She's probably bored brainless. Bet I can come up with something to keep her busy."

"Don't start, Rosie." He could practically hear the gears grinding.

"Start what?" she asked innocently.

"Whatever you're plotting. Call Rusty like you promised, then find me another waitress."

She waved him away, intent on her mission.

Soon, CJ was calling out orders. The poker players wanted double cheeseburgers all around, the cheerleaders BLTs, chocolate shakes and piles and piles of fries.

"No go on the fries," he told CJ. "All that's left is a torn bag with freezer burn."

"I can work with that," she said and dashed off.

A minute later, the fries were sizzling and she was making shakes. She'd figured out the timing on the finicky machine without wasting a drop of syrup, unlike Darlene, who ruined every third shake.

Rosie was right. She *was* good.

Jonah expected to be annoyed with her crowding into his kitchen, but she zipped and flitted like the sprite in that game, and she smelled so damn pink.

He shook his head at himself.

CJ caught his expression and stopped short. "Did I do something wrong?" She seemed hyperaware, as if braced for trouble.

"No. You're doing great."

"Good." She blew out a breath, then squeezed past him, just brushing his backside, setting off a reaction belowdecks, like he was a kid again, late for class because the sight of a bra strap had given him a hard-on.

When she returned to the fries, she shifted to avoid bumping him, lost her balance and would have landed an elbow on the hot grill if he hadn't grabbed her arm.

When he did, her face went ashen with fear.

"You were about to get burned," he explained.

"Oh. Right." She was too shook up to even fake a smile. He'd scared her. He hated that. It reminded him of that time with Jared, when Suzanne had covered her face, cringing, as if she thought Jonah would hit her next.

Shame surged through him, as fresh as that night. Like a wounded beast, he'd struck out in pain, done what he'd sworn never to do—behaved like his father.

More proof that he'd had no business getting married. He'd known already he wasn't built for it, that when the chips were down, he would fail the people he loved. After that, he knew he could do worse. He could hurt them.

"Try this."

He turned to find CJ holding out a fry. He smelled aged cheese, hot potato and corn oil. He pulled her hand closer and bit off the top, registering the contact and the taste at once, a one-two punch of pleasure.

Their eyes met and awareness burned between them. Cooks tasted each other's food all the time. But this felt more personal somehow.

Jonah released her hand and focused on the bite. "What'd you do?"

"Double fried them and coated them with parmesan."

"Not bad." The cheese made it tart and creamy, the double frying gave a crisp outside and a moist center.

"Not bad?" She ate the bottom half, eyebrows dipped in concentration. "It's delicious."

"The girls will just smother them in ketchup."

"We'll just see about that." She loaded a platter with the fries and carried them to the cheerleaders, hips swaying in a way that held his gaze until she reached her destination.

A few minutes later CJ bounded back for more orders. "They said the fries were *epic*. Totally too good for ketchup." Triumph shone in her eyes and made her smile. This one lit up her whole face, like in the video game when the character peered into the treasure box of powers.

A sight to see for sure.

It would stay with him, he could tell, the way the feel of freshly sanded wood stuck with him long after he'd left the shop.

"Don't gloat," he said.

"Can't help it." He liked the gleam in her eyes. It was sure and steady, not scared or jumpy, like when she first walked in. "I did want to thank you for that ketchup tip with my daughter. Bunny."

She turned to where the girl had been sitting. "Where is she?" Her eyes were wide.

He started to explain about Rosie, but she bolted for the hall.

He followed her.

She burst out of the ladies' room. "She's not there."

"I'm sure she's upstairs."

"Upstairs?" She was breathing hard, her eyes big and afraid.

"With Rosie. Hang on." He pulled out his cell and hit Rosie's speed-dial number. CJ watched, holding her breath.

"You got CJ's girl up there?" Jonah asked when Rosie answered.

"I told you I'd keep her busy."

He gave CJ a quick nod to relieve her. "You've got her mom worried sick."

CJ reached for the phone. "I need to know where my daughter is at all times," she said, clearly trying to hold down her anger. "I appreciate that, of course, but—" She listened. "And the mechanic is…what?" She frowned. "That's not good." She listened more. "That's kind of you, but I'm sure there's a motel in town we could—" Her eyebrows shot up. "Really? It does? I'll think about it…. Thank you." She handed Jonah his phone, looking dazed. She'd been run through the Rosie wringer.

"Rusty's got a bachelor party in Yuma," CJ said, "so he can't look at my car until tomorrow."

"You could try the mechanic at the Shell, but he's not that good. Small towns." He shrugged.

"Rosie invited us to stay with her. I hate to impose." She gave him a questioning look.

"She's got the extra beds." Though the last time

Jonah had seen the rooms they were crammed to the rafters with overflow from her vintage shop.

"She said the Sleep Inn has bedbugs. Is that true?"

Rosie. He had to laugh. "I doubt that. She probably figures if you stay upstairs tonight, you'll work downstairs tomorrow."

"I see." He noticed she had freckles like a shake of cinnamon across her nose and her blond hair had darker streaks like ray flake in an oak plank. "I guess it makes sense to stay really...."

"Up to you." But he felt a jolt of pleasure at the prospect. Maybe Rosie's schemes weren't *all* bad.

CHAPTER TWO

CARA STARTED UP the stairs to Rosie's apartment, the pleasant smell of old wood and fried food reminding her of Dolly's, where she'd worked in high school. She'd loved it there. She'd felt useful and competent and it had been her haven from her mother's constant boyfriend drama.

As soon as Cara had picked up the order pad, she'd felt a burst of the confidence she'd felt at Dolly's. She'd needed it badly.

She heard Jonah climbing behind her. She felt uneasy with him back there thinking the kind of thoughts men were hardwired to think when a woman's backside crossed their sightline. Since Barrett, men scared her, especially big men like Jonah.

Except there had been that *moment*. He'd zoomed under her radar helping Beth Ann and when their eyes met, she'd felt a hot twist of a feeling she hardly remembered: physical desire. She'd seen it in his eyes, too.

It had scared her a little.

She reached the top and turned to him.

"You okay?" he asked, evidently reading her tension.

He had kind eyes, she saw, and her anxiety faded.

"A little dazed," she said. "This happened fast."

"Rosie can spin you around, but don't worry. You're in good hands."

His words hit home. She had the stupid urge to cry. "Thank you," she mumbled, turning for the door so he couldn't see her so weak.

Entering the apartment, Jonah called out, "Rosie, don't shoot. It's me and CJ." He led her through a living room jammed with '60s furniture and knickknacks, then to the kitchen, where Rosie and Beth Ann were playing cards at a red Formica table with chrome legs.

The kitchen was done in '50s style, with black-and-white linoleum tile, a red sink and red appliances. Chickens and roosters decorated everything from the wallpaper to the refrigerator magnets. "Rosie taught me poker," Beth Ann said.

"Ante up, you little hustler." Rosie pushed five red jelly beans into the center of the table.

"What's a hustler?" Beth Ann asked.

"A pro who pretends she's never played the game. You're skinnin' me alive here." Rosie waved at her smaller mound of candies.

Beth Ann beamed.

The jelly beans reminded Cara of her grandmother, who used to bake jelly beans inside buns, with each color meaning a different fortune. She called them her "good-luck" buns and made them when she had a decision to make or just to cheer herself up.

Beth Ann turned her hand so Cara could see that she had a full house.

"Hell's bells, I fold," Rosie said.

"You're supposed to raise," Beth Ann said.

"Not when you've got a killer hand."

"You looked? That's cheating."

"I didn't have to. You need to work on your poker face, kid. No matter what you draw, you can't show it. Totally no emotion."

"I can do that easy," Beth Ann said. The truth of that made Cara sad. Her daughter had been a brave soldier since the attack.

"We're grateful to you for your hospitality, Rosie," Cara said.

"You haven't seen the rooms yet," Jonah said.

"Don't be so smart, Mr. Interior Design Star," Rosie said. "Move a few boxes to the laundry room if you have to."

"A few boxes?" Jonah chuckled, then led Cara to the end of the hall, where she saw what he meant. The room was crammed with furniture, boxes, '60s lamps and more knickknacks.

"Rosie has a vintage shop in town. This is the stuff she can't bear to sell." He went to the casement window and yanked up the blinds, letting the late-afternoon light wash the room in gold.

Cara went to look out the window. Below, she saw a huge vegetable garden, shaded by netting. "Is that garden Rosie's?"

"Yes. Not that she's happy about it. It was her husband Eddie's idea. Same with the café."

"Is he...gone?"

"Dead, yeah. Before I was born. Blood clot after a routine surgery."

"That's so sad."

"Rosie kept the garden, the café and the antique shop in his honor. If Eddie loved it, Rosie kept it."

"That's sweet."

"Sweet? God, don't let Rosie hear you call her that."

"She reminds me of my grandmother." She'd been brusque but tenderhearted, and Cara could tell that was Rosie's way. "She died when I was fourteen." Cara had been devastated. Her grandmother had loved her unconditionally.

"I'm sorry to hear that."

"I miss her."

Jonah looked at her in a way that made her feel really *seen*. Seconds passed like that and it happened again. *Zing.* Another jolt of desire. She caught an answering flare in his eyes. What was going on here? Sex was the last thing on her mind. Part of it was that Jonah was handsome, with longish dark hair, a square jaw and dark eyes. He reminded her of a young Russell Crowe.

He was older than her, maybe mid-thirties. *Barrett's age.*

Jonah had made her think of Barrett when he'd grabbed her arm to keep her from getting burned. Barrett had squeezed her arm so hard her fingers tingled, showing he had power over her, that he could hurt her if he wanted to.

The thought of Barrett snapped her out of it. Cara whipped her gaze to the window. "You don't use the vegetables in the café?" She could make out cabbage, peas, tomatoes and peppers, some low vines—melon or squash—and maybe strawberries.

"Rosie sells the stuff to a restaurant in town— one of those places with puny entrées, kitchen-sink salads and every cheese labeled *artisanal.* It's not a café, mind you. It's a *bistro.*"

She looked at him. "Not your kind of place?"

"Not even close."

She smiled, staring out the window. "I would kill for a garden."

"So plant one. Wherever you're moving."

"It's not that simple." Nothing in her life would be simple for years to come. Her mother's house had been a stopping-off place at best. Now they'd been set adrift, taking only the belongings they could fit in their bags.

Cara longed for a permanent home, safe and private, where a garden would be as easy as Jonah made it sound. Right now it seemed impossible.

Back near the trees, she saw a round-cornered silver trailer with a redwood deck, lots of furniture and strings of white lights. "Who lives out there?"

"Whoever's cooking. Right now that's me."

"Before you, your brother? The one who charred the hamburgers?"

"Yeah. He lives in town at the moment." He frowned and there was tension in his voice.

Why had Jonah taken over? Had they fought? She sensed he wouldn't welcome the question. Just as well, she guessed, since she couldn't say much about herself either.

"I thought the Quonset hut was an auto shop."

"Used to be one. Right now it's my woodshop." He turned toward the bed. "Let's clear a path to the door." He obviously didn't welcome more questions. He picked up a box from the bed. She did the same.

Together they cleared out boxes and furniture and rearranged what was left so she had room to move. The work forced them to be physically close, the way they'd been in the café. Each time their bodies brushed, Cara felt more tingles and jolts. By the time they were finished, she was out of breath and not from exertion. So strange.

It must be a primal drive sparked by being on the run.

Beth Ann's room was equally crowded, but what caught Cara's eye was a long shelf with toothpick structures—a fort, a biplane, an elaborate marble run, a bridge and more. "Who made all these?" she asked.

"My brother, Evan. This was his room for a couple years when we were kids." He surveyed the collection with a look that seemed both sad and wistful.

"So the room I'm staying in…?"

"Was mine, yeah." He shrugged. "Let's get to it."

When they'd finished clearing the room, Cara went to the window to open the blinds.

"Does Bunny like to read?"

When she turned, Jonah was so close that strands of her hair caught in his emerging beard. She brushed the hair away just as he did. Their fingers tangled for a second and she rocked into his chest. The chrome-stemmed floor lamp he held rattled. They both took shaky breaths.

"Y-yes. She loves to read." Her face felt hot.

"Good." He angled the shade so light would hit the green fake-fur pillow, then turned to her. "Is Bunny short for something?"

"No. Just Bunny."

He held her gaze. Didn't he believe her?

As they left the room, he bent to the plug by the door and flicked on a night-light. A peace sign lit up. "So she won't get lost on the way to the toilet."

Jonah was gruff, but thoughtful. He paid attention. She liked that. It made her feel better about her decision to stay. Maybe they *were* in good hands.

They returned to the kitchen. When Jonah offered to follow Cara to the auto shop to drop off her car so Rusty could get to it as soon as he returned from Yuma, Rosie asked him to pick up take-out chicken for supper on the way back.

Cara and Jonah left the café and headed for Jonah's truck. He put a light hand to the small of her back to guide her. Barrett used to do that. When they were first married, she had loved the feeling. It made her feel protected and cared for. But she'd been young and inexperienced. He'd been ten years older and a lawyer. She'd admired him, hung on his every word, tried to be the wife he wanted her to be.

As the years passed, she matured. The minute she began to make her own decisions and plans, she discovered the trap she'd fallen into.

Barrett hadn't been *protecting* her, he'd been *controlling* her, locking her away from anyone but himself, tearing down her self-esteem with every word he pretended was *for her own good*—

to keep her from failing, getting hurt, embarrassing herself.

Jonah's hand on her back felt nice, especially since Barrett's release had sent her self-confidence plummeting. She wanted to lean into it, let him take over, direct her steps.

But that was wrong, dangerous even. Leaning on a man had nearly gotten her killed. She walked faster, away from Jonah's hand. She traveled under her own power, on her own two feet and she didn't dare forget that.

"I'M NOT much for salads," Jonah said as CJ leaned over him with the bowl of greens, tongs at the ready, smelling so pink he could hardly see straight.

The chicken was soggy, the biscuits cold and the butter on the corn-on-the-cob congealed, all because CJ had made them wait for her to raid Rosie's garden and make a damn salad. She'd wanted to *contribute,* for hell's sake.

"It's not fancy, I swear. Fresh veggies and a simple vinaigrette."

"*Vinaigrette?* Isn't that French?"

She laughed—there was pure delight in the sound, as if humor were a rare and precious thing. Jonah liked it a lot.

"Might as well try it," he said.

As CJ loaded his plate, he averted his gaze from

her softly swaying breasts. The heavy locket hung in the air. What picture was inside? Her alone? Her daughter? Both of them? He was a live-and-let-live person, but this woman roused his curiosity.

And other parts.

Forget that, he told himself, relieved when she took her breasts and her pink smell over to Rosie.

"Salads make me feel like a cow chewing her cud," Rosie said.

"Try the ketchup cure," Bunny said, dipping lettuce into a puddle of sauce on her plate. "It works."

CJ smiled her thanks at Jonah, her blue eyes shining bright. He felt lit up inside. Jesus. Maybe he *had* been alone too long if a woman's smile could do that to him. He got another oil pop in the chest.

"Ah, hell. Give me some," Rosie said, watching CJ dish some salad out. "Lotta cars stacked up at Duvall's?"

"Some," Jonah said.

"No telling how long he'll take to get to CJ's," she said, way too pleased by the prospect.

"Rosie, would you let it go?" he said, though this was the liveliest Rosie had been in weeks. Some days she didn't even open the shop. Maybe she was depressed. She'd die before she would talk to him about what was wrong. She kept asking him about the furniture show he was getting ready for in New York, hinting that he should head there early and stay for good.

He couldn't leave Evan yet. And Jonah had a feeling he shouldn't leave his aunt either. Not until she was back to normal.

"I'm just being realistic," Rosie said. "They might not hold your job, you know, wherever you're going." She shot a look at CJ.

"Have you always lived in New Hope, Rosie?" CJ asked, clearly trying to steer the subject away from her destination.

"My husband, Eddie, grew up in New Hope. When we got married, he sold his business and moved us out here."

"Jonah mentioned that he died. I'm sorry you lost him."

"I didn't lose him. He croaked on me. Set me up with the café, then took a powder." She brushed her palms together, like clearing dust.

CJ blinked at the harsh assessment.

"It's not like he died on purpose," Jonah said.

"He might have just to see how I'd do on my own." Rosie shook her head, then muttered darkly, "It was the hospital that did it. All he had was a hernia, but once they sink a knife in you, you're done. That's how it was with my folks."

"They died of cancer, Rosie," Jonah said. "Your

dad had lung cancer from smoking like a fiend and your mom had—"

"It was the surgeries that killed them." She snapped her fingers. "Gone just like that."

"Eddie sounds like an interesting man," CJ said, obviously trying to lighten Rosie's mood. "How did you meet?"

"That's a great story." Rosie smiled. "He caught me stealing electric typewriters from his office. That was before computers were everywhere. Instead of calling the police or coming after me with a baseball bat, he asked me out."

"You're kidding," CJ said.

"Nope. I said yes out of pure shock. I was twenty, mixed up with druggies, on a bad path. Eddie saw into my heart. Of course it didn't hurt that I had a great pair of tits."

"Rosie." Jonah nodded at Bunny.

"You've heard *tits* before, haven't you, Bunny?" Bunny nodded eagerly.

"See?"

Jonah glanced at CJ, but she didn't look upset.

"At first I figured he was after you-know-what. But he was a complete gentleman. I had to make the first move. He was forty and thought he was too old for me. But I didn't care about that. I never looked back."

"And you've kept the café going ever since," CJ said.

"Forty years. A lifetime." She got strangely quiet. Jonah stared at his aunt. What the hell was up with her? She'd been reminiscing a lot about Eddie, too, now that he thought about it.

Rosie cleared her throat. "So, anyway, New Hope's a nice town. Friendly people, lots to do for such a small place. We've got a big old bowling alley, a couple bars and two movie theaters. Galleries up the ying-yang. Magazines are always coming out to do stories on us. The schools are decent. Because of all the artists who live here, the art teachers are great. Football team's for shit, but you probably don't care about that."

"You running for mayor, Rosie?" Jonah said.

"I'm just saying it's a good town. You liked when you lived here. Evan, too." She turned to CJ. "The boys stayed with me when their father had his troubles."

"Rosie, don't." Heat washed through Jonah. He did not want their private mess served up with supper.

"Your dad was my brother and I can talk about him as I see fit. He was an angry man and a mean drunk and we all suffered for it—especially Evan, who got the booze gene from him. The disease took my brother, God rest his soul."

"That's enough." The words came out harder than he'd intended.

Rosie shot him a familiar look. *Don't tell me*

what to do, young man. "What's the big deal? Evan's sober now. All's well that ends well."

But the fight was far from over. Alcoholics were always in recovery. *One day at a time* was what they taught in AA. Jonah had sat through plenty of meetings with his brother, learning all he could to stave off the next setback.

"Every family's got problems, right, CJ?" Rosie asked. "You're divorced, aren't you?"

"Leave her alone, Rosie," he said.

"Kids complicate things. At least you didn't have that, Jonah—" Rosie caught herself, remembering too late about the babies.

He wished to hell he hadn't told Rosie when Suzanne got pregnant. He'd been so proud he'd gone and crowed to her over the phone. *Twin girls.* He hadn't been able to believe it. For those months it seemed like he and Suzanne both walked six inches off the ground, grinning at each other like fools whenever their eyes met.

She was seven months along when it happened. Complications due to uterine crowding. Not uncommon with multiple births, the doctor said.

"Divorce is hard," Rosie mumbled. "That's all I'm saying."

"You managed to say a lot more than that." He grabbed his plate and stood, scraping his chair against the floor. "I apologize for airing our laundry in front of you, CJ." He took his dish to the kitchen sink and ran the water hard. He hated that she knew something so private and painful.

When he turned around, CJ stood there. "Fresh-picked strawberries for dessert. All I have to do is whip the cream."

"No, thanks."

"Okay." She colored. "I picked too many. I could bring them down to the café. I have a great French toast recipe, if you've got the bread I need."

"Just wait tables. That's plenty."

She blanched, so he knew he'd been too blunt. He was always saying the wrong thing the wrong way. When he'd told her she was in good hands with Rosie, her eyes had gotten so shiny he was afraid he'd made her cry.

"Night," he said, wanting to get out of there before he made it worse.

"When do you want me?" she said softly.

"When do I…" Her words caught him short, gave him that hot spark again.

CJ flushed. "In the café. In the morning."

"Sure. Yeah. Deliveries start at five, but I don't need you until—"

"I'll be there at five. And I can do more than wait tables, Jonah." There was that glint again. He had a feeling he hadn't heard the last of that French toast.

CHAPTER THREE

WHEN CARA WENT to say good-night to Beth Ann, she found her in bed staring wide-eyed at the ceiling, holding Bunny tight.

She took a cheerful approach, since her daughter wouldn't welcome sympathy or comfort. "Look at you, all cozy in the toothpick room." She sat on the edge of the bed and pulled the sheet up to Beth Ann's chin. "And *Star Wars* sheets. I've got race cars on my bed. It was Jonah's room. This room was his little brother's."

"It smells weird here," Beth Ann said in a scared voice. "Dusty and old."

"You're not used to it." Cara brushed her daughter's hair from her forehead—one kindness Beth Ann allowed her mother. "Remember the first night at Grandma Price's? You hated how it smelled like cigarettes and hairspray."

Beth Ann didn't look convinced.

"This smell is old wood," Cara said. "I like it. If you add in baked bread, that's how my grandmother's house smelled." She paused. "Rosie is kind of like her."

"Did she teach you poker?"

Cara laughed. "Nope. She taught me how to cook. She did like jelly beans though. She used to bake them into rolls. Each color meant a different fortune."

"Really?"

Beth Ann seemed cheered, so Cara kept talking. "Green meant good luck. Red meant you'd fall in love. Pink meant you'd make a friend."

"That's cool. Could you make those rolls?"

"When there's time, sure." She hadn't baked in more than three years. Barrett had poisoned that pleasure. His first act of violence had happened over a burnt batch of banana muffins.

He'd come home early and found her registering for college online. In her excitement, she'd forgotten the muffins. He'd thrown the blackened rolls at her, one by one, berating her for neglecting her family, for being selfish and foolish. That had been the beginning of the end.

"You used to let me cook with you," Beth Ann said.

"I did." Thankfully, Beth Ann had been out of hearing range for the fight. Barrett had swept everything from the counter, shattering Beth Ann's special cooking bowl.

Cara didn't want to think of that. "Anyway, my grandma was a great teacher. So patient. No matter what little dish I helped make, she always said it was the best part of the meal." Dinners at her grandmother's had been celebrations, warm with love.

"I wish I could have met her," Beth Ann said.

"She would have adored you." Cara swallowed against that sadness. Losing her grandmother had sunk her very low. It was only when she went to work at Dolly's that she bounced back. Dolly picked up where her grandmother had left off, teaching Cara tons about the restaurant business, too. Cara had soaked it up like a sponge.

"I miss Grandma Price," Beth Ann said. "I miss her disco songs." All those nights her mother spent with men in clubs had come to some good, Cara thought. At least her mother had been good to Beth Ann.

"And I miss Serena…so…much." Tears welled in her eyes, and Cara's heart ached for her. "Can I call her one time?" Beth Ann pushed up onto her elbows. "I could use the phone in Rosie's kitchen. Just for three minutes. Please?"

"You might slip and say something about where we are and Serena might slip and talk to Grandma Price or your father."

"We won't. We're good at secrets. Please, *please*." The agony in her daughter's face was almost more than Cara could bear. Beth Ann had lost so much already. She was so vulnerable, so shut down, unable to talk with Cara about what had happened.

What could it hurt? One three-minute call on a stranger's phone?

"We can't risk it." The domestic violence counselor had told her of women who'd made one quick phone call home and been caught. If Cara let Beth Ann break the rule once, her daughter would push for more. Better safe than sorry.

Before they left Barstow, she'd broken apart their cell phones and thrown the pieces in different Dumpsters because of the GPS locators. She'd closed out their email accounts, too.

"You're mean." Beth Ann flopped back into the pillow, angry now.

"I'm keeping us safe." Beth Ann didn't understand the extent of the danger. Barrett was a family lawyer. He hired investigators all the time. His wealthy mother would spare no expense in helping him track Cara down.

P.I.s had access to all kinds of databases and tricky ways to glean information. Barrett had once crowed that he'd located a deadbeat dad through the man's subscription to a hunting magazine.

She couldn't take a chance. They had to stay invisible. "Remember what we agreed. If you have to tell anyone where we're moving, say Denver, okay?"

Cara should have told Rosie that right off. Peo-

ple in small towns were nosy and Cara had roused
Rosie's curiosity by evading her questions.

She sighed and reached for the cord to close the
blinds. Out the window, she saw Jonah sitting on
a wooden swing on his deck. A black cat stalked
toward him.

"Look at that," she said, pointing. "A cat's
sneaking up to Jonah."

Beth Ann turned her body to look out the window.

"Jonah's pretending not to notice." He stared
steadily ahead.

The cat slinked up until its head was under
Jonah's dangling hand. Without looking, he
scratched the cat. From here, she could see he
was smiling. Cara felt a rush of tenderness.

"Do you think I can pet the cat?" Beth Ann
asked.

"You can ask Jonah tomorrow." She dropped
the blinds, then gazed at her daughter, who still
seemed nervous. "Would you rather sleep with
me?"

Beth Ann took a deep breath and made herself
be brave. "No, thanks."

It broke Cara's heart every time her daughter
refused her comfort. She'd never forget when Beth
Ann visited the hospital after Cara came out of
the coma. Cara had held out her arms and Beth
Ann had backed away.

Losing her daughter's trust felt worse to Cara than nearly dying.

"If you change your mind, I'm next door." She shut off the reading light. The peace sign sent a golden glow from the doorway.

"Jonah's kind of grouchy," Beth Ann said. "Maybe he won't let me pet the cat."

"I bet he will. He put in the night-light for you."

"He did?"

"So you could see your way to the bathroom. And he made sure you had this lamp to read by."

"So he's grouchy, but nice."

"Mostly nice, I think."

"I like the light."

"You can tell him tomorrow. When you ask about the cat."

"Okay." She sounded calm now, thanks to Jonah's thoughtfulness. "Good night, Mom."

"Good night, sweetheart."

Back in her room, Cara undressed and got into the bed Jonah had slept in as a kid. *When their father had his troubles.* With alcohol, she assumed. And Jonah had been through something awful related to children based on what Rosie had started to say. Had he and his wife been unable to have any? Had he lost custody?

Not her business at all, but she couldn't help being curious.

Cara closed her eyes. She needed all the sleep

she could get if she was to start work at five. She was glad, really. Staying busy slowed the churn of dread and panic in her head. Working at the café had distracted her from her troubles. For those hours, she'd felt more herself. She enjoyed meeting the customers, tracking orders, juggling tasks, timing her moves so no one waited too long for a refill or their tab.

She turned onto her side, hoping to fall right to sleep. Five o'clock came early. *What about Barrett?*

He would go to Cara's mother, of course, where he knew they were staying. Her mother would tell him anything she knew. She'd thought Barrett walked on water from the moment they met, when Cara was sixteen. He was the attorney who convinced her mother's unstable boyfriend to leave the state.

Her mother believed Cara had exaggerated Barrett's behavior, that Cara's injury had been an accident. But then Deborah Price believed men over women, even to her own detriment. Or her daughter's.

The betrayal hurt all the same.

Cara would have expected it from Barrett's mother. Alice Warner had despised her from the beginning. The punitive prenuptial agreement she'd insisted on should have been a clue, but Cara had been too blinded by love to realize it.

She would never forgive herself for being so trusting, so naive.

The divorce attorney Alice had hired had kept child support as low as possible. Alice had offered a "supplement," as long as Cara and Beth Ann moved into her guesthouse and complied with her "house rules." She was building a case to win custody of Beth Ann, Cara realized.

The worst blow of all, the most outrageous, was that Barrett had won supervised visitation rights with Beth Ann when he was released.

The judge's rationale was that Barrett had never harmed or threatened Beth Ann or struck Cara in Beth Ann's presence. So, in theory, Cara was breaking the law by keeping Beth Ann away from him.

As soon as she could save the money, Cara would hire an attorney to reverse that decision, but that was down the road.

Cara's mother would help Barrett however she could, Cara knew. She had told her mother nothing of their plans, simply packed up, traded Barrett's BMW for her mother's sedan, said goodbye and driven off.

What if her mother had overheard a phone call with the domestic violence counselor or peeked at Cara's laptop's browser history? She'd tell Barrett. What if he was on his way here?

The thought burned through her.

They were sitting ducks, trapped here, just off the highway, with a broken car. She gulped air and sat up, dripping with sweat, scared out of her mind. She felt small and helpless, like the mouse she'd been in the marriage.

Cara heard the whine of a saw. Looking out the window, she saw golden light glowing from Jonah's woodshop windows. He was working in there. It was a peaceful thought.

What had he said to her? *You're in good hands.*

The words had felt so right, she'd almost cried. Remembering felt like a cool cloth on a hot forehead.

She lay back down. Barrett couldn't know they were here. The shelter expected her sometime this week, so there was no urgency there. She'd already made over a hundred bucks, which would help pay for the car.

You're in good hands. Her muscles loosened, her mind let go, and the next thing she knew her travel alarm was giving out its high-pitched beep.

She dressed in stretchy capris, a cool yellow blouse and comfortable sandals, peeked in on her sleeping daughter, then followed the smell of coffee to the kitchen.

"Left you a mug's worth," Rosie said, not looking up from her paper.

Cara filled the rooster-shaped mug Rosie had set out for her and took a sip.

"Paper guy told me Rusty's still not back from the bachelor party," Rosie said, sipping from a matching mug. "Long drive from Yuma."

"That's not good."

"I don't know. You'll get a better price tomorrow. People with hangovers want someone to pay."

Her stomach burned. Another delay. Another day's wait and she still didn't know how much it would cost to fix.

Rosie leveled her gaze at Cara. "You've got your troubles. That's clear. I've been there. Like I said, I was swirling the drain when Eddie hauled me up."

Her words caught Cara short. She sucked in a breath, nervous about what Rosie had guessed about their situation. Would she tell anyone? The police? Barrett, if he showed up? Or an investigator he sent?

"I'll pay cash under the table and you can live here free. That's the deal."

"That's very kind of you, Rosie, but as I explained—"

"You've got a mysterious job in some secret city. Right."

"Denver. It's not a secret. And I do have a job. No mystery."

"Doing what?"

"Secretarial." She wasn't sure, but it was a good guess.

Rosie looked at her the way her grandmother would have—not buying it, but not minding the lie. "A job in the hand is worth one in the weeds any day. We both know that."

"I appreciate that. I do, but—"

"I can keep my mouth shut when it counts, if that's your worry."

"I'm sure you can, I just—"

"Think about it. That's all I ask." She went back to her paper.

"I will." Cara gulped the coffee, rinsed the cup and started to go.

"There are a hell of a lot of strawberries in the fridge."

"I got carried away, I guess." She'd had so much fun in the garden she'd lost track of all she'd harvested.

"You going to let them rot in there?"

"I thought I'd make French toast in the café and use them. Jonah said no."

"Your French toast any good?"

"Very. Plus, baked goods have a big profit margin."

"Is that so?"

"The lady who owned the diner where I worked told me that."

"Then get down there and get toasting."

"But Jonah said—"

"Hell's bells, he's all bark and no bite. Go down

there and tell him that junk about profit margin. Stand up for yourself."

"Okay. I will."

"Good. And remind him my sink needs fixing."

"Will do." She grabbed the gigantic bowl of sugared berries from the fridge and left. She liked Rosie. She'd taken the same tone that her grandmother would have. Her grandmother had overcome tough times, too. She'd been poor, done most of the raising of her five younger siblings, but she'd plowed ahead, no matter what. She knew who she was and what she wanted. Cara wished she were more like her grandmother. And Rosie, for that matter.

Rosie's offer was tempting, it was true. The Phoenix job would be minimum wage, so it would take forever to save for new IDs and legal help. And being around Rosie felt reassuring.

That was deceptive, though. It was a false sense of security. Phoenix was bigger, more anonymous. Safer. There was the shelter, too, with domestic violence counselors and kids Beth Ann could relate to, people who understood what they'd been through. She would stick to the plan. As soon as Rusty fixed her car, they had to go.

"WHAT THE hell is *challah?*" Jonah asked, adding a loaf of perfectly fine white bread to the stack that CJ had rejected for her blasted French toast.

She'd hassled him from the minute she stepped into the café and it was too damn early to be hassled. Rosie must have told her to kick his ass because she didn't back down one bit, no matter what he said.

He hoped to hell Rusty Duvall would choke down a raw egg and some Tabasco and get going on her car.

"Jewish egg bread," CJ answered, her voice muffled because she was between shelves, pawing through all the breads and rolls he had in stock, her spectacular backside close enough to grab.

Luckily, his hands were full of rejected bread.

She backed out with two loaves of thick-sliced French bread. "These will have to do."

"Look, this crowd just wants a hunk of bread to soak up their yolks. Don't expect many takers." But his words fell on deaf ears. Pretty, shell-like ears that peeked from beneath her flyaway hair, but deaf to good sense all the same.

She'd made real whipped cream because the canned stuff was *gross,* doing this really distracting wiggling and bouncing the whole time. He'd been so distracted he hadn't noticed he had scorched the back of his apron until he smelled burned cotton.

Now the bell jangled. "Customers." He bent to look out the pass-through at the construction crew heading for a booth.

"I need five minutes to get the bread soaking," she said. "Can you see what they want? Hold the breads until I tell them about the French toast." She scurried off. He couldn't help but watch that hitch and jiggle she had when she walked. It wasn't her fault exactly. What did they call it in the law? *An attractive nuisance.* Yeah. And he had the charred apron to prove it.

Soon enough she'd wiggled out with coffee for the workers and returned with a triumphant grin. "They all want French toast."

"What they *want* is *you,*" he muttered, turning back to the stove.

"What?"

"Nothing," he grumbled.

She slapped batter-coated bread onto his griddle, drips and splats flying everywhere. "Flip these when they're light brown, please. Also, you might use more butter on those fried eggs. The edges are crusting. Where's the powdered sugar?"

"Top shelf to the left. With the brown sugar."

She set off and he checked his eggs. They weren't crusty. Or not that crusty. Dammit. He added butter. Everybody was a critic.

"I don't see it," CJ yelled.

Hell's bells. He stomped into the pantry. She was reaching up from the ladder, her backside at eye-level, the edge of yellow lace panties peeking above her pants. Did her bra match?

Focus, man. He hauled his gaze to the shelf, where she had her fingers on the right sack. "You got it."

She jerked, surprised by his voice, he guessed, and a cloud of powdered sugar drifted onto him and the floor around them.

"You scared me." She scampered down the ladder.

"You called me in here." Powdered sugar puffed from his lips with each word.

"I'm sorry." She was clearly fighting a grin as she brushed the sugar from his hair, then his shoulders, her breasts swaying gently before his eyes. The woman had a million ways to drive him wild.

"There. All better." She met his gaze, mere inches away. Powdered sugar sparkled in her hair, on the pale down of her forearms, and on her lips. Could they be as soft as they looked? Would they taste like the cotton candy she smelled of?

"Something's burning," she breathed.

No kidding. If the powdered sugar were gunpowder, it might have blown them sky-high. Then he smelled what she meant. Scorched bread. Her damn French toast. "Hell."

They rushed out together, banging into the doorjamb, bumping shoulders, but they caught the bread while it was still dark brown.

CJ plated it with powdered sugar, strawberries

and whipped cream, added it to the egg dishes and danced out to the workers.

When she returned, she fixed a slice and held out a forkful for him.

"I don't have time to—"

"Try one bite." Her sky-blue eyes were lit with pride.

"If it gets you back on the floor." He dragged the morsel off the fork. Flavors exploded on his tongue. Tender bread, sweet with a zip of spice, tangy with strawberries and the whole effect made dreamy by the cream.

"Not bad, if you like dessert for breakfast."

"Come on. I can see your pupils pulsating."

"You can see my…what?"

"That's a sign of pleasure."

"It's a sign we need brighter lightbulbs."

"Don't be such a poop. Admit it's good."

"Did you just call me a poop?"

"Would you prefer grouch?"

"Yeah. More dignified."

"Deal. Not that you asked, but it's the flour that makes the batter richer. And the honey gives it that bite."

"Big hassle for a side dish. Would you get the sugar off the pantry floor before we get ants?"

"You're such a p—"

"Eh, eh, eh. Grouch, remember?"

Jonah turned back to his grill, grinning despite himself.

CJ pitched the new dish to every soul who wandered in and Jonah spent half the morning frying battered bread. The men, especially, went for it. But then what man could say no to CJ? He sure as hell couldn't.

He'd let her disrupt his kitchen, use up dozens of eggs and loaf after loaf of bread *and* pop the clutch on his sex drive.

She was far too pretty and way too bouncy, a temptation he didn't need. Casual sex was all he could offer anyone and CJ wasn't the type.

He'd been wrong to let Suzanne coax him into marriage and a family. He'd held it together okay until they lost the babies. Then he'd cracked like paper-thin veneer. *I'm lonelier with you than by myself,* she'd said. He hadn't blamed her for seeking solace elsewhere. What hurt was that she'd found it with Jared.

When his wife and his best friend and business partner had slept together, that had pretty much taken down all the load-bearing walls in his soul.

So, yeah, he'd be better off without a delectable pixie dancing around his kitchen making him want what he didn't dare have.

CHAPTER FOUR

BETH ANN STARED at the fried-egg sandwich her mother had ordered for her. It looked toasty, at least. *Eat one bite. Then one more. Then another.*

If she ate half, her mom said she could ask to pet Jonah's cat.

She lifted the sandwich to her mouth, but the icky egg smell made her gag, so she put it back down again. Eating had been hard since The Terrible Thing. The Terrible Thing happened because of how much Beth Ann loved ice cream on Family Night.

She glanced up and caught her mom watching her, looking all worried. She'd gotten worse since they'd left Grandma Price's. She wanted Beth Ann to be all right, to be better, to be happy and regular.

It made Beth Ann tired trying to pretend she was. Tired and mad.

Try again. She held her breath and brought the sandwich up, but her stomach heaved. She set it down.

"Psst, Bunny." Jonah called to her from the silver kitchen.

Bunny sounded so fake, so babyish. Whenever someone called her that, Beth Ann felt lonelier. She should have picked a better name.

Too late now.

Too late for everything she wanted.

"What?" she called back.

"Try the cure."

Oh, yeah. She squirted the bottle, smashed down the bread and took a bite. Her stomach jumped, but the ketchup hid the egg smell and the sweet taste made it easier to swallow.

Whew. When she looked up, Jonah wasn't there. Good. He didn't watch her like her mother did. She sighed and ate another bite. Four more and she could ask about the cat.

Serena had an orange cat named Chulita— Cutie in Spanish. When Serena watched TV, the cat sat on her lap, all puffed up and purring. Beth Ann had wanted a cat, too, but Grandma Price was allergic.

She wished she could tell Serena about the black cat here. She missed Serena so much she ached everywhere like when she had the flu.

They were like twins, the two of them. Sometimes they didn't even need words, which was good because Serena's English wasn't that great yet. They'd been teaching each other their languages.

Would Serena be mad that Beth Ann had disappeared? Or hurt? She'd be too shy to call Grandma Price and ask what happened.

That made Beth Ann ache even more. She had to explain to Serena. Her mom said no phone calls, but how could one hurt? There was a pay phone by the bathrooms. She could slip down here at night. Easy peasy.

Her mother zipped behind the counter to clip slips to Jonah's wheel. "Every single order has French toast," she told him in a bossy voice.

"Quit selling it so damn hard. We're low on eggs."

"Take the heat down a hair. The crust was a pinch too dark."

"A pinch? Really?" He held out his spatula handle. "Be my guest, Ms. Pinch. Grill as you will."

"I'm just giving you a tip."

"Save your tips for Rusty. You'll need them to pay for your car."

"I didn't understand what he was trying to say on the phone."

"I'll drive you over after we close. But not until you scrape the stalagmites of batter off the ceiling."

"You mean stalac*tites*. Stalag*mites* grow from the ground up."

"Scrape those, too."

"Oh, please. It's not that bad."

Her mom was way more cheerful in the café, almost like before they found out about Beth Ann's dad.

It was funny, but even when Jonah sounded mean, her mom didn't act afraid, not like she got whenever she talked about Beth Ann's dad.

That's why they had to move—because her dad was after them.

Beth Ann was scared, too, because her dad might tell her mom what Beth Ann had done and her mother would stop loving her like she'd stopped loving him.

The thought swelled in Beth Ann's mind, turning into the black blob and making her feel so bad she wanted to tear off her skin.

Think about the cat. You'll get to pet the cat.

She gulped down two bites at once and chewed fast.

"Look how much you ate," her mother said, so relieved it made Beth Ann's heart tighten. Her mother's worry felt like a pile of dictionaries on Beth Ann's head.

"It was the ketchup cure," she said.

Her mom's eyes shot toward Jonah.

They stared at each other like they were having a contest. Beth Ann couldn't tell if they wanted to yell at each other or laugh or talk or what.

Lots of the time, adults made no sense. She wouldn't be like that when she grew up. She would always say what she meant and mean what she said and never say, *you'll understand when you're older.* If a person knew enough to ask the question, she could understand the answer.

Her mom looked away first, losing the staring contest, and grabbed a bunch of dishes then ran off to serve customers.

Jonah watched her go, his elbows on the silver ledge, a funny look on his face.

"Can I pet your cat? Jonah?" He didn't seem to hear her at first.

"Huh? My cat? Louis isn't mine. He's feral."

"What's that?"

"Wild. He was born outdoors and lives there, too. He doesn't like people."

"But we saw you pet him."

"He's used to me because I took care of him after he got hurt. He's only got one eye and one leg's messed up."

"Would he get used to me?"

"That depends." Jonah studied her for a few seconds, then got a bowl and poured cream from a carton into it. "He likes to lie in the sun. Take this to the clearing just past the big pines. See what happens. Don't rush him."

"I won't. Thanks." She told her mom the plan so her mom wouldn't freak out and set off for the trees.

Beth Ann put the bowl in the middle of a sunny

circle and sat on the edge, half in the sun, half in the shade, feeling hot and cold at once.

The pine needles looked golden brown in the sun. They smelled like Christmas mixed with dust. Nearby, a creek made a friendly bubbling sound. No wonder Louis liked it here.

She held very still, since Louis was wild and quick moves would scare him off, ignoring the way the pine needles poked her butt and legs.

It was so hard to wait and hold so still.

Come on, Louis. Where are you?

She waited until her legs went to sleep. She was about to give up when she saw a flicker of blackness against the trees. She stared so hard her eyes watered.

Yes! There he was. When he saw her he froze, blinking his one golden eye, holding up his broken paw.

He looked so lonely. She felt the same way. He had secrets, too—where he lived, how he got hurt.

Would he go for the cream? She looked away like Jonah had when Louis had sneaked up to be petted, listening with all her might for the crackle of the cat's paws in the dry needles. She held her breath.

Come and get your nice cold cream, Louis. Please, please, please.

When she finally dared to look, Louis had run

away. Not even cold, fresh cream would make him get close to her.

Stupid loser girl. Not even a broken-down cat wants to be your friend.

Now the sun was too hot, the trees too scary and the bubbling creek seemed to be laughing at her.

Beth Ann's nose tingled. *Don't cry. Do not cry. You are no baby.* She told herself that all the time. She didn't deserve to cry after the bad thing she'd done, so she made herself be strong.

She went back to the café with the bowl of cream. Rosie was at the counter. "What's with the face? You look like you lost your best friend."

She *had* lost her best friend, but she told Rosie about Louis.

"Come help me at the shop. It'll be lots more fun than waiting on that god-awful cat."

It sounded boring, but she was too polite to say no, especially when her mom thought it was a good idea. She put books and drawing paper in her backpack in case she ran out of stuff to do. At the store, Rosie gave her a duster and lemon spray and told her to dust all the old furniture and vases and junk.

When she was done, she returned to Rosie, who sat at a black-metal desk clicking a calculator and grumbling. She balled up a paper, then noticed Beth Ann. "I'm not paying you to stand around."

"You're paying me?"

"That depends on the kind of job you did, Little Miss Speed Demon. Make yourself useful and bring me that trash can." Beth Ann liked that Rosie said stuff straight out, no puzzles or tricks.

When she picked up the can, she saw that a cell phone had fallen into it. She took it to Rosie. "You dropped your phone."

"I didn't drop it. I threw it where it belonged. It was a come-on. They loaded it up with minutes to start with, but then you pay through the nose. I'm already paying for too many phones."

Rosie had tossed out a phone with minutes on it! A phone that didn't belong to anyone. Beth Ann's heart turned over in her chest. She could call Serena and it would be totally safe.

When she could do it without Rosie noticing, she hid the phone in her backpack. Her mother would be mad if she knew, but she didn't understand how terrible this was for Beth Ann. Her mom wanted her to act normal. If Beth Ann could talk to Serena, she might be able to.

WHEN THEY GOT to Duvall's, Jonah opened his truck door for Cara and held out his hand.

She braced herself, then took it. *Zing.* Heat zoomed through her, head to toe. At least she was prepared this time. In the pantry, she'd been caught off guard. She'd been trying not to laugh at him with sugar puffing from his mouth, as she brushed the dust from his shoulders and hair. Then she saw his face, the tiny gold flames in the center of his dark eyes.

He wanted her.

She'd been thrilled…and scared.

Cara felt the same way now, holding Jonah's hand, as she stepped down from the truck. He gazed over her, head to toe, the same glow in his eyes. It was like the heat swooshed back and forth between them. Her stomach jumped and it was hard to breathe. She was playing with fire and she knew it.

Jonah let go of her hand, as if he realized it, too.

They turned at the same time and started for the shop. She saw her car was in the left bay. "Maybe it's fixed."

He gave her a skeptical look.

"It doesn't hurt to hope."

"That's later, after it fails."

"That's a pretty grim attitude."

"That's how my mind runs," he said as they stepped into the cool garage. "Rusty!" Jonah yelled. "Hello?"

"No need to shout." A man rolled out from beneath a red SUV in the other bay and got to his feet, wiping his hand with a greasy rag.

"What's the story on CJ's car?"

"Rusty Duvall," he said to Cara, ignoring

Jonah. "Nice to match the face to the voice. I'd shake your hand, but I'm a bit greasy."

"I understand. About my car, I didn't quite get what you were telling me on the phone."

"That's because the bachelor party threw my circadian rhythms off."

Jonah rolled his eyes.

"It's true. They've done studies. Daylight saving time lowers your IQ. Take SAT scores for instance—"

"The lady wants her *car*."

"No need to take a tone, Jonah," Rusty said, then turned to Cara. "On that, we've got a problem complex."

"A complex?" she asked.

"Interlocking issues." He laced his fingers. "You know *intermittent* problems are the worst. Real puzzlers."

"Intermittent?"

"On-again and off. I tried a few things. Some worked. Some didn't."

"What does that mean exactly?"

"It means we need a full diagnostic."

"How long will that take?" Her heart sank at another delay.

"Normally a day, but my unit's being recalibrated. It should get here tomorrow. Day after at the latest."

"You won't know what's wrong until tomorrow?"

"Or the day after, like I said. But then we'll get the full picture on your car's health. Kind of like a CAT scan for your auto." He grinned, pleased with the analogy.

She was stuck another day. At least.

"Say the unit arrives in the morning," Jonah said. "Can you fix it by day's end?"

"Here's what I tell all my customers. Fast… good…cheap. Pick two. I can do fast and good, but it'll cost you. Or good and cheap and it'll take time. Or fast and cheap and that'll be crap—"

"Just do your best as quickly and cheaply as you can," Jonah said. "Okay?"

"That's why people come to me."

"And you'll call as soon as you know anything?" Cara asked.

"You bet." He saluted her, leaving a smear of grease over his eyebrow.

They walked to Jonah's truck. "Circadian rhythms, my ass," Jonah groused. "Rusty Duvall likes to hear himself talk."

He held the door for her, then went around to his side and started the engine.

Cara was grateful that Jonah kept quiet as they started off. She was beside herself with frustration. Even if Rusty could fix the car tomorrow, it was starting to sound expensive. If it was too much, they'd have to give up the car and take a bus. Losing the car would hinder them in a town with as much sprawl as Phoenix. She sighed.

"Rosie will be happy to keep you longer," he said. "I could use you in the café…long as you leave my menu alone."

"Thank you, I guess." He was trying to cheer her up, but panic began to swirl in her head. *Barrett's after you, maybe closing in. You need to move, leave, hit the road.* He would be furious when he found they'd run. Just as he'd been when she said she wanted a divorce. She'd seen in his face that he'd rather kill her than lose her and she knew then she was in a fight for her life.

She still was.

"You're worried."

"A little," she lied, fighting for calm.

"How about we swing by the market for some of that bread you wanted? That *challah.* You can go to town on the French toast tomorrow. How's that for turning lemons into lemonade?"

The idea did cheer her a little. "Speaking of lemonade…the mix we use tastes awful. Let's get some lemons. Where I waitressed before, we made tons on fresh lemonade."

Jonah groaned. "Here we go."

She smiled. She felt better, she realized. The café had done that for her. All day she'd felt cheerful, energetic and useful. She was glad Rosie had pushed her to try the French toast.

She had another idea. "I spotted a coffee grinder in the pantry when I was looking for the sugar. Fresh-ground coffee would taste so much better. Cheaper, too, in the long run, because you can control the grind."

"This keeps up and I'll have to track down Rusty's diagnostic unit and drive it back myself."

She laughed, but she started a grocery list as they drove toward town.

"I THINK I nailed it." CJ held out another cup of coffee to Jonah.

"You said that last time." The woman had been trying out blends since five and now his head buzzed and his stomach burned from all the caffeine.

"But this is really it."

Resistance seemed futile, so he took the cup, his fingers brushing hers just enough to jolt his equipment the way the coffee had jolted his brain.

He sipped the brew. It was full-bodied with a hint of mocha, but he wasn't about to give her any more to crow about. "It's good."

"It is, isn't it?"

"Grinding the beans takes more time."

"It's so worth it."

"Coffee is coffee to our customers. They want hot caffeine, period."

"We'll test it. Let's see if anyone notices."

"No dropping hints now."

"I swear." She held up a hand.

"Or lingering looks. Or eyebrow shorthand."

"Eyebrow shorthand?"

"Yeah. You talk with your eyebrows." He cleared his throat. "You have…uh…talkative eyebrows."

"Talkative?"

"Yeah, like now. They're half up, half down and curvy. Just trust me. They talk." He felt like an idiot saying so and noticing in the first place.

"You want me to duct tape them?"

"If I have to keep you from cheating."

"I won't cheat. It'll be a true test. We seem busier today," she said, nodding at the packed booths. "Do you think it's the French toast?"

"I think it's the new waitress. The place is full of *men*." She looked so hot in short white pants and a yellow top that shivered over her breasts that he wished she'd worn a full apron again. And that pink smell was killing him.

"That can't be it…can it?"

Absolutely. Before he said that, he noticed the light in her eyes had faded. "Nah. You're right. It's gotta be the toast."

"Told you!" She beamed, then danced off, sashaying those hips of hers. She had no idea how sexy she was. She acted friendly, not flirtatious, but she had men hanging on her every word, tying up the booths forever, joking, laughing, showing off.

Smiling, he absently sipped more coffee. *Mocha notes...definitely....*

The bell clanged and Evan walked in. Automatically, Jonah scanned him for signs of inebriation. Steady stride...solid posture...clear gaze. *Sober still.* Ninety days this time. He knew because he'd slipped into the back of the meeting to see him get his chip. He was proud, but it was too soon to say so.

Evan took a counter stool.

"You hear back on that job?" Jonah had set him up with an interview about a marketing job for a national home-improvement chain.

"Could you grill my eggs before you grill me?"

"Coffee?" CJ asked, holding out a mug, a carafe in her other hand. She seemed to appear out of nowhere just in time to take an order or refill a mug.

"Please." He watched her pour. "You're the new Darlene, right?"

"Her name's CJ," Jonah said. "This is my brother, Evan."

"I'm so glad to meet you!" She shook Evan's hand vigorously. "We love your toothpick sculptures. My daughter's in your room."

"She's what? Wait. You're staying at Rosie's?"

"Our car broke down and she was kind enough to let us stay."

"Rosie was kind?" He turned to Jonah.

"Don't worry. There was something in it for her. She conned CJ into working here while she's waiting for her car."

"Now that sounds like Rosie." Evan sipped the coffee, then did a double take, sipping more. "What did you do to the coffee?"

"You like it?" CJ shot Jonah a look. "It's a medium roast from Costa Rica. We ground the beans ourselves."

"Damn." Evan sipped more. "This beats the house blend at Coffee Stop easy. You should offer it to go. You'd steal customers."

"Really? You think so?" She was so excited you'd think she won the lottery.

Jonah groaned. "I can't believe my own brother betrayed me." CJ would carry on about this all day now.

"What?" Evan looked puzzled.

"We had a bet that no one would notice the coffee," CJ said. "And I just won."

"Way to go." Evan held out a fist for a bump.

"I like the to-go idea," she said. "It would be easy to set up a station with carafes, cups, lids and condiments."

"Too much hassle," Jonah said. "People buy coffee by habit."

"Not these days," his brother said. "But then maybe my marketing degree was a waste of time." He studied Jonah over his cup.

"Whatever," he grumbled.

"What can I get you to eat, Evan?" CJ asked, pulling out her order pad.

"I hear you make killer French toast."

"You heard that?"

"Jesus. Don't encourage her," Jonah said.

CJ huffed a breath. "You are such a p—"

"Don't say it." If she called him a *poop* in front of Evan, he'd never live it down.

"I was just going to say party pooper," CJ said. She tore off the slip with Evan's order and held it out. "Give him double berries, okay? For the coffee tip? Thanks, Evan." She topped Evan's mug, then waltzed away.

"Party pooper, huh?" Evan grinned at him. "Look at you, big brother, all red and flustered. She's cute, for sure."

His face did feel hot. "She's gone as soon as her car's fixed." *Hurry up, Rusty.* He started Evan's order, then turned back to him. "So what about the job?"

"No word yet. It was a long shot. Plus, it's in Columbus. I don't know the music scene there."

"The last thing you need is a music scene." That

had been where the trouble started. "It would be a stepping stone. From there, you could—"

"You might as well know I took the job at the Wash-Bowl-N-Brew." He locked his jaw like he would as a kid when he'd done something dumb, but wouldn't admit it.

Jonah tensed. "Doing what?"

"Whatever they need. Work the car wash, the bowling counter."

"The bar?" Jonah snapped. "You're not working in the bar."

"If they need me to, I will. I'll be fine. It's time to rejoin the world."

Uh-oh. He sounded too confident. "What does your sponsor say?"

"If I stick with the program, keep up with meetings, he thinks I'll be good. Unlike you, he has faith in me."

"I don't want you to get lost again."

"I won't. I promise you."

He'd promised more than once.

"I saw you at the back of the hall when I got my chip," Evan said. "Ninety days. I'm good." Yep, he wore that *I-got-this* look that came right before he tumbled off the wagon.

"So far." Ninety days was barely a dent in all the days ahead.

Anger crackled in Evan's eyes. "Can't you be happy for me?"

Jonah tried a different approach. "Come with me to New York. We'll find a place to rent together, get you a job."

"I have a job, Jonah," Evan snapped. "Leave it alone."

Frustrated, Jonah went back to the grill and cooked up the waiting orders. He plated Evan's with extra fruit and brought it to him.

His brother dug in and Jonah went back to work.

When he returned, Evan was wiping his mouth. "That was amazing. I hope you get the recipe from her before she leaves."

Jonah shrugged.

"You set for New York," Evan said. "It's soon, right?"

"Six weeks. End of June. I've got a couple pieces to finish still."

"Rosie said someone wants to mass-produce your furniture."

"The gallery owner set up a meeting with a manufacturer while I'm there. We'll see. Think about coming with me, Evan. I mean it."

"Your grill's smoking."

Jonah turned back to the stove and saw the French toast would be *a pinch too brown,* as CJ put it. He flipped it over. He should stick with what he could control—the food on his grill and the wood in his shop.

People were too damned difficult.

He kept his focus all day until he found himself cleaning up with CJ, just the two of them. She'd sent Ernesto home early for some family deal. "I've almost got him talked into waiting tables," she said to Jonah, shoving plates into the dishwasher.

"How'd you manage that?"

"I found out the reason he didn't want to. His sisters told him his accent was bad and people would think he was illegal. Can you believe that?"

"That's why?"

"So I told him his English is as good as mine, which it is, and that his sisters were messing with him the way siblings do. Anyway, did you know he cooks?"

"He does?"

"Yeah. I sent him home so he can make the tamales for his cousin's *quinceañera* tomorrow. He makes his own tortillas, too. You should use him more."

"Yeah." The woman had been in his kitchen three days and found out more about Ernesto than he'd learned in eight months.

"Your brother was nice," she said. "Easy to talk to."

"He's everybody's best friend, all right."

"There's nothing wrong with being friendly."

"There is if you're a drunk. His best friends are

drinking buddies, okay?" He did not want to get into this with her. Already, he had a knot in his gut. "Look, could we just…work?"

"Sorry. Just making conversation."

He turned away to wipe down the front of the oven. He'd been harsh.

When he turned to apologize, though, she was happily bobbing her head, dancing as she carried pots to the sink, earbud cord leading to her back pocket. Guess she'd gotten over her hurt.

Damn, could she *move*.

He forced himself back to work, scraping the French toast crusts off his grill. That was her fault, too. She'd done nothing but make more work for him and—

She shimmied past him and his hand slipped and he jabbed his thumb with the scraper, drawing blood. "Dammit!" He shook the injured hand.

She whirled, her eyes huge. "Did I bump you? I'm so sorry. Is it bad?" She reached for his hand.

"I've got it." He squeezed the cut to stop the blood. "Just…don't be so…disruptive."

"Disruptive?" She stared at him.

"All that…" He made two fingers dance. What the hell was he saying?

"Hold it." She put her hands on her hips. "You're saying my *dancing* made you cut yourself?"

He cleared his throat, his face hotter than it got

when he had every inch of grill firing up beef. "You distracted me, okay?" he said in a low voice.

"Well, you distract me, too, but I don't blame you when I goof up."

"I distract you?"

Their eyes met and held. "You do." Her blue eyes sparkled, her lips parted and she heaved a sigh.

The hot pop of oil in his chest became a splash. In the steamy kitchen, he wanted to shove the soup-crusted pots to the floor and pull her onto the steel table and kiss her senseless.

What the hell? He shook his head to break the trance.

She stepped back, watching him. "Sorry you got hurt."

"No big deal."

"About your brother, I know how hard it is when someone you love has demons to fight and you're stuck on the sidelines."

Exactly. A connection snapped between them like a flicked switch. It wasn't sexual. It was personal. He felt less alone. Damn. "Yeah. Anyway, I need to finish up."

"I'll try not to be so disruptive. Wouldn't want you to lop off a limb." She grinned and hip-swayed away.

He turned and scraped the grill so hard he expected to raise curls of stainless steel. He should have let her shake her moneymaker until she wore it out. Torturing his libido was one thing.

Touching his heart was something else entirely.

CHAPTER FIVE

"Too bad about Rusty's unit," Rosie said cheerfully over the supper dishes that night. "We'll just make the best of it." The woman wasn't even trying to hide her delight.

Cara felt glum. They were stuck another day. *What if he had to order parts?* It made her heart race to think about it.

"Now that green sauce you put on the spaghetti," Rosie said, drying a plate. "What was it again?"

"Huh? Oh. Pesto. Throw basil, pine nuts, Parmesan, garlic and olive oil into the food processor and flip the switch. Really easy."

She'd brought up the food processor from the café pantry, where she'd found the coffee grinder, as well as an industrial citrus press she'd used to make fresh lemonade. People had loved it, which had really boosted her confidence. Rosie had inspired her.

"Too much fuss for one person."

"The basil's right in your garden."

"The garden's too much fuss, as well. I'm

too old to be crawling around in the dirt." She sounded depressed all of a sudden.

"You're not that old," Cara said.

"I'm sixty. That's plenty old in my family."

Rosie said it so ominously that Cara stopped washing and turned to her. "Are you feeling okay?"

"'Course I am." She slammed the cupboard door hard enough to rattle the china inside. "And when I'm not, there's nothing to be done about it." Rosie dropped into a chair at the table, tossing the red-checked dish towel over her shoulder. "Let the rest air dry." She sounded weak.

Like Grandma before her heart attack.

Cara put down her sponge, dried her hands and sat across from Rosie.

"Quit eyeballing me like that," Rosie said. "I'm fine. I'm about done with the café, too. Writing's on the wall. No one wants to sit down to a meal anymore. It's all fast-food, rush, rush, gulp it down. When a café's done, it's done." She shrugged, then tried to smile, but failed. "Besides, closing the place is about the only way I'll get rid of Jonah."

"What do you mean?"

"He came here to sort out Evan. Evan's sorted, but Jonah's still here."

"I get the feeling Jonah doesn't think Evan's okay."

"That's Mr. Doom and Gloom for you. His divorce ran him down and he hasn't peeled himself off the tarmac yet."

Rosie reached for the jelly bean bowl on the counter and set it in the center of the table. She fished out two black ones and popped them in her mouth.

Black meant *bad luck will befall you.*

"What happened? Do you know?" Cara ate a green jelly bean to reverse it.

"Hardly. The man's secretive as a spy. I have to think it started with the miscarriage."

"His wife lost a baby?"

"Two of 'em. Twin girls. Seven months along, I think."

"How devastating."

"Mmm-hmm." Rosie ate a yellow jelly bean, then tossed in a blue one. *You'll come into money.... You'll take a trip.*

"You should have heard him when she got pregnant. He was so amazed. It was like he'd won the lottery and a trip to the moon, like he couldn't believe his luck, even though millions of people have babies every day."

"But then he lost them." Cara couldn't imagine that heartbreak.

"He sent me a card. Couldn't face the phone, I guess. Wrote that the babies were gone. *Gone.* That was how he put it."

Thinking of Jonah, Cara ate an orange jelly bean, which meant *your wish will come true*. "When did that happen?"

"Two years ago. The divorce, I have no idea. When he offered to come out to help Evan and me, I said, *What about your business? What about your wife?* Know what he said?"

"No."

"Same thing he'd said about those babies—*They're gone*."

"His wife *and* his business?"

"That's all he would say."

"He seems to be a private person."

"And no good comes of that. Bottle it up and it just ferments. We have enough trouble with things that ferment in this family. He's still moping around, expecting the worst from Evan."

"Healing takes time." Cara knew that firsthand. She'd recovered quickly from her head injury, but the trauma to her soul had lingered for months and months. She'd been strong for Beth Ann, but inside she'd been a shaky mess. College had helped, given her a mission. She'd just begun to feel whole when the news of Barrett's release came and tore her apart again.

"Yeah, well he'll heal right quick if I close the café out from under him." Rosie picked up a few candies, frowned, then threw them back into the bowl. "Hell, we're eating up Bunny's poker pot."

She rose to set the bowl beside the deck of cards on the counter, then dropped heavily into the chair, staring out the window for a bit. "Forty years is plenty long to keep a promise, don't you think?" She searched Cara's face.

"You mean to Eddie? About the café? He'd want you to be happy. If you don't enjoy the café any longer, then—"

"Oh, I love the place. That's not it. Like I said, when the end's upon you, you surrender. I don't have time to—" She stopped abruptly. "It's just time," she finished, though that wasn't what she'd started to say, Cara could tell.

Rosie clearly didn't *want* to close the café, but she felt she had to. "It sounds like you lost customers to the fast-food places and maybe the bistro, but you can get them back. The French toast was a hit—receipts were up, Jonah said—and Evan had a great idea about selling the new coffee to go."

"You sound like Eddie. He was Mr. Never Say Die. The man saw what he wanted to see. In a way that's what saved me. He saw fire and spirit in me when I felt as dead and cold as a rosebush in winter. He loved me like I was worth it. After a while I felt like I was."

"That's how love is supposed to work," Cara said, her throat tight at the thought. It was what she'd naively hoped for when she'd married Barrett.

Rosie got a faraway look in her eyes. "I tried to be the woman Eddie saw when he looked at me. Not sure I succeeded." When she looked back at Cara her face was paler, the lines around her mouth deeper, her eyes rimmed in red. "It'd take more than good coffee to fix the café and Jonah's only marking time at the grill. You're running off, remember?" She shook her head. "I'm bone-tired, CJ. Think I'll turn in early." She started off, then braced herself against the refrigerator before stepping into the hall.

Something was wrong. Rosie would bite her head off for asking, but she intended to anyway. Cara's grandmother had ignored minor heart problems until a massive attack killed her. Cara didn't want that to happen to Rosie.

When it was time for bed, Cara was surprised at how cheerful and talkative Beth Ann was. She'd had fun at Rosie's shop. She'd told Cara that she knew how to miss Serena less. That was a relief. Maybe Beth Ann would adjust to Phoenix better than Cara expected.

Cara dressed for bed, but the pulse of a headache sent her to the bathroom for aspirin, then to the kitchen for a glass of water.

Moonlight cast the kitchen in silver. A metallic clunk drew her gaze to the floor. A barefoot man in jeans lay under the sink. Jonah. She gasped.

Jonah jerked up, hitting metal. "Damn!" He rubbed his head.

"What are you doing here?" she asked, though it was obvious he was fixing Rosie's sink. He was naked to the waist. Moonlight glinted off his chest and stomach muscles. The light he was using under the sink outlined him in gold. He looked alarmingly sexy, and her mouth went dry.

"I *was* changing the U joint. Now I'm seeing stars."

"I'm sorry, but I didn't expect to see you...like that." She waved her fingers at his bare chest.

"Same here." He looked her over like he could see straight through her dark silk robe to her cami and shorts and beyond. She clutched the lapels, but the idea gave her a charge that wasn't exactly unpleasant.

He touched his head gingerly. "There's a lump."

"Guess I disrupted you again."

"You did." He shot her a smile, his teeth flashing white in the dim room. She liked making him smile. It felt like a prize.

"Didn't mean to. I came for water, I swear." She held out the pills as proof.

"I'm almost finished, if you want to wait."

"Sure it'll be safe? I'm serious. I don't want you to lose a body part."

"If I keep my eyes where they belong, I should be okay."

Oooh. Another zing flew through her. She was almost used to the feeling.

Cara sat. On the table was a footstool with clamped legs that Jonah must be repairing.

There was something natural and homey about waiting while Jonah did a household chore. The silence settled around them, except for the clucking of Rosie's chicken clock. Cara didn't feel her usual compulsion to fill the void with words. Something about Jonah Gold slowed her down, steadied her.

She almost felt safe with him. That was an illusion, of course. She'd felt safe with Barrett and he'd turned out to be the most dangerous man she ever hoped to meet. You had to find safety for yourself, on your own terms.

She was glad neither of them had turned on the overhead light. It would be like the blast of a car horn on a quiet night.

There was plenty of light to see the way Jonah's pectorals quivered, his abdominals tightened and his biceps swelled as he twisted and hammered and pried. Cara couldn't help but sigh. In a few minutes, he emerged, crouched, reaching up to turn on the faucet. Checking for leaks, she assumed.

There was something extremely sexy about a man's back. Was it the shape? The rolling muscles? The taper to the waist? She wasn't sure, but Jonah's was mouthwatering. She was glad he couldn't see her staring.

Then he turned and caught her. Their eyes locked. Cara darted her gaze to the side, totally mortified.

He cleared his throat. "So…that's got it."

"Great. Good job. Glad you finished." What was she going to do, sign his work order?

Jonah put away his tools, washed up, then fixed two glasses of ice water. He handed her one, ice tinkling musically, then sat across from her. She took her pills. When she finished, she caught him staring at her. He shifted his gaze to the footstool.

"You're repairing that?" she asked.

"It's crap—laminate over plywood—but it was Eddie's, so it's a treasure to her. I've offered to custom build anything she wants, but no…."

Cara smiled. "She was talking about Eddie after supper. Something she said really hit me. She said he loved her like she was worth it and after a while she felt like she was."

Jonah was silent for a long moment. When he spoke, his voice was soft in the darkness. "You ever have that?"

She'd never talked about her marriage to anyone. Not really. The clock marked the seconds with soft clucks. In this dark kitchen, with this quiet, thoughtful man, she wanted to.

"At first, I thought so. But it was a trick." She

paused. "I was only eighteen when we married. I didn't know much."

"That's young."

"I would have waited, but he was already twenty-eight and he wanted to start a family, so I went along." She went along with everything, too timid, too uncertain of herself to disagree.

"Did you love him?"

"I thought I did. I admired him. He was brilliant and accomplished. I was flattered that he chose me." Barrett had seemed to adore her, so she hadn't minded when they stopped going out with other couples, when he discouraged her from making her own friends. After Beth Ann came, it was Family Time all the time. She was grateful for his devotion, flattered by his focus. She hadn't known that her isolation, his subtle but relentless digs, as well as his intense jealousy, were hallmarks of an abusive relationship. How could she have been so stupid, so blind, so slow to act?

Cara swallowed hard. She was too ashamed to say any of that, but Jonah's quiet attention made her want to keep talking. "Even when two people love each other—or think they do—it can go terribly, terribly wrong. You know?" She raised her gaze to his.

"That's true."

"For you, too?"

He nodded slowly.

She felt a rush of relief. He understood. He hadn't been through what she had, but his marriage had crumbled. Cara and Jonah inhaled as one.

"If I'd only figured it out sooner, you know?" she said. "If I'd paid more attention. If I known what to watch for, the warning signs. If I'd known *better*." Her voice trembled.

"Knowing better isn't enough. You have to act better. I knew I wasn't built for marriage, but I put us both through it." His voice was rough, his eyes burning with regret. "Whether you know better or not, people get hurt."

Their eyes met again. "I'm sorry that happened to you," Jonah said.

"Me, too. About you." For the first time, she didn't feel alone in her pain. Her whole body was alive to the moment, the man, what they'd shared. Without thinking, she pushed her hands across the table toward him. As if by reflex, he covered them with his own.

That touch turned the moment inside out, made it physical…intimate.

This time, the zing was a rush, a steady current that turned some places soft and others tight and hot. She hadn't felt this with Barrett, even at the beginning. She'd had a teenage crush. She'd hardly known her own body when they married. This was adult sexual desire. It came from deep within her. She ached to be touched and to touch him in return.

Cara lifted her eyes to meet Jonah's, his dark pupils wide and shining with desire. He was tense, hardly breathing, his jaw muscle taut, holding himself back from what he wanted to do.

And what was that?

To lean across the table and kiss her? Lift her from her chair into his arms? Tear off her clothes and make love to her?

Did she want that?

She wanted *something*. Not quite meaning to, she leaned in and tilted her head. Jonah did the same. When their lips met, an electric thrill coursed through her, a wash of heat and need that made her whole body shake.

It was too much, too intense. Cara feared she'd be swept under and drown. She broke away, yanking her hands from under his, jumping up so fast her chair tipped and hit the floor. "I have to go."

Jonah righted her chair. "I frightened you. I'm sorry." He looked stricken.

"No. It's just been a while…" *forever* "…since I felt…" *sexual. Say it, you idiot.* "…that way. I was…" *terrified* "…surprised."

He considered her words, but he didn't look convinced.

"Really, it was me," she said, backing toward the hall. "All me." She banged into the wall.

"Night." She took the corner so fast he said *good night* to an empty kitchen.

Cara leaned against the hall wall, cringing and dizzy, breathing in great gasps that didn't bring one molecule of oxygen into her lungs. He'd looked stunned and sorry. It was awful, awful. She was so embarrassed.

She listened for him to leave.

There was a long silence. Jonah had to be shaking his head over the crazy woman who'd bolted from the merest kiss.

Finally, he exhaled loudly. She heard a metallic rattle as he picked up his toolbox, then his slow tread to the door and the click when he shut it.

Cara rushed to her room and into bed. What had she been thinking? She'd forgotten who she was and what had happened to her. The thrill of desire was one thing, actual sex totally different.

Just the thought of it made her break out in a sweat.

Sex with Barrett had made her feel awkward. He'd showed her what he wanted and that had been fine with her. She satisfied her own needs in private moments.

When it got bad between them, Barrett's touch reminded her how dangerous he was, how ready he was to hurt her. She dreaded sex then, the way it made her feel powerless and vulnerable. Sex was an assault, an invasion, an unwelcome intimacy that sickened her. She made herself numb, hid away in her mind until it was over, welcoming the brutal cramps of her period because Barrett was so squeamish he would sleep in the spare room for those blessed few days each month.

She knew now that no matter how much she wanted sex, if a man touched her, his hands would become Barrett's, his body, too, and his voice. She would feel Barrett's grip, his threats, the way he made her feel like her body belonged to him and he could do with it whatever he wanted.

She couldn't imagine trusting a man again.

Forgetting all that, she'd kissed Jonah. Her lips still tingled. The backs of her hands felt warm. She had the feeling they'd stay that way all night.

CJ HUNG UP the phone, her face as pale as the powdered sugar she'd spread like fairy dust all over his pantry two days ago. "It's the transmission," she told him. "Two thousand dollars and that's with a break on labor because of the delay."

"I could loan you a grand if that gets you there."

CJ met Jonah's gaze for the first time that day. He'd scared her last night, no matter what she'd said, and she hadn't looked at him dead-on since. Now her talkative eyebrows shot up in surprise, then twisted with doubt. "That's far too generous. I don't know when I could pay you back."

"No rush. It's sitting in the bank."

He could see she wanted to accept, but she shook her head. "Thanks, but it wouldn't be right. I have to pay my own way."

That stung, being brushed off so quick.

"Rusty says the car can stay there until I decide what to do. Sell it for parts? I don't know. I just know we have to get going."

He had to admit it would be a relief to have her gone. She mixed him up.

Last night in Rosie's kitchen, they'd *connected.* Saying next to nothing, they'd talked up a storm about their bad marriages. Like when they'd talked about loved ones with demons that afternoon, only worse. He'd recognized her pain, felt the same regret and guilt she'd spoken of.

When their hands met, the moment flipped over, went sexual. He'd been so hungry for her, like he hadn't felt in years, wide open and raw.

He'd kissed her. He couldn't help it. What he wanted was to slide her out of that slinky robe and get skin to skin, run his hands over every inch of her tempting body.

She'd been *surprised,* she'd said, but she'd looked *hunted.* He was sick that he'd done that to her. He'd been a total ass. It had taken him a bit to pull himself together and get the hell out of there.

They spoke little for the rest of the shift. CJ's energy had been dampened like a drizzled-on campfire. She smiled for the customers, but it was the empty smile he'd seen the first day. He hated that.

They were finishing cleanup when Rosie and Bunny came in.

"Look what Rosie gave me." Bunny waved a red pogo stick with fringed handles, an aluminum hula hoop over her shoulder.

"You shouldn't have," CJ said, uncomfortable.

"I had to get rid of them anyway," Rosie said with a shrug.

"Yeah, I helped her clear out her inventory," Bunny said. "Watch me!" She managed a couple of bounces on the pogo stick before losing her balance.

"That's very good," her mother said, "but we can't take them with us."

"There's room in the backseat."

CJ took a deep breath before she spoke. "We're not taking the car. It's too expensive to fix, so we're going by bus."

"By bus?" Bunny frowned. "But we can't leave Grandma's car here."

"Bunny!" CJ said sharply, as if borrowing a car was something that shamed her.

"Sorry." Bunny cringed.

He could tell she'd known not to say that. Strange.

"That's a stupid move," Rosie said. "Stay here

and make the cash to fix your car. You'll need a car in Denver."

So Rosie had gotten her to reveal her destination.

"We're expected," CJ said. "We can't stay."

Bunny sighed, took the hula hoop from her shoulder and handed both toys to Rosie. "Thanks anyway." Her shoulders slumped and she went down the hall to the stairs.

"You're not making sense," Rosie said to CJ, then followed Bunny, the rejected gifts clunking into each other with every step.

CJ stared after them, upset. She was in a tough spot. He felt for her. He had the urge to put his arms around her and tell her it would be all right— hell, he wanted to *make* it all right.

Totally misguided considering his track record. The best he could do was give her practical information. "Not many buses on Sunday. Be sure to check the schedule."

"What?" She turned to him, her eyes red.

"If you need the cash, feel free to work breakfast tomorrow." He caught a flash of hurt in her face, so he added, "But not if it holds you up."

Now she looked irritated. "I get it. If I'm leaving, stop whining about it and do it. I'll be out of your hair ASAP." She whipped off her apron, slapped it on the counter and left him with his mouth hanging open.

What the hell? He'd tried to help, but he'd pissed her off. Should he run after her and apologize? Nah, he'd only make it worse.

Jonah finished up at the café, eager to get to his shop. Stepping inside, he felt better. The shop had always been his sanctuary. When they'd lost the twins, when his marriage had failed, the workbench had given him solace and satisfaction.

He ran his hand over the high-backed bench he was finishing. He'd had to wrestle the dense mahogany into the curves he wanted, but it had been worth it. Jonah tried to honor the wood, let it speak to him, guide him with its texture, its give and resistance, its grain like bloodlines.

Today, he would carve hearts into the flared corners. Hearts modeled after CJ's lips. *Forget CJ and her lips.*

Jonah retrieved the carving chisels his father had given him. *See the shape in the wood and set it free,* he'd said—something like what Michelangelo said about freeing the angel in the marble he carved. His father had been a patient teacher. Jonah's best memories of him were in his father's shop.

He'd noticed that since his dad died four years ago, Jonah's good memories of the man had begun to override the bad ones.

Jonah was halfway through the first heart when Louis whisked by, crackling the tarps over the pieces he'd finished, then disappearing in the lumber at the back.

"Louis!"

The shout made Jonah look up. Bunny stood in the doorway looking frustrated. "He hates me. He always runs from me."

"It's not personal. Louis is his own cat. He likes the shop for some reason."

"Probably because it smells like the woods where he lives."

"I hadn't thought of that."

"Will he ever come out of there?"

"Eventually. You have to be patient."

"I don't have time to be patient. We're leaving." She sounded resigned, like she was used to being disappointed. It was kind of pitiful the way an old pogo stick had thrilled the hell out of her.

"Can I wait for him in here?" she asked.

"Be my guest."

Bunny lifted a few tarps searching for the cat, then came over to him. "Is that hard to learn?"

"Carving? It takes practice. Patience."

"More patience? I hate patience." She sighed.

"Woodwork is a craft. You get better as you go along." He preferred furniture to cabinetry. More creative and he could work alone. Selling out to Jared hadn't hurt anything but his wallet.

Bunny wandered off and he half forgot about her, until a crash near the power saws sent him running back there. If she'd gotten hurt… He should have been watching her closer.

He found her at the jigsaw, bent over a sheet of veneer.

"Are you hurt?" he demanded, reaching for her.

"No. I'm sorry." Bunny backed away, her eyes big.

"Stay clear of the saws. You could lose a hand." He put the wood back, then noticed she'd run for the door. He'd scared her by yelling.

"Hold on," he called to her.

Bunny turned, wary as Louis, poised to fly.

"Sorry I shouted. I was afraid you'd gotten cut." She just looked at him.

"How about I show you how to build a small box with a lid? That was the first thing I made. A treasure box." That's what he should have said in the first place, instead of letting her wander off unsupervised. You had to keep kids busy.

"Really?" she asked. "Right now?"

"Right this minute." He went to the worktable where he kept his computer, pushed the monitor to one side, cleared away the papers, spun the stool to Bunny's height, then set her up with scrap wood, a few tools and basic instructions.

She got right to it, which he liked. He had figured on bringing his girls into the shop from a young age to show them the joys of making something with their own two hands.

But that was done.

Hell, he'd probably have barked at them, too. Made them cry without meaning to. Jonah doubted his dad had set out to be an asshole. He was simply built that way—moody, quick to anger, distant, harsh. Jonah was just like him, except for the alcohol problem. That was Evan's burden to bear.

Jonah and Bunny had been working in silence for a time when she said, "I like the quiet in here."

"Me, too. The din gets to me in the café."

"It's loud. Yeah. Plus, my mom watches me too much. She always worries." He'd noticed how CJ hovered over her daughter, almost as if she were afraid if the girl were out of her sight, she'd be lost forever. It seemed excessive, but what did he know about being a parent? He'd let the girl wander among power tools.

A few more minutes passed, then Bunny whispered, "Look. He's out."

Louis had curled up in a sunny spot between the work spaces.

"Is it too soon to pet him?" she asked.

"Probably."

"Patience is hard."

"If it were easy people wouldn't want it so bad."

She considered that for a few seconds, then they both went back to work.

Soon, he heard her humming. He recognized the tune: "Blackbird," an old Beatles song his mom used to sing to him. He felt a pang, remembering how he would picture the hurt bird singing in the dark, waiting to heal, finally soaring free. He almost sang along with her, but he settled for tapping his foot. Louis closed his one wise eye.

CHAPTER SIX

"WHERE'S BUNNY?" Cara asked Rosie. Rosie and Beth Ann had been playing poker when Cara had gone to call for the bus schedule. Panic flared. It always did when she lost track of her daughter. *What if Barrett grabbed her?* It was irrational, but always in the back of her mind.

"She went after Jonah's cat. Wants to make friends before she has to leave." She shot Cara an accusatory glare.

"Where would the cat be?"

"Out by the creek. Maybe Jonah's shop." Rosie shot her a look. "Bunny's not lost, if that's what you think."

Rosie had no idea what she was thinking.

Cara bounded downstairs, through the café and into the yard, forcing herself not to picture the worst. There was no sign of Beth Ann or the cat in the open areas. She ran for the shop next, gravel grinding beneath each flying step. At the doorway, she looked inside, spotting Jonah working on a bench, then Beth Ann. *Whew.* She sat at a drafting table hammering nails and...*humming.*

Cara hadn't heard Beth Ann hum in forever, not since…before. Relief rushed through her. Beth Ann was safe. Pausing to collect herself, she surveyed Jonah's shop. Through the windows, late-afternoon light lit up swaths of sawdust. One wall held a huge, tool-laden Peg-Board. Tarp-covered furniture or unfinished pieces lined the walls. Toward the back, she saw standing equipment and all kinds of wood in sheets and planks. It smelled pleasantly of fresh-cut lumber.

"Hello," she said, stepping inside.

In response, a cat leaped from the floor and galloped out the door, fleeing on three legs.

"You scared Louis," Beth Ann said, frowning.

"Sorry." Cara felt like an intruder now. "I was looking for you. What are you making?"

"A treasure box. It's the first thing Jonah learned to make. Woodworking is a craft. That means you have to practice a lot. The rule is *measure twice, cut once*. That's because wood doesn't forgive, right, Jonah?"

Cara smiled at the information her daughter had absorbed from Jonah. She looked at him. "I hope she's not keeping you from your work."

Jonah opened his mouth, but Beth Ann spoke first. "I'm not. We both like it quiet. The café's got too much *din*."

"Din?" Cara said to him. "I assume that's my fault? The din?"

"Some of it." He'd seemed eager for her to get on a bus and out of town earlier. Maybe all her din was the reason. She'd enjoyed their teasing banter, but maybe he hadn't. She was a people person and he seemed more of a loner.

She'd be gone soon enough. "There are no buses on Sunday, so the earliest we can leave is Monday."

"Sounds good."

"Right." He *did* want her gone. Her face went hot with hurt.

He frowned as if puzzled. "That's what you want, isn't it? To take the first bus out of here? I want what you want. For you."

"Then we agree."

"So can you work tomorrow?"

"Do you want me to?"

"Why wouldn't I?"

Stupidly, her heart lifted. "Because of the din."

"The more din, the more money in Rosie's pocket. How can I complain?" His dark eyes twinkled at her.

"So one more day then," she said. Beth Ann was hammering away on her box in the background.

"One more day," he repeated.

One more day and they'd never see each other again. For some ridiculous reason, the thought made her feel hollow inside.

Afraid Jonah would see her feelings on her face, Cara shifted her gaze to the bench he was working on. "This is beautiful." A dozen curved slats formed its high back. "So elegant."

"That's what I was going for."

"It looks comfortable."

"Try it out."

She sat. The shape perfectly supported her body. "It feels custom fit to me."

Jonah gave a short laugh. "To Rosie actually. I made the template tracing her lying on her side with her legs bent. It wasn't easy to get that kind of curve in mahogany, but it was worth it, I think."

"It was. It absolutely was." Cara ran her fingers along both sides of the bench, which felt so smooth it was almost silky. He was carving a corner of the back, she saw. "How pretty. The heart almost looks like…lips."

"Exactly." He gave her a funny smile.

"What?"

"Nothing. So…"

Cara looked around the shop. "All this is your work?"

"It is."

"Do you sell online?"

"Some. Most of this is for a gallery show in Manhattan at the end of June."

"Wow. Can I see?"

"Sure." He pulled back the closest tarp, revealing a three-drawer dresser in a pale, shimmering wood. The drawers curved outward, resembling liquid. She ran her hand over it. "This feels like butter."

"That's red-flame yellow birch. It's got a rich grain and polishes well. The inlays are various veneers."

"It's breathtaking."

Cara uncovered a boxy chair with narrow, sharply angled slats and wide armrests. "This looks like it belongs in something built by Frank Lloyd Wright."

"Good call. It's an Arts and Crafts piece. It went well with his architecture."

"The grain is so pretty."

"Quarter-sawn oak. Showing the grain on all four sides is tricky. It's a hallmark of Arts and Crafts." Jonah explained more of the distinctive style elements, then showed her a sideboard that resembled a tree trunk, with the top as flattened boughs.

"It almost looks alive. You're creating art, Jonah."

"I'm building furniture. It has to be useful. But I make it as beautiful as I can."

Their gazes locked again. Jonah smiled. It was a different smile than she'd seen in the café—more relaxed and open.

"You're happier here," Cara said.

"I'm at home here." His eyes pulled her close the way they had last night in the dimly lit kitchen. Her heart began to race and she could hardly breathe. He dropped his gaze from her eyes to her mouth.

"They're yours," he said softly. "The lips I used for the hearts."

"Mine?" She touched her mouth. "I didn't realize they were so...puffy."

"They are. I know from last night." His voice was low and each word registered inside her. She remembered that kiss, how powerful it was, the surge of desire that had washed over her. Here it was again, fainter, but unmistakable. It was always there when she was around him, waiting to flare.

"I'm ready for the hinges," Beth Ann called, snapping their connection.

"Be right there." Jonah sounded grateful for the interruption.

She was, too. At least she should be.

While Jonah helped Beth Ann, Cara uncovered more of Jonah's furniture. There were spare modern pieces, more Arts and Crafts style, others with complex inlays and carvings, each more beautiful than the last.

Toward the back she found a rocking chair that begged to be tried out. It was made of a golden-brown wood, with dark whorls, highly polished with more than a dozen delicate dowels bent like tree branches. The seat belled out and the armrests were indented as if to fit forearms. She pulled the chair away from the wall and sat, pushing off. The ride was silky smooth, like swaying in a hammock.

Cara heard footsteps. From the corner of her eye she saw it was Jonah. "You must have used an angel to model for this." She leaned back and closed her eyes. "I feel like I'm floating on a cloud."

JONAH'S HEART LURCHED at the sight of CJ in the rocking chair. She'd closed her eyes, so he had a few seconds to arrange his face.

Suzanne had been his model and he'd built it for her and the babies. He'd been varnishing it in the garage when she'd burst in, her face terrified. *I'm bleeding, Jonah. And I haven't felt them move all day.*

"It makes me think of my grandma," CJ continued as he drew closer, her eyes closed in pleasure. "She had a rocking chair. Not this great, but we spent a lot of time in it. She would tell me stories and sing to me."

She sounded so happy, lost in a good memory, her face serene. This was what he'd wanted from the chair, what he'd built into it with all his skill.

When he'd pulled into the garage after the hospital, after they had lost the babies, Suzanne had seen the chair and shrieked, *Get it out of my sight. Burn it. Break it to bits. I don't care. I never want to see it again.* He'd crated it away. He intended to put it in the show in New York and be rid of it for good.

"Can I try?" Bunny had joined them.

CJ opened her eyes and smiled at her daughter. "Sure."

Bunny climbed beside CJ, who set them rocking. "This feels peaceful," Bunny said. "The chair is like a hug."

Jonah's chest went tight, so moved he had to catch his breath. *Yes. This was why I built it. For this.*

"It does," CJ said. "How can wood be so soft?" She looked toward Jonah, then froze, stopping the chair with both feet. Something in his expression alarmed her. "Are we too heavy? Should we get off?"

"No. I built the chair for…mothers and kids." The words scraped his throat, dry as sawdust.

CJ's eyes widened and she put her hand to her mouth. "Oh, no. I'm so sorry."

With a start, he realized she knew about the twins.

Dammit, Rosie.

"Get off, hon." CJ nudged her daughter.

"But I just got on."

"Stay there," Jonah said. "Use the chair. That's what it's for."

"Are you sure?"

"Absolutely." He wanted a new memory of the chair he'd built with so much hope and joy. Bunny leaned down to start them rocking again. CJ sat straight, holding his gaze, not quite convinced by his words.

As he watched them, the knot in his gut loosened and some of that peace Bunny had mentioned rolled through him.

"Take your time," he said. "I'm going back to work."

Jonah returned to the bench and began chipping at the wooden heart, their quiet voices in the background. It was a damn good chair. He wanted it to be enjoyed, even if the family he'd built it for was gone.

They're gone. Suzanne. The babies. The life we had, the one we hoped for.

He braced for the usual knockdown blow of grief and regret that always followed such thoughts.

But it didn't come.

He felt…fine. Normal. Sad, but not ripped apart or wrecked.

With a jolt that made him put down his chisel, he realized he would be okay. Relief washed through him, warm as bathwater. Without realizing it he'd climbed out of the hole he'd buried himself in all these months.

CJ had showed him that. CJ and her daughter. By loving the chair he'd built, by feeling its peace, by reminding him of its beauty and worth.

He was so grateful to her.

And attracted, too. So strongly it alarmed him. That must be a sign of his recovery, proof he was coming back to life, getting the feeling back in *all* his parts.

He was surprised to notice it didn't bother him that CJ knew about the babies. He trusted her not to pry or pity him. She'd been leveled by pain, too. Her husband had broken her heart and her spirit and likely hurt her physically, but he didn't want to think about that. Their connection made him feel less...well, lonely.

If he could do it without making a fool of himself, he'd like to thank CJ before she walked out of his life for good.

AFTER SUPPER, Cara did the dishes while Rosie went through her mail. Beth Ann was in her room watching a rented DVD on Cara's laptop.

The kitchen was fragrant with the scent of lemon soap and the garlic she'd used on the sole she'd sautéed for supper.

It doesn't taste too fishy had been Rosie's take on the dish that melted in your mouth. Beth Ann, on the other hand, barely ate a bite. Not even the ketchup cure helped. She was too sad about leaving.

"You got any idea why my nephew skipped out on a home-cooked meal?" Suspicion laced Rosie's words.

"He said he had work." Grateful Rosie couldn't see her face, Cara burned with embarrassment. Jonah was avoiding her because of the rocking chair incident, she was certain. She'd blathered on about the *angel* he'd modeled it on, not realizing it had been his ex-wife. To make it worse, she'd let on that she knew about the babies, his deepest pain. He was so private and she was a near stranger. No wonder he'd disappeared so fast.

They'd stayed in the chair as he'd insisted, but Cara had wanted to melt into the concrete. She knew any apology would make it worse. Jonah would not want to be reminded. Now, for sure, he would be glad to see the last of her and her din. They had one more day to get through.

"I don't buy it. He always has work," Rosie said, but Cara heard an envelope tear, so she knew Rosie had gone back to her bills. Whew. Bad enough that Rosie had looked at her funny after Cara let it slip that she'd watched Jonah repair the sink last night. *You and Mr. Silence is Golden had a chat?* She'd blurted about waiting for the water, but Rosie seemed to have read between lines Cara preferred blank.

Cara put the salad bowl in the cupboard. A sharp gasp made her turn just as Rosie slid to the floor, spilling iced tea over the paper she clutched.

Cara dropped down beside her, adrenaline making her shake as she felt Rosie's wrist. *There. A pulse.* Rosie's skin was gray, her forehead clammy. "Rosie?" Cara patted her cheek. "Can you open your eyes? Can you hear me?"

"I hear you. Now stop slapping me." Rosie pushed Cara's hand away and sat up.

"You fainted."

"I'm fine. I got up too fast. No big deal."

"Has this happened before?"

"A few times. When you're old, shit happens."

"You should see a doctor."

"I will not be interfered with. If it's my time, it's my time." She pushed to her feet.

Cara stared up at her, stunned by her attitude.

"Don't look at me like that. People pass young in my family. I've had a good life." She wobbled, so Cara jumped up and helped her into a chair, ignoring Rosie's attempt to slap away her hand.

"You haven't even seen a doctor and you're giving yourself a death sentence. Maybe your thyroid's off or your blood pressure's wonky. Insulin issues make people faint. It could be a million minor things."

"Eddie's hernia was minor, but the surgery killed him like that." She snapped her fingers. "I know what I know."

"Rosie...that's crazy."

"No. What's crazy is running out on a good job with good money and free room and board."

"Don't change the subject." Cara grabbed a cloth to wipe up the spilled tea. "You need to get checked." She dabbed at the wet paper.

"I'll take that." Rosie tried to snatch it from her, but Cara held it long enough to read FORE-CLOSURE NOTICE in red letters. She handed it over. "Are you losing the café?"

Rosie balled up the paper and tossed it, missing the egg-basket-shaped trash can by a mile. "When something's done, it's done. That goes for people as well as diners. You take a dignified bow and let the curtain drop."

The double whammy of bad news left Cara speechless. Rosie was sick and at risk of losing her café. "But you live here. You'll be homeless."

Rosie's face went slack, her eyes distant, and she spoke softly. "My friend Frieda in Tucson will let me stay with her through the end if I need that. I might not. It takes a while to evict a person."

"Through the *end*? You seriously think you're dying? Does Jonah know this?"

"No. And don't you say one word to him or Evan." She jabbed a finger at Cara. "I want them living their lives when I clock out. They're not to spare me a thought."

"They're your family. You owe them."

"*You* owe *me*. Swear you won't tell."

Cara's mind reeled. It was Rosie's life, of course, but she was acting irrationally, wearing a bullheaded expression exactly like Cara's grandmother's the time a commercial for a new heart drug listed heart-attack warnings, which matched what her grandmother called *heartburn*. Cara had pleaded with her to get checked. *That's just drug company scare tactics. They want you to buy their pills for a hangnail.* That had been that.

Six months later, her grandmother was gone.

Not this time. Cara wasn't about to back off with Rosie. She had to get through to her. In an instant, she knew how.

"Okay," she said. "I won't tell Jonah under one condition."

"What's that?" Rosie said warily.

"You go to the doctor and get checked out."

"Shit." Rosie banged the table, making the jelly beans rattle in the bowl. "What's it to you anyway? You're on a bus Monday."

"I care about you," she blurted.

Rosie's face softened for a second, then she made herself glare. "Then you'll respect my wishes."

Cara's rebuttal popped instantly into her head.

"Eddie wouldn't want this. Mr. Never Say Die, right? You're not acting like the woman he believed in."

This time, Rosie took longer to get back her game face. Cara had made headway.

"Don't you dare wave my dead husband's flag at me." Her eyes sparked fire.

Cara went for the throat this time. "Jonah has lost too much already. He can't lose you, especially for no good reason."

Rosie opened her mouth, then closed it. They stared at each other over the soggy bank notice like two gunfighters, the chicken clock clucking down the seconds until the showdown.

Finally, Rosie blinked. "If I do go and I'm not saying I will—" she swallowed, then finished in a shaky voice "—you have to stick around for the verdict."

Cara considered that. She wanted to repay Rosie's kindness. Beth Ann did like it here. So did Cara. She loved working in the café. Jonah was here. But he was more of a reason to go than to stay.

Their future was in Phoenix—their future and their safety.

Always there was Barrett and the impulse that hounded her: *Run, run, go, get away, don't stop until you're truly safe.*

If she left, Rosie would not see a doctor. Cara

could tell Jonah, but she wasn't sure that wouldn't backfire. For Rosie's sake and in Cara's grandmother's honor, Cara had to stay.

It wouldn't take more than a week, maybe two, for an exam and lab results, right?

"As long as my job and the apartment in Denver will still be there, it's a deal." She was reasonably certain of that. Families cycled through the shelter and there were always minimum-wage jobs.

"You'll work in the café?"

"But Bunny and I leave the minute you get the results. And no putting it off." Jonah would ensure Rosie got whatever treatment was required. Hopefully, it would be minor. A pill. A change in diet.

"So, deal?" Rosie held out a hand.

Cara shook it. "You're doing the right thing."

"You just shoved the foul end of the stick at me. Don't act like you've done me a big hairy favor."

Cara fought a smile at Rosie being so Rosie.

She remembered the other problem. "Now what about the café? We can't let you lose it."

"*We,* is it now? *We're* going to save the café?" A wily look came into Rosie's eyes. "I might have an idea or two, but you'll need to figure out how to bring back the customers. Like the coffee and French toast and whatnot."

It was immediately clear that Rosie had it all figured out, but let her health troubles sink her too low to take action. The plan was to catch up on her mortgage payments by selling half the space in her shop to the owner of the gallery next door, who'd been after it for years. Rosie gave Cara free rein to make changes in the café.

Two weeks wasn't much time to turn around a restaurant, but seeing the new light in Rosie's eye, buoyed by Rosie's confidence in her, Cara would do her best. She felt similar to when she'd started college, like she belonged, she counted, she could make a difference. Maybe Barrett's release hadn't set her as far back as she had thought.

"I'm done in now," Rosie said when they'd finished talking. "Something tells me I should have sent you on your way that first day. If you hadn't flashed me those sad puppy-dog eyes…"

"Come on. You practically shackled me to the counter."

"Yeah, well I can be my own worst enemy." But there was new life in Rosie's face. *She had hope.* Cara had given her that and that made her heart sing. She couldn't wait to get to the café in the morning.

What about Barrett?

Panic caught her short, but Cara forced it back. He had no way of knowing where they were. A few more days couldn't possibly hurt.

Could they?

CHAPTER SEVEN

THE MOUTHWATERING scent of fresh-baked pastry hit Jonah's nose fifty yards from the café, making his stomach growl. It wasn't yet five and CJ had been busy, making the most of her last day, it seemed.

Inside, the smell was so strong and so good he felt dizzy with hunger.

He noticed she'd set up a cart with coffee fixings. That to-go idea Evan had suggested. What the hell? It was bad enough that customers would gripe when the French toast went away with CJ. Now this.

Frowning, he followed the sweet aroma to an even sweeter sight—CJ bent over, hauling a tray of whatever she'd baked from the oven.

"What are you doing?" he asked gruffly, covering for his dazed look.

"Oh!" She jumped, tilting the tray.

He caught the rolls that slid off. "Ow. Damn. Hot." He dropped them on the counter. "That makes three," he said.

"Three what?"

"Injuries you caused me." Blisters added to the scraped thumb and the lump on his skull. At least the powdered sugar hadn't *hurt*.

"That was your own fault. You made me jump," she said indignantly.

The sight of her backside had fogged his reflexes, but he wasn't about to admit that.

"Could you help me frost these?" She motioned at four trays, a bowl of frosting and two pastry bags. "They're pecan rolls for the express coffee service and a side dish for breakfast or lunch dessert."

"Hold on. You're *leaving*. I won't have a waitress, let alone time to run a coffee cart, squeeze lemons or bake any damn—"

"But I'm not. Leaving, that is." Her cheeks went as pink as she smelled. He noticed dots of dark blue in the pale sky of her eyes.

"You're not?" Despite the risk of personal injury that would entail, he wanted to grin. Maybe some football pads would help....

"Not for a week or so. It's better for my, uh, job. Plus, the money's good." She glanced down, so he knew that wasn't the whole story. What was up?

"While I'm here, I want to spiff up the menu." She picked up a roll, swirled frosting on it and thrust it at him.

"Spiff up the...what?"

"Taste first, bitch after."

He took a bite. *Wham.* Sweet, spicy, nutty glory, the dough so flaky it dissolved on his tongue.

"Tastes great, huh?"

He couldn't pretend not to agree. She'd no doubt seen his pupils pulsating again.

"It feels good to bake again." CJ sounded relieved, as if she'd been afraid to try. She frosted more rolls while he savored the rest of his, explaining how easy they were to make, that Ernesto could do the baking and they could freeze ready-to-bake trays.

Jonah reached for a second, but she slapped his hand. "No eating up the inventory. Start frosting. At a price point of $3.95, that's $3 profit. Rosie needs the cash."

"Rosie won't care. She's pretty laid-back about the café." He picked up the pastry bag. Whatever the reason, CJ was staying. He decorated the first pecan roll with a heart made of lips he could draw from memory.

BARRETT WARNER RAISED his face to the sun, soaked in the endless blue of the California sky and inhaled his first breaths of sweet free air. It was the same sun, sky and air he'd experienced in the prison yard, but the sky had seemed grayer, the sun dimmer and the air had tasted bitter on his tongue.

He'd endured three long years of gray sky, dim

sun and bitter air. Three years behind bars, each minute of each day a slow drip of acid on his soul. He'd felt like Prometheus—his liver plucked by talons from his stomach each day.

Three years for an *accident*. If Cara hadn't struck her head so hard on the washing machine, he would have apologized for losing his temper, held her, convinced her not to tear apart their family, and all would have been well.

Instead, she'd accused him of trying to *murder* her and the best his lawyer could get him was six years. *Six years*.

Anger flared, but he quashed it. In prison, he'd discovered it was a personality disorder that caused his rages. He'd learned to manage it with pills, mental tricks and the lesson of prison: patience.

It's over now. He was out. The horror was behind him. Soon he'd hold his wife and daughter in his loving arms again. They'd been a closed circle, inviolate, which he'd broken with his unknowing outburst.

When he'd married Cara, he'd sworn before God and man to love and protect her. Instead he'd attacked her. Even if he'd been out of his mind for that wild moment, he'd still committed the act.

Cara hadn't answered a single letter. She'd no doubt kept the ones he'd written to Beth Ann from her. How *dare* she? By what *right*?

Rage swelled, but he pictured a manhole cover dropped over bubbling magma. *Easy now. Slow down. It will be okay. You'll see them soon.*

Barrett couldn't wait to begin fresh, united as a family, never again to be parted.

The macadam grit crunched beneath his shoes as he crossed the street, leaving behind the clang of steel locks, the meaty stench, and the bellows and grunts of the animals he'd been forced to live with all these months. Barrett looked ahead toward his mother, standing beside the Range Rover, as elegant and self-possessed as ever.

As he reached the curb, her polished smile faltered. He'd changed. He knew that. He was all muscle now, his face gaunt and raw-looking, his lips red and chapped, his eyes haunted, circled in black.

His mother reached to embrace him, but he held up his hands. "Not while I stink of prison." He saw dry-cleaning bags through the window. She'd brought fresh clothes as instructed.

Barrett noticed tears on her cheeks. "No more tears. It's over."

His mother shook her head. "It's not over, Barrett. They're gone. I'm so sorry."

"Gone? What do you mean…*gone?*"

"Cara and Beth Ann took off. They wouldn't tell Deborah where they were going."

He felt like he'd been punched. His insides

seemed to collapse and his knees sagged. "She ran away? She took Beth Ann?"

Rage surged, rattling the manhole cover. "She can't do that. I have rights. She's breaking the law. I won't have it. I won't permit it."

His mother jerked back, frightened of his outburst.

"I'm not angry at you," he said. "It's a shock, that's all." Hands shaking, he took a pill from the envelope in his pocket and swallowed it dry.

"Cara has been so cruel," his mother said bitterly. "She refused my help, cut me off. She's probably brain damaged from the accident. She shouldn't be allowed to raise Beth Ann."

"Stop," he snapped. "Cara is my wife and I love her. Don't speak of her that way."

His mother's cheeks turned red at his rebuke.

"She's afraid," Barrett said. "She can't help that." He'd studied psychology in the prison library and identified Cara's condition. "It's part of her disorder to be paranoid and hysterical. When I find her, we'll straighten it all out." He'd get her the psychiatric help she needed.

"I'm sure you will." His mother was always on his side. He was grateful to her for that.

"First, I want to change my clothes, then I want prime rib and two martinis. Then I'll make some calls."

He knew exactly which investigator to hire.

Francis Malloy knew how to bend the rules when the case required it. Certainly this one did. They were putting a broken family back together. They were on the side of the angels.

He would let Malloy start skip tracing—using database searches and other means to track someone down—while he went to see Cara's mother. Deborah adored him. He'd bent the rules to handle her asshole boyfriend all those years ago. The creep had been stubborn, requiring an overnight in an emergency room to convince him to leave the state.

Deborah probably knew more than she realized about Cara's plans. Barrett was very good at ferreting out information.

"It will be all right," he said, unbuttoning his shirt, reaching for the fresh clothes. He would *make* it all right. He had to. If he didn't get his family back, all his suffering and sacrifice would have been for nothing.

Barrett would get his family or die trying.

Louis stepped slowly into the circle of sun where Beth Ann had put the cream. She held her breath, held still. Today was the day she would pet him.

Monday, he'd taken one sip before he ran. Tuesday, he'd drunk half the bowl, watching her with his one eye. Yesterday, he'd finished it, hardly giving her a glance. *He was used to her.*

She was glad they were staying long enough for her to make friends with Louis. It was because her mother had talked Rosie into going to the doctor, which was so dumb. Doctors helped you.

She wasn't supposed to know about Rosie, but Beth Ann was excellent at finding places to hear important facts adults wanted to hide.

Sometimes she was sorry later—like the night her mom and grandma had argued about Beth Ann's dad, with her mom saying he was mentally disturbed and Grandma Price saying her mom exaggerated. *It was an accident. You were both struggling. You hit your head.*

I know what I saw, her mother had snapped. *He had murder in his eyes.*

Murder in his eyes. That made Beth Ann feel as cold inside as if she'd gulped a whole ICEE at once.

Had her dad wanted to *kill* her mom?

But her dad *adored* her mom and Beth Ann. He used to say so constantly, his eyes all watery with love. Her mom said he'd hidden his bad side from them, and that was even scarier. Did everyone have a bad side?

That made Beth Ann's stomach jump, and it started the black blob in her brain that surged whenever she thought about The Terrible Thing.

She pushed it away and focused on Louis, who

walked right up to the bowl without even looking at her. He trusted her.

His pink tongue made a cute lapping sound. Her heart pinched with love. She couldn't wait to pet him. She longed to lift him onto her lap, brush the dust from his fur and make it shiny.

Beth Ann rocked side to side on her butt cheeks, inching forward. The pine needles crackled.

Louis froze and stared at her. After a few seconds, he went back to the cream, his tongue slow at first, then quick, quick, quick. She moved more. This time only his ear twitched.

Two more moves and Beth Ann was close enough to touch him, but she decided to be a bit more patient just in case.

She could do it. She had self-control now.

She hadn't had self-control when she was six. If she had, she wouldn't have been so greedy for ice cream that she'd let her dad in the house for Family Night and caused The Terrible Thing.

She pushed away that thought and stared at Louis. Before long, he'd cleaned the bowl. He looked straight at her, *thank you* shining from his one golden eye. She smiled back.

He licked his one front paw, then rubbed it over his face again and again, washing it. That was so cute her heart squeezed.

She let her hand come out slowly. Louis leaned

out and sniffed it, then licked her finger, his tongue like the scrub side of the kitchen sponge.

Then he rubbed his cheek against her finger and her heart melted totally. She wanted to hold him, to promise to protect him and take care of him.

Her mother was always trying that with Beth Ann, but Beth Ann couldn't let her. It would be cheating.

Sometimes, when the dreams got bad, Beth Ann had to fight hard to keep from throwing her arms around her mother's neck and crying and crying. She had to be strict with herself. She had to take care of her own sadness. She didn't deserve to be hugged and patted.

But here was Louis and she could help him if he'd only let her. Beth Ann reached out, but Louis shot off, a black blur against the trees, almost like he didn't think he deserved her hugs either.

That made her want to talk to Serena again. Rosie's throwaway phone had had fifty-five minutes of talk time. So far, Beth Ann had only used ten on two calls to Serena. *"No llores,"* Serena had said the first time. *Don't cry.* But Serena had been crying, too. Talking to Serena had made Beth Ann feel stronger and calmer, so she wasn't sorry she'd done it. Serena pinky-swore to keep the calls a secret and Beth Ann knew she would.

Beth Ann picked up the bowl and started for Jonah's shop. She'd already made one box. Today, he'd promised to show her how to make one with secret buttons to open it. She wanted to hide her phone in the box.

"Hey, Jonah!" she called, stepping into the shop. She liked being here. She liked the wood smell, the flecks of wood floating in the sunlight through the windows, the quiet.

"What's up, Squirt?"

She smiled. She liked that name better than *Bunny*.

"Louis licked my hand and rubbed it with his cheek!"

He turned to her on his stool. "I'll be damned. We'll have to call you the Cat Whisperer."

"I like *Squirt* better. I hate whispering."

"Squirt it is. But I put Bunny on your nameplate."

"My what?"

He held out a low sign with her name in wood letters. "Put it on your worktable."

She did. It looked nice. She only wished it said Beth Ann instead of Bunny. "Thank you." She noticed a stack of toothpick boxes and some glue.

"I was thinking you might want to try some toothpick sculptures," Jonah said. "I pulled up a website. Take a look."

She clicked the mouse and saw pictures of toothpick buildings and objects. "This is so cool." She clicked through the pictures, then stopped at the perfect one. "I'm going to make a castle," she announced. "With a drawbridge and everything."

"You need help, let me know."

"Thanks." But she thought she could follow the picture just fine. She liked Jonah. He was patient and kind and he made her feel calm. In here with him, she forgot to feel sad about Serena or lonely or afraid that her dad would find them.

Jonah's shop was like a castle, too. She felt safe inside. She kind of wished she never had to leave.

ROSIE IGNORED THE nurse at the checkout desk and marched right out the clinic door.

"Send the bill," Cara said, then hurried after Rosie, who was already at the car, her hands shaking so much she dropped her keys.

Cara picked them up. "I can drive," she said.

"Good for you." Rosie grabbed the keys, unlocked the doors and got behind the wheel, starting off the instant Cara shut the door. Rosie's eyes stared dead ahead, her mouth a grim line.

"It's just a mass, Rosie." *Tumor* sounded so much worse. "They need to take it out to see if it's benign." Cara had sat with Rosie for the talk after the exam, so she'd heard the doctor describe the required outpatient surgery needed on Rosie's stomach.

Rosie rammed the accelerator and they lurched onto Main, cutting off a car that blasted its horn.

"It's a shock, but don't assume the worst. The odds are in your favor."

Rosie slammed on the brakes yards before the intersection, earning more honks. "The odds? The odds are *never* in my favor. I'm not a lucky person. Never have been." She roared through the red light.

Cara decided to hold her tongue so they could make it through town without an accident. Once they were on open road, she said, "It's a simple outpatient procedure. You could visit your friend in Tucson."

"If they cut me open, I'm a goner. A deal's a deal. I got checked."

"You don't know what's wrong yet."

"Not part of the deal."

They pulled into the café lot and Cara beat Rosie to the door, blocking her way. "Even if it *is* cancer, it can be treated. Millions of people live long and happy lives afterward."

"Get out of my way." Rosie's eyes burned at Cara. Her grandmother had never been so ferocious, but Cara refused to quail.

"How about this? I'll stay until you get the procedure. A whole extra week with a waitress. You want that, right?"

"Move or I'll knock you flat."

She moved, letting Rosie lead the way upstairs. Logic, begging and bargaining weren't working.

She needed a new approach. There was always Jonah, but his blunt words might make things worse.

In Rosie's kitchen, Cara took a handful of jelly beans from the bowl, putting back all but her favorites—green. Green for good luck. What had Rosie said? *I'm not a lucky person. Never have been.*

That gave her an idea. What if she made good-luck buns for Rosie? She'd make sure Rosie got a green bean for good luck. It might not change Rosie's mind, but it would surely cheer her up, especially if Cara involved Beth Ann. Rosie had a soft spot for Beth Ann, and her daughter had wanted Cara to make the buns anyway.

At least the pecan rolls had gotten her past the bitter memory of Barrett and the ruined muffins, the sting as each one struck her face or chest, accompanied by a hateful insult. At first, the smell and feel of the dough had made her stomach roil, but she'd gritted her teeth and pushed on, determined to do what she could to save Rosie's café. By the time Cara pulled the first batch out of the oven, she was fine.

She took the bowl of jelly beans to the café kitchen, pulled out a selection of ingredients, then headed out to Jonah's shop to get her daughter.

Reaching the door, she started inside, then heard Beth Ann's voice and stopped to listen.

"Do I really have to wait for the glue to dry before I stand the castle walls up?" she asked.

Cara saw she was building with toothpicks. What a good idea. Cara should have suggested that. She'd been so preoccupied with the café and Rosie, she'd left her daughter to amuse herself. Not very responsible of her.

Jonah looked up from the mahogany bench he was sanding—the one with hearts modeled after Cara's lips. The thought made her face grow hot.

"If the sticks slip, the foundation will be unstable," he said. "Mistakes amplify. You know what that means? *Amplify?*"

"Get louder?" Beth Ann answered.

"Or bigger. Yeah."

Beth Ann sighed. "Then how do I make the drawbridge go up and down?"

"What would you guess?"

"A string? If I can poke it between the picks?"

"Worth a try."

"Do toothpicks forgive?"

Jonah chuckled. "Guess we'll find out."

"Guess we will." Beth Ann gave a contented sigh.

Cara felt a stab of envy at how comfortable her daughter was with Jonah. She hadn't been that easy with Cara in years.

Was it bad that Beth Ann had trusted him so readily? Was her daughter too trusting? Jonah was a good person, Cara was certain, but people could hide their true natures. Barrett was proof of that.

She didn't want her daughter to fear men, but caution was vital. Cara's own choices made her no role model. That made her stomach churn.

But that was a worry for another day. Beth Ann was content at the moment and that was good.

"Hey there," Cara said softly.

Jonah and Beth Ann seemed slow to turn away from their work, making her feel even more like an interloper than when she'd scared away the cat.

"You're building with toothpicks," Cara said, moving close to Beth Ann's stool. She saw a toothpick castle on the monitor. "A castle, huh?"

"Jonah got me the stuff. He made this for me." Beth Ann pointed at a nameplate with *Bunny* spelled out in wooden letters. "I can take it wherever I go."

"How nice." But she felt a twinge. When would Beth Ann have a permanent place she could mark as her own? Not for a while. Like Cara's garden, it was a distant dream.

"Thank you, Jonah," she said. "We know how busy you are."

"Bunny's good company," Jonah said.

"See?" Beth Ann beamed.

"I do. In fact, I'd like your company right now. Remember those good-luck buns I told you about? I thought we'd make some."

"Not today. Jonah's going to start me on my puzzle box."

"It's a surprise for Rosie. She's feeling blue."

"If I have to..." Beth Ann sighed, but she got down from the stool. "You promise we can do the box tomorrow, Jonah?"

"Swear to God." Jonah held up a hand.

Satisfied, Beth Ann started for the door.

"I see how I rate," she said to Jonah, joking, but a bit hurt by her daughter's rejection.

"Can I talk to you?" Jonah asked.

"Sure." She turned to her daughter. "Beth Ann, can you start sorting the jelly beans by color? They're in the café kitchen."

Beth Ann scurried off and Cara went to Jonah.

"Rosie'd rather swim in fryer oil than confide in me. You have any idea what's got her down?"

She cringed. She'd promised Rosie not to tell Jonah. "She'll tell you when she's ready, I'm sure." She hoped that would be soon.

"If anyone could drag it out of her it's you."

"I don't know about that."

"I do. You're good with people—customers, Ernesto, Rosie...even me. And I've heard that's no picnic." His smile was wry.

"You're good with my daughter," she said, feeling a stab of guilt that Beth Ann felt more relaxed with Jonah than with her own mother.

He shrugged that off. "She's easy."

"Not with me, she's not."

"That's because you're her mother. I'm a stranger she has to be polite to."

"It's more than that. You make her feel safe. Relaxed. When I saw her in here the other day, she was humming."

"Yeah. She does that."

"Not for years." Cara's throat tightened.

"You worry about her." It wasn't a question.

"She won't let me comfort her. She won't talk about what's troubling her. I don't know how to help her." She couldn't even make her daughter feel safe.

"You're a good mother," Jonah says. "She knows that. You'll sort it out."

"That's kind of you, but you don't know our… situation." He didn't know Cara had stayed too long after she'd seen the cold steel that lay beneath Barrett's loving mask. Beth Ann had suffered from Cara's bad judgment.

"I know what I see." His eyes were so steady, so certain. If only he were right. With all her heart, she wanted him to be.

"Thank you for that." She felt a little better, whether it was justified or not.

"Actually, I wanted to thank you. That day with the rocking chair."

"Really?" That surprised her. "I was sure I'd upset you."

"At first. But then it felt good to see you and Bunny enjoying it. I didn't build that chair to gather dust." He pressed a palm to his chest. "You showed me I'd gotten past this bad patch I've been going through."

He meant with his wife and the lost pregnancy, she was sure. Emotion tightened Cara's throat. "I'm glad then."

"Me, too." He held her gaze. The connection clicked between them, stronger than ever. Jonah didn't know her story, but *he knew her*. And she knew him. It felt good…important…right.

"I'm glad you're still here," Jonah said. Wham. Desire burned through her, hotter than ever and it lit those gold sparks in Jonah's dark eyes.

For a moment, she wanted more, to kiss and be kissed, to see what happened next, to—

"Mom!" Beth Ann's shout from the café door jerked her back to earth.

"I have to go." She nearly ran to the café. This longing was useless. Why couldn't she let it go? In some ways, she was as stubborn as Rosie.

CHAPTER EIGHT

"I WANT THE rolls to taste like all the jelly bean flavors at once," Beth Ann said. "Like a rainbow." Cara had told her what each color meant and they'd agreed to leave out the bad-luck black jelly beans altogether.

"A rainbow it is," Cara said. After some discussion, they decided to use cherries, blueberries, orange and lemon zest, cinnamon, nutmeg, vanilla, peanuts and cashews. They took turns stirring and adding ingredients. Cara was relieved to notice that Beth Ann was totally enthralled.

"One final taste before we bake," Cara said, holding out a dab on the rubber spatula.

Beth Ann licked it off and savored the morsel, eyebrows dipped in concentration. "It has all the flavors. I think it's right."

"Good. Let's ball up the rolls, put them in the muffin tin, then you can add the fortunes."

As Beth Ann poked jelly beans into the center of each roll, she said, "I wish we could put in real charms like on my bracelet. A heart for love. A coin for money. A clover for good luck. But they could break your teeth. Would plastic ones work?"

"No, but gummy candy would. Like the gummy worms I made for Halloween. I could make molds from your charms in an ice cube tray."

"Can we do that?"

"Absolutely. Next time." And there would be more baking now, Cara realized. The joy of it rose in her again like bread dough on a sunny counter. And it was such a pleasure to share it with her daughter.

"This is fun. We invented a food." Beth Ann looked so happy that Cara wanted to weep with joy. This was what she wanted for her daughter. Days full of fun and laughter, no pain, no fear, no sad shadows from the past. She would make it happen, no matter what.

Cara opened the oven door so Beth Ann could slide the tray inside.

"But what if they don't taste as good when they're baked?" Beth Ann asked.

"Then we'll try again. *Practice makes perfect.* That's what my grandmother always said. It took me forever to get pie crust right. It came out tough or soggy or crumbly. But she never gave up on me." Her grandmother had praised each tiny improvement, her love as thick in the air as the smell of pie in the oven afterward.

"That's what Jonah says," Beth Ann said. "He

says a craft means you make mistakes, but keep getting better." She pondered that for a moment. "Wood doesn't forgive mistakes. Does dough?"

"Depends on the mistake," Cara said. "A small one you can fix—say you forget the nuts. But add too much salt or bake it too long and you're done for."

"Like with Daddy's muffins," Beth Ann said in a low voice.

Ice froze Cara's blood. Had Beth Ann heard the fight? "You remember that?" she said warily.

"I saw them in the trash. My bowl, too. It got broke."

"It did. By accident," she said, relieved that Beth Ann didn't know more. It was a sobering thought that stayed with Cara as they cleaned up the kitchen and waited for the rolls to bake. Beth Ann seemed quieter, too. Would they ever get past the bad memories?

The rolls turned out perfectly, round and golden-brown. Cara tipped them onto a plate. Beth Ann tore open one and took a bite. "Mmm." Her eyes widened. "It's even better than the batter. It tastes just like a rainbow."

Cara took part of Beth Ann's to taste. It was tangy, sweet and nutty. "Yum."

"Here's Rosie's. Let's put it on top." They'd marked it with three blueberries.

Upstairs, Beth Ann fetched a grumpy Rosie from her bedroom.

"Good God, what's all this fuss over a roll?" Rosie groused.

Beth Ann held out the marked one. "It tells your fortune!"

"My what?"

"With jelly beans. Each color means something. You'll win money or fall in love or get lucky. We invented it."

"My grandmother used to bake them when she had a decision to make or a worry." Cara gave Rosie a pointed look. "She called them good-luck buns."

"See what you got, Rosie," Beth Ann said. "Here, Mom." She handed Cara a roll and took one for herself. "Ready, set, open."

They pulled their rolls apart, filling the air with the smell of spice, citrus and cherry. Cara's jelly bean was yellow—*you'll come into money.* If only that were true. Money would solve most of her problems.

Rosie's, of course, was green. But so was Beth Ann's.

"We *both* got green for good luck," Beth Ann said, eyes wide in surprise. "So we get double luck!"

"Yeah?" A smile flickered, then faded on Rosie's face.

"Taste it," Beth Ann said.

Rosie took a bite.

"Plus, now you don't have to be scared of the doctor."

Rosie stopped midchew. "Excuse me?"

"Because of the good luck you just got."

"You heard us talking?" Cara said, staring at her daughter.

"You were loud." Beth Ann shrugged. "Rosie made a deal to go to the doctor if we stayed longer."

At least Beth Ann didn't seem to know about today's appointment.

"When I had to get stitches," Beth Ann said to Rosie, "I was scared, too. I took Bunny with me so I wouldn't cry and I didn't."

Her daughter still clutched Bunny to keep from crying.

"That's good advice, don't you think?" Cara said, fighting emotions—sadness for her daughter and pride in her, too, for trying to help Rosie.

"You could bring that picture of Eddie on your nightstand," Beth Ann continued. "Anytime you get scared, just look at it."

Rosie seemed too stunned to speak.

"Don't you like the roll?" Beth Ann asked.

Rosie lifted it to her mouth, then set it down again, turning to Cara. "If I do this," she said slowly, "you have to stay until I…" She cleared her throat and looked away. "Until it's over."

Did she really think the surgery would kill her? Poor Rosie. Cara wanted so much to ease her worry, but the woman was a brick wall.

Except she'd crumbled just now. For Beth Ann. The two shared a similar bond to the one Cara had had with her grandmother.

"Can we stay?" Beth Ann asked, her eyes as big as Christmas morning. "For Rosie? Please."

How long would that require? A month maybe? And what about after? If the tumor were cancer, Rosie would be so scared. She would need all the support she could get. "We have commitments," she said faintly. "And then there will be school for you."

"Can we stay until school starts? Please? Please?"

Cara was startled by how much Beth Ann wanted this. She looked at Rosie. In her stubborn, gruff way, Rosie was pleading with her, too.

She blew out a breath, giving in. "If my job and the apartment will wait..."

"Yay! I get to stay!" Beth Ann jumped up and down. "We both got good luck, Rosie! *Double* good luck."

Rosie had gone slack with relief. "The rest of the deal's still on," Rosie said. "Jonah is not to know."

"You're kidding," Cara said.

"Not one word. And that goes for you, too,

young lady." Rosie turned her attention to Beth Ann. "This whole talk we just had is top, top secret. Got that?"

"I do. Pinky swear." Beth Ann crooked a little finger for Cara and Rosie to grip.

"Pinky swear," they all said together.

Rosie picked the jelly bean out of her bun and looked at it. "Good luck from a jelly bean. What are you two doing to me?"

Anything we can to help. Cara had her doubts about staying, but the fact that Rosie needed her meant a lot. Cara had a place here, a role to play, a job to do. All her life, she'd longed for that feeling.

That was why she'd wanted college in the first place. But Barrett had crushed that dream and nearly killed her for daring to have it. She'd rallied and tried again only to have him return and send her running for her life.

Cara would not give up. In the meantime, she would help Rosie with her health and her café.

She took a bite of her bun. It was really, really good. *Maybe they could sell them in the café.* They would bag them by the dozen and include a card explaining each fortune. What a great idea!

Every day she stayed here her confidence grew. The café had pulled her out of the tailspin of Barrett's return. *And, don't forget Jonah.* Jonah was good for her, too. Cara was glad she'd be seeing more of him. She couldn't deny that.

And what about Barrett? The thought came again, as it always did when she had a quiet moment. They were safe here. If they made no calls, stayed off the internet, opened no accounts, they should be okay, right?

A shiver ran down her spine, so she opened another bun for luck.

Red. *You'll fall in love.* Impossible, of course. But her heart turned over in her chest all the same.

BARRETT FORCED A smile, then took a sip of the foul-tasting powdered iced tea Deborah had insisted on serving him. She'd made him wait forever while she'd mixed it up and fixed a tray with a dozen stale, store-bought ginger snaps.

It infuriated him that Cara had chosen to live in this sad cracker-box of a house, which reeked of cigarette smoke and cheap air freshener, when she and Beth Ann could have lived in luxury at his mother's. He didn't dare think about that very long or his rage would flare. He had to focus on the future, start fresh, forgive and forget.

Barrett had a few final questions before he could escape the place. "You must see how painful this is for me, Deborah. All I live for is to see my wife and little girl again."

"Oh, I know, and it just breaks my heart." Deborah snapped up another cookie. She'd nervously inhaled six already, afraid Barrett might blame her for Cara's actions. "My daughter has it in her head that you mean her harm," she said. "She can be so *stubborn,* that girl."

"And you can't recall any friends Cara mentioned who might know where they've gone?"

"Not really, no." Deborah gave him a shaky smile and took another cookie. "She didn't confide in me. Never has."

Barrett knew Deborah was a narcissist, totally oblivious to her daughter or anyone else but herself.

He wanted to sweep the tray and its contents to the floor in pure frustration, but he forced himself to speak calmly. "And Beth Ann never received any of my letters, as far as you know?"

"Cara always got the mail."

And paid most of the bills, he assumed, based on Deborah's complaints about her living expenses *these days.*

"How about Beth Ann? Did she have friends?"

"She finally made one this year. Serena…Sandoval, I think. Little Mexican girl. Not much English, but she always put away her dishes and said please and thank you. They were thick as thieves, those two."

Barrett perked up. Maybe Beth Ann had told her friend their plans. "Does she live nearby? Serena?"

"No, no. They're out in a mobile home park. Desert Sands…Silver Sands…I don't recall."

That was a start, at least. He pulled out the check he'd prepared to cement Deborah's loyalty. "I want to thank you for all you've done for my family…and for your faith in me." He held it out.

"Oh, that's not necessary," she said, staring at the dollar amount, then taking the check. "You've always been generous."

"You'll call if you hear from her or remember anything else?"

"Oh, absolutely."

Deborah had always been his advocate. *Couples argue, accidents happen,* had been her take on the incident that had torn apart his family.

"Was there a memento you wanted from their room?" she asked.

"No, no. Just seeing where they slept helped me." He'd asked for a private moment so he could search for receipts, brochures, business cards, any clue to where Cara and Beth Ann might have gone or to whom they'd spoken.

Cara had been careful. Neither one had used Deborah's desktop computer. Cara had taken her laptop with her.

"What should I do with the rest of their things?" Deborah asked.

Burn them. They reek of you and this hovel. "I'll let you know," he said with feigned sadness.

He drove away, waving as she stood in the driveway. As soon as he rounded the corner, he pulled to the curb and released his fury in the safety of his car, bellowing and pounding the steering wheel until he feared he'd broken a knuckle. Then he called his P.I.

"What'd you get?" Malloy asked right off.

"Not much. Her mother's an idiot. She had to *look up* their cell phone numbers—both phones are dead, by the way. She barely recalled the name of Beth Ann's school, let alone the one where Cara worked. They left a week ago."

"That's when she closed out her checking account."

"No clues at the house. She left the BMW and took her mother's clunker. I've got the plate number."

"I'll check for tickets. It's a long shot, but worth trying."

"Deborah said the car's been acting funny," Barrett added. "If it breaks down, they'd be stranded. Cara's only got $500."

"It's possible," Malloy said, but Barrett knew Malloy was humoring him.

"Or she could have bought plane tickets," he said gloomily. "Face it. In a week, they could be anywhere."

"I'll pretext her principal with a job-reference inquiry and see what he knows, tap into her school email, see if I can connect with any colleagues. Don't worry. I have a trick or two up my sleeve."

"You'd better at the rate I'm paying you."

"Worse comes to worst, Cara will have to request school records in the fall."

"That's months away." He wanted his family *now*. "I'm going to talk to a friend of Beth Ann's. She's Mexican, possibly illegal. That will give me leverage with her parents if I need it."

"Hang tough. Cara will surface. It's impossible to truly disappear these days. She'll make a mistake and we'll catch her. Don't worry."

Easy for Malloy to say. Barrett needed Cara and Beth Ann like life itself. In fact, he woke at night gasping for air, still in prison until he was reunited with them. He wanted it to be how it had been at first, when Cara was sweet and eager to please. She'd needed him and he'd wanted to give her the world. When Beth Ann was born—their love made flesh—it had been perfect.

Until Beth Ann started school and Cara got bored and confused. He'd been too busy at work to catch the signs in time, but he'd learned his lesson. This time he'd have clear priorities and so would she.

Barrett was willing to forgive Cara for all of it—for putting him in prison, for turning his daughter against him, even for this betrayal, running away.

If he could do that, she could surely forgive him his part in the accident—his one mistake.

Forgiveness was the answer. Forgiveness would make them whole again.

If he knew Cara at all, she wanted what he did—to have their happy family back. And he did know her—better than she knew herself. This was his chance to prove it.

THE NEXT EVENING, the breeze lifted Cara's hair from her forehead, but it didn't cool her one bit as she crossed the gravel yard toward Jonah's trailer carrying the plate of good-luck buns she wanted him to try.

It wasn't the summer heat that made sweat trickle down her face, her ribs and the backs of her legs.

She was *nervous*. It wasn't her errand—to tell him she'd be staying the summer and her plans for the café—it was that she'd never been to his place before. Cara had taken extra care getting dressed tonight, without admitting to herself why, donning a red-silk tank and white denim skirt, earrings and full makeup. She'd even curled her hair, as if she were going to a party...*or out on a date*.

So stupid. What on earth would Jonah think?

Already, he would think her insanely ambitious with his aunt's café. Rosie had made her promise not to mention the foreclosure either.

The strings of white lights on Jonah's deck were bright against the newly darkened sky. Red geraniums in barrels and the homey wood furniture softened the futuristic effect of the silver trailer.

At the door, Cara paused to breathe in the smell of pines mixed with the warm yeasty aroma of the buns, which she'd wrapped in plastic and placed on one of Rosie's decorative plates, covered with baby chicks popping out of eggs. Wooden wind chimes clinked like a quiet xylophone.

It was some seconds before Jonah responded to her tap on his door. She saw that he'd come from the shower, and the sight of him nearly took her breath away. He wore a towel around his hips, and water gleamed from his bare chest, his hair wet and tousled. He smelled of a fresh application of that woodsy spice of his, and it hit her so hard, her knees gave way like a girl with her first crush.

"What are you doing here?" he asked.

It took a second for her to respond. "Oh. Uh. Bringing you these." She thrust the plate of buns at him.

"Thanks." He started to close the door.

"Wait. Can I come in?" Her face burned.

"Oh. Sure. Dressed like that, I figured you were going somewhere." He looked her up and down.

Cara flushed even hotter. "Just to see you." *And be alone with you in your tiny trailer barely big enough for a bed. Ulp.*

"Come in then." He held the door as she passed, looking her over again, making her tingle everywhere his gaze landed.

They had no choice but to stand close together in the small space. The low ceiling made Jonah seem larger than ever beside her. He was barely dressed, the towel hanging so low it seemed about to drop. Desire swooshed through her on its familiar path, setting off little fires here and there.

Jonah swayed, possibly feeling it, too. He cleared his throat. "I'll put some clothes on." He set the plate of buns on the small table that divided the tiny kitchen from the main room, then tromped down the short hall.

"I'll wait here," she called, long seconds too late.

When he turned toward her to close the curtain that marked off the bedroom, she caught sight of his bed. *Where he slept. Naked?*

Cara wished she had a glass of water. All the moisture in her mouth was gone. Maybe turned into the sweat that had made her top stick to her stomach. She pulled the fabric away from her skin and looked around the compact space. Everything was in miniature—sink, stove, cupboards, even the windows. Framed photos placed on ledges along both walls drew her attention. Each showed a piece of furniture with a hand-scrawled description. Jonah's work, no doubt.

She was studying a picture of some elaborate built-in cabinets when Jonah emerged, as sexy in a black T-shirt and cargo shorts as he'd been in nothing but a towel.

"You do cabinetry, too?" She nodded at the photograph.

"Not anymore." He frowned briefly. "A partner and I did high-end cabinetry. He found the clients. I built the cabinets. Furniture's more interesting."

She wondered what had happened, but knew better than to ask. He'd moved to the table, clearly to change the subject.

"So what's this you brought?" He peeled back the plastic and picked up a bun.

Cara joined him. "They're called good-luck buns." She reached past him to pick one up, vividly aware of how close her arm was to his chest. The chest that had been bare and water-dotted just seconds ago. She was here for business reasons, but they stood barely a kiss apart and his scent was turning her knees to wet noodles.

"So, what, you eat a bun and get lucky? Be great at pickup bars. Save on small talk." His eyes twinkled at her.

"Would you like that? Getting lucky without having to say a word?"

"I'm not much on the subtleties of banter, but I know a loaded question when I hear one, CJ. Let's move on."

"Good point. Open the roll and you'll find your fortune."

He tore the bun in two and picked out the candy. A heart glowed yellow in the center of the dime-sized red circle. She'd used yellow to color the shapes she embedded in the red candies. "A heart. What does that mean?"

"That you'll fall in love." Awkward. Maybe she should have marked a roll with a more neutral charm.

"What did you get?"

She ripped the roll apart and pulled out the charm. A heart.

"You'll fall in love, too. What are the odds?" He gave her a funny smile.

Did he think she'd set it up? That she wanted *them* to fall in love?

God no. "The charms must have clumped."

"Clumped, huh?" Jonah held her gaze.

"Definitely clumped." She took his charm and put it with hers on the table. "Anyway, taste the roll and tell me what you think."

He started to take a bite, then stopped. "Wait. You're not adding this to the menu, are you?"

"Actually, yes. Rosie thinks it's a good idea, too. We'll sell them by the dozen with little cards that explain the charms."

"We?" he said. "Don't you mean *me?* You'll be gone in a week."

"That's just it." Cara took a deep breath, knowing her face had to be as red as the gummy charm, then said what she had to say. "I've decided to stay for the summer."

Using the café's pay phone to call the center's blind number, Cara had confirmed that a two-month delay wouldn't lose her place in Phoenix. They had a protected way to get Beth Ann's records to her new school, too.

His eyebrows lifted. "What about your job? Your apartment? You were ready to tear out of here on the bus a few days ago."

"I know, but I make better money in the café, so I can pay for the car repair. Plus, Bunny likes it here. I'll still have the apartment and job." She tried to meet his gaze, hating that she had to lie about Rosie and their deal.

"If you say so." He blew out a breath, sounding unhappy. He wanted her gone? That hurt. Her cheeks stung with heat.

"You sound disappointed."

"No. It's good. I need a waitress." But he didn't look pleased.

"But you'd rather it wasn't me."

Jonah didn't confirm, but she could see it was true.

"Is it all my din? The French toast and pecan rolls and the coffee? My personality?"

"No. None of that." He dropped his roll on the

table. She set hers down, too, waiting for him to explain. "I was braced for you to leave."

"Okay…" Was that supposed to make her feel better?

His eyes dug in, dark with a golden glow. "Don't you get it? You…disrupt me." His voice was rough. "I can't think straight around you. More and more it's all I can do not to…" He tilted his head, shifted forward.

He wanted to kiss her. He could hardly stop himself.

The thrill of that zinged through her. The air between them nearly crackled with electricity. *Then do it. Kiss me. I want you to.* She angled her mouth, leaned in.

Jonah pulled backed. "But that can't happen. You don't want that."

Cara sucked in a breath. He was right. She knew it. Instantly, the rush stopped, the heat fled. A kiss would be just the start. After that came getting naked, touching each other in intimate spots. Then Jonah would be on top of her, weighing her down, overpowering her, and she would think of Barrett and panic.

That was the last thing she wanted.

They looked at each other for a long charged moment.

"I guess we'll have to be careful around each other," she said.

"Meaning?"

"You know. Avoid temptation."

"Like being alone with my bed close enough to fall into? With you in a clingy top and a short skirt? With those lips?"

"And you smelling so good you make me weak in the knees?"

"Yeah? I had no idea aftershave had that power."

"Yours does. On you. You disrupt me, too." She felt dizzy, like her words were spinning her in a circle, turning her and turning her until she didn't know what she was doing. "I'd better go. I have some ideas to go over with you. Tomorrow, we'll talk. In the café. With customers all around."

"Right," he said, looking a little dazed himself.

"Taste the bun, okay? Tell me what you think."

"I will."

"Good night." She went to the door and twisted the knob. Then she remembered Rosie's fancy plate, and turned for it, finding herself against Jonah's chest, looking up at him.

His eyes widened in surprise, then he enclosed her in his arms and covered her lips with his own. He'd thought she'd changed her mind.

It felt like she had.

He tasted of mint and man and his lips were gentle, but insistent, giving and taking at once. He teased her lips with his tongue, seducing them open.

Everything in her wanted this. This kiss, this embrace, this man.

Desire roared through her, blocking her hearing, stopping all thought. Again, she felt swept into wild waters.

Cara grabbed on to Jonah's back, digging in her fingers, holding on tight, trying to stay above the flood. He deepened the kiss, pulled her closer, making it worse. And better. She didn't know what was happening.

She felt his body against hers, his hardness. He was ready for her.

Was she ready for him? She felt tight and liquid between her legs. That part of her was ready. It would be normal and natural to keep going, take the next step. They wanted each other, they liked and trusted each other.

But Cara wasn't normal, and nothing about sex would feel natural to her. Not now. Not for a long time. Maybe never.

She couldn't do this. The part of her that was strong enough to leave Barrett, that had helped her find a way out with Beth Ann, knew that.

Cara broke off the kiss, pushed out of his arms, fighting to breathe, to think, to explain. "I just wanted Rosie's plate," she managed to say.

Jonah appeared stricken. "My mistake." He turned to dump the remaining buns from the plate, and they tumbled to the floor. He thrust the dish at her.

"I'm sorry, Jonah. It wasn't you." She'd said that before. How totally lame, so weak. She was a scared rabbit, and as soon as she got the door open, she ran like one all the way to the safety of the café.

She was so ashamed. The man had barely kissed her and she'd acted like he'd threatened her life. How could she face him again?

For a few minutes, it was only her promise to Rosie that kept her from packing up and taking the bus in the morning.

CHAPTER NINE

JONAH STOOD watching CJ cross the yard, feeling six shades of stupid. She'd turned back for *the plate* and he'd basically assaulted her.

She'd kissed him back, sure, but not for long.

Was he that desperate, that out of control?

CJ was running from her ex-husband, he was almost certain, and the man had likely abused her. God knows what he'd done to her in bed. The thought made Jonah see red, made him want to find the guy and beat him to a pulp. *Just like your old man. Solve it with your fists.*

Jonah shook his head. The point was some guy had given CJ trouble, and the last thing she needed was more from Jonah.

What she needed was a friend. What she needed was to feel safe. And he'd gone and scared her.

He made sure she got into the café, then shut his door.

What the hell was wrong with him?

CJ would be here all summer. He'd better fix it fast, be an adult from now on, keep his hands to himself, support her, listen to her, keep her daughter busy in the shop and say yes to whatever she wanted to do to the café.

She deserved a good man. Someone worthy of her trust, who would consider her needs first, let her call the shots, and always, always be there for her, through good times and bad. That was not Jonah. He'd proved that once and for all with Suzanne.

He found the torn roll on the table and took a bite. It was tasty. Complex. Tangy and sweet. Like a fruit muffin but airier. Even the nuts tasted better than usual. Peanuts...cashews, too. And CJ wanted to sell the buns in the café. More mess, more trouble. He threw out the rolls that had hit the floor, swept the candy charms into his hand. He started to toss them in the trash, but they glowed golden in his palm. CJ had gone bright red when their charms had matched. They'd *clumped,* she said. That made him smile.

What the hell. He'd keep them. He dropped them onto the windowsill next to the jade plant he couldn't seem to kill.

You're going to fall in love. Yeah, right. Did she have a charm for hopeless horn dogs?

Through the window, he spotted Louis slinking toward the trailer, so he went out to pretend he didn't notice when the cat tucked in for his nightly scratch. As far as dealing with needs and feelings, a cat was about his speed.

AT 5:00 P.M. the next day, Cara set two places on the café counter, wiped her palms on her apron and inhaled deeply. She was holding a tasting of the new menu ideas for Jonah and Ernesto. As soon as the café closed, she had started cooking. The pair of them were due any minute.

Sure enough, the door jangled and in came Jonah.

Cara's heart lifted at the sight of him. She couldn't help it. "Hey," she said, glad she could blame the steamy kitchen for her red face.

"Hey." He gave her that look, cool as the iced coffee they now offered, just like this morning's and all day when their eyes met. She'd expected awkwardness. She was mortified, after all. But coldness? Distance. That felt awful. The kiss had ruined their friendship.

"Ernesto can't make it," Jonah said. "Some family thing."

"Oh." They would need Ernesto as sous-chef if they added the menu items Cara wanted. "So it's just us then." She swallowed.

"You think that's bad? The two of us alone?"

She gave a wry smile. "After today, when you treated me like I had the plague? I doubt there will be a problem."

He frowned. "After last night, I figured you'd want me to steer clear. I attacked you."

"You didn't *attack* me. I wanted you to kiss me. I wanted to kiss you."

Jonah stared at her, not understanding.

"Look...I'm not in good shape for...intimacy." She couldn't even say *sex*.

"I pushed you. I saw your face."

"No, Jonah. I'm messed up. I wish I wasn't. I'm sorry."

"Don't be. I was out of line."

"I won't if you won't," she said. "Be sorry, I mean."

Jonah studied her for a long moment. "Okay," he finally said.

"So, we're good? Able to pass within a foot of each other without flinching?"

"Depends on how disruptive you plan to be." A smile flickered on his face and it made her feel so much better.

"Yes! That's what I missed today. The joking around, the teasing." She'd missed *him*. "We're back to being friends."

"Guess we are."

The surge hit again. *She wanted him.* She could see the same reaction in his eyes. That had to stop.

They *were* friends. They'd shared a little of their personal stories. Jonah had been good to her and kind to Beth Ann. He'd said Cara had helped him. They cared for each other.

If only they could try...

No. She forced her thoughts in line. No wishes. No if-onlys. Just here and now and how things were.

"So, let's get this done." Jonah gave a weary sigh and headed for the counter.

"You make it sound like torture."

"That's later when I have to cook it all." But his teasing smile was back. Much better. They would be okay. All she had to do was focus on doing her best for Rosie and the café. She was nervous about the ideas she had, whether they were good, whether they would work, but Rosie kept encouraging her.

Jonah's approval would help.

"Have a seat. I'll be right out."

CJ BUSTLED INTO the kitchen and Jonah climbed onto a stool to wait for her to turn his menu upside down. What just happened? She didn't blame him for the kiss. That was good. She wanted them to be friends.

Friends. Yeah, he could do that. She'd missed the teasing and joking. He'd missed *her.* Period. He wanted her in his arms and in his bed.

Can't happen. Forget it.

If she could, he could. So he sat there while she dashed out with dish after dish, explaining each one, sampling them with him, comparing opinions, deciding on spices and salt, leaning across the counter, giving him a way too tempting view of the tops of her breasts. Lace on the bra, too. Mmm.

"Well?"

"Huh?" She'd asked him a question.

"Is there too much tarragon in the green goddess dressing?"

He took a bite of lettuce and savored the dressing. "Tastes like licorice? Yeah. Too strong."

"That's what I thought. Okay. I'll back that down. The garlic parmesan dressing is good?" She seemed so nervous. Her color was high and she kept biting her lip and bobbing side to side. She was smart, she knew what she was doing, but she seemed to doubt herself.

"It's great, like I said. Looks like you've got plans for Rosie's garden. The bistro girls won't be happy to lose the produce."

"Can't be helped. Garden-fresh dishes will bring in more health-conscious patrons. We need another niche."

She went on about ads and specials and coupons and maybe a highway billboard until his head spun.

"You seem to know a lot about the restaurant business. You get your degree in that?"

CJ froze, then looked down at the counter. "I don't have a degree. Not yet anyway." She glanced at him, embarrassed, it seemed.

"Not a big deal," he said. "College doesn't guarantee much these days. People I know—"

"I'm halfway toward a teaching degree," she blurted.

He studied her. "Teaching, huh? You'll be good at that."

"I hope so. I won't really know until I student teach."

"Come on. You're smart, energetic, enthusiastic. You're good with people. You care. What else do you need?"

"A lot, trust me. I want to teach middle school. There's so much about psychology, how people learn, the curriculum, brain development." She'd flushed when he'd praised her.

"You're brave." He smiled. "Middle school is hormone hell."

"It's a crucial time. Kids solidify their beliefs about themselves during those years. I kind of got lost then. If a teacher had encouraged me, I might have pushed myself more, ended up less timid."

"Timid? I don't see that."

"You don't?"

"No. You gave me hell from the day you walked in here. Relentless is more like it."

"Really? That's good, I guess." Emotions swirled in her blue eyes, not all of them happy. "After I had my, um, rough patch, it took a while to build my confidence." She swallowed. "I've had a setback." CJ glanced at him. "But with you, here in the café, I think I've bounced back. It's been good for me."

For some reason, his eyes started watering. "All I can say is if you can get me frosting pecan rolls, you'll have seventh graders writing operas and acting out quadratic equations."

CJ smiled a big, bright, treasure box of a smile, and it lit him up inside. She'd been good for him, too.

She served him beef and chicken curry turnovers, home-style mac-and-cheese, fried catfish in panko crumbs, grilled zucchini in a peanut sauce, fried pickle chips and sweet potato fries.

Jonah savored every bite, snared constantly by the sparkle in her blue eyes, the soft fullness of her lips shiny with oil. It made him light-headed.

"Huh?" CJ had asked him another question.

"I said you're probably wondering how we'll prep all this."

"Sure. Yeah." But he'd been too distracted. "How will we?"

She told him she thought Ernesto could help, doing some of the baking, gradually taking over as sous-chef as they got busier and more money came in. Ernesto had a cousin, Hector, who could take over as busboy.

"You've thought this through," Jonah said.

"I had time last night. I didn't sleep well."

"Me neither." He'd relived that kiss a million times, then slapped himself down for taking advantage of her. She'd taken the guilt away, though, when she'd told him she wasn't sorry, that she'd wanted it, too, but had just lost her nerve.

"That's all I've got for now," CJ said finally. *Finally.* She'd wreaked enough havoc on the menu. "No dessert, but I do want to add more baked goods. So…what do you think?" She looked at him eagerly, excited about it.

What did he think? *My life would be so much easier if I'd closed up early the day you walked in smelling so pink.* But what he said was, "Long as we ease into it, dish by dish, I'm good."

"Really? That's so great. I'm so glad. Help me clean up and we can talk about the renovations."

"The…what?" But CJ had flitted off and he had no choice but to follow her. He washed dishes, while she put away food, and rattled on about painting the interior, reupholstering the benches and making a new sign to reflect the fresh new menu. Damn, what had he said yes to?

She reached over his head to put away the pepper jar. He steadied her at the hips, liking the weight of her in his hands, the curve, the give of her flesh. And she smelled so damn *pink.*

CJ turned to him, leaning against his arm. "So will you do it?"

"Will I…"

"Sketch the new sign. Weren't you listening?"

"Doing my damnedest." He blew out a breath. "Yeah. I'll sketch it. I'll build it. I'll reupholster the benches and get Evan to help me paint the place."

"But you have your show and all."

"I'll fit it in when I can."

CJ looked stunned. "Are you sure?"

Hell, no. But he was too far gone to back out now. He was under her spell, swept up in all her energy and fire. Whatever she needed, he'd do—bag her happy buns, frost her rolls and rinse grit from Rosie's greens. Hell, if she asked, he'd probably build a gazebo and a koi pond out back. "Of course I'm sure."

She squealed and threw her arms around him. Just like that he had her body against his, the soft give of her breasts, her warmth, the weight of her in his arms.

CJ backed away with a shaky breath.

It took Jonah a second to see straight. "If you're serious about all that baked crap, you'll need a display case. Lighted. Rotating shelves. I'll see what I can put together."

"That would be amazing." She stepped forward, as if to hug him, then thought better of it, bouncing foot to foot. Finally, she held out a hand for him to shake.

He linked fingers with her and gave her small

hand a squeeze. It seemed like the most natural thing to do.

She squeezed back. Her eyes flitted all over his face, similar to the way she zipped around his kitchen. When they let go, his hand felt too empty.

Jonah couldn't offer her much, but he could do this. Cook for her. Paint and build and sketch. *He'd need a small motor for the shelves...*.

"This will be fun, won't it?" she said.

"It'll be a hell of a lot of work." The fun would be being in the eye of her hurricane and watching her fly, seeing her zest for everything she did. "And fun. That, too."

Their gazes tangled. CJ looked so happy that he got another hot oil pop. By now his chest should look like a shot-up highway sign. She took a ragged breath and swayed closer. A few more inches and she'd be in his arms...

The pay phone by the johns rang. CJ jumped like she'd been bitten. Her eyes went wide. "I'll get it. You can go. I'll finish up."

She wanted him out of here. Was she expecting the call? On the pay phone? Why? There was the café phone and Rosie's upstairs.

He went to check the food order, then headed out, pausing to say goodbye to her. CJ stood in the hall, frozen and pale, her eyes blank.

"Who was on the phone?" he asked.

"Nobody. Nothing. I'll see you tomorrow." She turned for Rosie's stairs.

Something was wrong. The call had been bad. It wasn't his business. Rosie was nosy enough for ten people. CJ wouldn't want to talk about it. He knew that already.

Jonah stood, jaw locked, fists working. *Stay or go. Decide.*

It was the look on her face that got to him. She'd looked scared. Really scared. He turned on his heel and headed up the stairs after her.

CARA TOOK THE stairs on numb legs. *Barrett was after them.* The call from the domestic violence counselor confirmed it. When she'd arranged to get Beth Ann's school records, the secretary had told her that someone claiming to be from Beth Ann's pediatrician's office had called for her new address to send her immunization records.

The secretary had thought that odd. Cara confirmed that the doctor whose name the person used wasn't Beth Ann's. It had been a ploy by Barrett or someone he'd hired to locate them. It also meant Barrett had talked to Cara's mother and learned the name of her school. Probably Cara's, too.

She'd expected this. She knew Barrett would try every tactic, but now it was real. It was as if

Barrett's hand had reached through the phone and grabbed her by the throat. She felt faint.

"Wait."

Jonah's voice from the bottom of the stairs startled her. She turned and he took the stairs two at a time, stopping below her so they stood eye to eye. "You're in trouble. The phone call was bad news."

"No. I'm not. It's…okay."

"It's not okay. You're shaking. Let me help you."

"You can't help me." *No one can.*

"Try me," he said.

For a second she wanted to. She wanted to fall into his arms and let him tell her it would be all right, even if it wouldn't be. But the social worker had been firm: *Tell no one. People talk. They forget their promises. They slip. They get tricked.*

"I really can't."

"Are you in danger? Because I'll—"

"Stop. Please." She had to give some explanation or he'd keep pushing. "It's a mix-up at the school where Beth Ann—" She put her hand to her mouth, horrified that she'd used her daughter's real name. "I mean Bunny. Her school records are wrong and—"

"Her real name is Beth Ann."

"Forget I said that. It's important."

"Fine."

But Jonah now knew they had false names.

He suspected they were in trouble. Cara's heart pounded in her ears. This wasn't good.

"Please don't ask for more," she said. "I'm okay. Really." She did not want a man to take over her problems. Barrett had done that, made choices for her, decisions that should have been hers. Jonah wanted to take over, too. He already had guessed too much.

"I have to go." She ran up the last few steps and into Rosie's apartment without looking back.

Inside, the panic hit full force. Barrett was hunting them down. They had to run, catch the bus in the morning and just go, go, *go*. She'd saved nearly a thousand dollars. Maybe Rusty would let her owe him the rest on the car.

You're in good hands. Jonah's words offered a flicker of respite. Enough that she was able to think it through.

Nothing had changed. Barrett hadn't learned a thing from the school. There was no reason to run. She'd promised Rosie she would stay. She had to tough it out. *You can handle this,* she told herself. *You have to.*

CHAPTER TEN

SOMEHOW, CARA pushed through the week, determined not to let her worry show. At night, panic washed over her like a fever, but she forced herself to think about the café and the changes they were making, and managed to get enough sleep to function.

She was grateful that Jonah had taken her at her word, that she was all right, though she felt his eyes on her a lot. He wanted to dig, to help, to take some action on her behalf. But this was her crisis to survive.

The new dishes and the renovation plans kept them too busy for much personal conversation. Ernesto turned out to be a genius baker and a damn good sous-chef. He was a quick learner and he had a great palate.

By Friday, they'd added all but one of the new dishes and they sold decently. There'd been a trickle of new diners curious about the changes. So far, her ideas seemed to be working.

The café renovations were coming together, too. She'd consulted with Jonah and Rosie on the colors, deciding on lilac and mustard for the walls with white wainscoting to break up the blocks of color. Jonah had found the perfect fabric for the stools and booths—white vinyl with confetti polka dots. She loved the new sign he'd sketched—a whimsical teacup with a curlicue of steam spelling out *Comfort Café*.

Cara thought they made a great team, with Jonah's artist's eye and her instincts about the food and ambiance. Fighting the physical attraction was exhausting, but the work *was* fun, just as she'd hoped. She and Jonah clicked the way she'd always thought a married couple would, working together, facing life's challenges, with shared values, mutual respect and heartfelt support for each other.

Stupidly, Cara kept slipping into a fantasy that they *were* together. It was an illusion, she knew, but it felt so good to have a man who cared about her, listened to her, enjoyed her, *wanted* her. A man with no hidden agenda or ill intent. A *good* man.

They'd earned a break, so Saturday night they were taking Beth Ann bowling at the Wash-Bowl-N-Brew. Jonah wanted to ask Evan to help paint the café…and check up on him, though he hadn't said that out loud.

"I don't need camp," Beth Ann said from the backseat of the extended cab of Jonah's truck.

"It'll be fun," Cara said. She had signed her daughter up for the YMCA's day camp starting Monday. Beth Ann needed to be with kids her own age. Rosie would drive her there and Cara would pick her up after the café closed. "Remember the good-luck bun last night? Clasped hands for *You'll make a friend?*"

"You faked that," Beth Ann said.

"I swear I didn't."

"You fake the fortunes?" Jonah asked in a low voice. "I'm shocked."

"Only in an emergency," she muttered to him, then turned to Beth Ann. "You can invite kids out for good-luck buns in the café maybe. Or when your birthday comes, for a party."

"*You* invite them for *your* birthday," she grumbled.

"You've got birthdays coming up?" Jonah asked.

"Bunny's is in two weeks, mine's in three."

"Ah." He found Beth Ann in the mirror. "So, Squirt, how old will you be? Thirteen?"

"No, ten," she said, sounding annoyed, but clearly pleased he'd guessed she was older. "Rosie can't drive me those days she's visiting Frieda."

"We'll work something out, don't worry."

Rosie was having the mass in her stomach removed the following Monday in an outpatient surgery center in Tucson. Her cover story was that she was visiting her friend for a few days.

"Just how did you convince Rosie to be away for the big sale?" Jonah asked. Rosie's parking-lot sale was that weekend.

"I have my ways," she said, wishing she could tell Jonah the truth.

"Smart move. She'd try to buy it all back, no doubt. And what the hell got into her to sell off the store space?" He shot Cara another look.

Cara squirmed in her seat. Her promise to Rosie was killing her. "The café project energized her." That much was true. Every time Cara expressed a doubt about one of her ideas, Rosie nudged her on. When Cara had wavered on the billboard because of the six-month lease, she'd said, *Grow some ovaries, girl. I'm the one writing the check.*

Rosie believed in her. That truth lit a fire in Cara every day.

"Something's up with her. Out of the blue she books four days with a friend she says is a *bossy old bat?* Then she gives me this speech—*Leave the damn nest, Jonah. Fly to New York and, for God's sake, get on with your life.*"

"She did?" Her heart pinched. She was preparing Jonah for her death.

"I don't get it. You find out anything?" He shot her another look.

"No more than before." Her stomach clenched

at the half truth. And what if it turned out to be cancer? Rosie would probably start planning her funeral. And treatment? Forget it. Rosie would fight that tooth and nail. What would Cara do then? She would have to find a way to help her. Rosie was family now.

Jonah pulled into the lot of the sprawling Wash-Bowl-N-Brew building. The car wash was dark, but the neon *Bowl-N-Brew* sign glowed pink, blue and yellow with a pin that slowly fell, then righted itself.

Jonah held down the seat for Beth Ann to get out, then came around to where Cara waited for him. They watched Beth Ann run inside, then Jonah turned to her.

"You nervous?" he asked. "Don't be. I'll take it easy on you."

"They don't call me Gutter Queen for nothing." They were both pretending the tension in the air was due to bowling and not to the fire they stoked between them with every shared glance.

"You probably just need some help with your form." He paused. "Though I don't think God himself could improve on that." He looked her over in a way that made her perfectly decent black capris and simple white blouse seem far too short and way too sheer. She felt hot all over.

"You're one to talk. I've seen you in only a towel."

He colored, which charmed her. It was surprisingly easy for her to flirt with Jonah. They spent a lot of time together, for one thing, but mainly it was that she trusted him not to push her.

He looked sexy as hell in butt-hugging jeans and a dark blue golf shirt that emphasized the swell of his biceps. Did bowling qualify as a tempting situation? Lately, anytime she was around him she was tempted.

They went inside. The '60s-era bowling alley was in good shape, she thought. A singer belted Motown from the bar at the far end. Beth Ann was watching some teenagers bowl.

They found Evan behind the counter talking with a cocktail waitress who held a tray of beers. When he saw Jonah, he straightened. "You checking up on me?" he asked in a joking tone, but he looked wary.

"We came to bowl," Cara said in case Jonah was about to bristle. "My daughter's over there." She pointed and Evan smiled, more relaxed now.

"Later," the barmaid said. "I owe you, Ev."

"Anytime," Evan said, watching her walk away, a smile on his face. "That was Nicolette," he said. "She'll tell you I'm strictly seltzer and lime. Go ask her."

"I'll take your word for it," Jonah said.

"Good. So what size shoes?"

After Evan had rung up their game and brought

their shoes, Jonah said, "Any chance you'd be available to help paint the café interior?"

"Rosie says you've been turning the place upside down."

"She did? Was she upset?" Cara asked, suddenly worried.

"Don't you know her by now? The more she complains, the happier she is." He turned to Jonah. "Yeah, I'll help you paint. Long as I'm not on shift here. I can bring Nicolette, too. And, actually, I have a favor I want to ask you two."

"Certainly," Cara said.

"I've started doing some music promotion for the bar and I—"

"Yeah?" Jonah tensed.

"Yeah. Some big-name bands blow by here on the way to L.A., so I've started booking them for weeknight gigs. My boss likes the idea."

"You sure that's wise?" Jonah's voice was sharp.

Evan looked at him. "Music is where I want to be. You know that. I'll be making good connections. So anyway—"

"That's where the trouble starts, Evan."

"You worry too much."

Cara could see Evan was trying to stay light, but anger simmered under his words.

"As I was saying, I've booked Devil's Anvil Reborn for a Thursday next month. You heard of them?"

"No, but—"

"You will. They're getting famous. Anyway, I'd like to host a private dinner for them in the café before their show. It'd be about a dozen people—band, manager, crew. Is that possible?"

"I think so," Cara said. "The renovations will be done, so the place should look good. It'll be after we've closed, right?"

"Yeah. Five or six, I think."

"That should work, don't you think?" She looked up at Jonah, who was staring at Evan. "Jonah?"

"Uh, yeah. I guess."

"Great," Evan said. "Let me know the paint day. Enjoy your game."

They took their shoes to their lane and put them on. She could tell Jonah was working to get past his worry about his brother and enjoy the fun. When Beth Ann picked out a huge ball, he said, "Never bowl with a ball bigger than your head, Squirt," and traded hers for a smaller one. "Give this a try."

"Okay," she said and ran for their lane.

Cara's heart tightened at the obvious affection between the two. Every time Jonah called her *Squirt,* Beth Ann beamed.

She'll miss him when we leave.

Would it mean another setback? Cara couldn't

bear the thought. Any choice she made—to stay or go—seemed to have pain attached to it.

"See how this one feels." Jonah handed her a ball.

She slid her fingers in and hefted it. "Seems f-fine." She met his gaze and saw heat flare there. He was so close and he smelled so good that she swayed.

"My aftershave taking out your knees?" he asked.

"Plus you smell like your shop. Like fresh lumber."

"Sorry. I did some work after I showered."

"No, I like it. A lot."

"I like how you smell, too. You smell pink."

"Pink? And how does pink smell?"

"Like cotton candy. I figured it out that first day when you were flitting and darting all over the place."

"You make me sound like a hummingbird."

"More like a fairy."

"A what?"

"You ever play that video game *Esmeralda?*"

"The one where the boy knight conquers the evil wizard?"

"Yep. Helped by Esmeralda."

"And that's me? A ball of fluff with wings? Not too flattering."

"Are you kidding? Esmeralda is a warrior. She's fast and clever and brave. She's...*dazzling.*"

"*Dazzling,* huh?"

"Oh, yeah."

Her cheeks burned at the praise, but she loved it. Jonah found her *dazzling.* He was looking at her the way he always did, like he didn't want to miss a single word, look or move.

Being near him made her feel so alive, every nerve on fire, her senses wide open.

"Let's *play!*" Beth Ann called impatiently from their lane. They broke apart like children caught licking frosting from a cake, and joined her.

With Jonah's help, Beth Ann managed a wobbly split that made her squeal with pride. Cara's first throw was a slow gutter ball.

"You turn your body too much," Jonah said, standing behind her before she tried again. He shifted her hips, his hands warm and sure. His uneven breathing told her he was affected by the nearness, too. "Try that."

Dizzy, moving down the lane on rubber legs, she somehow managed a strike. She was shrieking for joy when she noticed Jonah staring over her shoulder, a frown on his face.

She turned to see Evan carrying a tray of beers to a group of bowlers. Jonah intercepted him on the return trip. "I thought you were working the counter."

"Nicolette had to leave early, so I'm filling in."

"You're serving booze," he said in a low voice.

"I have to live in the world, Jonah."

"Your sponsor okay with this?"

Evan pulled his cell phone from his shirt pocket, clicked a button, then held it out. "Ask him yourself."

Jonah ignored the phone. "You're early in recovery."

"I'm fine. Go to New York. You've done your job." He glared at Jonah.

"You're setting yourself up to fail."

Cara cringed. He needed to let it go. Evan was at work.

"And you'd love that, wouldn't you? You're dying to say *I told you so.* I'm supposed to be humble with those I've wronged, but I've had it with you. Right now the biggest threat to my sobriety is my own brother."

"I know you, Evan. You get cocky and then—"

"I hate to interrupt the party, but you've got pitchers losing foam at the bar," a Hispanic man said. His name tag read *Carlos Rivera, manager.*

"Sorry, Carlos. I'm on it." Evan put the tray under his arm and trotted for the bar.

Jonah watched him go. "Dammit," he muttered.

"Evan seems to know what he's doing," Cara said gently.

"That's how it starts," he snapped. "See those

guys he's serving?" He nodded to where Evan was setting down beers. "Those are his running buddies. The guy in the ponytail deals pot and pills."

"They're customers. He has to wait on them."

"Don't you get it? This bar and those guys are *triggers*. He's supposed to stay clear of triggers and he knows it."

She didn't appreciate his tone. "It's none of my business, but—"

"You're right. It's none of your business."

"You embarrassed him in front of his boss. Of course he'll be defensive. Maybe if you stepped back—"

"Step back? *That's* your advice?" He glared at her. "You have no idea what you're talking about. You don't know him. You don't know what I've been through with him." Jonah bristled, muscles tight, tensed for a fight, and he loomed over her, his fury building with each word the way Barrett's used to. Her skin prickled and her stomach twisted. She was scared.

"Please don't yell at me," she whispered.

Instantly, Jonah's face cleared. "I'm sorry." He looked away, the muscle in his jaw ticking. When his gaze returned, he looked contrite. "I shouldn't have yelled."

Barrett had always regretted his outbursts, too.

"It's okay," she said, but a chill had settled in Cara's bones. Jonah had a temper like Barrett's.

Men like that could explode in an instant with a slap, a shove, a punch, before you could escape or even protect yourself.

Jonah had caught himself quickly, responding immediately to her request, but this had been a minor incident.

That wasn't the only way Jonah reminded her of Barrett. He was protective of her and attentive. Barrett had been like that. And Cara liked that. She couldn't deny it. That was a weakness she had.

The incident brought her up short. Jonah had showed his dark side. It was a warning. She'd been *flirting* with him, acting like they were on a *date,* which was foolish. Had she not learned her lesson yet?

The argument ruined the fun, and they finished the game quickly, awkwardly polite, and drove home in near silence. Beth Ann had picked up the tension and peered from one to the other with big eyes.

Jonah dropped them off in front of the café and drove away.

Later, when Cara went to tell her good-night, Beth Ann said, "Is Jonah mad at us?"

"No. He was upset about his brother. I said something he disagreed with. We apologized and we're fine now."

"Are you sure?" Her daughter seemed hyperaware of people's moods. Did that come from the tension between Cara and Barrett? They'd both protected her, she'd thought, but children didn't miss much.

"I'm positive," she said. "Don't give it another thought." But she doubted it would be that easy for her. Another warning about Jonah she should heed. Her daughter was watching.

Cara was about to climb into bed when a rattling sound drew her to the window. Cupping her hands between her cheek and the glass, she saw Jonah below her window, moonlight shining on his upturned face. His arm was back, ready to throw more pebbles.

She cranked open the glass and stuck out her head. "What are you doing?"

"I didn't want to wake the whole house. I have something to say if you'd come down."

She looked at him, considering what to do, then nodded. "I'll meet you on the porch." She pulled on shorts and a jersey tank top, slid into flip-flops and headed downstairs. She found him on the steps, elbows on his knees, hands clasped before him.

She sat close by, her back against a post. A mild breeze whispered through the pines and lifted her hair so it tickled her cheek. Cars swished by on the highway. Crickets sang.

When Jonah turned to her, their knees nearly

touched. Moonlight outlined his square jaw, the muscle jumping with tension. "I shouldn't have yelled at you. I know better."

"You were upset about Evan," she said. "It's over."

"That's no excuse." He held her gaze. "Not with you."

What did that mean? Had he guessed she'd been abused? Had she acted like a victim? God, no. Shame burned through her. Cara did not want his pity. She wanted his respect. She wanted him to see her as capable and assertive, not a frightened mouse.

"No one likes to be yelled at in public," she said. "I'm not fragile or weak or whatever it is you think I am. You said you were sorry. That's enough."

Cara stood to go.

He blocked her way, his face confused. "I've offended you."

She had to erase the concern from his face. "No. You didn't offend me. I appreciate your apology. And you were right." She blew out a breath. "Evan's not my brother. I don't know him. I shouldn't have interfered."

He took that in before he spoke. "He gets a few weeks of sobriety under his belt and he thinks he's invincible. And he slips. And the next thing you know, I'm bailing him out of jail after a bar fight or dragging him from a fleabag hotel, scrawny and sick and dead broke."

"That would be hard."

"I can't lose him, too. I just can't." He gave her one last look, his eyes full of pain, then turned and strode away.

He'd lost his father, a wife and the babies. His aunt might be sick, too, and he didn't even know it yet. She couldn't leave things this way. He wouldn't want her pity, but she could try to be his friend.

Cara ran across the yard.

He heard her and turned. She caught up with him near his porch.

"Is something wrong?" he asked.

"No. I just…" She didn't know where to start. Behind him the lights lit the beautiful furniture on his deck. "Did you build all that?"

He turned to see what she meant. "Yeah."

"I can tell," she said, climbing the steps to the deck, then dropping into the swing. She pushed off. "Definitely a Jonah Gold."

Warily, he joined her, sitting in a wide-armed chair close by.

"That's Arts and Crafts style. I recognize the joints. Mortise and tenon, right?"

"What's this about?"

"It's a nice night to sit out and talk."

"I guess."

She kicked off her flip-flops and pushed off with her bare feet. They sat in silence for a few minutes, while she figured out how to start. "You said music was where it started with Evan…."

Jonah let a few seconds pass before he responded. "After high school, he went to L.A. to promote a friend's band and got into booze and drugs." His voice was distant with memory. "The music industry chews up and spits out sturdy people. It's brutal for addicts."

"I can imagine."

"Tonight he seemed on top of it, but I've fallen for that more than once—given him cash for studio time, or a publicist, but he spent it partying every time."

"That would be difficult."

"Yeah. A year ago I cut him off like they tell you to. So he could hit bottom and decide to make the climb for himself. Instead, he got Rosie to hire him as fry cook. When that went south I came out to get him straight."

"And took over in the café."

"I'd sold my business. I was at loose ends."

She remembered what he'd told Rosie about his business—and his marriage. *They're gone.*

"I got him into an outpatient rehab program in Tucson. He slipped a couple times. This time it's three months, but he's got that cocksure tone again."

"No wonder you snapped at me." She tried to smile.

"I was way out of line. I saw your face, CJ. You looked so…scared." He cleared his throat. "I wish I could take it back."

She hated the way he was beating himself up. "It's true that anger is…hard for me."

He leveled his gaze at her. "He hurt you, didn't he? Your ex."

So it was true. She *had* acted like a victim. She couldn't speak.

"That first day, when I caught your arm to keep you from hitting the grill, you looked at me that way. Terrified. Braced for a blow."

He was correct. She'd been so damaged it showed. It made her feel so desolate, so hopeless.

"You're running from him. That's why the fake names and the secrecy. And that phone call on the pay phone. Was it him?"

"No. It wasn't *him*."

"But it was about him."

"Yes. He's looking for us. Now I know for sure." Saying it out loud made it real and the fear poured through her again.

"Have you contacted the police?"

"They can't do anything. I don't have a re-straining order—not that that would stop him—he hasn't directly threatened me." And there was the matter of his visitation rights, which put her on the wrong side of the law anyway.

"New Hope is a needle in a haystack. You're safe here."

"No, we're not. We're not safe anywhere." Cara realized her teeth were chattering. She hugged herself.

"I'm sorry you're in this mess." Jonah moved to the swing and put his arms around her, tucking her into the cave of his body.

It felt so good, the words poured out of her. "I'm sick of being so afraid, of hiding, of watching every word, expecting him around every corner. We were okay for a while, but now that he's—"

Cara stopped. Already, Jonah knew too much. She wouldn't mention prison or even Barrett's name. "I'm just worn-out."

"And you'd like to grow a garden."

She nodded against his shirt. "And finish school and start teaching. I want a home where my daughter can make friends she can keep forever." The longing washed through her, stronger than ever.

After that Jonah simply held her, his heart beating steadily against her ear, his chest swelling and subsiding with each breath. He smelled of aftershave and wood and the cotton of his shirt.

Cara realized she'd never been held like this. Her mother gave quick impatient hugs. Barrett's embraces had been controlling or manipulative. Her situation meant that friendships were superficial, so those hugs were casual.

Jonah's hug was solid and caring and real. She felt sheltered from all harm. Her muscles loosened, her breathing slowed, her tension faded. When she'd soaked up the moment so long she was sure his arms were numb, she let go and looked up into his dark eyes. "Thank you. That helped."

"Good." He put his arm across the back of the swing, his hand on her shoulder. "For the record, I don't think you're weak or fragile, CJ. You're strong and brave and..."

"Relentless?" She managed a smile.

"That for sure."

"I'm glad that's how you see me."

"It's how you are." He linked his free hand with hers, squeezing to tell her he meant it. Warmth poured through her.

Maybe she was stronger than she realized. Maybe she would be okay. Looking at Jonah, she almost believed it. The swing swayed gently beneath them, lulling her.

"I want you to feel safe here," Jonah said.

Cara shifted to see his face. "I do. As safe as I ever feel. What you said that first day, that I was in good hands, it steadied me. It's funny, but at night when I see your shop lights or hear you working, it helps me fall asleep."

"I think about you at night, too, but it doesn't put me to sleep." Candle flames danced in his dark eyes, setting off her own desire. She pictured him, restless in tangled sheets, wanting her, thinking of her.

"That happens, too. For me."

He closed his eyes briefly, his breath a rasp. "I should have kept my mouth shut." He stopped the swing, squeezed her shoulder and let go of her hand. "We have to stop. My bed's too damn close and I know what it's like to kiss those lips." He stared at her mouth.

"You're right." Cara took a deep breath, but it only made her dizzier. Her arm felt bare without his around it, her hand empty. "I wish we could be together. I do. I just…"

He waited for her to explain.

She owed him that. "I'm afraid that it would be…how it was with him." She swallowed. "That I'll never be able to forget… That I'll never be able to…" She couldn't finish. "It's pointless to talk about it. I should go." When she stood, she wobbled.

Jonah rose and steadied her, his hands slow to leave her body. "It's not pointless. That's how you feel. That's the point."

Cara searched his face. His eyes held compassion, not pity. And desire.

"I want to be normal, you know?" The words were a whisper. *Not crippled forever by my past.*

"It's normal to want to take it slow. For anyone." He shrugged.

Jonah made her sound reasonable, and she felt a surge of hope. Maybe one day she would be able to love a man and be loved in return.

Why not Jonah? He was a good man. She trusted him. Why couldn't she try? When would there be a better time...or a better man?

She was stronger, right? When they'd kissed, she hadn't thought of Barrett. She'd felt swept away, but now she knew what to expect. If she focused on Jonah, how he made her feel, surely she could block out Barrett.

Cara looked up at him to explain, but the words were slow in coming, so she went with what her body wanted, put her arms around his neck, pulled him down and kissed him.

Jonah stilled against her lips, then broke off, taking her hands from his neck to tuck them into his chest between their bodies. "What are you doing?"

"I want to try, Jonah. I want this."

"Are you s—"

She shut him up with another kiss.

This time he believed her. He pulled her tight

against him and kissed her back. Oh, did he kiss her back.

Cara closed her eyes and let go, enjoying the glory of being in his arms, the way he kissed, his lips soft, then firm, slow, then fast. They kissed for a long time, lips sliding, tongues dancing, quiet sounds of pleasure floating away in the night. She could handle this. She loved this. It gave her courage to go for more, the next step. She would let this lead her on.

Jonah cupped her head and broke off the kiss to study her face. "You doing okay?"

"I'm doing great." She was determined to be. She didn't dare stop or think or look down. "Take me to bed," she said. "Now."

He sucked in a breath as if he'd been socked with sudden pleasure. "You got it." He swung her into his arms.

Alarm shot through her. She was off the ground, under his power. He could carry her anywhere.

Jonah saw her expression and set her back down. "Better?"

She nodded.

"You set the pace. Fast or slow, it's your call. You want to stop, we stop."

"Okay." Jonah understood what she faced. He was the perfect man to help her prove to herself she was no longer Barrett's victim. He held the door for her and she stepped inside, her heart racing but full of hope, her body trembling but eager. This was her moment. She was going for it.

CHAPTER ELEVEN

BE CAREFUL WITH HER, Jonah reminded himself, closing the door behind them. *No sudden moves.* She'd been terrorized by a man who was supposed to love her, so Jonah had to be certain she welcomed every kiss, every touch. CJ trusted him. He'd die before he'd make her sorry she had.

In the heat of the moment, he'd hefted her sweet body into his arms, but then saw right away it was too much for her.

Inside, CJ kissed him hard, digging her fingers into his back, as if to convince herself she wanted this, then yanked him toward his bed, that determined glint in her eye.

She was acting like this was a challenge—a walk over hot coals or a triathlon—which wasn't exactly his preferred approach, but he was too far gone to raise an objection.

In his room, he threw back the covers and she dropped onto his bed. He gave her a quick kiss, then ducked into the bathroom, praying he still had condoms in his kit. *There. A strip of three.* Hoping they weren't past their use-by date, he set them on the headboard ledge and lay down to one side of CJ.

She was so pretty, lying on his pillow, her pale hair a filmy halo against the blue cloth. Then he noticed her eyes were jumpy. "Second thoughts? Because we can—"

"No." She grabbed him by the neck and kissed him hard.

He broke off. "This isn't a test. It's supposed to be fun."

She cupped his face in her small hands, delicate and strong at the same time. "You're right." She blew out a shaky breath. "I can't believe I'm really here."

"You are," he said, kissing one of her palms. "I've dreamed of you a lot. I know the difference." He leaned down to kiss her amazing lips. They were even softer than they looked. She tugged at his tongue, coaxing him deeper. Lust surged through him. He wanted her naked. He wanted inside her.

Easy, cowboy. You gave her the reins. No fair taking them back.

He reached both hands under the thin cotton of her shirt to brush the smooth underside of her breasts. She moaned softly. He wanted to take them fully in his hands, kiss them, run his tongue around the nipples, but he made himself stay put.

To his surprise, she grabbed his hands and put

them dead center on her breasts. He cupped their impossible softness, ran his thumbs across her nipples. They tightened and she shivered.

"Too much?" he asked near her ear.

"No, no. Just…my top…off." She squirmed to get at the hem of her shirt. He helped her pull it off, then removed his own.

The sight of her naked to the waist in his bed was better than any dream of her he'd conjured. "You are so beautiful," he said, then took one of her nipples between his lips, pressing it against the roof of his mouth.

CJ shuddered, then moaned, rocking her hips as she would if he were inside her.

Stay with her. Don't lose control. She arched her back, offering more of her breast to him. He took it, tugging the nipple deeper.

She lifted her hips, making room for him to reach inside the elastic of her shorts to grab both sides of her ass. "Ohh," she moaned, tightening her butt muscles beneath his palms, bucking up against him, her eyes hazy with lust.

When she stopped to try to take off her bottoms, he helped her, uncovering a pretty triangle of straw-colored curls. He widened his fingers over her hips, stroking her trembling belly with his thumbs.

She inhaled sharply and pushed up onto her elbows.

"This okay?" he asked, aching for more, but determined to hold back.

CJ nodded, her eyes glazed, chest heaving.

Jonah widened the circles until his thumbs grazed her cleft, one after the other, watching her face. Her eyes glazed, her lips parted and she gasped out, "More…"

He slid his thumb over her slick and swollen lips, then slipped a finger inside her. She gave a tremendous gasp, bucked faster, then froze, crying out as her climax burst upon her. That nearly sent him over the edge, but he stayed with her through her release.

When she stilled, unleashing a shuddering breath, he kissed his way up her stomach.

"I'm sorry it happened too fast," she said.

"It happened just right," he said, kissing her throat.

CJ shook her head. "You've still got pants on."

"That's easy to fix." He took them off, tore open the condom, put it on and moved to her, dying to feel her tighten around him, to move with her, to rock to the top and over with her.

He rose over her, weight on his elbows, leaned down to kiss her, but her face was tense.

"There's no hurry," he said, rolling to one side. *Oh, yes there is,* his body bellowed.

"I want you to do it. Now. Please." She pressed

his backside with both palms and closed her eyes against him. Was she gritting her teeth?

No. Not like this. She was gone, locked in memories of the man who'd hurt her. The last thing she wanted was sex. He felt sick for her.

"That's plenty for tonight." Jonah kissed her forehead, frustration tight in every muscle. He did his best to hide it.

CJ's eyes flew open. "But we're not done.... You didn't…"

"I did plenty."

"But it was just me."

"And you were amazing. I had a great time."

"That can't possibly be true."

He looked into her eyes. "Do I want more? Yeah. But not when you're forcing yourself to take your medicine. You have to want it, too."

"I do want it." She bit her lip. "I got lost. I'm sorry." Her eyes were shiny with tears and regret.

"We'll try again when you're ready. It's okay."

But it wasn't okay. It never would be. Cara knew that, her heart sinking and sinking. When Jonah had climbed on top of her, she'd seen Barrett and felt small and scared and powerless. "I don't think I'll ever be ready."

To his credit, Jonah didn't flinch at her words. "Sure you will."

No, she wouldn't. She couldn't bear to look at

him again. She had to leave. How many times could she apologize to the man? Cara grabbed her tank top and yanked it over her head. It was inside out, but she didn't care.

She was so ashamed. She'd used Jonah and left him frustrated. So selfish. So mean. She patted the sheets for her shorts.

Jonah caught her arm. "Don't run off. Lay here and catch your breath. I'll hold you." He looked so good with the moonlight glinting off the curves and planes of his face and chest, making his tousled hair shine and his dark eyes glow. "No funny stuff, I swear."

Cara would love to lie against him, let him wrap himself around her, but it wouldn't be fair. He would want more. He *deserved* more. She'd tried to be normal and failed miserably. "I can't. I have to go." She found her shorts and stepped into them.

Jonah pulled on his jeans.

"What are you doing?" she asked.

"Walking you home."

"Please don't. I feel bad enough already. I basically *used* you."

"If that's being used, sign me up."

"It's not right." Cara looked down to slip into her flip-flops and when she glanced up, Jonah stood before her.

"You have no reason to feel bad." He pushed

a strand of hair behind her ear and cupped her cheek. "You need time, that's all."

He was being kind. She gave him a quick kiss. "Good night, Jonah."

As she ran to the café, she could smell Jonah on her skin—his cologne, his shop, him. She remembered how he'd looked at her, held her, *touched her*.

You need time, that's all.

But it wasn't that simple. She knew that now. She couldn't forget Barrett. He'd poisoned intimacy for her, possibly forever. If she couldn't get past that with a kind, patient man like Jonah, what hope did she have?

The minute she came through the door, she heard someone crying softly. *Beth Ann.* Her heart in her throat, she hurried to her daughter, who sat in the beanbag chair, clutching Bunny.

Cara dropped to her knees. "What's wrong?"

"I had a bad dream. I looked…for you…but you…were…gone." She gulped breaths between words.

"I'm so sorry." Cara leaned in to hug her daughter, but Beth Ann pulled back and brushed away her tears, refusing Cara's comfort.

"I should have left a note. I was…talking to Jonah," she said. Beth Ann hadn't waked from a bad dream in two years, but Cara should have considered the possibility. How could she have been so thoughtless?

"I'm tired now." Beth Ann pushed up out of the chair. Besides Bunny, she also held the puzzle box Jonah had helped her make, which seemed an odd item to bring her comfort.

In her room, Beth Ann put the box on her night-stand, got into bed with Bunny and turned her back to Cara. In the moonlight, Bunny's one eye gleamed in accusation.

"I'm sorry I scared you. I would never leave you. You know that, right?" But Cara *had* left her. After Barrett attacked her, she'd been in a coma for five days, in the hospital for ten. The therapist had said Beth Ann likely felt hurt and angry at Cara for abandoning her.

Beth Ann had always refused to talk to Cara about what happened and she'd barely spoken to the therapist.

Maybe this time…

Cara took a deep breath. "I know you were scared when I was in the hospital. That was a terrible experience for you, so it stuck with you. When you couldn't find me, you probably felt that way again. Scared and mad at me, too." She paused. "That's natural. That's how anyone would feel."

Cara waited for Beth Ann's reply. *Please talk to me. Let me help you.*

But Beth Ann hugged Bunny tighter and scooted closer to the wall, the message clear. Bunny she could count on. Her mother…not so much.

Cara's eyes burned with unshed tears. She felt hollow inside. Her top priority was to protect Beth Ann, keep her safe, make her feel as secure as possible in their unstable life. Instead, she'd left Beth Ann alone to cry in the dark. And why? So she could have *sex*. As far as priorities went, sex was so far down the list it didn't deserve a number.

What kind of mother did that? The one time Beth Ann had looked for her, Cara wasn't there. Cara longed for her daughter to trust her with her sorrow, her fear, her confusion. Instead, Cara had given her even more reason to be a brave soldier, hiding her hurt away. How could she repair this rip in the fragile gauze of their relationship?

Beth Ann came first. She'd forgotten. Furthermore, she'd let down her guard about the danger they were in, telling Jonah too much about their situation. He knew she was running from her exhusband. He knew Beth Ann's real name.

The longer they stayed here, the more likely they would be discovered. Highway travelers stopped at the café every day. The billboard would bring in even more. Barrett's investigators could be prowling the highways, showing their pictures at gas stations, motels, restaurants.

All it took was one careless word and Barrett would find them.

Cara pushed down the panic, vowing to be more careful, more watchful, and to stay out of Jonah's bed…and his warm and tempting arms.

JONAH WOKE EARLY in a bed that smelled…pink, and found himself grinning. He couldn't wait to see CJ. She'd be uncertain, but he'd tell her how sexy she was, that she could take all the time she needed, that he'd loved every minute they'd spent together.

She just needed time. Together, they'd replace her bad memories with good ones—kind of like she'd done for him with the rocking chair.

Jonah showered, dressed and headed early to the café. He would make French toast for her. She'd like that. Remembering her, how she'd felt under his fingers, the way she'd moved, her cries of pleasure, made him so hard he had to stop and adjust himself before starting for the café.

The sun had barely lit the sky and the air still felt cool as he strode across the lot, his heart thudding in his chest.

He smelled pecan rolls and knew she'd beat him up. Sure enough, she was pulling rolls from the oven, wearing a sexy white blouse and tight pants and he wanted to back her into the pantry and pick up where they'd left off. "You're up early," he said, smiling in advance.

She set down the tray and turned to him. She looked exhausted, her face gray, her blue eyes cloudy.

"What's wrong?" he asked.

"Nothing. Just tired." She gave him that awful fake smile.

"You have nothing to feel bad about. Last night was—"

"A mistake. These rolls need frosting." She tried to get past him, but he blocked her way.

"No, it wasn't. Next time—"

"There won't be a next time," she said, escaping him to grab the pastry bag. She squeezed, but nothing came out, so she banged the bag on the counter. "What's wrong with this?" She was shaking.

"Give it here." He cleared the plug, then handed it back.

"Thank you."

"What the hell happened? You weren't this upset when you left last night."

CJ frosted a roll before answering in a low voice, "When I got back, my daughter was sobbing in the living room. She woke from a bad dream and couldn't find me."

"Rosie was there. She wasn't alone."

She jerked her gaze to his, her eyes wet. "She

wanted *me*. Her *mother*. And I wasn't there. I let her down."

"You had no way to know she'd wake up."

"That's not the point. I was so caught up in… what we were doing…that I forgot about her. She needed me for once and I wasn't there. I broke her trust."

Jonah couldn't stand to see her so upset. "You get to have a life, CJ. Bunny wouldn't begrudge you that. She's pretty sturdy."

"No, she's not. She puts on an act. You have no idea how fragile she is, how vulnerable." She took a sharp breath. "I have to focus on her, watch over her, watch out for her. That's my job."

She was eating her guts out over this. Her daughter already felt too much pressure. "The last thing she needs is for you to hover over her more. It already weighs on her."

She homed in on him. "She told you that?"

"She says she likes being in my shop because you're not there worrying about her like you do in the café."

CJ looked like she'd been punched.

When would he learn to keep his mouth shut? "Forget I said anything."

"No. I should know that. I'm glad she confided in someone." But her cheeks had red blotches and she kept blinking. He'd hurt her. She squeezed the bag hard, making a huge blob on the roll below her.

Jonah picked up the other bag and started squirting. How could he fix this? Not with words. He'd done enough damage with them already. Trying to reassure her, he'd made her feel like a bad mother. He wrote *ass* in frosting on the roll.

How many times had he hurt Suzanne like that or worse? Tried to comfort her, but made her cry harder. Or gave her space when she was desperate for company. Then there was Evan. He'd fumbled with him, too, made him defensive, pushed him closer to the edge. *The biggest threat to my sobriety is my own brother.*

He'd stepped crosswise with Rosie, too, telling her to quit living in the Eddie Underhill Memorial Museum and get a life, meet men, visit friends, only to have her stop talking to him for days.

When it came to emotions, he was at sea. Like his dad, who'd shut down totally when his wife walked out. Jonah did the same with the miscarriage and Suzanne—shut down, backed away from her grief.

Maybe Rosie and Evan were right. Maybe he should move to New York. He wasn't doing much good sticking around.

CJ was right not to sleep with him, but not for the reason she claimed. If they got involved, she would expect more from him. It was only natural. And he would let her down, hurt her worse. Better to quit while they were ahead.

And he would back off on the personal talk with Bunny, make sure she took her problems to her mother. It wasn't much of a fix, but it was all he could do.

Jonah hoped to hell by the time he went to bed, the pink smell would be gone. Fool that he was, he'd miss her anyway.

"MY DAUGHTER...she talk to Beth Ann. *Anoche.* Las' ni'."

Barrett sat up in bed, fighting the fog of sleep to understand Estrella Sandoval's halting words.

When he'd visited the Sandovals, she'd promised to call if Beth Ann contacted her daughter Serena. It had happened. At last, two weeks after his release, Barrett had gotten the break he'd been living for.

Estrella told him that late last night, she'd found Serena talking with Beth Ann. Serena admitted they'd spoken before Saturday, but that she'd promised Beth Ann not to tell anyone.

Estrella's voice shook. Barrett's hints about *la migra* had scared her. He rushed to reassure her in the passable Spanish he'd used as a family lawyer. He told her he was grateful to Serena for being a good friend to his daughter and promised to thank them both in person as soon as he could get there.

He'd bring gifts, of course, and extract every detail he could from the little girl and her mother.

At last a lead. Barrett was beside himself with excitement. Malloy's pretext calls to Cara's principal and Beth Ann's school had netted nothing and so far Cara had stayed off the grid. She was smarter than he'd given her credit for.

Barrett jumped in the car, and drove for Barstow, stopping at the first electronics store he passed to buy a big-screen TV and the latest gaming system. By early afternoon, he again sat in the neat trailer, dense with the smell of fried cornmeal, religious pictures on the walls.

The Sandovals were thrilled with his gifts, but wary of him. He promised Beth Ann would visit as soon as possible—a lie, but it made Serena relax enough to repeat every word of each conversation the two girls had had.

Beth Ann had told Serena she lived above a café where her mother was a waitress. Cara's mother's rattletrap had broken down as he'd speculated, but Serena didn't know how long they'd been on the road when it happened or the name of the café or the town where it was located.

Interstates snaked in all directions from Barstow, but Malloy could earn his keep calling res-

taurants in an ever-widening radius, asking about
new hires.

Serena told him Beth Ann had made friends
with a wild cat with one eye, that she'd built a
wooden treasure box, that she loved ketchup and
that she missed Serena, her teacher and her school.

Barrett made the girl swear that, if Beth Ann
called again, she would keep his visit a secret so
as not to spoil the surprise, but if she learned the
name of the café or the town, she would call him.

Serena nodded yes, her eyes big and earnest.
Estrella would enforce the promise. The threat of
la migra hovered over her like the angels in the
painting above her head.

One thing Serena said had upset him. The reason Beth Ann had called so late was that she'd
had a bad dream and couldn't find her mother.
That made Barrett's blood boil. What the hell was
Cara doing? It had been a Saturday night. Was she
bar hopping? On a date? Had she turned into her
mother, constantly after male attention?

No. It couldn't be. Cara was too sweet for that.
He mentally slammed the manhole cover on his
roiling rage. This got harder each day that passed
without finding his family. He'd begun to exceed
the recommended dose of mood pills just to keep
from exploding at his poor mother over minor an-
noyances.

But now he was close. So close. Barrett burned

with adrenaline. He had half a mind to start hunting himself. The wait was killing him.

He tried to stay busy. He'd found a house and the sellers had accepted his offer. He would keep Cara busy decorating it. *Nesting,* they called it.

There was one other painful detail Serena had shared. Cara had been baking again. That was good, but it reminded him of when she'd stopped. Once she'd gotten it in her head to go to college, she'd had no time to bake. No time for him or Beth Ann or the ordinary joys that made life worth living.

She'd gotten lost, become selfish. It was his mission to help her find her way back to the contentment she'd lost in the fruitless search for external approval.

He would approach her with love.

Cara, my darling. If I could take back every hard word, every angry touch, I would. I support you. I respect you. I adore you. We need to be a family again. To be whole.

The words brought tears to his eyes. He hoped they'd do the same for Cara.

Soon he would have her at his side and his daughter on his shoulders—though Beth Ann was nine now, possibly too old for piggyback rides.

But no child outgrew ice cream.

They'd have Family Night at Carcher's every night if it made Beth Ann happy. He wanted to give her the world. He couldn't wait. It was hard not to call her right now. He'd programmed her number into his phone. Two clicks and he'd hear her voice in his ear.

Wait. Use caution. In his law practice, he'd dealt with fearful women. Barrett knew to proceed with care. Before he made contact, he had to locate them and assess their situation, determine the best approach. He couldn't afford one false step.

If he lost them again, he didn't know what he might be forced to do.

CHAPTER TWELVE

MONDAY, AFTER she got back from the first day of day camp, Beth Ann headed for Jonah's shop. She *had* to use his computer. *Had* to.

She hoped Jonah wouldn't be grouchy like yesterday. He'd showed her how to use the vise and a small saw to cut short legs for her castle stand, but he'd hardly talked to her. When he looked at her, he frowned. Had her mom told him about Beth Ann's crying fit the night before? Did he think she was a baby?

That idea made her feel sick. She hated for Jonah to think she was that weak. She would have stayed away today, but she had to find out what happened to Serena. Jonah's computer was the only way she could think of.

She'd called Serena Saturday night because she'd *had to*. First, she'd dreamed her daddy was chasing her with a knife and she woke up gasping for air. Then she ran to her mom's room, but the bed was made. *She's gone. She's gone. Daddy took her. I'm all alone.* It was how she'd felt when her mom got put in the coma. Her grandma had said she might not wake up ever.

Standing there so scared, Beth Ann's brain went black as midnight and she started to shake like that time she'd had the flu. She ran for her puzzle box and called her friend. She had to. It was an *emergency*.

And it helped. Serena calmed her down just talking about ordinary things. Chulita. The last days of school. The laptop she got to check out from school for the summer because of her good grades. She told her that Beth Ann *had* won the reading prize. But Serena hung up in the middle of telling her about Water Day. Then all day Sunday she didn't answer her phone. That was weird. Had her mom taken it away? Was Serena in trouble?

Beth Ann had to find out. Two girls she'd met at day camp had reminded her of a way to do it. They were the only other third-graders besides Beth Ann at the stupid camp, so they had to talk to her.

Amanda was kind of bossy and a show-off, but she included Beth Ann when she and Rachel started IM'ing each other with their iPads instead of making sock puppets like the little kids.

Beth Ann had used Instant Message at school. And Serena had a laptop now. She'd said it was because of her grades, but Beth Ann knew it was also because her family was poor.

Beth Ann would download the free IM program on Jonah's computer and text Serena. Instant Message would be good, too, since Beth Ann had used up half the minutes on the secret phone.

At the workshop door, Beth Ann took a deep breath and closed her eyes. She could hear Jonah hammering. *Please don't be grouchy at me. Pretty please.*

She opened her eyes and went in. "Hey, Jonah."

"Hey." Jonah gave a quick smile, then went back to work. So far, so good.

"Is it okay to use your computer?"

"Why wouldn't it be?"

Whew. She climbed onto the stool, clicked onto the internet, so nervous she felt sweat pop everywhere on her body.

In a few seconds, she had Instant Message loaded and she logged in, then clicked her friends list, her heart racing. *SerenaS* was offline. Darn, darn, darn. She wrote a message anyway so Serena would see it the next time she used WiFi in the rec center at her trailer park.

Now she had to wait. She logged out and scooted over to her castle so she could put the legs on the base.

"Drawbridge working okay?" Jonah asked.

Beth Ann pulled the string, but it popped out. "The knot won't hold."

He walked over and looked at it, then went

to get something from one of his drawers. He brought her back a spool of plastic thread. "This is thicker. Try it." He went back to work.

She cut some thread, knotted it and tested it. "It worked. Now all I have to finish is the base."

"You built a handsome castle." He was being nice. Maybe he'd forgotten about her being a crybaby.

"I like it." The walls were wavy and the towers didn't match, but she was proud of it. "I wish it could be real. I could pull up the drawbridge and be totally private."

"Yeah? I built a tree fort like that when I was a little older than you. Put the lowest rung too high for my little brother to reach. Mean, I guess, but I wanted a place of my own."

"That would be cool."

"It was." He looked over at her. "Was camp as bad as you expected?"

"Mostly, yeah. It was all little kids except for two girls my age."

"Did you like them?"

"They're okay. Amanda's bossy. Rachel's quiet. She likes cats."

"So you hung out?"

"We were stuck together. Their other friends are on vacation." Listening to them talk and joke made her miss Serena more than ever.

"You have to get used to each other. Maybe

invite the one who likes cats out to meet Louis or—no." He frowned. "That's up to you and your mom. I need to get this work done."

He *was* mad at her. Her cheeks felt hot, so she focused on finishing her castle. She measured the legs, then checked again before she cut, but when she glued them on, the base slanted down. She sighed.

"Troubles?" Jonah asked.

"The legs don't match. I measured twice and cut once."

"You can still make a mistake, Squirt."

"You don't."

"Sure I do. I just don't talk about it. I've redone the lip for this pastry display case twice now. You'll get better."

"I have to start over, right? Since wood doesn't forgive?"

"You've got plenty of scrap. It's good practice."

"The reason wood doesn't forgive is because it's hard." Beth Ann measured and marked the skinny board. "My grandma says my mom's heart is hard. That's why she doesn't forgive." She'd said it during that bad argument. Saying it out loud now made her throat ache.

Jonah put down his hammer and turned to her. "That's baloney. Your mom has a big heart." He paused. "She loves you like crazy. In fact—" He frowned. "Just talk to her. I've got work to do here."

She sucked in a breath. She'd made him angry. She couldn't stand it. "Is it because I talk too much? Is that why you're mad at me?"

"Mad at you? I'm not mad at you. You can talk all you want about woodwork. I'm no good at the personal stuff. That's for your mom and you."

Her cheeks felt hotter than ever.

Serena was gone and now Jonah didn't want to talk to her. She didn't feel like being in the shop anymore. She got off her stool.

"You heading out?"

She nodded.

"You get what I said? About talking to your mom?"

She nodded again, but it wouldn't work. Her mom would just feel worse and worry more. And Beth Ann had already hurt her mom enough.

"And there isn't one thing you could do that your mom wouldn't forgive, Beth Ann. That's the last I'll say about that."

"Okay," she said to be polite. She was almost to the café when she realized he'd called her *Beth Ann*. Not *Bunny* or even *Squirt*. How did he know her name? It was probably a mistake, but she didn't care. It felt like a hug for her heart. It almost took away the hurt of him not wanting to talk to her anymore.

TUESDAY NIGHT AFTER supper, Cara headed to Jonah's woodshop. He wanted her to approve the colors he would paint the new sign. Otherwise, she wouldn't have entered his sanctuary. The disagreement about Beth Ann had put distance between them. The easy teasing was gone, along with the intense looks, the secret smiles, the thrill of casual touches, the intimacy and connection. She missed that. She missed him.

They worked together still, but it wasn't the same. Cara felt alone.

She was determined to get back to being friends again. Surely, they could get past her bad judgment. They'd come so far. She'd brought a peace offering—a puzzle box with *Jonah's Treasures* burned into the lid she'd found in a crate she'd emptied for Rosie's yard sale. She hoped looking through it would get them talking like they used to.

At the doorway, she stopped to watch Jonah work. He was hammering nails into the pastry display case. Watching him doing the work he loved put butterflies in her stomach and made her pulse race. But that happened every time she caught sight of him—standing, sitting, walking around, flipping burgers on the grill.

Cara steadied herself, put the box on a shelf just inside the door for when they'd finished with business, and stepped into the lovely sawdust smell and cozy golden light of Jonah's haven.

"Hey," she said softly.

He turned to her, hammer in hand. "Hey." He looked delighted to see her. His gaze stayed on her, drinking her in. *He misses me, too.*

That gave her hope as she walked closer. "Looks like you're nearly done," she said, touching the corner of the case.

"Just need to put in the rotating racks, lights and the sliding glass doors."

"It's beautiful." She ran her hand over the curlicues he'd carved into the borders. "This is like the teacup steam, huh?"

"That's the idea."

"You added so much detail."

He shrugged. "I wanted it to be right."

"It's like everything you build—functional and beautiful."

He looked down, embarrassed by her praise. "The sign won't take me long once you approve the colors. I'll install the case once we finish painting on Monday."

"That's perfect. Darlene said she'll help us paint. She's going to cover my shifts while I run Rosie's sale. She wants any extra shifts we can give her. I guess her boyfriend's not working much."

"Construction's down."

"I hired him to hang the sign, by the way. His boss has a cherry-picker."

"Good. You haven't missed a detail, CJ."

"So far," she said, but his admiration warmed her. His admiration and the way he kept drinking her in.

"You even got Rosie out of town until the dust settles."

Rosie. Her stomach clenched. Monday was her surgery. Cara was so scared for her.

"We're going to have to start calling you Rosie Whisperer."

"I don't know about that." If Rosie did have cancer, it would take more than whispers to get her to cooperate with treatment.

"Something up?" he asked.

"Just that we have a lot going on." She didn't want to have to fib about Rosie any more than she had already.

"Let me show you the sign." He led her to his computer on Beth Ann's worktable. She sat on the stool and he leaned past her to click the mouse. She closed her eyes and breathed him in, grateful she was sitting so her knees couldn't buckle. Being this near him was a guilty pleasure.

"What do you think?"

She opened her eyes to see the sketch colored in. The teacup was lilac with mustard accents. The letters were in red with black shadows.

"I love it," she said. "It's friendly and festive and fresh. Exactly the feeling I want for the café."

"Then I'll go with that." He turned to her, so close it was almost an embrace. His breath hitched. Hers did the same. She noticed flecks of latte in the espresso of his eyes…and the golden glow in the center. Desire.

It flickered, then went out, like a failing fluorescent bulb. That was proper, but it made her sad.

She turned away and noticed Beth Ann's castle. "It was a good idea to get her building with toothpicks. So was inviting Rachel out to meet the cat."

"On that, I didn't mean to interfere."

"You didn't. I also thought about what you said. Maybe I do hover too much."

"No. I put my foot in my mouth and—"

"That's part of why she won't confide in me, I realized. She's afraid I'll worry more. So I'm glad you said what you said."

"I made you feel worse. I didn't intend that." He paused, his jaw locked, his gaze fierce. "You matter to me. Both of you. That's why I overstepped."

"You matter to us, Jonah. To me." Their connection snapped into place. She was glad. She felt instantly better.

"Good. I'll try to keep my foot out of my mouth here on out. Shoe leather tastes nasty."

"Try rosemary," she said. "Maybe a bay leaf."

"And a red wine reduction?"

"Perfect." She laughed.

"We're good?" he asked.

"Better than ever, I think." She remembered the treasure box. "I found something of yours."

"Yeah?"

Cara retrieved the box from the shelf and held it out. "It was in one of Rosie's crates. It's like the puzzle box you helped Bunny make, but bigger."

He grinned. "I thought this got tossed." He ran his fingers over the top, making her think of the way he'd touched her. She almost shivered.

"Let's see what's here." He motioned for her to take the stool and pulled up his own, setting the box on Beth Ann's worktable. He pushed a spot on one side, then one in front and the lid popped up.

"So that's the secret," she said.

He put a finger to his lips. "Don't tell her you know."

Cara pretended to turn a lock on her lips.

He set the lid aside and rummaged inside, picking up a scuffed baseball. "Caught this at a Cubs game. My dad took us. Best day ever, except Evan ate too many hot dogs and puked on the way home."

She leaned in to see, their heads nearly touching. Jonah pushed aside a blue ribbon, a pellet gun, a couple of action figures, then picked up a block of pale wood with a paper wrapped around it. "Damn." He sat back, holding it.

"What is it?"

"Piece of birch my dad gave me after he taught me to carve."

"Were you close? You and your dad?"

"In the shop." He peeled off the rubber band and uncurled the paper. "I went through an Indian myth phase. This lists all the spirit animals and what they represent. I did a spirit quest in the woods to find my animal guide. I took a tent, a notebook, some water and a couple granola bars and waited for a vision."

"And?"

"All I got was stomach cramps and bad dreams. I was too attached to choosing, rather than being chosen. I wanted the eagle for power or the hawk for truth."

He set the list and the wood on the table. Cara picked up a pink valentine heart that said *be mine* and showed it to him.

"That was from Linda Latham. She had incredible lips."

"You kissed her?"

"Are you nuts? I was nine. Girls had cooties. She blew the best bubble-gum bubbles."

"You've had a thing for lips for a while."

"Only the exceptional ones." His gaze dropped to hers, making her stomach flutter.

Cara put back the heart and picked up a photo.

It was two boys and a woman standing with Mickey Mouse.

"Is this you and Evan?"

"Yeah. Disneyland. I was ten, he was six."

"Is this your mother? She's very pretty."

"She was."

"*Was?* Did something happen to her?"

He didn't answer immediately.

"I don't mean to pry."

"It's okay." Jonah seemed to force himself to say more. "She left right after this trip. Couldn't take our dad anymore."

"But what about you two?" She'd abandoned her children. Cara couldn't imagine doing that, though she knew better than to judge. Many women couldn't imagine doing what she'd done either.

He shrugged. "She wrote to us for a while. I think she went to Chicago. That was where her family was from."

"You don't know where she is?"

"Don't look so stricken. Families break up all the time. We survived."

"It would still hurt." Though Beth Ann wouldn't talk about it, losing her father had been hard for her. He'd adored her. No matter how Cara explained Barrett to her, Beth Ann had to be confused.

"She did what she had to do," Jonah continued.

"Everybody does. It was harder on Evan than me. He was only six."

The same age Beth Ann had been.

"Evan thought Mom left because of him. Plus, Dad went downhill after that. I'd spent time with him in the shop, where he was patient and friendly. Evan only knew the bitter, brooding drunk he became."

"You were so young."

"We managed. I made sure Evan ate breakfast, had clean clothes, got to school, did his homework. The practical stuff." He looked past her, lost in thought. "That had to leave a huge hole in the kid—thinking it was his fault Mom left and Dad fell apart. He filled it with alcohol." He took a breath. "If I'd explained it more, maybe he wouldn't have gone that route."

"Alcoholism is genetic, Jonah. You couldn't have controlled that. You were a kid, too, remember."

"I never handled Evan well. I still don't. I make him feel small." Jonah's eyes held anguish. "I miss the mark when it counts. That's how I am."

"I don't believe that." Cara picked up the curled paper and thrust it at him. "Which spirit animal carries the weight of the world on his shoulders?"

He took it, half smiling. "Let's see... Looks like...bear. Yeah. *Guardian of the World*. I'm too much of a grumpy hermit to protect the world."

"Let me look." She took it from him, her fingers brushing his, sending heat along her nerves. "That's not all it says about the bear." She read, "'The bear is brave, strong, industrious, protective, strong-willed and a healer.' That's exactly you, Jonah."

He shook his head, not buying it one bit. She had to get through to him.

"It's true. I've seen it. With Beth Ann. With me. You've made me feel safe. You've given me hope that…one day…I might heal."

"You will. Don't doubt that." His gaze was fervent. "Give yourself time. Find a solid, steady guy who'll be there for you, thick or thin, who'll give you what you need when you're ready. You deserve that. You'll get it."

Cara was so moved tears pricked her eyes. "You don't know how good you are." Who could be more steady or solid or patient than Jonah? Her heart swelled with emotion. She cared about this man and he cared about her.

Maybe she'd given up too soon.

Her gaze landed on the name plate Jonah had made. It didn't even say her daughter's real name. *None of this is real.* They were on the run, in hiding. This was no time to explore pointless hopes. She had to fulfill her promise to Rosie and get on with her plan.

She picked up the piece of birch and held it out.

"Carve the bear, Jonah. That's your spirit animal. I'd stake my life on it."

That sounded pretty dramatic, but it felt somehow right.

CHAPTER THIRTEEN

"I'LL GET IT!" CJ dashed for the café phone, trailing drips of purple paint from her roller. Jonah watched her go. What the hell was going on? It was Monday. They'd closed early to paint the café, everyone intent, pushing to finish as soon as possible, yet CJ lunged for the phone each time it rang.

It wasn't her ex. He knew that because she seemed nervous, not terrified, as she'd been the day the pay phone rang.

Jonah turned back to his work, nodding at Hector and Ernesto, who were masking the front windows. They'd hired Hector as full-time busboy since Ernesto had begun doing more cooking. They got busier every day, thanks to CJ. She was a wonder.

They had a good crew today. Hector, Ernesto, Darlene, Evan and Nicolette, with Charlie, Darlene's boyfriend, outside changing the sign. Even with CJ stopping every ten minutes for the phone, they should finish by nightfall.

CJ returned from the call, so pretty, even in paint clothes and a bandanna, she made him ache.

He almost wished he'd never had her naked in his arms. He couldn't forget the look of her, her sweet cries, the velvet of her skin, the way body heat had intensified her pink smell. It was all fuel for restless nights. More than once he'd given up on sleep and gone to his shop to lose himself in wood and work. The extra hours hadn't hurt, considering the new projects he'd taken on for her. He still had three pieces to finish for his show, three weekends away.

This *thing* he had for her should pass soon. The intensity was due to him waking up again, the way a numb arm tingled when the blood returned in a rush. He'd be happy when he got past it.

"Was it the call you're waiting for?" he asked her.

"The what? No. I wasn't…" She blushed, flustered that he'd caught her out. "It was an order. Two dozen good-luck buns." They'd been doing a brisk take-out business on the fortune rolls. CJ knew her stuff, for sure.

"The machine could have taken that." He opened his mouth to ask her what she was up to, but Evan interrupted.

"Check the wainscoting," he said. "Does it look straight to you?"

"You measure it?" Jonah asked. "Use the level?"

"Yeah, but—"

"Then it's straight."

"Okay." Evan seemed surprised Jonah had taken his word for it. Since he'd talked to CJ about his brother, Jonah had been trying to see things through Evan's eyes more.

"This is really coming together, huh?" CJ said.

"It'll look great for Devil's Anvil Reborn," Evan said. "Next Thursday."

"Right," CJ said. "That'll be fun."

"I was thinking maybe you could make a special batch of those lucky rolls?" he said. "With only coins and clovers? They're going to L.A. to meet with a record label and tape an *E!* segment about bands on the verge, so I figured the good luck would be a nice touch."

"That's clever," CJ said.

"You think so?" Evan wore the painfully eager look Jonah remembered from after their mother left. He'd craved approval, but their moody father had been oblivious.

"It's smart. Yeah," Jonah said, his voice rough. *It wasn't your fault Mom left.* He wished to hell he'd said that to the poor kid.

Evan did a double take at the compliment. "I'll get back to it."

"That was a nice thing to say," CJ said when Evan was out of hearing.

"I don't give him enough credit," Jonah said.

"You're not the only one who hovers too much." It was funny, but since that moment with the rocking chair, he'd been noticing changes in himself. The talk about Evan added to that. Now his brain felt like Rosie's spare bedrooms after they'd taken out the last of the junk for the parking-lot sale—full of light and air, with space to breathe and move and think.

The door jangled and Beth Ann stuck her head in. She was riding a bicycle with high handlebars and a banana seat. "Charlie says to come check the sign angle."

"Ooh, let's go see," CJ said to him, her eyes huge with excitement. That fake smile hardly ever made an appearance these days. He liked that.

The sign looked damn good, he had to admit. CJ was thrilled.

Bunny rode past on the bicycle.

"You stay clear of the highway," CJ called to her.

"Rosie give her the bike?" he asked.

"Yes." She sighed. "An early birthday present, she said."

"That was nice of her." Since he'd heard about the upcoming birthdays, Jonah had been working on gifts for CJ and Bunny. He hoped the one for Bunny would make up for her hurt feelings. She'd barely spoken to him since he'd told her to lay off the personal talk. She'd only been in to use the computer, then left. "Rosie thinks the world of your daughter."

"I know. She also gave her a giant dollhouse, a sewing machine and lawn darts, for God's sake. Those things are deadly. I don't know how kids survived the '60s."

"Little higher…to the left," he yelled up at Charlie.

"Got it!" He made the shift and started securing the bolts.

"Rosie seemed glum when I talked to her about how the sale was going," he said "You think she's having second thoughts?"

"We made more money than she expected," CJ said. "She has things on her mind, I guess."

She seemed nervous, too.

"I feel bad about all those gifts," CJ said. "We can't take any of it with us. It's more to say good-bye to."

They'd be saying goodbye to him, too, in a few weeks. That gave him a sinking feeling. "You pay Rusty to fix your car yet?"

"In two weeks. It'll be my birthday present to myself."

"A transmission is a pretty sad gift."

"Has to be done," CJ said.

"If you're going to leave, yeah."

Once the sign was set, they went back inside.

"You got a call, CJ," Darlene said. "Someone

named Frieda." She held out a napkin with a number on it.

CJ snatched the paper and ran for the phone. That was clearly the call she'd been waiting for. Frieda was the friend Rosie was visiting. Why would she call instead of Rosie? His scalp prickled. Something was wrong and this time he wasn't letting it slide.

He caught up with CJ as she was picking up the phone. "Hold on," he said. "You need to tell me what's going on with Rosie. Right now."

She searched his face. "I can't." She bit her lip. "I promised her."

"I don't care. I need to know." What the hell was it?

CJ bit her lip, then spoke. "She had surgery this morning. They're taking out a tumor in her stomach. It's just outpatient, but—"

"She has cancer?" He felt like he'd been dropped into ice water.

"They're doing a biopsy to find out."

"Jesus Christ. When did this happen?"

"It started three weeks ago."

"Three weeks? And no one told me?" He couldn't wrap his mind around that.

"I wanted to, believe me. I begged Rosie to tell you, but I had to promise to keep it a secret to get her to go to the doctor in the first place."

"But she told you she was sick?" He fought to keep his voice low.

"By accident. She fainted in the kitchen. Scared me to death. She said it had happened before. I told her to get checked, but she was going to just wait to die."

"That's Rosie."

"I couldn't let her do that, so I made a deal to stay until she went to the doctor."

"That was why?"

CJ nodded. "Also, I found out the café was in foreclosure. She dropped the letter from the bank when she fainted."

"She's losing the café?"

"Not anymore. She thought she was dying so it didn't matter."

"Why didn't she tell me? I could have helped with the money. Dammit."

"We worked it out. Selling off the shop caught her up with her mortgage and we've been making more money in the café, so she should be okay."

"That's what the new menu was for? And the renovation?"

She nodded. "She wanted you and Evan to be off living your lives when she died. She wanted to protect you, so she didn't want you to know."

"Protect me from what? From being there when she needed me?"

CJ took a step back and he realized he'd raised his voice.

"Sorry." He took a breath and spoke in a lower voice. "I've been frying burgers and sanding furniture like any other day while she thinks she's at death's door—*and* losing her café."

"You know how stubborn she is. So she went to the doctor and when he wanted to operate—"

"She refused. 'Once they sink a knife in you, you're done.'" He shook his head over his aunt's fatalism.

"Exactly. So I made another deal. I said I'd stay for the surgery. She agreed as long as I kept it secret from you."

"Damn." Jonah was disgusted that this had been going on and he'd been clueless. "I knew something was up, but I let it slide."

"You asked me, Jonah, and I had to lie."

"I should have asked *her,* made her tell me."

"You said she'd rather boil in fryer oil than confide in you."

"Doesn't matter. I'm family. If I can't be there for her when her life's on the line, what's the point?" He fought to rein himself in. He'd failed Rosie without even knowing it.

Jonah thought about what CJ had done. "You gave up so much. You put your plans on hold."

"It wasn't a sacrifice. I love it here. So does Bunny."

CJ was such a good person. "I can't believe you did all you did for Rosie. For us. I think you're the one whose spirit animal is the bear. You sure as hell have been the guardian of Rosie's world."

"It meant a lot that Rosie needed me. When I left, I let people down where I worked. This makes up for that a little. And Rosie reminds me of my grandmother. I love her, Jonah."

Emotion welled in his chest. He was so lucky to know this woman. He wanted to say that, but he wasn't sure how, so he stuck with what needed to be done. "Guess you'd better call Frieda."

CJ dialed the number and put the call on speaker. Frieda told them the surgery had gone well, Rosie was in recovery and the biopsy results would take a day or two.

"That's that," CJ said, hanging up. "Rosie will kill me when she finds out I told you."

"She'll get over it. I needed to know."

"Hopefully, the café being painted will cheer her up. She'll love the sign you made."

Jonah had to laugh. "You save her life and I paint her a sign. Sounds about right." CJ was the heart of things. The least he could do was be the muscle.

WEDNESDAY AFTERNOON, Cara pulled up a chair between Jonah and Rosie in the café kitchen. They sat shoulder to shoulder waiting for the doctor to call with the results of Rosie's biopsy. They'd given the doctor the café phone number so Beth Ann wouldn't hear. She was safely upstairs.

When the phone rang, all three jumped. It rang again.

"Pick it up, for God's sake," Rosie finally said.

Cara pushed the speakerphone button. "Hello? Dr. Randolph?"

"This is he. Who's this?"

Cara told him and explained that Rosie and Jonah were also present.

"Glad you're all there," he said. "I'll get right to the point. The tumor was cancerous, Rosie. The good news is we believe we got it all, the danger of metastasis is slight with this tumor type...."

Cara's mind shut down at the word *cancerous*. The doctor's words went muddy, as if she were listening under water. Rosie had cancer. *Cancer.* She looked at Rosie, who sat as still as stone.

Jonah blew out a breath and turned his head to the side.

She managed to tune back in to the doctor as he said, "Harvey Royce is a superb oncologist. He'll want to start chemotherapy right away. We've had excellent results with an aggressive treatment plan. Do you have questions?"

Cara and Jonah looked at Rosie. Silence.

"Mrs. Underhill?" the doctor said.

Rosie cleared her throat. "That's all I need to know."

"If you'll hold, I'll have my nurse give you Dr. Royce's number."

"No, thanks. I'm set. Goodbye." Rosie pushed the end call button.

"We need the number," Cara said gently.

"No, we don't." Rosie folded her arms, and Cara's heart sank.

"You're getting the treatments if I have to drag you there myself," Jonah said, his eyes on fire. He looked afraid for Rosie.

Rosie stabbed a finger at Cara. "I blame you for this. We had a deal. But you went and blabbed to this bulldog."

"I made her tell me," Jonah said. "Deal or not, you don't keep life-and-death secrets from your family."

"You worry about your own life and death and leave mine to me."

She got up.

"Where are you going?" Jonah said. "We need to discuss this."

"We're done discussing. No treatment. I'm done." Rosie got up and stomped off, thudding up the stairs to her apartment.

"I shouldn't have threatened her." He was pale as death. "I got her back up."

"She needs time to adjust to the idea."

"She's got cancer." He looked devastated. "Rosie's got cancer." He swallowed hard, clearly battling emotion.

"I know. But we'll talk to her. She'll come around. The doctor said they get good results when they're aggressive."

"What the hell does he mean by *aggressive?* You got the guy's number? Rosie might not have questions, but I have plenty."

AFTER SUPPER, Cara opened the apartment door to let Jonah in so they could talk with Rosie, who sat gloomily watching TV in the living room. Beth Ann was in her room watching a movie on Cara's laptop with headphones so she wouldn't overhear.

"I'm armed." Jonah waved a thick stack of paper. "Internet research."

Rosie looked over at them. "Go home, Jonah."

"Not until you listen to what we found out," he said.

Rosie huffed a breath, but she stayed in her recliner, legs up, hands clenched on the armrests like stubborn royalty. Cara and Jonah took the beanbag chair and fuzzy mushroom ottoman, subjects at her feet.

"The doctor told us that with chemotherapy and radiation, the long-term survival rate is eighty percent," Jonah said.

"That's drug company PR," Rosie snapped.

"No, it's not. I looked it up." He put the print-outs on her lap. "Read it."

"No need." She handed it back.

"You are a stubborn old goat."

Cara cleared her throat. "What Jonah means is that he loves you and doesn't want to lose you."

Jonah looked chagrined. "Right. That's right." He exhaled. "You're all we've got." He paused. "Do it for Evan. He's barely sober. You croak on him and he'll sink into booze."

"Don't you dare play the booze card." Rosie slammed down the footrest and stood. "It's too late. Don't you get it? They opened me up. That's lighter fluid on a bonfire. I'm done for." Her voice shook. "This is my life and I'll end it with dignity. Now leave me the hell alone."

"Good-luck buns for dessert!" Beth Ann's cheery voice from the kitchen doorway made them all turn. She walked to them and held out the plate of four rolls. "Everybody take one."

The adults glanced at each other.

How much had Beth Ann heard? "Honey, we were just talking about—"

"Rosie has cancer and she won't get it fixed. I heard you."

Once again, Cara had failed to protect her daughter from hard truths.

"Take one and check your fortune. I already buttered them."

There was nothing to do but pick up the rolls, so they did.

The smear of cold margarine disguised a rip in her bun, Cara saw. When all four held good-luck clovers, she knew Beth Ann had made sure the charms matched.

"Wow!" Beth Ann said with feigned surprise. "That's good luck times four. You'll be safe for sure, Rosie."

Cara's heart squeezed. Her daughter was trying to help.

"First off, you rigged the rolls." Rosie slapped hers back on the plate. "And second, luck won't fix me."

"Because you don't need luck," Jonah said. "The odds are in your favor."

"Like poker odds?" Beth Ann asked. "Does she have the odds of a full house? Or three of a kind? Or—"

"More like a pair," Jonah said.

"You said any idiot can draw a pair, Rosie."

"You're too smart for your britches, young lady. I'm going to bed." Rosie stomped off.

Beth Ann's face crumpled. When Cara reached for her, she gave her the plate and ran down the hall.

"Go talk to them," Jonah said. "I've done enough damage for one night."

"Rosie just needs more time," she said.

"I hope you're right. Call me if there's anything I can do that won't make it worse."

"I will."

He looked at her for a few seconds, then pulled her into his arms. "I'm sorry we dragged you into our mess."

She felt better just being in his arms. "I'm sorry there's a mess in the first place."

"If there's a hope in hell of fixing it, you're the one who can do it." With a last comforting look, Jonah left.

Cara found her daughter sitting up in bed, Bunny held tight, eyes full of worry.

"Did I make her so mad she won't get fixed?" Beth Ann asked.

"She'd not mad at you. She's scared about being sick."

"Are you sure?"

"Absolutely." Cara sat beside Beth Ann with her back against her daughter's pillow. "She's just scared. She needs time to decide to get treated."

"Oh." Beth Ann sighed with relief, surprising Cara by resting her head against Cara's shoulder.

Cara brushed a strand of hair from her cheek. "I'm proud of you for trying to help her. You have such a big heart."

"I do?" After a pause, she added, "Jonah says you have one, too."

"Yeah?"

Beth Ann shifted to look at Cara's face. "He said you would always forgive me, no matter what I did." Wary hope flickered in her blue eyes.

Cara's breath caught in her throat. "He's right. I always will." She paused. "Is there something specific you mean?"

Beth Ann thought for a few seconds, then said, "Not really. But what you said, the night I cried, about how I felt when you almost died?"

"Yes?" Cara held her breath. Beth Ann had never spoken of this with her.

"I did feel like that. Scared and mad at you. And that night…I felt that way again. My brain went, like, black. It was dumb. I acted like a scared baby."

"It wasn't dumb. And you weren't a baby. You experienced a trauma. Doctors know that trauma stays with people for a long time. You're very grown-up and brave, Beth Ann. Almost too brave. You hold in so much."

Cara swallowed before continuing, "I know I let you down. Maybe you're not sure of me yet, but I want you to trust me, to talk to me about what bothers you."

Beth Ann studied her. She didn't speak, but there was relief in the way she lay back against Cara's shoulder. This was a breakthrough. Beth Ann had talked for the first time about what had happened. Cara swallowed back the tears that would spoil the moment.

"Did you tell Jonah that I cried?" Beth Ann asked abruptly, turning to look at her. "Does he think I'm a baby? Is that why he won't talk to me anymore?"

"What?" That made no sense. "What exactly did Jonah say?"

"He said to talk to you not him about personal stuff. He said he's not good at it, but that's not why. I know it."

As her daughter spoke, it all became clear. Jonah had heard Cara's concerns about Beth Ann not confiding in her and tried to fix it in his own clumsy way. "I think what Jonah was trying to do was help you and me talk about our feelings more. Like we did just now."

"What?" Beth Ann wrinkled her forehead, confused.

"He likes you a lot. He likes talking to you, but he feels like you talk to him more than to me. He wanted to help us."

"That's dumb," she said. "Are you sure?"

"Almost positive." Cara's heart seemed to break open in her chest. "But I'll go talk to him and be certain."

"Will he get mad that I tattled?"

"Absolutely not. I'm sure of that."

"Okay." Beth Ann sighed. "I'm tired now." She scooted down under the sheet, ready to sleep.

Cara kissed her forehead. "If you wake up and want to talk, you can call me at Jonah's. The number's—"

"In Rosie's book. I know," she said sleepily. "Good night."

"Sleep tight." At the door, Cara looked back at her daughter, lit by the softly glowing peace sign—one more gentle gift from Jonah—and smiled.

Then she ran to Jonah's trailer and knocked on the door.

He threw it open. "Did something happen? Is it Rosie?"

"Rosie's the same. Something happened, but it's a good thing. Beth Ann and I had a breakthrough and it was because of you."

"Because of me?" He looked puzzled.

"You told her I had a big heart and that I would always forgive her."

"I said that, yeah."

"Because of you, she opened up to me for the first time in a long time."

"So I didn't step in it for once."

He seemed so relieved she almost laughed. "You spoke from the heart. And no one's heart's bigger than yours. Don't doubt that."

He turned red. "Thanks, I guess."

Standing there on his porch, she realized how much she cared for him.

And wanted him. This was more than desire. This was *yearning*. She *had* to be in his arms again, to feel what she'd felt before.

Cara had stopped them because she thought she was hopeless, and because of Beth Ann, but she knew better now. She could hold Beth Ann in her heart and still be with Jonah.

"I want to try again," she blurted, not thinking it through first. "You gave me hope. I don't want to lose that or give up."

"You want to... I gave you...what?"

Her words weren't sinking in for some reason, so she went to kiss him, but he caught her arms. "We can't do this. You were right to end it."

"But I thought you wanted..." *Me*. She couldn't say it. Hot shame poured through her, making her want to melt into the deck.

"I did. I do, God help me, more than ever. But it won't work. It sounds simple, but it won't be. There will be snarls. It would kill me to hurt you."

Cara stared at him, stunned, unprepared to argue, not sure she should. Was he right? Would this be a mistake? Did she really know him? She'd been wrong before. Dangerously wrong.

"Have a glass of water with me." He held the door for her and she followed him to his tiny kitchen while he poured their drinks. The moonlight made the water glisten and turned the ice cubes to silver.

As she accepted the glass, her glance landed on his windowsill, where two yellow hearts glowed up at her from circles of red. The good-luck charms from three weeks ago. "You kept these?" She put them on her palm.

"Didn't seem right to toss them." He smiled faintly.

"Because it would be bad luck?"

"I think people make their own luck, so no."

"Why then?"

"Because you got so embarrassed when they matched, had to explain that they'd *clumped*."

"I was afraid you'd think I set it up, that I wanted us to fall in love."

"That would have been crazy. You were on the way out of town."

"But I didn't go."

"No. You stayed for Rosie."

"And I was glad to see more of you."

"Same for me."

"Despite the din…and the disruption?"

"Maybe because of that." Jonah's eyes held hers close, as if understanding her was all that mattered to him in the world. Shadows made his strong jaw stronger, the bones of his face crisper, his straight nose straighter.

Cara studied the hearts glowing in her palm,

and her doubts melted like the ice in her glass. She wasn't wrong to try again. She knew this man. She'd seen him with Evan and Rosie and Beth Ann. He could be gruff at times and clumsy, too, but he did his best for the people he cared about. And he cared about her. He'd told her so. And she believed him.

Cara set down her water glass and locked gazes with Jonah. "I *do* believe in luck. I believe we're lucky to meet at this moment in our lives, when we're both coming out of—what did you call it, a rough patch? We can help each other."

"Yeah?" He put his water glass beside hers.

"I don't want to waste this good luck. We can keep it simple. We won't be together long enough to hit any snarls."

"Damn, I hope you're right," Jonah murmured, "because I'm only human and you're too damn close and you smell too damn pink for me to resist you one second longer."

He leaned in and kissed her. She met his tongue with her own. This time when the wave came, she let it take her, tumble her, make her tremble. She pressed her hands to his back, letting the gummy hearts drop to the floor. They'd served their purpose. They'd reminded her of Jonah's good heart, of their good fortune.

Cara was determined this time, sure she could power past her doubts and fears on the strength of her feelings for this man and his feelings for her. If she weren't half his size, she would have carried *him* to bed.

Instead, she backed him into the living room, down the short hall, so narrow they bumped both walls, then to his bed. He turned her at the last second and lowered her first, lying at her side, looking down at her, eyes burning.

She would think only of Jonah, a man who respected her, cared for her, even admired her. A man she cared for and respected.

He edged his fingers under her shirt, stopping at her bra, waiting for her signal. His jaw was tense, his muscles tight. He was holding back, following her lead. He would go slow, touch her first, patiently wait his turn.

But she didn't want that this time. She didn't want to be fragile or tentative or nervous. She didn't need to be. This was Jonah, not Barrett. He would never trap her or try to own her or make her act against her better judgment, let alone against her will.

"I want you with me," she said. "I want us to be together. Let's get undressed." They took off their clothes and Jonah pulled the sheet over them, which made her feel less exposed.

He shifted his leg so it was between hers, the soft friction of his hair delicious against her thighs, the pressure on her sex just right. She felt him, hard against her stomach.

Jonah cradled her head in his hands and lowered his mouth for a soft kiss. "I thought I'd never have you like this again."

He deepened the kiss, his tongue more insistent, and she kissed him back the same way. He shifted on top of her body. Bad memories teased at her, but she forced them back. *Be here. Feel this. Jonah. This is Jonah.* She gripped his butt with both hands, feeling the curve of muscle, noticing how she ached for him, her body rocking toward him, wanting him, ready for him, as he was ready for her.

This is good...so good... She was doing fine until Jonah stopped moving and reached past her. "Condom," he said, giving her a quick kiss.

It was only a few seconds, but it was long enough for her focus to slip. Now he loomed over her, so heavy, so much stronger than she was. He could overpower her so easily. Panic made it hard to breathe, and she knew it showed on her face. She was glad Jonah was looking elsewhere, parting her legs, easing into her body.

Cara had wanted this so much, longed for it, but her body had gone numb.

She closed her eyes to fight her way back. *You want this. This is Jonah. Forget Barrett. Barrett's gone forever. Think about Jonah, only Jonah.*

Jonah stopped moving.

She opened her eyes.

"I lost you," he said.

"I'm here. I just…" Shame washed over her. "Don't give up on me." If she didn't push through, she might never have the courage to try again.

CHAPTER FOURTEEN

NOT LIKE THIS. Not with that haunted look in her eyes. CJ was lost in the past, reliving whatever her ex had put her through in bed. He hated that she'd been hurt in such a personal way.

If he stopped, she'd be embarrassed and disappointed.

He had an idea. Holding her tight, he rolled over and put her on top. CJ's eyes widened, looking down at him. "What are you doing?"

"Letting you take the wheel," he said, hoping to hell this worked for her.

She sat up slowly. Damn, she was beautiful above him. Her cheeks were flushed, her lips swollen. The heavy locket rested between her pale breasts. He wanted to press his mouth to those breasts, run his tongue over her nipples and—

It's her show. Let her run it. Jonah rested his hands lightly on her hips, determined to follow her lead, pick up her rhythm, not grab what he wanted. He wanted it all.

She blinked at him and took a shaky breath. Had she never been on top?

"You okay?"

She nodded, adjusted her knees and lifted herself, then wiggled lower on his shaft. He ached to catch the down stroke hard, but he resisted, letting her test-drive the position.

She repeated the move, a smile stretching, slow and sexy. "I like this. This feels good."

"Oh, yeah."

"I'm back," she said, leaning down for a slow kiss while her hips rocked.

"Good to know," he said, relief easing his tension.

She sat up and began to ride him in earnest, her breasts bouncing gently, her back arched, bucking against the base of his shaft. He slid a finger into her cleft. She was so wet and swollen he almost came himself.

CJ's eyes flew open. "Oh, oh. That's, oh…" She began really moving now, giving out little cries. He stayed with her, riding her rhythm, watching her face. Her eyes were glazed, her mouth slack, her cheeks bright with color. What had she said about pupils pulsating? Hers were doing that for sure.

"It's… I'm…" she gasped. "Oh…I'm… I'm… oh…" With a sharp cry, she dropped onto his chest, jolting and trembling.

"…coming. You're coming," he breathed. "So am I." His release came from somewhere deep, bringing with it old sorrows, old pain, washing it all away in wave after wave, leaving only soft pleasure shuddering through him.

When they'd both stilled, he wrapped his arms around her, breathing her in—sweet pink, night air and woman. He stroked her hair, feeing her heartbeat slow, her breathing settle. He felt good. He felt...*happy*. He would remember this for the rest of his life. "CJ," he breathed near her ear.

She pushed up to look him in the eyes. "It's Cara. Cara's my real name."

"Cara," he repeated, touched that she'd told him. He noticed her locket resting between her breasts. He picked it up. "Can I see?"

She nodded. He opened it and held it so they could both see the picture. It was a blonde toddler holding a stuffed rabbit.

"This is...Beth Ann?" He knew their real names. That felt good.

"Yep. And that's Bunny." She pointed at the stuffed animal.

"The grubby thing she was carrying the day you came into the diner?"

"Yes. She hangs on to him when she's insecure."

He closed the locket. "Speaking of that...you leave her my number?"

"I didn't have to. She knew where it was all along."

"Good."

"Thank you for this."

"Don't *thank* me, for God's sake. I was there, remember? Enjoying every minute."

"Being on top was a good idea. It brought me back and gave me control. Thank you for staying with me." Tears shone in her eyes.

"You pushed through, Cara. You did it." He brushed her hair from her eyes, filled with tenderness for this woman who'd been broken, but was coming back strong. He thought about the two hearts winking golden on his windowsill and this soft and sexy woman in his arms. *If that wasn't luck, what was?*

CARA JOLTED AWAKE. Where was she? The low ceiling made her remember. Jonah's bed. She'd drifted to sleep.

"What's wrong?" Jonah said foggily.

"Nothing." She squinted at the clock. "It's late. I should go."

"Not yet." He pulled her back against him, his fingers barely caressing her skin. That felt soo good. "Mmm, Cara," he said, sniffing her neck. "You smell even more pink now."

Alarm flickered. He'd called her by her real name. "You have to call me CJ in the café and everywhere else. And Beth Ann is—"

"Bunny. Got it. Sure." He kissed his way to her shoulder.

This was heaven, lying here. She was so happy, so relieved. She'd shoved Barrett out of her head—and her bed—she hoped for good, with the help of the wonderful man curved around her body, his fingers now busy...*Oh, what was he* doing *to her?*

Despite how late it was, and how satisfied she'd been, she wanted more. She rubbed herself against him.

He groaned. "If you're going to go, you'd better stop that."

"Maybe I can stay a little while longer."

He chuckled against her throat. "Good decision." He reached past her, then held out the condom packet. "Last one. Should I buy more?"

"Enough to last the summer," she said, not hesitating one bit.

Afterward, she headed for the café, the moon bright, the air soft on her skin. Her feet seemed to barely touch the ground.

As she reached the porch, doubts flickered. What if she was wrong? What if her panic returned? What if they got snarled up? What if someone got hurt?

Cara glanced back at the trailer. As if in answer, Jonah stood on his porch, a sheet around his hips, her big protective bear of a man, making sure she got safely home. He raised a hand. She waved, her doubts completely erased.

WITH ONE GIANT breath, Beth Ann blew out all ten of her candles, filling the air with waxy smoke. "I did it!" she said. "Now my wish will come true, Rosie."

Cara guessed Beth Ann had wished for Rosie to get chemo. In the four days since they'd heard the diagnosis, Beth Ann had been engaged in a quietly persistent battle to convince Rosie to do the right thing.

They'd made headway—Cara had seen Rosie reading Jonah's research, hiding it in her news-paper—but Rosie was stubborn.

"It's a party, for God's sake," Rosie said. "Cut the damn cake."

Rachel gasped at Rosie's language. Beth Ann had invited her favorite friend from day camp to spend the night with her.

"Rosie swears a lot," Beth Ann said. "You'll get used to it."

Beside Cara, Jonah squeezed her hand under the table, which gave her butterflies. She strug-gled to keep her face normal. Already, Rosie had asked her twice if she felt faint. They'd agreed to keep their relationship private, but Cara knew it was hard to hide her glow, or how often their eyes met.

Cara served the cake Beth Ann had "invented"—cherry-chocolate-chip with lemon-blueberry frosting, which turned out to taste delicious—then Beth Ann opened her gifts. Rachel's present was a beading kit, which Beth Ann loved. Cara's gift was practical—new school clothes.

"Clothes?" Rosie said disgustedly. "That's not a birthday gift. Here." She shoved a newspaper-wrapped box toward Beth Ann, who tore it open, then gasped.

"It's the *Wonder Woman* comics. But you said I couldn't touch them."

"Not until your birthday, of course," Rosie said. "Now that's a proper present."

"Thank you so much." Beth Ann left her chair and threw her arms around Rosie, who turned bright red.

"They're collectible so take care of them," she said gruffly, but her eyes shone with emotion.

"Let's go upstairs and read them," Beth Ann said to Rachel.

"I have something for you," Jonah said, standing. "It's outside."

"Outside?" Cara looked up at him.

"You'll like it," he said with a wink. "Let's go." He started for the door.

"I've already seen it," Rosie said. "I'm going to eat another piece of that god-awful cake, then go to the TV and watch the Beverly Hills house-wives bitch at each other."

Jonah led the rest of the party across the lot. As they neared the stand of trees, Cara caught glimpses of boards in the low boughs of a huge pine.

"You built my castle!" Beth Ann shrieked, then ran there, Rachel at her heels.

"You built a tree house?" Cara tried to keep the dismay from her voice.

"She said she wished her castle was real." He shrugged.

"But we'll be—" *Leaving soon.* She couldn't bring herself to say it out loud. "It was so much work for—" *so little time.*

"There's still eight weeks, Cara," he said in a low voice. "That's a lot of time to enjoy the tree house and everything else."

He meant the two of them, she knew. They'd only been together four days and already she dreaded the goodbye. She'd get a preview when Jonah went to New York for his show in two weeks.

In the meantime, Cara loved every minute they spent together. Each time they made love, her bad memories faded further. Sex was amazing with a man she trusted. Every night they tried some-thing new. Jonah made her feel so attractive, so desired, it made her shiver just thinking about the way he looked at her.

"Come check it out," he said to her, guiding her with a hand to her back.

The gesture no longer made her nervous. Not with Jonah. He wouldn't push her anywhere she didn't want to go.

When they reached the tree house, Beth Ann leaned down from the opening. "We're going to sleep out here tonight, okay? With flashlights and sleeping bags?"

"I don't see why not." Her daughter's joy was a delight to see.

"You have to come up here, Mom," she said.

"Go ahead," Jonah said. "There's room."

Cara climbed the rungs he'd hammered into the trunk and lifted herself into the "castle." There was plenty of room for her and the girls and a small table on low legs. Jonah climbed the ladder so his head and shoulders were visible. "This is nice," she said.

"Just the basics," he replied, but she could see it had the polish and beauty of all Jonah's work.

Beth Ann exclaimed over the shelves, the windows and tiny curtains, the ledge to sit on, complete with round orange pillows that Rosie had contributed. She'd made the curtains, too, from tie-dyed cotton.

"I love it so much." Beth Ann lunged to hug Jonah.

"Glad to hear that." Jonah cleared his throat.

"Can you get Louis up here?" Rachel said.

"Sure, I can," Beth Ann said. "Jonah says I'm the Cat Whisperer."

The girls spent the evening running back and forth between the apartment and the castle, gathering toys, snacks, pillows and flashlights.

Finally, at ten, Cara called up to them from the base of the tree house, "Permission to say goodnight to the fair damsels?"

She'd tucked Bunny discreetly into a pillowcase to give to Beth Ann, since she'd want it to sleep with, but might not want Rachel to know.

"You may enter, mi'lady," Beth Ann said.

Rachel giggled.

Cara found them reading comic books by flashlights, eating birthday cake.

"Everything okay?"

"Yeah," Beth Ann said. "It's great."

She slipped the pillowcase to her daughter, who looked inside. "No, thanks," she said, handing it back.

Beth Ann didn't need her comfort object. Wow. *Meow.*

Cara did a double take. Louis was curled up on Beth Ann's sleeping bag. He looked at her with his one good eye. *I've got this,* he seemed to say.

"Don't stay up all night now. If I'm not in the apartment, I'll be at Jonah's for a bit." They would stay dressed until she was certain the girls were asleep.

Cara climbed down, smiling. Beth Ann was bouncing back. She'd made a friend. That was wonderful, but also sad. She'd have to say good-bye to Rachel, too, along with the tree house, the cat, Rosie and Jonah.

She stopped to let the breeze lift her hair. The white lights of Jonah's deck seemed to welcome her. She loved being with him. She loved the café. Beth Ann was happy here. It would be so hard to leave.

What if they stayed? According to Rosie, the schools were good. Beth Ann already had a friend. Cara could follow through on the café improvements. And she could be with Jonah. The idea quickened her pulse.

All she'd wanted was a safe home. Why couldn't it be here?

She started toward Jonah's, then remembered she wanted to show him the new staff uniform shirt she'd ordered—yellow cotton, the logo in purple, to be worn with purple shorts, a skirt or slacks—so she headed back to the apartment, her steps light, feeling happy, thinking that maybe they could stay in New Hope for a while.

The uniform box was empty, and Rosie told

her she'd washed the shirt to be sure it wouldn't shrink, and it was now in the dryer.

In the laundry room, Cara opened the dryer door. The scent made her instantly sick. She glanced up at the shelf and saw a new box of dryer sheets—the brand she'd used three years ago. She backed out of the room, leaning on the wall to wait for the nausea to fade.

The day Barrett attacked her, she'd been drying one last load before she and Beth Ann left for Barstow. Barrett was living in a hotel at the time to *wait for Cara to trust him again.* But that wasn't going to happen. The black rage that came over him when she even mentioned divorce told her he would hurt her, so she knew she and Beth Ann had to get away.

She had changed the locks, and started packing, placating him on the phone to buy enough time to organize their departure.

That morning, she'd turned to get the laundry basket and found Barrett in the doorway, his face a mask of cold fury.

How had he gotten in? In her haste, she must have forgotten to lock the door after Beth Ann went next door to play with a friend.

Slowly, Barrett closed the door, a sick smile on his face, a predatory look in his eyes.

You promised me time, he said in a slow, hypnotic voice, *but I see packed bags. I won't have that, Cara. I won't let you destroy our family. I love you too much for that.*

When she tried to push past him, he grabbed her arm, knocking over the box of dryer sheets, spilling them everywhere. She twisted away, but slipped on the dryer sheets and hit the floor. He was on her, choking her. She gasped, blacking out, smelling the sweet powder of the fabric softener. She scratched his face and he let go for a second, then yanked her to her feet and threw her against the wall. She tried to reach the door, but he grabbed her again. He looked here and there. *For a weapon,* she realized. He wanted to kill her.

Finally he gave up and threw her against the washing machine with all his might. Her last thought was of Beth Ann. She had to stay alive for her daughter. Pain flared and everything went black.

Cara had survived to protect her daughter. And that was still her mission. Barrett was after her again. If he found her, he would finish what he'd started. He would kill her. And Beth Ann? What would become of her?

You can't stay here. You're not safe. Not yet. Never forget that.

The sickening smell faded from her nose, but she didn't dare let her fear fade. Again, she'd dropped her guard. The joys of living here had pulled her in. Two months was as much time as she dared risk here.

They needed the safety of an anonymous city and a shelter designed to protect families like hers. And that was only a way station until she'd paid for new identities and truly started over.

Even then...would she ever truly be safe?

THE FOLLOWING THURSDAY night, Cara stood at the back of the crowded bar with Jonah, applauding Devil's Anvil Reborn as they finished the first set. It was eleven and she was wiped out, her legs aching, her head full of sawdust.

It had been a full day, including a private dinner for the band and crew, who'd stumbled out of the big black tour bus into the café at 5:00 p.m.

Jonah studied her face. "Let me drive you home. You need sleep." It still startled her how closely he watched over her. She had to admit she loved being so precious to him.

"I want to congratulate Evan."

"Then it's straight to bed. *Your* bed. So you'll sleep."

"I'll just lie there wanting you."

His sharp inhale gratified her. It was almost scary how a mere look or touch could set them both on fire. The heat built all day and by the time they got to bed, it was a wildfire that all but consumed them.

Since that moment in the laundry room, she'd tried to keep her head on straight. She didn't dare get so wrapped up in Jonah, in the life they shared here, that she forgot the danger. She could feel herself leaning into him, depending on him. That was how she'd been with Barrett when they were first married. That thought chilled her, as it should. She made herself think it often.

Evan strode up to them, clearly proud of himself. "What did you think?" he asked eagerly.

"They're great," Cara said. "You filled the place."

"Yeah. Carlos is seeing dollar signs. Thanks for the dinner at the café. The food was great."

"They seemed to go wild for the good-luck buns," she said.

"I know. The band's manager was impressed. He says if they score a contract in L.A., he might have a publicity job for me."

She felt Jonah go still beside her. He worried about Evan's sobriety if he got too deeply into the music industry, but he'd been trying not to criticize him.

Evan was waiting for Jonah's reaction. Cara crossed her fingers that he'd say something helpful.

He glanced at her, then seemed to dig deep before he spoke to his brother. "I hope you get the job you want."

"Yeah?" Evan looked stunned. "You mean that?"

Jonah nodded.

"I know you're afraid I'll relapse," Evan said, "but I'm not cocky like I was. I check in more with my sponsor. I watch myself. I'm different, I swear."

"I've been in your face your whole life, Ev. It's time I stepped back." Jonah paused. "I'm there if you need me. No questions asked."

"I appreciate that," Evan said, his voice shaky. Abruptly, he threw his arms around his brother and hugged him.

Now Jonah looked stunned. "I'm proud of you," he said huskily.

"I won't let you down, Jonah."

They broke apart. Neither could meet each other's gaze.

"Gotta check the sound," Evan mumbled and slipped into the crowd.

"I hope I did right," Jonah said to Cara. "He's walking a wire with no net."

"You're his net. He knows that."

"In AA they call that enabling." He smiled wryly.

"You're telling him you trust him. That's what he needs from you."

"He's a grown man, not a kid I have to nag to brush his teeth. He's got to make his own way."

"You've changed your attitude."

"You started me thinking that day we looked through my box of childhood crap. I'm about ready to track down our mother, see what she has to say for herself. It would help him to hear it wasn't his fault."

"And for you?"

"It might be good for me, too." He gave a swift smile. "Looks like you renovated me along with the café."

"It wasn't me. *You* made the changes, not me."

"You showed me things I've missed." He shook his head. "Jesus, enough. I sound like I'm on a talk show." He gazed at her with so much tenderness her heart felt like it might burst in her chest.

I love you, Jonah.

Cara almost said it out loud, but caught herself in time. Not saying it didn't change how she felt, or how much it would hurt to leave when it was time. Talk about a snarl.

She refused to regret it, despite the pain to come. They were helping each other heal at a crucial moment in their lives. When it was time, they would send each other off on their separate journeys with champagne and confetti, high spirits and hopes.

And a broken heart. Maybe two, if Jonah felt the same.

"Surprise!" The shout was so loud it seemed to make the helium balloons sway over the café tables. Jonah grinned as Cara turned his way, her jaw hanging open, her blue eyes huge.

"You said a quiet birthday dinner!"

He laughed. "That's why they call it a *surprise party.*"

"Oh, my goodness." She turned back to the people gathered around her—a bigger crowd than he'd expected, but Cara warmed everyone she met. Of course they'd want to wish her well on her birthday. "I'm… I don't know what to say. Just…thank you."

"'Bout time you got here," Rosie said. "They've about scarfed up the pantry waiting on you." Rosie had made most of the calls, surprising Jonah with her enthusiasm. She loved the hell out of Cara.

Jonah couldn't take his eyes off Cara as she moved through the café, mingling, touching a shoulder, sharing a laugh, accepting a hug. She meant so much to him. She'd turned him around, eased his grief, filled his life with warmth and laughter and life.

And desire.

Lots of that. All he could think about was getting her alone again. He wanted to give her his birthday gifts and then he wanted to take her to bed.

It almost hurt to look at her. He had it bad.

He went to get a pitcher to refill people's glasses with the fresh-squeezed lemonade Cara had insisted they offer. She'd been right about that. And the changes to the café. It looked new, fresh and bright. But then so did the world now that he'd been sleeping with her.

Colors were more vivid. Sunset burned his eyes. Food tasted richer. Smells knocked him dead. The wood he worked felt alive.

And Cara. Cara hit him hardest of all. A glance across the café made his knees cave, the brush of her hips in the kitchen electrified him.

They couldn't keep their hands off each other, sneaking into the pantry for stolen kisses when they could, exchanging hot looks when they couldn't. He didn't think he'd felt like this with Suzanne, not even at the beginning.

Every time he kissed Cara, he got the same rush, as strong and fresh as the first time their lips had met. He was glad they'd worked out a way to be together. He felt good. He felt…happy.

And uneasy as hell.

If it hurt to take his eyes off her now, he didn't want to think how he'd feel when she left for good. What would he do with himself? Hide in his cave, pull the covers back over his head?

No. The whole point was to enjoy what they had, then move on, all the better for the time they'd spent together.

Still, he felt like he walked on loose boards. Any minute, he'd crash through to the basement below and break a leg...or worse.

An hour later, Cara blew out the candles on the cake Beth Ann had made her, Rosie at her side. "Pay attention, you all," Rosie barked out. "Now I got you hostage to the cake, I want to say a few words. Lift your damn drinks."

Around the café, glasses rose. No one argued with Rosie Underhill.

"Here's to CJ," Rosie said, raising her lemonade. "Who has messed up my life, plain and simple. Taken over my spare rooms, made me eat salad and forced me to sell off half my inventory and most of my heirlooms."

"You mean that sad pile of junk?" Carver Johnson called out amiably. Laughter rippled through the room.

"You shut up, you old goat. Then there's her daughter. Not only can she whip me in poker, she's got me hooked on these housewife reality shows. I never saw so many fake boobs in my life."

Everyone laughed.

"And don't get me started on this café. Lord God what CJ's done in here. Painted it up like Disneyland, filled it with sweet rolls, pissed off the bistro girls by using up my garden...and stealing their customers."

"Hear, hear!" Carver called.

"Now we're so damn busy we had to hire back Darlene and start serving out on the patio."

Jonah had laid down flagstone and they'd set out colorful umbrellas over the tables.

"Yay, Darlene," someone called.

"But that's not the worst. The absolute *worst* is how she bosses me around. I believe they call that *elder abuse*."

More laughter.

"She dragged me to the doctor, forced me to have surgery and nagged me about more medicine. Her daughter wasted her birthday wish on me." She gave Beth Ann a soft look, then cleared her throat.

"Basically, she's been another Eddie Underhill. And, trust me, no one needs two of that man."

The crowd hummed quietly.

Rosie turned to Cara. "If I had the brains God gave a beagle, I would have paid you for that first shift and sent you down the road to a real mechanic."

"Hey, now," Rusty hollered. "Fast, cheap and good. Pick two."

The laughter was quiet, as people sensed Rosie was going to announce something. Jonah hoped like hell she'd decided on chemotherapy.

"But I let you stay, sad to say. And now, it looks

like I have no choice but to get shot up with poison and strafed by lasers."

"You'll get treated?" Cara asked. "Really?"

"If that's what it takes to get you and your pit bull of a daughter out of my personal business."

Beth Ann threw her arms around Rosie's waist and hugged her.

"Hey, now. You're spilling my lemonade." But when Beth Ann let go, Rosie put her arm around her and held her close as she lifted her glass. "So, a toast to CJ on her birthday. And good luck to the poor sucker she picks on next."

Shouts of "Hear, hear" filled the room, along with applause and whistling. Rosie cut the sheet cake, handing the plates to Beth Ann and her friend Rachel, who carried them to the guests. Jonah stood toward the back of the room.

"Here." Beth Ann thrust a paper plate at him. "Is it okay if me and Rachel use your computer?"

"Sure. The Instant Message shortcut is on the desktop, since the task bar was so full."

Her eyes shot to his, alarmed.

"It's fine that you added it."

"Please don't tell my mom, okay? She won't let me be online, but I'm always safe and I only talk to friends. Please."

"Sure," he said, but he didn't think Cara would mind. It was probably leftover hovering.

After the cake had been eaten, the guests trailed

out. Darlene, Charlie and Ernesto had cleanup duties, so Jonah and Cara went to say goodbye to Rosie. "You made the right decision," Jonah said. "Eddie would be proud."

"How would you know? You never met the man." She patted his cheek so hard it hurt, the way she used to when they'd lived with her, the mother they'd needed at the time.

"Then *I'm* proud of you. I want you around."

"God knows why. All I do is give you hell."

"It's good for me. Keeps me in line."

"And don't you forget it." She studied him. "I have to stick around a bit longer to see what comes of this." She waved her hand between Jonah and Cara.

"What?" Jonah said.

Cara gulped.

"Oh, cut it out. Like it's not obvious the way you moon over each other. Bunny says it's nice that you both like movies so much, since you watch them almost every night."

Jonah swallowed. Cara turned pink.

"Far as I know there's no DVD player in that trailer."

Cara gave a nervous laugh.

"Just take care of each other," Rosie said in an uncharacteristically tender voice. "That's all I'll say on that."

When Jonah looked at Cara, it hit him like a

punch. He was in love with her. He'd fallen for the sprite who'd danced into his diner over a month ago to dazzle him and bring him back to life. So much for keeping it simple.

CHAPTER FIFTEEN

Take care of each other.

Rosie's words caught Cara totally off guard. She sounded so sincere, so tender, so not like Rosie that Cara almost blurted, *Yes, of course. That's what people in love do.*

But she couldn't say that and it made her ache, turned her joy bittersweet. They told Rosie goodnight and headed for Jonah's place, where he had her birthday gift.

"Thank you for the party," she said, as they set off.

"Rosie did most of it. She's gone soft on us, thanks to you."

"I'm so glad she decided to get treated."

"Me, too. You worked your magic on her—you and Beth Ann."

"What she said meant a lot to me." She'd been so touched by Rosie's praise she'd had to dig her nails into her palms to hold back the tears.

The feeling kept coming: *You belong here, with these people. This is home.*

It couldn't be. *You can't stay. You're not safe.*

Barrett's after you. She made herself repeat the mantra, but it sounded weaker and weaker.

"It was all true." Jonah put his arm around her. Cara made sure no one could see.

"The secret's out," he said. "No use pretending."

"I guess not."

Jonah kissed her hair and held her close as they climbed the steps to his deck. He bent to pick up a box lying on the bench and handed it to her.

She read the label. "Nails? A do-it-yourself gift?"

"That's just the box. Open it."

She shook the box over her hand, and out fell a keychain with a wooden bear attached. It stood upright, its fur, snout and eyes so precise it seemed alive. "You carved your spirit animal. It's beautiful."

"To keep you safe wherever you go." His dark eyes held her close. He was preparing them for when she had to leave.

"I'll cherish this forever." She rose to kiss him in thanks.

"Hang on. That's not all. Close your eyes."

She did and he led her into the trailer. "Now open them."

Cara saw the rocking chair, gleaming in the lamplight. He'd folded back the table to make room for it.

"It's yours," he said.

She looked up at him. "But you made this for…" Cara couldn't finish. "This is too personal. You must have…memories."

"You showed me I'd pushed past the worst of them. You gave me back the beauty of the piece. I want to think of you and Beth Ann using it."

Tears sprang to her eyes. "I don't know what to say."

"Sit." He picked up a camera from the bench. "I need a photo to hang."

Cara sat and he snapped a picture. "Got it," he said, putting down the camera.

She leaned back and pushed off, floating on air. "This is an amazing chair." The seat hugged her bottom, the slats her back, the armrests her arms. "I can feel the love you put into it."

Sadness flashed in his eyes.

"Was that the wrong thing to say?"

"No." He sat on the bench and motioned for her to give him her foot, so he could rub it as he did most nights. She kicked off her sandal and put her foot in his hand.

"Rosie told you about the miscarriage." He shot her a look.

"She mentioned it, yes."

He nodded, using his thumbs to stretch her instep. Warmth poured through her. "I was finishing the chair when Suzanne started bleeding." He kept his head down as he talked. "Seven months. We were so close." He swallowed, shook his head. "They induced labor. The birth was hell. I've never seen anyone suffer like that."

"You don't have to tell me, if it's too hard."

Jonah raised his eyes, a determined expression there. "It's the story of the chair. I want you to know." He shifted his grip to her heel. The pleasant sensation contrasted with the sadness of his story.

"Suzanne was devastated. I held her and told her it would be all right, but it wouldn't and we both knew it. They were empty words."

"It's hard to know what to say."

"After a while I stopped trying. I took care of the practical stuff—the bills, the burial arrangements, the sympathy calls. I fixed meals neither of us ate, washed clothes when we ran out of clean ones, went to work."

He looked at her again, his dark eyes anguished. "I escaped in my shop. I told myself I was giving her space, but I was running from her pain." He motioned for Cara to lift her other foot. He cupped his hand around it.

"You were grieving, too."

"I was her *husband. For better or worse,* remember? When life was easy, I managed to fake it. But when it got bad, I failed her."

"I'm so sorry." Cara wanted to ease his guilt, but he'd built a wall against her words.

"Eventually, Suzanne found the comfort she needed." He gave a brief, bitter smile. "The problem was she got it from my best friend and business partner."

"How awful." Talk about a betrayal.

"It started out innocent. Suzanne did our books and answered phones, so they were around each other. Jared's like Evan—good with people, easy with small talk." His voice was so rough it seemed the words hurt his throat.

"I was relieved to see her happy, so I didn't question it. Until the morning they met me in the office to tell me they were in love."

"What did you say?"

"I didn't *say* anything. What I did was punch Jared in the face."

Cara sucked in a breath, picturing Jonah raising a fist. It was a terrible image, reminding her of Barrett so much she felt ill.

"The worst was Suzanne. She cowered like she expected me to hit her next. The look on her face will stay with me until the day I die."

She'd experienced what Suzanne had. She'd faced a violent man. She knew that helpless terror. *Jonah's not Barrett.* Cara tried to say something reassuring, but the words wouldn't come.

"The minute my arm cocked back I felt it—my

father's rage. I was acting the way he would have. It scared the hell out of me. I knew I was like him, but I'd never hit anyone before."

It scared her, too. That's how she'd felt when Jonah yelled at her at the bowling alley. She pushed back that thought. "You didn't hit her."

"I didn't have to. The damage was done. And being sorry didn't fix it."

Barrett had been sorry, too, when he lost his temper, grabbed her, threatened her. *I would never hurt you. You're my life. I'll do better.*

And Cara had believed him too many times. He'd almost killed her.

This is different. Jonah's not Barrett. He's a good man.

"I'm sorry to frighten you," Jonah said, "but you should know who I am and what my limits are." He put down her foot and took her hands, pressing them between his own. "I need the reminder. When I'm with you, I forget." He paused. "Especially lately. I'm in love with you, Cara."

Her heart leaped in her chest. *They were in love.* That didn't happen every day. Couldn't they find a way to be together? Didn't love conquer all?

In movies and books. Not here, not in her life. The part of her that had kept her and Beth Ann safe so far told her that. "I love you, too. I do." She took a deep breath. "That only makes this harder. I have to leave."

"I know." He looked sad, but resigned.

She gripped the chair arms. "But I'll always have the bear you carved and this chair to remind me of you, of how happy I was. Will you help me strap it to the roof of the car?"

"I can do better than that. I've got a small trailer you can take."

"That'd be great. Maybe we can take the bike Rosie gave Beth Ann. Something for her to remember, too."

"Happy birthday, Cara," he said, pulling her up and into his arms.

She did feel happy. But sadness had leaked in through the cracks and when they made love, Cara memorized every touch and feeling, as if it were the last time they'd be together. They had two more months, but they were already saying goodbye.

"TELL CJ to slap on some lipstick and fluff up her hair," Evan said to Jonah on the phone. He'd called in the middle of breakfast service.

"What are you talking about?"

"A TV crew from Tucson's doing a story on the good-luck buns. They're coming here first to talk to me, then out there. Noon or so."

"How'd this happen?" He looked out at Cara who was darting booth to booth with a plate of apple crumb cake she was trying out.

"From the *E!* segment. You saw it, right?"

"Not yet. Rosie recorded it. We haven't sat down to watch yet."

"Jesus, Jonah, keep up. Devil's Anvil Reborn told the *E!* host that the buns gave them the luck that got their record deal."

"You're kidding."

"Nope. I've been pitching the story ever since. TV 6 is the first nibble. It's local, but it's a start. The publicity should be great for the café."

"I'll tell CJ. She'll be thrilled."

But when Jonah told her, she nearly dropped her tray. "Are you crazy? I can't be on TV. I have to stay invisible."

"It's a local station, what's the big deal? It'll bring in more customers."

"What if it gets picked up by other affiliates?"

"That seems like a long shot to me."

"I can't risk it. Rosie has to do the interview. Darlene can cover my tables."

"I think you're overreacting," he said.

"You have no idea what my husband is capable of." She was pale and trembling. She looked like a hunted animal. Cara ran off to tell Rosie, leaving Jonah holding her tray.

What the hell had her ex done to her? He wanted to erase that look forever. He wanted to make her feel safe, to protect her. He wanted her to stay and be with him. That was the truth of it.

So you can fail her, too? Hurt her?

He knew better. So did she since he'd told her he'd hit Jared and made Suzanne cower. The look on Cara's face afterward...

It was the same one she'd just showed him. She'd been as afraid of him as she'd been of her ex. That truth crushed any hope of a future with her he dared have.

"THIS IS it. That's the café!" Rosie stabbed a finger at the TV screen. Cara sat with Rosie and Jonah to watch the news story about the good-luck buns.

Please let it be okay, Cara prayed. *Please, please.* She felt Jonah's eyes on her. He thought she was being paranoid, but he was wrong. She knew that for sure. All her instincts told her so.

They started with footage from *E!* where Devil's Anvil Reborn declared the good-luck buns had won them their contract. Next, Evan told the reporter he'd had calls from bands all over the country wanting to play at the bowling alley and buy the lucky buns. That sounded like an exaggeration, but it made for good publicity for him.

Then they shifted to the café to interview Rosie, who stood stiffly in front of the counter wearing a ruffled dress and too much makeup.

"God, I look like a hooker. And in that dress... make that a *fat* hooker. Why didn't you tell me, Jonah?"

"I was in the kitchen," Jonah said. "You look fine."

"Shh," Cara said, leaning in.

The reporter said, "I'm here at the New Hope Café talking to—"

Rosie yanked the microphone from her hand. "You mean *Comfort* Café. New Hope's the town." The reporter seemed taken aback.

"She kept calling it that," Rosie said now. "Where do they get these idiots? Airhead Academy?"

Rosie told the reporter the baker preferred to remain anonymous, as Cara had asked her, then talked about how popular the buns were. Whew. Cara relaxed a little.

The scene changed to the patio. "Even kids love the special rolls," the reporter said. She thrust the microphone in front of a girl. Amanda, one of Beth Ann's camp friends.

"They're awesome," Amanda said. "Bunny's mom invented them." The shot widened to include *Beth Ann,* who smiled shyly.

"You let her be interviewed?" she demanded of Jonah.

"I didn't know. I was at the grill."

"So how do you feel about your mom's baking?" the reporter asked.

"Good." Beth Ann ducked her head.

Amanda pushed into the shot. "The rolls were

good luck for Bunny 'cuz she got me as a new friend."

The reporter finished with directions to the café and the phone number.

Cara froze. If Barrett saw this, he'd know where they were down to the highway marker and hours of operation.

The phone rang from the kitchen. "Here we go with the orders," Rosie crowed, going to answer it. Beth Ann came from the hallway. "You missed it, young lady," Rosie said to her. "You were on the news talking about your mom's lucky buns." Rosie turned the corner and picked up the phone.

"I was?" Beth Ann turned frightened eyes toward Cara.

"Why did you do that?" Cara said. "You know we have to be careful." Her ears were ringing and her brain buzzed with static. She couldn't think straight.

"Amanda made me." Beth Ann sucked in a breath. "Will he find us now? Do we have to leave?"

"I don't know. I have to—"

Jonah cut her off. "Of course not, Squirt. There's nothing to worry about."

Cara stared at him.

"It's true," he said. "It was ten seconds."

Cara forced herself to speak calmly to her

daughter. "Go back to your room for now. I'll decide what we need to do and come talk to you."

"I want to stay here," she said.

"I know you do. But if we have to leave, we will."

Beth Ann turned for the hall. Cara didn't trust her not to eavesdrop and Rosie might return any minute. "Let's talk downstairs," she said, starting for the door. When they reached the café, she turned on him.

"You had no right to contradict me with my daughter."

"You were scaring her. She's only a kid."

"She needs to be scared. We're in danger. One slip and he'll find us. She knows we have to be vigilant."

"Trust me, she's already plenty vigilant. She was terrified I would tell you she's been using Instant Message."

"She what?" Cara froze. "She's been online?"

"She uses my computer to text her friends. She told me she's safe about it."

"Safe? Are you kidding me? It's not possible to be safe online. My ex-husband has flagged our internet IDs for sure. What friends? Was one of them Serena?"

"I don't know. I didn't look."

"Serena is from where we were living before. Barrett would have talked to her. The TV spot is nothing compared to this." Cara could hardly breathe. Fear poured through her. "I can't believe you didn't tell me," she said, her mind spinning with the implications.

"You were getting along better with her and I didn't want to mess that up."

"So you put our lives in danger."

"That's extreme, Cara."

"When she said I didn't want her online, you should have known I had good reasons. You should have told me, Jonah."

"Your ex isn't a superspy. He can't be every-where."

She glared at him. "My husband is a family-practice lawyer. He knows police, prosecutors, judges. He hires investigators to track deadbeat dads. He's rich and ruthless." She paused for air. "On top of that, my own mother is helping him."

That hurt more than she'd let herself know.

Jonah looked chastened. "You should have told me."

"The less anyone knows about us, the safer we are. You should have trusted me."

He thought about that for a moment. "You have to be careful, sure, but it's far-fetched to think that a few text messages and a ten-second TV shot will bring the guy here. Beth Ann's been online for weeks. If your ex was that diabolical, wouldn't he be here by now?"

She hated the sneer in his voice, the condescension. *That was how Barrett talked to her.* A chill made her spine tingle. "Don't you dare mock me. I'm not a child afraid of the bogeyman."

"I'm asking you to be reasonable. You can't jump at every shadow. That's no way to live."

Cara was so angry she saw red. "Listen to me. I know what I'm talking about. When I tried to leave him, he nearly killed me. He slammed me into a washing machine and left me for dead."

Jonah paled. "My God."

"If my next-door neighbor hadn't checked on me, I would have been. As it was, I was in a coma for five days." The words seemed to tear at her throat as she said them, making it burn.

Jonah stared at her, horrified.

"He's obsessed with us. He wants us back. He wrote letter after letter from prison saying that without us he can't go on living."

Cara swallowed hard. "Am I getting through to you? Can you see the tabloid headline in the making? *Abusive husband fulfills prison vow—shoots wife and daughter, turns gun on self.* It happens every day to women like me."

The words made the danger real. They echoed in the air. They made her shake. "I do not intend to be a statistic, Jonah. If that makes me paranoid, then so be it."

She felt so betrayed, so alone. She knew what

she had to do. She had to leave. She'd known that from the beginning, but she'd been seduced into a sense of false security, lulled by the comforts of the café, the people, the joy of being needed... loved.

"What can I do to make you feel safe?" Jonah said.

"Make me *feel* safe? You think that's all I need? *There, there, little lady, don't you worry. I'll scare away that nasty monster you think is under the bed?*"

"That's not what I meant and you know it."

"Then what did you mean? You'll guard us? Stand outside our door at night with a rifle? And even if you wanted to, you leave for New York Thursday, remember?"

"So come with me." His eyes raced back and forth. He was thinking out loud. "We'll rent a place. That was my plan anyway. You'll be safe in New York. I'll come back to get Rosie through her treatments and make sure the café's staffed properly, then join you for good. You and Beth Ann."

She stared at him, totally blown away. "You would do that?"

Jonah would throw his life into chaos to save her from what he saw was unnecessary panic. Her fury melted instantly, replaced by relief and gratitude.

New York was huge, totally anonymous. The

headquarters of the domestic violence network was there. Surely she'd be safe. She'd be far away from Barrett. She'd be with the man she loved.

"I love you," he said. "I need to take care of you."

Need to. The words pulled her up short. So did the determined set of his jaw. This was his *duty* as her guardian, the way he saw it. He no doubt wanted to make up for how he thought he'd failed Suzanne, too.

"Jonah..." She felt so sad she almost couldn't say what she had to say. "No. You don't." Then she realized something more important than Jonah seeing her as a responsibility.

"You can't rescue me," she said, ashamed that she'd even for a moment considered that. "That's my job. Handing over my life to a man is what got me in trouble in the first place. I got myself into this. I have to get myself out of it."

Cara had let herself lean on Jonah just as she had with Barrett. Jonah wasn't Barrett, but there were too many echoes, too many similarities— Jonah's strength, his temper, his protective nature, his urge to ease burdens that were rightly hers to carry.

If she went with him to New York, every time he raised his voice, she would be reminded of Barrett. Every time they argued or she felt belittled or patronized, she would become the timid girl she'd been in her marriage.

Maybe all men would become Barrett for her. Maybe she'd wanted so much to be normal that she'd fooled them both into thinking she was.

"I want to do whatever you need me to do," he said stubbornly.

"I need you to step back," she said levelly. "You can't make up for what happened with Suzanne. You think you failed her. I don't believe that. You haven't failed me or anyone else here—Evan or Rosie or Beth Ann."

Her words hit home. She could see it in his face. He *was* trying to make up for his past and her refusal had hurt him, but it couldn't be helped.

"You don't have to do this alone."

"Yes, I do. And staying here with you makes it worse. It's time for us to leave." She knew it with everything in her. It was the TV segment, Beth Ann's texts to her friends, possibly Serena, and it was Jonah. Being with him had healed her in some ways, but it had also set her back, made her weaker, more dependent.

He stared at her. "You don't mean today."

"As soon as I can arrange things at the café. Rusty's working on my car, but I'll have to tell him to make it *fast* and *good* instead of *cheap* and *good*." Her mind raced with the details. "Darlene can take over for me. Charlie can take the extra shifts she had. She said they're low on cash. I'll try to get a part-time baker to help Ernesto."

"You're serious." It wasn't a question.

She nodded. "Before you go to New York, could you take the trailer to Rusty's and hitch it on? For the chair?" She swallowed against the sudden sadness that hit her.

"You're leaving before I get back?"

"As soon as we're able to, Jonah." Tomorrow would be their last day together. The thought made her feel so faint she grabbed the counter to keep her balance. Early Thursday morning, Rosie was taking Jonah to the airport. She had chemotherapy that afternoon and would stay the weekend with Frieda, returning Sunday after she picked up Jonah from the airport.

"Why drag this out?" she said.

Hurt flew across Jonah's face, but it turned to anger. "It's your call. It always has been. I'll get the trailer to Rusty." He turned and walked out, his stride angry. He shoved open the door so hard she feared the glass would shatter. Then he was gone.

Cara felt so alone, so scared. She wanted to run after him, take it all back, tell him they'd go to New York, that she couldn't do this by herself. *You can handle this. You have to.*

She had bags to pack and arrangements to make. She took a deep breath and headed upstairs to talk to Beth Ann.

CHAPTER SIXTEEN

THE NEXT AFTERNOON, Jonah flipped the café sign to *Closed,* ending the last day he'd ever work with Cara.

They'd been too busy to talk much. Evan had shadowed him, since he would be covering the grill while Jonah was in New York. When Cara wasn't waiting tables, she was making lists for him, Darlene and Ernesto or calling part-time bakers.

It was stupid for her to run off like this. Beth Ann swore her friend Serena had never gotten her messages. The TV spot brought in new customers and phone orders, but there was no way her ex-husband had seen it.

But she was determined to escape. There was panic in her blue eyes, her pink smell had gone sharp with fear and her fake smile was back. Bigtime.

She couldn't wait to get away from him. That was the truth of it.

He walked toward her. She stood behind the

counter, keeping her distance as she had all day. She gave him that false smile. He hated that.

He didn't bother to fake one back.

"I think I found a baker," she said with false cheer.

He didn't reply.

Cara twisted the towel in her hand, looking uncertain. "Guess this is it. Last day in the café."

"Last day," he echoed, his throat tight. He would see her briefly in the morning before he left, but Evan would be there and Rosie. This was it. Goodbye forever.

She came around the counter. "I don't know how to say goodbye to you," she said, her eyes shimmering like wet varnish.

Don't go. Stay with me. We'll build a life together. Impossible with his stunted soul, but he couldn't help wanting that.

"Come see me tonight," he said. They could make love one last time, part with that memory, at least.

She shook her head. "It would hurt too much."

"Dammit, it already hurts too much." He pulled her into his arms, tucking her head under his chin, feeling all of her against him, memorizing her shape, her smell, the weight of her. He felt so empty.

Cara broke away. "This is for the best, Jonah. I was wrong to think I was better. The specter will always be there. I'll spend my whole life afraid that any man I love will turn into Barrett." She swallowed hard.

"You just need time."

She shook her head. "I'm broken." Then she got a fiery look in her eye. "But you're not. You need to know that. You are a good and loving man who does all he can to help the people he loves. You haven't let me down or Beth Ann or Rosie or Evan or—" She started to cry. "Oh, Jonah…" She threw herself into his arms.

He couldn't stand to see her cry. Hell, he felt like crying, too—big gulping sobs, as if he were a kid experiencing his first heartbreak. He felt like he was about to lose his last chance at happiness.

Jonah pulled back and wiped the tears from her cheeks with his thumbs. "Wait for me," he ground out. "Be here when I get back from New York."

"I can't…." But he could see she wanted to.

"Sure you can. We'll have a farewell dinner. You can make a kitchen-sink salad for Rosie, hear how her chemo went." By then maybe he'd have figured something out, found the right words, found a way to fix this. Hell, he wasn't ready to let her go.

"That would be nice." She held his gaze and he felt the rush of desire again, stronger than ever. How would he ever get over her?

"Do you regret us?" she said in a trembling

voice. "Because I don't. Maybe it was a cheat, but it was good for me. *You* were good for me."

"You're the best thing that's happened to me in a long time," he said. And losing her would be the worst.

"BE REASSURING and calm," Barrett said to Deborah, holding the phone over the gearshift box. "Whatever you do, don't frighten her." He wished he could do the talking, but Deborah would be a more familiar voice to Beth Ann. Foolish and clumsy as she was, Deborah would pave his way.

"I know how to talk to my own granddaughter."

He just hoped to hell she wouldn't babble like she'd done nonstop since he'd picked her up in Barstow.

After dozens of calls to highway-side restaurants, Barrett's P.I. had hit pay dirt in an Arizona tourist town, where he'd talked to the owner of a bistro who'd mentioned a diner with a new waitress who'd been in the news for baking special dinner rolls.

To be sure it was Cara, Barrett had found the news clip on the TV station's website. When Beth Ann appeared, with her soulful blue eyes and button nose, his heart almost stopped.

Barrett had wanted to grab them immediately, but he knew if he pounced, Cara would flee. She had histrionic personality disorder, he'd discovered, which predisposed her to paranoia and panic, so he needed a good plan.

Now he had one. First, he'd called the bowling alley bar guy interviewed in the story, pretending to be a travel reporter doing a follow-up story.

Evan Gold had been delighted to tell Barrett all he needed to know about the café, the baker and her daughter. They were going by ridiculous aliases—*CJ* and *Bunny Peyton*.

Barrett and Deborah had reached New Hope Thursday night. He'd spent Friday and Saturday putting his plan in place and observing Cara and Beth Ann as best he could from the parking lot.

The plan had come together, the timing tight, but doable. In some ways it was perfect. According to Gold, Cara and Beth Ann would be leaving town tomorrow morning.

Instead, they'd leave today with Barrett—departing before the café's cook and owner got back, saving all those awkward questions.

A half hour ago, Cara had driven off on a wild goose chase he'd sent her on, so he had time to connect with Beth Ann. Cara was on her way to meet with a commercial bakery she thought wanted to sell her good-luck buns wholesale. His P.I. had been quite convincing on the phone.

Commercial Kitchens only leased kitchen space, however, and by the time the misunderstanding was sorted out, Barrett and Beth Ann would be happily reunited and eager for Cara's return.

Thinking about it gave Barrett a rush of pleasure. He loved when a plan came to fruition.

Watching Cara through the café window these past two days made him remember Dolly's, where he would drink cup after cup of coffee just to watch her move and smile, to hear the sweet ring of her laughter.

To be proper, he'd waited until she was eighteen to ask her out. It had been torture, but worth the wait.

It would be worth the wait now. Worth every desperate, agonizing day he'd spent behind bars. The six weeks he'd been searching for them had seemed even more excruciating.

Now he faced the crucial moment—talking to Beth Ann. He'd seen her in the window of her room with that ugly black cat. She'd spent the previous day playing in a tree house with it and a little girl, but she was alone now.

He ached to feel her arms around his neck and hear her say *I love you, Daddy, so, so, so much* like she used to. All the years he'd missed with her, all the little moments, the gestures, the shared secrets and jokes. Fury spiked in his head. *Stop. Think. Be still.*

It wasn't *fury.* It was *hurt.* For people with his condition, *hurt* became *anger* became *violence,* like flipped switches. The little white pills broke the circuit. They made him dizzy and foggy, but that was a small price to pay to be worthy of his family again.

"Here we go," he said to Deborah, pushing Talk, ringing Beth Ann's phone. If she didn't answer, he'd have to be more aggressive. He hoped it wouldn't come to that, but he'd do what he had to do.

He would not lose them again.

BETH ANN'S FACE hurt from trying not to cry. She sat on her bed holding Louis beside her empty suitcase. She was supposed to be packed when her mom got back from the bakery meeting. They were leaving in the morning.

She was too sad to pack.

It felt like they were already gone. Evan was at the grill instead of Jonah and Darlene was doing her mom's job. Yesterday, when Rachel had to go home, it had felt like leaving Serena all over again.

They had to run again and it was all Beth Ann's fault.

She gritted her teeth, so mad at herself for letting Amanda pull her in front of the TV camera. Plus, Jonah had told her mom about IM'ing Serena. Her mother had been so scared and disappointed in Beth Ann that Beth Ann had felt like throwing up. No way could she tell her about the phone calls after that.

The Terrible Thing was her fault and now this was, too.

Beth Ann buried her face in Louis's fur. "I wish you could come," she whispered. But the apartment was no-pets. Louis wouldn't understand why she'd gone away. He would just feel lonely again and lost. That made her heart ache and her stomach burn.

She hugged him, but he squirmed away, going to the door to shake himself and wait for her.

"Want to go to the castle?" She had to get her comic books anyway.

Just as she reached for the doorknob, she heard a buzzing sound from her bed. It was the secret phone in her puzzle box.

Was Serena calling her at last? She pushed the hidden latches and picked up the phone, her heart pounding. *Private name, private number.* Did Serena have a new phone? She clicked Talk. "H-h-hello?"

"Beth Ann? It's Grandma Price. Surprise!"

She was so shocked, it took her a long time to speak. "Grandma?" Her skin tingled all over and she felt like she had to pee.

"We got your number from your little friend Serena. Such a nice little girl and so polite. Are you glad to hear my voice?"

"Y-yes," she said, but she was too dizzy to know for sure. Why would Serena tell Grandma Price about the phone? It was a pinky-swear secret.

Her grandma's voice sounded too cheerful, like when the nurse said the shot would be just a pinch, when it was really a long, burning stab.

"You sound so grown up," her grandma said. "I've missed you like crazy. My poor shoulders are in knots. You are the best shoulder rubber...."

In the background, a man grumbled.

"Okay, okay," her grandma said crossly to the man. "I have another surprise," she said into the phone. "Guess who wants to talk to you?"

"Serena?"

"No, silly. Your daddy."

"What?" Her entire body turned to hot liquid. Her dad was in her grandma's house. He wanted to talk to her. Her mom would be crazy mad. "I'm not supposed to have this phone. I have to hang up." She felt like crying.

"Don't do that. Your daddy wants to ask you to forgive him and for you to have a fresh start as a family."

He wanted *her* to forgive *him?*

"You want that, don't you?" her grandma said. "To have your family back? He's not mad about prison. He's just glad to be home. And your mom wants to be a family, too, I'm sure."

"No. She's scared of him." She felt hot all over, caught and pulled apart. She took gulping breaths, holding back her sob.

"Well, that's just stupid. Your mom has a rock-hard heart. I've been through this and through this with her. It was an *accident.* It takes two to tango. Now quit crying, for heaven's sake, and—"

"It's all right, Beth Ann."

The man's voice was so strong Beth Ann jumped, nearly dropping the phone. It was her dad. *Her dad was on the phone.* She couldn't breathe.

"Sometimes your grandmother doesn't choose her words well." He sounded so close, almost inside her head. "I love you so much. And your mom." His voice shook like he was going to cry. "I hate that you're afraid of me."

It was all too much, like the blackness in her brain times ten. She didn't want it to be real.

"I can't talk. I have to go. Bye." She held down the end button until the phone went totally black, put it in the box, then threw it in the trash can by the door. She should never have taken it out of the trash in the first place.

Calm down. They don't know where you are. She'd never told Serena, so they couldn't know. She had to get away from the phone, so she picked up Louis and went out.

Downstairs, Evan saw her and yelled, "Where you headed?"

"Out to the tree house," she said. Her mom had asked Evan to keep an eye on her until she got back. Beth Ann didn't need a babysitter, but once her mom saw Beth Ann on TV and learned about the messages, she'd been punishing Beth Ann, treating her like a baby, worrying and always watching.

It's your own fault. If only she'd run from that reporter, none of this would have happened. Sometimes she was so dumb she hated herself.

Beth Ann was in her castle, reading a comic with Louis on her lap when she heard the click of a shoe on the ladder. She looked over, expecting Rachel, but a man's head popped up through the hole. Louis hissed. Beth Ann yelled.

"It's me, Bethie. Don't you recognize me?" It was her dad. His face was thinner and his black hair was gray, but it was him. Her whole body tingled. Was she dreaming? This couldn't be true. Her dad had found her. Her mom would be so mad. She shouldn't have answered the phone.

Her dad climbed into the fort. Louis ran up Beth Ann's body and flew out the window. She wished she could go with him.

"I didn't mean to scare you." Her dad sat cross-legged on the floor in brown pants too dressy for the castle. So was his silk shirt. Why was he here? This was wrong, all wrong.

"I'm not mad that you hung up on me. It was because your mom would be mad about the phone, right?"

She nodded slowly.

"So we won't tell her. How's that?" He put a finger to his lips.

"Okay." Her heart was beating so fast it hurt.

"You got scratched." He pointed at her arms.

Beth Ann looked at the bloody marks. She was so upset she hadn't even felt Louis claw her trying to get away.

"That's the trouble with a feral cat. They're always wild inside. They'll turn on you like that." He snapped his fingers, the noise sharp as a gunshot.

She jumped.

"Serena told me you made friends with it. You're a kind person to do that. You've always been kind." He peered at her so closely her cheeks got hot.

"How did you find me?" Her throat was dry and scratchy.

"Serena said you lived in a diner near the highway. We called around and found out about the lucky buns and I saw you on TV."

"You did?" This *was* all her fault. She felt sick.

"We'd better keep that secret, too, huh? Let's

tell your mother that Grandma Warner was at
Canyon Ranch—that's a famous health spa near
Tucson—and saw the news."

Beth Ann nodded. He was helping her get out
of trouble with her mom. That was nice of him.
He seemed to know what was in her mind.

"It's so good to see you." He smiled the warm
way she remembered. She used to jump into his
arms and wrap her legs around him and he would
squeeze her tight and say how much he loved her.

That good memory mixed her up so much. She
was scared and worried, but also glad.

"I bet you don't know what to think, do you?
Your mom said some bad things about me, I bet.
But that's in the past. I'm a better person now.
Once she sees that, she'll take it all back, don't
worry."

His words sounded kind and relaxed, but his
body seemed tense, like how she was with Louis
at first, trying to pet him without scaring him.
Her dad was treating her like *she* was a feral cat.

"In prison, I found out I have a condition that
makes me get angry. There's a pill that fixes it,
so now I'm fine."

He was pulling her in with his eyes like he used
to do. It had made her feel special and important.

"When I got out of prison, I was so excited
to see you that I filled my car with flowers and
presents and drove straight to Grandma Price's

house, but she told me you'd run away. You were so scared of me you ran." He sighed and hung his head.

Beth Ann felt bad for him and embarrassed, too.

"You know what I did? I got back into my car with balloons bobbing every which way and I cried like a baby. That's how sad I was."

She felt even worse.

"Can you imagine how glad I was when Serena's mom told me you'd called Serena? I told Serena to talk more to you, but her mother threw away her phone. Can you believe that?" He shook his head. "I found you after all, so that's old news." He smiled like he'd won a prize. "It wasn't your fault your mom made you run, Bethie. She didn't realize that I'm better. I'm not mad about prison either because the judge saw the mistake and let me out. So that's all over and we'll start fresh."

He made it sound okay, and she felt a little less scared. Her arm began to sting from the scratches. Her body wasn't so shocked now.

"Feel better?" he asked.

She nodded. He could see her fears and feelings so easily.

"I wrote you a lot of letters in prison, but your mom kept them from you."

She didn't know about any letters.

"I was afraid of that," he said, reading her face.

His eyes got angry, but he smiled at her. "But it's okay now. I can say it all in person now. The first thing—and I didn't put this in my letters because it's just between us—is about the night of the accident."

She sucked in a breath, scared of what he would say.

"You left the door unlocked for me when you went next door so I could talk to your mom and we could have Family Night at Carcher's. Do you remember that?"

She nodded, her heart jumping into her throat.

"Except your mom wouldn't listen to me and she fell and bumped her head." He looked hard at Beth Ann. "Did you tell your mom that you let me in the house?"

She shook her head.

"Because you were afraid she'd be mad, that she'd blame you for the accident, right?"

"Yes," she whispered, feeling dizzy and nervous and scared.

"She might blame you, but *I* don't. You did what I asked you to do to help our family. So don't give that one more thought."

"Really?" It was like he'd gotten into her brain and saw the blackness about The Terrible Thing and washed it all away. Tears made it hard to see.

"You poor thing. I want to hug you, but I bet you

need more time to get used to me." He sounded so sad, but he was right.

He even understood *that*.

"We'll just keep this our little secret, okay? Mommy can be unforgiving at times. So, that's two secrets I'm keeping for you, isn't it?"

There was a funny look in his eyes, like he'd cheated and seen her poker hand and knew he could beat her. That made her uneasy.

"How about you pay me back a little? Can you do that?"

"I guess." What did he want?

"All I need you to do is help me to talk to your mom, let her know that you trust me and want us to be a family again. She'll be jumpy at first, you know, but if you show her everything's fine that will help all of us."

"I'll try," she said, taking a jerky breath. Maybe it would be okay once her mom knew about the pills and how her dad wasn't mad about prison.

"Good. Because I have so many great plans for us. I found us a new house. It's not quite ready, so we'll stay with your grandmother until then."

"We're going to Grandma Price's?" That would be amazing.

"Grandma *Warner's*. Grandma Price's house is too...well, small."

"Oh." Her heart sank. She didn't like Grandma Warner. She had mean eyes and made *sugges-*

tions that made Beth Ann feel small and stupid and clumsy. Maybe they wouldn't stay there long.

"Is the new house near Grandma Price? Can I go to my old school?"

"No, no. It's in Sacramento."

"Oh."

"But you'll love it. And you can pick out your furniture and decide what colors to paint your room. Won't that be nice?"

She nodded, looking down.

Her dad was silent for a moment. "Would that make you happy? To live in Barstow? Go to your old school?"

She raised her eyes to him.

"Maybe I'll see if there's a house there we might like."

"That would be great!" It made her want to sing. She'd have her old life back, but in her own house with her mom *and* her dad.

Then she thought of something else. "Can I bring Louis? The cat?" That would make it almost perfect.

He hesitated. His eyes went back and forth, but he said, "If it makes my little girl happy, it makes me happy, too."

"That's so great." She almost wanted to hug him now. She'd have Louis and Serena and her old school and a new house with furniture she picked out and they'd never have to run again.

"And tonight, we'll stay in a resort with a water slide. You still like water parks, don't you? You're so big. I miss the little girl you were." He looked so sad that her stomach jumped.

"I like water parks a lot!" She used to ride on his shoulders as he walked into the deeper part, so she felt like she was flying over the water.

"Good." He looked at his watch. "Okay. The diner closes in an hour. Your mom should be back around then. Here's the rest of how you'll help me. You can tell time, right?"

She nodded.

"We want the cook and dishwashers gone, so let's make it four o'clock. I'll be waiting on the porch at four for you to come get me and we'll go up and surprise your mother."

"Surprise her?" Her mother might freak out.

"Don't say a word now. You keep my secret and I'll keep yours."

"Okay." She swallowed over a dry throat.

"That's my big girl. Are you all packed to go?"

"Not yet."

"Get to it before your mom gets here. And don't forget your swimsuit."

Beth Ann climbed down from the tree and went to the café, a fluttery feeling in her stomach. He'd made it sound so easy, but it didn't feel easy.

How did she know when her mom would be

back? And that they were packing to leave? Her
fluttery stomach turned upside down.

She wanted to lock the café and never let her
father inside. *Keep my secret and I'll keep yours.*
She had to do what he said.

CHAPTER SEVENTEEN

EVAN WAS WAITING for Cara at the café delivery door when she got back from her wasted trip to Tucson. He handed her the keys and took off for his shift at the bowling alley.

Inside, she saw he'd left buns to be bagged and a messy kitchen.

She blew out a breath, irritated all over again. She'd wasted an entire afternoon on a fool's errand. Commercial Kitchens leased kitchen space, period, the leasing agent told her. He seemed honestly puzzled by the claim that someone had told her they wanted to sell her pastries. If someone had scammed her, it wasn't him.

Since she was there, he gave her a tour of the facility and she talked to a woman who rented space to make fruit tarts she sold wholesale. The idea had gotten Cara thinking. She'd need a business loan, but someday she might try to sell her good-luck buns herself.

That would have to be down the line. Right now she needed to pack before Jonah and Rosie returned in a couple of hours. She trudged up the stairs, dreading the goodbye supper she'd promised Jonah. She should have said no, but there'd been this look on his face, as if when he returned he would have figured out how she could be safe and they could be together.

Which was impossible and they both knew it. She wasn't sure she had the stamina for another goodbye. She already felt raw and lost and alone without him.

Up in the apartment, she put the café keys on the kitchen table, then removed Rosie's apartment key from her keychain. Her fingers tightened around the bear Jonah had whittled. It was always warm to the touch, as if he'd embedded his love into its very grain. It had a calming effect on her. So did the rocking chair. If the bear was Jonah's protective spirit in her hand, the rocking chair was his loving arms wrapped around her.

They would load it into the trailer tonight and in the morning, she'd drive away from this place and the people she'd grown to love forever.

Cara ate a green jelly bean for luck. She would need it. She went down the hall to check on Beth Ann. Her daughter jumped up from the bed like she'd been caught doing something wrong.

"What's the matter?" Cara asked.

"Nothing. I'm all packed." She looked feverish.

Cara touched her forehead. Clammy. "You sure you're okay?"

"I'm going to watch a show, then go out and get Louis and be right back."

"Okay…" What had gotten into her? She'd been sad about the move, not jumpy like this.

Rosie's chicken-shaped kitchen timer was clucking on Beth Ann's nightstand, set to go off in fifteen minutes. Cara looked at her watch. What would happen at four o'clock? Maybe the show Beth Ann watched?

Very weird.

She noticed a plastic sack next to the clock. Inside, Bunny sat on top of the comic books Rosie had given Beth Ann. Bunny was back, signaling Beth Ann's need for comfort.

It couldn't be helped. Cara would make it up to her once they got to Phoenix. As she left, she noticed the peace-sign night-light. *That might help.* Bending to get it, she saw Beth Ann's puzzle box in the wastepaper basket. Why had she tossed it? The box rattled, so she clicked the secret buttons, opened it and found…*a cell phone and power cord.*

Beth Ann had a phone? Why? And why didn't Cara know about it? Her heart racing, Cara powered it on and scrolled the calls, finding Serena's number more than once. *Beth Ann had talked to Serena.*

Furious, Cara took the phone into the living room to confront Beth Ann, but she wasn't watching television. Cara went downstairs after her. She was heading for the café door when she heard voices. Through the glass, she was horrified to see Beth Ann looking up at *Barrett,* who was holding her hand.

Cara's heart lurched in her chest and her legs turned to liquid. She shoved the phone into her pocket just as they entered.

"Cara!" Barrett said. "You spoiled our surprise."

"What are you doing here?" she choked out.

"I came for my family," he said cheerfully.

He'd aged dramatically. His hair was gray, his face gaunt and lined, his eyes sunken. He was thinner, but she could see huge biceps under the half sleeves of the silk shirt he wore.

"It's okay, Mom," Beth Ann said. "He takes pills so he can't get mad. And he forgives us and everything."

Barrett gave a false chuckle. "Let's not blurt out all our news at once, Bethie. How about we sit?" He motioned toward a booth. Hearing him use that nickname made Cara feel ill.

"Go on upstairs, Beth Ann," she said in as steady a voice as she could manage. "So your father and I can talk."

"She needs to be part of this," Barrett said, steel lining his words. "She's been left out too long." He led Beth Ann to a booth and she scooted in.

Barrett motioned for Cara to sit opposite her, his smile as bright as the polka dots of the new upholstery, but cold as ice. His gesture caused the hem of his shirt to snag on something.

A handgun in a holster.

She gasped.

Barrett noticed and adjusted his shirt, looking to be sure Beth Ann hadn't seen. "You can't be too careful these days," he murmured to Cara. "Please…sit."

Cara crossed in front of him, her blood slowing to sludge. She was in a nightmare trying to run in quicksand. She sat down and Barrett hemmed her in, an arm across the back of the bench.

"Now isn't this better?" He squeezed her shoulder, a gesture that he meant to appear affectionate but was intended to show her his power over her.

Cara's head felt as though it floated six inches above her neck. Her heart pounded so hard it hurt her ribs. The rest of her had gone numb.

She forced herself to think, to analyze escape options that wouldn't frighten Beth Ann. She had the phone in her pocket. She could call for help.

For now, she would go along with Barrett. As long as they didn't cross him he should remain calm.

"Don't be mad, Mom," Beth Ann said in a small voice, looking at her with worried eyes. "Please."

Cara managed a smile. "I'm not mad. Just shocked."

"We expected that, didn't we, Bethie?" Barrett shifted his body so he could look straight at Cara. "On the other hand, I was disappointed to learn that you hid my letters to my daughter." He made a tsk sound. "Not kind. Not kind at all. She was frightened of me."

Cara didn't speak. Didn't dare. She needed to orient herself, prepare for what came next.

"But I forgive you," Barrett declared smugly. "For all of it—for prison, for never writing back, even for running away. You're breaking the law, you know, keeping my daughter from me. I could have you arrested."

"No!" Beth Ann's eyes went huge. "Please!"

"I'm just making a point," Barrett said. "As I said, it's all forgiven now."

He was manipulating Beth Ann to control Cara. It was outrageous, but she forced herself to speak calmly. "Isn't it risky for you to leave California while you're on parole?"

His face went very still, like it had before he slapped her the first time. Had she gone too far?

He closed his eyes, then opened them. They burned with rage, but he smiled. The effect was chilling. "I appreciate your concern, but I obtained permission to travel to Arizona to assess a business opportunity. It was for you, as a matter of fact. I'm investigating ways for you to sell your famous rolls."

"It was you? You set up the meeting?"

To get her away while he talked to Beth Ann. He was cunning. She knew that. How could she ever outsmart him?

"That's how we found you. Your lucky rolls." He babbled on about how his mother had been at a spa and seen the news, but he was clearly lying. She realized Barrett had probably lied constantly when they were married, but Cara had been too naive to see. At least she'd matured that much.

"Kudos on your success," he continued. "I want you to know that I can support you in your little hobby, as long as it doesn't interfere with our family."

She could hardly believe this was happening. Barrett sounded like they'd had a minor spat and would go on as before.

He no doubt wanted to take them with him. If she could delay until Jonah and Rosie got here, there should be enough confusion to allow her to get Beth Ann away from him.

"I've changed, Cara. That's what you need to understand…." He kept talking, his voice hypnotic, explaining that he had a condition that made him lose his temper, but he had mental techniques and pills that corrected it.

She didn't buy one word. She'd seen the malevolent predator behind the charming facade, like a dark figure passing a lit window. She would not be fooled again.

"Now he can't get mad," Beth Ann threw in.

Barrett chuckled. "Not quite, Bethie, but close. I also discovered what you have, Cara. I had lots of time to read in prison, as you can imagine." He paused and fury flashed like lightning in his eyes. "You have histrionic personality disorder, characterized by excessive emotionality, hysteria and paranoia. That's why you see danger where none exists. It wouldn't be fair to blame you. Just like you can't blame me for my condition."

"He can't help it, Mom. But he fixed it."

Barrett smiled. "Very good, Bethie. And Cara, I will pay for your therapy and the medicine you need to manage it. All's well that ends well."

Meaning he would drug her into submission.

Despite the horror she felt, Cara kept a neutral face while Barrett spun his twisted tale. If anything, he'd become more dangerous, pretending forgiveness when what he had to want was revenge. Her poor daughter didn't have the tools to realize that. For her sake, Cara had to placate the armed monster at her side.

She flashed on a memory of Jonah's eyes, full of warmth and kindness. So different from Barrett. How had she ever compared the two men?

Her time with Barrett had made her doubt

her own instincts. Jonah had helped her see her strengths.

"Beth Ann and I want us to be a family again," Barrett said. "I know that's what you want, too. So, will you give us a fresh start?" He gave her that sunny smile she couldn't believe she'd ever fallen for.

She had to buy more time. "This is a lot to think about. How about I fix us some supper? We can catch up while we eat."

"I'm afraid we don't have time." He glanced at his watch. "In fact, your mother's waiting for us just outside town in a rental car."

"My mother's here?"

"Certainly. She missed you both terribly."

Cara's blood ran cold. The ground seemed to tilt beneath her. Barrett had an accomplice—her own mother.

"We get to stay at a hotel with a water park," Beth Ann said, her voice high. "Daddy remembered how much I liked water parks."

Cara sucked in a breath. "That sounds lovely, but we can't leave this minute. We need to pack."

"Cara," Barrett said in a disapproving tone. "Beth Ann told me you're packed and now so is she."

"Daddy said to leave a note for Jonah and Rosie," Beth Ann chimed in.

Cara's heart sank. Beth Ann had told him too

much. Barrett wanted no witnesses to their kid-napping.

"And I can bring Louis. We're getting a new house near Grandma Price."

"In Barstow?" she asked Barrett.

"I said we'd see. Otherwise, I've found a lovely home in Sacramento." He winked at her. He'd lied for Beth Ann's benefit.

"I get to pick my furniture," Beth Ann said in a hollow voice.

"So, let's get your bags and go," Barrett said. "If we're late for check-in we'll lose the lovely casita I booked for us. Bethie, lead the way."

Beth Ann scooted out of the booth and headed for the stairs, looking back at them nervously. Barrett held Cara by the waist, so they walked side by side, the gun digging into her hip.

Despair washed through her. He'd planned care-fully. How could she best him?

You're strong and brave and relentless, Jonah had said. *You gave me hell from the day you walked in here.* Jonah had held up a mirror and showed her what she'd become. *Dazzling.* He'd called her *dazzling.*

She'd survived a coma, made a life for Beth Ann, managed her difficult mother, started school again and gotten help when they needed to run. She'd found work and a home when their car failed, she'd renovated a café and convinced a scared and stubborn woman to get treated for cancer.

She could beat Barrett Warner at his own game. She had to. Their lives depended on it.

In twenty minutes they were on the road in Cara's car minus the trailer—too much trouble to load, according to Barrett. Cara was driving, Barrett at her side, Beth Ann sobbing quietly in the backseat.

"Hey, hey, no more tears." Barrett turned to look at her. "I promise we'll get the cat shipped to us." Beth Ann hadn't been able to find Louis fast enough to suit Barrett. "Crybabies don't get to stay in resorts with water slides, now do they?"

Beth Ann wiped her face, gulping for air, her shoulders heaving.

"You've spoiled her," Barrett muttered to Cara. "We'll have to correct that." She hated his superior smirk, the way he'd lied to Beth Ann about moving to Barstow, about the cat, about himself.

Cara wanted to slam the brakes and put him through the windshield, but she didn't dare. Not with the gun at his waist. She would bide her time, watch for her chance to make a call. She had the phone in her pocket and had managed to slip the puzzle box into the sack with the comic books and Bunny, so she had the cord.

Barrett had dictated a note about hating long

goodbyes. She hoped to hell Jonah wouldn't take it at face value. Surely Jonah knew her better than that. Barrett had even insisted she include a smiley face like she used to do in high school.

The fact she'd left the rocking chair she'd sworn to keep forever should tell him something was wrong. She'd also set the bear on end in the middle of the seat. He couldn't miss that message.

As they drove, Barrett spun a sticky-sweet web around them, talking about the new house, the private school for Beth Ann, couples' tennis lessons, a less demanding job for him, family fun nights, on and on, until she felt like she was suffocating.

"Nothing matters more than our family," he continued. "Not hobbies, not classes, not friends, not relatives. We'll devote more time to each other, not get foolish about *our selfish whims, right?*" His glance was the lash of a whip.

Barrett's fury was a ticking clock. He was holding it together now, but soon enough he would explode, punish her, hurt her, possibly kill her. How much time did she have? And how could she be sure Beth Ann stayed safe?

It was hard not to lose hope. Even if Jonah did figure out she was in trouble, he didn't know where they were headed. He didn't know Barrett's name or her last name. The plates she'd put on her mother's car were from California, but that wasn't much to go on.

No, she was likely on her own. Maybe that was how it should be.

JONAH READ CARA'S note again. *Long goodbyes are hard.* She'd promised to stay until he got back. And a *smiley face?*

Really?

Rosie sat glumly at the table. "She ran off so she wouldn't see a grown man cry," she said, but her feelings were hurt, too. Her first chemotherapy had been less miserable than she'd expected and she wanted to tell Cara. "They didn't even take Bunny's bike."

"The trailer was hitched. All she had to do was throw it in. That makes no sense. What about the chair?" He tromped down the hall and found it sitting there. He wanted to toss it out the window. It had caused nothing but pain in his life.

Then he noticed the bear he'd carved. She'd put it in the chair on purpose. It was a message. That she didn't need his protection? She'd said he couldn't rescue her, but this was a pretty harsh way to make the point.

Maybe she meant it hurt too much to keep it.

So say so in the note, dammit. And with a frownie face at least.

He tromped back down the hall.

"It's too quiet around here," Rosie said. "Maybe I need a boarder. You'll be gone soon, too."

"Not for a while." Not until her treatments were over. The furniture show had gone great. He'd sold most of his pieces and the deal with the manufacturer was percolating. He'd even checked out a couple apartments, thinking about Cara and Beth Ann the whole time.

"I'm going down to check the kitchen," he said.

It was a mess. The back of Jonah's neck began to prickle. This was not like Cara. There were even trays of buns waiting to be bagged. She'd worked hard to make sure the café would run smoothly without her. She would have cleaned up after Evan, no question.

That wasn't like her.

None of this was like her. Not the lame note, the smiley face, the abandoned gifts. What had she said about the chair? *I'll keep it forever.*

She wasn't rejecting his help. She was *asking* for it. She was in trouble. Had her ex-husband found them? Kidnapped them?

Jonah dialed Evan, who'd been the last person to see them today.

Evan told him Cara had gone to Tucson to meet with a bakery about selling her buns, returning a little over two hours ago. They hadn't talked. Evan had been in a hurry.

"Did she seem rushed? Or scared? Was she alone?"

"She seemed tired, not rushed," Evan said. "What's going on, Jonah?"

"I'm afraid something's happened." He took a deep breath. "Her ex-husband just got out of prison for trying to kill her. She's afraid he's after her."

"Is that why she was freaked out about the good-luck buns story?"

"Yeah. I'm afraid he's kidnapped them."

"How did he find them?"

"I have no idea. That bakery visit seems odd. On a Sunday?"

"They called her yesterday. Word's getting around about the buns. In fact, I expected a reporter from *World Traveler Magazine* to show up here by now. He called and got a lot of background from me."

"A reporter?"

"Don't worry. I told him the baker wouldn't talk to him. He didn't care. He said he'd cover how fame affects a small town. He asked for a hotel, so I gave him the Sleep Inn's number."

Jonah went on full alert. "Did you verify who he was?"

"No. He sounded legit. You think he was her ex?"

"Maybe."

"He asked a lot of detailed questions about the café. Jesus. If it was him, I helped the guy. Lee Schmidt was his name. My laptop's on. Let me check." Computer keys clicked. "I'm on the site. Checking… *Jesus Christ.* There's a Lee Schmidt, all right. Picture's right here. It's a woman."

"Damn." Electricity shot through him. Cara had been right to be afraid. "I need to call the sheriff's office. Hell, I don't know the guy's name or Cara's real last name. I'll get the plate number from Rusty. California tags, so that's probably where he came from."

"If he was here, he stayed at the Sleep Inn. I know a couple clerks. I'll find out and get back to you."

"Okay." He made the calls to Rusty and the sheriff's office, but Cara's car was a nondescript white sedan and unless they were speeding, the Highway Patrol was unlikely to catch them.

Dammit. Cara and Beth Ann could be terrified hostages on the highway somewhere right now. The man had nearly killed Cara before. What if he wanted to finish the job? Jonah's gut clenched.

He went out to the café porch to pace, while he waited to hear from Evan. They could have been gone for almost two hours. That's a lot of highway miles. Every second took them farther away. Jonah was about to get in his truck and start driving, when his brother pulled up and ran up the steps to him.

"They came in a rental, California plates, and stayed three nights. White car. I got the plate number."

"They?"

"Yeah. There were two of them. A middle-aged blonde named Deborah Price checked them into a suite and got two keys. A much younger guy joined her each night, using the back entrance. The maid thought it was creepy, like he was a gigolo."

"We need to call the sheriff's office with the rental car plates," Jonah said.

"Already did."

"I'm going after them."

"That's crazy. They have two cars. They could split up. California is a big-ass state, Jonah."

He stared at his brother. "I have to do something. I'm losing it." He ran his fingers through his hair, wanting to jump out of his skin.

"I can see that. Let's go in and talk this through. Maybe you know more than you think you do. I'm friends with one of the dispatchers. She'll feed us any information they get, like where they rented the car. That's likely where they'll head from here."

"Okay. Maybe you're right." Jonah blew out a breath. He needed to know more before he took off.

Inside, Evan said, "You eaten anything?"

"Not really."

"I'll fry you some eggs." He went into the kitchen.

Food would help, too. "Keep the burner low and use plenty of—"

Evan turned to him.

"Right. You know how to fry an egg. Sorry. Weren't you working?"

"I told Carlos I had a family emergency." He slapped down butter and grabbed eggs. "I'm sick to death I helped the guy. Me and my big, damn mouth."

"If it weren't for your big damn mouth, we wouldn't know as much as we do. You talk to people. That's a good thing. I'm the one who screwed up. Cara kept telling me the guy was capable of anything, but I treated her like she was crazy. I should have stayed here, watched out for her."

"You couldn't know any more than I could. Forget laying blame. Let's figure this out. The guy was in prison in California, right?"

"That would be my guess, yeah."

"I bet there was plenty of news coverage of his trial. Newspapers subscribe to fancy clipping services. Call the *New Hope News* and ask for Tina. She'll search the archives with whatever keywords you can come up with."

"Someone else you dated?"

"What can I say?"

Jonah grabbed the newspaper from the rack and located the number. "At least it's a place to start," he said. "Thanks, Ev."

"I've got your back. You always have mine."

Evan was acting as big brother at the moment and Jonah needed that. If Cara hadn't helped him see Evan with new eyes, that might not have been possible.

When he found her, he would thank her.

And he would find her. Or die trying.

WHEN BARRETT GOT out of the car to pump gas, Cara slipped the cell phone from her pocket, her heart in her throat. She smiled through the windshield at him, powering up the phone without looking.

She'd wanted to warn Beth Ann to be ready to run, but Barrett had sent her with Deborah to buy snacks.

When Barrett turned to put the nozzle into the tank, Cara looked at the phone. The battery was scary low. She pushed 9, then 1, then stopped. If police descended, sirens blaring, Barrett might pull his gun and they'd become hostages. That would be a disaster.

The rescue had to be controlled. She punched in Jonah's cell number. She would give him the basics and he would call the police.

Hurry, hurry, answer. Barrett was pulling the nozzle from the car. She had a few seconds while he put in his card and paid.

"Hello?" Jonah said.

She wanted to weep with relief, but she spoke quickly, the words bursting like bullets from her mouth. "We've been kidnapped by Barrett Warner. He has a handgun. We're headed to a resort, probably Tucson. My mom's following us in a rental car. The resort has a water slide. We're in my car."

"We've got the plate numbers."

"You figured out my message."

"Absolutely."

Barrett started to turn toward her, but Beth Ann ran up to him, holding out candy, buying Cara more time.

"Call the police, but no sirens. Whatever we do has to be quiet, so Barrett doesn't panic and Beth Ann doesn't get hurt or scared."

"We'll get you out of there. Don't worry."

"I'm powering off the phone. Leave a message with the plan. I'll call when I can." She slid the phone into her purse just as Barrett opened his door. "Bethie remembered I like red licorice," Barrett crowed, waving a piece.

"I got your favorite, too," Beth Ann said from the backseat, setting a Heath bar on the console. "Are you mad at me?" she asked plaintively.

"Of course not," Barrett snapped. "She couldn't be mad at a girl who wants the best for her family, could she?" He shot Cara a look.

"It'll be okay," Cara said to Beth Ann, who looked dazed and jittery. "I promise." Cara had to get her alone and tell her what was going on so she wouldn't freeze at the crucial moment.

Meanwhile, Barrett gnawed on the licorice whip, content as a child. He thought they were a happy family making a fresh start.

That was his weakness. She would use it, wait for him to let down his guard and then escape. It sounded much easier than she feared it would be.

CHAPTER EIGHTEEN

CARA FIGURED A busy resort would offer many chances to escape.

Not so. Barrett sent her mother to register so all they had was a short walk to the secluded casita. Not a soul saw them.

The casita was roomy, with a full kitchen and a separate bedroom.

"You and I will share the foldout, Beth Ann," Cara's mother said, "so your mom and dad can have their privacy. We'll have a slumber party, you and I!"

"Sounds perfect," Barrett said. Cara's heart sank. Alone in a bedroom with Barrett. She couldn't bear for him to touch her. She had to escape before then.

"I have an idea," Barrett said. "Why don't you and Grandma check out the water park, Bethie, while Cara and I catch up." He winked at Cara.

He wasn't waiting for bedtime.

Cara's blood ran cold. She'd come too far to endure that horror. "Let's all go," Cara said. "Let's get our suits on, Beth Ann." In the bathroom, they could talk and Cara could check for messages, maybe make a call.

She started for the bags, but Barrett caught her arm. "After supper we'll all go. You and I will stay here." There was steel in his voice.

Beth Ann's eyes shot to Cara, who managed a smile. "All right."

"We'll scope out the fun parts," Cara's mother said. "Get your suit."

Beth Ann did as she'd been told, but she was clearly nervous. When they were gone, Barrett drew Cara to the sofa. "Isn't this better?"

It couldn't be much worse. She was alone with the man who'd tried to kill her. She couldn't help trembling.

"Quit that," he snapped. "There is no need for hysteria. I love you. I would never hurt you." He seemed to calm himself and continued in a more wistful tone. "Every night in prison, I dreamed of us in bed the way we used to be. You were so sweet to me. Remember?"

She had to handle him carefully. She had to be loving but firm. "A lot has happened since then. With my condition, you must realize that I need time to trust you again."

"I've waited three long years, Cara." His eyes burned at her.

Stay strong. Be confident. Dazzle him. "I know you want things to be right. You were a gentleman from the beginning, waiting for me to turn eighteen. You want me to be ready." Her heart beat wildly.

Her words registered, but not deeply. Lust was lighter fluid to his banked rage.

She needed more. Then it came to her. "I have another problem." She ducked her head as if embarrassed. "It's that *time*."

Barrett's head jerked back. "Oh."

"In fact, I need to change my...you know..." *And use the phone.* Before he could object, she got up, grabbed her purse and made it to the bathroom, locking the door. Her heart racing, she got out the phone and a tampon, tearing the paper near the door, so he would hear. When she turned on the phone, it died. Damn, damn, damn.

She'd have to get the charger and try later. Aching with frustration, she applied the tampon she didn't need, washed her hands, then started to leave. What if Barrett searched her purse? To be safe, she tucked the phone behind the trash basket before she stepped out.

Sure enough, he reached for her handbag.

"What are you doing?" she said.

Barrett didn't reply, just pawed through it, setting it down with a sour smirk. "I guess I need time to trust you, too." He studied her, angry suspicion in his eyes. "In fact, I think we should go straight home. We need a more controlled environment to get reacquainted." With doors he could lock, she thought. And tranquilizers he could force down her throat.

They couldn't leave. Not with the police on the way and a plan in the making. A plan she didn't yet know.

The door rattled, then opened. Beth Ann ran to Cara and threw her arms around Cara's waist. Her grandmother wore a disagreeable expression. "It was crowded and Beth Ann did nothing but whine and pout."

"I wanted you to come." Beth Ann raised desperate eyes to meet Cara's. Cara hated to see her suffer this way.

"You baby her," Cara's mother declared with a sniff.

Her impulse was to defend Beth Ann, but she realized she could use this moment to good advantage. She dropped to Beth Ann's level. "I know you're upset. This has been *soo* hard on you. You need your Bunny, don't you?" She was almost baby-talking. Beth Ann looked puzzled.

Cara went to the plastic bag, hid the charger in her palm before she grabbed the rabbit and carried it to Beth Ann. She hugged her daughter, looking up at Barrett. "She's exhausted, Barrett. We all are. We've had a long, stressful day. Leaving again will be worse."

"We're leaving?" her mother said. "We just got here." For once, she was being helpful.

Cara realized how she could ease Barrett's fears. "How about if we *all* have a slumber party? We'll open up the sofa, order room service and watch pay-per-view movies until we fall asleep. *No one leaves except to use the bathroom.*" She emphasized the last words, looking straight at Barrett, promising him the controlled environment he was after.

"Won't that be fun, Beth Ann?" she said, squeezing her arms, begging her to agree with her eyes. Beth Ann looked confused. "How about a big order of chicken nuggets covered with the ketchup cure?"

Beth Ann's lip trembled at the reminder of happier days, but she nodded, a brave trooper once again.

"Sound good?" she said to Barrett.

"I suppose." He sounded weary, too.

"Would you order for the two of us, Mom, while I help Beth Ann change and wash her face? I'll have a salad."

She practically shoved Beth Ann into the bathroom, her heart pounding, praying Barrett wouldn't stop them cold. She locked the door, dropped to her knees to plug in the charger, then the phone.

"That's my—"

Cara put a finger to Beth Ann's lips. "Get dressed. We're making a plan to get away from Daddy. You need to stay calm and do exactly what I say. Can you do that?" She handed Beth Ann her clothes.

Fear sparked in her daughter's eyes. "He'll be so mad at me."

"He's using your feelings to trick you into doing what he wants. He's not better, Beth Ann. He's dangerous. I won't do anything until it's safe, okay? Will you do what I say?"

Beth Ann gave a miserable nod and started to dress.

"We'll pretend-talk while I call Jonah." The phone showed two missed calls and one voice mail. To save time, she called Jonah so she could tell him where they were and hear the plan. She flushed the toilet for sound cover.

As soon as he answered, Cara told him the name of the resort and their casita number.

"That's the place we figured. The police are on their way," he said. "The plan is to send in a female officer as a maid with towels. When she knocks, you two answer, then run. Deputy Collins left you a message."

"I don't know if he'll allow that." She stood and turned on the faucet for more noise.

"It's the best they can offer. If it doesn't work,

it becomes a hostage situation and they follow protocol."

"I'll try. When?"

"An hour, maybe less."

"Thank you. I love you."

"Cara?" Barrett rapped on the door. "What's going on in there?"

Adrenaline rushed through her and the phone slipped from her fingers, clattering to the tile floor.

Beth Ann gasped.

"What was that?" Barrett rattled the door.

"Soap dish!" Cara said, bending to hide the phone. She smiled at Beth Ann, put a finger to her lips, then grabbed her hand and stepped out of the room. She forced herself to return Barrett's suspicious glare with a smile.

He pushed past her into the bathroom and shut the door. Cara held her breath, her heart pounding. Maybe he just had to pee.

She heard him moving around, opening the medicine cabinet, the shower curtain, looking through the toiletry basket.

Please don't let him find the phone.

After a few seconds, the door whipped open. Barrett grabbed her arm, his face red, holding the phone in his other hand. "What did you do?"

"Don't, Daddy!" Beth Ann squeaked. "It's my phone. I had to charge it."

Barrett ignored Beth Ann. Holding on to Cara, he clicked buttons with his free hand, then put the phone to his ear.

He was listening to the message from the deputy. She hadn't had time to hear or delete it.

As Barrett listened, his face changed, his eyes going hard, his mouth tight. He squeezed her arm so tightly it tingled. He snapped the phone shut and stuck it in his pants pocket. "Deborah, get your bag and Cara's. Beth Ann, take your own. We're leaving."

Holding Cara, he put his bag strap over a shoulder and went for the door. Cara spoke so only Barrett could hear. "Don't do this. It's kidnapping. You'll be in prison for the rest of your life."

"We need more time, that's all," he said grimly, squeezing her arm so tightly she cried out. "Guess I don't know my own strength," he said. He would soon lose control of his rage. Could they escape before then?

Beth Ann started to cry.

"Shut up!" he yelled, then spoke calmly. "I can't think with you shrieking, sweetheart." He reached into his shirt pocket for a pill bottle, thumbed the cap, popped a pill into his mouth. He chewed and swallowed. "That should help. Now go ahead with Grandma to the car."

Beth Ann shook her head, Bunny tight in her arms.

Barrett went very still and he spoke in a low,

threatening tone. "Did you forget about ice cream on Family Night?"

Beth Ann shot a scared look at Cara, then bolted to do what her father had said. He'd threatened her with *ice cream?*

While Barrett marched them to the car, Cara looked right and left for someone to signal—a gardener, a maid, a hotel guest—but no one appeared.

In the parking lot, Barrett switched cars with Deborah and sent her off in the opposite direction to the one they would take.

Cara pulled out of the lot.

Barrett turned to Beth Ann. "All set?" He frowned. "You're too old for that ugly thing." He took Bunny from her, leaned way back to shove it onto the back window ledge. "There. Now he can see out."

As he did that, Cara saw the phone he'd taken from her tipping out of his pocket. She tried to reach for it, but he sat down too soon. He popped another pill and they drove in frightened silence, Beth Ann staring back at Bunny, tears rolling down her cheeks.

"I'm sorry that I panicked," Cara said to calm Barrett. "You're right about my condition. Sometimes it takes over. That was why I made the call. What I really want is our family to be the way it was. I just need time, like you said."

She talked on and on and she seemed to be succeeding because Barrett didn't argue with her. Then she noticed that his eyelids were drooping.

From the pills. Maybe he would drift off and she could stop the car, grab his gun and Beth Ann and run. That only worked in the movies, she feared.

Barrett cleared his throat and blinked. "I need coffee." He looked at a billboard. "Look there. The Date Shake Ranch is the next exit. We'll have family ice cream after all, Bethie."

"I don't want ice cream," Beth Ann wailed.

"Sure you do. You love ice cream."

"No, I don't. I hate it," she shrieked.

He leaned into the backseat. "You wanted it then, though, didn't you?" His tone was pure evil. "More than anything. Didn't you?"

Beth Ann went silent instantly.

Then? What was he talking about? Cara thought back to the attack. It had been on Sunday. *Family Night at Carcher's.*

With a jolt, it hit her. Barrett must have promised Beth Ann ice cream. She'd told Beth Ann not to answer the phone, but if she recognized her father's name on the display, she might have been tempted. It was Beth Ann who left the door open. When she went next door to play.

That was why Beth Ann hated ice cream and why she wouldn't talk about what had happened.

She didn't want Cara to know what she'd done. And Barrett was blackmailing her with the secret.

He was a monster.

As Barrett leaned back, the cell phone stuck out even farther. Holding her breath, she pushed the call-back button, hoping the microphone would pick up their conversation for Jonah.

"It's okay, Beth Ann," she said as loudly as she dared. "The Date Shake Ranch is famous for its ice cream. Just one more exit." She had to remind Jonah about the sirens. "We'll go inside, slow and quiet, so no one gets hurt."

"Stop scaring her," Barrett snapped. "I told you I'm not angry. I can't *get* angry."

"Sorry." She glanced down and saw the phone was black. The battery must have died. Had Jonah heard anything? She felt more scared than she'd ever been in her life. Her one chance at getting help had gone black.

THANK GOD FOR Beth Ann's ratty stuffed rabbit. It caught Jonah's eye in the rear window of a sedan pulling out of the resort parking lot just as he was pulling in. He'd whipped around to follow and verified the plate number matched the rental car from Barstow—the city where Warner had rented the car, according to Deputy Collins, the officer handling the case.

Getting closer, he saw that Cara was driving,

her ex-husband beside her, Beth Ann in the back. He called Collins and informed him, warning him again against marked cars and sirens, which would enrage Warner, who'd somehow gotten wise to the plan or simply decided to run for it.

Staring at the car, praying Cara and Beth Ann would get away safely, he vowed he would never let them out of his sight again. Specters faded. He could become a better person. He was not giving up. Not this time.

A few minutes later, his phone rang. He recognized the number as the one Cara had used. He pushed speakerphone and heard crackling, then a muffled voice. No way she could have called him with her ex sitting beside her, so it had to be a pocket call. A few seconds later, the call died.

Checking the phone, he almost missed seeing them take the exit. Whipping across two lanes, and swerving to miss the barrier, he made it, following them into the parking lot of the Date Shake Ranch, a road-stand-turned-market. He called Collins, who told him to stay back, that he was calling in every available officer.

Jonah ignored him and slowly trailed the car across the huge parking lot. If there were a chance he could rescue them before Warner heard a siren and pulled his gun, he had to try.

They made the turn to the back of the lot and parked near a Dumpster. Jonah stayed back,

parked his truck and crept his way along the wall.
When he risked a look around the corner, they
were all out of the car.

Barrett gripped Beth Ann's shoulder and had
an arm at Cara's waist, holding her close. Where
was the gun? *There*...a bulge at his waist.

Jonah braced himself against the wall to wait.
His plan was simple. As soon as they passed him,
he would lunge at the guy, grab for the gun and
yell for the girls to run like hell.

He listened to their steps on the gravel. Closer...
closer...*now*.

When he stepped out, Cara saw him and yelled,
"Run," to Beth Ann, then ran herself. Warner
grabbed his gun.

Jonah swiveled, putting himself in front of the
gun. He heard a pop, felt the burn of a thousand
bee stings, then slammed Warner to the ground.
The gun flew across the gravel.

Warner scissored his legs, and twisted in a
grappling move Jonah was in too much agony to
counter. Warner then jammed a heel into Jonah's
ribs. A bone snapped and pain ripped through
him. He couldn't breathe. Punctured lung, he figured, gasping like a beached fish.

Barrett kicked again and everything went black.

Jonah woke to the sound of Cara's voice. "Let
her go, Barrett."

He looked up and saw she'd pointed the gun at

Barrett, who held Beth Ann before him, an arm across her body.

"Give me the gun," Barrett said, inching closer, hand outstretched.

The gun wavered in Cara's hand. "Stay where you are."

Jonah fought to stand, but his vision grayed, threatening to go black, so he only made it to his knees. He had to save them.

"What kind of mother points a gun at her daughter?" the man said, advancing on her. "You're mentally ill. We'll get you the help you need. Just give me the gun."

Cara stepped backward. She looked uncertain. Then she noticed Jonah and her expression became determined. She separated her legs, added her other hand to the gun grip and stiffened her arms. "Stop right there or I *will shoot you*," she said in a tone indicating she meant it.

Warner stopped moving. "I can see you're too far gone now." He glanced to his left where the car was parked. "Beth Ann and I will get into the car and leave. We'll straighten things out once you've gotten the help you need."

He backed toward the car, taking Beth Ann with him.

Jonah crawled toward him, stopping when his vision wavered.

"You can't take her, Barrett. I promised to keep her safe." Cara lunged closer.

"You're the one aiming a gun at her."

"You promised her Family Night at Carcher's, didn't you? You talked her into leaving the door unlocked."

Beth Ann sobbed.

"It's not your fault, Beth Ann," Cara said. "He tricked you so he could hurt me. He used you. That was cruel of him."

"That's enough!" Barrett snapped.

"I'm not done. You can't bully me anymore. I'm too strong for that. So is Beth Ann. You said she's part of this, so let Beth Ann decide. She can come to her crazy mother with a gun or she can go with you."

"You truly have lost your mind," Barrett said.

"You choose, Beth Ann. Choose who you want to be with and we'll respect your decision."

"Your mother is sick, Bethie," Barrett said.

"Choose, Beth Ann," Cara said levelly. "Trust your good heart. Be your brave self."

Jonah gathered what was left of his strength to stand, hoping that when he passed out, his momentum would take him into the guy.

"I want my mom," Beth Ann said in a steady voice. "Let me go."

"You don't mean that," Barrett said.

"You said you'd let me choose," she said, leaning away from him.

"You did this!" Barrett screamed at Cara. "You made her afraid of me."

In the distance, Jonah heard sirens. Barrett heard them, too. His hesitation was enough for Beth Ann to twist away.

Jonah lunged. The last thing he saw before it all went black was Beth Ann in her mother's arms. He passed out smiling.

CARA HELD BETH ANN'S hand as they watched the ambulance take Jonah to the hospital. The bullet had passed through muscle, according to the EMT, so there wouldn't be much nerve damage. His other injuries included a punctured lung and at least one broken rib, but he would be fine.

She sank down to talk to Beth Ann, praying she could say what her daughter needed to hear.

"I'm sorry I didn't keep you safe," Cara said, her throat tight. "I know I broke my promise, and—"

"I was greedy," Beth Ann choked out, tears streaking her cheeks. "I wanted ice cream. It was my fault. I'm sorry."

"It wasn't your fault," she said. "Of course you wanted ice cream. Your father tricked you because he knew that. It was not you. Never you."

Her daughter searched her face, her blue eyes swimming in tears. "Do you forgive me?"

"There's nothing to forgive."

Beth Ann burst into tears and threw her arms around Cara's neck, nearly knocking her over.

Cara squeezed her eyes shut, tears spilling down her own face. She had her daughter back to comfort and care for. "We'll get past this, Beth Ann. We will. We'll talk about it until it makes sense and then we'll talk some more. Okay?" She leaned back to look at her daughter.

"I let Daddy find us. I lied about Serena. I didn't warn you that he was here."

"It's okay. I asked a lot of you, taking you away from your friend and making you keep so many secrets. You made some mistakes, sure, but so did I."

"Really?"

"Oh, yes. And I'm so proud of you for standing up to him. You were brave and confident."

"You were, too."

"I was. I'm proud of us both."

"Did Grandma Price get tricked, too?"

"She did." Cara wasn't sure she'd ever forgive her mother for her part in this, but she was Beth Ann's grandmother, so Cara would keep that to herself.

"Ms. Price?"

She nodded at Deputy Collins, then spoke to

Beth Ann. "The police need to talk to us for a bit. Can you answer some questions?"

Beth Ann nodded. She seemed much calmer now.

"After that, we'll go see Jonah in the hospital."

"Then what will we do? We don't have to move to Phoenix now, right?"

"No, we don't. We can live where we want." Barrett would be in prison for a very long time. She studied her daughter. "What do you think about staying with Rosie for a while longer? Maybe even go to school in New Hope."

"Can Serena visit?"

"She can stay the rest of the summer if she wants. I'll pay for her ticket."

"That's great." Beth Ann sighed. "I can be Beth Ann again?"

"Absolutely."

"Bunny was a dumb name." She blew out a breath.

"Tell the police everything, Beth Ann. No more secrets."

Her daughter nodded and Cara knew that she could finally do what she'd sworn to do three years ago—help her daughter heal.

TWO HOURS LATER, Cara and Beth Ann met Rosie and Evan in the hospital reception area, then rode the elevator to Jonah's room.

He was propped up in bed, his shoulder bandaged, his arm in a sling, but he looked so good to her she wanted to throw her arms around him and cover him with kisses.

Beth Ann ran to Jonah and started to hug him.

He held up a fist. "Fist bump for now, Squirt. Until my ribs heal."

Beth Ann gave him a careful tap.

"So cancer wasn't hair-raising enough, you had to go get yourself shot?" Rosie said, her voice husky.

"What can I say?" Jonah said. "That's how I roll." He smiled crookedly. The morphine must be affecting him.

"You saved my life," Cara said.

"I backed your play. You saved yourself." His eyes shone with love.

That was what he'd done, she realized. He'd let her take the lead when Barrett kidnapped them. He hadn't tried to take over. Cara stood on her own two feet, but that didn't mean she couldn't accept a supportive hand at her back.

"Which reminds me…grab my jeans out of that bag, would you, Squirt?" Jonah said. "In the pocket's something that belongs to your mom."

Beth Ann did what he asked, holding out the carved bear.

Cara took it. "I missed this," she said, looking at him. "I missed you."

"Me, too," Jonah said.

"Jeez, it's getting goopy in here," Rosie said. "You hungry, Bunny? Let's hit the cafeteria."

"Call me Beth Ann," she said solemnly. "And can I have ice cream?"

"Absolutely," Rosie said. Cara's heart was full to bursting.

When they were alone, she moved closer to Jonah, who gave her a goofy smile. "They give you something for the pain?"

"Oh, yeah. You might have to remind me what we said afterward."

"Don't you dare say you let down the people you love. You took a bullet for us. Literally. I'd say that's taking *guardian of my world* too far. I don't know what I would have done if you'd been killed."

"Better me than either of you," he said and she knew he meant it.

Careful not to bump any injured part, she leaned down to kiss him, breathing him in, welcoming the familiar rush of desire. She never wanted to lose it. Or this man.

When they broke apart, Jonah said, "When I was chasing after you, afraid that maniac might hurt you, I realized I couldn't live without you, Cara. Wherever you move, I'll be there. I'll hook up that Airstream and drive it all the way to Canada if that's what it takes for you to feel safe."

"I'm not running anymore. I know you plan to move to New York, but—"

"I can work wherever I want. Wherever you are, Cara, that's home to me. You and Beth Ann."

Tears filled her eyes. "I'd like to see Rosie through her treatments and Beth Ann through a school year. After that, how about we figure out a life that works for all of us?" Maybe she'd apply for a loan to sell her good-luck buns. Maybe they would move to Tucson so she could finish her teaching degree. Maybe they would go to New York. She was free. She could make any choice she wanted.

"Sounds good." He grinned crookedly. "Really good."

"Morphine makes you less grouchy, for sure."

"That's all you, Cara. You woke me up, turned on all the lights. It's like what Rosie said to you about Eddie, that he loved her like she was worth it and after a while she felt like she was. You do that for me."

"That's how it's supposed to work, I think."

"You make me want to be a better man, Cara. You make me think I can be." His eyes shone at her, full of compassion and respect and love.

"You do the same for me. I stood up to Barrett. You helped me see I was strong and smart and—"

"Relentless. Don't forget relentless."

"Apparently, you won't let me." They grinned at each other, teasing again like every day in the café.

"Barrett's out of my head," Cara said. "He's gone. So is the girl I was with him. You're all I see, Jonah. All I want to see. And I know who I am and what I want."

"That's good. As long as I'm on the list of what you want."

"Oh, yeah. You're right up there with fresh-squeezed lemonade."

He laughed. "Ow." He grabbed his side. "No more jokes for a while."

"You know how that reporter kept calling us the New Hope Café? From the minute I walked through the café door, that's how I've felt about it."

"Maybe we should change the name. Rosie's pretty hopeful herself these days."

"You'll have to make a new sign."

Jonah groaned. "Here we go again." His eyes searched hers. "I'll likely screw up, you know—raise my voice, say the wrong thing, let you down—but if you'll stick with me, give me a chance, I'll do better, I swear. I'll do my damned-est to be the man you need me to be."

"You already are." Cara leaned down for an-other breath-stopping kiss.

"Mmm," Jonah said in a sexy growl. "How long

do you figure we have till they get back from the cafeteria?"

"Are you crazy? You're injured."

"No problem if you stay on top. If I recall, you *do* like to steer." He gave her a slow smile.

"You're terrible," she said with a giddy laugh.

"Those candy hearts clumped for a reason, I guess," Jonah said. "Right now, I feel pretty lucky."

"You should. We got double hearts, you know." What charm could she make that would mean *you will live happily ever after?*

Maybe they didn't need a charm. Maybe they would just make it happen.

* * * * *

LARGER-PRINT BOOKS!
GET 2 FREE LARGER-PRINT NOVELS PLUS
2 FREE GIFTS!

Harlequin®

Super Romance®

Exciting, emotional, unexpected!

YES! Please send me 2 FREE LARGER-PRINT Harlequin® Superromance® novels and my 2 FREE gifts (gifts are worth about $10). After receiving them, if I don't wish to receive any more books, I can return the shipping statement marked "cancel." If I don't cancel, I will receive 6 brand-new novels every month and be billed just $5.44 per book in the U.S. or $5.99 per book in Canada. That's a saving of at least 16% off the cover price! It's quite a bargain! Shipping and handling is just 50¢ per book in the U.S. or 75¢ per book in Canada.* I understand that accepting the 2 free books and gifts places me under no obligation to buy anything. I can always return a shipment and cancel at any time. Even if I never buy another book, the two free books and gifts are mine to keep forever.

139/339 HDN FEFF

Name _____ (PLEASE PRINT)

Address _____ Apt. #

City _____ State/Prov. _____ Zip/Postal Code

Signature (if under 18, a parent or guardian must sign)

Mail to the **Reader Service:**
IN U.S.A.: P.O. Box 1867, Buffalo, NY 14240-1867
IN CANADA: P.O. Box 609, Fort Erie, Ontario L2A 5X3

Not valid for current subscribers to Harlequin Superromance Larger-Print books.

Are you a current subscriber to Harlequin Superromance books and want to receive the larger-print edition? Call 1-800-873-8635 today or visit www.ReaderService.com.

* Terms and prices subject to change without notice. Prices do not include applicable taxes. Sales tax applicable in N.Y. Canadian residents will be charged applicable taxes. Offer not valid in Quebec. This offer is limited to one order per household. All orders subject to credit approval. Credit or debit balances in a customer's account(s) may be offset by any other outstanding balance owed by or to the customer. Please allow 4 to 6 weeks for delivery. Offer available while quantities last.

Your Privacy—The Reader Service is committed to protecting your privacy. Our Privacy Policy is available online at www.ReaderService.com or upon request from the Reader Service.

We make a portion of our mailing list available to reputable third parties that offer products we believe may interest you. If you prefer that we not exchange your name with third parties, or if you wish to clarify or modify your communication preferences, please visit us at www.ReaderService.com/consumerschoice or write to us at Reader Service Preference Service, P.O. Box 9062, Buffalo, NY 14269. Include your complete name and address.

HSRLP11B

The series you love are now available in

LARGER PRINT!

The books are complete and unabridged—
printed in a larger type size to make it
easier on your eyes.

Harlequin *Romance*

From the Heart, For the Heart

Harlequin
INTRIGUE
BREATHTAKING ROMANTIC SUSPENSE

Harlequin *Presents*

Seduction and Passion Guaranteed!

Harlequin *Super Romance*

Exciting, emotional, unexpected!

Try **LARGER PRINT** today!
Visit: www.ReaderService.com
Call: 1-800-873-8635

Harlequin

A *Romance* FOR EVERY MOOD™

www.ReaderService.com

HLPDIR11

Born in Tynemouth in 1919, C. L. Skelton's varied career has included stage and film acting, war service in the RAF, seven years as a lay brother with a religious order, hunting the Loch Ness monster and selling insurance and brushes door-to-door in the Scottish Highlands.

Other novels by C. L. Skelton in Grafton Paperbacks are *Hardacre*, *Hardacre's Luck*, *Sweethearts and Wives* and *Beloved Soldiers*.

C. L. SKELTON

The Maclarens

GRAFTON BOOKS

A Division of the Collins Publishing Group

LONDON GLASGOW
TORONTO SYDNEY AUCKLAND

Grafton Books
A Division of the Collins Publishing Group
8 Grafton Street, London W1X 3LA

Published by Grafton Books 1980
Reprinted 1986

First published in Great Britain by
Hart-Davis, MacGibbon Ltd 1978

Copyright © The Regiment Publishing Co. (Jersey)
Ltd 1978

ISBN 0-583-13076-3

Printed and bound in Great Britain by
Collins, Glasgow

Set in Linotype Plantin

AUTHOR'S NOTE

This book is a work of fiction. The 148th Regiment of Foot never existed. However, the campaigns which occur in the story are fact, though the actual manner in which they were conducted has been fictionalized. The history of the regiment and the attitude of those serving in it are fairly typical of the attitudes of men serving in the British Army, where they never joined the army as such; they joined the battalion.

Among the many people who have helped me in the research which went into the writing of this book, and to whom I owe much, there is one whom I would like to mention, and to whom I would wish to offer my gratitude. He is Major Hugo Macdonald-Haig, M.C., who served for many years in one of the great Highland regiments.

Finally, I dedicate this book to my father, Clement Skelton, M.C., who was a professional soldier for much of his life, and who served his country and his regiment through three major wars and many small campaigns.

C. L. Skelton

Drumnadrochit,
Scotland
August 1977

1

It was hot. It was as hot as the hell through which they had just lived and died. He looked around the square in which he stood. It was all yellow-brown dust and mud buildings, the high sun giving only a foot or two of shadow along the blank anonymous walls, concealing interiors like dry, stinking ovens.

The men, those fortunate enough to have been given a stand-easy, lay tucked up close to the walls, keeping their bodies within what little shade there was and hating the merciless heat of that sun. At least they were free from the torturous weight of their Enfield rifles and the fifty pounds of full marching order – packs, blankets, ammunition pouches, and the rest – which had torn at their backs over the last few days. The square blocks of buildings and shops which formed the uninspiring centre of the native quarter offered no solace or comfort. Any form of movement brought forth a cloud of the brick-dry powder which choked the nostrils and cemented itself into their throats and the sweat which covered their aching bodies.

With whatever voice they could muster they shouted for the *bhisthi* who padded around barefoot in the dust, filling their canteens with a pint of brackish water from his goatskin bag, grinning stupidly at the sahibs as they cursed him for his tardiness, not understanding what it was that they said in their strange language, and wondering why they had ever left that cold, wet country from which they had come. Every fumbling delay as he tipped the water from his *mussak* was greeted with another grin as he stepped quickly and easily out of the way of the halfhearted blows that were aimed at him.

In the middle of all of this stood Andrew Maclaren leaning heavily on his broadsword. He had neither the heart nor the energy to try and avoid the sun beating down on his feather bonnet. Beneath the grime which encased him, Lieutenant Maclaren was a good-looking youth. Tall, he had the Maclaren red hair and blue eyes, a legacy of his Pictish ancestry. His nose was a little too thin and his jaw was a little too square. On his left cheek there were two moles, one above the other, the victims of a thousand cuts since he had started shaving at the age of fifteen.

He was a boy who had suddenly become a man. A few days ago he had been a youth of twenty-one; now he had been baptized an adult. The blood of his baptism was caked on to his sword, cemented with the same yellow-brown dust which covered his uniform, his men, and the whole bloody country for as far as he could see. The once-white tropical tunic which he had been issued with on his arrival in India and which his servant had dyed to a blotchy khaki was now stained with the sweat which tried to rid his body of the heat. He was wearing the Maclaren kilt, the deep blues and the greens and the yellows, the colours and the sett of the tartan no longer distinguishable under the grime. The dust penetrated through his uniform and deep into his skin and made his body feel as if he had been invaded by a million minuscule creatures. He had an almost overpowering desire to scratch, to tear at his flesh with the ragged nails of his fingers, restrained only by the knowledge that if he broke the skin, the dust would work its way in, bringing with it creatures smaller and more virulent than the grains of sand and powdered clay, to feed on his flesh. There were creatures already feeding on his flesh, small winged creatures that took their fill and then moved on, each one making room for two more. Then there were the flies, fat blue-green-bodied ones that crawled presumptuously across his face and body. Now and again he would shake himself in an endeavour to rid himself of the current crop, only to have them immediately replaced by a new and more ravenous contingent.

Every bone ached, every muscle begged him for rest. His body could not understand the mind that drove him on. His throat was dry and parched by the same muck that covered his face and hands, save where globs of sweat had turned it into a muddy mortar which dried, caked, and fell from him as his skin twitched under the constant irritation.

Andrew was the fourth generation of Maclarens to serve with the 148th Foot since the regiment had been raised by his great-grandfather to fight the French, over fifty years ago in the Napoleonic Wars. And Andrew was wishing with all his heart that he was back at home in Scotland with his regiment.

'How in God's name did I get myself into this?'

He was addressing the air and the question was rhetorical. He knew the answer. On his promotion from ensign, instead of taking command of a half-company, as was his right, he had volunteered for service with the army in India. Not with the East India Company force, for he held the Queen's commission, and *that* he was not prepared to surrender. The added financial advantage of the Company force with double the pay of the Queen's soldiers meant nothing to Andrew, whose family estates in Scotland and investments in rapidly industrializing Britain provided the Maclarens with wealth in plenty.

Andrew was here because he had taken this course in order to avoid the iron hand of his father, who commanded the First Battalion at their permanent headquarters at Perth. Not that Andrew disliked his father; they got on very well together and shared a mutual love of their regiment and the traditions already created. But his father was a strict and fearsome disciplinarian who Andrew knew would rather have seen his son dead than be himself accused of nepotism. Besides, Andrew believed that his father had doubts about him, about his manhood, about how he, who hated to shoot a stag, would react under fire and in the stress of battle. He believed, with some justification, that his father considered him perhaps too gentle to be a *real* soldier.

So Andrew had decided, and his father had readily agreed, that a year or so away from the regiment and the chance of

9

seeing some action would be a good thing for both of them. It would be especially good for Andrew's formation as a soldier, who was by right of birth one day destined to command the regiment.

And that was why, on that sixteenth day of July in 1857, Andrew was standing in the middle of the square, in the middle of the native quarter of Cawnpore, weeping.

They were not embarrassed tears, but they were real tears. Tears that made little rivulets down his dust-encrusted face. They were not tears of pity, though pity was there. They were not tears of grief, though grief was there too. The Maclarens did not weep for grief or sorrow; they were tears of anger. Anger, frustration, and a deep, deep, bitter hatred. He felt emotions that he had not known he possessed. Cold, cold fury. He wanted to kill, not in the heat of battle as a soldier should, but slowly and without compassion. Not the way the men he had killed that morning had died, swiftly and cleanly; but in drawn-out agony as their lives were tortured from their bodies.

'What dae I do wi' it, sir?'

Andrew forced himself to look again at the bloodied, ragged cloth bundle in the man's arms. The corporal who stood before him was a hard-bitten Highlander. A Seaforth who had fought in a dozen campaigns, rough and unimaginative, a man to whom death and mutilation were no strangers. But as he spoke, his words were choked from between tense lips as he too forced back the tears. The small mutilated bundle of flesh that he held had been a baby. A little girl, not more than a couple of years old, with soft clear white skin and golden hair. And there it lay, its skull crushed and two of its tiny limbs torn from their sockets. A harmless, innocent little body, savagely defiled.

'Put it —' Andrew choked back a sob as he tried to form the words. 'Put it with the others.' And he turned his face away, more to hide the sight of the child from himself than to hide his emotion from the soldier.

It was not the first pitiful sight that he had seen in that pitiless land. He had seen infants left to starve on dungheaps, little children with distended bellies and fleshless limbs, holding out emaciated hands as they begged for the food that would enable them to continue their shabby existence. He, they, had always tried to help with food for the hungry, and shelter in convent or

10

institution for the abandoned. Not that the
scratch the surface of a problem that was ju
they tried.

He had seen a little of what this count
whom the accident of birth had condemned to
were the rajahs, the princes, the wealthy me
believable luxury of the rich; but they were fe

Against this, the grinding poverty of the poor
water wheels, and scratched the earth with wo   ough-
shares, knowing that if the next monsoon were to fail, then
starvation would inevitably follow. Hundreds of millions,
packed into that vast subcontinent of plain and desert and
mountains and forest, living only by the law of survival of the
fittest, and knowing that when things went wrong, the very old
and the very young would not survive. Those who did live were
condemned to spend their lives bending their backs in servi-
tude to support the massive wealth of the few.

Most of them lived in little villages consisting of mud and
straw huts where their inhabitants slept on mud floors, or, if
they were lucky, on cots of woven string which served as tables
during the day. Their household articles were few, mostly pots
made from clay in which they cooked, carried water, and stored
their food. There was no sanitation, the water was probably
brackish, disease was a way of life, and a full belly was a great
and infrequent luxury. There was no way out, for most of
them were condemned to live within the caste to which they
had been born.

The rule of the East India Company, now shaken to its foun-
dations by the Sepoy rebellion, was tottering. Back home in
Britain, the prime minister, Viscount Palmerston, was aware
that the rule of the Company must end and direct control must
be imposed on British India. And all of this because someone
had decided to wrap some of the bullets supplied to the Company army in paper greased with pig's fat.

But these things meant nothing to the poor, for nothing
would help the poor, and the British government would treat
only with the princes and the rich, for they were the ones who
owned the masses, and the masses would do as they were bid.
And the poor would be left, as they had always been throughout the long history of their land, to be born and, if they were

rvive in that same poverty which was the only
ew.

ew was not the only one who had wept that day. There
others, many others, from highly bred officers of crack
fashionable regiments down to the coarsest and most illiterate
of the common soldiers, the men whom Wellington had described as 'the scum of the earth', men to whom emotion, if it
existed, was just another bodily function. They too had wept
and vomited from empty stomachs as they looked upon the
horror that was Cawnpore.

Why? On the tenth of May in 1857, at Meerut, a town about
thirty-eight miles from Delhi, and after about two months of
scattered unrest brought on by the rumour that the cartridges
issued to the native troops were encased in pig's fat, eighty-five
of the men of the native cavalry were court-martialled for refusing to fire with those cartridges. These men were sentenced
and marched off to jail. The court-martial was held on a Saturday, and on the Sunday evening, the native regiment suddenly
rose and fired upon their officers and released the prisoners.
After burning the prison and setting free more than a thousand
convicts, the first of the massacres which were to become a horrible feature of the mutiny began. Of the European residents
few survived, women and little children being put to the sword
without mercy.

At that time, the garrison at Cawnpore was under the command of Sir Hugh Wheeler, a seventy-four-year-old Bengal
officer. He realized that the situation was dangerous and began
to form an entrenched camp around the hospital barracks between the soldiers' church and some unfinished lines which
were being constructed for European troops. The position was
not a good one militarily speaking, and by some incredible over-
sight, he failed to guard the magazine which contained the vast
majority of their ammunition. It was after this that Sir Hugh
asked the aid of the Chief of Bithoor. This man, Doondhoo
Punth, or as he was more frequently called, Nana Sahib, had a
carefully concealed grudge against the British authorities. He
claimed that he had been robbed of an inheritance of some eight
hundred lacs of rupees. He had mixed much with the European

community and though he did not speak English, he had acquired a superficial refinement which distinguished him as a native gentleman, and as such he was regarded as a friend of the British residents.

He had been allowed a princely house and a retinue of two hundred soldiers and three field pieces. As soon as Wheeler applied for his aid, he came promptly with his guns and his men to Cawnpore. On his arrival in that city, however, he placed himself at the head of the mutineers and demanded that Sir Hugh Wheeler surrender his entrenchments. The surrender was refused and the entrenchments were assaulted. Inside these entrenchments were 465 men and 280 women and children.

As the forces of the defenders became depleted, the forces of Nana Sahib became stronger. He was joined by a large body of fine soldiers, Oudh natives, and again and again they assaulted the garrison, which was daily diminishing in numbers. The defenders knew that there was no hope unless some sort of compromise could be reached, and they received with great relief an offer from Nana Sahib that those who were willing to lay down their arms would receive safe passage to Allahabad. To that offer was added a promise of food and boats to carry them all – the garrison, the women, and the children.

They had no alternative, they had to accept. The men were required to leave first. They laid down their guns and were put aboard the promised boats. The boats moved out into the Ganges and as soon as they were into the stream of the river, Nana Sahib's artillery and infantry opened fire on them. Four men survived to take the message of Cawnpore to Allahabad.

Andrew had joined General Henry Havelock on the latter's arrival at Calcutta, whence he had been rushed at the outbreak of the mutiny. Sadly, Havelock had not arrived at Calcutta in time to avert the tragedy of Cawnpore. However, immediately on their arrival on July 7, they had gone to Allahabad to organize the troops who had been gathering there in small detachments from various garrisons in the neighbourhood.

Andrew's chief was well known in India as a somewhat staid puritanical type of soldier, reminiscent of Cromwell's Ironsides.

He was over sixty and had served in the East for thirty-four years, a fact which Andrew regarded with some awe. Included in his campaigns were the Burmese war of 1824 and the Sikh war of 1825. He was a serious, sober-minded man, fierce in battle and gentle in victory, who would permit no blasphemy or drunkenness among his soldiers.

In Allahabad they were given orders to take a relief column to Cawnpore, and then on to Lucknow. With only 1,200 men hastily assembled, Havelock pushed forward at once, leaving Allahabad on July 12 and heading northwest along the fertile plain along the Ganges, now baked dry in the Indian sun awaiting the monsoon which would flood the river and bring the latent life back to the land. They were in a hurry and proceeded by a series of backbreaking forced marches through the mean little villages and across the now-dusty plain.

They had travelled some sixty miles when they were joined by a force of about 800 men under the command of a Major Renard, bringing their force up to 1,400 British bayonets, eight guns, and about 500 loyal native troops. At Futtehpore, just after Major Renard had joined them, their van fought an engagement with some 3,500 mutineers and took the town. Andrew was not involved in that battle, being in the rear in the company of the general.

It was after this that, without pause, they took to the Grand Trunk road and marched to within eight miles of Cawnpore. Here forward pickets came in with the news that Nana Sahib had taken up positions across the road, entrenched and covered by his artillery.

After Futtehpore, Havelock had pressed on, leaving his mule-drawn artillery, a mixed bag of eight twelve- and eight-pounders, to catch up as best they could, so great was the urgency with which they regarded their task. Tired and weary, they would have been an easy prey to any major ambush set along their path, but apart from minor skirmishes, none came.

It was just before midnight on the fifteenth when they bivouacked, and exhausted men freed themselves from the sixty pounds of oppressive weight of their packs and blanket rolls, shed their ammunition pouches, dropped their rifles, and slept wherever they stopped. But not for long.

At three o'clock in the morning the bugles, which had sounded so sweet only a few hours ago telling them to rest, broke the silence of the night and ordered them to arms. By the flickering light of the dying campfires, General Havelock addressed his men.

'You all know why we are here,' he called. 'There are about two hundred women and children still in Cawnpore. They are British women and British children, and it is our job to get them out. I have little idea of how strong the enemy is, how many men he has, or what cannon he can bring to bear. But I tell you this, if there are a hundred of them to each of us, we will still give them the hiding of their lives. If they have cannon, and I suspect they have, we will take them and turn them on to the mutineers. There will be no pause to mop up isolated pockets. The objective is the city itself and those women and children, and remember that every moment of delay could cost them their lives. I know that we have had little rest, but I pray that the Lord will give you strength for the fight. Keep your powder dry and God save the Queen.'

The men replied with a cheer and then set about the business of checking weapons and striking camp.

Andrew had been at his place at the general's side during the short speech, and as Havelock got down from the makeshift rostrum from which he had addressed the men, he turned to Andrew.

'Well, Mr Maclaren, will this be your first battle?'

'Yes, sir.'

'Have you the stomach for it?'

'I hope so, sir.'

'Aye, lad, you wouldn't be a Maclaren if you hadn't.' The general paused and became thoughtful. 'I hope to God that I'm doing the right thing. I wish that those damned guns were here. I know that Nana Sahib has at least three field pieces. They'll be seven-pounders, accurate up to a thousand yards and still effective for another five hundred. He'll be sitting across the main road. You see those mango groves just ahead of us?'

'Yes, sir.' Andrew looked in the direction the general was pointing. He could just make out in the half-light the groups of tall evergreens with their slender pointed leaves, obviously

15

carefully tended by someone long since fled. 'Yes, sir, I see them.'

'We'll go through there and try and get round his flank. But I fear that we are going to have to shift them with cold steel and pray that we can take his guns quickly. We're going to lose a lot of men today.' He took a deep breath, and then, catching sight of something hanging from Andrew's belt, changed his tone. 'What the devil have you got there, lad?'

'It's a revolver, sir. A Colt.'

'Let me see it.'

Andrew handed the weapon to the general. 'It's called the Navy Belt Model. My father made a present of it to me just before I left for India. He believes that it will revolutionize close combat.'

'Hrrumph!' said Havelock. 'It's heavy.'

'Only four pounds, sir, and it takes a thirty-six-calibre bullet.'

Havelock held the gun for a moment, swinging out the rammer and poking it into one of the chambers.

'How long does it take you to load?'

'About five minutes, but you've got six shots.'

'And then?'

'I don't know, sir.'

'And then you need your broadsword. I know your father, lad. Damned fine soldier but a bit too keen on newfangled ideas. Wouldn't trust the damned thing meself. It'll never replace the bayonet or the broadsword.'

'Yes, sir,' replied Andrew dutifully.

'Go and get yourself a glass of claret from my tent before we start, and good luck to you, lad.'

Havelock watched him go. That was going to be the new army. New young men with new ideas and new weapons.

It was time that the Company was kicked out anyhow. They had made a real mess of things. No one but an idiot would demand that a native soldier should bite a bullet that he believed was greased with pig fat. The Sepoy would die first. Things were changing and India would never be the same again. But this was no time to reminisce. There were women and children at risk, and subordinate commanders to brief. But first he would pray.

16

He looked around at the men preparing to move, smelling of sweat and leather in their stained uniforms and tarnished brasses, their webbing, cross belts, straps, and packs still bearing the scars of the march. Soon they would be fighting and dying, but first Henry Havelock would go down on his knees before his Maker and beg for their lives.

Less than an hour after Havelock had finished speaking, they were advancing on the city in a wide arc which they hoped would take them on to the enemy's flank. Their lines of communication were stretched for sixty miles and they were pretty fragile at that. They were tired from the long marches of the previous days and they knew that the guns were not yet up with them. But as the sun rose and they headed through the geometric lines of mangos, the knowledge of where and why they were going straightened their backs and gave them strength. A piper from the Seaforths, bearded and in blue tunic and kilt of the regimental tartan, spurning both cover and camouflage, played a march and gave Andrew a moment of nostalgia for other times and other days in the hills and glens of home. So, spurred on by what their commander had said, they strode bravely on towards Cawnpore.

It was to be no set-piece battle. The British did not form the traditional square and face a suicidal rush from an undisciplined foe. The Sepoys were British-trained – men who, but for the mutiny, might have been marching by their side. As they emerged from the mangos, where the ground was released from the restraint of the roots of the tall trees, the yellow dust started to rise again as they advanced – now by companies in open order.

The Sepoys held the advantages that always go to the defending force, advantages of cover and of high ground. The old city, the native quarter, formed the centre of town. The outskirts were dotted with the homes of the European community, each a little fortress surrounded by a stone wall. Andrew spotted one; a bodhi tree stood in the centre of a green lawn, and from its branches hung a child's swing gently swaying, but there was no wind. Why? As he asked himself the question, the answer came. From the gardens, from behind the hillocks, from the windows of houses built of solid masonry, the firing started and the enemy began to cannonade the advancing British infantry.

Men started to fall; they were still too near the enemy's centre. Havelock, sizing up the situation, galloped on his charger through the advancing companies turning them out on to the enemy's flank; and aided by the range and accuracy of their new Enfield rifles, accurate over distances which would have been unthinkable a few years ago when they would have been equipped with the old smooth-bore Brown Bess, they began to take their toll of any Sepoy foolish enough to expose himself for more than a second.

At long last they were among them, each man with fifty pounds of weight on his back and ten pounds of rifle in his hands. Thrusting into the brown masses for nearly three bloody hours they fought hand to hand and, as Havelock had predicted, it was the bayonet and the broadsword which carried the day.

Andrew had amazed himself. It was as if he were standing outside his own body and watching some demoniacal being which had taken possession of him. Before him was a brown and grey rocky outcrop with a tuft of parched grass sticking out from its head. Suddenly a face appeared from behind. It was a young face, little more than a boy. He remembered how the thick lips had curled into a smile as he watched the musket come up pointing towards him. Then he heard an explosion and felt his right arm wrenched up from the recoil of the Colt that he had fired instinctively. He saw a bloody hole appear in the Sepoy's head and looked at that thing which had been a man and was now just a mass that twitched and spasmed at his feet.

It gave him a wonderful almost Godlike feeling as he looked down at his victim, totally unaware of the battle that was raging around him. It was only when a soldier screamed in his ear, 'You'll get bloody shot standing there, sir!' and then died himself, that he returned to reality. Intoxicated by his kill, he shouted and cursed as he cut and shot his way through the mass of brown bodies. And when the silence came, when the last shot had been fired, the last agonized scream stilled, he stood silent on the battlefield, knowing what he had done, looking at the blood on his sword, and then at his own body, untouched, bearing not even a single scratch to remind him of what he had been through. And in that moment, the words of another

Henry, Harry Hotspur, came to him, out of time and into mind:

> But I remember when the fight was done,
> When I was dry with rage and extreme toil,
> Breathless and faint, leaning upon my sword ...

In the stillness that followed the battle, the bugle had sounded, plaintive and weary. The men had slowly and with aching limbs formed columns. Stretcher parties were detailed off to carry those wounded who could not walk, and what was left of them marched into the town.

The city that they entered was silent. Not a single soul to greet them. No cheers, not even a curse, the only sound the battle-weary tramp of their boots puffing up little clouds of yellow dust with every step. The thing of which they were most conscious was the smell – the smell of recently burnt buildings, a pervading odour of decay, but most of all the stench of the sweat of their own tired bodies as the temperature rose to over a hundred. They marched on through the European quarter towards the centre, past the burned-out lines of the garrison. There was one house, a pretty little white bungalow surrounded by trees. It looked intact, until you looked again and saw the broken door and the smashed verandah, a doll's pram, new and shining, split into two, and the flagstaff with the barely recognizable remains of a Union Jack half burned, lying drunkenly across the lawn.

On they went through the streets, past the deserted dwellings and into the native quarter where the buildings were all square blocks of clay, and straw, mean little houses surrounded by the litter of insanitary living. Then towards the market square; shops and stalls began to appear, their goods in disarray, their owners fled. A mangy dog, its ribs delineated sharply against patches of bare skin, crept towards Andrew, gazed at him for a moment with lacklustre eyes and then slunk quietly away through an open door. Was this to be the only living thing in Cawnpore?

At last they arrived in the square where a couple of oxen were helping themselves to the mangos, maize, sugarcane, rice, and other vegetables which were piled in an untidy mess from the overturned counters where they had so recently been neatly displayed. The beasts standing up to their bellies in the mess of fruit and vegetables barely moved as two soldiers broke ranks and slit their throats.

Well, thought Andrew, at least the troops would have fresh meat tonight. In the square they halted and the command was given to fall out. The men went only as far as the nearest shade, slipped out of their packs, dropped their rifles, and lay exhausted on the dusty ground.

For Andrew there was, however, to be no rest.

He reported to the general as soon as the stand-easy had been sounded.

'Get me Colonel Hamilton,' demanded Havelock.

Andrew found him, the commanding officer of the 78th, the Seaforths, and together they reported back to Havelock.

'Willie,' said Havelock, 'your chaps put up a great show today, but I still need some of them. Detail a couple of your junior officers to take squads and search the European quarters. There's got to be someone alive somewhere.'

They had erected Havelock's tent, a simple, spartan ridge tent with an awning outside. Havelock was seated at a trestle table with Colonel Hamilton and Major Barrington, the brigade major. They were deep in conversation. Andrew, as was his duty, stood a little apart from them out of earshot and ready to intercept anyone who wished to approach the general. It was while this conversation was in progress that the first squad returned from their search. Their officer stood them easy, but the troops did not move; ashen-faced under their grime, they just stood there as if in shock. Their subaltern, a tall pink-faced youth wearing the Seaforth kilt and red double-breasted jacket with Inverness skirt, approached Andrew.

'Ensign Campbell, 78th,' he said. 'I have to see the general at once.'

'Sorry, he's in conference,' said Andrew. And then, seeing the man's obvious distress, 'What is it?'

'Holy Jesus, we've found them,' he blurted out and pressed his hands to his temples. 'For God's sake, man, get the general!'

'You've found who?'

'Get him or I'll go myself.'

'Wait here,' said Andrew and went over to the tent.

Havelock looked up, irritated at the interruption. 'Mr Maclaren, this had better be important.' An expression of astonishment crossed his face as he looked past Andrew. 'What the—'

Campbell had followed Andrew to the table. Hamilton and Barrington rose to their feet glaring at the presumption of the young man.

'What the devil are you doing, here, sir?' demanded Havelock.

'Come with me, sir, please,' said the young ensign. 'I can't explain. It's too horrible. You'll have to see it for yourself. Please.' Without waiting for a reply, he turned and left them.

Havelock was impressed. Without another word he followed Campbell out, and together with Andrew and the two field-ranking officers, they set out through the town.

'Not so fast,' shouted Havelock to the disappearing figure of Campbell.

'Hurry, sir. Please hurry,' was the reply.

They followed to the edge of the native quarter and then they saw it. It was a waterhole, or a well; it was surrounded by a low crumbling mud wall. There were caked patches of mud all around it and it stank. It stank with the sweet, sickly-cloying smell of death. They stopped and gazed in horror at the sight before them. Over the edge of a broken piece of wall, upside down, its hair brushing the dust beneath it, a rag doll still clutched in a small hand, was the body of a child. Beyond this, piled high, were mutilated corpses, women and children, more than they could count, the women and children they had come to rescue. One hundred and twenty miles they had marched, exhausted they had fought a battle, one in every three of them had died or been wounded, and they had achieved nothing.

Havelock stood silent for a moment and then turned away from the sight as though he could bear it no more. Andrew, after one glance at the carnage, kept his eyes fixed on his general, because had he not, he would have had to look again.

'Mr — er — what's your name?'

'Campbell, sir.'

'You stay here.'

'But, sir —'

'Sorry, but it's an order.' Havelock turned to the others. 'Come with me, all of you.'

They went back to the square in silence, each alone with the image of what they had seen. At his tent, Havelock leaned heavily upon his table. Andrew and the other two waited for their chief to speak. Finally, Havelock rounded on them, his lips trembling and his hands clenched so that the knuckles showed white through the bronzed skin.

'Colonel Hamilton, as soon as we can, tomorrow if possible, we march to Lucknow.' He paused. 'We will take no prisoners.'

'We already have taken prisoners, sir,' said Major Barrington.

'You know what to do.'

'Sir?'

'Organize an execution detail at once. Take them to that waterhole, show them what's there, then shoot the filthy lot of them.'

'And the wounded, sir?' The Major was surprised at the vehemence of his chief's reaction. He knew him for the staid, grave, but kindly puritan that he was.

'And the wounded,' snapped Havelock.

The major saluted and left on his grisly errand. Havelock turned to Andrew.

'And now, Mr Maclaren.'

'Sir?' replied Andrew. He was still shaken by the memory of what he had seen. His gentle, bookish nature violated by the bestiality of it all, he felt sick and angry, and yet he was afraid that he might be given the same job as Barrington. He was not sure that he would have the guts for it.

Havelock's voice was toneless, the voice of a man of iron control fighting back his emotions. 'You can take a squad and carry on searching the town. If you find any Sepoys, shoot them. I want to be sure that there is not a single one of them left alive when we move out.'

Andrew left the group and started out across the square to seek out some men to come with him. Released from the gaze of his superiors, he became aware of his own weariness. His shoulders slumped; how he envied those men who lay asleep in the patches of shade, who had not had to see what he had seen. But for Andrew there was no rest. He held the Queen's commission and he was under orders; he had a job to do. Never in his life had he felt so weary, so sick at heart. He had to rest, if only for a moment. Exhausted, he leaned on his broadsword. He felt that he could stand no more. That was when the corporal came. That was when the tears came.

He looked blankly at the pathetic little bundle that only a couple of days ago might have been lisping out its first words to its mother, that mother who now lay in a festering, fly-covered heap at the well.

'Take it to the waterhole and lay it with the others.'

'Them's rotten bastards, sir.'

'What's your name, corporal?'

'Jones, sir, eighteen years with the colours, sir, and I ain't never seed anything like this.'

'None of us have, corporal, but you must do as I say.'

Andrew had neither the wish nor the energy to continue the conversation.

'Yessir.'

The corporal left him and still he did not move. He stood there sweating in the silence, his eyes beginning to droop. There were limits. Suddenly a cannon boomed, jerking him back to consciousness. He straightened up, grasping firmly on his sword, and then he realized what was happening. Barrington was blowing the prisoners from the mouths of their own guns. He looked across the square at the retreating figure of Corporal Jones, thought of the baby, and allowed himself a grim smile. According to the Sepoy's religion, if his body was dispersed, his future state of existence was in jeopardy. They would not die happy.

Andrew had a job to do. He walked over to where a small group of men were relaxing in the shade.

'Not more bloody fighting, sir,' said one of them, a grizzled old veteran with a sabre slash down his right cheek. 'We've only just got stood easy.'

They were English and the speaker viewed the young Scot with an experienced eye. He reckoned he could smell out a soft officer a mile off. 'Look, sir, can't you get some from the 78th? They've been fell out longer than us.'

Andrew drew a deep breath. He did not like pulling rank. It always made him feel inadequate.

'You're coming with me, rifles loaded and bayonets fixed. Who's the senior man?'

'I suppose I am,' said the first speaker.

'Name?'

'Smithers.'

'Sir!' snapped Andrew.

'Smithers, sir.' He got to his feet. He had been beaten, but only just, and he bore no grudge. 'Orlright, you lot, you heard what the officer said. What's the job, sir?'

'We're going to look for survivors. If we meet up with any Sepoys, we have orders to shoot them on sight.'

'Too good for them buggers, sir,' said a lean youth with a Yorkshire accent.

'Leave your equipment here,' said Andrew as one of them started to struggle into his fifty-pound pack. 'Smithers, detail one of them to stay and guard your gear.'

While the men loaded their Enfields, Andrew heaved out his Colt and carefully measured the powder into each chamber, pushing in the wad and ramming home the bullet. Then he gently fitted the percussion caps to the nipples at the rear of the cylinder and reholstered it. The six weary men got to their feet and he led them through the main street and towards the European quarter.

To Andrew, it was all so incomprehensible. They were searching through a part of town that had been touched by neither shot nor shell. Yet the buildings, homes, and gardens had been burned and wrecked. He could have understood an enemy that had taken over the town and held it, using what facilities were left intact for their own use. But this wanton destruction seemed so useless. It gave him a vision of the expression of anger and hatred of the mob which must have surged through, bent only on destroying for destruction's sake. Many of the houses were just ashes lying in smouldering heaps among scorched lawns. Others, those which had not been burned, had verandahs smashed, verandahs where ladies and gentlemen had gathered after dinner dressed in cool white linen, and sipped cold drinks before retiring, safe and comfortable under the protection of the East India Company. Doors and windows ripped out, roofs at drunken angles where a gable end had been hammered to matchwood, and personal belongings, toys, and furniture heaped in broken mounds of rubbish over the lawns. He could see no reason for it. Anything they could go into, they entered, and found nothing but destruction. He could envisage them all as they had been, neat, white-painted, and smart with evenly cropped, well-watered lawns, children's playthings, swings, and sandpits. How delightful they must have been before all this.

The house they were approaching was not all that different, except that it did not seem to have been quite so vandalized. The line of the roof was straight, there was the inevitable litter of furniture and personal possessions around the lawn which had a series of massive fig trees creating shady oases. The house itself had had its pale-grey wooden verandah splintered, and the mosquito screens torn and ripped. Two pairs of large French windows which had opened on to the verandah had been half torn from their hinges and swayed drunkenly outward. It was obvious from its style and layout that it had been the home of a fairly well-to-do European family.

'Haven't we done enough?' said Smithers. 'We're not going to find anybody.'

Andrew was sure the man was right and was very tempted to agree with him. All of their fruitless searching was not going to help morale any, but he had his orders.

'We'll go in and look,' he said.

Smithers compressed his lips and for a moment was inclined to carry on the argument. He looked at the others, who seemed to be in a state of bored resignation. Right little bastard, he thought. Still, he'd try again at the next one.

Rifles at the port, they went in through one of the pairs of French windows. They were in what had been the dining room. The heap of scarred mahogany had once been a carefully polished dining table. Broken glass was everywhere; some of it had been fine crystal, some frames which had held the daguerrotypes that littered the floor. With little more than a glance, they moved on through the house. They had done it all a couple of dozen times in the last three hours. They had been tired when they started, now they were tired and bored and hungry. They trod over the remains of lace curtains, picked their way through broken furniture until they came to what had been the with-drawing room. An engraving of the Queen lay on the floor, glass smashed and stinking with human excrement which smeared it. The room was dominated with the remains of a grand piano, battered and broken and tipped against the wall.

'There's another door there, sir,' said one of them. 'Behind the piano.'

'Shut yer gob, Wilson,' hissed Smithers.

If Smithers had not spoken, Andrew might have ignored it. But the uncertainty of his own authority made him act. 'We'll look,' he said. 'Get that piano shifted.'

They heaved it away from the wall, and Wilson, proud of his discovery, tested the door.

'It's locked, sir. I think it's bolted from the inside.'

Their interest quickened; even the reluctant Smithers wanted to know. He swung back the butt of his Enfield. 'Shall I, sir?'

'Yes, break it down,' said Andrew.

It was a heavy door, panelled and strong, the sort of door one found at home, not like the flimsy structures that had been smashed throughout the rest of the house. They stood back as Smithers thumped a hole through the panel and put his hand through.

'Wilson's right, sir, it's bolted from the inside.'

'Open it and stand back,' said Andrew. 'There's just a chance that there's somebody in there. I'm going in. Cover me.'

With the chance of some action, the lethargy had gone. The men stood at the door, tense, their rifles primed and loaded. Andrew drew his revolver and cocked it. Then he walked silently through the open door.

It was dark inside, dark and cool. He waited just inside the door for a full minute to allow his eyes to become accustomed to the darkness. He could hear nothing but the breathing of the men grouped behind him. He felt forward with his foot and found a step down. He tapped it; it was stone. Beyond it was another, and another. He reached out with his hand and found a wooden rail. It must be a cellar. As he cautiously descended, vague shapes started to appear, a couple of long, shadowy shelves. A wine cellar? As if in confirmation, as he reached the bottom he kicked against something which tinkled away with the unmistakable sound of glass on stone.

In the silence he held his breath. He was sure that he could hear the sound of heavy breathing, and it was not coming from the men at the top of the stairs. He paused, trying to locate the sound. It appeared to be coming from the farthest corner, beyond the rows of shelves. He stopped again, feeling forward with his left hand. He touched the racks and felt the cool dusty neck of a bottle. It was certainly the wine cellar. He stood silent; yes, he was not alone down there.

'Come out,' he called. 'I know you're there, whoever you are. Come out and show yourself.'

There was a gasp. A quick frightened intake of breath. There was no reply.

'I am a British soldier, and there are six men at the top of the stairs, all armed. If you do not show yourself, I shall open fire.'

'Have pity!'

It was a small frightened voice. A woman's voice. Then there was a long silence, punctuated only by the sound of her breathing. Slowly Andrew discerned a shadowy figure emerging from behind the wine rack. It stopped.

'*Are* you British?' It was barely a whisper, but it was a cultured English voice. It did not have the clipped accent of the English-speaking native.

'Yes, I am.'

'Oh, thank God, thank God.'

He caught up the dim figure as she started to fall, fainting into his arms.

He picked her up, amazed at the lightness and softness of her body. He carried her back up the stone steps and into the light, where the men moved silently aside to let him pass. Without pause, he walked straight out of the house on to the road and towards the square.

His lips compressed and with an illogical feeling of embarrassment, he looked down at his burden, a woman, little more

27

than a girl. She was wearing a torn, once white linen skirt and a silk blouse which had ripped under her arm, revealing the smooth white flesh beneath. She had no shoes, and her stockings peeping out from beneath were worn and dirty. Her eyes were open, large and blue, but not seeing. Her long blonde hair was matted and filthy. Through the rips in her skirt and on her legs there were smears of blood. As they left the house, one of the soldiers, a burly Scot, grabbed one of the discarded curtains. He ran to Andrew's side and covered her with it.

'Ye canna tak the lassie oot like that,' he said.

Andrew looked at the man's honest, grimy face. 'Thanks, Jock,' he said.

Andrew had never held a woman before. To him they were strange and mysterious creatures. Almost another species. He felt this strangeness in the soft thighs which lay across his right arm, and the thin gentleness of the arms and shoulders against his left.

As they walked, a silent little procession grouped around him. Andrew kept glancing down at her face. Her eyes flickered and blinked. For a moment they were still, and then they focused on him, and suddenly she started to scream and struggle. He held her easily; there was little strength in that small body. But before her eyes closed and she lapsed again into unconsciousness, he noticed that they were terrified.

As they neared the square, about a mile and a half from where they had found the woman, they heard the rattling and rumbling of the guns arriving, the teams of mules straining under the load of the twelve- and eight-pounder field pieces and their ammunition limbers. With them came the baggage mules carrying loaded packs or hauling wooden-wheeled carts piled high with stores of food and ammunition, tents, and all the impedimenta of war; the clatter of the cannon and the mule train, the cursing of the muleteers, the clouds of yellow dust, all bringing the dead city to life.

Andrew was barely aware of the commotion as he carried his burden across the square. He called to a passing N.C.O.

'Where will I find the surgeon, sergeant?'

'Over there on the other side,' said the sergeant, pointing to a large ridged marquee of grey canvas with a white flag flying

28

from its front pole, from which men were emerging bandaged and limping, and one, his eyes covered with a dressing, being led across the square by a comrade.

He carried the girl over and found the surgeon sitting on a three-legged stool outside the tent, shoulders slumped in utter exhaustion, trying unsuccessfully to light his pipe and flicking flakes of tobacco off his blood-spattered rubber apron.

Captain Higgins was not a young man and he had never been a successful doctor. He had spent the first part of his practising life in the poorer quarters of Liverpool and then he had joined the army. He had seen it all before in the Crimea, and seven years in India; until now it was all just another job. As Andrew approached, he raised his greying head and drew the back of his hand across his brow, where the sweat was pouring into his bushy eyebrows.

'Not another one,' he said wearily. And then looking again, 'What the devil have you got there?'

'It's a woman,' said Andrew.

Captain Higgins took his pipe out of his mouth. 'Good God!' he said in astonishment. 'Where in the blazes did you find her? No, don't tell me, it's none of my bloody business. Better take her in.'

Wearily the surgeon heaved himself to his feet and followed Andrew into the tent. Andrew picked his way carefully through the two lines of seriously wounded lying on straw paillasses. There must have been over fifty of them there, and they were only the worst cases. He came to a table, a few planks spread across a couple of rude trestles and stained with blood, some of it not yet dry. Next to it were Captain Higgins's instruments – saws, scissors, chisels and knives, needles and thread. It looked like a carpenter's shop which had got itself mixed up with a seamstress.

'Stick her on there,' said the surgeon.

'Haven't you got anything to cover it with?' Andrew was shocked.

'No, I haven't, unless I take a blanket from one of them,' was the reply. 'And I'm buggered if I'm going to do that. Put her down.'

Andrew did as he was bid. 'I'd better report to the general,' he said.

Higgins was looking at her; he looked up and smiled. It was a nice smile, revealing a row of tobacco-stained teeth. 'Come back when you can. I don't think there's much wrong with her, and she *is* your prisoner.'

Andrew left them, found Major Barrington, and was taken immediately to General Havelock.

'Woman?' said Havelock after Andrew explained. 'That's deuced awkward. Still, we had better go and take a look at her.'

Andrew led his commanding officer across the square in the direction of the hospital tent. It was quieter now, the guns having gone through, headed for the banks of the Ganges where they would camp for the night. Still the bustle of activity was there, quartermasters checking and rechecking stores. Marquees in various stages of erection, and men carrying loads of ammunition to points where it was being issued to queues of troops. Havelock was anxious to move to Lucknow, fifty miles away, at the earliest possible moment. As they arrived at the tent, the surgeon led her out. She was wrapped in a grey army blanket.

She stopped as they approached, tugging the blanket around her, her arms crossed and her hands holding the edges of the blanket pressed tight against her shoulders. She stood motionless, like some stone statue over which someone had thrown an old rag. Captain Higgins was a man of average height, and she was nearly as tall as him. Andrew saw again the long fair hair falling below her shoulders, the finely drawn features, tight clear skin over the high cheekbones, the blue eyes set wide apart, staring but not looking, and he realized that beneath the grime and the unkempt hair, she was beautiful. He looked straight at her, wishing that her eyes would answer his glance, but they looked straight through him with no sign of recognition.

Havelock looked at her and pursed his lips. He glanced at the surgeon, who nodded slightly and took his pipe out of his mouth as if in deference to his general. Then he stepped aside and allowed Havelock to approach.

'Good day to ye, ma'am,' said Havelock.

The girl started, and it seemed to Andrew that she tightened her grip on the blanket, trying to draw it together around her body. But she looked straight past both of them.

The general continued, 'I must apologize that there is so little that we have to offer. We'll do what we can, though. Mr Maclaren will arrange some sort of a bathhouse for you, and I'll send some of the men through the houses to see what they can find in the way of clothes.' He paused, but there was no reply. 'Hrrumph. Perhaps we might have the pleasure of your company at dinner tonight?'

'You are very kind.'

It sounded so ridiculous. The tone of her cultured voice was abnormally normal. A formal invitation formally accepted in a voice that was low and calm.

Havelock grunted. He felt that there was more that he should say, but for the life of him he could not think what. Finally he grunted again and turned to leave. The girl still had not moved.

'What happened to her?' asked Andrew of the surgeon who was now by his side.

'Shock mostly. Physically, as far as I can tell, she seems to be all right, but she's had a damned rough time.' He was trying to get his pipe going again.

'You'll join us this evening,' Havelock spoke to Andrew as he passed.

'Oh, yes, sir, thank you, sir,' replied Andrew. He turned to Captain Higgins. 'Did you find her name?'

' 'Fraid not. Those are the first words I've heard her speak. Perhaps if you tried?'

Andrew hesitated for a moment and then went over to her. 'I'm Andrew Maclaren, ma'am.'

'How do you do, Mr Maclaren.' She spoke without looking at him and again there was that eerie formality and the low, even voice. It seemed to Andrew that the hands – which apart from the face were all that was visible of her outside the blanket – tightened and trembled slightly.

Andrew tried again. 'We are going to try and find you some clothes, and then we will see what we can do about getting you out of here.'

'The other officer already told me, but really, I have a very

31

ample wardrobe of my own,' she replied calmly. Then, still without looking at him, she turned away and walked unconcernedly back into the tent.

In the dusty square, a white marquee had been erected next to the general's tent. The fall from the canvas roof had been rolled up and covered with mosquito netting. It was divided by a canvas curtain into two rooms, in the larger of which the Indian servants were preparing for dinner – simple by regimental standards, but none the less it would be the best meal they had had for nearly a week. Freshly squeezed fruit juices to start, and a roasted saddle of mutton whose succulent smell came from somewhere in the rear.

A long table, improvised but hidden by a starched white linen cloth, dominated the room. On it was the general's silver, including a pair of ornate four-branched candelabra, all of this having been brought in by the supply train and arranged in military precision on the table. The claret, port, and madeira stood in their jugs and crystal decanters on a sideboard constructed from the general's packing cases. These cases were exquisitely carved of Indian rosewood and had been used to transport the general's dinnerware. The four stewards, immaculate in their white jackets, turbans, gold shoulder straps, white gloves, and gleaming brass regimental buttons, were all Sikhs, a sect who had remained loyal throughout the whole period of the mutiny, and were under the command of the general's personal servant, a mountain of a man with bright eyes and gleaming teeth shining through and over a shining black beard. Not that they were only servants; every one of them was a fighting man and all of them had taken part in the engagement less than twenty-four hours ago, though looking at them now it would have been hard to guess.

The other portion of the marquee had been set aside as an anteroom. The guests, a select body, consisted of Colonel Hamilton, Major Barrington, the brigade major, Major Sutcliffe, who had commanded the artillery, and Andrew, who had already arrived; the surgeon, Captain Higgins, and the mysterious lady were expected momentarily. They were all resplendent in full dress, Andrew and Hamilton wearing the kilt and red tunics with braided Inverness skirts, Barrington in the blue-and-gold frock coat of the Bengal Lancers, and Sutcliffe in red tunic and the tight blue trousers of the artillery. It was a colourful sight made incongruous by the scene outside in the square, where the men were clustered in little groups around campfires roasting on sticks their pieces of the two oxen that had been slaughtered that noon.

Sergeant Gundah Singh, the general's servant, had detailed one of his men to hand around drinks as soon as the guests had started to arrive, and the conversation, helped by the whisky-and-sodas, was beginning to flow.

'Thank God the mule train got here intact,' said Major Barrington to Andrew. 'Can't bear to fight and eat in the same clothes. Having that woman you found to dine with us, I hear. Bit odd, what?' he grunted. 'Can't say I approve of women in a regimental mess.'

'It's not quite a regimental mess, it's the general's dining room,' replied Andrew.

'Wonder if she'll retire when the port goes around?' asked Sutcliffe.

'I expect the general'll make her an honorary man for the occasion,' said Barrington, and they all laughed.

Andrew tried to change the subject. He did not want to make jokes or small talk about the day's happenings, least of all about the girl he had found. 'The men seem to be enjoying themselves,' he said, and they gathered around him looking out into the square.

There was some singing coming from the other side as the men tucked into their ample food supply. For the first time in nearly a week they were filling their bellies with good fresh meat and the vegetables that had been lying around for the taking. They were drinking, too. Andrew was pretty certain that the cellar where he had found the girl had been revisited. But over the rough, bawdy soldiers' songs he could hear the sound of the piper playing a lament. It was quite emotional and he thought of the men who had fallen that day, and he thought of home.

'How do they do it?' he said quietly.

Barrington was standing at his elbow. 'They've got their

boots off now, they're relaxing and wriggling their toes. They're very basic. The British soldier is the scrapings of the jails and gutters of the country. There isn't one in twenty who joins the army because he wants to. But once he has enlisted, the army does something to him. It makes him a man.'

'It isn't even one in twenty,' said Sutcliffe, who had a passion for statistics. 'When I was an ensign, I did a little exercise. I took a hundred men and found out why they had joined.'

'What was the result?' asked Hamilton.

'Sixty-six were out of work and hungry. Two were, or had been, gentlemen. Thirteen were looking for an easy life; they were disappointed. Nine were criminals or wanted by the police. Another nine had joined to spite either parents or girl friends. And only one really wanted to be a soldier.'

'You may be right,' General Havelock said, coming in unannounced. 'But they're all soldiers now. They'll most of them get drunk tonight. Can't say I approve, but if it's what they want, they've earned it. There's about a hundred men in that square and another seven hundred scattered around the town, and they're tired and battle-weary. But at six tomorrow morning they'll be on parade, cleaned up and ready for another hellish march. And when the fighting comes, there is no one in the world I would rather have at my side than those men out there. Hrrumph.' The general had embarrassed himself. '*Chota peg*, steward. By the way, where's the lady?'

'The surgeon's bringing her over, sir,' said Andrew.

'Ah, well, there's time yet. Ten minutes before we sit down. Do any of you know her name?'

There was a general murmur of no, and Havelock turned to Andrew. 'Maclaren, you are to leave for Allahabad at first light tomorrow. We've managed to find you a boat, and I can spare you four men. Perhaps Colonel Hamilton will oblige with four of his jocks.'

'I thought we were marching on Lucknow, sir.'

'We are. You are not. Can't take a blasted woman with us. You found her, so you can take her to Allahabad. It's reasonably safe now between here and there and you should make good time on the river. After dinner you can organize your stores for the trip, and make sure that you can provide some sort of privacy for the lady, if you take my meaning.'

As the general finished speaking, Sergeant Gundah Singh came into the anteroom. 'The doctor sahib is here, sir, with the memsahib.'

'Ah, good,' replied Havelock.

She came into the flickering candlelight wearing the sort of plain linen dress that might have been worn by a maid or a nanny. Her fair hair, now clean and sparkling in the light, had been parted in the centre and hung in soft, shimmering ringlets down to the white yoke of her dress. As they rose to greet her, she smiled slightly and inclined her head a little, allowing the ringlets to fall forward and then immediately back into place. Not one of that company would have questioned the fact that they were in the presence of a lady. And then Andrew saw it. It was so out of place that he almost laughed: her feet were bare.

She spoke as calmly and assuredly as if she were in a London withdrawing room. 'I am sorry if I have kept you waiting, gentlemen, but I was unable to find either Mamma or Pappa. However, I have no qualms at assuming their consent to my dining in such gallant company.'

There was an awkward silence for a moment, and the men looked from one to another. Havelock cleared his throat. 'Ahem, can I offer you a glass of sherry wine, ma'am?'

'Thank you, no.'

'In that case, if you have no objection we shall go in. I fear you will find our dinner a little spartan; soldier's fare, you know, ma'am. May I?'

Politely she laid her hand on his and together they went into the dining tent. After seating her on his right and saying grace, Havelock rang a small silver handbell and the stewards started to serve the first course.

Throughout the meal, Andrew kept glancing at her. She obviously had no memory of what had happened. He kept thinking of her parents, her Mamma and Pappa. Outside, he knew, the burial parties would still be working at their gruesome task, perhaps at that very moment consigning to the earth the mutilated remains of what had been her mother. As for her father, unless he had been one of the four survivors from the massacre on the river, it was equally certain that he, too, was dead. These

35

were known facts, but what had happened to this girl? How much had she seen? How long had she been in that cellar?

After dinner when they retired to the anteroom, Havelock talked to the surgeon for a while and then came over to Andrew. He drew him to one side.

'You're going to have to try and talk to her on your trip to Allahabad. The doc doesn't seem to have found out anything. He thinks that she is probably the daughter of an East Indian Company official, but that's a guess. He doesn't know who she is or where she comes from, or anything about her. The only thing that we can be sure of is that she was living with her parents and that they are both dead. But it might even be worse than that. Doc thinks she might have been raped.'

'Oh, God!' Andrew was shaken. 'How sure is he, sir?'

'He's not. Just says that it's possible. She can't remember anything; shock, and all of that sort of stuff. See what you can find out on the trip, but don't press matters. When you get her to the Resident, he can handle that. They'll make arrangements to have her shipped home. She's obviously a lady and must have relatives somewhere. The adjutant's arranging quarters for her, and he'll post a guard over her tonight. You had better be off and get your men and stores organized, and then turn in yourself.' He pulled out his watch. 'It's nearly nine and that lot'll take you a couple of hours. Good luck, lad.'

Andrew went over to the girl. 'I have to say goodnight now, Miss – er –'

'You seem to have a very short memory, Mr Maclaren. My name is Westburn. Maud Westburn.'

And with that, she turned and left him standing with all the assurance of a hostess in her own withdrawing room in her town house in London.

2

Andrew was up before five the next morning and had walked the half mile or so from Havelock's headquarters down to the river to have a look at his boat. He regarded the river with some distaste. It was July, and at that time of year it was a series of muddy pools and shoals which wound their way reluctantly through the one hundred and twenty miles of parched country-side southeast to Allahabad, waiting for the monsoon, which would turn it into an eager, raging torrent. He walked across the caked and cracked mud of the riverbed down to the water's edge, where he found the craft.

It was not hard to find. It was the only one which seemed to be in one piece. It had a pointed bow, but that apart, it looked more like a punt. Flat-bottomed, it was about twenty-four feet long with four to five of beam. A crude mast had been rigged and a lateen sail lay across the thwarts. Andrew was no sailor, but he realized at once that his boat had one great advantage. In that dry and parched time of the year, a boat that would draw only inches of water would stand a much better chance of navi-gating the shallow river than a more conventional craft.

One thing did strike him as incongruous. Here he was a regu-lar officer in the army, and his first command was a boat.

He had put as much as he could of his personal possessions into the pack of a soldier who had died the previous day. It was necessary to travel light. Apart from the pack, his broadsword, and his revolver, he had abandoned the rest of his belongings.

At the boat, he found a young private from the 78th standing guard. The craft already contained three Enfields and an assortment of packs of gear.

'I'm Lieutenant Maclaren, 148th,' he said. 'Are you coming with me?'

'Private Grigor, sorr,' was the reply from the rosy-cheeked youth who could not have been more than nineteen. 'Yes, sorr.'

'How many of you are there?'

'Four, sorr. Corporal MacKay and two other privates.'

'Where are they?'

'Weel, sorr, they put their own stuff in the boat and they've gone off to get the stores. Colonel Hamilton's arranged the food for the trip.'

'Right, Grigor,' he said. 'You can put my pack into the boat and I'll go and see if I can find the lady. We want to be off as soon as we can.'

He was about to leave when a thought struck him and he turned back to Grigor. 'By the way, do any of you know how to handle this thing?'

'Och, aye, sorr, Corporal MacKay kens fine. He's put two long poles and four oars on board. He says he might need the poles to push us off the shoals.'

'Thank God for that,' said Andrew.

He picked his way back towards headquarters through the turmoil of troops, now awakened, some having breakfast from tin plates and others striking camp and preparing to move out.

He found the small ridge tent which had been reserved for Miss Westburn in the square. Outside, a burly sergeant with huge muttonchop whiskers was standing guard.

'Ser'nt Evans, sir, artillery. The lady's ready.' He spoke with a soft Welsh accent. 'She keeps asking for her ayah. Seems to think that she's coming with her.'

'Oh, dear,' said Andrew.

'Is the lady all right, sir?'

'I wish I knew, sergeant,' replied Andrew.

At that moment, Maud Westburn came out of the tent. She was wearing the dress she had worn at dinner the previous night, but from somewhere she had obtained a pair of soft leather button boots and a pith helmet.

'Good morning, Mr Maclaren,' she said. 'I would like to point out that my quarters were quite unsatisfactory.'

'I'm sorry about that, Miss Westburn,' replied Andrew. 'But I am afraid it was the best that we could manage.'

She still spoke in the same low, formal, natural tone, which sounded as incongruous now as it had done the night before.

'I shall be ready as soon as my ayah arrives,' she announced. 'Would you mind waiting?'

Andrew exchanged a glance with the sergeant, who shrugged his shoulders and raised his black eyebrows.

'Your ayah is meeting us at the boat,' Andrew lied.

'How very foolish of her. Has she dealt with my luggage? And I shall need proper travelling clothes.'

'Everything is down at the boat,' said Andrew. 'I'm sorry, but we thought that you would like to get as much sleep as possible before we set off, so we packed and loaded everything.'

'This is rather inconvenient. But I suppose that there is nothing that can be done about it now?'

'I'm afraid not,' said Andrew.

'Then we may as well leave. Goodbye, sergeant, and thank you.'

'Goodbye, ma'am,' said Sergeant Evans, trying to keep up the play-acting. He turned to Andrew. 'If there's nothing else, sir, I'd better report back to my battery.'

'Of course, sergeant,' replied Andrew, and the man saluted and left. 'Can we go now?' he asked.

'One moment, Mr Maclaren,' she said, and went back into the tent and came out again carrying a small valise. 'I don't recognize this, but it does contain some toilet articles which I will need. Do you think I should bring it? Or will my own be at the boat?'

'I think you had better bring it with you. Here, let me carry it for you.'

'Thank you, but I am quite capable,' she said. 'And now, as you seem to be in somewhat of a hurry, we had better leave.'

'This way, Miss Westburn,' said Andrew, not wishing to risk saying more.

Together they headed for the river through the organized confusion of an army preparing to march. The wounded had been moved out, the dead had been buried, and the survivors were sweating it out again as the sun rose in the east and the temperature started to climb. They arrived at the boat where the four soldiers were waiting for them. When she saw the boat, Miss Westburn gazed at it with an expression of disbelief.

'Is that it?' She was obviously appalled.

'I am sorry, but it is the best we can manage,' said Andrew.

'And who are these gentlemen?'

'These are your crew,' said Andrew. He searched out the corporal. 'This is Corporal Mackay, who is an expert sailor.'

'Guid day, miss,' said MacKay, a small man, bronzed and weather-beaten by years of service in the East. He was obviously surprised at being presented as a naval expert. 'Privates Grigor, MacDonald, and Murray, Miss.'

'How do you do, gentlemen,' she said. 'And now, Mr Maclaren, where is my mamma? And where is my ayah?'

Andrew was in trouble. Here was a young lady who had undoubtedly never set foot outside her home unchaperoned, and he was asking her to get into an open boat with five soldiers for what would be at least a three-day journey through possibly hostile country.

'They are coming on the next boat,' he said. 'They particularly asked that you should come with us.'

He held his breath as, for a moment, she hesitated. And then to his utter surprise, she seemed to accept his statement, and stepped into the bow of the craft where some tattered cushions had been arranged to give her some little comfort. He followed her on board and told Corporal MacKay to cast off and get them into midstream.

MacKay ordered MacDonald and Murray to the oars, while Grigor busied himself attaching the rope, which ran through a pulley at the top of the mast to the centre of the gaff of the lateen sail.

'Anything I can do?' called Andrew.

'Ye look to the lady, sorr,' called MacKay. 'We can handle her. Grigor, keep your eyes open for shoals. Ye'll see them from the wee ripples on top or the driftwood stuck on them.'

Slowly, through the muddy water, they pulled out into the stream. There was a light breeze and they hoisted the sail which promptly filled, and they shipped oars and started on their journey.

As they headed downstream, Andrew sat beside Miss Westburn in the bow. Just aft of them stood Private Grigor, looking for those shoals. Charred pieces of wood, packing cases, and other debris floated past them, the legacy of the fighting and destruction of the last few days.

Andrew could not take his eyes off Maud Westburn. She stood up in the bow like a statue, never glancing at him. She just stared straight ahead at the muddy brown water slipping past them.

For a little while nothing happened. They got well under way with a few cautionary shouts from Private Grigor. They were approaching a bluff which stuck out into the river. On top of this was a small fort, brown and uninspiring, with castellated battlements and slit windows of a bygone age. At the same time, a bloated, disgusting corpse that had once been a man floated by. The effect on Miss Westburn was electric. Andrew watched her body suddenly stiffen. She went down on her knees, grasping the sides of the boat convulsively, still rigid, still staring straight ahead. Suddenly she screamed:

'They're shooting! They'll all be killed! Daddy! Daddy!'

She whipped around on Andrew, who was already reaching for her. 'Can't you stop them? Turn back. We're all going to be killed!'

Her face was contorted with fury, anger, or grief; which it was, Andrew could not tell. The river was calm, silent, and peaceful; nothing had happened. And then he realized what it was that she was seeing. She was seeing the boats carrying the men towards what they believed to be safety, seeing Nana Sahib's troops opening fire from that fort just as it had happened only a week ago.

He leaped forward and caught her. She fought him, struggling with a strength and ferocity that he could scarcely believe.

'For Christ's sake, sorr, ye'll ha' the bloody boat over!' shouted MacKay.

She clawed at him, trying desperately to get free. The muddy water was slopping over the low freeboard as for a moment she succeeded, and in a flash was halfway over the side, before he got hold of her again.

'Slap her face, sorr!' yelled Grigor.

That was it. His mind told him that he had heard somewhere that that was the thing to do. He hit her hard across the face with his open hand. The result was dramatic and instantaneous. The struggling stopped and in a moment she was lying limp on the cushions, sobbing quietly.

'Want help, sorr?' shouted MacKay.

'No, no,' said Andrew. 'It'll be all right now. See to the boat.' He arranged the cushions and made her as comfortable as he could in the bow, and sat down watching her.

'Is it all right to gae on, sorr?' asked MacKay.

'Yes, yes,' he snapped back impatiently. Dammit, what the hell else could he do?

'Aye, aye, sorr,' called MacKay, naval fashion.

Andrew returned to his vigil. She lay there motionless for what seemed like hours. He did not try to speak. Alone with his thoughts, he did however try to understand.

When he had found her, there had been a closed door in her mind, shutting out the horrors that she had been subject to. Now that door had opened and she lay there, a prisoner of her memories, confined by the thoughts of what she had lived through.

But this was no time for philosophizing. As they sailed on, the sun rose higher, and with it the heat. It was not too bad in the middle of the river, but hot enough to be uncomfortable. Andrew gave the men permission to remove their tunics, and the ever-resourceful Corporal MacKay found, in the box seat under the stern, a length of sail-cloth. With this and some rope, they rigged an awning over the bow to give Miss Westburn what shade they could. They tied one end of the rope to the mast, just below the foot of the sail, nailed an upright to the bow to which they attached the other end, and spread the canvas across it, securing the edges to the gunwales.

It was just after they had completed this task that she turned and spoke to Andrew.

'Mr Maclaren,' she said. Her voice was even and normal, solemn and lacking the strange formality which had characterized her previous conversation. Her face was serious and sad.

'Yes, Miss Westburn,' he replied.

'They are dead, are they not?' She hesitated. 'Both of them?' And then, as though she were forcing out the words, 'I am talking of my parents.'

It was a while before he replied, searching his mind for some way of softening the blow, yet knowing that she knew the answer. Finally he said simply, and with a little nod of his head, 'Almost certainly.' It was the only way. After all, what was there that he could possibly say that might bring her comfort?

'I know,' she replied calmly, looking straight at him for the first time. 'I can remember all of it now, right up to the moment when my ayah pushed me into the cellar and shouted at me to bolt the door. I do hope that she is all right. She wasn't young, and she loved me very much. She had looked after me since I was born. She would never let me do anything for myself. In a way, I spent my whole life depending on her, and now I suppose I owe her my life.' She stopped.

Andrew waited to see if there was any more that she would add. 'Do you want to talk about it?' he asked.

'No,' she replied. 'Not now. Later perhaps. If you don't mind, I think I should like to sleep a little. I am very tired.'

With that she closed her eyes. Andrew did not reply to her. He just sat there watching the tortured expression on that beautiful, delicate, fair-skinned face. Gradually, her facial muscles relaxed and her breathing took on an even tenor. She was asleep, safe at last from the horrors that beset her mind.

During the remainder of the trip, she talked a little. Andrew never tried to lead her into conversation, but he did manage to find out a little more about her. It seemed that she had an aunt in Surrey whom she hardly knew, but who would no doubt provide a home for her until such time as she could get herself settled. She seemed quite determined to have a home of her own. He gathered that she was by no means poor, so that the question of financial assistance did not arise. The one thing she never discussed was her experiences in Cawnpore. Not once did she give the slightest indication of the assault on her own person at which Havelock had hinted. This gave Andrew hope – hope that it had never been. After all, the surgeon had not been certain.

There was a sameness about the country through which they passed. All of it was brown and scorched by the summer sun, waiting for the monsoon to revitalize the land. The only relief was the occasional mango grove whose long roots dug deep down beneath the parched surface to where the damp soil was still surviving. And here and there, they would see a man treading a waterwheel, coaxing a trickle from what was left of the river on to his crops of maize or rice.

They reached Allahabad and put ashore at that point where the Ganges is joined by the Jumna. Here the pools and shoals disappeared, and beyond, the river assumed its latent grandeur. They were safe now, lying under the guns of the extensive fortifications which commanded the junction of these two mighty rivers, between which lay the most fertile and productive land in the whole of northern India.

Miss Westburn obviously knew the place well and chattered excitedly about the city, pointing out to Andrew the old fort beneath which it was said the Saraswati united with the Ganges and the Jumna. She told him that it contained an underground temple which held a sacred tree stump known as the undying banyan, and that the fort was nearly three hundred years old, and suggested that, should he find time, he should visit the mausoleum and the gardens of Khusru which surrounded the fort. He listened politely to her chatter, knowing that she was forcing herself to act normally and trying not to think of those matters which must be uppermost in her mind.

They found a young artillery officer who proved most helpful and provided them with a mule-drawn cart to transport them to Government House in the city. At the entrance to the house, guarded by two turbaned Sikhs of the Bengal Lancers, they bade farewell to their four companions and headed down the drive, through the parkland to the pillared and porticoed building itself.

Inside, they were intercepted by a cavalry officer wearing the tight pink breeches and silver spurs of the Eleventh Hussars. Lieutenant Watkins-Percival viewed the pair with some distaste. 'Scruffy, doncher know,' he said later in the mess. 'Not the sort of thing you expect to find wandering about Government House.' He enquired of them what their business might be.

After Andrew had explained the situation, Watkins-Percival agreed that it would be necessary for Miss Westburn to remain at Government House until the Resident could make the necessary arrangements for her transport back to England. He said rather pointedly that it would not be necessary for Andrew to remain, and that he had better report to the commandant who he would find at the military cantonments. He, Watkins-Percival, would see to all the needs of Miss Westburn.

Andrew turned to her. 'Well, Miss Westburn,' he said. 'It looks as if this is goodbye.'

'Goodbye, Mr Maclaren,' she replied. 'I owe you a great deal. I want you to know that I am deeply grateful to you for all you have done. I doubt that we shall ever meet again, but if we do not, it would please me to know that you knew that I shall never forget your kindness.' She offered him her hand.

He took it and for a moment their eyes met. Then she looked down and he left her.

Andrew left the House, not without a tinge of regret. What she had said was probably true. It was highly unlikely that they would ever meet again.

He went straight to the cantonments, finding the sight of the familiar military surroundings pleasing and reassuring. The neat lines of brown hutments which housed the European troops, each exactly like its neighbour, surrounded three sides of the barrack square. Across the square from the guardroom, where he made himself known to the sergeant of the guard, stood a square stone building. This the sergeant informed him was headquarters block, and there he would find Major Gifford, the camp commandant.

'Maclaren, eh?' said the major as Andrew saluted and introduced himself. He was an elderly man, balding, red-faced, with a purple bulbous nose. One of those soldiers who opted for a desk job when he could have retired years ago, but knew no kind of life to which he could retire.

'Sit down, lad. I'm glad you've shown up. Got some orders here for you. Arrived the day after you had left. By the way, how did things go up there?'

'Pretty bloody, sir.'

'I imagine it was. Things are quiet enough here now. We blew the last of the bastards off a cannon this morning. I'm going to have his skull made into a cigar box if it's still in one piece. Good idea, what?'

'You said that you have some orders for me, sir,' said Andrew, not wanting to continue that particular line of conversation.

'Oh, yes, of course. Now where the devil are they?'

He rummaged through a pile of papers on his desk, finally coming up with an official-looking document on heavy paper bearing an embossed stamp, and a sealed envelope. 'Here we are. Go ahead and read it. I already have.'

The orders came from the commander in chief, Great Britain, and had been signed by a member of his personal staff. The substance of them was that he was to return to Britain forthwith and rejoin his regiment at their headquarters in Perth. The sealed envelope contained a letter to him from his father. It seemed that the colonel had changed his mind about his son's secondment and had pulled the necessary strings in order to have him recalled. His father had decided that he would retire from active duty within the next few years, and he wanted his only son back to serve in the family regiment which, in the natural course of events, he would one day command.

'Well,' said Major Gifford, 'you're a lucky devil to be out of this lot. Which way do you want to go? There could be trouble between here and Bombay, but it'll save you a fortnight.' He looked up at Andrew. 'Or you can go by Calcutta. Things are pretty quiet that way.'

Andrew thought it over a moment. He was a good soldier, and good soldiers are neither heroes nor cowards. There was no point in running the risk of 'trouble', as the major put it, just to be able to save two weeks.

'I'll go by Calcutta, sir.'

'Sensible fellow, do the same myself,' said the major. He was rummaging again. 'Ah, here we are.' He produced a printed leaflet. 'There should be one of those newfangled steamers, an East Indiaman, leaving Calcutta in about a fortnight. I'll arrange passage for you; you had better be ready to leave at any time after about three days.'

'That'll suit me fine.'

'Pop over to the mess now, it's just behind H.Q. I'll arrange quarters and a servant for you, and join you there.'

An hour later, Andrew was in his room meeting his servant, a wiry little Indian who introduced himself, 'Maclaren sahib, I am your very good servant. I not let any bad man steal from you. I am Ahmet. You want something, you just shout.'

Andrew demanded a bath and Ahmet dragged in an army-issue zinc tub, which he proceeded to fill with buckets of hot water. Andrew lay and soaked his aching limbs for the best part of an hour, occasionally shouting for Ahmet to top up his bath with boiling water.

When he had dried himself, he found his uniform cleaned and neatly pressed and laid out on his bed. There were three rupees missing from his sporran, but that was the way of things; if Ahmet ran true to form, he would steal in small amounts from Andrew, and if Andrew did not complain, then Ahmet would guard his possessions from all others.

'Ahmet,' called Andrew when he had finished dressing. The little man appeared instantly. 'I need some clothes, lots of clothes.'

'Ah, yes, sahib,' replied Ahmet. 'My cousin, he is the very best tailor in Allahabad, possibly in all India. I get him here for you.'

A little later, Ahmet returned with his cousin. Every Indian servant could produce a 'cousin' capable of doing anything that his sahib demanded.

'This is Gopal,' said Ahmet. 'Very good tailor, make shirts, suits, everything.'

Gopal, who looked incongruous dressed in white jodhpurs and a frock coat, pulled out a tape measure, and after noting a multitude of measurements asked Andrew what he wanted.

Andrew ordered a full wardrobe: pyjamas, dressing gown, slippers, a couple of suits, and a half-dozen shirts. After the inevitable argument about price, Gopal left. He returned the following morning, having, with that incredible industry of the Asiatic, completed the entire order; and after a last vain attempt to up the price from two hundred and twenty-five rupees to two-fifty, he left completely satisfied, for he would have done the job for a hundred and fifty.

For the next couple of days, Andrew did not leave the cantonments. Several times he thought about going over to Government House and finding out what had happened to Miss Westburn, or even wandering over to the old fort in hope of finding her in the gardens which she had praised so highly. But he did neither. Her farewell to him had had an air of finality, and he felt that he would not be justified in pursuing their acquaintance.

In the mess, he kept very much to himself, finding very little common ground between himself and the smart cavalry officers who seemed to constitute the bulk of its inhabitants. So it was with some relief he got the news from Major Gifford that he would be leaving, and that his passage had been secured.

Two weeks after his arrival in Allahabad and only an hour before she sailed, Andrew was boarding the PS *Indian Enterprise* at the Calcutta docks on the Hooghli River.

She was an enormous ship, nearly three hundred and fifty feet long and weighing almost three thousand tons. Midships and standing out from her hull were a pair of gigantic paddle wheels. She had a square-rigged foremast with jib halyards running down to her bowsprit. Behind the foremast there were two thin funnels, both already belching forth black smoke, one forward and one aft of the paddle wheels. At the stern was the gaff-rigged mizzenmast, which would hold a giant staysail. Behind the after funnel, a long oak structure, highly polished, ran aft towards the mizzenmast. This had a series of doors and windows, the doors in panelled oak, which provided the cabins and dining saloon for the passengers and ship's officers. The passengers were limited in number, as the *Indian Enterprise* was mainly a cargo liner carrying raw cotton to the mills of Lancashire.

There was a gangway leading up over the paddle housing and on to the deck. Andrew went on board and a seaman directed him to his cabin, which was towards the stern. It was a small room about ten feet square. It contained a writing desk, a chair, and what appeared to be a washstand, all secured to the deck. There was a built-in wardrobe, and against the wall opposite the door, a bunk was recessed between the wardrobe and a series of drawers. Under the bunk, there were more drawers, the smallest of which contained a chamber pot. His tin trunk containing his clothes had arrived, and he set about unpacking into what was to be his home for the next several weeks.

He had not been long at this task when there was a tap at his door. 'Come in,' he called.

A merchant navy officer entered and introduced himself.

'I'm the second mate, the captain cannot call on you at the moment as we are preparing to sail. You nearly missed her, sir.'

'Yes, it was all rather a rush,' replied Andrew.

'My name's Jarvis, sir, and the captain asked me to show you the passenger list in case there is anyone on it that you know. We're arranging seating in the dining saloon.'

'Thank you, Mr Jarvis,' said Andrew as the latter handed him a sheet of paper. 'Good heavens!'

At the bottom of the list of names was 'Miss Maud Westburn.'

'Someone you know, sir?'

'Yes, Miss Westburn.'

'I'll see that you sit next to her at meals, sir. Sorry I can't stay longer. We've got to get to sea.'

Before Andrew had time to protest, he had gone. Not that Andrew really wanted to protest. He just felt that it might seem a little forward, sitting next to her at meals. And it was not really too surprising to find Miss Westburn among the passengers. After all, there were not a lot of ships sailing at that time, and doubtless the Resident had been making reservations at the same time as Major Gifford.

After Jarvis had left, Andrew finished putting his things away, and as he did this, he felt the throb of the engines beneath him, and that almost imperceptible sense of move᙮᙮ ᙮᙮se the ship pulled away from the quay. It was about f᙮ afternoon and he went out on to the deck to watch ᙮᙮ rama of the teeming masses of Calcutta scurrying about ᙮᙮

daily occupations. There were about ten other passengers on deck; he knew that the ship carried only fourteen. But there was no sign of Miss Westburn.

It was not until he had seated himself in his appointed place at the long polished oak table at seven that evening that they met for the first time. She came into the wood-panelled room which spanned the breadth of the vessel, with windows looking out on to the river shore on either side, and he rose as she started to take her place beside him.

'Miss Westburn,' he said. 'This is quite a surprise.'

'How do you do, Mr Maclaren,' she replied formally. 'I was aware that you were coming. I saw the passenger list when I came on board this morning.' She looked beyond him. 'The lady on your right is Mrs Wilberforce, and her husband, the Reverend Wilberforce.'

Andrew smiled a greeting at the rather dumpy Mrs Wilberforce, who was about to become effusive, when the captain tapped on the table with his spoon and asked the Reverend Wilberforce to say grace.

'My napkin is wet,' said Miss Westburn.

'Haven't you sailed before?' asked Andrew.

'I hardly remember the first time.'

'Well,' he said, referring to the small square of linen which lay before each diner, 'they wet these so that if the ship is moving about, your plate will not slide off.'

'Thank you,' she said, and her tone indicated that she regarded the conversation as closed.

'Ladies and gentlemen,' said the captain, 'I am Captain Hogg, master of this vessel, and there are one or two details which I feel I ought to give you before I return to the bridge and leave you to your meal. First of all, you will find all relevant information about emergency drill and mealtimes and such like posted in your cabins. Secondly, we are fortunate in having with us the Reverend Wilberforce and Doctor Adams, the gentleman on my right. They have both kindly offered to place their services at your disposal for the voyage. So all our needs, both spiritual and temporal, are well catered to.

'We are at present in the Hooghli River some seventy miles from the open sea, which we should enter at just after dawn.

So I am sure that you can count on a quiet first night, and I would suggest early bed, during which time I hope that all of you will become accustomed to the motion of the ship. In the event of rough weather, the ship's officers will ask you to remain in your cabins, and I count on you, for your own safety, to obey their instructions. And now, ladies and gentlemen, if you will excuse me, my first mate will be getting very hungry. Goodnight to you.'

As soon as they had finished their meal, Maud Westburn turned to Andrew. 'Excuse me, Mr Maclaren, I shall go to my cabin now and rest.'

'May I escort you?'

'That will not be necessary, thank you.'

She left him with the feeling that she had no desire either to further their relationship, or to recall in any way their recent experiences together. This attitude he accepted; after all, theirs had been a strictly professional acquaintance, brought upon them entirely by force of circumstances.

The other passengers appeared a pretty dull lot. Mostly they were Company officials and their wives who had decided to get out of India before the mutiny caught up with them. Dumpy little Mrs Wilberforce was obviously one of those women who spent her life 'doing good works'. Already during dinner, she had given Andrew a dissertation on her 'poor, dear little native children'. No doubt she did do a fine job, but there was equally no doubt that she was determined that everyone should know about it. As for her husband, an angular undernourished-looking individual with greying hair, he hardly said a word, and Andrew felt that he must have become a parson in order to give himself the chance of getting a word in, at least on Sundays, from the pulpit.

The doctor appeared to be a reasonable sort of chap. Andrew supposed he would be in his late forties. He had a heavy tropical tan, and from what little Andrew could gather at table, he was returning home after some fifteen years in the East. However, he, like Andrew, seemed a quiet individual, not given to socializing, and did in fact return to his cabin as soon as the meal was finished.

It did not appear that the voyage would be in any way a

social occasion. Not that this worried Andrew; he was not gregarious by nature, and apart from Miss Westburn, had little in common with anyone on board. He found a well-stocked library in the saloon which adjoined the dining saloon, so at least he would be able to read. And that apart, he enjoyed the sea for its own sake.

Andrew selected a book – *Pilgrim's Progress*, which he would now be reading for the fourth time since childhood. He walked out into the darkness on deck, went into his cabin, where a hurricane lamp had been lit over his desk, and settled down to half an hour's reading before turning in.

When he awoke, he could feel the movement of the ship much more vividly than when he had retired. He went out on deck and found that they were in open sea. It was calm and the ship heaved gently in the long ocean swell. India was just a smudge on the horizon.

It took them five and a half days to sail through the Bay of Bengal. There was nothing to see, just the calm waters and the thrashing of the paddle wheels churning up a long, frothy wake behind them. During all of this time, he hardly exchanged a dozen words with Miss Westburn, apart from the formalities which politeness demanded.

On the sixth day, they entered the Palk Straits, that fifty-mile-wide stretch of water which separates Ceylon from mainland India. He could tell this by the two smudges of land that appeared on either side of the ship.

They had just finished lunch, and Andrew, who had by this time got into a routine, was about to find some shade on deck and relax with his book, when Miss Westburn spoke to him.

'Mr Maclaren,' she said, 'I hope you will not consider this forward of me, but I have a mind to take a turn around the deck and I should be most grateful if you would be willing to accompany me.'

Andrew was delighted. It was a most unexpected request. 'It would give me the greatest of pleasure,' he replied, and he meant it.

They strolled around the deck for about half an hour, and though they said little and certainly nothing of any conquence, he did not feel embarrassed in her company. They spent most of the time gazing across the calm waters at the thin grey line of the subcontinent to the north. Their walk ended with her heading wordlessly in the direction of her cabin. He accompanied her to the door and she turned to him.

'Thank you, Mr Maclaren,' she said. 'I enjoyed that. You were most understanding.'

Spurred on by her recognition of him, he managed to discover that there was a pianist aboard. It was the captain's steward, a perky little cockney called Turner. There was a piano in the saloon, and Andrew persuaded Turner to play for them after dinner that night.

When the meal was finished, Miss Westburn rose to leave.

'Won't you stay a little longer?' said Andrew. 'I have arranged some entertainment next door.'

Smiling, but not comprehending, she agreed. They went into the other room, which Andrew had now discovered was called the smoking saloon, with its leather-covered seats built against the bulkheads, and small tables in front of them, but still leaving a clear area in the centre.

Only one other couple followed them into the saloon; that was the doctor and his wife. The redoubtable Turner was waiting for them, and as soon as they entered he commenced to play. They sat for a little while on the bench seats under one of the windows and then the doctor went over to Turner and asked him to play 'See Me Dance the Polka'. As the music started, the doctor and his wife rose and began dancing.

'Do you dance the polka, Miss Westburn?' asked Andrew.

'I have done, Mr Maclaren,' she replied.

'Then may I have the pleasure?'

She hesitated for only a second before saying, 'Why not?'

'You must forgive my ignorance of modern dancing,' said Andrew. 'But watching the doctor, I think it should not be too difficult.'

'It is really very simple,' she replied. 'Just one-two-three-hop, one-two-three-hop, and so on. Do you really want to try?'

'Indeed I do,' said Andrew, 'if you will be so kind as to bear with me.'

They rose from the table and he took her hand, putting his

right hand gently against the small of her back. As he did so, he felt her body stiffen and saw her eyes go wide as if with fear. But it was only for a moment, and then she danced happily, and even smiled at him a little.

A day later, the ship called at Colombo, tying up at the south end of the bay and under the lee of a peninsula which stuck out northward into the sea. From where they were they could see the business quarter of the city. The captain had advised them that as they would be coaling, it might be in their own interests if the passengers went ashore for the afternoon. Lines of ox-drawn, wooden-wheeled carts were drawn up on the quay, some carrying their coal, and some containing cases of tea which was to provide the remainder of their cargo.

'Perhaps,' said Andrew, 'you would care to come ashore with me and see the native quarter? I am told that it is most colour-ful.'

'No!' she snapped back at him with considerable vehemence. 'I have no desire to see the native quarter.' Then, recovering her calm, she said, 'But I would quite like to see that large building over there. It appears to have very pleasant surround-ings.'

The building she indicated was, in fact, the Queen's House, a large new colonnaded structure which housed the govern-ment offices. It stood a little back from the quays. Beyond it, they found a large lake and a park, all essentially British in character.

They spent two or three hours in the park, enjoying the sight of the many colourful birds that seemed to be its principal in-habitants. They saw Lady Amherst pheasants with their long black-and-white striped tails walking sedately across the green lawns, and they laughed when Andrew likened a red hornbill, which they saw sitting in a tree not twenty feet away from them, to Mrs Wilberforce. Peacocks there were in plenty, but, to their disappointment, none of them obliged with a display of their magnificent tail feathers. Andrew would have rather taken a look at the native bazaars, and possibly purchased a few gifts, but he respected her abhorrence of mixing with the native population, and her unstated reasons, and did not bring the matter up again.

During the whole of their walk, she never left his side for an instant, staying almost embarrassingly close to him, obviously nervous and not very communicative. But they did manage some conversation, and to establish a rapport that had not existed before. They returned to the ship for dinner just as the sun was beginning to set.

By that time, they were calling each other by their first names, and Andrew was falling more and more under the spell of the woman he had saved.

The same pattern was followed when they called at Zanzibar and Capetown. On several occasions, Andrew tried to broach the subject of the future, but she would hear none of it, and always shied away from the issue. Only once did he try to discuss her aunt in Surrey, but again she would not be drawn.

She became gay, unrealistically gay, when he tried to be serious. Once when he asked her directly what she was going to do, she replied, 'Eat, drink, and be merry, for it's a long way home.' There was almost a touch of hysteria in the way she said it, and Andrew, unwise in the ways of women, let the matter drop.

This really set the pattern of their journey. So long as he made no attempt to be serious, he found her a delightful and charming companion. But at the merest mention of anything concerning the future, she would laugh and change the subject.

They rounded the Cape and stood well out into the Atlantic in order to take advantage of the southeast tradewinds. They made very good time, their engines thrusting them through the doldrums and across the Equator for the second time, and soon they picked up the northeast trades, and their sails filled again as they headed on the last long leg of their journey.

If she was reserved about her own background, he never hesitated to answer her questions about his own. He talked with pride of his family. They would spend many hours sitting on deck when the weather was fine and the sea was calm. They had deckchairs which they always positioned on the leeward side of the cabins.

'Tell me about you Maclarens,' she said teasingly.

'Well,' he said, 'I suppose I really have two families, both of which in a way I was born into: the regiment and my home.

We are not terribly popular at home among our lordly neighbours. We fought on the wrong side in the forty-five, you
know.'

'The forty-five?' she enquired.

'Yes, Bonnie Prince Charlie and all that. I apparently come
from very staunch Presbyterian stock who would have nothing
to do with Catholic Charles. It was after the forty-five that they
made one of my ancestors a baronet. If I survive, I shall hold
that title myself one day.'

'What about your regiment?' she asked. 'That seems very
important to you, and yet you run away from it and go and
serve in India.'

'I think I probably did that because it was important to me;
regiments can become very parochial. I have known since I
was able to understand, that this was to be my life, just as it
was my father's and my grandfather's. You see, we have always
been the Queen's men, or the King's. My great-grandfather
raised the regiment to fight in the Napoleonic wars with Wellington. I suppose we were a little out of step even there, the
'auld alliance' and all that sort of thing didn't really mean very
much to us. In a way, the regiment itself became a sort of extended family. I like to feel that we are a cut above most of the
regiments in the British Army. Nearly all of our men come
from the estate and the surrounding villages. We know them
all personally; and our womenfolk know all the wives and the
sweethearts of the men who serve with us, and any man who
joins us knows that, if anything should happen to him, his
family will be cared for. I suppose that if I was honest, I
wouldn't claim that it was a very important regiment, but it
matters a great deal to us. It means a lot to be a Maclaren and
to be in the 148th.'

She let him chatter on and teased him gently about being in
love with a thousand soldiers.

'No,' he replied, 'it's much more than that. In many ways,
we are fortunate. Both my grandfather and father invested
heavily in cotton and railways, all that sort of thing, none of
which I really understand. My father tells me that it doesn't
matter; financially, the future is secure so all that need matter
to me is the regiment. We shall never be poor. You may have

heard of this terrible business which has been going on in the Highlands. People having their houses burned down and being cleared off the land that they have called home for all of their lives to make room for the Cheviot sheep. They are a money crop, all right, but we never did it. I think that my father is content with what he has. As a matter of fact, he took in several families who had had their farms burnt by neighbouring landlords. That didn't increase our popularity with the Establishment. I think, though, that I can say that my family is held in real affection by the ordinary people around us. Do you understand?'

'It all sounds so very nice,' she said, and her voice sounded a million miles away. 'I envy you, Andrew.'

'There's really no need to,' he said.

They were silent for a little while and then he said, 'Maud, I want to talk to you seriously, about the future.'

The old barrier came down between them. 'Not now, Andrew,' she replied quickly. 'I really must go and change for dinner.'

He waited a long time before he tried to talk seriously with her again.

As they sped northward, her gaiety seemed to increase, but to Andrew it seemed even more unreal. Sometimes he wondered if she ever slept. They would say goodnight in the small hours of the morning after drinking a midnight bottle of wine, and when he came in to breakfast, no matter how early it was, he would find her there before him. Andrew did not mind. All he now wanted was to be in her company.

As they entered the Bay of Biscay – which, contrary to its reputation, was smooth and calm – it was late, approaching midnight. Off the starboard bow, they could see the winking of the Corunna Lighthouse. They were sitting together, an empty wine bottle between them. He looked at her, still gazing out the window of the saloon at the reflection of the light in the water, and he saw for the thousandth time that she was beautiful.

'Are you thinking of England?' he asked gently, for he could see that she was troubled.

'Yes,' she replied.

'It won't be long now,' he said. 'In a couple of days, we'll be into the Channel.'

'I wonder what it would be like,' she said, and her mood seemed dark and thoughtful.

'What? The Channel?'

'No, I was thinking, suppose someone were to fall overboard? It would be quite simple, especially at night, and if the sea were at all rough. I doubt if anyone would see them go. Go out on deck and look around you, there's no one about. And then you would be in the water, and you would see the lights of the ship as it went away from you. And that would be the end of everything.'

'That sounds pretty horrid,' said Andrew.

'Oh, I don't know. There are worse things in life than death. You must believe that or you would not be a soldier.'

'That's different.'

'I know,' she said gently, 'that's the regiment.'

'I suppose that it is.' He was not liking the turn that the conversation had taken. It was morbid. 'Can't we talk about something else?'

'Later, perhaps, when we meet again,' she replied. 'I would like you to take me to my cabin now.'

They went out on deck and he escorted her the short distance to her cabin. When they reached the door, she paused and turned to him. 'Goodbye, Andrew,' she said, and then suddenly, 'dear Andrew.' And she kissed him on the lips, went inside, and closed the door behind her.

Andrew stood for a moment looking at the closed door. He put his fingers to his mouth where her lips had touched his, and then, not understanding, turned and went back into his own cabin a few yards away.

He undressed and got into his blue Indian silk pyjamas, sat down on his bunk, and smoked a small cigar. It was no good. There was no point in going to bed when he knew that he would not sleep. He put on his heavy quilted dressing gown and slippers and went to the chair by his desk. He sat there for a while doing nothing, leafing through a book but not reading it, looking up at the hurricane lamp swaying gently with the motion of the ship. Finally, he got up and went out on to the deck.

He walked towards the stern near to the helm, but not so near that he could be drawn into conversation with the man at the wheel. He wanted to be alone with his thoughts.

He had been standing there for some little time when he noticed a movement up forward near the lee rail. Someone else could not sleep, he thought, and then he realized that it was a woman. He started towards her, and as he got closer, recognized Maud. She was standing against the rail near where the foremast shrouds joined the hull. He was only feet away from her when he realized who she was, and he paused, not wishing to intrude.

She was standing very still, looking straight out across the sea. She remained motionless for some time, her long hair blowing back in the wind, when suddenly he realized that he had seen it all before, on the little boat in the Ganges. He started towards her, and as he did, she began to clamber over the rail. He sprang to her. She was nearly over when he grabbed her and dragged her back inboard.

She fought and struggled with that same mad strength which had amazed him on the Ganges. Fingers tore at his face, ripping the top off one of the moles on his cheek. A crazed screaming of words poured from her as she tried desperately to free herself. At last he got her arms pinioned to her sides and held her fast.

'So that's what you were talking about tonight.'

'Let me go! Let me go!' she cried, and suddenly her shoulders went limp, the tension went out of her body, and she gave up the struggle.

'Maud, Maud,' he said, 'how could you do this to yourself? How, why do you want to do this to me? Oh, my darling ...'

'*Mister* Maclaren,' she hissed his name. 'You shouldn't be touching me. You shouldn't be wanting to touch me.' Her voice became calmer. 'I'm not a very nice person, you know – don't you know that there's something inside of me? An animal, growing and growing, and that one day it will be born – and it has no right to be born!'

At last he understood. The compulsive gaiety of the past few weeks suddenly made sense. The surgeon's fear, related to him by Havelock, had been all too well founded. Not knowing what else to do, he released her, and then as he did so and she started to move away from him, he reached out to stop her.

'Don't touch me,' she said, her voice now completely calm. 'And don't worry, I shall not try to do it again. Mr Maclaren, I hope you are aware that you have ruined everything, including my life.'

She turned away from him and he watched her dejected figure all the way back to her cabin.

He stood for a long time looking towards that closed door, and suddenly, angrily, he said aloud, 'What the hell is she to me, anyway?' And he went to bed.

It was three days before he saw her again. In spite of his outburst, he spent every waking hour watching her door. Not once throughout his vigil did she come out. He saw Turner come and go, carrying trays. On two occasions he wrote a little note begging to be allowed to see her, but both were ignored. However, he maintained his watch. He was not sure whether it was because he wanted desperately to see her or just that he was afraid that she might try again.

They were into the English Channel now. The ship was to unload the tea at London and then sail to Liverpool with her cotton. They passed Torbay at dusk, the flashing light on Berry Head warning of the treacherous rocks which snaked out from the cliff on which it stood. Inshore of them, a group of Brixham trawlers were busy on their fishing ground, drifting slowly along as their trawls gobbled up their catch. They would be out all night and then race home the following morning to land and sell.

The next morning he breakfasted and took up his position on deck outside her cabin. Turner passed him with her finished breakfast tray.

'How is she this morning, Turner?'

'Seems a bit better, guv'. She's got dressed.' And he went on his way.

Andrew stayed there till one o'clock, but there was no sight of her, and finally he went in to lunch. The sea was choppy and he had to struggle with his cup of soup. He had just finished when she walked in. She was wearing a brown woollen travelling outfit. She had done her hair with care in two buns, one over each ear. As she entered the saloon, the men rose to greet her.

'Miss Westburn, I trust you are feeling well now,' said the Reverend Wilberforce.

'I was not aware that I had been ill, Mr Wilberforce,' she replied coolly.

Her face was pale and her eyes looked tired, and the tone of her voice seemed to preclude conversation. She took her place beside Andrew, who half-turned to speak to her and then thought better of it. They passed the rest of the meal in silence.

They were in the Straits of Dover when he found her alone on deck. She was standing gazing expressionless towards the white-grey cliffs which rose through the thin rain. He stood watching her for a while as they ploughed on past the green-capped cliffs and the grey misty dampness of the town and fort. He realized that she was crying quietly, and he went over to her.

'Miss Westburn,' he said very gently. 'Are you absolutely sure that there is nothing I can do which might be of some help?'

'You have tried, Mr Maclaren,' she replied, not looking at him. 'And for that I thank you. But there is nothing that you or anyone can do. I fear very much what the future holds for me, and we dock the day after tomorrow.'

'But you have your aunt. Surely she will provide you with a home?'

'Mr Maclaren, my aunt is sixty. She is a spinster and a pillar of the society in which she lives. It is a small village, and though I myself have never been to England since I was a child, I have learned sufficient to know something about the narrowness of village society over there.' She nodded in the direction of the English coastline. 'I have no doubt that she would take me in. But you know what would happen. I would become an object of pity and of village gossip. I am certain that when she knows the circumstances I will be regarded as an embarrassment and my welcome will be very cool.'

decreed that

'But you have done no wrong. You are a victim in exactly the same way your poor parents were. Surely no one will blame you for your condition.'

'That is not how gentlefolk will see it. You are not a woman, Mr Maclaren, so you cannot understand. My parents have the dignity of death. I am soiled and would be better dead. An accident at sea would have been forgivable. Mr Maclaren, I do not doubt your motives, but it was most unkind of you to have prevented me from going over the side.'

'That is foolish talk,' said Andrew.

'Perhaps, but when you stopped me, I knew that I lacked the courage to try again. So your vigil outside my cabin, though kindly meant, was quite unnecessary.'

On the spur of the moment, he took her by the shoulders and turned her towards him. 'I want to say something to you, and I want you to do the kindness of hearing me out.'

She looked up at him.

'Will you promise?' She nodded her consent. 'If you have any fears regarding your reception in England, and I know that you have, I suggest that you travel to Scotland with me and not go anywhere near your aunt.'

She was about to protest, but he carried on. 'Remember, you promised. Your aunt doesn't even know that you are here. Now let me finish. As I have already told you, we have two homes. A town house in Perth and the estate in Strathglass. I am certain that, knowing your circumstances, my mother would make you most welcome in our homes. These things are viewed somewhat more tolerantly in the Highlands.

'You have no need to think of it as a permanent arrangement, but at least you could stay with her until your present difficulties have been resolved. Remember that my mother is a soldier's wife and is not easily shocked. I beg you to consider this course most carefully. What is your answer?'

Andrew knew what he was offering. He was pretty confident about his mother's attitude. She would do all that she could for the girl, of that he was sure. As for his father? That was something else, but he had no doubt that his mother would deal with any objections which came from that quarter. But most of all, he did not want Maud Westburn to pass out of his life.

'But I couldn't —' she started.

And the hope in her voice told him that she would

3

Andrew paused for a moment as he strode up the road which snaked its way up the hill towards Fort Bruce. There in front of him stood the grey granite arch, the entrance to the headquarters of the 148th Regiment of Foot. It was flanked by high walls of the same stone. He looked up at them. In an earlier age, sentries would have been pacing the top, fully armed, and on the lookout for any intruder. Today he was coming home. It was as a baby that he had first been carried across the barrack square which lay beyond the arch to be presented to the officers of the regiment.

As he entered the arch, he squared his shoulders and smartly returned the salute of the guard on duty. He emerged from the gloom and back into daylight between three-storey barrack blocks to his right and to his left. Down both sides of the square which confronted him, an ancient cannon standing in each corner, were more identical barrack blocks, each of which housed eighty men. Facing him were two buildings, both severe and grey, one the H.Q. block, and the other, with its pillared portico, the officers' mess. It all looked so solid and everlasting; there was an air of permanence about the whole complex.

He glanced at the clock tower standing under its little slate pyramid over H.Q. It was six-fifty-two, and the Law, in the person of his father, whom he h...

all officers would be present at table when the commanding officer arrived in the dining room at seven o'clock precisely. The men, he knew, would be at their evening meal of soup and bread and jam or cheese, and a mug of beer. The officers and the sergeants would be gathering in their respective messes, and that was why the square was deserted. Well, practically deserted.

There was one splash of colour in that grey arena. He was small. Had he been only an inch shorter than his five foot six, he would have been rejected by the army, and the 148th would have been the worse off for it. He was smart, straight-backed, and he never walked anywhere; he marched. At the moment when Andrew spotted him, he was striding across the square, darting glances this way and that, like a robin in search of a worm, as he headed towards the sergeants' mess. His feet were encased in boots which gleamed and twinkled like mirrors under the evening sun beneath the snow-white of his spats, topped with the turn-down of his red-and-black-diced hose. His kilt, the pale-green and blue tartan over-checked with lines of yellow and red, the tartan of the Maclarens, had been pressed so that you could cut your finger on every crease. His immaculate braided red tunic, with its scalloped Inverness skirt and the turned-up cuffs of blue and gold, seemed redder than red. His brass buttons gleamed like little lamps, and his feather bonnet with the white and yellow hackle of the regiment was set squarely upon his head.

'Sergeant Major!' Andrew called.

'Sorrrrr!' came the thundering reply.

Sergeant Major Mackintosh stamped to a halt, and then in military double time, trotted towards Andrew. Andrew watched him approach, wondering, as he had so often before, how so small a frame could contain so enormous a voice.

The sergeant major reverberated to attention and saluted.

'Welcome back, Mr Maclaren, sorr!' he roared, convincing Andrew that all of Perth must now know of his arrival.

'Is the colonel in his office?' he asked.

'He is, sorr, but I wouldna fash him. His lady is wi' him.'

'And?'

'And there would seem to be a wee disputation, sorr.'

'I see. Thank you, Sergeant Major.'

'Sorr!' bellowed Sergeant Major Mackintosh, then saluted, about-turned, stamping the ground as if determined to do it an injury, and marched off.

Andrew welcomed the warning. He had a pretty shrewd idea of what was causing the 'wee disputation'. His mother must be telling the colonel about the arrival of Miss Westburn.

He had taken her to their house that morning, where she had been warmly and sympathetically received by his mother. When he had mentioned that he was a little worried about what his father might say, his mother had simply replied, 'Don't you bother about him. This is not a military matter and you can trust me to deal with it.'

And that was that, and that was undoubtedly also the cause of the 'wee disputation'.

Andrew went in through the line of smooth columns and into the open oak door of the mess. It was nice to see that just inside the entrance, the stuffed wildcat was still standing there in its case, as he handed his sword and feather bonnet to the mess steward and carried on into the anteroom on his right.

There were nearly a couple of dozen officers already present. Andrew realized that he must be about the last to arrive. It was a Tuesday, and Tuesdays were dining-in nights in the mess, when all officers who could not show good reason were required to be present.

Amidst the chorus of greetings brought about by his arrival, one burly figure unfolded himself from one of the massive leather armchairs which flanked the fire, above which in the place of honour hung a portrait of the Queen, signed in her own hand.

'Andrew, my boy,' he said, 'it's good to see you back.'

Andrew smiled with the genuine affection in which he held this man – Quartermaster Lieutenant Angus Cameron, risen from the ranks.

'Hello, Angus,' he said, warmly taking the proffered hand.

Cameron found the going in the officers' mess a little hard financially, though the mess president, Major Campbell, always made sure that his mess bills were not too outrageous. But he loved the life and he loved the regiment and he loved Andrew.

He had grown up with Andrew's father on the estate. Now approaching retirement, and knowing that he would never rise above the rank he now held, he was none the less a contented man.

'Hello, Andrew, old boy,' called another voice. It was Ian Chisholm, tall, dapper, baby-faced, looking about eighteen though he was at least five years Andrew's senior. Captain Chisholm came over to Andrew and greeted him. He was another odd man out, another friend of Andrew's. He hailed from a large estate in Kinross-shire, the most southerly member of their company and probably the most wealthy.

Andrew looked around, smiling and happy to be back. The smell of the old leather of the furniture. The walls panelled half way up, pale lemon above that up to the decorated plaster ceiling. The wall were hung with polished targes and claymores, relics of days and battles long since gone. Nobody knew where they had come from. They were certainly not regimental trophies, though everyone knew that the Cossack hat worn by the bust of Andrew's great-grandfather had been brought back from the Crimea by their present commanding officer. The glass cabinet at the far end of the room held the regimental trophies, cups and shields awarded for various regimental activities. But lovely as it all was, Andrew appreciated most of all the feeling of belonging.

'Come on, chaps,' called Chisholm. 'Down drinks.' He turned to Andrew. 'You haven't time for one, father will be in soon. Andrew, we'll find out all about your adventures after dinner.'

So they trooped out, across the hall and into the dining room.

It was grand to see the old dining room again. It was a magnificent, timeless, unaging sight. Longer and narrower than the anteroom, it had the same half-panelled walls and large oblong windows, heavily curtained in brown velvet, looking out across the barrack square. Through these, the troops could be seen returning to their barracks for their 'bull' session of blacking and blanco and brasso, preparing their equipment for inspection the following morning.

A little squad of about seven men was doubling around the

square in full marching order: defaulters, miscreants who had committed some minor offence and been duly sentenced by their company commanders.

Heavy gold-fringed pelmets crowned each window, and between the windows and around the other walls were sconces of beaten iron, candles flickering in their holders. Trophies hung around the walls, too; a Russian officer's sword that Andrew's father had brought back from the Crimea, a pair of assagais, a tattered French cavalry pennant from Waterloo, and so on.

The room was dominated by a long, polished mahogany table gleaming under the cut-glass chandeliers, outshone only by the lustre of the regimental silver, donated by Andrew's great-grandfather, which graced its surface. The place settings, eleven on one side, eleven on the other against the wall, and one at either end for the mess president and the adjutant, lay in precise order. The cutlery and blue-and-gold-rimmed crested plates lay exactly equi-distant from each other, and aimed directly at the place setting opposite. Three massive silver candelabra were set at equal intervals down the centre of the table, gifts of Captain Chisholm, and the light from their candles twinkled merrily, reflected in the polished silver claret goblet which stood at each place at the tip of the entree knife.

These goblets, like the rest of the silver and china, were engraved with the head of a snarling wildcat, the regimental crest, beneath which was a scroll engraved with their motto: *Si Vis Pacem Para Bellum*. The colours – the Queen's Colour, a gold-fringed Union Jack with the legend *148th Foot* inscribed across its centre, and the regimental Colour, a gold-fringed buff flag dominated by their crest and motto, flanked by six scrolls embroidered with their battle honours, Peninsular, Waterloo, Aden, India, Balaclava, and Gwalior – hung on their gold-mounted staffs behind the carver's chair in the centre of the table against the wall.

The officers themselves were hardly less colourful than the room they were in. Their kilts were of Maclaren tartan, their scarlet full-dress tunics were double-breasted with gold diamond-shaped buttons, embossed with the regimental number. The slashed flaps of their cuffs were dark blue and picked out in gold braid. The jackets ended in an Inverness skirt, braided flaps of scarlet in front and behind, decorated with button loops and buttons. They wore red-and-white-diced stockings and light silver-buckled shoes. Heavy gold epaulets and a high collar, again fringed in braid, bore their badges of rank. Their sporrans were of white winter hare pelts with a silver clasp and silver-mounted tassels arranged in two rows of two and three.

As they entered the dining room, the clock in the square started to chime the hour. As the third stroke of seven clanged out, Colonel Sir Henry Maclaren, Bart., strode into the dining room, arriving behind the carver in front of the colours as the seventh chime struck.

Like all the Maclarens, the colonel was tall and slim. His heavy sideburns, greying slightly, swept around and over his upper lip. His hair, or what remained of it, circumvented the burnished dome of his balding pate like a pelmet. A tinted monocle was screwed firmly into his right eye which had been nearly blinded by a powder flash at Sevastopol, and his pale-blue good left eye traversed the table without expression as he waited for his officers to take their places.

'Gentlemen,' he grunted by way of greeting.

He never looked at Andrew, who was waiting for the order which would seat him on his father's right – not because of his relationship, but because, as a returning officer, it was customary that he should take that place at his C.O.'s invitation for his first dining-in night in mess. The command did not come. There was not even the faintest flicker of recognition when finally Sir Henry's good eye looked straight at him. Andrew compressed his lips; that augured no good. Ignoring him, the colonel came smartly to attention behind his chair, and addressing his Maker as if the Lord was facing him on the parade ground, barked:

'For what we are about to receive, thank God. God save the Queen!'

The colonel did everything at attention. It was rumoured in the barracks that should he ever stand easy, he would disintegrate. He took his place and they all sat down. The colonel's hand hovered over the small silver bell which would be the signal for dinner to commence and conversation to begin.

Andrew was sitting next to Captain Chisholm, their backs to the windows. Chisholm returned Andrew's glance with a compression of his lips and a raising of his eyebrows, drawing a glare from the colonel opposite. Sir Henry transferred his glare to his son.

'Andrew!' he barked.

'Sir?' replied Andrew.

The colonel tapped the vacant chair on his right.

'Join me.'

Andrew breathed a sigh of relief, and Chisholm whispered, 'That was a near thing,' and was rewarded with another glare.

'Thank you, sir,' said Andrew, getting up to join his father.

Whatever it was, it was not going to be too bad. At least not in military terms. For his father would never allow domestic matters to interfere with those which concerned the regiment. It was now quite certain to Andrew that his father's disapproval was aimed at his having brought Miss Westburn home, but on that score, at least, he would be able to argue his case on more or less equal terms, and not as subaltern to the commanding officer.

'Well, lad,' said the colonel as soon as Andrew was seated, ignoring the convention that matters military should not be discussed at table, 'how are things in India?' He rang the bell and stewards started to serve the soup. 'Did you know that Havelock had fallen back on Cawnpore?'

'What happened at Lucknow, sir?'

'Couldn't take it. Insufficient force after the hammering you got at Cawnpore. He was down to less than half his strength after he had had a go at Lucknow. Colin Campbell is taking a column up, though. He's got the 93rd Highlanders with him.'

'I pray that they won't be too late, sir.' Andrew spoke soberly as a vision of the carnage at Cawnpore flashed through his mind, the wrecked assembly hall where the massacre had taken place, with its bloodied floor and the pathetic litter of personal possessions, daguerrotypes, children's toys, the rag doll by the waterhole, locks of hair, one in particular, long and blonde and bloodied – it might have been Maud's – and then the waterhole itself. He looked at his soup with distaste. No, he did not want to talk about India.

'You'll be glad to hear that you've got a company now,' his father said. Thank God, he had changed the subject.

'A company, sir?'

'Aye, lad, you've been gazetted captain. You take over command of C Company tomorrow. Good news travels slowly, eh?'

'Thank you, sir,' replied Andrew. He accepted the news of the promotion both with pleasure and as a matter of course. In spite of the fact that he was well aware that several subalterns were senior to himself, he was a Maclaren. 'Who is my colour-sergeant?' he asked.

'Willie Bruce,' was the reply.

Andrew could not complain at that. Sergeant Bruce was a year or two older than himself, the son of a worker on their estate at Strathglass. Willie was one of that rare breed of men who had joined the army because he really wanted to be a soldier. All of his life he had wanted nothing else. When they had been children together, Willie had been Andrew's hero. He had taught Andrew how to use the land, how to see and not be seen – skills which were second nature to a countryman like Willie, who could stalk a stag and get within twenty-five yards of the beast before he was spotted. Andrew could still remember the time that Willie had shown him his first bird's nest, a blackbird's with a clutch of four green eggs mottled with reddish-brown spots. It was in a hawthorn bush. Willie had taken Andrew down to a burn, and after lying patiently for half an hour with his hand in the water, he had suddenly lifted it, holding a fine brown trout. Andrew tried, but was never able to do it. Andrew was always the amateur and Willie the professional. And in the army, in a strange way, that was still true. Officers in the British Army were with very few exceptions not professionals; they were gentlemen, amateur soldiers. As children, they had played army games together. Of course, Andrew had always been the officer and Willie the N.C.O. As a child, he had learned a lot from Willie, and now as men they would be working together again. And Willie would be able to teach him, and he would be able to listen and learn, just as he had done as a child. It was good to know that he would have Willie to rely on.

'And you will no doubt be glad to know that we are

re-equipping with the new Enfield rifle,' the colonel said.

This was more good news, even though it was no more than justice. When Andrew had left for India, the 148th was still equipped with the old Brown Bess, the same smooth-bore which had been used at Waterloo. The Enfield would be a terrific improvement. He had seen the Enfield and the slightly older Minie rifles in action in India with Havelock, and there was no doubt about the superiority of the Enfield. Weighing just under nine pounds against the Minie's fourteen, it was accurate up to nearly a thousand yards. With the Brown Bess, you would be lucky to hit the side of a house at a hundred yards. There had been the usual mutterings at regimental H.Q. about favouring English battalions when the Maclarens did not get the Minie, but now they were getting the even better Enfield. So national pride was assuaged and all would be forgiven.

The meal proceeded slowly on its well-ordered and dignified way. Conversation was subdued, as it always was when the colonel was present. Most of it was small talk, talk of sport, hunting, and the regimental football team, which was to play the opening match of the season the following Saturday.

The grouse, which was the main course, had come from Captain Chisholm's estate. He had taken a party of brother officers out a week ago, and the bag from the day's shoot had been gifted to the mess. After the dessert, fresh strawberries and cream, the table was cleared and the decanter of port was placed in front of the mess president, and the madeira in front of the adjutant. When the decanters had completed their clockwise circuit, never touching the table in the process, they drank the Loyal Toast. Andrew was given the honour of proposing The Regiment, and then Ensign Smith, the youngest officer present – who had purchased his commission for four hundred pounds only six months ago, just before the colonel decreed that commissions would no longer be available for purchase in the 148th – proposed Sweethearts and Wives, and Andrew thought about Maud.

After the toasts they relaxed a little, though really they were all waiting for the colonel to go. Cigars were handed round and the colours in the room became subdued in a haze of blue smoke.

'Andrew,' said the colonel, puffing at his cigar, 'your father would like to have a word with you after dinner.'

'Of course, sir,' replied Andrew. 'Where?' His father always referred to himself in the third person when in his role of commanding officer.

Sir Henry pulled out his watch. 'It's about eight-thirty now; come along to my office in about ten minutes.' He rose to his feet. 'Goodnight, gentlemen.'

They all rose as the colonel made his exit. Now, relieved of their C.O.'s august presence, what had until then been muted conversation became a noisy babble as they trooped into the anteroom. In the anteroom, Major Scott, the mess president, called Andrew to one side.

'Just a quick word, Andrew,' he said. 'It's highly confidential. It's about the quartermaster.'

'Angus?' said Andrew. 'No trouble, I hope.'

'Well, he's getting a bit behind with his messing. I haven't told him yet, but you know the way things are. He's got nothing except his pay.'

'How much is it?' asked Andrew.

'About forty pounds.'

'I'll let you have it tomorrow,' Andrew replied, glad to be able to help his old friend. 'Don't say anything to Angus.'

'Naturally, and now if you'll excuse me, I'm going to escape before things start to hot up.'

Major Scott, Angus Cameron, and one or two of the older officers were drifting out as the younger spirits gathered around the mess piano, where Ian Chisholm had started to play Samuel Wesley's 'Arelia'. Irreverently they started to sing:

> We are MacLaren's army,
> The Highland Infantry,
> We cannot fight, we cannot sing,
> What bloody use are we?
> And when we get to India,
> We'll hear the Viceroy say,
> Hoch, hoch, mein Gott,
> What a bloody fine lot,
> To earn sixpence a day.

The statement regarding their income was rather pessimistic. An ensign received five shillings and threepence a day, but he needed at least another two hundred pounds a year in order to be able to live in mess.

Chisholm swung around on his piano stool. 'Andrew,' he shouted, 'I've ordered a case of champers to celebrate your return. Tonight we will all get drunk in your honour.'

'Sorry, Ian,' replied Andrew, 'I have to go and see the old man.'

'Let him wait.'

'Would you?'

'Maybe you're right. Well, we'll have a wake for you instead. Steward!' he roared.

Andrew slipped out of the mess. The big parade ground was empty. Lights were beginning to come on in the barrack blocks where the men would be bending to their tasks. He walked the few yards to the headquarters block and down the long corridor towards his father's office.

He knew that his father wanted to talk to him on a domestic matter. Had the subject been military, he would not have referred to himself as 'your father'. And Andrew was certain that the subject of the talk was going to be Maud Westburn.

This was not going to be easy. He tried to sort out his own feelings in the matter. With the sole possible exception of his mother, women were strange and alien creatures to Andrew. He had two sisters, but even they were beyond his understanding. All his life had been directed towards the army and the regiment. He could not comprehend this compelling urge to be with Maud, to touch her. Perhaps this was what people meant when they talked of love. After all, he believed himself to be in love while they were together on the ship. Perhaps he should ask for her hand, even though she was, to use her own words, 'a soiled woman'. Could she be blamed for her condition? He was absolutely certain that she was an innocent victim. Perhaps this talk with his father would help to sort things out; after all, the old man was no fool. He tapped on the door of his father's office.

'Enter,' called the familiar voice from within.

The office was sparsely furnished, reflecting the spartan

character of the man who inhabited it. There was a large desk on which lay inkwells and pens, paper with the regimental crest, a copy of *Queen's Regulations*, and that morning's issue of *The Scotsman*.

There was a small bookcase which contained a selection of books, all on military subjects: things like the record of the Peninsular War and Waterloo, and several manuals on arms and ordnance. There was one large window which looked out on to the barrack square, hung with heavy brown curtains. Two portraits dominated the walls. They were of the preceding Maclarens who had commanded the regiment, both of them in uniform and both of them looking uncannily like his father. In the other wall was a fireplace with a cheerful coal fire burning in the grate. This was flanked by two leather chairs, between which was a small table containing a bottle of The Glenlivet and two glasses and a jug of water. In one of these chairs, Colonel Maclaren was sitting, his tunic collar undone.

'Sit down and help yourself to a dram,' he said.

Andrew poured out a generous helping of whisky and waited for the older man to speak. He glanced up at his ancestors glowering back at him from their gilt frames.

'Cigar?'

'No, thank you, sir,' Andrew said, anxious to get to the point.

The colonel sipped his whisky. 'Had a rather tedious chat with your mother before dinner.' The remark was casually made, but its implication did not escape Andrew.

'So I heard, sir.'

'The devil you did. Who told you?'

'I was on my way to see you when I met Sergeant Major Mackintosh. He told me you were having "a wee disputation".'

The colonel almost smiled. 'It wasn't all that wee,' he grunted. 'You know, boy, your mother can – but that's something else. I want to hear your story. I want to know about this Miss Westburn.'

Well, it was better to have it out in the open. 'The history, sir,' he said, 'is simple and very tragic. Both her parents were killed in Cawnpore, and either before or after that, I don't know which, she was assaulted.' Strange, he thought, he could not bring himself to use the word 'rape'. 'I'm not really sure of the details, as you can understand. It was not the sort of thing she would want to discuss, especially with a man. But I do know that the only reason she herself was not killed was because they didn't find her. Her ayah hid her in a cellar when they were rounding up the women and children and locking them in the assembly hall. That was where we found her.'

'In the cellar?'

'Yes.'

'And then you brought her home.'

'It wasn't quite like that, sir. The Resident arranged her passage, and it was quite coincidental that we were on the same ship. It was not until a couple of days before we docked that I really became aware of her distress and offered her the hospitality of our home.'

'Distress? How do you mean?'

'She was frightened. Terrified. One night she tried to jump overboard. She was alone. She had nowhere to go. There is a spinster aunt in Surrey, but she was afraid to go there in her condition. Besides, I – er . . .' He became silent.

'Go on. You were about to say that you found her attractive or something like that.'

'Yes, I did. I was very much taken with her. At the time, I couldn't bear the thought of losing touch with her.'

'I see,' said the colonel. He sipped his whisky in silence while Andrew waited for him to continue. 'This is more serious than I had thought. Your mother insists that she is a most personable young lady, and no doubt when I meet her, I shall agree.' He paused again. 'Come now, Andrew, I want the truth. Where do you stand? What is your relationship with this young woman?'

'I haven't got one, father.'

'Come now, you know what I mean.'

That was the trouble. He knew exactly what his father meant, and the colonel was entitled to an honest answer. Unfortunately, Andrew did not know the answer himself.

'Supposing,' he said after a long hesitation, 'and only supposing, I said that I wanted to marry her.'

Sir Henry gazed at his son with an expression of incredulity. The boy must be out of his mind. Even to contemplate the possibility of such a course was unthinkable. He looked at Andrew as if he were trying to determine that he really was his son. 'Good God!' he said slowly and quietly, sitting back in his chair and staring at Andrew. 'You have just told me that the woman is pregnant. You cannot possibly know what it is that you are saying.'

'She is pregnant through no fault of her own, you must remember that. If I were to marry her, I could claim the child as my own.'

'Have you gone off your head, boy?' The colour had risen in the colonel's cheeks. He was really angry now. 'Just you try and imagine your mother agreeing to anything like that.' And then with a note of anxiety, 'You haven't mentioned this to her?'

'Of course not, sir. I was only speculating.'

'I hope that you damned well are. It is quite apparent to me that you have not given this any serious thought at all.'

'I've thought a great deal about it, sir,' Andrew replied defensively.

'Poppycock! And what would happen if the child were to be a boy? Tell me that? You'd sit back and watch it inherit the estate and the title and the regiment, even though you had a son of your own?'

'I hadn't thought of that.'

'I'm damned sure that you hadn't. Apart from being a bastard, that child will be Eurasian. Can you imagine a half-caste bastard commanding this regiment?'

Andrew was silent and the colonel, calming himself with an effort, continued. 'My boy, up to now you have behaved exactly as a gentleman should, given all the circumstances. But this talk of marriage ... Do you mind if I ask you a very personal question?'

'What is it, sir?'

'Have you ever been with a woman?'

'But I'm not married, sir.'

The colonel's jaw dropped as he stared at his son in amazement. 'Seems to me that I've neglected your education. You're nearly twenty-two. Great Scott, I'd had a couple of dozen by the time I was your age. You might even have a half-brother or half-sister living on the estate at this very moment.'

'Does mother know?' It was the first thought that entered his head.

Suddenly the colonel laughed. 'Heavens above, man, yes! Marriage is for breeding, for the family. The others, all of them, are for pleasure. Men born to your station take mistresses. You're more than ready for that. God alone knows when you'll be ready for the other. If you feel attracted by this girl, why don't you take her as your mistress? No one will mind that.'

Andrew was visibly shocked at the thought. 'I am sure that Miss Westburn will never agree. And I would certainly never dream of putting such a proposition to her.'

'More fool you, then. But be that as it may. As your father, I strongly advise you against even contemplating marriage with this young lady. And as your commanding officer, I would like to point out to you that it is contrary to Queen's Regulations for any officer to marry before he has attained the age of twenty-six. On those grounds if on no other, I positively forbid it.'

'I could resign my commission, sir.'

'You could what?!' the colonel exploded. 'No son of mine would ever do such a thing. For if he did, he would cease to be my son.'

'What does that mean?'

'It means, Andrew, that I would disinherit you. It would break my heart, and it would break your mother's heart, too. She would hate me for the rest of my life. But I'd do it.'

'But I don't understand, sir,' Andrew pleaded. 'Why is it so important?'

'I'll try and explain, lad. On one hand you have a woman. I won't name her because it could be any woman. On the other hand,' he paused and waved his hand in the general direction of the barracks, 'out there, there are twenty-four of your brother officers and nearly a thousand men. They may not all be gentlemen. A lot of them were the sweepings of the gutter when they joined the army. Many of their families thought that they had brought terrible disgrace on to their name when they enlisted. But they are our men. They are all Maclarens. They are all, even the meanest of them, our family. They may not love you as an individual, and they're not all heroes, not by a long chalk. But there is not a man Jack of them who would not die to protect you and your honour. Tell me if you think you could give up all of that simply because of a woman!'

'It would be hard.'

'It would be bloody impossible.'

There was a silence, and then the colonel got up and refilled their glasses. He handed Andrew his.

'My boy, I want you to drink a toast with me. Look.' He pointed to the portraits. 'One day, my picture will be there, and then God willing, your own. Will you drink with me – to the regiment?'

Andrew hesitated. It was not going to be an easy decision. There was wisdom in what his father had said, and he did not really know how he felt about Maud. It would have to wait. Maybe it would go away. He could not decide, not now anyhow. Slowly he rose to his feet.

'Well?' said his father.

Andrew raised his glass to his ancestors. 'The Regiment!'

4

'As you were!' roared Colour Sergeant Willie Bruce. 'Call yourself sodjers?' He glared at C Company with studied contempt. 'Teuchters, the lot of ye! Now,' he continued with withering sarcasm, 'if ye'll oblige wi' a wee bitty effort, we'll try again.'

Momentarily he turned his back and there was a mutter from the ranks. He whipped around. 'Wha said that?' There was no reply. He expected none. He walked menacingly up to one private. 'Wha said that, I said!'

'Naebody, sergeant.'

'I canna teach ye bugger all. Nobody! Now just remember, I've got eyes in the back of ma heed and I can see round corners. We'll try again.'

He paused to fill his lungs. 'C Company, 'tand a' hease. Attennntion! Stand at ease. When I say attention you bend your right leg till ya foot is fifteen inches above the ground and then ye bring it doon *seventeen* inches. Attennnnntion! Sloooop – you there, hald ya heed up or I'll stick ma bayonet up your left bloody nostril. Slooop – wait for it, wait for it!' he barked as one overanxious private twitched an anticipatory muscle. 'Slooop harms. Open order march!'

The men's feet crashed to the ground with a single satisfying thump. Willie paused, glowering at the motionless files in front of him and then walked slowly down the front rank. He inspected each white buff crossbelt from which was suspended the bayonet frog and scabbard with its polished plate bearing the number 148 hanging over the man's left shoulder. Twice he berated men who had failed to polish the back of the plate. Three times he found a speck of dust on a waistbelt held by a polished buckle bearing the regimental crest. One of these buckles had a tiny spot of verdigris; he pronounced that it was a field fit to grow tatties in. He paused in front of one man and stuck his finger at the small pocket on the man's right chest.

'What ha' ye got in there, lad?' he demanded.

'Nothing, sergeant.'

'Open it up!'

Inside he found a cigar butt. 'I suppose ye think you can fire your rifle wi' one o' these?' He pushed the offending object under the man's nose. 'That pooch is for percussion caps. Company office for you, me laddie.'

So he continued down the second file, stopping here and there, adjusting a crossbelt which had moved a fraction out of true, or reprimanding some unfortunate whose rifle sling was not as white as driven snow, or whose boots had not been polished to a degree where he could see his own face in them. He stopped before one man in the rear rank and straightened his feather bonnet.

'Macbeath,' he said despairingly, 'when am I going to make a sodjer oot o' ye?'

'Rome wasna built in a day, sergeant.'

'Only because I wasna there!' snapped back Willie, and passed on.

It was rumoured behind closed doors in the sanctuary of the barrack room that Williewaught, as he was known by the men when he was out of earshot, ate a bag of rusty nails for breakfast, a gleckard private for dinner, and drank a barrel of ale for his tea. The men, many of whom were little more than boys, took an inordinate pride in Willie. It was a distinction to be singled out for his wrath on the parade ground. They feared him and they cursed him, but he was theirs. No man who was not a member of C Company was allowed the privilege of uttering a word against him without the risk of a bloodied nose.

They were honoured to be in the same company as a man who had gone out three times under fire and, single-handed, carried wounded comrades back to their lines. And it was said that he had then lambasted them for daring to get themselves shot.

Willie Bruce stood six foot two inches, weighed nearly a hundred and eighty pounds, and there was not an ounce of spare flesh on him. He was a big man in every way, loud of voice, strong of arm, able to bend a six-inch nail with his bare hands; and under it all, gentle of heart. He had the red Pictish hair and heavy eyebrows overhanging pale blue eyes, and a long, thin nose which, it was said, could smell out a defaulter a mile away. His skin was weather-beaten and tanned with the suns of half the world, and he was what he had always wanted to be, a Scottish soldier.

Willie had joined the regiment ten years before as a drummer boy and had been under fire before his fourteenth birthday. He had been wounded in the arm in the Kaffir wars in South Africa in 1850. He was twenty-four now, but in spite of his youth he had that strange maturity which comes to a man who had been under fire and looked on death, not without fear – for no one but an unimaginative fool does that – but with courage and an unshaking faith in himself and the men around him. If they were proud of him, he was no less proud of them. After South Africa, when he had returned home to Strathglass, he had shown his scar to Andrew, visible proof that he was now a man. Andrew, reared as he was in an environment which revolved around the regiment, listened to his stories with envy. Willie's mother also listened to the same stories in the confines of their little house on the hill, near the big house, and she listened, not with envy but with sadness, fearing the day that might come when someone else would walk up to her door to tell her of Willie's deeds, because her son would not be coming home anymore.

Willie's mother was a big-boned Highland lassie, who always wore her mutch, the linen cap which was the mark of the properly wedded woman. She wore simple dark clothes, invariably covered with one of the voluminous aprons of which she seemed to possess an inexhaustible supply. Her sleeves were always pushed up to her elbows as she strode around her everyday tasks of caring for her men and their small holding. Her face shone as if it always had been recently scrubbed.

Willie's father was a small and dark man, a true Celt, smaller even than his mother. He was one of Sir Henry's two shepherds. In return for this task, he received a small wage, his house, and a few acres of land on which he kept the family cow, their Highland pony, and a few sheep, and grew oats for their porridge and the winter feed.

They always had plenty to eat, porridge every morning, a good bowl of steaming broth at noon, cooked in the cauldron hanging over the peat fire which never went out; and in the evening, a full meal of meat or fish. Sometimes there would be a stag hanging in the steading, or a salmon fresh from the Glass. And if the summer was bad and the crops were poor, if there were any problems like someone being ill, then Lady Maclaren from the big house did not have to be asked. She always knew and was there with help, just as she would be to any other home on the estate, to make sure that none of them ever went hungry or lacked medical attention.

As for Willie, he never thought about these things. He was a man content with his lot. He had all that he wanted from life in being a soldier. On this he had always insisted, even when the dominie at the local school said that it was a waste of one of the brightest boys he had ever taught. Not that he did not appreciate his home. The fact that he had a comfortable but-and-ben to come home to was an added bonus. If anything, the regiment meant more to Willie than it did to the Maclarens, and C Company meant more to him than the regiment.

Today, he was in high spirits even though his emotions were somewhat mixed. Young Master Andrew had been made a captain and given command of Willie's beloved C Company. That pleased Willie. It would be their childhood all over again. In that egalitarian Highland society which overflowed even into the regiment, they would continue their respect for each other. Once again they would be able to play at soldiers, only now they would have a real army to play with, and Willie would make Andrew the best company commander in the regiment. For if he failed in this, it would be a criticism of his own professionalism.

There was a snag though. Willie very much wanted to break Andrew in himself, but that would have to wait. In a week's time he would be leaving Perth on a month's detachment and would have to hand over C Company, albeit temporarily, to Sergeant Fraser. The sergeant major had told him only last night that he was to travel north to Strathglass, recruiting. It was all very necessary, of course. Just now, the regiment was some two hundred under establishment, and Willie had been detailed to put that right.

The thought of going home appealed to Willie. He would be able to stay with his parents, and of course the big house would supply him with a saddle horse whenever his duties required one. It would be nice, too, to earn the bounty which each new recruit would bring him. He would tour the villages and the courtrooms and the jails. Many a good soldier came directly from prison to the army. He would be singing the praises of the regiment. He would stick his posters in village halls and institutions – posters featuring the head of the wildcat which exhorted:

All lads of true Highland blood willing to show their loyalty and spirit may repair to the village hall at —— where the recruiting sergeant will see that they receive high bounties and soldierlike entertainment. The lads of the 148th Regiment of Foot will LIVE and DIE together. They cannot be draughted into other regiments. Huzza for the Scottish Soldier, God save the Queen.

He finished his inspection and took up his position in front of C Company.

'C Company, 'tand a' hease!' he roared. 'Stand easy.' And the men relaxed.

The whole regiment was drawn up in open order and ready for the morning colour-hoisting parade. The officers were marching in little groups of twos and threes, up and down the edge of the parade ground in front of headquarters block. Sergeant Major Mackintosh was pacing in front of the flagstaff, and the colour sergeants were reporting to him one at a time as they finished their preliminary inspection. Willie came to attention in front of the R.S.M.

As he approached R.S.M. Mackintosh, Willie glanced up at the sky. There had been a threat of rain earlier. That would have been unfortunate; feather bonnets did not take kindly to a Scottish downpour. But the cloud was now broken and the shadows of the barrack buildings were etched across the square in the early morning sunlight.

'C Company present and correct, sir.' The R.S.M. acknowledged with a grunt and Willie returned to his place.

When all the companies had reported, the sergeant major took a last professional look around the regiment, then strode over to the adjutant, roared something at him to the effect that the parade was in order, and marched back to his position in front of the flagstaff.

'Parade!' The precautionary word of command brought the regiment to the proper 'at ease'. 'Parade —'shun!'

There was a satisfying single crash as nine hundred hobnailed boots thundered down simultaneously. Now the clan, the regiment, the family – call it what you will – was ready to receive its officers.

'Fall in the officers!' called the adjutant in a weak, high-pitched voice many decibels lower than the sergeant major's.

The officers broke from their pacing and took their positions in front of their companies and half-companies. R.S.M. Mackintosh, all the time eyeing the immaculate files, marched around to the rear and the adjutant spoke again:

'Fall out the Roman Catholics and Jews.'

About thirty men took one pace forward, turned right or left, and marched to the side of the square nearest to them. The adjutant stood the parade easy, and the minister of the local kirk – the 148th did not boast a chaplain – roared a few platitudes at his Maker. The men who had fallen out pretended not to hear, and when the minister had finished, they were recalled to the ranks. The parade was then brought to attention and Colonel Maclaren, having been assured that all were present and correct, took over the parade.

'Battalion, general salute, present arms.'

The men brought their new Enfield rifles to the present, the officers drew their swords and held them at the salute, their gleaming basket guards obscuring the lower parts of their faces, and the bugle sounded the stirring, almost gay notes of the salute. The colours were broken at the gaff of the flagstaff, which stood a few yards inside the grey stone arch, the camp entrance, in its own little square of bright green lawn.

The colonel turned smartly under the flagstaff, facing the battalion, and by companies they all marched once round the square and back to their starting points, while the colonel took the salute.

The colonel and the adjutant left the parade ground. Andrew turned and dismissed his subalterns and stood staring at Willie as he marched round to the front of the company towards him. He had his mind on something, but he could not quite formulate his thoughts.

Willie came to attention and saluted. Andrew returned the salute absentmindedly.

'Is there something wrong, sir?' asked Willie after a long pause.

'Oh, no,' Andrew replied quickly.

'Good to have you in C Company, sir,' said Willie.

'Yes,' replied Andrew. 'It'll be like old times.' He smiled. 'I suppose that you will be going to breakfast now, sergeant?'

'Aye, sirr,' replied Willie.

'What's the form for the rest of the day?'

'Kit and barrack inspection at ten, sir. Company office at eleven-thirty, two defaulters. Route march after dinner at two o'clock, full marching order.'

'What about after breakfast?'

'Spot of square bashing wouldna dae them any harm, sir. Then gi' them half an hour tae get ready for kit inspection.'

'That sounds all right, sergeant. Tell them to drill by half companies. Don't go on yourself. I'd like you to come over to the company office after breakfast and give me a rundown on the men, especially the N.C.O.s.'

'Yessir.'

'You can dismiss them now, sergeant.'

'Sirr!'

Willie turned to face the men. 'C Company, attention! Officer on parade, to the right, dismiss!'

The men right-turned, saluted, and broke ranks. Andrew returned their salute, then headed off in the direction of the mess. It was all so familiar, and so right, he thought. Back to the old routine of parades, marches, musketry. He wondered if they would change the name, now that they were equipped with rifles. 'Riflery' – that didn't sound too good. He went into the mess and sat down to a huge platter of ham and eggs, and started to wonder again.

It was his father's remarks last night which had set his mind buzzing. There were so many people in the glen, back home, who looked like Maclarens; some of them, quite a lot, bore the same name. But then it was not really surprising. For hundreds of years, the clan had inhabited the glen with little or no communication with the outside world. In such an enclosed society, it would have been remarkable if many of them had not looked a bit alike, just as he and Willie did. They not only looked alike, they felt the same about the army and the regiment. Andrew was happy to have Willie to rely on. He was a damned fine soldier, one of the best. He would be R.S.M. one day. They had been friends all their lives, and Andrew was glad it had worked out this way. Childhood friendships did not always mean the best for army discipline, but that would not apply to Willie and himself. No, it was going to be all right. He felt warm towards Willie. After all, he had no brother, and if he had, he could think of none that he would prefer to Colour Sergeant Willie Bruce.

5

Maud Westburn walked out of the entrance of Culbrech House. The ancestral home of the Maclarens stood in a small glen near the Crasks of Agais, that beautiful valley which followed the River Glass from Cannich to Beauly. She walked along the green lawns towards the drive that ran straight as a die for nearly a mile from the main door of the south front to the huge wrought-iron gates on the Cannich–Beauly road. The east wind which brought with it the chill of autumn had left the sky clear and bright in that cold, damp, alien land. The lawn was a vast expanse of bright green grass, dotted here and there with an ancient oak or elm.

She looked back at the great pile of pink Moray sandstone that the local people called the castle, though castle it was not. Culbrech House was a fortified house, a creature that had evolved in the fourteenth or early fifteenth century and through the generations to protect those who dwelt within its walls. It was a minor fortress, alone. Not a community surrounded by walls and battlements, but a family dwelling, structurally guarded against the intruder, and it had fulfilled its purpose. A Maclaren had built it and the Maclarens still occupied it and called it home.

Maud had been left in little doubt as to the antiquity and nobility of the Clan Maclaren; the whole domain breathed its history. They were descended from those warlike chieftains who until not so very long ago had ruled the Highlands of Scotland for hundreds of years. But though there had been change, perhaps it was not for the better, at least not all of the time. They were a proud strong people, more alien to Maud than the Indian native society into which she had been born. They were kings, safe in their mountain fastness – men who feared God, but the Deity apart, acknowledged no master who did not wield a stronger sword. They were hard men and women, too, even now, not given to sentiment or pity, and still marked by the genteel savagery of their forebears.

The society in which the Maclarens lived had in it the remnants of the feudal culture that it once was. It could not have existed in her aunt's village in Surrey; Maud was sure of that, though she had never been there. It was not like India either, where everything was governed by class or estate. Maud knew that she could not fit into either of those, the middle-class gentility of Southern England, or the pomp and circumstance of upper-class India.

Here the family who inhabited the big house were supposed to be the first among equals. Once upon a time they probably had been; but not any more – if for no other reason, the clearances on the neighbouring estates had developed a sense of insecurity reflected in the attitude of the ordinary folk. They knew now that theirs was no longer an interdependent society. All who lived and worked on the estate knew that they were utterly dependent on the will of the Laird. They were slaves to their chief.

Maud understood this, the vulnerability of being at the mercy of other people. If you broke the rules, even innocently as she had done, you were either discarded or imprisoned in a vacuum.

She had accepted Andrew's offer of hospitality because at the time she had felt that there was nothing else that she could do. But she was still trapped, a slave to her condition. No normal life was open to her. She was a lady, with all the restrictions and privileges that name implied. Worse than that, she had been brought up in India, where she never had had to do a single thing for herself, not even to lift anything heavier than a teacup. Unequipped for anything other than marriage to one of her own station in life, now here she was, alone in a strange, cold, alien land, wearing heavy clothes to guard against the elements which had bred people like the Maclarens. She looked back on the house with distaste.

It was the wrong shape for a start, higher than it was wide. The huge iron-studded oak door wasn't the entrance at all. That led to the kitchen and the servants' quarters which occupied the whole of the ground floor, ill-lit by slit windows through walls six feet thick. The entrance to the house was in the west wall, a much less distinguished portal. This led up a flight of stairs to the first floor which contained the dining room, the library that also served as Sir Henry's study, the gunroom, and in the southeast tower, the morning room.

There were two towers, the one on the southeast corner and another on the southwest corner. Each contained a narrow stone spiral staircase which wound its way to the floors above, right up to the top, where the entire area of the main building was taken up by the banqueting hall. Maud had never been present at a banquet; not yet, anyway. But how on earth, she wondered, did they manage to get hot food up to that height? The room was certainly magnificent, there was no doubt about that, with its huge black oak rafters and beams sweeping away to the gabled roof above. But in spite of its magnificence, Maud thought of it as an attic.

The towers themselves were occupied by the bedrooms, most of them not very large but each with its coal fire and little alcove containing a polished copper bathtub. And when you wanted a bath, it threw the whole house into turmoil as relays of solemn, grey-faced servants carried up the hot water in buckets to fill the tub.

Below the banqueting hall were the two master bedrooms with their adjacent dressing rooms, and the floor between them and the dining room was occupied mainly by a spacious withdrawing room.

Everywhere throughout the house there was militaria, even in her own bedroom at the top of the southeast tower, where the fireplace was dominated by crossed lances and a polished targe. This room had, jutting out from it, two little baby turrets which hung on to the walls under conical slate roofs. She discovered these when she moved a heavy velvet curtain and found a gap about eighteen inches wide. She squeezed through and found herself in a dimly lit circle some five feet in diameter. She stayed but a moment; the dim light and the cold stone walls were too reminiscent of the cellar thousands of miles away across the oceans.

Had she stayed a little longer and looked out of the narrow windows, she would have seen a sight so beautiful it could easily have changed her feelings towards this land. To the right, she would have looked up Glen Cannich and Glen Afric with its island-dotted lochs and high mountains beyond. Nearer she would have seen the Crasks of Agais, where the Glass had cut itself a deep gorge, and where the water rushed and tumbled through while the salmon fought against its flow, leaping their way to the spawning grounds. But she did not look.

The last few generations of Maclarens had tried to convert what had been a fortress into a stately home. The furniture was all massive. Most of the beds were four-posters. Oak panelling was everywhere, hiding the pink stone beneath. The ceilings were high and recently adorned with ornate plasterwork, and carpets and rugs lay in profusion over the floors.

Whatever else, it seemed that the Maclarens were determined to achieve at least one form of immortality, for wherever she turned, there she would be confronted by the portrait of an ancestor frowning or simpering at her from its heavy gilt frame. The line ran true, if the pictures were anything to go by. They all had the thin Maclaren nose and the red hair. One could have been Andrew dressed in the fashion of a hundred years ago and sitting astride a white charger with dilating nostrils. Another, a demure creature, looked like Jean, the older of the Maclaren girls, sad and wistful. But it wasn't her; the oil paint was already beginning to show the cracks of age. Targes, claymores, suits of armour seemed to be everywhere. The gunroom contained a small arsenal of comparatively modern weapons, clean and lovingly cared for. But the library, dominated by a large oak desk, seemed to be filled with leather-bound volumes which Maud suspected had not been moved for many years.

Maud looked back again at the house. She did not belong

there, she felt it. But then she did not belong anywhere. And it was not fair, or even just, to think like that.

She had been made welcome. Almost too welcome. On their arrival in Perth, Andrew had taken her straight to their town house, where she had been handed over to his mother, Lady Maclaren, who had given no indication of surprise at having Maud thrust upon her without warning. Within forty-eight hours of her arrival, she was on the train with Lady Maclaren heading northward along the Tay Valley and towards Dundee and Aberdeen, that city of grey granite with its harbour cluttered with the masts of the fishing fleet. There they had changed trains and carried on along the coast of Elgin on the Moray Firth. It was harvest time and they had passed through field after field of golden barley and oats, watched the farm workers as they scythed and stacked their crops, and here and there a couple of heavy horses already ploughing to open the ground to the coming winter frosts. At Elgin, the railhead, Lady Maclaren had made a point of the tediousness of the journey and how much easier it would be when the railway came through Inverness. They were taken by carriage to Inverness, where they spent the night at the new Station Hotel that had been opened in anticipation of the railway's imminent arrival.

The drive from Inverness had opened a whole new vista. Here the cornfields and the arable farms gave way to mountains and glens, hillsides dotted with sheep. Little houses with roofs of peat, with an eternal wisp of smoke rising from the centre. A hard country, though Maud was seeing it at its best, populated by a hardy people, solemn-faced and stern in their outlook, who scratched an existence from the hills.

She had been welcomed into their home as if she had been a member of the family. Even when all the circumstances of her situation had been made clear, her ladyship had shown no sign of shock or disapproval, and had been all sympathy and kindness. This had been backed by a series of assurances that she was not to worry, as everything would be taken care of. In fact, the generous acceptance of her situation was one of the things she found most galling.

Jean and Margaret, Andrew's elder sisters, had both accepted her in their different ways. Margaret, of whom Maud saw very little, had shrugged the matter off as no concern of hers. Her only interest in life was the running of the estate, at which she was most competent. She spent most of her time in the company of Richard Simpson, Sir Henry's English factor, and out on the hill. Jean, on the other hand, was quite different. She welcomed Maud as a confidante. In the man's world in which she lived, and lacking the mannish abilities of her sister, she was a lonely person. There had been one great event in her life. She had fallen in love. He was a banker from the south, a personable and pleasantly spoken man who had looked enviously upon the obvious wealth of the Maclarens and decided to carve out a slice for himself in the form of plain, simple Jean. It had not worked. Sir Henry had had enquiries made into his background and discovered that he had amassed considerable debts through various unsavoury dealings, and when he had asked for his daughter's hand, had booted him out of the house. Poor Jean felt that her entire life had been ruined; at the first opportunity she blurted out the story to Maud, feeling that in Maud she had found a kindred spirit. Maud for her part warmed to Jean. Here at least was someone whom she could feel sorry for; this plain, lanky, honest girl who had resigned herself to permanent spinsterhood.

Lady Maclaren must have been in her youth a neatly rounded beauty. She was small, not above five feet two inches in height, and towered over by her menfolk and even her daughters. The years had, however, added somewhat to her figure, and with her shiny round face and plump little body, she exuded an aura of happiness and good living. In Perth she had looked out of place. She had worn the fashionable crinoline, which did not suit her at all, but here in the Highlands, in homely tweeds and woollens, she seemed to fit into the country. Her skin was clear and bore hardly a wrinkle. But her hair, always worn in a large bun at the back of her neck, was now quite grey. She had a habit of gently twisting the broad gold wedding ring on her finger whenever she had something important to say. Her voice was soft, but cultured and precise. When she spoke, she always knew exactly what she was going to say. She was a practical woman, warm and gentle by nature, but always ready to face the realities. Separated for quite long periods from her men, she had had to be able to run her own household.

She showed her practicality and her grasp of the situation when, on the journey north from Perth, she turned to Maud and said, 'Now my dear, we have to decide just what we are going to do with you.' The question was, of course, rhetorical. Lady Maclaren had already made her decision.

'How do you mean?' asked Maud.

'You must excuse an old woman for being frank' – and she started turning her wedding ring – 'but the situation is such that it must be faced immediately. You are carrying an unwanted child. Now there is nothing we can do about that, other than an act even more barbarous than the one by which it was conceived.' She patted Maud on the knee. 'I know that you are completely blameless in this whole sorry business, but you must also be aware, as aware as I am, that it will carry a social stigma. If you had had the good fortune to be a crofter's daughter, it would not have mattered. Your baby would be born and taken into your family without so much as a raised eyebrow. But,' she said firmly, 'you are not a crofter's daughter. You are a lady. You have social standing and position, and we – I include myself – we are not nearly as broadminded and sensible in these matters.'

'But there's nothing we can do.'

'Of course there is. In fact, I have already decided. You will give birth to your child in a convent in Ireland, away from tittle-tattle and local gossip. Don't worry. I can arrange that quite easily, though it will have to be without my husband's knowledge. He does not approve of the Roman Catholic Church. Then, as soon as the baby is born, we will set the necessary wheels in motion to have it adopted.'

Maud had received this with strange emotions. True, she hated the manner in which the child had been conceived, and loathed the creature who had violated her body. But did she hate this infant in her womb? She thought she did. She felt that she ought to, but . . . and it was not a small but. Doubting apart, she had found some comfort in the fact that the practical details pertaining to her position should be dealt with by another, and by now she was finding the beginnings of resignation in accepting what appeared to be inevitable.

She continued her stroll across the lawn in the soft autumn air, delighting in the spring of the close short-cropped turf. The lawn was that type of carpet which can only be produced by planting good seed and rolling and mowing and rolling for hundreds of years. Its permanency matched the permanency of the house itself. Even so, it still bore the hallmark of the martial environment. The drive so straight, the edges so precise, each tree standing in its own little circle of black earth surrounded by a nine-inch wrought-iron fence. It was all straight lines and perfect circles. She wrinkled her nose in slight distaste; yes, the lawn was perfect, too perfect.

She looked up towards the wrought-iron gates and saw a figure of a man on horseback just turning into the drive. Even at that distance she was sure that it must be Andrew. She had been told that he would be coming home on leave at any time now. Strangely, she felt a little frightened at the sight of him. Not that she was really afraid; she was just a little worried at the thought of meeting him again. She had no way of knowing how she really felt about him, though there would always be gratitude towards the man who saved her life.

The man was in army uniform, with red dress doublet and feather bonnet nodding in the slight breeze. He was tall and fair, and he presented a magnificent sight against the grey background of the craggy cliffs on the other side of the River Glass.

She smiled and half-waved a greeting as her pace quickened and she hurried across the lawn towards the drive to meet him. The closer she got, the more sure she was. Twenty yards away from him she stopped and waved again. He had certainly seen her and he reined in his horse and tilted his head on each side, looking at her quizzically. He returned her wave and broke into a broad grin that creased and wrinkled his face with mocking good humour. Suddenly she blushed violently. It was not Andrew.

'Guid day tae ye, ma'am.'

'Oh!' she gasped. He did not sound like Andrew, either; his voice was deeper, there was a relaxation about him, a casualness of manner which she had never seen in Andrew. 'I'm so sorry,' she continued, 'I thought that you were somebody else.'

'You thought I was Master Andrew, did ye no?' He slipped easily out of the saddle and saluted her. 'Well, ye need na fash aboot that. You are no the first to make that mistake, and you will no be the last.'

She smiled at him. She liked the deep, soft, precise English of the Highland burr of his voice. 'Then who are you?'

'Sergeant Bruce. Willie by name, C Company, the 148th Regiment of Foot, and at your service, ma'am.' He grinned and saluted again. 'I apologize for wearing the kilt on a horse but I'm recruiting, and for not being Captain Maclaren.'

'You know Andrew then, Mr Bruce?'

'Och, I ken him fine. We were laddies together. He's just been made ma company commander, a verra satisfactory arrangement. But you'll oblige me, ma'am, by no referring to me as mister. That is a title borne with pride by only the regimental sergeant major and with contempt by junior officers and civilians. I am Sergeant Bruce, or, if you're of the family, Willie.'

'I'm not of the family, but I'm staying here.'

'Then you shall call me Willie, for you are a handsome lady, ma'am.'

She could not help smiling in spite of his impertinence. He was certainly a most attractive man. She could see now why she had first mistaken him for Andrew. They were very alike, but Willie was obviously harder, and there was a greater maturity about him. The corners of Willie's mouth turned up, making it seem as if he was always slightly mocking. He was relaxed, lacking the strained stiffness of Andrew, and he seemed much more assured.

As for himself, Willie was in high good humour. He had been to Dingwall for the first two days of his recruiting drive, and in that time he had managed to increase the strength of the regiment by twelve. Of that twelve, four had been genuine volunteers, seeking him out in response to his recruiting poster. They were Highlanders who genuinely wanted to be soldiers – a very high proportion. He had listened to the sheriff give a couple of the others the option of prison or army, and as they had seemed fairly strong and their offences minor (one was poaching and the other drunk and disorderly), Willie had taken them and they had taken the Queen's shilling. As for the rest, he had bought beer and whisky in a pub and offered homes to the homeless and food to the hungry, and six had taken the shilling – trading their present misery for the harsh discipline, and quite probably short life, which he offered.

Of course one got a better type of recruit in the Scottish regiments than they did south of the border, where the mill towns ground men into human trash. Especially now when so many had been thrown off their land by landlords more brutish than the severest discipline the army could offer, there were plenty who chose the security of army life. And over and above that was the personal popularity of the Maclarens throughout the district, and the knowledge that Sir Henry was a people's laird.

And now Willie returned to Culbrech and was greeted by a bonnie lassie with a wave and a smile. What could be better?

'I don't think I should call you Willie, Sergeant Bruce,' Maud spoke severely, but there was a slight smile in her eyes.

'Oh, do not worry about it, you are quite worthy of the honour.'

'I am to consider it an honour?'

'Naturally, for that is what it is.' He felt that perhaps he had gone far enough for a first encounter, so he abruptly changed the subject. 'Has Master Andrew arrived yet?' he asked.

'Not that I know of. He is expected, though.'

'Then I'll awa' to the stables and return her ladyship's mare,' said Willie. 'Perhaps if you see her you would be kind enough to tell her that I have done that.'

Without waiting for an answer he mounted and trotted off in the direction of the house. Maud watched him go as his horse's hooves crunched on the gravel drive and the sun glinted on his brasses and brought out the deep green and purple sheen of his black feather bonnet. She felt that she would have liked to continue talking to him, and she continued to watch until he disappeared out of sight around the back of the building.

So Andrew was due back today. Her drawn face mirrored

the turmoil of her emotions. She could not explain it, but she was afraid of meeting him again. They would be strangers here once more.

She was now under the protection of Andrew's mother, and dependent on the Maclarens to see her through the months ahead. What could she do if Andrew continued to make advances to her? Would it not be an abuse of his mother's hospitality if she were to encourage him? Still, whatever happened, should the situation start to prove embarrassing, it could not be for long. Very shortly – possibly within a matter of days, for she would have to leave before It started to show – she would be off to Ireland.

She turned back towards the house. As she was about to go in she was aware of a man looking at her. It was Willie Bruce. He had stabled his horse and come back from the stables at the rear. He was standing at the west corner, watching her, smiling. She looked straight at him for a moment and returned his smile. His look made her feel uncomfortably nice; it also made her feel naked. Then quite suddenly she stopped smiling. Her face hardened, and Willie, thinking he had offended her, withdrew. But it was not Willie at all: just for a few happy moments, she had forgotten the whole set of circumstances which had brought her to Culbrech House.

Andrew arrived home the following day. He stood in the small hall on the first floor of Culbrech House, his Harris tweed suit steaming from the slight October drizzle, surrounding him with that musty smell which only Harris tweed can produce. MacKay, their butler and one-time batman, then senior mess steward to his grandfather, had greeted him and gone off in search of some of the family to announce his arrival. Smiling, Andrew watched the retreating figure of MacKay. That man must have been sixty, but he was still more soldier than butler. Straight-backed, white-haired, and with a limp that he refused to acknowledge, he always addressed the male Maclarens by their military rank. Andrew was glad to be back. He was happy to be among things familial and surrounded by the hills and glens he loved. Of course he was also surrounded by women – his sisters, his mother, and now Maud. Maud was one problem.

Moreover, he never really understood his own mother. Women were strange and different – and now one of them came into the hall to greet him, his sister Jean.

'Andrew, whatever are you standing there for in all those smelly clothes?' She kissed him on the cheek.

'Hello, Jean, it's good to be back. Where's mother?'

'In the morning room, I think.'

'Is Miss Westburn with her?'

'No, she's out walking somewhere. I say, Andrew, she's a delight, isn't she?'

He wished that he could readily agree, but he could not. His mind was thoroughly confused where that lady was concerned. His father's talk had had its effect, and he had spent most of the journey up from Perth thinking about her. Had he made a mistake in asking her to stay with them? Did he really want to see her again? Somehow, her intrusion into his life – and it was an intrusion – had disrupted the easy, even tenor of his existence, and he did not know whether he liked it or not. But things were as they were, and it was no use trying to imagine that things would have been easier had he never made his offer of hospitality to her, or indeed why he had done so in the first place. He supposed that had he not done so, he would by now have forgotten all about her. But now he was living under the same roof with her, wanting to be with her, wanting to avoid her, and above all, seeing her as a threat to the regiment.

Whatever happened, it was not going to be easy, unless she made it obvious that she wished to have no more to do with him. This thought made him smile; at least it would solve all problems. 'Take her as your mistress,' his father had said. But you could hardly take a pregnant woman as your mistress – it made the whole idea seem sordid. However, he would have to see her soon, and alone, if possible. He wished he could, but he honestly could not say how he hoped that meeting would turn out.

He went along with Jean to the morning room, where they found Lady Maclaren sitting on a chintz-covered sofa with an embroidery ring in her hand and surrounded by a heap of coloured silks.

'Andrew's back, Mummy, and he smells.'

'Don't be rude to your brother, Jean. Hello, Andrew, darling. Did you have a good journey?' She gave him the perfunctory familial kiss. 'My goodness, those clothes *do* smell. You had better go and change them, then we can have a talk.'

'Hello, mother. What on earth do you want to talk about?' It's only a week since I saw you.'

'Oh, things,' she replied vaguely. 'Now be a good boy and run along and change. I'm busy.'

It was late afternoon when he eventually found Maud. He had changed into a grey frock coat and spotted cravat, and wandered down to the withdrawing room in search of one of his father's cigars to smoke before dinner. She was seated on a velvet-covered sofa, wearing a modest green-velvet crinoline that almost seemed to match. Half a dozen deep scalloped flounces descended from her still-small waist. The bodice was cut in a deep V with large lapels, and decorated with brown silk braid. Beneath, she wore a blouse of fine lace which revealed the rise of her breasts. It was drawn tight around the neck, and terminated in a tiny velvet bow. Her fine, fair hair was drawn back from a centre parting and arranged in two coils over each of her ears. To him she was achingly beautiful. At the first sight of her he felt that stirring in his loins and the dryness on his lips, making it hard for him to say anything. He nervously passed his tongue over his lips as she recognized him and gave him that strange, solemn smile of hers in greeting.

'Miss Westburn.' He had stopped just inside the door looking at her.

'Surely I'm Maud by now,' she smiled at him again.

He stood in silence. Quite suddenly he could find nothing to say. He searched his mind for conversation, but the words would not come.

'It is nice to see you again, Andrew,' she said.

She stretched out her hand to him and he moved over to her and took the tips of her fingers for just a moment, but still did not speak.

'I hope you had a pleasant journey north?' she said.

'It was very nice, thank you,' he replied. Really these empty pleasantries were quite absurd, but he could find nothing else to say, nothing that mattered. 'I hope that you are comfortable and being well cared for.'

'No one could be kinder than your mother, or, for that matter, your sisters and everyone in the house. I shall always be in your debt.'

Andrew gave an embarrassed, deprecating grunt. There was another long silence.

'Shall I ring for tea?' she asked.

'Please, that would be nice.'

Tea arrived and the conversation staggered on its halting way. She suggested that he might smoke, remembering that he enjoyed a cigar. He lit one gratefully and puffed away at it while they discussed the weather and the estate. He was quite surprised to find that she already knew quite a lot about the estate. He assumed she had got that from Margaret, and he was quite at a loss when she asked him for his opinion of the relative qualities of the Cheviot and the black-faced sheep, both of which breeds grazed in vast numbers on their land. But Andrew was only mildly interested in the details involved in running the estate. He knew that they had enough to support the family in the regiment, and as far as he was concerned, that was all that mattered.

The conversation sank into awkward silence yet again, when suddenly she said, 'I met Willie Bruce yesterday. I think that he admires me.'

Andrew looked at her hard and long. 'He'd be a fool if he didn't. You are a very beautiful woman, Maud.'

The compliment embarrassed her. 'I leave for Ireland soon.' Why she should want to remind him of her condition, she did not know. 'Your mamma has made all the arrangements.'

'Yes, I know, she told me. I'm sorry. I had hoped that I might see quite a lot of you during my leave.'

'Well, I'm not going immediately. Not tomorrow.' She looked up at him. 'I had hoped so, too.' Then she looked down at her hands.

'Do you realize something?' Andrew asked.

'What?' His tone had indicated a change of subject and she was glad.

'This is the very first time that you and I have been in the same room together and alone.'

'Do you think that is why we are both feeling so awkward?'

'You, too?' he asked.

She nodded. 'It's silly, isn't it? After what we've been through together.'

'Bloody silly,' and they both laughed. The ice was well and truly broken.

The conversation carried on in the same inconsequential way, but different in that they were now at ease in one another's company. They still kept up some pretences; they talked of Ireland, but as if Maud was going on a holiday. The real reason was never mentioned. They chatted through two cups of tea each when Maud suddenly changed the subject.

Outside, the glowing October twilight had burnished the copper beeches, turning the park into an Edenlike setting in which all time had stopped.

'Who *is* Willie Bruce?' she asked.

'Willie?' Andrew was a little surprised at the question. 'He's my colour sergeant. He's a local fellow. Why do you ask?'

'When I saw him, I thought he was you.'

'You're not the first. Tell me, were you disappointed?'

The question was pointed, and she paused before replying. 'Yes, until I found out it was him. Are you related? You're very alike.'

To Andrew the question was not easy to answer. Related to Willie Bruce. The thought was neither unpleasant nor an impossibility, though one did not tend to jump to conclusions no matter how apparent they might be. He compressed his lips, not wishing to deny and yet not wishing to admit his own innermost suspicions.

'I don't know,' he said after a long pause. 'You see, people around here, most of them at any rate, have families who have lived in these parts for hundreds of years. I should think that more than half of them have never left the glen. We used to steal women from the Frasers – they hold the next glen – and they used to steal from us, but nobody went much further than that. We are a very small community, and I have no doubt that if you go back far enough, we are all related in one way or another.'

He left it at that. He had no intention of telling her how close his relationship with Willie Bruce could be.

'I liked him,' she said. 'He was quite rude, but rather nice.'

'He's a damned good soldier,' said Andrew, giving Willie the highest accolade of the clan.

The 'damned good soldier' was at that moment sitting on the grass outside the Dores Inn, a small, whitewashed, slate-roofed tavern, one storey high, with small square windows set into the thick stone walls. It was situated on the northeast corner of Loch Ness, about five miles from Inverness.

He had had a heavy day and had landed up at Dores for no good reason that he could think except that he wanted to get away and into the clean air after the stench of the unwashed, unwanted, and unloved whom he had been trying to persuade to join the army.

However, the weather was fine and he was hungry, so he decided to have his meal of bread, cheese, a raw onion, and a pint of best ale. Most of the day he had been at the Sheriff's Court in Inverness, but it had been remarkable for its lack of success. Three miscreants whom he had regarded as possible recruits had opted for prison rather than take the Queen's shilling. Two more had been unsuitable by reason of their age, and he had ended the day with only two. One was a burly tough who had been charged with smashing up his home and beating his wife, and the other, a man he might not have taken had the day been more successful, was a weedy character of about twenty-three charged with vagrancy. This latter, however, possessed one not too common virtue. He could read and write, an ability possessed by well under fifty per cent of the members of the 148th Foot.

The lawn behind the little pub backed right down to the shore of the loch, and after finishing his pint, Willie wandered down to the water's edge to relieve himself. He was just about finished with this operation when a small voice interrupted him.

'Hi, mister, are ye a sodjer?'

Willie looked quickly around and saw no one until he glanced down and espied a diminutive figure at his right elbow. He dropped the edge of his kilt and glared at the boy.

He had a figure like a matchstick, bony elbows poking through the torn sleeves of his shirt. Trews hung in rags around his bare feet. They were tied at the waist with a piece of greasy string. The little thin pinched face and pallid lips were the legacy of years of grubbing around the dustbins and back alleys trying to scratch enough food to keep body and soul together so they could suffer another miserable day. But his eyes had a brightness and spirited look that set him off from the usual urchin. There were so many of them; they had no hope beyond prison, transportation, or the gallows.

'Hi, mister,' the boy repeated. 'Are ye a sodjer?'

'I'm a sergeant,' he growled.

'Polismen's sometimes sergeants; yer no polisman, are you?'

'I'm a soldier, a colour sergeant.' Willie was offended at the inference.

'Youse a real sodjer, then?'

'That I am.' He turned away.

'Dinna go awa', mister. Have you been to the wars?'

'Hundreds of them,' growled Willie.

'I want to be a sodjer.'

'Away, laddie, you're no old enough.'

'I am so. I'm thirteen. A man told me you could be a drummer boy when you was thirteen.'

'You shouldn't listen to everybody who tells you things, and you're no thirteen.'

'I am so, and ye canna say I'm not.'

'What does your mam say about it?'

'I have na got a mam.'

'Well, your da then?'

'He's deed. They hanged him, I think.'

Willie compressed his lips. It was true that the child could be a drummer boy at thirteen. He was quite sure that he was not thirteen, but the army would not question that. He looked at the thin, emaciated, strangely appealing little figure before him.

'What's your name?' he demanded.

'Alex Maclaren.'

Willie raised an eyebrow. The name did not mean anything. There were several Maclarens in C Company alone. There weren't any Maclarens this side of Strathglass, however.

'How do you come to be called Maclaren?' he asked.

'How do you come to be called whatever you are?'

'Don't be cheeky. Are you from Inverness?'

'Och, no. I come from up there somewhere.' The boy waved his hand in a general northerly direction.

He was probably one of the clan, then, thought Willie. That was important. It made it right for him to be in the regiment. Not that the name implied any blood relationship; the nameless ones on the big Scottish estates usually adopted the surname of the chief. Also, they really could use a drummer boy; C Company did not possess one. He looked at wee Alex and decided he'd be doing him a favour by taking him into the regiment. The life was hard and sometimes brutal, but he would get enough to eat. And the boy would stand a decent chance of not ending up in prison or on the gallows as a pickpocket, or worse. Above all, he said that his name was Maclaren, and that he came from up there; that counted for a lot.

'Have you eaten today, lad?' The boy shook his head. 'Here, get this inside you then.' He fished a chunk of cheese out of his sporran and watched as the boy ate ravenously. 'Are the police after you?'

'I don't know.'

'It wouldn't make any difference, you know.'

'You're all right, mister,' said the boy, stuffing the last piece of cheese into his mouth.

'And if you're going to be a soldier, you'll need to learn to stand to attention and call me "sergeant" when you speak to me.'

'Aye, sergeant.' He brought his thin little body to a parody of attention.

'I'll tell you what I'm going to do. I'll take you to ma hoose. It has a fine steading and you'll be able to sleep there. We'll get you some boots and see if with good vittles you can put on a bitty flesh. You can help me da in the field, and if you're a good worker, when I go back to the regiment next week, I'll take you with me and we'll see if we can make a soldier out of you.'

Richard Simpson ran his fingers through the thick black mop of hair that covered his head. He was seated at his desk in the estate office in the factor's house. This house was his home, a pleasant little six-room dwelling of harled stone. It had been recently built about a mile from Culbrech House and provided more than ample accommodation for his bachelor needs. It lay close to the main road between the big house and the tiny village of Crasks of Agais, where a number of the estate workers lived.

Dick Simpson was an Englishman, something of a rarity in those parts, the youngest son of a large family, who had taken up estate management as one of the few ways that a gentleman of limited means could with dignity earn a living.

His devotion to the Maclarens was beyond question, and he had taken it upon himself to try to hold together as much of the family fortunes as Sir Henry's generosity and Andrew's lack of interest would allow. They seemed to think that their investments in the railways and in Lancashire cotton would maintain their wealth for the foreseeable future. That was as might be, but the estate itself ought to be a viable unit, and to maintain it as such was no simple task.

Quite a lot had happened on the credit side. They now ran the Cheviot and the blackfaced sheep. These were beasts which could be handled in large flocks by a single shepherd and a couple of dogs. The old, small highland sheep would not herd, and would not respond to dogs. The labour requirements for hill farming had, by the introduction of these sheep, been cut as much as eighty per cent. Had Sir Henry behaved as most, but by no means all, of the lairds, and cleared his lands of unnecessary labour, then all would have been well. This Sir Henry would not do. Most of the families in the glen had men in the regiment, and Sir Henry would rather beggar himself and his own family than see them suffer. But each of these families needed about four acres in order to survive, and while that might be morally good, it was not economic sense.

Richard Simpson had seen several of the lairds go to the wall for these reasons and was determined that he would not allow it to happen here. Just now they were all right, they could get by. But the long-term future was very shaky. That was why he was sitting and gazing at a large-scale map of the estate and marking off sections of about twenty to thirty acres. Some of these areas were already wooded with tall, bushy-topped Caledonian pine, and these he was in the process of harvesting. He was, however, sure that there was a great future in timber, and that it lay not in the native Caledonian but in the faster-growing and hardier Norwegian variety, and for several years now he had been reforesting with Norwegians as an investment against the future.

Of course, there was another way. If a good marriage could be arranged for Andrew, then all would be well. It was unfortunate that Maud Westburn had appeared on the scene. Obviously she was in comfortable circumstances, but she did not strike Richard as being sufficiently wealthy to fill the bill. He was unaware, of course, of the cause of her arrival at Culbrech, but her presence there worried him none the less. The important thing was that the family should survive. After all, it was a noble and ancient clan which Richard Simpson served, and into which he had been accepted as one of them. Only a few weeks ago he had been down to the borders buying a couple of breeding rams. There he had been offered the management of a massive estate near Peebles. This he had refused without a second thought. Factor he was and factor he would remain, but advancement was not important to him, and the Maclarens *were* – especially one of them, Margaret. He and Margaret always saw eye to eye about the running of the estate, and though it was not very likely, perhaps one day ...

But there was work to do. He turned back to his maps just as she walked into the office, seating herself beside him at the desk, ready to discuss the autumn planting.

That evening after dinner as the darkness was gathering through the long, slow twilight, Andrew suggested to Maud that she might care to take a walk outside. Even though autumn was upon them, the evening was warm, bearing a reminder of the summer that had not so long passed. Together they strolled out on to the lawn and among the scattered pines.

'Funny how everyone always seems to think that it is cold up here,' said Maud. 'I know I always did.'

'The frozen North,' replied Andrew smiling. 'You know, you and I have not done this since we were on the ship together.'

He had mentioned the ship deliberately, but she did not seem to mind. 'That was only a few weeks ago,' she said in reply.

They walked on in silence for a while, and then, hesitantly, he took her hand. She accepted the gesture without demur, her hand soft in his, feeling the pressure of the heavy gold signet ring which he wore on his little finger. The night was coming soon and the stars were beginning to appear in the sky. Somewhere a blackbird called, and a sheep bleated plaintively. Away over the other side of the hill, someone was playing the pipes. The setting, the gentle contact, the whole atmosphere gave them both a feeling of peace and warmth and well-being.

In the withdrawing room, Lady Maclaren went over to the French windows and looked out over the balcony. She stood for a moment, and then her face hardened and an expression of determination set upon her mouth. She turned quite quickly and went directly to her sitting room, where she took notepaper, pen, and ink. She started to write in her firm copperplate hand:

Dear Reverend Mother,
    I feel that it is time ...

6

The two weeks he had spent with Willie Bruce's parents had been a revelation to wee Alex. Every day had produced its new experience. Every day had been so full that his fortnight had seemed like two months, and yet the time had flown. For the first time in his short life he had discovered that there could be order and peace and happiness, and not the hunger and brutality which had scarred his preceding days. He had found himself among people who knew who they were and where they belonged and were proud of it, and for the first time he realized that there was something in life called security. The manner in which he had been accepted by the people, not only the Bruces but also their friends and neighbours, had amazed him. He was one of themselves and accepted as himself.

He had settled happily in the but-and-ben which Willie's parents called home and which lay on the hill rising gently away from the big house about a mile away. It was a small dwelling, but to the boy, it was luxury beyond his wildest dreams. It was the first real home he had ever lived in. There were only two rooms; the but, or kitchen, small, though spacious by his standards, all clean and shining where Mrs Bruce prepared the morning porridge and the main evening meal of meat and tatties and neaps. The living room, the ben, where the family lived and slept, was comfortable and furnished with good, solid pieces, nearly all of which were gifts of the laird. Here, too, there were personal mementoes like the old foot plough which had been cemented into the wall above the fireplace, and the Russian officer's sword above the sideboard – symbols of the two ways of life of the Maclarens and their people. Ever present, too, lay the huge Bible open on the table.

Of course Alex did not sleep in the ben, but the steading was almost as comfortable; plenty of clean straw and a clean blanket, and the warmth of Mr Bruce's Highland pony with which he shared it. He slept better there than he had ever done in his short life, and even when the cat decided to stroll across his dormant form in the middle of the night, perhaps to share his bed, it never disturbed Alex.

Willie's mother had taken the boy in with typical Highland hospitality, pressing his head between her ample soft breasts and making motherly noises almost as soon as Willie had brought him over the threshold. After her greeting, however, she had taken him outside to the tin tub by the burn, stripped him, and gone over his shivering body with a hard scrubbing brush and a vast amount of MacFarlane's Carbolic Soap. Then she burned his rags and supplied him with an outfit from the box in which she kept all of Willie's cast-off childhood clothes.

Alex soon settled down to the routine of the crofting life. He was up at dawn and worked until dark, but for all his small frame, he was tougher than he looked and he revelled in it. He worked out in the fields, those four or five acres which sloped above and below the but-and-ben and which provided the Bruces with their vegetables and winter feed for the cow. There was good topsoil on their little piece of land – good, that is, for the Highlands – and it had to be turned over now to catch the winter frosts so that it was ready for the sowing in early spring. He worked on until it was dark, returning to the croft in the evening, ravenous, to a huge meal of broth and meat. They seemed to have meat, mostly venison, almost every day, which was unusual but which could be put down to the fact that Willie's father was a better poacher than most of the estate workers – or perhaps the ghillies had instructions not to catch him.

Alex learned quickly. They had burned the brush and started

the ploughing, and he was handling the horse and the heavy share with confidence beyond his years. Within a few days, Mr Bruce was able to leave him alone at that task.

It was the middle of the afternoon when Willie found him still at work. He watched him for a while, until he had finished a furrow and raised the share to go to his marker and start another.

'Alex,' he called.

'Yes, sergeant,' he replied, coming strictly to attention and letting go of his plough.

Willie grinned. The boy was trying to be a soldier already. 'You still want to join the army, eh?'

Alex looked worried. 'You are taking me.'

'Aye, if you still want it. Ma mither says that you can stay here if you'd rather.'

'I want to be a sodjer, sergeant.' He stuck out his chest, looking Willie straight in the eye as his horse dragged the plough over to a patch of green grass under the dry-stone wall of the field.

'Look!' Willie said, pointing to the horse. 'It's a good job youse are not going into the cavalry.'

'Sorry, sergeant,' said Alex, abashed, and he ran over to secure his horse.

'Well, if you're still of a mind, we'll be leaving tomorrow. There's another sergeant coming today, and he'll be taking the new recruits down. You can come with me if you like.'

'Thank you, sergeant.'

'We're going to take a lady on the steamer to Fort William, where we leave her, and then catch the train to Perth.'

Willie had seen Lady Maclaren earlier that day, and she had suggested that he might escort Maud as far as Fort William and see her safely aboard the packet for Larne in Ulster, where she would be met by the sisters. As the other sergeant and a couple of trained soldiers who were arriving would be quite capable of handling the eighty or so recruits Willie had managed to gather in his campaign, he agreed most readily.

Andrew would not be returning to the regiment for a few days, as he would be required at home for the ball the Maclarens gave each year at the beginning of autumn. He was needed because his father might not be able to attend. At least, that was the reason given.

Willie was surprised to learn that Maud was to leave for Ireland before the ball. There had, of course, been rumours, but that was none of his business. And anyway, he was glad of the chance to avoid the journey to Perth with the recruits, especially as it would not affect the bounty of two shillings and sixpence he would receive for each one of them. Another advantage was that there would certainly be a few deserters en route, and it would not be up to him to explain them.

At six o'clock the next morning their carriage pulled away from Culbrech House to catch the steamer which would leave Muirton Lock at Inverness at eight-thirty. Miss Westburn and Willie rode inside, while a very jubilant and excited wee Alex rode with Donnie Driver on the box. The coachman was known as Donnie Driver because, like so many in the glen, his surname was Maclaren. Also, like so many, he was retired from the army and the possessor of a glass eye which, under his grey hair and beetling eyebrows, gave him a most fearsome aspect. Wee Alex was quite terrified of Donnie and he rode in silence as they drove through Strathglass, and then across the river at the little village of Kiltarlity, all grey and damp from the haar, that dampness somewhere between mist and rain, which had drifted in from the sea. Then they headed away to the shores of the Moray Firth and drove down the old coaching road to Muirton Lock, just north of the city of Inverness. They arrived just in time to board the steamer before it cast off and headed out through the first of the lock gates and on into the Caledonian Canal. The weather was pleasant and mild, and so they stayed on deck. The trip would take most of the day. It would be about five in the evening before they arrived in Fort William, and Lady Maclaren's cook had laden them with a hamper of cold chicken, meat, and a liberal supply of beer from the big barrel in the kitchen.

Alex was fascinated by the steamer. It was small, in reality – about seventy-five feet overall – but to him it seemed enormous. Of course, he had seen it before, but never as close as this. It was driven by two great paddle wheels, and black coal smoke was belching from its thin, smutty funnel. It was comparatively

new and the line of red paint between the hull and the water-
line showed bright in the morning sunlight which had burnt
off the haar. But already there were streaks of rust dripping
away from the anchors and around the portholes. They cast off
amid a great deal of shouting and were soon heading for the
first of the lochs which formed the Caledonian Canal.

As the little steamer emerged from Bonar Narrows and
headed out in Loch Ness, Willie pointed to the little village on
their left.

'That's where I met wee Alex,' he said.

'It looks different from here,' said Alex, who had never been
on the water in his life. 'It's afu' big.'

'Do you mean the Loch, Alex?' asked Maud.

'Aye, Miss. I hope the Kelpie is no aboot.'

'Kelpie?'

'There are tales of a great beast in the Loch, but nobody
ever proved anything,' said Willie.

'Not so very long ago, I was on a river that was bigger than
this,' said Maud.

'Was that in India, ma'am?' asked Willie, who had seen the
sadness come into her eyes. 'I shouldna talk aboot it if I were
you. Anyhow, it was no as beautiful as Glen More; there's
little in the world that is.'

She was surprised to hear such a remark from him, and her
curiosity overcame the black thoughts which had entered her
mind. 'But you're a soldier,' she said. The remark was an in-
voluntary expression of the strictures of class and ignorance
which lay between them.

'Aye,' he replied, 'I'm a soldier, but I'm a mannie, too. So
what do ye mean?'

'Your business is war and guns and being away in foreign
lands. You must have seen a great deal, and yet you still see
the greatest beauty here in your own home?'

'A man that canna see beauty canna live.' He held out the
palms of his hands for her to look at. 'These hands know how
to hold a gun or a sword, and they know how to use them when
they must. But they find more joy in the tight-knit wool of a
newborn lamb, or a smooth stone in a fast-running burn, or ...'

He stopped and looked hard at her. 'Or in the softness of a lassie's cheek.'

She coloured slightly under his gaze. 'You are a remarkable man, Willie Bruce,' she said.

'What are yees talking aboot?' asked Alex. 'Lookee, they're putting a coo on the boat.'

They had stopped at Temple Pier in Urquhart Bay, the first fourteen miles of their sixty-mile journey completed. They stood in the bows and watched the loading and unloading of passengers, goods, and livestock. Among that livestock was Alex's cow. It perhaps realized the fate that was in store for it when it arrived at Fort William, and was objecting strenuously to being forced up the narrow gangway and on to the boat. All of this was sheer delight to the boy. He danced up and down recounting every action of the drovers and their reluctant charge, and crying encouragement to the beast. But of course the animal lost, and a pair of somewhat battered cowmen returned to shore, signalled to the boat, and the gangway was slid away as they cast off again into the loch. They rounded Strone Point, where stood the majestic ruins of Urquhart Castle, and down Loch Ness towards Fort Augustus with its towering mountains sweeping upwards in scree-covered slopes on either side.

After going through the locks at Fort Augustus, they sailed through Loch Oich and into Loch Lochy. Here the south-westerly wind started to rise, and soon little splashes of spray began to come up over the gunwales. The water was different now; they were in a sea loch, and the tang of salt in the air seemed suddenly to emphasize to Maud that fact that she was leaving the sheltered security of the Maclarens' home and heading towards the unknown.

Alex wandered off. He had found an open door which looked down into the engine room and he stood by it, his dark brown eyes wide with amazement as he watched the rods and wheels and levers clanking away, turning the steamer's paddles.

There were two men working down there. One was shovelling coal into the open door of what appeared to Alex to look like the gates of hell. The other was wandering around with an oil-can in his hand, his overall shining with the saturation of oil. He looked up and saw the boy gazing, enraptured, down at him.

'Awa' doon wi' ye and we'll mak a sailor o' ye,' he called.

'Ye no will. I'm going to be a sodjer.'

'More fool you!' And the man went on with his oiling.

There was a decided air of tension between Maud and Willie. Perhaps he had gone too far when he had talked to her of beauty. The simple fact was that they were young, and they had each found the other attractive, and this made them both feel guilty; he because of the social barrier between them, and she because of her condition.

'No doot you'll be sorry to be missing the ball,' said Willie at length, in an attempt to make some sort of conversation. 'It's the great night of the year in these parts.'

'But you will miss it as well,' she responded.

'Och, no, miss. The ball's no for the likes of me. We have the estate party at Hogmanay; everybody goes to that, even the colonel and his lady. The ball is for the quality, and I think it is sad that you should miss it.'

There was a long silence before she replied. She was standing looking straight ahead over the bow, the wind catching little wisps of hair under her bonnet and her face damp with spray. Or was it tears? Willie could not be sure.

'I suppose you know why I cannot stay for the ball,' she said.

'I've heard rumours, miss, but then there's always so many rumours in the glen, nobody minds them.'

'This one is true, Willie.'

She turned to look at him and there were tears in her eyes.

'I thought it might be,' he said casually. 'Though why certain kinds of folk mak such a fuss about these things, I just dinna ken. Look at me. I was eight months old when my parents invited me to their wedding, and who thinks the less of me or them for that?' That was not quite true, but he thought it would help.

There was nothing more that needed to be said; the barriers were down. Maud looked at this big, solid, gentle man and smiled. She reached out towards him.

'Take my hand, Willie Bruce,' she said.

115

'I couldna do that, miss.'

'And call me Maud. I want you to be my friend.'

He took her hand and turned his head away from her towards the shore.

7

Mr MacKay, ex-colour sergeant of the 148th Foot, and now butler to Sir Henry Maclaren, was in the midst of his preparations for the Autumn Ball at Culbrech House. This was the major social event of the year, and MacKay treated it as he treated everything else, as a military operation. Belowstairs, the footmen in green baize aprons were busy polishing the already immaculate silverware. Up in the banqueting hall, he had impressed Donnie Driver and Iain Doig, who worked in the stables under Donnie, into erecting the dais where the orchestra would play throughout the night. Below them, in the dining room, Morag and Grizel, the two upstairs maids, polished furiously at the already gleaming, long, dark dining table; while Elizabeth, Lady Maclaren's personal maid, rushed around with a feather duster, dusting where no dust lay.

Rooms were being prepared for the houseguests, the MacDonalds from Strone and the Worthings from England. A carriage had already arrived containing the Worthings' luggage, and General Worthing and his wife and daughter, accompanied by their personal servants, were expected at any moment. They would be lodged in rooms in the west tower, where coal had already been laid in the grates ready to light upon their arrival.

Amid all of the preparations, Lady Maclaren was fussing about like a mother hen who had lost her chicks, interrupting the well-ordered plan of MacKay and oblivious to his glowering looks whenever she entered a room where he was working.

As for Andrew, he was really not interested; not after what had happened. To begin with, he had not said goodbye to Maud. He had slept in on the morning of her departure, and had rushed downstairs in a dressing gown just in time to see her coach disappearing along the drive. He found himself suffering from cross-currents of emotion and of feelings of a kind that had never before troubled the tranquil flow of his growing up.

The immediate effect of Maud's departure had been to leave him lonely, morose, and introspective. He knew that he was desperate to get back to Perth and lose himself in the old familiar military routine. Suddenly, here in his own house, he felt a stranger. He wanted to avoid everybody, and during the following days he took to walking the hills alone. He especially wanted to avoid meeting his father when he heard that the colonel would be arriving on the morning of the ball with General Worthing and his family. On that day, he dressed in old tweeds, packed some sandwiches and a flask of brandy, and fled to the hills. That was how he met Maggie Buchannan.

It was warm. All in all it was a wonderful October, and he first caught sight of her walking purposefully along the skyline on the crest of the hill behind the house. She was wearing a brown homespun skirt, a black knitted blouse, and a tartan shawl. Her brown hair hung free, blowing softly in the breeze. She was not wearing the mutch, that white frilled linen bonnet which was the mark of the married woman.

He watched her as he climbed the hill, watched her as the little gusts of wind blew her skirt against her body, displaying well-rounded buttocks and tapering thighs. She saw him coming and stopped, waiting so that he could not fail to meet her without being deliberately rude.

'Good day to ye, Master Andrew,' she said when he had arrived within a few yards of her.

'How do you do,' he replied formally. 'I don't think that I know you, miss?'

'Maggie,' she said. 'Och, youse seen me before, I've lived here all my life.'

'Where? On the estate?'

'Aye, over yonder,' she replied vaguely.

'Of course,' said Andrew, enlightenment coming to him. 'Of course I remember you. Now don't tell me, it's – it's, I've got it, Maggie! Wee Maggie.'

'That's right, Master Andrew. And thank you for remembering me, especially now that you have got so big and grand and me still a simple lassie.'

'Oh, I remember, all right. There were others, too —'

'Aye, Willie Bruce was one of them. Then you all went awa' and joined the army and forgot all about the lassies.' Her tone was mocking, friendly.

'Willie's been here, you know.'

'Aye, I ken fine he's been here,' she replied.

'Will you walk with me awhile, Maggie?' he asked, glad of the company.

'Indeed I shall, Master Andrew. It will be like old times.'

He smiled at her and they strode out across the patches of purple heather.

'And what is it that you are doing up on the hill, with the ball and all the fine people at the big hoose tonight?'

'The house is no place for me, not at a time like this,' he replied. He was already beginning to enjoy her company, and she was beginning to fit into his memories of childhood. A friend, someone he had played with. She had sometimes been the nurse who tended himself and Willie when they were wounded in their mock battles.

'Do you remember —' They had started speaking simultaneously; they both stopped and laughed.

'What were you going to say?' he asked.

''Twas nothing,' she replied. 'I was just remembering.'

'So was I,' said Andrew, and he felt embarrassed. 'Would you like something to eat? I have some sandwiches with me.'

'Aye, I will share your piece with you.'

'I think,' he replied, 'we had better find somewhere sheltered.'

For though the day was pleasant, there was a little chill in the October breeze.

'Over there looks like a nice spot,' she announced and headed in the direction of a rocky outcrop cradling a sunlit, heather-

and-bracken-carpeted bowl shielded from the wind. She sat herself down and grinned up at him. 'Well, now, where's the piece?' she demanded.

As he opened his sandwich case and shared its contents between them, she sat, knees up, her chin cupped in the palms of her hands, gazing down the hill.

' 'Tis a grand sight,' she said.

'What?' asked Andrew. 'Oh, the house. Yes, I suppose it does look good from up here.'

And indeed it did, standing there beneath them and surrounded by the bright green of its lawns, solid and timeless.

'But,' she continued, 'I dinna think I should like to stay there myself. It is too big.'

'There are a lot of people live in it,' said Andrew.

'I ken that, but they'd all be strangers to me.'

They munched away at their sandwiches for some time. Andrew kept glancing at her, but she seemed oblivious of him. He watched the turn of her head as she followed the path of a black-headed gull.

'It's gone,' she said sadly, and their eyes met.

He moved over towards her because it was the only thing he was capable of doing, and slipped his arm around her waist. Her lips parted and he kissed her. He felt her body straining against his, and then suddenly they were apart.

'I'm sorry, Maggie,' he said. 'I had no right. What can you think of me?'

'I think you are just a laddie who is needing to take his lassie. Come Andrew, it will be right for you. It is time you know.'

Gently and tenderly, for she instinctively knew that she was his first, she let him take her. When it was over, he wanted to speak, but she put a finger to his lips. 'No. It was good for me, and I want that it should have been good for you, too. And now, perhaps it is time for you to go back to your big house and for me to be away to my little house.'

He nodded, not able to speak, but he tried to take her hand as they walked away from their little hollow.

'Oh, no, Master Andrew, you must no take my hand. What would people say if they saw us?'

'Look, Maggie,' he said, 'if there's anything I can do for you, if there's anything you want, well, you only have to ask.'

Suddenly she became serious. 'There is something, Master Andrew, though I ask it only because of what you have just said.'

'Tell me.'

'My husband —'

'Husband!'

'Och, aye, I'm a married woman. Did ye no ken?' And she pulled the mutch out of her pocket and tucked her long brown hair under it. 'I've been married to Angus Buchannan for three years now.'

'Oh, my God!' said Andrew.

'You've done nothing that any other man would not have done under the same circumstances. Now don't you be silly about it, Master Andrew. What we did was for me every bit as much as it was for you. I need a man, Master Andrew, and that is what I wanted to ask you about. You see, Angus got drunk the other night wi' Willie Bruce, and the fool went and took the Queen's shilling, and the ploughing still to be done.'

'But what can I do?' Andrew was even more horrified to discover that he had had relations with the wife of one of the men who would be serving under him.

'Can you no get him out of the army and send him home to me?'

'That would not be easy.'

'Please, Master Andrew, I want ma mannie back.'

'But suppose he doesn't want to come out?'

'What man in his right mind would want to stay in the army? But will you do what you can?'

'All right, Maggie, I'll do what I can.'

'You promise?'

'I promise, Maggie.'

'Thank you, Master Andrew. And now we had better be awa' home, you to yours and I to mine. And thank you, Master Andrew.'

He turned away from her to go.

'And Master Andrew, don't ye look so sad. Ye mind me of the time when you were fourteen when you took your father's favourite mare wi'oot permission and brought her back lame.'

He laughed. The tension had gone.

When he got back to the house, his feelings were of happiness tinged with guilt. He did not want to see anybody, so he went in through the iron-studded front door and through the servants' hall. He had just reached the stairway to the east wing, which would lead him to his room and safety, when MacKay called his name.

'The colonel is back and wants to see you, sir.'

'Oh,' said Andrew, 'when did he get here?'

'An hour or more ago, sir. He came with the Worthings.'

'What are the Worthings like, MacKay?' asked Andrew.

'That is not for me to say, sir. But I would say that they have a great deal of luggage, and each one of them has brought along a personal servant, thus providing us with an accommodation problem.'

'Which you will solve.'

'Only because I have no option, Captain Maclaren. I think that you had better go and see the colonel. I think that you will find him in the library.'

He had barely arrived at the library door when the familiar voice barked out:

'Andrew, come here.'

He went into the dark, oak-panelled room with its mountainous shelves. His father was standing with his back to the fire, a whisky in one hand and a medical journal in the other. Sir Henry had been most impressed by the behaviour of the nurses under Miss Nightingale in the Crimea, especially with their hygiene, and had as a consequence developed a consuming interest in medicine, especially as it applied to the military.

'Have a dram, boy,' said Sir Henry. 'I want to have a talk with you.'

Andrew poured out a large one. He felt that he needed it.

'Sorry to have to spring this on you, but we've got to go back to Perth tomorrow.'

'Oh, good,' said Andrew.

His father looked at him quizzically. 'Not enjoying your leave?'

'Oh, yes, sir. But I really would like to get back,' he replied.

'In that case, you're getting what you want. We're off to China in a couple of months. That means an intensive training programme for the new recruits. China will be quite an experience for you.'

It struck Andrew as strange that his father had bothered to come all the way up from Perth if he was going to return the next day.

'Didn't want to miss the ball, you know,' said Sir Henry in answer to his son's unspoken question. 'Besides, I promised General Worthing that I'd bring him up. He wants you to meet his daughter.'

The implication of his father's remark was completely lost on Andrew. 'That will be nice,' he said lamely.

'You'd better get packed and ready before dinner tonight. We'll be leaving tomorrow morning. The Worthings won't be coming with us; they're going to stay on for a few days.' He paused, and when Andrew made no remark, he continued, 'Well, I suppose I'd better take you along and introduce you. They're in the morning room with your mother.'

'Father,' said Andrew as the colonel started to move, 'before we go, can I ask you something?'

'Of course, what is it?'

'Actually, it's about women. I don't think that I understand them.'

Sir Henry laughed and put his arm around Andrew's shoulder, a rare paternal gesture on his part. 'If you did, you'd be the first man ever. I've been married to your mother for getting on to twenty-six years, and I'm damned if I understand her yet. No, Andrew, what little you learn about women before they push you into your hole in the ground, they'll teach you themselves. They're not the same as us, quite a different animal. They're born fourteen years older than men. You stick to the regiment, boy, and you'll be all right.'

'Yes, but—'

'What's on your mind, Andrew? Is it Maud Westburn? She's gone, hasn't she?'

The mention of Maud brought a feeling of guilty nostalgia

to Andrew. It made him feel dirty. 'No, sir, it's not Miss Westburn,' he said.

'Thank God for that,' said his father. 'What is it then, a woman, or just women in general?'

But Andrew could not reply. All he could think of was that he had promised Maggie that he would try to get Angus Buchannan out of the regiment.

'Is there something wrong, lad?' his father asked.

'Oh, no, sir. Really there isn't. Nothing, nothing at all.'

'I wish I could believe you. Still, we'd better go and take a look at this Worthing filly. See what you think of her, eh?'

He accompanied his father into the morning room. This was dominated by a massive Raeburn portrait of his great-grandparents. There was also a collection of Raeburn miniatures which Lady Maclaren had recently taken to collecting. This was really his mother's room. The whole feeling of it was feminine. It was situated at the corner of the house and the windows opened to the east and the south, so that on a pleasant day such as this the sunlight streamed in, picking out the flowered chintzes of the comfortable furnishings, and gleaming off the polished mahogany of the small tables scattered about the room. It was also the only room on the first floor which was not wood-panelled, and the light-coloured drapes and the blue and gold of the striped damask wall covering gave it a spacious, gracious air.

Andrew's mother was pouring tea for the other two ladies, the younger of whom was sitting demurely, hands folded on her lap, eyes downcast, and blending into the chaise longue on which she was seated, so that it was difficult to separate her from the furniture.

General Worthing was stocky, grey, and moustachioed, his huge head seemingly out of proportion to the rest of his body. Like most of his breed, he had not pursued his military career without it leaving its mark, both physical and in the shape of a pronounced limp, and more obviously in his abrupt and often embarrassing directness of manner.

As they entered, the general cleared his throat and, without waiting for formal introduction, said, 'Grrumph, so this is the young fellah-me-lad?' He looked Andrew over as if he were a horse in the sale ring. 'Worthing,' he announced, offering Andrew his hand.

'How do you do?' replied Andrew, taking the proffered paw.

'Firm grip, that's a good sign. Me wife; me daughter, Emma,' he said, indicating each in turn. 'Sit with the gel. Like to see what you look like together.'

Andrew acknowledged the ladies, and feeling slightly uncomfortable, did as he was bid.

'What a charming place you have here,' said Emma, and that remark set the tone of the conversation. Stilted and as formally choreographed as Chinese theatre.

Later that evening at dinner, Emma Worthing turned to Andrew, who was seated on her left.

'I suppose it is quite obvious to you why we have been seated next to each other?' Emma Worthing was unmistakably English, tall, fair, blue-eyed, and attractive in a formal sort of way.

'Probably just the way it worked out,' replied Andrew, raising his eyes from the soup and gazing at the expanse of white female flesh which rose from the pink rosebud-studded satin of her décolleté bodice.

'Oh, you cannot possibly be so naive,' she said. 'They've decided that we are a good match. Makes one feel like a cow on offer. Still, you had better have at least three dances with me tonight or they'll be furious.'

'They' were, of course, their respective parents, who, after discussing the matter at some length, had come to the conclusion suspected by Miss Worthing.

As the main course was being served, Emma turned to him again.

'Does all this embarrass you, Captain Maclaren? We shall not meet again until you return from China, you know.'

Andrew sliced his venison ruthlessly. It did embarrass him. Besides, he was remembering Maggie, and thinking of Maud.

8

The Earl of Elgin had been chosen for his diplomatic skill. He had been described in Parliament as 'a man with the ability and resolution to ensure success, and the native strength that can afford to be merciful'. He had been sent to China early in 1857, and was currently negotiating the Treaty of Tientsin. This was intended to secure the China trade so essential to Empire. But peace in China could never be secured by a piece of paper, and the British government, in cooperation with the French, were waging constant battles with the insurgent native population in order to keep the trade routes open. This applied especially to those which covered the river approaches to Peking. So in spite of the diplomatic activity of the noble Earl, the government was taking no chances. It was British bayonets which would maintain the peace, and they were strengthening their garrisons on the China mainland. The 148th Foot had been designated for part of this work, and this was the job to which Sir Henry had referred when he told Andrew of their imminent departure for the Far East.

Before they had left and amidst the intensive training programme which had been drawn up for the new recruits, Andrew, conscious of his promise to Maggie, had sent for Private Angus Buchannan.

The man who had come into his office and stamped to attention before him was every inch a soldier. Smart in his uniform, cross belts blancoed to a snowy, spotless white, ammunition pouches gleaming black leather, buttons shining, kilt pressed, and sporran brushed and combed, Buchannan still had the thick neck and near-purple bulbous nose and cauliflower ear which had marked him as a drunkard and a troublemaker when he had first reported to the regiment. But troublemaker he had not been. Andrew had kept an eye on him, hoping to find a reason to have him discharged, but no reason came. So, after putting the matter off until it was almost too late, he had at last decided to talk to the man.

'Ah, Buchannan, I called you in here to find out how you were getting on.'

'Sirr!' replied Buchannan.

'I, as you know —' Andrew was searching for words '— I take a very personal interest in all the men in my company, and a very special interest in those who come from the estate.'

'Yes, sirr.' Buchannan did not sound very impressed.

'They tell me that you are a married man.'

'Aye, sirr, that's right.'

'As a married man, I should imagine that you would much rather be at home with your wife than stuck out here in the army.'

'What for, sirr?'

'Do you mean that you would rather be in the army?'

Andrew swallowed hard. This was not the way he had rehearsed this conversation. 'What about your wife, how about her feelings?'

'Maggie's all right, sirr. She's getting her allowance and living at home wi' ma faither and mither. Och, sirr, she's better off than she's ever been.'

'I see,' said Andrew. 'But what about yourself?'

'Weel, sirr, I look at it this way. I don't have to worry about Maggie, and I get four shillings a week to spend on meself, and I'm a man who's never had more than maybe a couple of pence before and it's gie seldom I've even had that.'

'Am I to understand that you like the army?'

'I like it fine, sirr. 'Tis a guid life for a man; I've known no better.'

'You have heard that we are going East soon?' Maybe the threat of overseas would work.

'And that's another thing, sirr. How would a body like me, who's got nothing, get to see anything of the worrld except in the army?'

'You mean that you'd rather go to China than go home?'

'Och, home's fine, sirr, but it's afu' crowded in oor wee hoose, what wi' ma folks and Maggie and the bairns.'

'You have children?' This was news to Andrew, and it gave him a twinge of conscience.

'Aye, sirr, two, a boy and a wee girl, and there's another on the way.'

'What!'

'Aye, Maggie's due in four or five months,' said Buchannan unconcernedly.

Andrew heaved a sigh of relief. At least it was not his.

There was, he decided, nothing that he could say. He knew from Willie Bruce that Buchannan had the makings of a fine soldier, and that C Company would do well with him, and here was the man himself confessing that he liked the army and wanted to have one last go.

'If I were to offer you your discharge, what would you say to that?'

'I'd ask you where I'd done wrong, sirr.'

'There's nothing like that; you've done very well,' replied Andrew.

'Then, sirr, I'd say no thank you, sirr.'

So that was it. He had tried, and honour (if you could call it that) was satisfied. Andrew sat, not saying anything for a time.

'Is there anything else, sirr?' asked Buchannan, uneasy at the long silence.

'No, Buchannan, you can go now,' replied Andrew.

'Thank you, sirr.' Buchannan saluted and marched out of the company office.

So that was it. Andrew could not and did not try to understand either Angus Buchannan or his wife. He had enjoyed his experience with Maggie; though it had seemed at the time pretty quick, and he had wondered if that was all there was to it, and though it had worried his conscience, he soon found himself wanting to do it again. He did not really know whether Maggie had seduced him or he had seduced Maggie; or perhaps he would not admit to himself that it was she and not he who had taken the initiative.

Over the following weeks and during the voyage, he thought a lot about women. He thought about them in a way in which he had never considered them before. They had become sex objects in his fantasies. Not all of them, of course; Emma Worthing, for instance. She was like so many of the young ladies he met on social occasions. She was attractive, well groomed. But when he tried as he did occasionally to imagine them lying on their backs, naked, and taking their bodies, it did not work. Somehow they all seemed to be sexless. In a strange way, they did not seem to have material forms beneath their expensive, beautifully cut gowns. Perhaps it was because he assumed them all to be virgins and therefore untouchable. He was well aware that his parents wanted him to marry Emma, and that financially it would be a very good thing to do. He was surprised at his own complete indifference to the whole idea.

Then there was Maud. Maud was different. The thought of her never failed to arouse him, though if he had been able to be honest with himself, he would have admitted that he usually thought of her body and not her person. Her past, even her present condition, had no effect on his desire for her. He had resolved that he would not lose contact with her, and had written to her the day after the ball. He had a good reason; he wanted to apologize for not being present when she took her departure from his home, but he would have written anyway.

She had replied to him. It pleased and surprised him a little. The letter was formal and told him that the weather was nice, the home in the convent was nice, the sisters were nice, that she was well, and very little else. Still it had been a letter, and had indicated that she would be quite willing to continue corresponding with him. He and she both realized that it was extremely doubtful they would meet again for several years.

And so they had gone to China to sweat it out while the Treaty of Tientsin was made, and then broken a hundred times. It seemed like another world, a world that was without end. After

129

Rear Admiral Hope had failed to take the Taku forts, they had been moved to bivouac some eight miles north of them at Pehtang in northern China, on the banks of the river of the same name. They had been allocated the task of garrisoning the town and manning the batteries that covered the entrance to the river, from which it was rumoured that another assault on the forts would be launched. But that was only at the beginning, and as the months dragged by; they became convinced that they had been forgotten.

Cholera and venereal disease had taken their toll, and about two hundred men had fallen to one or the other of those scourges. But a greater menace than either of these was the boredom which sapped the morale of the men. Colonel Maclaren had offered awards to those who could devise new and popular ideas to keep his men occupied, but few were forthcoming. Life resolved into a ceaseless round of drills, parades, inspections and the occasional game of football, devised by officers and N.C.O.s who could think of nothing better to occupy the time of the men under their command. Keeping the men out of the brothels which had proliferated since they arrived proved a full-time occupation, and it was seldom successful. Morale was low, and the forts to the south were still there, held by a large force of Chinese. They were only eight miles away, but they might have been a hundred, as the land between them consisted mainly of marsh and salt flats.

It was not until the end of July 1860 that things began to change, and an air of expectancy began to pervade the garrison. First a new general officer had arrived, General Sir Hope Grant who was the brother-in-law of the Earl of Elgin, but a good soldier for all of that. Mysterious meetings and conversations took place between himself and the commanders of the two battalions which were garrisoning the town, giving rise to massive speculation in the bivouacs. And then one morning, while Willie Bruce was walking around the fort inspecting pickets, accompanied by Colour Sergeant Donald Murray of the H.Q. Company, Murray suddenly stopped and pointed out to sea.

'Willie, what in the name of God is all o' that?'

Willie looked where his stocky, black-bearded companion

was pointing. There on the horizon were ships. Not just one or two ships; you could count them by the dozen.

'There must be a hundred of them,' said Willie.

'Aye,' replied Murray, 'and they look as if they're coming this way. Shall we call the colonel?'

'Och, bide a wee,' said Willie. 'Unless I'm mistaken, yon is a twenty-two-gun frigate and she's one of ours.' He was indicating the nearest ship.

'Ye know, Willie,' replied Donald, 'I think you're right. There's a hell of a lot o' them. Surely there canna be any more.'

But more there were. In all, there were forty-one men-of-war and one hundred and forty-three transports. Slowly this armada, a mass of billowing sails and smoking, grimy steamers, made its way towards the mouth of the river. Over the next few days, they disgorged some eleven thousand men. British, French, and Indian, including Sikh Irregulars from the plains of the Punjab. It was obvious that something immense was about to happen, and of course, rumour was rife throughout the tents of the 148th. The speculation did, however, serve one useful purpose; the men had something to talk about, and this gave an immediate lift to morale. With their years of sweating and freezing it out behind them, they felt superior to the 'new boys.' A certain swagger appeared in their bearing, uniforms were a little smarter, and they were quick to pick a fight, especially with the French around the brothel quarter, where trade had blossomed and there were not enough women to go around.

C Company had remained relatively unscathed from the attentions of most of the evils which had beset the regiment. Most of this was due to the ministrations of Willie Bruce. He never let a day go by without seeing to it that at the end of it his men were too exhausted to go further than the wet canteen when the day's duty had been completed. Cholera he could do little or nothing about, apart from seeing that the men were clean, but it took its toll. As regards the other scourge, V.D., C Company, with very few exceptions, did not frequent the brothels. This was not out of lack of desire or any high moral sense. It was more in fear of Willie, who announced that any man who caught a packet would have his name and the nature of his disease forwarded to his minister at home. It took a very hardened individual to risk having himself denounced by name from the pulpit of his local kirk in front of his family and friends.

Unknown to each other, both Willie and Andrew were corresponding with Maud. Her letters to each of them were formal and polite, and she never mentioned Willie to Andrew nor Andrew to Willie. Her letters were prompt in reply, and to Willie there was a certain warmth in her language which was lacking when she wrote to Andrew. There was one matter on which she wrote which was of concern to both of them. She had given birth to a baby girl and called her Naomi, and she had decided that she would not have it adopted but keep her daughter for herself. For Andrew, this served only as a barrier to the possibility of any really serious relationship developing between them. Willie was not surprised. It seemed to him that it was the natural thing to do. He had expected it, and by his standards, she had behaved absolutely correctly. After the birth of Naomi, Willie, who until then considered himself so much the social inferior of Maud as to have no hope in that direction, and had couched his letters in the terms of a devoted servant, now began to believe that there might be a chance for him. His letters took on a much more friendly and intimate style; he started to write to her as an equal. Andrew, for his part, took her desire to keep the child as a personal slight, and though he did not, because he could not, stop writing, his letters became more and more formal in their content.

In 1862, General Sir Hope Grant had been given command of the expedition which was now massing at Peh-tang, and on the first of August he called his battalion commanders to conference. Among those present was Sir Henry Maclaren as commanding officer of the 148th Foot. As for the rest of them, they were a mixed bag of French, Indian, and British. The general surveyed the assembled company, all seated around a large trestle table. Dammit, he wished that he could speak French, but he could not and had to have an interpreter standing by to translate his briefing. They made a colourful sight, the French in blue, the British in red, and the Indians – there were only two of them – in braided tunics, jodhpurs and immaculate turbans. There were too many of them for the task in hand, but after the failure of Admiral Hope two years ago, there was no point in taking any chances. Still he could not help feeling that he had been given a sledgehammer to crack a nut. Hope Grant cleared his throat and rose to his feet.

'Gentlemen,' he began, 'the purpose of our expedition is to take the Taku forts by storm. If we succeed in this, the road to Peking will be open and the end of the current unrest here in China will be in sight. Once those forts are in European hands, the whole of the Pei-ho River up to the northern capital will be free and navigable by our shipping.

'Apart from the forts themselves, the Chinese have a considerable force some eight miles upriver at Sin-ho. This position can be reached by a causeway which runs southwest from our present base. I intend to march to Sin-ho, defeat this army in the field – we will outnumber them by about three to one – and then proceed down both banks of the river to take the forts.

'There are four of these forts, only three of which are of consequence. The Great North Fort and the Great South Fort, which lie either side of the river mouth, are the key to the whole situation, but they themselves have a key, and this is a fort about a mile inland, much smaller, but well garrisoned. It lies on the north bank of the Pei-ho River and covers the rear of the two large forts, which have all of their cannon pointing seaward. These will be in any case engaged by the navy, and our own force should be able to take them from the rear without a great deal of difficulty.

'The small fort could, however, prove to be a problem. Well manned, and tenaciously held, it could hold up our advance. This must not be allowed to happen. Therefore, I propose to take it while our main body is dealing with the land army at Sin-ho.

'The fort is small and of the usual mud construction. It is, as I said, well garrisoned and has some cannon. I am detaching one battalion from our force, which will proceed independently.

'They will leave camp ahead of the main body. They will storm this fort and hold it while we are at Sin-ho. This will enable us to pass that fort in safety and, as I have already said, take the Great Forts from the rear.

'For this important part of the operation, I am detailing

the 148th, which will be reinforced by a number of guns and eight-inch mortars, and a half-company of sappers.

'Colonel Maclaren, I shall discuss your part in this operation in greater detail immediately after the conclusion of this briefing.'

Two days later, C Company was drawn up on morning parade being addressed by Andrew. They had been standing there for some half-hour, standing easy, relaxed and yet with an undercurrent of tension as they chatted quietly among themselves while they awaited the arrival of their company commander. Rumour, of course, was rife. It was obvious from the comings and goings of the top brass that some form of action was imminent. Private Buchannan turned to his companion in the ranks, Hughie Gibson, still a private after ten years service, a man with the reputation of being able to 'take a good dram', and who had spent a fair proportion of his service on defaulters.

'What's going on?' asked Buchannan. 'Do ye ken where we's going?'

'Och, aye,' replied Hughie. 'We're awa' to Peking and there we'll shoot all the Chinks and tak' the toon for Her Majesty.'

'Will there be any fighting?'

'It's aboot time there was. Nearly two years noo we've been sitting around on oor arses. A guid fight and awa' home to bonny Scotland. That would suit me fine.'

'Hey, serge!' Another man in the ranks called to Willie Bruce, who was pacing slowly between the files.

'What is it, Smith?' said Willie.

Ian Smith, a thin, wiry little man on his first campaign, and showing just a touch of nervousness – the nervousness that comes upon a man who does not know where he is going but fears the worst – repeated, 'Hey, serge, what's going to happen?'

'How the hell do I know?' said Willie. 'The captain's coming to talk to us and no doubt he will tell us that which is good for us to know.'

'Will there be fighting, serge?'

'Och, aye, there might be a wee skirmish.' Willie, seeing the fear in the man's eyes, continued, 'But it will be nothing to worry aboot. Our Enfields shoot straight and true and they'll aye be deed before we're in their range.'

'Where are we going to?' asked yet another.

'Hell and back, if necessary,' replied Willie, and then his tone changed. 'Stop chattering in the ranks.' He marched out to the front of the company as Andrew approached them across the parade ground. 'C Company, attention!' called Willie, saluting.

'Stand easy men,' replied Andrew, after returning the salute. The troops relaxed again. 'In a few moments you will be dismissed. There will be no further parades or duties for the rest of today. After you have been dismissed, you will all go to your bivouacs, where you will spend the remainder of the day dirtying your equipment.'

C Company looked at each other, wondering if their company commander had gone mad.

'Cross belts,' continued Andrew, 'and any other articles of white webbing will be blackened with mud or dye or whatever you care to use. Buttons and badges and sporran clasps will be smeared with a similar substance, so that nothing you carry has any shine on it at all. We will parade in full marching order at four o'clock when I shall expect to see no sign of anything light in colour, or shining, on any man. Dismiss the men, sergeant.'

'C Company, officer on parade, dismiss.'

The men turned right, saluted, and wandered off in the direction of their bivouacs, and there was a great deal of shaking of heads and muttering as they went. One, however, remained.

'Sergeant Bruce.' It was wee Alex, now resplendent in kilt and scarlet tunic, who had been standing by the colours. 'Sergeant, what aboot this?' He held out his bugle, a gleaming piece of copper and brass, and Alex's pride and joy. 'Dae I really have ta mess this oop?' he asked.

Willie grinned. The boy had taken so much pride in everything that he did, it must have been like asking him to throw mud at his grandmother. 'Aye, laddie, you do,' he said, and then, seeing the dejected look on the boy's face, he added, 'But I'll gi' ye a wee tip.'

'What, sergeant?'

'Just cover it nice and thick wi' brass polish and leave it on.

Then, when it's all over, all ye'll need to do is to gi' it a wee rub wi' a clean cloth and it'll come up as good as it is the noo.'

'Thanks, serge,' said Alex, and he scuttled off.

'Sergeant Bruce.' Andrew was speaking.

'Sir?'

'I had better put you in the picture, sergeant,' said Andrew.

They went over to Andrew's tent, outside of which was a small trestle table on which Andrew spread a map.

'The regiment,' he said, 'has been given the job of taking this fort here.' He stabbed the map with his finger. 'It is only eight miles south of us, but there are marshes and salt flats between us and the target. We will be on our own. We are being detached from the main force and will be leaving two days ahead of them. They seem to think that, having been here all this time, we must know the country. We start tonight at dusk so that we can cross the salt flats during darkness and take up siege positions, under reasonable cover, about half a mile from the fort. I don't know yet what is to happen after that. I'm seeing the colonel in a few minutes, and I should have more information when I get back. The only thing you have to worry about at the moment is to see that the men are ready to move out by nightfall.'

'Rations, sir?'

'Three days' rations and fifty rounds per man.'

'Sir.' Willie went off in the direction of the men's bivouacs and Andrew headed in the direction of his father's tent.

They started at dusk. For the first mile and a half it was easy going and then the ground beneath them began to soften, and the air began to fill with the fetid odour of rotting vegetation. Their boots began to sink into the mud and each step became a physical effort. Sometimes there was a thin layer of water, stagnant and stinking, over the mud, and here and there a pool into which a man would sink up to his neck and have to be dragged out by his comrades. Sharp thorns tore at their bodies, and the air was filled with living, buzzing winged things, each one seemingly more ravenous than the last. Conversation soon died as they concentrated on the sheer effort of keeping going and not losing sight of the man next to them. Occasionally a cry would ring out and Andrew and Willie would pause, but they never saw anything. At last the ground began to harden again. It had taken them over four hours to drag themselves across about three miles of swamp, but their troubles were not yet over. They were now on the brown salt flats, and salt invaded the cuts and insect bites which covered the exposed parts of their bodies. At last, aching and sore, they arrived at their objective, and C Company took up their position opposite the west wall of the fort. They made camp and called the roll. Three men failed to answer their names. There was no point in searching for them; they had just disappeared, undoubtedly sucked down into the slimy depths of the swamp as they stepped unsuspecting into one of the numerous deep holes. As for the rest of them, their bodies were caked with filth. The kilt is not the ideal garment for wading through mud, and their genitals were glued to their thighs as the mud dried to bricklike hardness. The injunction to 'dirty up' had proved totally unnecessary; not one of them was recognizable under the batter of grime which caked their bodies and their weapons. One wag had announced that if the Chinese saw them like this, they would probably frighten them to death. Once the sun got up, the mud dried and at last they were able to scrape and chip away the thickest of it, particularly from the pleats of their kilts which must have weighed a hundredweight with all the mud which was clinging to them.

Andrew posted his sentries under cover before first light. By the time the sun was up, they were all well down, concealed by the hillocks and scrub vegetation which dotted the landscape about a half mile from the fort. Andrew grieved silently. His father had told him gravely that C Company was to get the task of 'Forlorn Hope'; they would be sacrificed that the rest might succeed. Sappers were to work through the following night mining the west wall with slabs of guncotton. At dawn, the company would advance towards the fort in open order. When they were about twenty-five yards from the wall, the sappers would blow their charges, hopefully breaching the wall. This would be the signal for C Company to charge. It was their job to storm the breach and hold it while the remainder of the battalion forced their way through and took possession of the fort.

It was a good plan. Militarily it could not be faulted. But Andrew knew that if they came out of the action with less than fifty per cent casualties, they would be damned lucky. Last night he had dined with the colonel, and after dinner his father had embraced him. It had been embarrassing, like saying goodbye. He could not remember when last his father had so displayed his affection for his son. Neither could he criticize the choice of C Company to storm the breach. Any commander would use his best troops for that task, and C Company was not only the best in the regiment, but it was almost up to strength. After their years of sweating it out in China, it was the obvious choice.

As daylight came, he looked around the eighty or so men with whom, in twenty-four hours' time, he would fight, and he knew that many of them would die. He realized that they mattered to him. Most of them came from the estate at Strathglass, most of them had wives and families that he knew, but they were the regiment's men. What his father had said was true: the regiment was a family, bound together by blood and sweat and sometimes fear, but they were all one. And tomorrow, as a family, they faced certain bereavement. Wee Alex was the youngest, fifteen perhaps, if he had not lied about his age. But his two half-company commanders, Ensign Doig and Ensign Wallace, could not have been more than five years older; they were boys, immortal in their own minds. The men were mostly a rough and unimaginative lot, but they were loyal, tough, hard-bitten Highlanders, and he knew that they would follow him through hell and back again. But how many would come back?

John Maclaren, Donnie Driver's son – it would not be easy to go back to Culbrech House and have to tell Donnie that his tall red-haired soldier laddie would not be returning. And Angus Buchannan – how Andrew wished that he had been able to make good his promise to Maggie. Angus was big and tough, but it took only a tiny piece of lead to fell the strongest man. Now Andrew was on his own; there was no one to call on. The decisions he took in the next few hours would mean life and death to these men around him. He looked up and spotted Frankie Gibson, the best poacher on the estate; many was the time that Frankie had gone back home with a fine salmon stuffed up his sweater. His sister Margaret did not approve of Frankie, but his father always said that if they were clever enough to catch it, they deserved the eating of it.

And then there was Willie. Willie Bruce was probably the best soldier in the regiment, and perhaps something more than that. Somehow he did not worry about Willie. Willie really was indestructible.

Lastly, he thought about Maud. She would be at home now, back at Culbrech House, with warm fires and clean sheets. Would he rather be there with her? He looked around at his sleeping men again, and could not answer.

On C Company's right lay the river, so their flank was protected, unless the Chinese had a gunboat. They were not supposed to have one, but if they did, it would be a massacre. A Company covered the left flank and the north wall of the fort, with B Company covering the east wall. Behind him was Headquarters Company, who were to provide support fire and cover their advance. Andrew hoped that the bastards had improved their musketry; otherwise there were going to be more casualties inflicted by the Chinese. The plan was that A and B companies would advance towards their walls at the same time as C Company. This would serve to spread the enemy fire around the whole of the perimeter. As soon as the breach was blown, A and B companies would change direction and follow C Company through and into the fort. That was how it was supposed to work.

Willie Bruce did not think of any of these things. He spent his day creeping from man to man, inspecting rifles and ammunition, and lambasting them if he found a speck of dirt remaining on any weapon. Willie knew that it was going to be a tough show, and he was bloody well determined that every man would go into it as prepared and as well equipped as it was possible to make him.

'Clean the bloody thing, I could grow tatties in it!' he snarled at one. 'I'll be back, and if it isn't right, ye'll be square-bashing for a week.'

As he passed each man, he was roundly cursed, but not until he was out of earshot. Only when he got to wee Alex did his manner soften.

'Well, laddie, are you scared?'

Alex shook his head, but his lips were tight and Willie could see that he was.

'Dinna worry yoursel'. We're all scared, even me,' said Willie.

'I havena got a gun,' said Alex. 'I wish I had yin.'

'You've got your sword, and you know how to use it.'

'Och aye, serge.'

'And ye have your bugle. You are just aboot the most important man in the company. When you blow your bugle, every one of us has to do what it tells us. You stick close to Captain Maclaren. He needs you to protect him after you sound the charge. Just you take care of yourself, laddie, and maybe you'll be a general one day.'

The boy's eyes glowed with pride. 'Could a laddie like me really get to be a general?'

'And why not?' Willie said slowly and solemnly. 'It could happen. You know, Alex, I've half a mind to become a general myself,' he grinned. 'Now get as much sleep as you can, you'll need to be rested and have your wits about you when the shooting starts.'

'Sergeant,' said Alex as Willie was about to move on.

'What is it, lad?'

'Could I come wi' you noo?'

'I'm finished,' said Willie. 'I'm going to get ma head doon noo.'

'Serge,' said Alex nervously as Willie again started to move, 'you could sleep here, could you no?'

'All right, laddie, one piece of hard ground's verra much the same as another.'

Willie stretched out his great length on the ground and lay there silently. The boy did not dare to move closer to him, but he reached out with his hand so that he was touching the edge of the older man's kilt.

Willie lay on his back looking up at the night sky. There was no moon and the millions of stars twinkled brightly out of the velvety blackness. The air here was as clear as the air in the glen back home, but there the similarity ended. Here it was hot and hostile and never silent.

They had been lying there about an hour, when suddenly there was a fusillade of shots. Alex leapt up into a sitting position, and moving just as fast, Willie dragged him down again.

'Never move quick or sudden,' he hissed.

'But they're shooting, serge,' said Alex nervously.

'Don't worry aboot it, it's our own lads. A and B Companies are trying to keep the Chinks away from our wall while the sappers get on wi' their jobs. Don't let it worry you, lad, they'll be at it most of the night.'

And so it was. Intermittent firing continued, and Alex, feeling a sense of security in the nearness of the big man, lay back and was soon asleep.

9

'Stand to in five minutes, pass the word.'

Angus Buchannan grunted and rubbed the sleep from his eyes. It was still pitch-dark and had become very silent and still. He sat for a moment scratching himself and then searched around in his sporran for a biscuit. He took the thing out. It was hard as a brick and square and unpalatable. Angus fingered it with disgust and dearly wished that he was sitting at home with bonny Maggie placing a bowl of steaming porridge before him. He located his tin canteen and poured some water into it out of his water bottle, spilling some of the precious liquid in the process. Then, dipping the biscuit into the water, he had breakfast. Somewhere on his right, someone struck a match.

'Put that fucking light out,' hissed an angry voice.

Angus, gasping for a cigarette himself, wondered if he could possibly light up without drawing attention, decided that he could not, and continued to munch away at his tasteless meal. Thank God that it was dark, he thought, and you were unable to see the living creatures that inhabited the biscuit. So he gave himself over to cursing the world in general and junior N.C.O.s in particular. Like most private soldiers, he blamed most of the unpleasantries of life, even the waging of war, on his immediate superiors.

C Company was awake now, and with their waking the

silence had vanished. All around, there was to be heard the clink of metal upon metal as they prepared to do battle, the occasional muttered curse or the grunt of satisfaction as the quartermaster's orderly issued the rum ration. Andrew had made a point of seeing that the rum had come up. It was a tradition in the 148th that no man died without a tot of rum in his belly.

'I dinna tak strong drink,' said Alex when he was offered his tot.

'Drink it doon, laddie,' said Willie. 'It'll put fire into your belly.'

'Yes, serge,' said Alex obediently, and he swallowed the liquid, spluttering as it went down. 'It burns ma gut.'

'Aye, that it will,' said Willie, grinning. 'Well, you'll ha to see to yoursel' noo. I've got to report to the captain.'

Andrew had his two ensigns with their sergeants and Willie grouped around him for a last-minute briefing.

'At first light we advance, under cover, for as far as we can,' Andrew said. 'I've had patrols out and we should be able to get to about a hundred yards from the wall. There we will lie low, fix bayonets and wait until the sun is up. We don't want to start too soon, as we shall be advancing straight into the light. My bugler will sound the advance and we will walk, I repeat, walk, in open formation. Officers will lead their halves, and senior N.C.O.s will back up. The sappers are dug in and lying twenty-five yards from the wall. When we are level with them, they are going to blow their mine. That is the signal to charge. Every man must then change direction and make directly for the breach. When the breach is taken, we hold it but go no further. Our job is to let the other companies through. Any questions?'

'Sir,' said Ensign Doig.

'Yes, Charles?'

'What about casualties on the advance?'

'No one is to stop at any time. Stretcher bearers will follow H.Q. Company and they will deal with the wounded,' replied Andrew.

'Sir,' said Ensign Wallace.

'Yes?'

'When the wall is blown, there should be some cover from

fallen masonry or whatever it's made of. Do we use that?'

'Not unless it is actually in the breach. Our orders are to hold the breach from within. With any luck, we could be there before they realize which wall has been blown.'

'I think, sir, that we should make it an order that no one is to fire at distant targets,' said Wallace.

'Good point. There probably will not be time to reload, so no firing until we are in the breach, and then only at those of the enemy who are attacking us directly.'

Willie had waited his turn until the officers had had their say. 'What do we do, sir, if the wall doesna blow?' he asked. 'Guncotton doesna always go off when you want it to.'

'I'll have to see the colonel about that one. Have you any suggestions?'

'I think, sir,' said Willie, 'we should retire. Wi'oot the breach, we'll be sitting ducks.'

'You're probably right,' replied Andrew. 'Anyway, I'll talk to the colonel, and hopefully, if the breach does not blow, we'll be allowed to signal retire.' He paused. 'If that's everything, you'd better get off and brief your own troops. We'll pass the word.' He looked at the sky. 'In, I think, about fifteen minutes, we move off to our first position.'

Fifteen minutes later, as the first grey streaks began to appear in the eastern sky, and the shadowy outlines of the fort became visible, C Company began to crawl towards their target. Within another quarter of an hour, they were in their forward positions, poised for the attack, watching as the shape in front of them began to take form, now finely etched against the greys and pinks of the dawn.

Andrew lay at the head of his men, taking what advantage they could of the sparse cover available. At his side, Alex watched the fort which, now that they were no more than a hundred yards from it, appeared massive and impregnable as it stood there in the shadow of the sun rising behind it, black and menacing.

There were shots. They came from far in front of them. That would be B Company trying to draw the fire of the occupants. Then more shots, now from their left, where they could see A Company already on their feet and moving slowly towards the fort. Still there was no command to move, and the tension they were feeling had become an almost tangible thing. Slowly, the blood-red arc of the enormous sun began to show as it started to creep up from behind the fort.

'Stand by, bugler,' said Andrew.

'Ready, sir,' replied Alex, and he licked his dry lips and prayed that he would be able to sound the advance.

Little by little, the disc of the sun became fuller, and the colour of the fort began to change from black to dirty brown. At last the yellowing sun was clear of the battlements.

'Bugler.'

'Sir?'

'Sound the advance.'

This was it! Alex ran his tongue across his lips again and raised the bugle to his mouth. The notes rang out clear and sweet on the morning air, and all around him, kilted figures rose reluctantly from their places of safety, their Enfields, bayonets fixed, held across their bodies at the port. Andrew stood up and tugged his Colt from his belt, drew his broadsword, took a deep breath of the fresh morning air and, closely followed by Alex, started to walk towards the fort.

The whole line of C Company followed, moving slowly, step ... step ... step. Everything seemed to have gone quiet again as they moved inexorably forward to cover the seventy-five yards of open ground which lay between them and the charge. It seemed to Willie, in his position at the rear of the company, that the fort had suddenly been pushed back and away from them. It seemed that they had miles to go. He waited for the first shots which he knew had to come. A and B Companies must, by now, have drawn most of the defenders to the other walls, and with reasonable luck, they might get halfway before the real shooting started. He looked at the men in front of him and knew that they shared the tension he was feeling. He saw one hesitate and another straining to stop himself from breaking into a run; a run which would have brought him to the breach exhausted, and he understood. It had started. From the parapet, he saw a series of puffs of smoke followed by the crack of firing, but no one fell. Muskets, he thought, smoothbores, thank heaven for that. Rifles would have decimated them before they had got twenty yards. He grinned grimly, because he felt that they would do it.

On their left the firing started up again with increased fury. They heard the sound of a distant bugle as A and B Companies renewed their diversionary assaults. Willie glanced behind him. Headquarters Company were starting to move up some hundred yards to their rear. More shots came from the parapet and a man fell. Two of his comrades lowered their rifles and started towards him.

'Leave him for the bearers!' shouted Willie. The men hesitated a moment, and then continued on their way towards the fort.

Andrew too had seen that the Chinese were firing with musket, and there was no cannon. That was a blessing. Before they had time to drag one from another wall, they would be among them, or at least too close for them to bring the cannon to bear. He looked back.

'Not too close,' he said to Alex, who was less than a yard away from him. Two men together presented an easier target than one alone.

Dutifully Alex moved away. With no one nearer to him than two or three yards, he felt alone and frightened. He walked automatically, only half-conscious of what he was doing, offering his small body as a living target to the enemy, unseen behind the brown wall.

The firing was continuing and beginning to tell. Three more men went down. The fort loomed large now; it looked so safe and secure and indestructible. Thirty-five, forty paces. It could not be long now. Hands gripping rifles showed white knuckles through the suntanned flesh. Though it was still not warm, they sweated under the tension that was building up with every step. C Company was like a spring being wound ever tighter, waiting for the release which would hurl them forward into the breach.

Willie could see the muskets now. They were being poked over the parapet. Then a figure would rise for a moment and there would be a puff of smoke and a crack before the figure would disappear to reload. Still C Company moved forward, their rifles held at the port, ignoring the fire. By now there must be a good half-dozen of them lying either dead or wounded, but Willie was proud of them. The months of training and discipline were paying dividends.

Suddenly, one of the figures rose from the parapet, fell forward, and crashed to the ground in front of the wall. Willie cursed and glanced along his line. Bob MacDonald was fumbling with his rifle, trying to reload as he moved on. Willie made a mental note that Private MacDonald would face his sergeant's wrath that day.

Andrew was near to the point of ordering the retreat. They were getting too close, too damned close to the wall, and more of his men were falling. Then it happened. Accompanied by a huge explosion, a large section of the wall crumbled and fell away before them. Dust and smoke were everywhere mixed with the smell of the exploded guncotton, and for several moments the fort was blotted out from their vision.

As the last pieces of masonry were crashing to the ground, Alex raised his bugle to his lips and sounded the charge.

In ten seconds they were scrambling into the breach, firing at the grey-brown figures who were massing to repel them.

In fifteen seconds, their rounds fired, they were locked together in bloody hand-to-hand combat. The screams of the dying and the wounded filled the air, the victims lying disembowelled and trying to shove their guts back into their bellies, bleeding from the thrust of bayonet or broadsword, retching from fear or pain.

In twenty seconds, the enemy had started to pull back and away from the breach in a desperate search for cover. This gave the members of C Company who were still on their feet time to reload and fire after them.

In thirty seconds, Headquarters Company was charging past them through the breach, and for C Company it was all over.

Two minutes later, a white flag was fluttering over the keep of the fort and the firing had stopped. Andrew looked around him in disgust. Bodies of his own men lay piled in the breach. He could see Willie Bruce – thank God he was safe – kneeling on the ground just inside the fort. Andrew went over to him.

'What are you doing, sergeant?'

Willie was cradling a Chinese man in his lap. 'I think he's

dead, sir. I just gave the poor sod a drink of water.'

Andrew compressed his lips. He could not understand Willie, the real professional Willie, who had no animosity towards anyone, no hatred of the enemy. Willie just did his job.

'Better fall the men in and call the roll. Then we'd better take up defensive positions in case they counterattack from the big forts.'

'I doot that will be necessary, sir,' replied Willie. 'Listen.'

Andrew heard it, faint on the morning air; it was the sound of the pipes. It meant only one thing. Hope Grant had kept to his timetable and was on his way to the big forts with the bulk of his force and his artillery.

'All right, sergeant,' he replied. 'Fall the men in, roll call, then burial parties and assist with the casualties.'

'I doot we'll find thirty of oor lads still standing,' said Willie. 'What's yon stupid wee bugger doing?'

Alex was standing in the breach, his face flushed with excitement. He was dancing up and down and blowing a series of discordant notes on his bugle.

'We's won! We's won!' he shouted. 'Hurrah for the Fighting Hundred and Forty-eighth!'

'Get doon oota that!' bellowed Willie.

But he was a second too late. As Alex heard his voice and looked over towards him, a huge piece of masonry jutting out from the jagged hole in the wall cracked away from its tenuous anchorage. Alex knew nothing about it.

And that was why, after a roll call, Willie gently laid what was left of wee Alex into a shallow grave and cursed the God who had allowed the boy to survive only long enough to strike him down.

10

Lady Maclaren tapped the envelope against the fingertips of her left hand. She had recognized the writing. It was Andrew's. This whole business was disturbing. She should not have the letter; it was addressed to Miss Maud Westburn. Maud was a charming girl, and but for her Eurasian daughter – or niece, as she was known at Culbrech House – would have made a quite suitable match for Andrew. With the child, however, any such thought was completely out of the question. Indeed it was the very reason that she had produced Emma Worthing before the regiment had sailed for China. If only Maud had been willing to have the child adopted before returning from Ireland, then all might have been well. But all was not well, and it had taken quite a lot of persuasion to get her to present Naomi as her niece rather than her daughter.

If only she knew what Andrew was saying in his letters to Maud, then at least she would know if her fears were well founded. And Maud was receiving letters not only from Andrew; someone else in the regiment was also writing to her. Who that was, Lady Maclaren did not know, though she had seen the envelopes and had not failed to notice the low standard of penmanship in the address. A thought struck her, and she found it worrying. Supposing Andrew and Maud suspected, and Andrew was getting someone else to write the address on

149

the envelopes? That would be most disturbing, for she had already intercepted three letters from her son to Maud and thrown them, unopened, on to the fire.

She had not acted out of any spiteful motive; she was genuinely fond of Maud. But she had to protect Andrew. An alliance with Maud would have unquestionably ruined his whole career. Her husband had said as much. On the other hand, she had no desire to ask Maud to leave Culbrech and find a home elsewhere. That would have been unkind, and Lady Maclaren was not an unkind person, though if it became necessary for the sake of the family, she would not hesitate. It was also true that, having Maud here under her own roof, she was much more able to keep an eye on things than she would be if Maud was to go and live elsewhere. It was all very difficult, and now here was this other letter.

Could she look at its contents? She felt, knew rather, that she had no right. But then neither had she the right to burn it as she had done the other three.

At last she came to a decision and ripped open the envelope. Then, feeling all the while afraid that someone would come into the morning room and find her with the letter in her hand, she read it as quickly as possible and threw it on to the fire.

The first part told her nothing that she did not already know. The regiment was leaving China and would by now be approaching New Zealand. They had been reduced to a strength of two and a half companies after the battle of Taku, where Andrew had lost both of his ensigns and over half of his men, including that nice boy who had stayed with the Bruces. It was the latter part of the letter which gave her both satisfaction and some little cause for concern. Andrew had finished by pointing out that he had not heard from Maud for several months and had said, as any gentleman would, that if she did not reply to this letter, he would, out of respect for her feelings, discontinue their correspondence. This Lady Maclaren regarded as very satisfactory. What she had not liked was the manner in which her son had signed himself, 'With much love, your devoted friend, Andrew.'

Love? Devoted? That would not do. No, it would not do at all. She would have to talk to Maud. She went over to the fireplace and tugged at the tapestry bell pull. A moment later MacKay came into the morning room.

'You rang, my lady?'

'Yes, MacKay, I wonder if you could find Miss Westburn and ask her if she would be kind enough to join me here,' she said. 'And perhaps before you do that, you could send in some tea.'

At the mention of Maud's name, MacKay stiffened. He did not approve of Miss Westburn. She had returned to Culbrech House with this beautiful dark-haired child after an absence of several months. Her niece, she called it. Well, it was, he supposed, as good a name as any, but MacKay had his private doubts. It seemed to him that Miss Westburn had probably behaved in a manner unbecoming a lady, and while that sort of behaviour was acceptable belowstairs, it really should not be tolerated above.

'Miss Westburn,' he replied, as coldly as politeness would allow, 'is in the nursery with Miss Naomi. Nanny is in her room having a cup of tea, but I'll send her along to look after the child. Tea for two, my lady?'

'Yes, please.'

MacKay withdrew and Lady Maclaren hoped that he had not noticed her confusion when he had entered the room. A minute or so later, the tea arrived, closely followed by Maud.

'You wanted to see me?' she inquired as she entered.

'Yes, Maud, do sit down and make yourself comfortable while I pour you some tea.'

'Thank you,' replied Maud, seating herself beside the fire while Lady Maclaren busied herself with the tea things.

'Now, my dear,' said Lady Maclaren when they were both seated and sipping their tea, 'what I want to talk to you about is not easy for me, but this has been on my mind for some considerable time. First, let me ask you, are you happy here?'

'Why, yes, of course I am. Everyone here has been so kind. Especially Jean. She has proved to be a real friend.'

'My daughters,' said Lady Maclaren, 'have little to do with what I want to talk to you about. Jean, as I am sure she has told you, feels that she too has been a victim of the male sex.' Maud nodded. 'And therefore identifies with you in your own problems. Margaret too has problems. I have persuaded her to wait until her father returns home, but I fear that she will probably go through with the match. I cannot say that I blame her, or Jean, for that matter. They are neither of them beauties, and both are soon going to be of an age when marriage becomes nothing but a remote possibility.' She paused. 'But to continue with what you were saying, are you sure that you are happy here, or at least as happy as you would be anywhere else?'

Maud thought for a moment before she spoke. 'I feel that I owe you and your family everything. Was what was worrying you that you wished me to leave? If that is so, please do not hesitate to say so. It would not affect my affection for you, nor the love I have for your family in the least. As you know, I am well provided for financially, so you need have no worries on that score, and I would be most upset to feel that I had outstayed my welcome here.'

'My dear child, it is nothing like that,' replied Lady Maclaren. But Maud had said 'love,' and that worried her just a little. 'I want you always to regard this as your home for as long as you wish to do so. We are all very fond of you, all of us.'

'Then?'

'Well, my dear, I must confess that there is one matter that has me a trifle disturbed.'

'Then please tell me what it is so that I can rectify it. Be assured that I shall not be offended, whatever this matter may be.'

'I am worried about Andrew.'

'Dear God, he has not been hurt!' Maud responded quickly. Too quickly, thought Lady Maclaren. 'Nothing has happened to Andrew. What I am worried about is Andrew's relationship to you.'

Maud sat silent, and then said, 'I am to understand that you would find that unacceptable, you would not approve?'

'Maud, what do I not approve of?'

There was no point in talking around the subject. 'You would not approve of me as a daughter-in-law. That's it, isn't it?'

'My dear,' replied Lady Maclaren, and now that Maud had brought the subject out into the open, her tone became gentle and sincere. 'You have said that you are fond of us here. I do not need to assure you that the feeling is quite mutual. You are already one of the family and, for myself alone, I should be very happy to see you married to my son. In fact, I find my own feelings in this matter every bit as much as your own, and, for that matter, Andrew's.'

'I'm sorry,' replied Maud. 'I cannot understand your argument. I could understand a complete opposition to my presence here with my child. Naomi is, of course, a social barrier. I knew that when I decided to keep her. Yet I could not bear to part from her. Until the first moment I saw her, until I held her in my arms for the very first time, I had really hated her and dreaded the moment when she would be born. She was, until then, a living cancer within my body. Unwished for, and uninvited, and no part of me. But when she came out of my body, she became suddenly two things, a living person and a part of myself. What had gone before and the manner of her conception became remote and irrelevant, and no longer had anything to do with the infant I held in my arms. Can you possibly understand that?'

'Of course I can understand. I am a mother myself. I agree with you. You are right in what you say, but it is not possible to judge the situation from our point of view. You and I are both women and mothers.'

'What other way can we judge it?'

'Tell me first about Andrew, about your feelings towards him. Please, this is not the idle curiosity of an older woman. This is a very important question and I ask it as his mother, who once held him as you held Naomi, and lived through the same emotions as you lived through in those first minutes of his life.'

'I am very fond of Andrew.'

'You know that that does not answer my question.' Lady Maclaren smiled at Maud. It was a gentle smile, full of understanding. 'I must know the whole truth, whatever it may be, in so far as you know it yourself.'

'That is not easy, and I am not trying to evade a direct answer when I say that I cannot be sure. Of course, I am bound to him by gratitude; he did save my life.'

'No, Maud, in that at least you are wrong. Andrew did not save you. He was a soldier, acting under the orders of his commander. The credit for your rescue belongs to the army. The army and the regiment which brought Andrew to the army. It might have been any soldier. Any soldier could, by a similar accident, have been the instrument. It might just as easily have been Willie Bruce or someone like that.'

Willie. Maud thought about Willie. Lady Maclaren had mentioned him in a tone which assumed that she would never have considered Willie in the way that she thought about Andrew. But that was not true. She thought about the man who had accompanied her to Fort William, a contented man, a man whose strength of body was matched only by his strength of mind. He was forthright, too; he had not been ashamed to be obvious in his admiration for her, sergeant and common soldier though he was. She felt a little thrill of pleasure when she thought of Willie and how much less complicated than Andrew he was. But she still had to answer Lady Maclaren, if that was possible. She tried to think: what precisely were her feelings towards Andrew?

'I'll try and be as honest as I can, Lady Maclaren,' she said. 'I had thought of your son as a husband and I believe that he had thought of me as a wife. I believe that that is past. Both of us were acutely aware of the social problem of Naomi. As a matter of fact, that was the reason that I agreed to present her here as my niece. It was not to my taste and I did not want to, but at the time, it seemed a small enough price.'

Lady Maclaren compressed her lips. 'You do know, of course, that no one believes that Naomi is your niece. It is just a convenient device to make both of you socially acceptable, and everyone will be quite happy to continue to play out the fiction unless ... unless ...' And here Lady Maclaren stopped.

'You were about to say, unless I marry your son.'

'Yes, I was. You see, if that were to happen, there would be talk.'

'Does that matter?'

'To me, personally, no. But the regiment would not stand for it. They, I fear, would never accept it. You see, unless he is very foolish, he will one day command the regiment.'

'And he would be very foolish to marry a woman with an illegitimate daughter,' said Maud. 'Lady Maclaren, does it really matter?' she repeated her question.

'To me, as I said, no. Especially knowing the circumstances as I do.'

'But supposing he did marry me, what then?'

What then indeed! Lady Maclaren found it difficult to answer. This girl had done no wrong. Her greatest misfortune had to be that she had been born into a stratum of society which treated innocent victims of such happenings as if they were criminals. She knew that Maud, comfortable though she was financially, would never be able to find a family who would accept her. She wanted to embrace the girl and say go ahead and marry my son, but she knew the consequences, not of her doing, but imposed by the world in which they lived. There would be forgiveness and pity, yes, but acceptance, never. Women were chattels, and if the chattel were stolen or besmirched, it was discarded. That was the way it was, and there was nothing that anyone could do about it.

'Then he would be finished,' she said at last. 'He would be asked to resign his commission, and his career in the army would be over for all time.' Lady Maclaren paused. 'It would hurt Andrew, and it would hurt the regiment – the regiment to which you owe your life. I know that it sounds hard, but we Maclarens, because it is our regiment, must always be above suspicion, and any form of scandalous gossip. Don't ask me why. It is just the system under which we live.'

'Lady Maclaren.' Maud took a deep breath. 'For considerable time, I corresponded with your son. It is now over three months since I heard from him last. Ours were not lovers' letters, but they were warm and friendly. I have kept all of his letters; there is nothing in any of them which could give you cause for concern. I would be quite willing to allow you to read them if you wished to do so.'

'No, thank you,' said Lady Maclaren, and she coloured slightly at the mention of the letters.

'So be it,' said Maud. 'Nevertheless, it is apparent to me that I should be very wrong to allow matters to continue the way they are, especially as I am living under your roof. I shall not promise never to write to Andrew again, for if he should write to me, I shall reply. I have not written to him since I received his last letter, and I shall not write unless I hear from him again.

'As for the rest, I feel that it might prove easier for us all if I were to find a place of my own.' And then, as Lady Maclaren started to protest, 'No, I mean it. I will not be leaving Culbrech with any thoughts other than those of gratitude for all the kindness that has been shown me. But if I am to live my own life in my own way, then it is only right that I should live it in my own house where I should be answerable only to myself.'

Maud was as aware as her ladyship of her own circumstances. She bridled at the unfairness of it all. She had made up her mind that she was not going to spend the rest of her life a slave to the system, end up a pathetic old maid with nothing but the memory of one terrifying incident that was already becoming remote. She knew that she ought to feel grateful to the Maclarens, but her feelings belied her words. She was not grateful, because they were holding her within the ironclad conventions which, if she allowed them, would ruin her life. So when she said this, her mind was already made up. She did not give a damn about social life or position, but she gave a damn about having the right to live her own life, and that was what she intended to do.

Lady Maclaren protested. She really did want Maud to stay, but she was aware that after the business of the intercepted letters, she would always feel guilty in the girl's presence. So it was that with genuine sorrow she agreed that this might be the best thing to do.

It took some little time, but eventually Maud found what she was looking for: a delightful little house called Cluny lying in the Glen near the river. Her two acres marched with Culbrech's twenty thousand, so she was near enough to call and to be called on.

She moved in about a month after her long talk with Lady Maclaren. Her ladyship had been most helpful with bits of furniture and carpets and even in finding a girl whose husband was in the regiment. The girl moved into Cluny, having left her children with her parents, a couple of days before Maud arrived with Naomi. She had spent those two days getting the house ready for her new mistress. Her name was Maggie, Maggie Buchannan, and her husband was, much to her annoyance, serving in Andrew's company.

11

In London, at the War Office, men in bright cavalry uniforms gaudy with the scarlets and blues of the crack regiments, faceless ones who had never seen a shot fired in anger, decided the fate of the common soldier. These were men who by power of birth or influence of social position – sons of the elite aristocracy of the home counties – treated the army as a social occasion. They served their few years by warming their backsides at a fire in one of the high-ceilinged rooms in the massive grey buildings of Whitehall, dining in superb messes, escorting débutantes through the season, and spending a minute proportion of their time gazing at maps of the world in which various-coloured pins denoted the locations of units throughout the ever-expanding British Empire.

One of these pins, a yellow one, represented the 148th Foot. After Taku, referred to by one scion of London society as a 'jolly good show', one of this nameless number took out the pin, wondering what to do with it, and then found an empty troopship lying off the China coast. So, as he had an urgent luncheon appointment, he stuck the yellow pin into the ship, Her Majesty's Troopship *Himalaya*.

When the repercussions of this casual act reached them in China, there was much rejoicing among the men.

'We're awa' hame,' said Frankie Gibson, for what else could

a trooper mean? And he thought of his wee house up in the hills of Strathglass, close to the deer forest, secluded in a little valley seven miles from Culbrech House. The wee burn which ran from the lochen at the top down to the Glass was where the salmon came to spawn, and Frankie came to the salmon. He thought, too, of his wife Betty and the bairns, five of them, one for each campaign. And he dreamed of the nights at home sitting in his chair by the fire puffing at his clay pipe, with a bottle of whisky, a hundred proof or more, which would make your back hair curl, illicitly distilled by Peter 'Mannie' somewhere on the other side of the hill. It was a wonderful thought, and his spirit was high as the ship put out to sea, the land slipped away below the horizon, and the men fell to their tasks.

Sir Henry had spoken to the master of the vessel and demanded that they be given work and plenty of it, that the ship should be kept scrupulously clean, and that no effort should be spared in the fight against the disease and boredom which were the paramount threats against the successful conclusion of any long voyage with an overcrowded vessel.

Many days out from China, they were still heading south, though it had taken some considerable time for this fact to filter through to the soldiers in their unfamiliar environment. For one thing, they had been kept busy. They had been divided into messes and watches; they scrubbed the ship from stem to stern every day, learned to haul and slacken lead ropes at sail drill, and of course grumbled, as soldiers will, as they paraded every afternoon for kit inspection. Sleeping, too, was a communal affair. There were half as many hammocks as there were men, slung between decks and seldom unoccupied. They were hot and uncomfortable in the equatorial sun, and many a man dreamed of sleeping on deck. But this was forbidden, and the one or two who tried were summarily dealt with. The lash was an ever present threat.

It was Jamie Patterson who first brought the matter up — the taciturn alcoholic whom Willie had recruited on the same day that he had recruited wee Alex.

'Serge,' said Jamie.

'Aye,' said Willie. 'What is it?'

'We're not going home.'

Willie looked at Jamie, puzzled. The man was a gentleman, there could be no doubt about that. He did not fit, not with the common soldiery who were his comrades. Yet he tried to be one of them. He kept a diary and wrote it up every day. But in the tightly knit group that was C Company, Jamie was the enigma. Nobody knew where Jamie came from. Nobody knew anything about his background. He did not come from the estate; in fact, it was whispered that he was an Englishman. His speech was cultured, he was obviously well read, and almost certainly Jamie Patterson was not his real name. All of this was of no concern to Willie Bruce. Jamie was turning into a fine soldier and that was all that mattered.

That morning, Jamie had written in his diary:

The lads are all convinced that we are going home. I now have grave doubts, for if we were, we would now be sailing southwest across the Indian Ocean. But as far as I can ascertain, our course is still due south. Before us lie only Australia and New Zealand, and I cannot but feel that our destination is one of these lands.

'We're not going home, are we, sergeant?' he repeated.

'Do ye think that they would tell me?' Willie Bruce replied, brushing the question aside.

'That I do not know,' said Jamie. 'I only know that we are sailing south.'

'Aye,' said Willie, who was as aware of this fact as Jamie. 'You may be right.'

'Don't you think that the men ought to be told?'

'They will be told when the colonel decides that it is time to tell them, and not before. Have you no got a job to do?' Willie was getting fed up with this conversation.

'Not before we muster on deck in half an hour,' was the reply.

'All right, then awa' wi' ye. And don't talk about this,' said Willie.

What had in fact happened was that the faceless ones had stuck another pin in the map and the 148th was on its way, as Jamie had so rightly guessed, to New Zealand. Historians delighted in dividing the Maori Wars into the First, the Second, and so on. But during that period, the Maoris were fighting a guerilla war almost without ceasing. They were defending their homeland against the incursions of the white man who had found, in that beautiful country, that he could grow sheep quickly and efficiently. And as more and more settled there, they wanted more and more land, and more and more the Maori resented it.

Their destination was Wellington. There they disembarked and did nothing but receive another directive. Someone had moved that yellow pin again. So they re-embarked and there they sat for long, hot days, cooped up in the ship lying within sight of land awaiting orders which finally came; though what those orders were, no one but the master and Sir Henry knew.

Again they put to sea, and some two days later, Her Majesty's Troopship *Himalaya* lay wallowing in an ocean swell some hundred miles north of the Cook Strait which separates the North and South Islands of the New Zealand colony. When the ship had finally stood out to sea, leaving Wellington behind, rumour and speculation began all over again. Surely this time, at last, they were really going home.

It was 'make and mend,' and young Murdoe Campbell, son of Sir Henry's head gamekeeper, was darning a pair of thick woollen stockings and thinking about the glen and his father and home. It was just another little house, like so many of the houses on the estate, a little bigger than most, as befitted his father's position. They had four rooms, twice the norm, and Murdoe even had a room all to himself with a brass bedstead and a hair mattress; but it was home. Murdoe's father was proud of his son who, only twenty-four years old, was already a corporal, and still in the family, the regiment, the clan – call it what you will, but it was theirs and it belonged to all of them. And Ghillie Campbell would welcome his son home and show him off in his fine uniform, much to the boy's embarrassment. And the ghillie would think of Frankie Gibson up the hill, the old and much-loved enemy, and all the extra vigilance that Frankie's return would entail. Anyhow, for Murdoe, you were never really away from home when you were with the battalion. The laird himself was there, and there were cousins and second cousins scattered throughout the regiment. But it would be so nice to see Scotland again.

Taku, sickness and all the rest, had taken its toll, so many of them would not be going back. But the regiment itself had survived, though it needed respite; needed to pause and lick its wounds, and to rise again from what was left of it, rerecruited, reequipped, and revitalized. The voyage itself they knew would not be pleasant, with its diet of rotting biscuits and stagnant water, and the limes which the colonel insisted that each man consume every day to ward off the chance of scurvy. But the breath of home was once again in the air, and perhaps, just perhaps, all that were left would get back to see Scotland again.

Familiar faces were missing, never again to be seen in barrack room or mess, and C Company with only thirty of their men left had suffered more than most. It had been necessary to reorganize the regiment into two companies only. A and B Companies had disappeared. C Company had been permitted to retain its identity as a mark of approbation for its historic storming of the breach at Taku. Andrew had been given a Lieutenant Farquhar and two ensigns to replace the officers he had lost. The surviving members of B Company and a dozen men from A Company had brought him up to establishment, and he now had one hundred and twenty men under his command.

This did not altogether please Willie Bruce, however. He was not happy to have men thrust upon him whom he had not trained himself, and whom he had little opportunity of licking into what he considered satisfactory shape. Ever since they had re-formed and left China, they seemed to have been at sea with absolutely no chance of field training and drill. True, they had had strenuous physical exercise on deck when the weather was calm, but that was no real substitute for the barrack square. Until they had sailed from Wellington, it had looked as if there was some other task for them, and Willie did not relish having to go into action with a group of men who had not been properly moulded into an efficient fighting unit. Willie hoped that the rumour was right – that they were going home and that he would not have to put that rag-tag of a company to the test.

The whole operation was a boredom of being shunted around

the oceans, not knowing what they were going to do next, and even when they did arrive in port either for coaling or disembarkation, finding that it was not the end, but just a pause until they were back on board and out to sea again. It would all have been a terrible disaster as far as morale was concerned, but for one man: Regimental Sergeant Major Mackintosh. As a boy, he had walked from Glasgow to the barracks at Fort Bruce in Perth and presented himself to the 148th and told them that he wanted to be a soldier. He had come from a slum home, where his mother, a prostitute, had thrown him out of their room whenever she had a customer to entertain. As to the identity of his father, he had no idea; it could have been any one of a hundred. In spite of his background, he was a neat and tidy lad, almost fastidious, and the squalor and the filth and smells finally drove him away from that city and into the army. He took to the service with a dedication and a will until it became his whole life, his whole reason for existence. He had never married, he had no family, but he was complete in himself. Now, second only to the colonel, the most important man in the regiment, he had fulfilled his every ambition. Like all of his breed, he was feared and he was respected, and secretly loved, by every man in the battalion, not one of whom did not envy the man who stood next to him in battle.

Among his other duties, he was administering H.Q. Company, which was in a rather better situation than the other companies. He still had the bulk of his company intact and had managed to ensure that the best of A Company had found their way into its ranks. However, he had lost three colour sergeants; Taku had taken one of them and cholera had accounted for the other two, along with about forty men and three officers. He, too, was worried and had suggested to the colonel that in view of their diminished strength, it might be more effective if he were to take over the direct running of H.Q. Company, rather than risk promoting an unknown quantity before getting home where they could fully assess the situation. Colonel Maclaren had readily agreed to his R.S.M.'s suggestion. The colonel was also left with the problem of finding a new adjutant, the previous one having been a victim of cholera while they were in China. He approached Captain Chisholm and asked if he would care to take on the job. Chisholm, whose background fitted him more for the cavalry or the Guards, had demurred slightly. He had joined the regiment because he wanted to serve with the Maclarens, but it was as a line officer not as a pen-pusher that he wanted to see out his service. Chisholm was a man of great wealth who did only what he wanted to do. Behind him were his estates in Perthshire and the entree to any house in the land. However, as senior captain it was really right that he should take on the job, and he finally agreed provided that it should be regarded as a temporary expedient until their return home.

Thus the battalion had been reorganized in a make-do manner and everyone hoped that they would not be tested in action until they had returned home for that very necessary breathing space.

They had re-embarked at Wellington after bivouacking ashore for only a matter of days until someone moved the yellow pin again. While they had been there they had listened to many stories of 'trouble up north', and for a little while it seemed as if there was a real chance of them having to march up country to deal with this situation. But apparently it was not to be. They had been bundled back into the ship and now, once again, they were out on the open sea, sailing west between New Zealand's two main islands. Again spirits began to rise as the ship turned northward, and yet again it began to be whispered that they were going home.

The seamen on board, ever anxious to show their superior knowledge once they had the army out of their environment, fed them with stories of destinations as far apart as South America and the Arctic Ocean. This did not worry the 148th unduly. After nearly three months at sea, they were beginning to get used to sailors' stories. The truth was that no one other than the ship's master, a retired naval officer who went by the name of Glover, and Colonel Maclaren himself, had any inkling of what was to be their ultimate destination. These two gentlemen, with that unnecessary secrecy so beloved throughout the services, kept their own counsel.

Privates Angus Buchannan and Donald Munroe, the son of the pawnbroker from Inverness who scratched a living out of the pathetic pledges of the poor of that city, and who himself indulged in a loan business throughout the battalion – illegal of course, but quite profitable – were on deck. They were exercising along with half the members of C Company, having spent an uncomfortable night crammed together in hammocks forward on the lower deck, and currently occupied by the other half of their company. They were glad of the chance to breathe fresh air untainted by the smell of their comrades' sweat. It was their second day out of Wellington.

'What's yon?' demanded Angus, pointing off the starboard bow to where a low grey streak had appeared on the horizon. 'There's no land that we should be seeing noo. What do ye say, Donnie?'

'I think we're turning,' replied Donnie. 'See the wake?'

It was true. The ship was heading for land. It could only be another part of New Zealand.

Belowdecks, speculation flared up once more. Two hours later, the *Himalaya* dropped anchor just outside the harbour of New Plymouth. Within the hour, a lighter had drawn alongside. It was loaded with coal and the men were 'stood to' to top up the ship's bunkers. Coaling was a filthy business, but every man bent to his task, happy in the thought that this could only mean one thing; they were really going home.

Almost unnoticed, a pinnace, flying the white ensign, came alongside, and a young naval officer clambered aboard the *Himalaya*. He was taken immediately to the captain's cabin. A few minutes later, Colonel Maclaren was summoned to the captain. When he arrived, he found the captain and the young naval officer deep in conversation.

Captain Glover looked up as the colonel entered.

'You wanted to see me, captain?'

'Thank you for coming, colonel. May I present Lieutenant Arkwright.'

'Good morning, Mr Arkwright.'

'Sir,' replied the lieutenant.

'Lieutenant Arkwright has brought us a present, a bottle of whisky.'

The colonel smiled at the sight of the bottle of his beloved Glenlivet gracing the captain's table.

'Help yourself, colonel,' said Captain Glover. 'Arkwright here has a request to make.'

'Of me?' said the colonel, raising his eyebrows. 'What is it you want, Mr Arkwright?'

'Well, sir,' said Arkwright, 'as you command the only British force nearer to us than Wellington, I cannot but feel that your arrival was most fortuitous. You see, we need the army to help us; and we need them now. Immediately.'

'Is there no naval garrison?'

'No, sir, only myself and four seamen.'

'I think you had better explain yourself,' said Colonel Maclaren. 'My men have had a pretty rotten time, and though they do not yet know it, they are on their way home.'

Arkwright digested this information for a moment, rubbing his thumb slowly over his lower lip. 'Do I understand, sir,' he said, 'that you don't want to help us?'

'I think,' replied the colonel, 'that you had better give us all the details. Until I know them, obviously I cannot make a decision.'

'Well, sir, have you heard of Kingi?'

'Who is Kingi?'

'He's a Maori chief. He's really a first-class chap, and in many ways one sympathizes with him and with what he is trying to do for his people. But recently, he has been taking the law into his own hands, and of course we cannot allow that to continue. There are, as you probably know, very few troops in New Zealand, British troops, I mean, and we have asked for assistance from Australia. But that, of course, is going to take a long time. The settlers here have been pushing inland, looking for fresh grazing for their sheep. That was all right to start with, and they didn't have much trouble with the Maoris. But as the operation got bigger, resentment began to grow. Kingi has taken it upon himself to start raiding the sheep stations.'

'Can't the settlers look after themselves?' asked the colonel.

'Only to a very limited extent,' replied Arkwright. 'Of course, the Maoris are not well armed. They have no artillery, and they only have common muskets, fowling pieces, and double-barrelled guns. But now Kingi has built a *Pa*.'

'What's a *Pa*?' asked Glover.

'That, sir,' said Arkwright, 'is a fortified village. It's built behind a heavy wooden palisade. From there, he sends out raiding parties at night to kill a few sheep, or even a settler should one get in their way. They are never seen and always return to the *Pa* before dawn. It is not possible to deal with the Maoris in the bush; the bush is so large, and the Maoris know the bush so well. A couple of them working together can pin down a force of twenty men and possibly even destroy them. They do what they intend to do and you never see them. Of course, they are gentlemen in their own way. They will never attack a man whom they know to be unarmed. There have even been incidents where they have offered us ammunition to ensure a fair fight.'

'Is that true?' asked the colonel, showing his surprise.

'I know it is,' said Glover. 'This is not the first time I have heard of such happenings.'

'Go on, Mr Arkwright,' said Sir Henry.

'Well, the Maoris are not very numerous, but there might be a hundred or so in a *Pa* and we have not got the force to deal with that number and destroy their base. That is the reason I am asking for your help.'

The colonel thought long and hard. He saw it as the clearances all over again, and just as he had sympathized with those who had lost their homes in Scotland, he felt a sympathy towards the Maoris who were losing their lands so that the sheep might graze. However, that was not a military consideration and he could not allow sentiment to interfere with his judgment of the situation. Arkwright was well within his rights in asking for his aid, and he would have to produce a damned good reason for withholding it.

'I'm sorry,' he said at length 'I don't see that we can be of very much help there at all. You see, we have not got the means to breach any form of fortification. We have no artillery and no sappers.'

'But we have, sir,' said Arkwright. 'We have got one cannon, and myself and my ratings are able to operate it. I was hoping that we might be able to attack the *Pa* during daylight and subdue Kingi and his men.'

Colonel Maclaren leaned back in his chair as he digested this last piece of information. He did not want a repeat of the affair at Taku which had already so reduced his force. 'How urgent is this?' he asked. 'What I'm getting at is, cannot you wait until such a time as you get reinforcements from Australia, or must the matter be dealt with at once?'

'Well, sir,' said Arkwright, 'we could wait. I have no doubt that our casualties would be light in the time between now and when the Australian force arrived. But it's the sheep we're worried about. We haven't got a lot, and what we have are mostly breeding stock. If Kingi can destroy the majority of these, it will set us back for years. Until we can get fresh stock shipped out from England, or possibly Australia, we would be at a complete standstill. Whether the settlers would be able to survive that is highly improbable.'

'If we did this,' said the colonel, 'how long do you estimate that the operation would take? And have you got a plan?'

'Kingi's *Pa* lies on the north side of the Waitara River, about twenty or twenty-five miles east of us here. The river is fordable at that point, especially at this time of the year. So it would be a day's march. With reasonable luck, we should have the action completed and be back in New Plymouth within the week.' He paused. 'What do you say, sir? Can you help us?'

'Perhaps,' replied the colonel. 'I think I had better have a word with my company commanders and then I should be able to give you a definite answer. One more thing,' said the colonel as he rose to leave. 'Do you have mules? Your cannon isn't going to be of much use to us if we can't shift it.'

'I am certain you will have no problem there, sir,' replied Arkwright. 'The settlers have mules, and they'll be more than keen to move the cannon for us.'

Neither Captain Chisholm nor Andrew could find any logical reason to refuse Arkwright's request, and so it was decided that the regiment would take on this commitment. Andrew suggested that it might be a good idea if the colonel were to put the men into the picture. The reaction from Chisholm to this suggestion was quite spectacular. He went almost purple. The very idea of telling the men why and where and how long they were likely to fight, and for what reason they might even have to die, was unheard of. Colonel Maclaren, however, took a different view. He knew that once they disembarked and started marching inland, the morale of his battalion would take a terrific knock. They had not been told that they were going home, but that peculiar bush telegraph which works throughout all military establishments had told them that they were. He ordered Sergeant Major Mackintosh to fall the men in on deck, and when this had been accomplished, he, Chisholm, and Andrew went out on to the quarterdeck and the colonel addressed the men.

'Men,' he said, 'I have called you together to tell you that we are going home.' His voice was drowned in a resounding cheer. 'But —' he cried.

'There's always a fucking but,' said a voice from somewhere down among the throng.

'No talking in the ranks!' growled Sergeant Major Mackintosh.

'But,' repeated the Colonel, 'we will not be leaving for a week; we have a task. It is not a very difficult task, but it must be performed before we can sail. We are to march to a spot about twenty-five miles from here, and there we will destroy a wooden, fortified village which the Maoris have been using as a base from which to raid the settlers in this area. I doubt we will have any trouble. We shall be dealing with about a hundred men, equipped with ancient muskets and fowling pieces. We will march tomorrow and be back as soon as we can. Captain Glover has promised that he will remain here until we return. The moment we have re-embarked, we will sail for Scotland. I promise you that. Carry on, sergeant major.'

When the officers left the quarterdeck, Sergeant Major Mackintosh turned on the battalion.

'Now, you horrible lot!' he roared. 'Rifle inspection at six o'clock and you're all to be in full marching order, and ready to disembark, at seven o'clock tomorrow morning. Parade ... Parade, dismiss!'

The following day, they covered almost twenty miles, until they were within four miles of their target. The going had been comparatively easy – rolling green moorland with patches of scrub or small copses scattered about it. It was reminiscent of the border country between England and Scotland, and the rich green of the pasture through which they marched gave many of them thoughts of home.

It was as they approached the river which lay to the east and slightly north of New Plymouth that they began to find more in the way of vegetation. Of wildlife they saw nothing. The pastures had been cleared, and it seemed that the inhabitants of the scrub and the woodland which was left had at last realized that man was not the type of being with whom one associated.

They marched on ahead of Lieutenant Arkwright and his cannon and made camp, waiting for him to catch up. The cannon proved to be a muzzle-loading field gun with its limber containing the ammunition. It was drawn by six mules and accompanied by Lieutenant Arkwright and two naval ratings.

Before settling down, the colonel sent out a forward picket of three men under the command of Corporal Campbell to scout the land ahead of the main body. They returned and announced that they had seen the *Pa* and had found a good site for the cannon near the riverbank. The colonel sent for Arkwright and told him that he was to go on ahead with the picket and get his gun in position before dawn the following morning. He was to camouflage his site, and then, having posted sentries, he could lie up until the battalion arrived.

'But, sir,' said Arkwright, 'we're pretty well all in. Is it not possible to delay the action for twenty-four hours?'

'Listen, Mister Arkwright,' said the colonel, 'we're doing you a favour, at least that's the way I see it. I want to get my men back on to that ship and on their way home just as soon as I possibly can. I am not going to ask them to sit around on their arses for twenty-four hours, when they could have the job over and done with and be on their way back by then. You can have a meal, then you will collect field rations and out you go. And remember, the sooner you get there, the longer rest you'll have. You had better send the mules back as soon as you get there. You don't want them hanging around and giving away your position.'

Arkwright was not very pleased at this, but he went. He really had very little alternative, having placed himself under Colonel Maclaren's orders. So the mules were again hitched up into the limber and Arkwright was on his way.

The troops were given a stand-easy, and rations were issued. Half a loaf of bread, a hunk of cheese, and a piece of cold mutton per man. Water was the only drink they had and they took this from their canteens. The colonel had decided against lighting fires. Even though they were in open country, he did not want to advertise his position, if it had not already been noticed, though it almost certainly would have been.

The men sat around in groups eating and talking and smoking. In one of these groups, Angus Buchannan was holding forth on the tribulations of army life; he who had insisted on joining the army could now find nothing right with it.

'I'll tell ye all one bloody thing,' he said. 'I'm going to get meself a woman. I've no been near one since we left China.'

'Aye,' replied his section corporal, 'and you can count yourself bloody lucky that you didn't get the pox there. These native pushers are riddled with it.'

'Who cares?' said Angus. 'We're going to be weeks on that fucking ship and I'm going to get one before we go back on board.'

'Ye'd be better off wi' a sheep,' said the corporal. 'Or away into a corner and wank yoursel'.'

'I'm going to get a woman before we go back. I'll bet you a week's pay that I do,' said Angus.

'You're on,' replied the corporal. 'It'll be the easiest money I've ever earned. Man, you won't have a chance.'

'I would na mind one of these Maori women,' said another.

'They're too fat,' said the corporal.

'Aye, I ken that, but they're comfortable. I'll bet ye that,' said Angus.

They were interrupted by the arrival of Sergeant Major Mackintosh.

'Corporal MacMilan,' he roared, 'take half a dozen of these men and relieve the sentries.'

'Sir,' replied the corporal. 'Come on, you'll do for one,' he said, indicating Buchannan.

Angus spat and muttered something about being picked on.

'Watch what you're saying, sodjer,' said the corporal, who proceeded to detail off the other five men he required and marched his little squad off to relieve the sentries.

Angus complied with the order with ill grace. His mind wa
on other things. He was thinking of Maggie and her plump littl
body; what would he not have given to have her there jus
then. They had one thing in common, Angus and Maggie; the
both loved sex and in this each had found a satisfactory partner
It held them together when there was little else that they had
in common, and Angus was feeling the ache which the long
years of near-celibacy had produced. 'I fancy that the wee
whore isn't going short of a man,' he would mutter to himself.
And this was unfair, for Maggie had settled down at Cluny and
was proving a most efficient housekeeper to Maud Westburn.
and though they never spoke of it, they both spent many hours
dreaming of their men across the seas. Andrew, of course, was
in both their thoughts; Maud still trying to decide whether she
loved him or no, and Maggie working up an increasing resentment towards him for failing to keep his promise and get her
man out of the army.

Angus, of course, knew nothing of this as he marched off to
spend a dreary four hours staring at nothing in the moonless
blackness of the night.

The colonel had decreed that they would leave a dozen men
to guard the camp and march the remaining four miles to the
Pa, carrying only rifles and ammunition. Headquarters Company led by Captain Chisholm and the R.S.M. would make the
initial assault, C Company being held in reserve with orders to
back up five minutes after Headquarters Company had entered
the village. Once the village had been taken and casualties had
been dealt with, they would have a break for rations, and if the
village was in reasonable condition, they would spend the night
there. The following morning, they would burn the village and
march back to New Plymouth and their ship.

Reveille was sounded at five-thirty the following morning,
and within an hour, they were on their way. It was an easy
march over the pleasant green rolling meadows of the New
Zealand countryside. By eight o'clock in the morning, they
had arrived at the river facing the *Pa*. Lieutenant Arkwright
had uncovered his gun and as soon as the battalion got there,
he opened fire. After some fifteen or twenty rounds, there was

a sizeable breach in the stockade surrounding the village, and Colonel Maclaren gave the order for Headquarters Company, with Captain Chisholm at their head, to advance in open order.

Andrew stood with his men watching as Headquarters Company made their way across the river and up the far bank. The distance they had to cover was no more than a couple of hundred yards. But it was quite eerie; not a single shot was fired until they arrived on the opposite bank. There was a volley, and as far as Andrew could see, three men of Headquarters Company fell, and then silence. He watched them as they went, with bayonets fixed, cautiously through the battered stockade and out of sight into the village.

He checked his watch as the last man disappeared inside. In five minutes, his men had to start moving in. A kilted figure appeared at the gap in the wooden wall and waved to them. It was an obvious request for C Company to move up. Andrew gave the order to advance. He checked his Colt, drew his broadsword, and started to move forward cautiously. One could never be sure. The stillness and the silence reminded him of the day they had entered Cawnpore, and he started to think about Maud. Almost before he realized it, they were fording the river. It was not deep; at no point did the water come above knee height. And then they were scrambling up the opposite bank.

'The colonel says to bring in the casualties,' shouted a voice from the stockade. 'There's nobody here.'

Andrew ordered Willie Bruce to detail a few men to bring in the three casualties, and went on ahead himself and through the gap in the wall. There he was greeted by his father.

'All right, men,' called the colonel. 'You can relax, there's no opposition.' Then he turned to Andrew. 'Andrew, I want a thorough search of the whole village. If they find any food that's worth eating, they can bring it back here, and if we get enough, they can have a meal. Then we can start moving back. It looks as if we're going to get home a day early.'

The village itself consisted of a cluster of houses, one in three of which seemed to be used as a food store. Most of the houses seemed to have only one door and one window. The whole village was encircled by not one, but two palisades, both of which had been breached by the cannon fire. There was no sign of any pots or pans or any form of cooking implements. In the centre of the village, there was a shallow hole in the ground filled with the dying embers of burnt wood on top of which were piled red-hot stones. On some of these stones, strips of mutton had been laid, and the men were picking off the pieces of hot meat and cursing as they burned their fingers in the process.

Andrew went to the colonel. 'Sir,' he said, 'where have they gone?'

'What are you talking about, Andrew? Where have who gone?'

'When you went in, there was a volley of shots fired, but there's nobody here. The place seems deserted.'

'Yes,' replied the colonel. 'I'm damned if I know what's happened to them. They've just vanished.'

'It often happens,' said Arkwright. He had joined them unobserved. 'They just seem to disappear. They won't come back. They won't build here again once we have burned the place.'

They looked out over the rolling moorland. 'But where the devil could they go?' demanded the colonel.

'They'll not be far away,' replied Arkwright. 'They'll be behind one of those ridges, watching us.'

'Oughtn't we to go after them?' said Andrew.

'Not really much point,' said Arkwright. 'Besides, there'll be women and children with them.'

In all, there would have been between twenty and thirty houses in the compound. Andrew started to wander around these, glancing into each one as he passed. They were, as Arkwright had indicated, completely deserted. He was about to give up his search – it seemed a waste of time – and return to the colonel for further orders, when he heard a muffled cry.

It seemed to be coming from one of the huts in the far corner. He ran over towards it, tugging at his Colt as he went. He burst through the door of the hut from which the sound seemed to be coming. The sight that met his eyes was not a very pretty one. The body of a dark-skinned man dressed in a feather cloak lay in one corner of the hut. His throat had been slit, and there were bayonet wounds in his chest. He lay there on a mattress of his own blood. A rifle with a bloodied bayonet lay near to him. In the opposite corner of the hut was a half-naked woman struggling fiercely as one of the Highlanders tried to mount her.

The man struck the woman across the face. 'Take that, ye bloody bitch. I'll slit your bloody throat, too, if you don't fucking well open up,' he snarled.

Andrew rushed over to them and kicked the man's bare behind as hard as he could. 'Get up, you filthy swine!' he shouted.

It was Angus Buchannan, trying to win his bet. Andrew aimed his Colt at the man.

'What are you going to do?' Angus panted, and there was real terror in his eyes.

'I'm going to shoot you, you bastard, and that's more than you deserve!' Andrew hissed the words at him.

'Why do ye wanna do that, sir? She's only a nigger. She doesna matter.'

Slowly and deliberately Andrew cocked his revolver.

'Don't do it, sir,' said a voice. 'Don't do it.' It was Willie Bruce, who had entered the hut unnoticed.

'You keep out of this, sergeant,' said Andrew.

'No, sir,' replied Willie. 'There's no use in getting yoursel' into trouble over that,' contemptuously indicating the cowering Buchannan. 'There's a law that takes care o' this kind. I have him covered, sir. You'll no need your gun. Come back beside me.'

Andrew lowered his revolver and stepped back to where Willie was standing, holding his rifle.

'Buchannan,' said Andrew, 'you are under close arrest.'

'I think we'd better do something aboot the lady, sir,' said Willie.

There were a few blankets lying in the hut. Andrew took one of these and handed it to the girl. Then he took another and covered the body of the man. He was all right now, the sudden anger had passed. He went to the door of the hut and called to two men who were passing. When they came in, Willie turned to them.

'This man is under close arrest. You two bring him wi' me. We'll find a hut to keep him in until we're ready to move out.'

As they left, Andrew turned to the woman. 'I'm sorry,' he

said. 'Is there anything I can do to help you? The man who did this dreadful thing will be punished.'

The woman, cringing against the far wall of the hut, pointed at the blanket-shrouded figure on the floor. 'Me husband, very sick, man kill,' she said. 'Not speak English.'

Andrew made signs to her indicating that she should wait. He had had an idea. It was possible that either Arkwright or one of his ratings would be able to converse with her and make arrangements to get her back to her people. This proved to be true. One of the ratings, a petty officer, said that he could speak a little of the language. Andrew took him to the hut. When they got there, the woman had gone. The body of the man still lay where they had left it, but there was no sign of her.

'She'll have gone back to her people, sir,' said the petty officer.

'But how did she get out?' asked Andrew.

'Same way they did, sir. They always seem to have an escape route.'

Andrew went in search of the colonel to report. He found him grim-faced and solemn.

'The sergeant major's stopped one, Andrew,' said Colonel Maclaren before Andrew had a chance to speak.

'Mr Mackintosh?' said Andrew. The thought of that inde-structible little man ever becoming a casualty had occurred to none of them. 'Is it bad, sir?'

'I'm afraid he's dead.'

'I'm sorry,' said Andrew. 'Damned sorry. What about the others? I saw three go down.'

'They'll be all right. Nothing serious there. I think you had better organize a burial party.' And then as Andrew hesitated, 'Get on with it,' said the colonel and he turned to go.

'I'm sorry, sir,' said Andrew stopping him, 'but there is something else. Sergeant Bruce has just placed Private Buc-hannan under close arrest.'

'Oh, my God,' said the colonel. 'What has he been up to?'

'I think the charge will be murder and attempted rape, sir,' said Andrew. 'I'm sorry, but I cannot discuss it with you, as I shall probably be the principal witness.'

The colonel looked grim. This was no slight matter and he

had no desire to set his mind to it at that moment. 'Very well,' he said. 'I'll get Captain Chisholm to take the summary of evidence. It will have to wait until we are on board ship; I cannot convene a court martial here. Where is he now?'

'Sergeant Bruce has placed him under guard in one of the huts, sir.' Andrew could have wept. He was aware of the almost inevitable consequences of Angus's action, and yet he, who had almost shot the man in cold blood, could not feel totally without responsibility. If only he had been able to fulfill his promise to Maggie. If only he had managed to get Buchannan out of the army.

'Stop daydreaming, Andrew.' The colonel was speaking to him again. 'There's work to do. Carry on and organize that burial party.'

Somehow the rifle party had managed to make their weapons a bit brighter; somehow the battalion had managed to give their buttons and their boots an extra shine. There had been no orders issued, but the parade which assembled was complete, not a man was absent, and every one of them could have been mounting guard at Buckingham Palace, so immaculate was their turn-out. It was as if they wanted to tell their R.S.M. something; they wanted him to be proud of the men he had trained and forged into a fighting unit.

They laid him to his rest in a deep, deep grave, where no animal or vandal, human or otherwise, would desecrate his bones. They buried him in his kilt and feather bonnet and wrapped his hands around his broadsword, and as they lowered him into that dark hole, the piper played 'The Fleurs o' the Forest.' As those plaintive notes rose on the New Zealand air, there was not a man who was not back home again in Scotland.

The colonel opened his battered Church of Scotland prayerbook and read, 'I am the resurrection and the life, said the Lord, he that believeth ...'

And the men held back their tears. And when the colonel had finished, the rifle party fired a volley over the grave, and someone, no one ever knew who, started to sing:

The Lord's my shepherd, I'll not want,
He leadeth me down to lie . . .

And they all joined in, five hundred Scottish voices softly, and with the magic which springs from great emotion, sang the Crimond.

When it was all over, they marched out heading for New Plymouth with Angus Buchannan in chains. Andrew could barely look at the man as they led him out. He was thinking of Maggie again, and that he might have to be the one to tell her, and he felt sick at heart.

Thirty-six hours later, they boarded the *Himalaya*. The ship cast off as soon as they were aboard, stood out to sea, and pointed her bow towards Scotland. At last they were going home.

Three days out from New Plymouth, they hanged Angus Buchannan from the foremast yard.

12

During their absence, great things had been happening back home in Scotland. The most important of these was that new barracks had been constructed. After the railway line had reached Inverness, many of the labourers who had hacked and hewn the track through the Grampian Mountains had been engaged for the task of building the new headquarters for the 148th. They built it only three miles south of Beauly with huge blocks of pink Moray sandstone piled and mortared and trimmed. This was their basic building material.

There had been some argument as to whether the barracks should not have been built to cover the approaches to the Beauly Firth, but with the knowledge that Fort George did this quite adequately, and that the railway would soon wind its way north from Inverness, on through Beauly up to the very tip of Scotland, expediency had prevailed. The buildings were constructed close to the proposed tracks.

This then would be the permanent home of the 148th. A great wall surrounded it, cocooning the rest of the buildings and cutting them off from the outside world. The arched entrance was commanded by the guardroom with two sentry boxes standing outside, where, hail, rain, sunshine, or snow, two men would stand and suffer for four hours at a stretch. Inside the wall, the barrack blocks had been built as barrack blocks always were, squat and rectangular, around the parade ground. They were four-storey buildings, each destined to house a full company with little rooms at the end of each barrack room for the N.C.O.s. The sergeants' mess and H.Q. block covered the far side of the square, differing only from the barrack blocks by the fact that they each possessed a porticoed entrance. Behind these, and set apart by a pleasant green lawn, stood the most ornate building of them all, gable roofed, white pillared, with large sash windows. This was the officers' mess. Next to it in a corner of the area surrounded by the outside wall, there was the garrison church; the only place in the entire complex where all men were, theoretically at least, equal.

In the town of Beauly, there had been considerable discussion and argument, and many passionate outbursts among the town dignitaries. These had occurred in two stages; first the building of the barracks themselves, about which the town could do nothing, and secondly, about the return of the 148th, about which the town could do a great deal. The town had been split into two factions, those who considered the invasion of the 'licentious soldiery' an affront to the ordered tenor of their lives, and those who waited with joy and pride for the return of their 'brave lads'! After all, these men were their men, men from the glens and villages which spread out beyond the town itself, and there were great advantages in having the regiment here within its own catchment area instead of a hundred and forty miles south.

Men would be available for special leaves and working parties. They would be able to help with the ploughing and the harvesting and the shearing, and all of those tasks that occur every year and always find a rural community short of manpower. Moreover, if things went well and recruiting was good, there would be a second battalion, and that would mean that there would always be a corps stationed at the barracks and available to help the civilian community, for any commanding officer was always only too ready to find work for soldiers employed in the dull and unexciting task of garrisoning their home base.

Most of these meetings had been presided over by Lord MacDonald of Strone. A Catholic, and one of the lairds who had ruthlessly cleared his lands, he was not one of the most popular men in the area, but none the less his position and influence were great. He had decided that the whole conception was a 'first-class idea'. Against him were ranged the minister, staunchly anti-Rome, and his elders who also sat on the town council. However, without any increase in his personal popularity, MacDonald had carried the day. He, of course, was thinking in terms of cheap labour, but those who supported him were thinking only of the proximity of their menfolk.

And now the town had been informed that the 148th was on its way. News had reached them that the *Himalaya* was due to dock at Greenock and that the regiment, as soon as it had disembarked, would be travelling to Inverness overnight by train. Beauly itself was an independent burgh and proud of its status, and the vast majority of its inhabitants were proud of its regiment; after all, most of them had at least one relative who served in the 148th. So had it been proposed that special privileges should be granted to their battalion, these Highland men, on their return. Therefore, it was decreed within the council chambers that this regiment of theirs should be accorded the honour, to be shared by no other, of entering and marching through the town, with bayonets fixed, drums playing, and banners flying. After all, if Edinburgh could do it for the Scots Guards, then Beauly could do it for the 148th Regiment of Foot. So all was made ready; the strings of bunting were strung across the streets, the Union Jacks and St Andrew's Crosses were flown in equal profusion from every flagstaff, genuine and improvised, throughout the town. And a rostrum was erected in the town square in the shadow of the ruins of the ancient priory where monks had once, centuries ago, walked in the now-crumbling cloisters and prayed in the church which now had no covering save the temperamental sky above.

At last the great day arrived. The men had slept well; after about nine weeks of sea travel in the crowded conditions on board the *Himalaya*, a seat in the train was a luxury. When they arrived in Inverness, they were greeted by the provost and the pipes of the town. They were marched to the Town House and there given a huge breakfast of porridge and bacon and eggs, as much as any of them could eat, and after a mercifully short speech of welcome from the provost, they set out on the nine-mile march to Beauly.

In the hills around Strathglass, there were very mixed feelings among the crofting community and the estate workers. Many of them who had waved and cheered goodbye as their men had marched away five years ago would have no man to welcome home. There were other worries, too. Mothers spoke firmly to their daughters of the dangers of associating with soldiers who had just returned from overseas. Men went to great lengths to conceal the fact that they had 'caught a packet,' and the older women were aware that in more than a few of the men returning, there would be lurking the dread syphilis which they had brought home from the brothels of the East, and for which there was no known cure. Worse, it might so easily be transmitted to the children who would be conceived in the next few months.

News had been hard to come by in Strathglass. Certainly the long casualty lists from Taku had been published in the *Inverness Courier* and many names were listed as 'died on active service' – these last being the victims of disease and accidents, greater scourges to the fighting man than the risks of battle. But there was little known of the happenings of the last year, so most of the families of the men waited and prayed for that moment of physical reunion, hoping desperately that it might come to be.

The state of the regiment was known mainly through rumour and invention. Quite a few of the homecomers would be due for discharge. Some would take it, while others would sign on for a further six years. All the married men would be given leave almost as soon as they had arrived in Beauly, and in little over nine months from now, there would be a new crop of children in the glen.

Today was the day of the parade. The women and the old men would line the High Street from the town boundary, where there was already work starting on the railway, down the little slope, past the shops, all whitewashed or neat sandstone with grey slate roofs, and on to the red-brick hotel, the largest building in Beauly, and finally into the village square. There, surrounded by the principal shops – the apothecary's, the tobacconist, the butcher's, the hardware and farm-implement store – and the old priory itself all strewn with bunting, the regiment would march to be greeted by the town fathers. The streets would be crowded, the children pushed to the front, where they could have a better view and cheer and wave flags as the soldiers marched by. The people, the young especially, would dance along the sides of the column, stealing kisses and thrusting little gifts of sweetmeats or flowers into the hands of the returning warriors. Those of them who had loved ones would be scanning the faces anxiously as each filed past, praying that they would find the beloved and familiar face, and until they did, fearing that something might have happened that had not yet been reported.

At Culbrech House, Lady Maclaren was fussing. That night she was to be hostess to the officers of the 148th. Of the twenty-four who had left, only fourteen would return. But she was an army wife and accepted these things, especially when they did not touch her personally. For her, there was no tragedy. She knew that both of her men were safe. She had received a letter from her son only that morning which told her that all was well.

Lady Maclaren would not go into Beauly to see the march. It would not do for the colonel's wife to wave a paper flag and cheer, and she could not wait for them at the barracks where her presence would only serve to delay their arrival at the house. No, it was better that she stayed at home and waited for her men to arrive. Dinner would be at eight, and after dinner there would be all the stories to listen to.

Of course, they would stay the night in barracks, but hopefully her husband and her son would be able to stay on for a few days. Especially she hoped that Andrew would be given leave immediately, for it was with that in mind that she had again invited the Worthings to Culbrech. It really was high time that the boy started thinking seriously about marriage, and Emma was, to Lady Maclaren, a most suitable match in many ways. For one thing, he would not have to break her in to army life; she had known no other. Yes, thought her ladyship, eminently suitable. Not that she expected them to fall in love with each other. As far as that was concerned, Andrew would undoubtedly have his mistresses, and hopefully Emma would be kept too busy bearing children to worry about her own desires in that direction. Ladies were born to breed and keep house; men had mistresses for their pleasure, but discreetly, and on the side.

At Cluny Cottage, Maggie Buchannan tapped on the planked door which led to the sitting room.

'Come in.'

Maud was seated in a polished oak wheel-backed chair by an octagonal bamboo table covered with a blue velvet tasselled cloth. She was intent on her embroidery, a pinafore for her small daughter. The room faced south, and the morning sun which had broken through after the threat of rain had just begun to filter through the bow window, picking out the heavy gilt framed oil painting of Highland cattle standing eternally by a burn. The soft golden tints of Maud's hair as she sat in the bow of the window were framed against the neat little front garden with its early roses still wearing their diamond drops of early-morning dew.

Maud had expressly not been invited to Culbrech House and the celebratory dinner, nor had she expected to be. She had not been there for a long time, and in fact the only member of the family whom she had seen to talk to since she had moved to Cluny had been Jean. Jean had paid her several visits and spent most of the time talking to her about God and how they, herself and Maud, would find refuge and solace in Him – refuge from a masculine world and solace for the hurt that they had both suffered at the hands of the opposite sex. Maud had borne Jean's well-intentioned ramblings with patience, knowing that the girl wanted to be her friend. But she had always been glad to see her go. There was no animosity between Maud and Lady Maclaren, but after she had left Culbrech, their relationship had been allowed to atrophy until now it was as if it had never existed. If they should chance to meet, they would smile and murmur a greeting to each other, but they were not friends, only acquaintances. The impossible friendship had sadly died an inevitable death on the day that Lady Maclaren had decided that Maud represented a threat to her son.

Maud looked up as Maggie entered the room.

'What is it, Maggie?'

'Please, Miss Maud, are you going to Beauly today? To see the regiment, I mean?'

'I don't know,' said Maud. 'I've thought about it, but I can't really make up my mind. Do you want to go?'

'Oh, yes, miss,' replied Maggie. 'Ma mannie's coming home.'

'What about your children?' asked Maud.

'They'll be fine wi' their gran',' said Maggie.

'I suppose you'll want some time off to be with your husband when he arrives?'

'Aye, miss, I would. Would that be all right?'

'Of course.'

'We'd better wait to find out when he's getting his leave,' said Maggie, and Maud smiled agreement. 'Are you going into Beauly, miss?'

'I don't know,' replied Maud.

'You could take the bairn, she'd like it fine, and she's old enough now. Och, miss, she'd love the flags and the colour and the pipes, and all the cheering and the shouting. The whole town'll be there.'

And Andrew and Willie, thought Maud. She would like to see them again. In her mind, and in the solitude of the life she had created for herself, she had confused images of both of them. It was mostly Willie that she thought of. This was natural, she supposed, since it was Willie who had kept writing to her. His letters had never been long, and had never been very informative. Just a few lines telling her that he was all right, Master Andrew was all right, and he hoped that she was all right. She had written little notes in reply, assuring Willie that she too was all right, and that everybody else in the glen was all right. The letters had stopped about three months ago, but then she knew that they were on their way home, and that she would soon be seeing him again. She came to a decision. After all, they had come across twelve thousand miles of ocean, and here she was wondering whether or not she should travel the five miles into Beauly to greet them on their homecoming. Yes, she would go, and she would take Naomi with her, and she would give Naomi a little flag to wave while she cheered as she watched the soldiers march by.

For herself, she did not really mind whether or not she spoke to them. Willie knew where to find her. And if Andrew wanted to, it would not be difficult for him to find out where she was. So it was arranged that they would have an early lunch, then take the gig, Maggie driving with her firm, well-practised hands, and drive into Beauly – Maud and Maggie and Naomi.

'Och, I'm so glad,' said Maggie. 'Thank you, miss.'

'A moment, Maggie.' Maud was rummaging about in her work basket. 'Ah, yes, here it is. I thought I had it. Take this and tie it around your bonnet.' She handed Maggie a wide piece of scarlet velvet ribbon.

'Thank you, miss,' said Maggie, delighted. 'But if you dinna mind, I'll make a bow of it for ma dress. For it is ma mutch I shall be wearing on ma heed.'

'Battalion, atten – shun!' The newly appointed Regimental Sergeant Major William Bruce gazed critically at the men drawn up by half-companies in columns of four.

There were just over four hundred of them left out of the thousand who had left Scotland five years before. But they were still the 148th, and they bore themselves proudly as Highlanders should. They stood on the outskirts of Beauly preparing to march into the town which was to be their home.

'Parade will fix bayonets. Parade fi-i-ix bayonets! Keep your heads up there. Don't let me catch you looking down. Sloooop arms!'

The rifles clattered in unison as the battalion came to the slope.

'Now you horrible lot!' roared Willie. 'Try and get this into your thick skulls. Oor toon has made us their regiment. Youse are going to be allowed to march through Beauly with bayonets fixed, colours flying, and band playing. There are no other sodjers in the whole British army who can dae that. So ye'll remember the honour that has been done tae ye and for once in your scruffy, clarty lives, ye'll be smart, ye'll be respectful, and ye'll be proud o' the uniform that yees are wearing.'

Willie walked over to Andrew, who had just put up the crown of a major. He had been appointed adjutant just the day before, Chisholm having taken over B Company.

'Hundred and forty-eighth present and correct, sir.'

Andrew returned Willie's salute. 'Fall in the officers,' he called, and then marched over to where his father was standing. He came to attention and saluted.

'Yes, Andrew, what's left of them.'

'Beg pardon, sir?' Andrew did not understand his father's tone.

'It is a long time since someone first stood before me and told me that the 148th were present and correct.'

'Yes, sir,' said Andrew, still bemused.

'Thank you, Andrew,' said the colonel.

Andrew raised his eyebrows slightly. There was a gentleness in his father's voice that he was not accustomed to hearing. He marched back to his place.

The colonel looked down the ranks of the regiment. There were under half of them left, only half of those men who had sailed from Scotland all those years ago. The rest would never be seen again. Of those who remained, possibly up to forty per cent would claim their discharge, and that would bring his strength down to one and a half companies. But they were a fine one and a half companies, blooded under fire, bonded together as only fighting men can be, comrades, brothers-in-arms. The nucleus was still there, and from it the regiment would blossom as from a single seed, back to its full power and strength.

They were a brave sight, their kilts, the multicolour of the tartan, the diced tops of their stockings over snow-white spats, boots gleaming, bayonets glinting in the sun, and the breeze gentling their feather bonnets, making them look like living things. And now, all that was left, this pathetic remnant, were returning home; these who had been spared from the battles they had fought and the tropical diseases which had accomplished much more than any human enemy they had encountered. They were going on leave. And in the bars and around the peat fires throughout the Highlands, there would be much talk, and tales would be told of great deeds. Not many of them would be true, but it would not matter. They would be soldiers' tales. Soldiers who had come home from the wars. Then the colonel thought of those other hearths, those desolate hearths which would never see their men again. He would do whatever he could about that, to soften the agony, to assuage the loneliness.

Tonight he was going to announce his retirement. Then he would be able to devote more time and solace to those who had suffered the loss of their men. It was a good thing to have their new headquarters here at Beauly. The men would be near to their homes, and they would be able to be released to go and help with the harvest, and where they could inspire fresh young blood to take the Queen's shilling.

For today, though, there was this parade. They were to show themselves to their town and to their womenfolk, who had waited so long for this moment.

Today he would not ride his charger, he would march at the head of his men. He wanted them to feel that he was their brother, that he was proud to be numbered in their company, and in the company of those who would not return but whose spirits would undoubtedly be at their side at this moment. It was the last time and he wanted them to know that he was one of *them*. He took his place at the head of the column and squared his shoulders.

'Pipe-major!' he called, and as the pipes played the first plaintive notes of the regimental march, he continued, 'Battalion will advance in columns of four. By the right quick march.'

They had assembled only a couple of hundred yards from the boundary of the town. Before them lay the earthworks of the new railway line which they would have to cross before entering High Street, which would lead them down the last quarter of a mile to the market square. In the street and square, they would be greeted by a mass of colour, of silks and prints and taffetas, of kilts and tweeds and homespun dresses, of the good and the bad, of the whole population who had turned out to greet them. Even Jimmy Henderson would be there.

Nobody knew how old Jimmy was. He might have been anything between forty and seventy. He never washed and seemed always to have a four days' growth of black beard on his craggy grey face. Invariably, in the pocket of his tattered tweed jacket, there would be the ubiquitous half-bottle. From somewhere Jimmy had found a stick and he was marching up and down in front of the crowd, swaying and shouting. As he passed them, matrons tucked their small children behind their skirts, men turned and looked the other way for fear that Jimmy would come to them and demand that they take a dram from him. For Jimmy was drunk. Not that that was anything strange, for Jimmy was always drunk.

'Huzza for the 148th!' he called, and promptly sat down in the middle of the road, where after a moment, he lay back and fell asleep, snoring violently. Jimmy had no home. Winter and summer alike, he slept in hedgerows or empty barns, and worked at anything that was going whenever he ran out of whisky. He was a good worker, when he was sober, and no one disliked Jimmy, but no one sought his company.

Two men among the crowd lining the street came out into the middle of the road, picked Jimmy up, snores and all, and deposited him gently in a shop doorway. There they knew he would sleep it off, and upon waking, reach for his half-bottle and wonder what the hell had happened to the procession.

While this was happening, the battalion had entered High Street and were approaching the square, where they formed up on three sides of the rostrum. Lord MacDonald spoke briefly of their bravery, and how they were all grateful to see their return. And then the minister spoke at length of the devils which might beset the town if they did not behave themselves. Not that he said it in so many words; it was more subtle: 'I know fine that these brave lads will respect the honour of their new home. They will not get drunk! They will observe the Sabbath, and only the married men will have any contact with the women of the town, or all of them will face the wrath of the Lord.'

They listened to the haranguing with patience, because they had to. And then Colonel Maclaren thanked everybody and it was all over. Then they marched off again, back the way they had come, to enter their new barracks.

This time as they marched down the High Street, it was different. Many, mostly women, broke through and ran alongside the file where their loved one marched, pressing little gifts and bunches of flowers into the men's hands.

There in the crowd, Maggie had looked earnestly and long as they had passed the first time, peering and searching for a glimpse of Angus. By the time they had started their return, she was convinced that he was not there. As the head of the column reached the point where she was standing with Maud and little Naomi, she ran out into the road alongside Andrew.

'Where's me mannie?' she demanded of him.

Andrew did not reply. He kept on marching, looking fixedly ahead. He had feared something, he knew not what, if ever he saw Maggie again. He had prayed that it would not happen. He would rather have stormed the breach at Taku again than face her.

'Where is he?' she yelled again, tugging at his sleeve and he shook her off.

'Awa' wi' ye, woman,' said Willie.

'I want ma mannie!' shouted Maggie. 'Where is he?'

Andrew glanced down at her only for a moment, and tried to fight the thoughts that came flooding back to him – thoughts of that afternoon in the heather; thoughts of standing in the Maori hut; and thoughts of Angus swinging from the yardarm.

'He's not here,' he snapped.

She tugged at his arm. 'Where is he, then? Is he ill? I want to know what you've done wi' ma Angus.'

Andrew tore her hand from his arm and looked appealingly in the direction of Willie Bruce.

'All right, sir,' said Willie, 'I'll take care of this.'

Breaking ranks, he took Maggie by the elbow and steered her to the side of the street.

'I ken ye, do I no?' said Willie, 'You're Maggie Taylor.'

'Aye, *you* know me, all right. You're the one that took ma mannie awa'.'

'What's your name now?'

'Buchannan, Maggie Buchannan, and I want ma Angus.'

So that was it, thought Willie. 'Your mannie's dead,' he said. 'Like many more who went wi' us.'

Maggie stood for a moment, her lips quivering. 'Deed, you say?'

'Aye,' said Willie. 'I'm sorry.'

'Then why was I no told like the others?'

'He died on the voyage home. There was no way to let you know before we got back.'

'How — how —' She was holding back the tears that were trying to flood through.

'I canna tell ye that,' said Willie.

'Why can ye no tell me?'

'Does it matter?' he replied. 'I'm no medical man. I do not understand these things.' And then as she became silent, 'Have ye got a place to go?'

'Oh, aye,' she said, and her voice was toneless. 'I have a place to go. But who do I go to?' she wanted to cry.

'I'll mention it to Major Maclaren.'

'No!' She spat the word. 'I'll ha' nothing to dae wi' a man who canna keep his word!' And she started to cry, silently.

Willie looked at her for a moment, but could find nothing else to say. 'I must get back to ma place,' and he trotted away towards the head of the column, leaving her, a forlorn and dejected figure in her homespun skirt and blouse.

Maggie walked aimlessly away to the back of the crowd who, sensing that there was something wrong, parted to let her through. She took off the scarlet bow which she had pinned to her dress and let it fall from her hand, and then she pulled the mutch from her head, that proud and now meaningless sign of married respectability, looked at it for a moment, and threw it into the gutter.

'Care and maintenance party, attention! Present arms!'

The command to salute the colours was given by Major Macmillan as the battalion marched on to the parade ground of their new home for the first time. Major Macmillan had been left behind in Scotland when the battalion had gone overseas. With him were forty-eight men and one senior N.C.O., Sergeant Grant. They had been responsible for the equipment and regimental treasures left at Perth and the transfer to Beauly when the new barracks were completed. Macmillan had been given the task because he was the oldest officer in the battalion, over fifty – really past the age at which a man should be ordered on to active service. At first sight, he was a most fearsome individual, mainly because of a deep scar which ran from his left ear right down his cheek, the legacy of a sabre slash he received as a cornet. This scar had the effect of making his smile – and he smiled frequently, being a man of amiable disposition – look like a fiendish grin.

Colonel Maclaren returned the salute and the two ensigns bearing the colours turned smartly in the direction of the officers' mess, where they would place the colours in their position in the dining room. The colonel then dismissed the officers and handed over the parade to R.S.M. Bruce to deal with the allocation of barracks.

The building which was to house C Company was like all the others, divided by a central staircase, one half-company being housed on the right and the other on the left. On the ground floor there were two rooms for the sergeants in charge of each half-company. The men were detailed off, twenty to a room. The ground floor left contained such worthies as Frankie Gibson, Alex Munroe, and Corporal Campbell. The corporal occupied the bed nearest the door because this was the way it was always done, the man in charge of the room always taking that position. The beds themselves were in two rows, leaving a central area, and in the wall on the side opposite the barrack square was a large black iron fireplace beside which stood a highly polished zinc coal bucket. Gibson and Munroe claimed the beds which were two removed from the fire. There was reason in this. In the winter it was a great advantage to be near the fire, but not too near, as every man was responsible for the cleanliness of his own bedspace as far as the centre of the room, and those nearest to the fire always collected a much higher proportion of grime than the others. So about two away from the fire was about the best compromise. Above each bed was a green tin locker with double doors in which kit was stored strictly according to regulations, and on the bed, a rolled straw palliasse, a hard canvas-covered cylinder which passed for a pillow, and four neatly folded coarse brown blankets. This was home, the home they had dreamed of throughout the long years they had sweated it out in the east and far south.

It was a busy time for Willie Bruce, inspecting billets, settling arguments about bed spaces, making sure that each man had his entitlement of bedding, soap, and towels. The latter were to be used in the ablution block at the rear of the barrack block – a row of zinc basins and a hand pump for cold water at one end. Hot water was of course an unheard-of luxury.

Willie reported to the individual company commanders as soon as he was sure that each company had been satisfactorily billeted. After inspecting C Company, he reported to Andrew.

'They seem to be settled, sir,' he said.

'Good,' replied Andrew. 'By the way, sergeant major, I have a request to make.'

'Sir?' said Willie. He was enough of a soldier to realize that a request usually meant work.

'You must understand that this is not an order, but ...'

There was always a but, thought Willie.

'But the junior officers have asked me if I would ask you if you would do orderly officer tonight. We have all been invited to Culbrech House for a dinner, and naturally everyone would like to be there.'

'Och, aye, sir,' said Willie. 'I doubt I would be able to get awa' from camp tonight, anyhow. I'll do it.'

Of course, he had treated the request as a command, even though it was not his turn. But on the other hand, he would not be sorry to spend the evening in the bar of the sergeant's mess, and getting acquainted with his new surroundings.

In the mess, he sought out Sergeant Grant, the man they had left behind. Grant, like Major Macmillan, was an older man who had become a senior N.C.O. more by virtue of his long service than by any special aptitude on his part. He was fat, and viewed from the side, his sporran seemed to be well in advance of the rest of his figure. He was no athlete, but a slow painstaking plodder who could be counted on to get the job done if he had time enough, and of course he had plenty of time to prepare for the arrival of the battalion.

'You did a good job, Charlie.' Willie addressed him by his Christian name, as was the mess custom.

'Thanks, Willie,' he replied. 'Ye've had a rough time? What happened to R.S.M. Mackintosh?'

'Naebody kens. It was just aboot the only shot fired in that action. He was a guid man.'

'Aye,' said Grant, sipping his beer. 'He was a guid mannie, all right. And wee Alex, too?'

Willie did not want to talk about wee Alex. 'Aye. Well, they're all bedded down, and now I suppose that the recruiting will start. Will you be on that?'

'Nae,' said Grant, looking down at his great girth. 'I'm no the sort of figure that's gonna inspire young lads to tak the shillin'.'

'Well,' said Willie, grinning as Grant patted his belly. 'I'd best be awa' to the men's mess. What's for supper here?'

'Venison. The colonel sent us a beast.'

'That was nice o' him. I'd better not tell the men.'

They both laughed and Willie went off on his rounds.

The great banqueting hall at Culbrech House was always a magnificent sight. Its plain whitewashed stone walls, its blackened oak beams and pillars arching away into the high ceiling gave an almost cathedral-like atmosphere. There were huge black iron sconces with their great guttering candles set into the walls, and a massive fireplace surmounted by the inevitable wildcat's head. The great black oak doors, made of timbers that were older than the house itself, were studded with iron bolts and huge brass fitments. The floor and the long refectory dining table were of polished oak, the table too beautiful ever to be shrouded by a tablecloth. This evening, the room looked even more magnificent than usual. The regimental silver had been delivered to the house direct from Perth; and Sergeant Watt, the senior mess steward, a man whose fastidiousness and attention to every little detail belied his origins in the slums of the Gorbals district of Glasgow, had spent the whole afternoon preparing the banqueting hall for the dinner. The silver had been polished until it shone like mirrors. The crystal gleamed and sparkled as the light danced off its cut facets. Fresh roses had been gathered from the garden and spread in profusion on the long polished table. Each place setting was exactly eighteen inches from the beginning of the next. Sergeant Watt had measured this in each and every case with the ruler he always carried on these occasions.

Everything had gone extremely smoothly, apart from one slight altercation between the butler MacKay and Sergeant Watt, both of whom claimed seniority. But as in all the best arguments, it was settled by compromise. MacKay would be concerned only with the wines, while the stewards and maids would be under the command of Sergeant Watt who would have responsibility for the serving of the meal. When the subject of carving was broached, it was decided that the chef who had been brought in from Inverness for the occasion should be allocated this task, thus saving another argument.

Lady Maclaren had resolved that this would be a day to remember. Apart from anything else, she was determined to impress the Worthings. She was well aware that the great country houses of England and the Highlands were two different animals. There was an easy social atmosphere in Scotland which was never apparent in England. Social divisions were not in any way so clearly delineated. The clan and the estate were one, and in the case of the Maclarens, that also included the regiment. Whoever belonged to any one of those three establishments was, irrespective of birth or wealth, a member of the family. So she had planned an evening more formal than most, but not so formal that the Worthings might feel that they were at just another English country house. The last few years had increased her desire to see Emma and Andrew matched. Richard Simpson, it seemed, would marry Margaret, and she could not really oppose that match. Simpson was invaluable to the estate, especially as none of the Maclaren men seemed to have any real interest beyond the regiment. No, she could not complain about Richard, nor Margaret, for that matter. If they married, they would undoubtedly remain at Culbrech, and the estate could not fail to benefit from their union. Emma, of course, was another matter. Her father was an extremely wealthy man and would no doubt provide a most welcome infusion of capital into the estate should his only daughter marry her only son. Yes, she thought, it would all be very suitable.

She had little doubt that the match could be arranged and that the young would do as their parents bid them. Andrew would obey because marriage with Emma Worthing could only increase his prospects in his military career, and she had already gathered from the rather cold, emotionless Emma that she at least was sufficiently satisfied with the idea.

In that torpid half-hour before dinner was served, when guests all hang on to their drinks waiting for the happening to begin, Emma Worthing turned to Andrew, who had been presented to her as her escort for the evening.

'Well, Andrew,' she said, 'I think that our parents have made up their minds.'

'I beg your pardon,' replied Andrew. 'I don't understand.'

'About us, I mean,' said Emma. 'They are determined that we shall get married. What do you think about it?'

Andrew felt the blood rising up from under his collar. 'Well, I – er – that is, I hadn't thought about it very seriously yet.'

'Oh, but you should have,' said Emma. She had thought about it very seriously indeed. She was over twenty-four. Five years ago, she had decided that Andrew Maclaren was worth waiting for and she had waited. Above all, she had let other opportunities pass her by, and now, at her age, there would not be so many more. She had gambled and she was fiercely determined not to lose. 'After all,' she continued, 'we *are* what is called a good match,' and she smiled.

It was quite an attractive smile, and Andrew was rather surprised to find it so. As a matter of fact, Emma Worthing was by no means an unattractive woman. Tall and slim, bright-eyed and clear of complexion, she was a typical English thoroughbred, and had the confidence and assurance that went with her breeding. Also, she had no illusions about her future. She accepted the fact that it was her destiny to become a brood mare to an aristocratic family other than her own. If she failed in this, there would be absolutely no purpose to her life. She had decided that Andrew was most suitable, and in her abrupt and forthright manner, was determined to settle the issue immediately.

Andrew, for his part, wondered whether there was any passion under that cold and superbly controlled exterior. But he also knew well that if he was ever to find out, he would have to marry her.

He returned her smile. 'What do you suggest we should do?' he asked.

'Man proposes, woman disposes,' she replied, still smiling.

'I see,' said Andrew. 'Do you think we ought to get to know each other a little better first?'

'I don't see much point in that,' said Emma. 'After all, however well one knows someone before marriage, they are different people after the event, or so I have been told.'

'Yes, I see what you mean,' said Andrew. He paused; he was thinking of Maud. Was what Emma said true? Was the illusion just that? Not that it mattered now; the die was cast. He knew that, and in another moment he would be committed to this stranger who sat beside him. Yet he could not help comparing the two women in his mind. Maud he could think of in no terms other that that of womanhood. Emma? Perhaps it was better not to think, just to let matters take the course which had been ordained for him.

'Well, then,' he said. 'Shall we?'

She looked at him and raised one eyebrow quizzically. 'Major Maclaren, are you proposing to me?' she said, and there was a touch of banter in her tone.

'I'm not quite sure – yes – I suppose I am—'

'Very well, then,' she replied. 'I accept. Now we can tell them and they can make the announcement at dinner, and they'll all be happy. Whether or not *we* shall be is entirely in the lap of the gods, but I know we'll try.'

'I suppose that I should go and ask your father's permission.'

'Oh, fiddlesticks!' she replied. 'Our possible engagement is the only reason that we are here. Daddy has always wanted to be a Scottish laird, and if I marry you he'll succeed, even if it's only second hand. Also, he knows that the Highlands are uneconomic, but he's prepared to pay for that, and we can well afford it.'

'Really!' Andrew was shocked at hearing the truth he knew so well put into words.

'Don't worry, I wouldn't marry you if I didn't like you. I'm only for sale on my own terms. Anyway, Daddy will be delighted; he's absolutely set on it. I believe that your people are too.'

Andrew was at a loss for words for a while, and then he said, 'Oughtn't I to kiss you or something?'

'Well, you can if you want to. It's not necessary,' and suddenly her tone became serious. 'Andrew, I shall try to make you happy, and I shall try to be a good army wife. I do know the form. I suppose you will probably find me a little direct, but I'm a great believer in arranged marriages, and I also believe that two normal, reasonable people, man and woman, can make a go of marriage. I think also that they have to be determined that the basis of their marriage is going to be friendship at best. I don't believe in what the novelists call love. I think that romance is more like a disease, and I am absolutely certain that infatuation is the worst possible basis for a life-long union.' Emma preferred Jane Austen to the Brontës when it came to romance. 'I have studied you. I have studied your background. I think you are young for your age, but I like you as a person, and I'm sure that you and I will make a go of it.'

'I'll try,' said Andrew, and he kissed her lightly on the cheek.

'Well,' she said, smiling at him, 'I suppose I had better go and tell Mummy and Daddy that their plan has reached fruition. And I suppose that you had better go and do likewise with yours. Shall we tell them that they can announce it to-night?'

'I suppose it's as good a time as any,' said Andrew, and they wandered off in the direction of their respective parents.

Dinner was, as intended, a magnificent affair. Lady Maclaren had determined to give the returning warriors a real taste of Scotland. They started with cock-o-leekie soup, then fresh salmon from the Glass, and of course haggis. This strange 'thing' which Burns had described as 'great chieftain o' the puddin' race' proved something of a chore for the Worthings. The general attacked it in soldierly fashion, refusing to be intimidated by the speckled brown lump on his plate. His wife took one forkful and pushed it aside, and Emma secretly resolved that it would never appear on her table. However, there was better to come. The haggis was followed by a huge saddle of mutton from their own hill, and each course was piped around the table by the regimental pipe major. It was then deposited on the massive oak sideboard where the Inverness chef carved and portioned at a speed and with a dexterity to watch and admire.

Just before the ladies retired, the colonel rose to his feet and made his speech. He announced his retirement and told them that the command of the regiment would now fall on Major, shortly to be Lieutenant Colonel, Macmillan. This was greeted with polite applause, everyone realizing that the appointment was primarily that of a caretaker until Andrew was old enough to take command.

'And also,' the colonel continued, 'I have the greatest pleasure in announcing the betrothal of my only son Andrew to Emma, daughter of General and Mrs Worthing. I know that you will join with me in wishing them all future happiness in the years ahead. I am sure that that will give the ladies something to talk about.'

There was a burst of applause, and some good-natured laughter, and it was just as the ladies were rising to retire to the withdrawing room that she appeared.

She had got in through the front door, along the passage by the kitchens, and up to the banqueting hall by way of the stairs in the deserted east tower. She stood there like a wrathful angel, just inside the door in her plain homespun skirt and cotton blouse, her brown hair loose and untidy and her eyes red with crying.

'Andrew Maclaren,' she shouted. 'I want Andrew Maclaren.'

Everyone stopped and stared at Maggie Buchannan, too shocked to utter a word. She pointed at Andrew.

'You,' she said, and there was venom on her tongue as she hissed the word, pointing at Andrew. 'You're the one. You're the one that murdered ma mannie.'

General Worthing was the first to find his voice. 'Is this a madwoman?' he called.

Andrew rose to his feet. 'No, Maggie, it is not true.'

'I heered it all. Frankie Gibson told his wife and that bitch came to gi' me her sympathy. You hanged him, did ye no? You made me a promise, that day that ye took me in the heather.

You promised you'd get him oot o' the army. You lied to me, Andrew Maclaren.'

'No, Maggie, I tried, believe me, I tried.'

She spat on the floor. 'Dinna lie nae mair. I ken it all. I ken weel what ye did. I ken what it was you told them and how they hanged him for it. I curse you, Andrew Maclaren, you and all your bloody regiment. May ye never know a day's happiness, as I never shall.'

At last she was silent, and the colonel nodded to MacKay. 'Take her out,' he said gently.

'Dinna touch me,' she said through her tears. 'I'm awa'.'

Suddenly she held her head up proudly and walked from the room.

There was a long silence.

'Who was that person?' said Emma calmly. 'And what was all that about?'

Andrew looked at her, expressionless. What could he say? He was not a coward, he had proved that on the battlefield. But this was something very different, something beyond his comprehension. He could not fight back. He could only wish that it had not happened, that somehow it would go away.

'Andrew.' The voice of his father, who leaned across the table, spoke to him quietly. 'That was Buchannan's wife?'

'Yes, sir,' replied Andrew. 'Her name is Maggie.'

'Poor woman, I'm sorry for her,' said the colonel. Then he turned to the others and, raising his voice slightly, said by way of explanation, 'You must understand, that woman's husband was hanged on the ship on the voyage home. Just before we left New Zealand, he was caught red-handed by my son here and Sergeant Major Bruce. He was tried by court martial and found guilty of murder and the violation of a native woman. Andrew was in no way culpable. At the court martial, I was very conscious of Andrew's reluctance to give what was inevitably damning evidence. Not that it mattered. All of Andrew's evidence was fully corroborated by Regimental Sergeant Major Bruce. There could have been no other verdict and no other sentence; it was a harsh moral and military necessity. I am sorry that she had to find out. It would have been so much better if we could have left her with the illusion that her husband had died on active service. But unfortunately, in a community as tightly knit as ours, secrets are very difficult to keep.' He tried to put the facts before his guests calmly, and with dignity, hoping that the matter could be let rest. Conversation had died, the officers were embarrassed, and the others, including the ladies, just did not know what to say.

After a long awkward silence, the colonel turned to Lady Maclaren. 'I think, my dear—' he said.

'Yes, of course,' she replied. 'Ladies?' and she started towards the withdrawing room.

In silence, MacKay solemnly placed the decanter of port in front of Sir Henry. He removed the stopper, filled his glass, and sent the port on its way around the table. Conversation after the loyal toast was halting and embarrassed. The officers, who had formed the majority of the guests, and most of whom had actually witnessed the execution of Angus Buchannan, did not want to talk about it. The other guests did not want to ask. But it was the only subject that was on everyone's mind. Chisholm tried.

'Pity we didn't get back in time for the twelfth,' he said. He was referring of course to the opening of the grouse season on the twelfth of August, and it was now well into September.

Someone replied, 'Yes,' and the conversation died again.

Sir Henry realized that it was no good. There could be no after-dinner conversation and he was rightly sure that his guests would rather leave than continue in that awkward atmosphere. Only about ten minutes after the port had made its first circuit, he suggested that they join the ladies, and within minutes of their entering the withdrawing room, guests were already making their farewells and leaving.

It was much later that evening, the guests had gone, and only the Maclarens and the Worthings were left in the house. General Worthing, who had been ominously silent since dinner, came over to Andrew.

'Andrew,' he said, 'I want to know the whole truth about this business. If I am to let you marry my daughter, I have got to be assured that you are a gentleman.'

Andrew had had a miserable evening, knowing well that he was the subject of every whispered conversation in the room.

'I really don't know what to say, sir,' he said. 'You heard Mrs Buchannan and my father. I think that you must draw your own conclusions.'

'Humph!' said the general. 'I can only draw the obvious, and I don't want my daughter married to a whoremonger.'

'Sir,' replied Andrew, 'you are a stranger to our glen. No Englishman can understand the relationship that exists within a Scottish clan. It is a family, and Maggie Buchannan is part of that family, just as the regiment is an extension of that family. There are no whores in our family, and no whoremongers, and I find your remark extremely insulting.'

'And so do I,' said Emma, who had joined them unnoticed. 'Daddy, I am not going to marry a whoremonger. I am going to marry Andrew, with or without your blessing. I think we are going to be very happy together. I have no interest in the past, only in the future.'

Andrew looked at her in amazed admiration. He was pleased and reassured, and at that moment he knew that he was now committed to this woman who was to become his wife. Here was a greater strength than his. 'Thank you, Emma,' he said. 'But—'

'No buts, Andrew,' said Emma. 'And Daddy, we will not refer to this matter ever again.'

Suddenly the general broke into a broad grin. 'By gad, Emma,' he said, 'I admire your spirit. Go on, then, marry the lad. But don't blame me if—'

'I shan't.'

General Worthing looked at them for a moment and then said, 'I suppose that if you two are going to get married, you are entitled to some time alone. I'll take myself off to bed. Goodnight.' And, without waiting for a reply, he left them.

After her father had gone, Andrew turned to Emma. 'What she said was true, you know. Most of it, anyway.'

Emma ignored the implication that her fiancé had had another woman. 'Did you really try to get her husband out?' she said.

'Yes,' said Andrew, but there was some hesitation in his reply.

'You mean that you could have tried harder?'

'Yes, I could, but how was I to know?'

'Naturally. And I think that the matter is best forgotten. I am going to bed. You may kiss me goodnight if you wish.'

She held up her face and Andrew kissed her lightly on the cheek.

'Goodnight, Andrew,' she said, and left the room.

Andrew stood for a moment looking at the closed door through which she had gone, and then he went over to the sideboard and poured himself a very large whisky.

13

The September rain, urged along by the near gale-force wind, was rattling against the windows of Cluny Cottage, where Maud Westburn was making her pot of afternoon tea. The events of the previous day had left her as confused as ever. She had not wanted to go and watch the parade, and yet she had been unable to keep away. She had seen Willie and Andrew in all their regimental finery as they had marched past her, and the sight of them had stirred her emotions, dragging back memories and crowding her thoughts with a mass of feelings which she could not analyse.

Maggie was not with her. She had not seen her since she had dashed out of the crowd and run alongside Andrew looking for Angus. Maud had not been surprised by this. She rather expected that Maggie would be spending the next few nights at home with her husband. She of course had heard nothing of the occurrences at Culbrech House the night before. She had allowed Maggie to persuade her to go to the parade, but she knew that she would have gone anyhow; at least she knew that now. Having seen them, and knowing that they were safe, there was nothing left for her to do but wait, wonder, and hope that at least one of them would call.

On the other hand, perhaps she almost hoped that neither one would come to see her. She did not know. It had been such a very long time, and she did not know if her mental images of the two men were real. They inhabited her dreams. Things happened when she was asleep, or daydreaming, which made her blush; or, remembering the horror of Cawnpore, filled her with revulsion. They were persons created in fantasy and demanding the materialism which would either confirm or destroy her images.

She carried a tray of tea things into the sitting room and placed it on a small table in the bow window. Just as she was about to sit down, she looked through the net curtains and saw a man walking down the garden path. It was the barely discernible figure of a soldier in uniform, his head bent low against the driving rain. She felt very weak and very excited all at once.

She hurried over to the mirror and straightened her hair, listening for the knock on the door. She stood for a moment, and then started down the passage towards the door, so that she should not keep him waiting. She was almost there when the knock came. She flung open the door.

'Andr —' she started, and stopped.

The man looked up at her and grinned. 'Sorry, Miss Westburn, it's me, Willie.'

It was indeed a very bedraggled Willie Bruce. The rain was bucketing down and Willie's feather bonnet looked rather like a cat that had fallen into the rain barrel. There were little globules of water dripping off the end of his nose, but he was still smiling.

'Welcome back, Sergeant Bruce,' said Maud, and then seeing the royal coat of arms, his new badges of rank, added 'Sorry, it really is Mr Bruce now?'

Willie nodded his head.

'I'm sorry, that was silly of me, Willie! You had better come inside.' And she took him by the elbow and steered him into the little hall.

'I'm afu' wet, miss,' said Willie as he came into the house dripping water on to the carpet.

'You'll have some tea,' she said firmly, ignoring his remark and leading him into the sitting room.

He looked around at the neat chintzes and said, 'I'd love a cup of tea, Miss Westburn, but should we no have it in the kitchen? I don't want to be spoiling your pretty furniture. Just look at me.' He glanced down at his dripping form and then repeated, 'I'm afu' wet.'

'I can see that,' said Maud. 'But don't bother about it. We have clean rain in the Highlands. That, at least, I have discovered.'

Willie sat gingerly on the edge of one of the chintz-covered armchairs while Maud hurried to the kitchen to get another cup. He sat there, acutely conscious of every drop of water that fell from him, until she returned.

'Thank you, Miss Westburn,' he said as she handed him his cup.

She sat silently watching him as he drank his tea. When he had drained his cup, she offered him another.

'Thank you,' he replied. 'You thought I was Major Andrew again?'

'Yes,' she said. 'I remember the first time.' And then with forced casualness she added, 'He was a captain then, so you have both come up in the world.'

'You'll no be seeing the major for a while. He got himself engaged yesterday, and his lady's staying at the big hoose, a general's daughter, I'm told. He'll be spending his time wi' her.'

'Oh,' was all Maud could say. It was strangely surprising to her how little effect the announcement seemed to have, but she stood silent for a moment, looking out the window.

'Is there something wrong, Miss Westburn?'

'Er – no.' And then, realizing that she really meant it, she added, 'No, there is nothing wrong.' She turned to him, changing the subject. 'You know, if you do not call me Maud, I cannot possibly call you Willie.'

'Och, I couldna do that,' said Willie.

'I'm sure you could,' she replied. 'Just try it.'

'Well,' he said doubtfully, 'Maud. How's that?'

'Much better,' she smiled. 'It was kind of you to write,' she said. 'And it was very kind of you to come and see me.'

'Well, Miss – er – Maud,' replied Willie, 'I have no exactly come to see you. As a matter of fact, I really came over to see Maggie Buchannan. I was told that she was staying here.'

'Oh,' said Maud, and she was disappointed. 'Well, she's not

here. She'll be over at her mother's cottage with her husband.'

'No,' said Willie. 'No, she's not with her husband.'

'Didn't she meet him at the parade yesterday?'

'She couldna have done that. You see, her husband's dead. I thought that somebody should come along and talk to her.'

Maud was silent for a moment. 'Poor Maggie, what a terrible thing to happen. How?'

'If you'll forgive me, that's not for me to say. But it's nice to have found you.'

She smiled at him and started sipping her tea to cover her embarrassment. 'Well, Willie Bruce, tell me what you have been doing. You're not married yet, are you?'

'Me married?' Willie laughed. 'A man would be a fool to get himself married while he was on active service.'

'Have you ever thought about marriage? Seriously, I mean?' She did not know if she was making small talk or not. 'Is there no one?'

'Aye,' said Willie, 'there is a lassie, but she doesna know. Anyway, she wouldna look at me.'

'Why ever not?' said Maud. 'You've never spoken to her?'

'Not about such things,' said Willie. 'You see, I'm just a common soldier. She's a lady, a proper lady.'

'There's nothing common about you, Willie Bruce. I can think of no woman who would not be proud to call you her man, unless she was a fool.'

'Are you sure that you mean that?' he said.

She realized that he was looking at her with a peculiar intensity, and she realized in that same moment that she was the woman to whom he was referring. She coloured slightly and looked down. She had to gather her thoughts. 'Yes, Willie,' she said in a very small voice. And then she looked up at him, this great bear of a man overflowing her armchair and making it look small and insignificant against his massive frame. She was very solemn and looked him straight in the eyes as she said, 'Yes, I mean that.'

'And you know who ma lassie is?' he said.

'Yes, I know who she is.'

'Oh, ye bonny wee thing,' said Willie, rising and standing over her. 'You've had ma heart since the first day I clapped eyes on you. I never believed that this was possible, but I want you for ma woman. I'm no an expert at the gentle ways of gentle-folk, but I can think of no higher calling than to guard and protect you for the rest of ma life. What do ye say, Maud? What is your answer?'

She did not reply immediately. He watched her as she moistened her lips with her tongue. He knew that there was something else that she had to say and he waited respectfully for her to say it.

'Before I answer,' she said, 'there is something you must know.' Maud walked to the door and turned back to him. 'Something I must show you. I shall only be a moment.'

Willie watched her leave the room, his thoughts in a turmoil. He felt that he had gambled all on a single throw, but somehow, he sensed that he had won.

In less than a minute she was back, accompanied by a child. The girl was about five years old, rather dark-skinned with straight black hair and deep brown eyes. She stared at Willie as she came into the room and hid behind Maud's skirt.

'Naomi,' said Maud, 'this is Mr Bruce. Say how do you do.'

'Hello,' said Naomi, taking a quick peek from behind Maud.

'Hello,' said Willie. 'The poor wee thing's shy, let her go.'

'She is my daughter,' said Maud, and waited for Willie's reaction.

There was none.

'Och, I know that,' he replied casually. 'Is that all you had to tell me? It's no verra much.'

'It doesn't make any difference?' There was wonder in her voice.

'What difference? Why should it? There's many a lad or lassie in the glen who doesna ken his father. I could be one of them. Would that matter? Does that make any difference? As far as I can see, I'll be getting twa for the price of one. That is, if —'

'Mummy, can I go and play now?' said the small voice behind her skirt.

'All right, darling, run along and don't forget to shut the door.'

They were alone again.

'Well, Willie, I think the question is, what do you say?'

'Nay, lassie. You've told me nothing I didna already ken. I still want ma answer. What is it to be?'

'I think,' she said, 'we had better go and see the minister. I think that I should like to be your wife.'

And then she was in his arms. He kissed her long and hard. She drew back, and looking into his face, just for a moment she saw Andrew.

14

It had arrived. Awkward and clumsy, it stood incongruously in the middle of the barrack square, looking for all the world like a bundle of sticks hanging between a pair of coach wheels. Soldiers off duty stood and stared at it and guessed its purpose. A farm implement perhaps? Some new device for the battalion kitchens? Many and farfetched were the theories as to its purpose. Corporal Campbell had been given the task of guarding it and, very conscious of his position and the fact that *he knew*, had allowed no one below the rank of sergeant to approach it. It was in fact a Gatling gun. This was the new American invention which was being tested, with a view to adoption, by the British army, and the 148th had been issued one of the test models for trials.

Sir Henry, who had had prior knowledge of its coming, had arrived from Culbrech House early in the morning, and anxiously awaited its uncrating like a child eager to find out what Santa Claus had brought him. When he had finally got to see it, he had enthused at great length, assuring everyone within earshot that it would undoubtedly revolutionize warfare. Colonel Macmillan, who did not share his faith in modern gadgetry, had remarked that the damned thing would probably never work, or if it did, it would break down.

Anyhow, they had all had a cautious look at it and taken a

walk around it; some of the more adventurous had even touched it. Then Corporal Campbell, being within earshot of most of the conversation, had ventured the suggestion that they might possibly fire it. Major Chisholm had resisted this idea out of hand. He maintained that such a machine would make war like a Lancashire cotton mill; no place for a gentleman.

Colonel Macmillan looked at his new charge sadly.

'I suppose that we ought to take it down to the butts and fire the damned thing,' he said.

The quartermaster, Captain Angus Cameron, who had been chatting to Andrew, came over to the C.O. 'I'm sorry, sir, but you can't fire it.'

'Why the devil not?'

'They haven't sent us any ammunition, sir, and they don't know when they will be getting any.'

'Sounds like the War House to me,' said Macmillan. 'Good. We can lock the blasted thing up and hope that they forget all about it. Sergeant major.'

'Sir,' replied Willie.

'Find this thing an empty hut and lock it up.'

And thus the machine gun was disposed of, at least for the moment, though Sir Henry went back to Culbrech House sad that he had not been able to have a demonstration.

The new arrival provoked a deal of discussion and speculation, all of which proved of little interest to the C.O. who, as soon as the opportunity arose, changed the subject to that of recruiting. They had formed four companies out of the remnants of their force, and the recruiting drive to get more men was in full swing. They were not doing badly, either; with the exception of H.Q. Company, all of the rest were increasing almost daily. The officer shortage had been eased, too, with the arrival of three ensigns, Farquhar, Grant, and Murray, from the Royal Military College at Sandhurst. These youngsters, their enthusiasm as shining as their bright new uniforms, had been shared out between A, B, and C Companies, where they supervised the training of the new recruits with a mixture of keenness and amateurism that resulted in a great deal of scathing comment in the sergeants' mess. However, as always, these three were rapidly summed up by the senior N.C.O.s. Farquhar and Grant, it seemed, would provide little trouble. They were typical of the young subalterns of the day – young, but not too bright, and willing to learn. A good sergeant would soon make a good officer of those two. Murray was not in quite the same class. He was a reflection of the changing times. He did not come from one of the landed families; in fact, his people were lawyers in Inverness and members of related professions. Donald Murray had joined the army intending to make it his career. Without ever being popular he had done well at Sandhurst and he had arrived at the 148th with a disconcerting knowledge of military law and tactics. Disconcerting, that is, to any N.C.O. who hoped to put one over on him.

In the officers' mess, the three new ensigns were accepted and Farquhar and Grant were soon at home. Murray, who was not wealthy by regimental standards and was unused to the boisterous behaviour of his younger comrades, kept very much to himself. He did, however, form one friendship and that was outside the mess – with Willie Bruce, who, like Murray, had his eyes set on a field marshal's baton.

It was a dull September evening. Dinner was over and most of them had left the mess. Chisholm was standing over by the fireplace in the anteroom nursing a glass of brandy and chatting to Murray.

'By the way,' said Chisholm, 'did you know that the R.S.M.'s getting married?'

'I knew that there was something in the wind,' replied Murray. 'He hasn't told me anything.'

'Is it true?' asked Farquhar, who had just joined them.

'Yes, he told the colonel today and his orderly told my batman, and my batman told me, so it's got to be true. Andrew,' he called.

Andrew was sitting smoking over on the other side of the room looking disgustedly at the weather outside. 'What is it, Ian?' he replied.

'You must have known about this, you might have told us.'

'About what?' asked Andrew. 'What's he talking about?' He turned to the small, dark, dapper figure of Donald Murray.

'About the R.S.M. getting married,' said Murray. 'He's a chum of yours, isn't he?'

'I promise you that this is the first I've heard of it,' said Andrew. 'Good luck to him, though, and I suppose we ought to have a whip round for a present.'

'Surprised that you didn't know. Anyhow, you do know his lady.'

'Do I?' said Andrew.

'Good Lord, yes, she's that girl you brought back from India. Westburn, isn't it? He saw the C.O. this morning and got the go-ahead.'

Andrew was not a little shaken by this piece of news; he resented it, though he knew that he had no right to do so.

'But I thought she had left the district,' he remarked, feeling irritated at the casual way Chisholm was nursing his brandy instead of answering.

'Not a bit of it,' said Chisholm, swallowing at last. 'She's got a cottage up the glen. Not short of money, I gather. Willie Bruce has done all right. Anyway, he's been seeing a great deal of her. Hasn't slept in barracks for nearly a month, except when he was orderly officer.'

The laughter which greeted this last remark angered Andrew. As soon as he could, he left the mess and went to his quarters to change, then down to the stables for his charger, and rode off home.

Even there, there was no respite for him. He was greeted by his mother, who also had just heard the news and was bursting to share it with him. Lady Maclaren was delighted. She had never been quite sure about her son's relationship with Maud Westburn, and she had gone to great lengths to prevent her son finding out where that lady had moved to. But now at last, she felt sure that the woman had been placed beyond Andrew's reach.

The Worthings were not at Culbrech House. They had left for London to prepare for the wedding. Andrew and his family would follow in a few weeks. General Worthing, being a personage of no little influence, had arranged that his daughter's marriage should take place in St Margaret's Chapel, Westminster, and the guard of honour would be provided by his old regiment, the Life Guards. The social implications of this were of course quite startling. Though no one had said it in so many words, it was not regarded as beyond the bounds of possibility that royalty might be present at the service.

Lady Maclaren prattled on, and Andrew wished that she would stop. Marriage was not in his thoughts at that moment. He knew now that he wanted Maud Westburn. He realized that as soon as he knew that she had given herself to another man. He wanted her, and marriage had damn all to do with it. He hated the thought of Willie Bruce lying beside that soft, cool body that he wanted for himself, and he hated himself for his hatred of Willie. He knew only one thing: he would have to see her. He would have to see her and hope that the sight of her would drive away the fantasy from his mind.

He regarded it as strange that he had not been told that she was still in the district, until he realized that the few people who would know would have been warned by his mother to keep quiet about her whereabouts. Still he believed that finding her would present no great difficulties. MacKay, their butler, was sure to know, and though MacKay would not willingly betray his mother, he would tell Andrew where Maud lived.

He wanted to go right away, but he could not. He would have to wait until the day after tomorrow. Then, he knew, Willie Bruce would be orderly officer and not able to leave camp for twenty-four hours. He would not dare take the risk of running into Willie there. Not that Willie could have done anything about it; after all, Andrew was his superior officer, and though Willie had the Queen's warrant, he would not be able to challenge Andrew as he was not commissioned, and therefore did not qualify as a gentleman.

Andrew wanted to be fair. He tried to argue with himself rationally. Rationally there was no reason why Willie should not have done that which he had done. Willie had approached Maud in the full knowledge that Andrew was already spoken for. Yet Andrew knew that he would never forgive him, and in his heart hated him for what he had done.

They had a quiet dinner the following night, just the family and Richard Simpson. Andrew felt, unreasonably, a growing dislike for Simpson. It seemed that this man, with his thinning hair and receding chin, was going to marry Margaret. It had, of course, been in the air for some time, and Sir Henry had given his consent, subject to a year's delay, believing that it would be good for the estate. But it was not fair; his sister could marry a nobody and no one questioned the propriety of this. Dinner was a bore to Andrew. Margaret and Richard talked about the estate, and Jean talked about God, and no one else said more than the odd word, except that his father did ask him to join him in the library afterwards to discuss 'a matter of mutual interest'.

The library was one of the most comfortable rooms in the house. It smelled of the leather of its comfortable chairs and heavy bound volumes. The big desk had its usual litter of papers dealing with medical matters and hygiene, subjects which were occupying more and more of Sir Henry's time now that he had retired from active duty.

They settled down and Sir Henry poured out a generous dram of whisky for himself and his son. Andrew sat obediently, watching his father and realizing that he was getting old. The back was not quite so straight, the fringe of hair was now completely grey, and there was a looseness in the skin around the neck which he had never noticed before. Also the hand which handed him his dram was not as steady as it had been a couple of years ago.

'Well, Andrew,' he said, 'you know, of course, about Willie Bruce's marriage.'

'Yes, father,' replied Andrew trying not to show any emotion in his voice. 'Ian Chisholm told us in the mess.'

'Didn't Willie tell you himself? I rather thought you would have been the first to know.'

'No, sir, he didn't.'

'That's odd,' said Sir Henry, and stroked the side of his nose with the forefinger of his left hand. 'Anyhow, no matter, I want to talk to you about Willie, though it has nothing to do with his prospective marriage.'

'I see,' said Andrew, not seeing at all.

'What,' asked his father, 'would you feel about Willie as a brother officer?'

'A commission, sir? You can't be serious.'

'Of course I'm serious. He's a damned good soldier.'

'None better,' said Andrew. 'But an officer —'

'You know, Andrew, we have to move with the times. Several regiments down south have commissioned men from the ranks, and from all I hear, it's been a great success. There is one colonel I know for a fact who started life as a private soldier.'

'But sir, I don't see what this has to do with Willie Bruce. It is something we have never done apart from quartermasters, not in our regiment. Why should we start now?'

'Because times are changing and we have to change with them. Anyhow, it's a good thing for youngsters joining the army to know that even the highest ranks are not closed to them?'

'Have you discussed this with the C.O.?'

'Of course; I would not have mentioned the matter until I had done that.'

'What did he say?'

'You know Macmillan. A bit of a stick-in-the-mud. He puffed and blew a bit, but he couldn't deny Willie's qualities. Then he said that he'd make a damned good quartermaster.'

'Yes, of course,' said Andrew.

'Quartermaster? Bah!' said his father. 'Willie Bruce will make a damned fine line officer. He'll have a company inside of six months, and I'll warrant it'll be the best company in the regiment.'

What could he reply? What could he say? Willie Bruce, the true professional soldier. Willie Bruce, now to become his social equal. Willie Bruce, who did everything better than he did. Willie Bruce, who was going to marry his woman and was already violating her. It made him feel physically sick, but all he replied to his father's statement was: 'He might not take it. I doubt that he would be able to afford to. Look what a hell of a job Angus Cameron has.'

'Don't worry, I'll see to that. I'll settle three hundred a year on him the day he is commissioned.'

If only he could think of a genuine, valid reason to object. If only he could think of some lie that he could believe himself.

'Why should you do that, sir?' he asked, searching his own mind for the answer.

'I have my reasons,' said Sir Henry. 'Reasons which I do not propose to discuss with you.'

So that was that. Andrew knew better than to press his father further on that point, but there was still the question of Maud. He, Andrew, could not continue in the regiment if he married Maud Westburn. Yet his father was proposing to have Willie Bruce commissioned with the foreknowledge that he was marrying Maud Westburn.

'You can't have doubts about Willie Bruce's ability.' Sir Henry was somewhat surprised that Andrew had not given his wholehearted approval of the idea.

'No, sir,' was all he could reply.

Sir Henry continued, 'I'm glad you agree with me that Willie Bruce is a good soldier, and I am sure that as an officer he would be a credit to the regiment. I think it is worth three hundred a year to have a man like him in a position of responsibility. I would like you to regard that part of the matter as closed.'

Again the nagging thought came to Andrew. Why was it that Willie was able to marry Maud Westburn?

'Father,' he said, 'all this I can understand. I may not agree with you, but I assure you that I do understand your reasoning. However, there is one thing which I find very odd. Some years ago, I suggested that I might marry Maud and you told me that I could not do that and continue in the army. You know that Willie Bruce is doing just that, yet you suggest that he should be commissioned.'

Sir Henry laughed. 'The circumstances are quite different. For one thing, he will be already married to her before he is commissioned, and certain things which would be socially unacceptable in yourself, or to a person of your social standing, would be quite acceptable in the case of a person of Willie Bruce's background.'

'You mean that he is not a gentleman?'

'I mean no such thing. Willie Bruce is in truth as fine a gentleman as you will ever meet. Well, Andrew, your opinion is important to me. What do you say?'

What could he say? He could not refute the logic of his father's arguments, or the right of his father to make Willie an allowance. He knew that but for the circumstances, it was something that he would have welcomed enthusiastically. He found himself at odds with his own nature. A few weeks ago, less than that, he would have had no doubts. Reason told him that Willie marrying Maud was not a personal affront, that to be jealous of it was wrong and illogical. But it was true. He was well aware that he should turn to his father now and tell him that it was a great idea and offer all his support, but he could not do that. He could not drive the dark thoughts of Maud from his mind. Instead, he turned to his father and said, 'You must do as you think fit. I can say no more than that.'

Sir Henry looked at his son. He was disappointed. He had been so sure of his support. This was not the reaction he had anticipated and hoped for. But his mind was made up.

'Yes, Andrew,' he replied. 'I must do what I consider right, what I consider best for the regiment. I am sorry that you have chosen to adopt this attitude, and for the life of me I cannot understand your reasoning.'

Andrew was silent for a moment, and then his father stood up, indicating that the discussion was over.

'I am sorry, too, father. I have to accept your decision, and I suppose that there is an end to the matter.'

Sir Henry stared coldly at him but made no reply, and after a short pause, Andrew rose and left the library.

For the next forty-eight hours, Andrew fought a losing battle against his emotions. Irrational it all was, but then rationality had nothing to do with it. He tried; he tried with all his might to be 'reasonable and civilized', but it did not work. He could only think of Maud and Willie, Willie and Maud, and the things they did together, the intimacy of their relationship, their closeness, their touching – like animals. He wanted to turn his mind away but could not. In his dreams, he watched them copulating and was disgusted, and when he thought about those dreams, he began to hate more and more. He did not return to barracks; he could not stand the thought of meeting Willie. Secretly he found out where she lived and felt ashamed. Secretly he determined that he would not go and see her, and knew that he would. He walked the hills alone, hating his loneliness, and yet terrified that he would meet anyone. He tried to conjure up pictures of Emma, but they would not come. She who was going to be his wife was not a reality. Then he thought of Maud whom he had known as a woman, who had drawn back in terror at the very touch of a man. In his mind, he saw Angus Buchannan rutting in the Maori hut, and sickeningly the image changed and it was Willie and Maud.

He would see her, he knew that. But why? He knew that, too, though he would not confess it, even to himself.

The torturous hours dragged slowly by until at last it was time to go, and go he must. Cluny Cottage was over five miles from Culbrech House, but he decided to walk. A vehicle or a horse would be an encumbrance. He set out and walked slowly, not wanting to get there, and the journey took him nearly two hours. He was afraid of how it would end and at every step he thought of turning back, but he did not.

He arrived at the gate to the cottage and thought how like her it looked. Like a picture postcard, the grey slate roof still gleaming from a passing shower, the white-painted harled walls brilliant in the fitful sunlight, and the neat little garden, bright and colourful in its profusion of late roses in a multitude of colours, tall lupins in blues and violets and reddish purples, and little patches of carefully tended green lawn separating the flower beds. He put his hand on the green wicket gate and stopped.

'No,' he said aloud, 'this I must not do.'

He took his hand from the gate and was about to turn away, but it was already too late. She was there, standing at the open door and smiling a welcome.

'Why, Andrew, how nice to see you!' And there was genuine welcome in her voice. 'I thought that you would never come.'

'Hello, Maud,' he said, still standing outside the gate and not trusting himself to say more.

'Well, don't just stand there; come in. Andrew, it is so good to see you.'

And she was halfway down the path towards him before he finally opened the gate and walked towards her.

She was smaller than the woman of his fantasies had been. Smaller and more delicate, more vulnerable, more feminine. The fair hair, which he had first seen in Cawnpore, seemed to have taken on an added lustre, tinged with gold and shimmering in the sunlight. She was wearing a green silk afternoon gown and no jewellery, and her eyes, her smile of welcome, seemed innocent beyond belief. She held out her hand as she came to him. Should he kiss her? Perhaps lightly on the cheek? But no, he drew back from that and simply took her hand.

'I'm sorry I did not come earlier,' he said as they started back up the path towards the house. 'But I've had so little time.'

'Yes, I know,' she replied. 'I did hear about your —' And she stopped.

'You mean about Emma Worthing,' he said.

'Yes.'

'Both our families consider it a most suitable match.'

'And you, Andrew? Are you happy with that?'

'Oh, yes, of course,' he replied as she led him into her sitting room.

Andrew looked around him. The room *was* Maud, gentle and feminine like herself. Then he saw the pipe lying cold in the ashtray, the big carpet slippers on the hearth, and for a moment he had a vision of Willie Bruce there. But he banished it from his mind. Willie did not belong there. He, Andrew Maclaren, did.

'You'll have tea?' Maud was speaking. 'Or a drink perhaps? It's late for one and early for the other, so you must choose.'

'I'll have a drink, if you don't mind,' replied Andrew.

'Sherry wine?' she said. 'I fear that is all I have.'

'Sherry would be wonderful. Can I get it?'

'Thank you, it's in the decanter on the sideboard.'

Andrew poured out two glasses of sherry while Maud settled herself in one of the armchairs. He took the wine over to her and paused for a moment, looking into her eyes as she took the glass. She lowered her gaze and he turned away. He sat down and there was silence between them.

'It has been a long time,' he said at length.

'A very long time,' replied Maud, and then, 'Why did you stop writing? It hurt me, you know. It hurt me a lot.'

Andrew looked at her in astonishment. 'But I didn't stop writing. I wrote at least three letters after the last time I heard from you, and you never replied to any of them. I felt that it would be ill-mannered of me to continue.'

'Three letters?' And she was as amazed as he had been. 'But I received none of them.'

'At least three,' he answered. 'It may have been more. I do remember that in my last I said that, if I did not hear from you, I would have to assume that you had no desire to continue the correspondence. How could this be?' He paused, but she made no answer. 'I did not hear from you, so I had to accept what I assumed to be your wish. Was it?'

'Oh, Andrew,' she said in a voice heavy with emotion. 'That was never my wish. I waited months, hoping that I would hear from you again, but the letters never came. How could that be possible?'

He could not answer, because he knew just how this thing was possible. It had to be someone at home, and that someone had to be his mother. An enormous feeling of hatred welled within him. The injustice and the heartlessness of it all appalled him. One day he knew that he would have to forgive her, but not now. But he had to confirm what he knew to be true, and he asked her how it was that she came to leave Culbrech House.

Maud smiled. 'I think that your mother was worried about us, and I felt that my continued presence there might be an embarrassment to her. She had been so kind, and I could not impose on her. So I left. We didn't part on bad terms, but I knew that she was afraid and I understood her reasons. As I had not heard from you for so long, I saw no point in increasing her worry by staying on.' Andrew was about to speak, but she continued, 'Please understand that she never asked me to leave. It was entirely my own decision.'

'I see,' said Andrew slowly. 'What a pity.'

'A pity?'

'Yes,' he said, 'that it had to happen like this.' His tone changed and he tried to appear light and conversational. 'Anyhow, that's all water under the bridge, and now they tell me that you are going to marry Willie Bruce.'

'Yes, yes, I am. Next week. You will be coming, of course.'

'Of course,' said Andrew, wondering whether he would be able to face the event. 'Willie is a very fine person, but he's – he's —'

'He's not you,' said Maud.

She looked at him, and he met her gaze, and that strange primeval thing happened, that thing that can only happen between man and woman when they look hard into each other's eyes, and beyond into the depths of desire. Though neither of them spoke, question and answer were both there. That strange instinct which strips away the veneer of civilized social behaviour, and makes even speech an unnecessary affectation, took command of them both. The animal cast out the rational, a thousand years of civilization vanished in an instant, and their bodies demanded that they unite and procreate. The spoken word, even if it could have been spoken, meant nothing.

Together they rose, and never for an instant taking their eyes from each other, as if fearing to break the spell, they came together in the centre of the room.

Andrew put an arm around her waist and started to caress her breast with his other hand. He moved his arm down her back until he could feel the softness of her buttocks. He clutched at them and pressed her body hard against him.

There was no tenseness, no struggle, and still she gazed on him. At last she spoke.

'Now,' she breathed, and he could feel the rise and fall of her breast against him. 'Now.'

Her lips were parted as she thrust her body still closer to him and they kissed for the very first time, drawing the breath from each other and impatient for that greater intimacy which had to come.

He started to fumble with her dress, and she drew back just a little. 'Not here, my darling. Upstairs. Take me now.'

He took his hands from her and allowed her to lead him towards the door, still staying close enough to her to feel the movement of her hip against his thigh.

The door opened.

'Mummy, you promised to come and play with me.'

It was Naomi. Small, dark, beautiful, and a picture of aggrieved innocence.

The spell was broken.

15

The wind had moved to the northeast, bringing with it the chill of autumn and the promise of winter to come.

Maud was alone in her house. Her husband Willie, now Lieutenant Bruce, had left some hours earlier in order to get to the barracks in time for the morning parade. The sky was overcast, and it was starting to rain. Maud kept glancing at the clock. It was almost eleven, and in her mind she saw the little medieval church lying under the shadow of the massive bulk of Westminster Abbey. She knew what it would look like; she had seen it all before when, as a little girl, her parents had taken her to a fashionable wedding at St Margaret's. Of course that was many years ago, and on one of her rare visits to England. But she knew; she saw it all again in her mind. Only the *best* people got married at St Margaret's. Only the quality could walk from their carriage between the gleaming breastplates of the Household Cavalry. Only the elite – and them; damn them!

She saw the guests being silently ushered into their places, waiting. Waiting for the moment when the organ would strike up the wedding march and Emma Worthing, an unreal person whom she had never met, would walk down the aisle on her father's arm. There Andrew would be waiting for her, to take her hand and approach the altar where she would say those words, which she herself had said such a very little while ago to Willie Bruce in the parish church at Beauly.

She looked out of the window and wished that the rain that was now falling on her garden would also be falling on the bride. She prayed that something, somehow, might have gone wrong – a quarrel, an illness, anything would do. Prayed that Andrew would realize their love and that even now, at this eleventh hour, would find the courage to run away. To run back to Scotland, and to her. But the eleventh hour was already upon her. The marble clock on the mantelpiece, Andrew's wedding present to her, had started to chime.

She did not hear its insipid bell. She heard only the notes of the organ as that other woman started down the short path which would remove Andrew for ever from her life.

When it was all over, they would step outside beneath the glittering crossed swords of the Life Guards.

Damn the army! Damn the whole bloody self-centred crew! Damn them for their morals, their ethics, and their traditions. Damn them for giving her life and denying her all that she had ever wanted from it.

She put her hands over her ears, trying to shut out the sounds that were not there. She grabbed the marble clock and flung it across the room, and then the tears came.

They were not tears of sorrow. They were tears of rage and frustration. Rage at what was happening, and frustration at what she had done when she had married Willie, and what she had failed to do in not following Andrew to London. There she could have put up a fight. There, she was sure, even at the very last moment, she could have taken him away from that creature.

And what of Willie? Did he know? Did he suspect? Did the man who had held her in his arms and called her his bonny wee thing realize that it was another she wanted? That other who was the image of himself? She had tried to keep it from him. She had used her pregnancy to stave off intimacy. She had tried to be interested, tried to show delight on the evening that he had come home and told her that he was going to be an officer.

He had come in that night and picked her up and swung her round in circles. 'It's great news I have,' he said. 'Great news.'

'Willie,' she replied, 'put me down. Remember ... remember my condition.'

His face fell. 'Oh, I'm sorry, lassie,' he said, looking into her face and thinking of that which was happening within her body, a thing so wonderful as to be beyond his ken. He put her carefully in an armchair. 'How could I forget? That was stupid of me. I didna think. Are you sure you're all right?'

'Yes, Willie, I'm all right,' she said, straightening her dress. 'What is this news that you have to tell me?'

'Well,' he said, his enthusiasm returning, 'you'll never believe this, but I'm going to be a general.'

'Don't be ridiculous, Willie,' she said, and her voice was cold. 'What do you mean, you are going to be a general? Have you been drinking?'

'Not a drop. And I'm not going to be a general right away, but I am going to be an officer. The colonel sent for me this afternoon and he told me that I had been offered a commission. Everything had been arranged, and it was only for me to say yes.'

'But Willie,' she said, 'you cannot possibly afford to be an officer.'

'Oh, don't you worry your bonny head aboot that. And I shall not need a penny of your money. It has all been taken care of by Sir Henry.' He paused, but she did not reply. Willie was too excited to be really aware of her lack of enthusiasm. He continued, 'You know, Maud, I'm going to prove that Napoleon was right when he said that every soldier carries a field marshal's baton in his knapsack.'

'I see,' she replied.

'Are you not pleased? Do you not understand what this means to me? To us?'

'Of course I'm pleased. I am delighted. I – I congratulate you.'

He sensed her lack of concern, and put it down to her condition. 'Is it tired you are? Perhaps all of this news has been a bit much for you and you would like to lie down?'

She made one more effort. 'You'll be a gentleman at last.' And she tried to smile.

'Aye, that's what they say, an officer and a gentleman, though it is not always true. You know, Maud, the R.S.M. is the most important man in the regiment next to the colonel, and when I become an officer, I become a nothing all over again. But I shall be a nothing who knows the ways of the army and the ways of the men he commands. I shall have knowledge that no other officer in the battalion has. I'll go a long way in the army, my darling, and you shall be proud of me.'

'When does this happen?' said Maud, trying hard to show some sort of joy.

'Right away. I have to get a uniform and all the bits and pieces that go with it. I have one week's leave and then I report back to the regiment as Lieutenant Willie Bruce.'

'You won't be an ensign?'

'Och no. Not after being a regimental sergeant major; they couldna do that to me. I start as a lieutenant and verra soon I'll be a captain, and from there, you see, I'll be a general one day.' He looked at her sadly. It did not seem to mean anything to her. 'Are you sure you had not better lie down?'

'Perhaps I shall, Willie. I find this excitement a little exhausting.' And she left him.

And Naomi. How she had resented that intrusion the last time that she and Andrew had been together, and there was still all to play for. But for that, at least she might have convinced herself that it was Andrew's child that she now carried in her womb. But no, even that small comfort had been denied her and denied her by a child of five.

They would have started by now. What was it he would be saying? 'I, Andrew, take thee, Maud —' No, not Maud – *Emma*. It would be something like that. 'To have and to hold ... for richer, for poorer ... till death us do part.'

Blast them all! Damn, and blast them all! That whole smug, self-righteous lot of them. Love, honour, obey. What did honour have to do with love, and what could that woman possibly know of love?

She picked the clock up from the floor. The glass was broken, but it was still going. It would be nearly over now. Was it finished? Not if Maud Bruce had anything to do with it; not by a long way.

Jean Maclaren walked into the sitting room.

'Maud, dear, is there something wrong?'

Maud glared at her, the calm, cool, self-righteous little prig that she was with her Maclaren nose and her mannish jaw, her head tilted to one side, wide blue eyes and a forced smile of sympathy on her lips. Jean, plain, pathetic Jean. What the hell was she doing here, anyway?

'Wrong? Why should there be anything wrong? And why aren't you in London? You may not have heard, but your brother's getting married today,' she snapped.

'I do not want any part of that. I do not approve of marriage. No woman should give herself to a man, not even to my brother. But Maud, dear, you are distressed, I can see it. I am so glad that I came; perhaps I can be of solace to you.'

'You? Solace to me?' Maud laughed, and there was a touch of hysteria in her laugh. 'Just who the hell do you think you are, anyway? You are a meddling bitch! That's what you are!'

'Maud, I am certain you are distressed; otherwise you would never say such things.' Jean refused to be ruffled.

'Listen to me! Just you listen to me! I don't want you, I don't want any part of you or your bloody family. I'd be a damned sight better off today if your damned brother had left me where he found me. Don't just stand there looking at me. Don't you dare pity me! I don't want you or your pity, or any of you.'

'I'll make you a cup of tea,' said Jean, 'and then perhaps if we said a little prayer together —'

'Shut up! Shut up and get out of my house. Nobody asked you here and nobody wants you to stay. Just get out and leave me alone. That is all I ask of you. That is all I ask of your whole bloody family.'

Jean finally got the message. 'Well, perhaps some other time.'

'There's the door,' said Maud

Jean squared her shoulders and left the house, tut-tutting as she did so.

Maud watched her going down the path from the bow window, then threw herself on to the sofa and burst into tears. 'Oh, Andrew ... Andrew ...' she sobbed.

A little crowd had gathered outside St Margaret's, drawn by the red awning and the shining carriages gathered nearby waiting to collect the 'happy couple' and their guests. It was the usual bunch of gapers who came to leer at brides and grooms as they left the church and passed on their way to bed together for the first time, while they themselves fantasized upon the virgin, or the rapist, and the joy or hurt of the impending copulation, according to their own experience.

They came out of the church and stood for a moment beneath the swords, Andrew solemn, almost grim-faced, and Emma with a smile that could have been cynical amusement playing around her mouth.

The bridal landau drew up and Andrew helped Emma into her place. A moment's pause, a little wave to the emerging guests, and the pair of gleaming black hackneys set off down Victoria Street and up Constitution Hill, on to Piccadilly and the Ritz Hotel where the reception was to be held, and where all the pointless speeches would be made.

The bride's mother, who was nothing if not a social organizer of distinction, had dealt with all of the arrangements, and the whole affair was carried through with a precision which would have done credit to the Brigade of Guards. A good time was had by all – all, that is, except Lady Maclaren. She alone had not enjoyed herself, and not because she felt she was losing her only son. There was something subtly, terribly wrong with Andrew, and she was well aware of it. For several weeks now, he had barely spoken to her, and when conversation had been unavoidable, he had conducted it in monosyllables and terminated it at the first opportunity.

She could hardly help but be aware that he was avoiding her, but she had not the courage to ask him why. She could not get it out of her mind that he had in some way found out about the letters. Not that he had mentioned them to her, not that he had even mentioned the wedding to her. But it was over now, and though his attitude had given her great pain, she could not help feeling great relief at seeing him finally married to the woman of her choice.

There had been some private talk about the honeymoon, and on this matter Emma had been quite adamant. It would not be Paris or the Riviera, or any of the fashionable continental resorts. The London season was just beginning, and Emma had no intention of being anywhere else.

Bowing to his daughter's wishes, General Worthing had placed his own town house, which lay just off Piccadilly in Mayfair's Grosvenor Square, at their disposal, fully staffed and provisioned.

It was there that they went as soon as they could, with dignity, leave the reception. The house was tall and terraced and modern, overlooking a quiet square where elderly matrons walked their Pekingeses, and uniformed nannies parked their prams and gossiped. It was built of red brick and fronted by iron railings, behind which steps led down to the basement where there were servants' quarters and the kitchen. The front door was of polished oak with a gleaming brass doorknob and bell pull, sheltered from the elements by a stone canopy supported on twin rounded pillars. It was like all the other houses in the square, opulent, and the town dwelling of a wealthy family. Inside was a large reception hall with a sweeping curved staircase leading to bedrooms; and heavy doors led off into the library and drawing room and dining room. Everything had been cleaned and dusted, the front steps newly pumice-stoned, the brasses polished throughout the house to greet the bridal couple.

They had left the Ritz in a closed carriage, and when it drew up outside the house, Andrew helped his bride down.

They were halfway up the steps when the door opened and they paused. Andrew looked at Emma in surprise.

'That will be Blundel,' she said, 'my father's butler. He'll have been looking out for us.'

'I suppose that I ought to carry you over the threshold,' he said.

'Please don't,' replied Emma. 'You don't believe in all that nonsense, do you?'

'Well, actually no.'

'Besides, I want to get out of this damned thing.'

The damned thing that she was referring to was her magnificent white satin wedding dress, the provision of which had cost her mother a great deal of time and her father a great deal of money.

Before he had a chance to say more, she had walked past him and into the house. He followed her just in time to see her disappearing up the broad curved staircase.

'I'll be down in half an hour,' she said over her shoulder as she vanished from his view.

'Ahem.'

Andrew turned. It was the butler.

'May I offer my congratulations, sir?'

'Oh – er – thank you,' said Andrew, handing him his feather bonnet and his gloves. 'You are —?'

'Blundel, sir. I am your butler. Would you care to have me show you over the house?'

'Not just at the moment,' replied Andrew. 'Is there a sitting room, a library? Somewhere I can get a drink?'

'Might I suggest the library, sir? There's a pleasant fire there. You will find it most comfortable, and well stocked with a variety of refreshments.'

He led Andrew into the room and Andrew thought it was strange how all libraries looked alike, book-lined, heavy with the smell of leather, and uninhabited.

'I'll have a brandy and soda,' said Andrew. 'And when Miss – I'm sorry, Mrs Maclaren comes down, I think you might send up some tea.'

'Very good, sir,' replied Blundel, pouring the drink and handing it to Andrew. 'Is that all, sir?'

'Yes, thank you,' said Andrew. 'Unless my wife wants anything. I'll ring if she does.'

'Thank you, sir,' said Blundel, and withdrew.

Andrew sat for some twenty minutes sipping his drink. It was not a large one, but even in that time he didn't finish it. He didn't really want it; as a matter of fact, he felt quite peculiar. And then she came in.

He stood up as she entered, and an expression of genuine hurt crossed his face.

'Andrew,' she said. 'Is there something wrong?'

'No, nothing wrong,' he said, lying. How could he possibly tell her? How could he possibly ask her why she had chosen to wear a green silk gown? That was Maud's special colour. 'You look lovely,' he said without enthusiasm. 'I've ordered tea. Unless you'd prefer a drink.'

'Tea will be fine.'

She sat down on the club settee which lay at right angles to the fireplace, and Andrew, after a moment's hesitation, sat in the armchair opposite. She looked at him, again the slightly cynical smile on her face.

'Don't you want to sit beside your wife, Andrew?' she said.

'Oh – yes – yes, of course. I'm sorry – I —'

'Andrew, are you frightened?'

'Yes, I am a bit. I've never been married before.' And he sat beside her.

'Well, neither have I,' said Emma. 'But I know what is supposed to happen. I hope you do?'

'You mean —' She nodded. 'Oh, yes, of course.' He was finding her direct manner somewhat unnerving. 'When?' he said.

'Whenever you like,' she replied. 'But I would like a cup of tea first.'

'All right,' said Andrew, glad of the delay. 'I'll ring.'

'I'll do it,' she said, and now she was really laughing at him.

They drank their tea almost in silence. Andrew took one sip and then watched his cup get cold, while Emma did not seem in the least perturbed. She had two cups and nibbled at a biscuit.

'Your tea must be cold,' she said. 'Shall I throw that away and give you a fresh cup?'

'No, thank you,' he replied. 'I didn't really want any.'

'All right,' she smiled. 'Now I'll tell you what we'll do. I'll go upstairs to our bedroom, it's the white door on the first landing. There's a lovely fire in there, and you come up in about fifteen minutes.'

'Don't you think it's a bit early?' he said.

'Oh, no. We can try now, and then if we like it, we can do it again tonight.' And before he could reply, she was gone.

He decided he needed another drink, so he poured himself a brandy – a large one this time – and drank it at a single gulp. He could not keep his eyes off the clock on the mantelpiece as he watched the minutes ticking away. Then it was time to go, and slowly he walked up the stairs and into the master bedroom. He looked towards the bed expecting to see her there, but she was not in it. She was standing in front of the fire, completely naked.

He gasped at the sight of her. He had never seen a naked

woman before except in his dreams and fantasies, but this was magnificent. She had let her hair fall down her back, and the creamy skin, the full breasts and delicate curves of her body, culminating in the triangle of soft curls beneath her navel, banished everything but desire from his thoughts.

She saw it in his eyes, and what she saw stripped her emotions until they were as naked as her body. The brittle veneer of sophistication was gone, and the fear which had left him came to her.

'I thought that you had a right to see me first as I really am,' she said, and her voice was softer than he had ever known it.

She crossed her arms over her breasts and hurried over to the bed and got between the sheets. He still stood just inside the door, not knowing what to do next.

'Andrew,' she said, appealing, 'your dressing room is through that door there. Will you close the curtains and then go in there until you are ready? and then come to me.'

'Yes, of course,' he replied. 'Anything.'

He did as she had bid and returned to the darkened bedroom.

'Can I come in beside you?' he asked.

In reply, she folded down the covers at the other side of the bed. He got in, being careful not to touch her, and then she found his hand.

'Andrew, I have never done this before; please be gentle with me. I have been told that it hurts the first time.'

'Would you rather wait?' he said, knowing that he didn't mean it, and that his body was crying out for her.

'No, Andrew, you must take me now. We cannot wait. Come, my dear, we must help each other.'

She moved towards him so that they could feel each other's nakedness. As he entered her, she gave a gasp and a little cry of pain.

'Maud, my darling,' he cried, not realizing what name he had used, 'did I hurt you?'

She neither replied nor reacted to the word. Instead she thrust her body closer to him, and when it was over, they lay together in silence for a long while.

It was not until they had dressed and gone downstairs that she mentioned the subject.

'Who is Maud?' she asked, and when he made no reply, she continued, 'Andrew, when we were in bed, you called me Maud. Maud must be someone who is very important to you. No, don't answer. Perhaps it is better you do not tell me. Ours is not a love match and there is little point in trying to pretend that it is.'

'But Emma —'

'Wait, I haven't finished. Perhaps I shall become pregnant very soon, and that will fulfil the purpose of our union. Then perhaps it will not matter. But let me tell you one thing, my dear. I do not mind if you look for solace among other women as long as I know nothing about it. If ever I find out who they are – and I include this Maud among them – I give you my solemn word that I will destroy them.'

16

The Himalayas, the vast mountain barrier which protected British India from the savage inhabitants to the north and west, is pierced where it turns sharply southward by a number of passes, the best known of which is the Khyber. This rises only to thirty-three hundred and some feet. Flanked by the huge mountains, it winds its way through the homelands of the Pathans and on into Afghanistan.

The Pathans are an ancient, unruly, independent, and proud people, not unlike the ancient Scottish clans, who had never submitted to the British Raj or to any other. Whenever the opportunity arose, they would sweep through the mountain passes and raid the fertile plains below.

The British army had built an elaborate system of defences to control the entry through the gaps in the mountains, and it was here, in the Khyber, that the 148th Foot sweated it out for nigh on three months.

Since the punitive expedition of Brigadier General Wilde the Khyber had been comparatively quiet. This did not mean that there was no action. Small-scale raids and counter-raids continued sporadically. The Pathans were covetous of the new Snider rifle, a breech loader with which the army was now equipped, and would take enormous risks in order to lay hands on one. Companies manning the forward positions would live under canvas. They slept in bell tents, fourteen to a tent, feet towards the pole around which their rifles were securely locked by means of a chain passed through the trigger guards. But even with all these precautions, occasionally one was stolen; and when that happened, the battalion could not rest until it had been retrieved.

But most of the time, nothing happened. For in the army, the fighting men, the soldiers of the line, spent over ninety per cent of their time in a state of boredom. Some of them took to drink, some of them gambled. The ordinary soldier talked about women and beer and bragged of his prowess in both fields. The young officers indulged in childish parties and pranks – anything in fact to relieve the monotony and the tedium of their day-to-day existence. But any of them who had a home, and in the 148th that meant most, spent a great deal of their time thinking about it.

Andrew spent many long hours gazing at the brown, barren, rocky hills with his thoughts in Scotland, remembering. He remembered how they had gone north after their short honeymoon, and how he and Emma had set up house. Sir Henry had given them the dower house, a comparatively recent structure, which had been built a mile or so from Culbrech. It lay on a south-facing hill overlooking the Glass and the hills beyond. It was not large by country-house standards. There were six bedrooms, and the ground floor had a drawing room, a dining room, and a study-cum-library. It had been built initially for Andrew's grandmother after his grandfather had died and Sir Henry had inherited the estate. His grandmother had lived in it only a couple of years, a broken-hearted recluse, before she too had died, and the house had remained silent and empty ever since. But while the family had awaited his return from New Zealand, it had been restored and modernized, and prepared for possible occupation by Andrew and his hoped-for bride.

The house was built of red brick, an unusual material in that part of the world, which had been shipped by sea from the south. It had French windows which led out on to the lawn and the gardens beyond. When Sir Henry had given it to Andrew and Emma, it had been absolutely devoid of furniture. With the help of a large cash settlement from her parents, Emma had furnished it herself, allowing no one to interfere with her fixed ideas of what a home should be. The result had been quite spectacular, if not in the vogue of the era. It lacked the clutter and the dark velvets and the heavy, heavy curtains so popular at that time. Instead, everything was light. She had discarded the conventional mahogany and heavy oak furniture and had used light-toned walnuts and rosewood. The rooms themselves were wall-papered in delicate blue and pale gold stripes, or painted in Adam green and white, and picked out with shining gilding. Where she had used velvets, as she did in the withdrawing room, instead of the sombre browns and greens, she had chosen pale salmon pinks and gentle yellows. She had left space, open spaces in all of the rooms, so that one could walk around and not be confronted every two paces with another piece of furniture.

Lady Maclaren had viewed the final result with slight disapproval. In her heart she felt that it looked more like a French salon than a Scottish country house. There was no denying this, the French influence was there all right. For Emma had engaged a French girl to be her personal maid. As for the rest of the staff, she engaged a butler, groom, two footmen, a cook, a scullery maid, and an upstairs maid. With the exception of the cook, they were all English and had all been vetted by her own mother before being sent up to the Highlands.

Andrew had had nothing at all to do with this, but he had admired his wife's efficiency in organizing their new home, and living in it, he could not deny the success of her efforts. It was comfortable, and pleasant, and easy to live in. A place to relax, if only he had been capable of relaxing and accepting his lot; if his mind had not been constantly drawn to that little cottage only a handful of miles away beside the river.

But out there in India, it was all so far away. Scotland and home. It was a period of great boredom, interspersed with spells of high tension. Tension because there could be fighting at any time to break the boredom of constant patrols, guard duties, and sheer inactivity, when men saw nothing but mountains and rocks and a dusty, barren land. There had been casualties, not many of them from the guerrilla actions of the Pathans. In three months on the frontier, they had lost one man killed, and two wounded; disease had taken a much higher toll, and they looked forward longingly to the relieving battalion which was soon due. Then they would move eastward to Lahore, and the officers and some of the luckier N.C.O.s would get a period of rest in Simla, where their wives and families would be waiting for them.

One night, sitting out there in the Khyber, Jamie Patterson, who had been sober longer than he could remember, wrote in his diary:

Life here is intolerable. There is nothing to drink except water, and very little of that. I never believed that the time would arrive when water would be the most precious thing in my life. I have not seen alcohol for over a month. We are camped at the foot of a long, narrow pass, down which the wind will suddenly blow at gale force and the sandy soil will rise in masses so that you cannot see the tent next to your own. And when the wind dies down, everything is coated with a fine dry dust and we have to spend hours cleaning our rifles and equipment, being sent out on guards or pickets, which time we spend hiding, for the Pathan is so much better at seeing us than we are at seeing him. We parade every morning at six o'clock and the colonel sometimes gives us a talk. He is trying to keep up our morale, but I fear that he, poor soul, finds this depressing as we do. I wonder sometimes that the men do not go out of their minds, but they are a hard lot, and though in the past I would not have associated with them, I am now proud to be numbered among them.

None of them had seen their womenfolk for many months, not since they had sailed from Tilbury on a three-year overseas tour. Britain and their Highland homes seemed like another world. Oh, there were mountains, but they were not green and beautiful and living; they were grey and brown, dry and dead.

Their few casualties had all been incurred at night. All of them had been among the forward pickets, that outer ring of the double circle of sentries which was posted around their camp every evening as the sun went down. No one liked the job, and in the confines of their quarters in the fort, the old sweats who had been there before would advise the youngsters to spend their time on guard lying down, keeping still, and waiting for their relief.

'It really was the damnedest thing,' said Lieutenant Farquhar.

He was speaking in the marquee which served them as a mess. He was referring to the unfortunate Major Chisholm.

'As orderly officer I was about to make my rounds of the forward pickets, and Ian said he was coming along with me. A Company were on pickets today. Just as we were approaching the second post, there was a single shot. Nothing else, just the one. There was no one in sight and the poor chap went down. Of course, I ducked and crawled over to see what I could do. He was bleeding quite a bit and I strapped him up with my field dressing, got hold of the sentry – Patterson from A Company – and we carted him back here to have the surgeon patch him up. The bullet had gone clean through his left lung. He was out most of the time, but he came round for a couple of minutes, looked at Patterson and said, "James, what the devil are you doing here?" Just as if he knew the fellow. The rest you know; they shipped him straight to Lahore this evening. Anybody heard anything more?'

Nobody had. This was the first major casualty that they had had, and the incident was immediately followed by a column at company strength going out to search the area. They all knew that this exercise was a waste of time. They did not see anybody and they knew that they would not see anybody. They came back empty-handed, of course, but with the knowledge that they had done their duty.

A week later, they heard that Chisholm had been ordered back home and that he had announced that he was resigning his commission. In a letter to the colonel, he explained that he really had no military ambition and he would be much happier back on his grouse moor near Perth. But he did promise at the same time to offer shooting to the officers of the 148th whenever they were in Scotland, and to keep the mess supplied with grouse whenever it was in season.

This happening created a vacancy in the regiment for a major, and back in Scotland, as soon as he got the news, Sir Henry pulled strings in the War Office and got the appointment for Willie Bruce.

Each casualty or attack was followed by a punitive expedition into the hills, mounted by two companies. There they selected a village, usually at random, and burned it. But it was always the same. When they arrived at the village, it was empty, and within an hour the crude dwellings had been razed to the ground. The men detailed to do the job then marched back to their frontier post wondering what the hell they had accomplished.

At long last their relief arrived. The 33rd Foot, a Yorkshire regiment, took over from them and they set out on the journey east. The first night, they bivouacked outside Peshawar, and three days later arrived at Rawalpindi. Another month passed before they arrived in Lahore and were established in the cantonments where they would be performing garrison duties for the ensuing months. It was the beginning of August when they got there, and the ladies had already left for the hill station at Simla. It was arranged that the officers would take leave in groups, those who had wives in the hill station being allowed to go first.

It was not without a feeling of guilt that Andrew looked back upon the period between his marriage and their arrival in India. Both Maud and Emma had produced sons for Willie and himself. The babies, only four months between them, looked so alike that they could have been twins. Andrew had grudgingly presented himself at the christening of Donald Bruce and had given Maud twenty sovereigns for the child. Not that he had any desire to increase the Bruces' fortune, but he felt that he had to do it.

Andrew had discovered, almost to his surprise, that he enjoyed sex, and that while he and Emma were no experts in the matter, they had managed to make their bed a satisfying experience. But then she was six months pregnant and had, some time ago, taken to sleeping in a separate room, which she would occupy until three months after the confinement. As for

Andrew, he had accepted Emma as a relief and comfort, despite the fact that he was still beset by fantasies of Maud. He believed that the pleasant physical relief which he experienced with his wife would become an ecstasy beyond description if he could only ... But that was another story.

As for Willie and Maud, they had married and their child had been born as predicted, less than eight months after their nuptials. Willie had been commissioned shortly after their marriage and had been accepted in the officers' mess as something of a novelty, their first ranker officer. Even Colonel Macmillan had gone out of his way to make Willie feel at home. Only Andrew had remained cool in his manner towards him.

Willie's gentleness towards Maud expressed itself in many small ways. He would pluck a flower on his way home from the barracks, whenever possible a single rose, and he would hand it to her shyly as he came through the door. At first, he accepted her pregnancy as a valid reason why she found sex abhorrent, and after Donald was born, he understood that a waiting period was necessary. Maud was distressed because in her more rational moments, she knew that she could not find fault with her husband and she did try to please him. Occasionally, she would offer him her body, and when he took her, she would lie there gritting her teeth and praying for the act to finish. Willie was all love and kindness towards little Naomi, for whom he had developed a great affection, and with the help of Sir Henry's lawyers, he had arranged that she take the name of Bruce. There was no apparent reason why both marriages should not have been successful, each in its own way.

Maud was totally devoted to her new child, but had regretfully been unable to breast-feed the infant. Not that this had proved any great problem. Among the ladies of the Establishment, wet nurses were de rigueur, and it had been a simple matter to find one on the estate for the baby Donald.

Little Donald was over two and a half months old when they took him to the church at Beauly and gave him his name, and after the ceremony they repaired to the local hotel to pay homage to the time-honoured custom of wetting the baby's head. It is probable that that was where it had all started. Emma, of course, was not present, and Maud had looked at Andrew and

Andrew had looked at Maud too often and too long, and though no word passed between them, Willie Bruce had seen them as they gazed at each other.

He was surprised to find that he was not surprised. He knew what he had subconsciously suspected, ever since Maud had agreed to be his wife, that she had taken him because she could not have Andrew.

The first time it had happened had been on the hill in the heather. Their meeting had been accidental, or almost so. Andrew, who had spent a great deal of his free time walking the hills, had almost instinctively tended to take his walks in the direction of Cluny Cottage, and it was on the fourth or fifth occasion that he had actually met Maud. She was alone; he knew that Willie was orderly officer that day and consequently could not be in the vicinity, and they had recklessly and unreservedly made love.

The following night, when Willie returned home and approached his wife, she had a headache. The next night she had a headache again, and then again, and then Willie began to wonder. In the mess, Andrew began to avoid him even more than he had done previously, and when he spoke to him, he never looked him in the eye. However, the thrill of illicit love drove Andrew to seek out Maud more and more. He used his position as adjutant to issue an order that no officer could exchange duties with another, a common practice, without Andrew's prior knowledge and approval, and this was never easily obtained. Somehow Willie always found himself on duty on those days when Maggie Buchannan would not be at Cluny, for Andrew still avoided Maggie.

This state of affairs could hardly go on for ever. One evening, Willie returned home after a spell of duty. Maud was sitting in the bow window watching the fine rain which was making little rivulets on the panes.

'Do I no get a greeting from ma wife?' he asked tersely.

'Oh, hello, Willie,' Maud replied tonelessly and held her cheek up so that he could kiss it.

Willie seized her by the chin and kissed her full on the lips.

'Willie, please! Maggie might come in.'

'Where's Naomi?' he asked, ignoring her.

'It's eight o'clock; she's in bed. Willie, have you been drinking?'

'I had a dram before I left the mess. What's for supper?'

'Lamb chops. Maggie couldn't start cooking until you arrived, so they'll be about ten minutes.'

'Just time for a dram, then,' he said, going over to the sideboard. 'You want one?'

'Don't you think you've had enough?' she asked, ignoring his offer.

'When I think I've had enough, I'll stop. I dinna need any advice.'

Willie took his whisky, watching Maud intently and in silence as he sipped it.

'Willie, is there something wrong? You seem to be behaving rather strangely tonight.'

He was about to say something, but Maggie came into the room to tell them that supper was ready.

They ate their meal, as had become their habit, almost in silence. When they had finished and Maggie had cleared away, Willie went through to the kitchen.

'Maggie,' he said, 'awa' home to your ma. You can come back in the morning.'

He went back to the sitting room and poured himself a large whisky.

'Where's Maggie?' said Maud.

'I've sent her home.'

The children were upstairs in bed and asleep, and for all practical purposes, he was alone with Maud. He drank his whisky and then returned to the decanter and poured out another. All this time he was watching her, never taking his eyes off her. She, embarrassed by his scrutiny, tried to take refuge in sewing, and when that failed to work, picked up a book, opened it, and pretended to read, but all the time she was aware only of his stare. He did not seem angry; if anything, he seemed cynically amused. But he did not speak, and she felt that she wanted to scream if only to break the silence.

'You've had a hard day, I suppose,' he said, echoing the words with which she had greeted him.

'Well – you know . . .' she replied.

'No, Maud,' he said. 'I don't know, and I'd be grateful if ye would tell me.'

'There's nothing to tell,' she said, afraid of his tone. 'Not really.'

'Did you see Andrew Maclaren today?'

His tone was casual, but she started at the mention of Andrew's name. 'Why do you ask?' she said.

'No reason. I ken he's in the habit of walking a great deal and just wondered if he might have wandered in this direction.'

'Why this way rather than any other?'

'I think,' said Willie, 'that ye should be the one to tell me.'

'There's nothing to tell, nothing. I have had enough of this ridiculous conversation. I think I shall go to bed.'

'Aye, lassie,' said Willie. 'You'll go to bed, all right.'

'What do you mean by that?'

'You'll have no headache tonight.'

'I – I – haven't been very well lately.' She was getting frightened.

'I'm well aware of that,' he said. 'And I think I know the cure. Stand up.'

'Please let me go to bed.'

'Stand up.'

'Don't you start ordering me about, Willie Bruce; you don't own me.'

'Oh, but I do. Stand up or I'll drag ye up.'

'What are you going to do?'

'Well,' he replied, and his tone was casual, 'if ye must know, I'm going to fuck ye.'

'How dare you talk to me like that!'

Willie did not reply. Instead he got up, walked across the room, and stood towering over her. 'Get up, Maud,' he said.

'Willie, please – please – you've had too much to drink. You – you're not sure what you're doing, you —'

'I ken exactly what I'm doing and so do you,' and he grabbed her arms and dragged her to her feet. 'First,' he said, 'we'll have a look at what I'm getting.'

'Willie, you can't do this, you're mad!'

'That is quite possible. Take your clothes off.'

'I'll do no such thing,' she hissed.

'All right,' he replied. 'I'll help.'

He took her dress by the shoulders and with one powerful movement spread his arms wide. The thin silk garment ripped down the middle and fell to the ground. She tried to get away. She tried to struggle, but her puny strength was no match for this great man. One by one, he tore the clothes from her until they were lying, a heap of rags, scattered about the floor, and she was standing naked, outraged, and terrified of what was to happen next.

'Now,' he said, and started to unbuckle his kilt.

As soon as he released her, she ran to the fireplace and grabbed the heavy brass poker. 'If you come near me, I'll kill you,' she screamed.

'No, you won't,' he said calmly, walking towards her, and as she raised her arm to strike, he seized her wrist and twisted the poker from her hand.

She fought and scratched and spat at him like a wild animal.

'A little discipline first would no do you any harm,' he said, and he laid her across his knees and pounded her buttocks until they were scarlet and she was crying out with the pain.

Then he took her.

At first she continued the fight, scratching and clawing at him until suddenly her body went limp beneath him and she started to moan, quietly, and then louder, with her breath coming in great gasps. This was something that she had never experienced before. She never knew that it could be like this, brutal, animal, and voluptuous rapture.

When he had finished, she lay there on the floor gazing at him, unable to speak, triumphant in her defeat. He left her and went over to the decanter and poured out another whisky.

'Now's your chance,' he said, and he stood facing the wall. 'If ye want to hit me wi' yon poker, ye can do it while ma back's to you.'

'Oh, Willie,' she said. 'Oh, my darling.'

'If ye dinna,' he said, 'get upstairs and into bed. Maybe I'll want more.'

'Don't be long, my darling. Please. Hurry.' And she went out of the room.

Half an hour later, he came upstairs and took her again. Then he got out of bed and started to dress.

'Where are you going?' she said. 'Can't you stay with me?' She was lying there, soporific, satiated, and sensually satisfied as never before. 'Come back to bed, Willie.'

'If ye want me, I'll be in the mess.'

After he had gone, Maud lay in bed luxuriating. She was not worried. He would come back, he had to come back. He had to do it again. She lay there trying to recall the passion of that which she had never experienced before, wondering how her body could be capable of such joy, until finally she fell into a deep dreamless sleep.

But Willie did not come back. Not the next day, or the next, or the next, or even the day after that. It was over a week before he set foot in the house again. When eventually he did, his manner was cool, correct, and offhand. Maud, who had welcomed him without a word of reproach, was worried. She was worried because at last she really wanted him as she had never wanted any other man in her life, and there he was, her own husband, making no approach to her.

Perhaps, she reasoned, he was ashamed of his behaviour. Perhaps if she could show him that there was no resentment on her part, then it would be all right. As they sat together, alone in their gas-lit sitting room, he reading with a glass of whisky at his elbow, and she with an open book on her knee and not looking at the words, she knew that she must try.

'Willie,' she said, 'shall we go to bed?'

'Awa' you go if you're tired,' he replied, not looking up.

'I'm not tired,' she said. 'I wasn't thinking of sleep. I thought you might like to come with me.'

He smiled, that slightly cynical smile which he seemed to reserve for her. 'I didna have that in mind.'

Then she tried to be frank with him. 'Willie, it's all right, you know. I'm not annoyed about what happened last week. It was wonderful.'

'I'm glad you enjoyed it,' replied Willie, and turned a page of his book.

'Put that damned book down!' she almost screamed.

'No,' he replied calmly. 'And this book is no damned; it is *Pilgrim's Progress*.'

She stood for a moment breathing heavily, and then snapped

at him, 'If you don't want me, then why do you bother to come home at all?'

He laid his book down and looked at her. 'I'll tell you, Maud. Firstly, because it is my home, too, and secondly, there's another reason. If I don't spend time here, if I am not with my wife on off-duty nights, there will be talk. Mind you, as far as I am concerned, I don't give a damn what they say. It doesn't worry me. But I do give a damn about the good name of the regiment. I'm an officer now, and one day I am going to be a general, so I'll have no scandal attached to my house.'

The hurt was greater than if he had struck her across the face. Without another word, she gathered up her things and went to her room, knowing that he would not follow.

It was a couple of months before he, at last, took her to bed again. He did it because he loved her and could no longer take the sight of her pain, and because he wanted her.

They made love. Gently and tenderly this time. And she found that the pleasure could be just as intense as it had been when he had raped her. Afterwards, when they lay together in the dark, relaxed and on the edge of sleep, she turned to him and gently took his hand.

'Willie,' she murmured, 'I'm going to have another baby.' There was no reply.

'Willie,' she said again, 'are you asleep, did you hear me?'

'Aye.' And all the old jealousies flooded back into his mind as he drew his hand away. 'Aye, I heard you.'

'I'm going to have a baby, Willie,' she repeated.

'Then no doot we'll be able to pass it off as mine. For if yon is the father, there's no man living who could tell the difference.'

She started to sob silently and he turned away from her, gazing wide-eyed into the darkness and praying for the sleep and its attendant oblivion that would not come.

Months later, when the child was christened, Willie named it Gordon Maclaren Bruce. This made Sir Henry and Lady Maclaren delighted, it made Andrew ashamed, and it made Maud furious.

17

The train rattled and clanked and puffed its tortuous way up the winding branch line that climbed another five thousand feet into the foothills of the Himalayas en route from Ambala to Simla. Its occupants were a fair smattering of the Indian Establishment, army officers, and high government officials going up to the hill station to avoid the worst of the summer heat. The train did not hurry; it stopped several times on the sixty-mile journey, once when a sacred white Brahman bull had decided to lie on the track chewing its cud. The driver, faithful to his beliefs, had waited until, half an hour later, the animal decided to move on.

As they climbed, the brown earth started to give way to patches of green, and here and there they would pass near a village where men spent their days treading a waterwheel to bring the precious liquid to the miserable patch of earth on which their survival depended.

Willie Bruce and Andrew Maclaren shared a compartment. They did this not out of choice, but because it would have been improper for two officers of equal rank and belonging to the same regiment to travel apart. In any case, it was the movements officer at Lahore who had made the travel arrangements.

Their compartment was upholstered in purple plushy velvet cloth, deep comfortable seats buttoned back against their frames of figured walnut. Above them a fan turned lazily, drawing the hot humid air away from them and out through the two ventilators in the roof, only to have it replaced by air that was equally hot and humid.

The only other occupant of their compartment was an older man, a typical product of the Indian Establishment of the seventh decade of the nineteenth century. He was a civilian in white ducks who had joined them at Ambala and carefully placed his pith helmet, attaché case, and gold-topped cane in the luggage rack. He took the window seat opposite Andrew with his back to the engine, Willie being on the same side and by the corridor, as far as possible from his brother officer.

'Been up to the hills before?' asked the stranger, obviously intent on making conversation.

'No, sir,' said Willie, and Andrew merely shook his head.

'You've got a treat in store for you. Simla always reminds me of Brighton. No beach of course, what?' He laughed, and Andrew suppressed a sigh.

'I've never been to Brighton, either,' said Willie.

'Good God! Thought everybody went to Brighton. You're Scotch, aren't you?'

'Scottish,' corrected Willie.

'First tour in India?'

'Aye.'

'You'll like it. I think we've got the native where we want him now. They were gettin' a bit uppish before the mutiny. Company made a bit of a hash of things. But it's all right now, thanks to you fellahs.'

'There are no many of us,' said Willie.

'Aye, lad, but you're British. Thirty thousand troops, three hundred million natives, and you can handle them. That's what being British means.'

'You mean looking after the likes of you?'

'And why not?' replied the man, stroking his immaculate greying moustache. 'I grow cotton in the Punjab. Cheap labour, high profit. Good for the Empire. Take that fellow, for instance,' he stabbed the window with a soft, manicured finger. Outside there was another waterwheel with a ragged, ill-nourished youth treading wearily away at it. 'So long as he's got his rice, and he can breed, that's all he needs. Why give him more?'

'You don't think of him as human, then?' said Andrew butting in. 'I mean, you'd do as much for your dog.'

'Human, yes, I suppose he is. But he's not British. He'll never be a gentleman.'

Andrew looked across at Willie. This man was an insufferable bore and even though, since their arrival in India, theirs had been a strained and purely professional relationship, this was too much for both of them. 'Let's go and get a drink,' he said.

Willie glanced at him, surprised, but almost anything was better than this. 'Aye,' he replied.

They edged their way along the corridor to the next carriage, which was equipped with a small bar where several other officers were already ensconced, sipping their 'pegs', and Andrew ordered.

Even before leaving for India, the only conversation that had passed between them was on matters military. However, they had been travelling many hours, all the way from Lahore, and it was just not possible for them to sit and glower at each other for the entire journey. So once at the bar they talked, taking great pains to mention neither Maud nor Emma, though both were very much on their minds, as they would both be waiting for them in Simla.

Until Willie had attained his majority, they had ignored the custom that in the mess all officers except the C.O. referred to each other by their Christian names. Willie had always said 'sir' when speaking to Andrew, and Andrew had always said 'Captain Bruce' when speaking to Willie. Now that they were of equal rank, they referred to each other only by their surnames.

Andrew opened the conversation by asking Willie what he thought of the Gatling gun. This had been shipped to India with the regiment, much to the colonel's disgust. But people in high places had decided that it would be a good idea to try the thing out in the field. This was to be a final trial before deciding on its adoption by the army as a standard weapon.

On this subject, Willie and Andrew were professionally divided.

Andrew had inherited his father's enthusiasm for gadgetry and treated the Gatling rather as a child would treat a new toy. Willie's approach was more practical. First of all, it was his company that had been given the gun, and if anything went wrong, it was his men who would suffer. Willie complained bitterly about the ammunition which had been supplied – thin copper cartridges packed with black powder which gave off vast quantities of heavy smoke. In thirty seconds, by which time a hundred rounds had been fired, it was impossible for the gunners to see the enemy, and you had by then provided your opponents with an excellent aiming point. Under pressure from above, the colonel had decreed that for their next stint on the frontier, they would take the thing with them.

'I wish we hadna brought that bloody Gatling,' said Willie, sipping his drink contemplatively.

'Why not? It's a good weapon. It's worth a hundred men.'

'When it works. I tell you, Maclaren, it was the last thing that your father did to us. Arrange for that. He did us nae favour. Ye canna rely on a contrivance. It's men that count.'

'Well, I admit it isn't perfect, but we have been promised better ammunition, and when that arrives —'

'Och, mannie, de ye think it will arrive? We're thousands of miles awa'. They'll forget all about us until the day that it does us a real hurt. That day will cost us men.'

'I'm not suggesting that we should rely on it.'

'I should bloody well hope not, for we'll nae get any help from Whitehall. We're too far away to make a nuisance of ourselves.'

Their argument became quite heated, and in a strange way the disagreement brought about a certain rapport between them. But as the train rounded the last curves and Simla came into view, and they gazed out the windows at that city of brick bungalows and towering greystone hotels, they became silent again.

Simla, sitting in the middle of India, might indeed have been Brighton. Set against a backdrop of the snow-capped Himalayas, it clung to the sides of the cliffs some seven thousand feet

above sea level. Here, apart from the eastern quarter which held
the native bazaars, was the home of the sahib. It even had a
brewery – discreetly tucked away, of course, but with high
chimneys – where it was said that the best beer outside of England was brewed. With a year-round temperature in the low
seventies, it made an ideal spot for the military sanatorium
which had been established there. Green lawns and rosebushes,
elms, and oaks were everywhere. It was so like England, but
just a little larger. The houses were bigger because they had to
accommodate the staffs of servants which were so cheaply come
by. Living was cheap, so the dining rooms were a little grander
than they would have been at home, because people could
afford to entertain much more lavishly than in Britain.

They looked out the windows as they drew into the immaculate new railway station with its pale, gilt-topped columns sup-
porting the iron frame of a sparkling glass roof, and the curtain
of discomfort in each other's presence descended again. In a
way, their thoughts were very similar. Each was joining his
wife and would spend a month with her. Both of them were
making the journey out of a sense of duty, and both of them
would rather have been back in Lahore with their men.

The women were both at the station but standing far apart,
waiting at opposite ends of the platform, both dressed in what
was almost a uniform for ladies – white cotton skirts and
jackets over pale silk blouses, with pith helmets tied under
their chins with bows of white muslin. Beyond them, waiting
for their customers, stood rows of hansom cabs, such as one
would have found at any London terminus.

Emma and Maud were apart because they had never really
got to know each other. Maud's husband, though of equal rank
with Andrew, was still a ranker officer, which placed him considerably lower on the social scale than Andrew. Emma was
naturally somewhat suspicious after what Andrew had said on
their wedding night, but Maud was a fairly common name. She
could number at least four among her own circle, and Emma
was not prepared to make a judgment. Not yet, anyway.

After the birth of her child, Emma had remained in the dower
house until the regiment had moved overseas, and then Lady

Maclaren had invited her to come and stay at Culbrech House.

'I am sure that you will find it a deal less lonely, my dear,' she had said. 'And it will not be for long. You will, of course, be joining Andrew shortly.'

Emma was waiting the required three months before sailing, in case she should find herself again pregnant.

'Moreover,' Lady Maclaren had continued. 'I am getting old, and there are duties with which I would very much appreciate your help. You know the sort of thing I mean.'

Emma knew well what she meant. So she had become the Lady Bountiful, visiting the workers who toiled for long hours for the betterment of the estate. She always carried with her a basket of good things to eat whenever she visited any of the cottages. She gave graciously, as she had been trained to do, and her gifts were accepted with courtesy and thanks from a people who had been trained to respect the *quality*.

When Willie had been commissioned, she had accepted it, though she did not approve. Rankers did not fit into the social life of the regiment. After all, officers' wives were officers' wives, and rankers might marry anybody. She did not learn the story of how Maud Bruce came to be living in the Highlands. Those who knew the story considered it better that Emma did not know, and those who did not know the story didn't really care.

The first time they had met socially, she had been formally introduced to Mrs Bruce by Sir Henry at a luncheon he was giving for officers and their wives and sweethearts at Culbrech House.

'I do hope,' she had said, 'that you are managing to settle down into your new life.' She was referring to Willie's recent advancement to commissioned rank, and was somewhat surprised to discover that his wife seemed to be perfectly at ease and quite accustomed to all the social graces.

Willie, on the other hand, had been a little awkward at first, but his own native confidence had soon carried him through that somewhat difficult transition of being accepted as a guest, and an equal, in a house where previously he had been on a social level with the servants.

It was later, after lunch, that she had the opportunity to talk to Mrs Bruce. She felt that it was her duty to put her at her ease and to be friendly.

'You really must let me call you by your first name,' she said. 'Mine is Emma.'

'That is kind,' was the reply. 'I am Maud.'

Maud! Emma looked long and hard at her. 'You know my husband?'

'Oh, yes, we met in India.'

After that, she had treated Maud correctly, but with a touch of condescension, and without any warmth, and always with the nagging thought that this was *the* Maud. She had come out to India some months prior to Maud and had spent some time with Andrew at Lahore before the regiment's first spell of duty on the frontier. Her child she had left in the care of her old nanny at her father's home in Dorset. Raised in that strict school which taught that duty superseded love, desire, or emotion, she had, as soon as she could, followed her husband east. She did this because it was right that she should be with her husband and bear him more children.

The train stopped and the passengers started to alight. Willie and Andrew separated as soon as they had got on to the platform. Andrew saw Emma standing near the barrier and headed towards her. She greeted him by perfunctorily brushing her lips against his cheek.

'Did you have a nice journey, dear?' she asked.

'It was all right, I suppose,' said Andrew. 'A bit dull.'

'Well, I have a carriage waiting. The bearers will bring your luggage. Come along now and I'll show you the house.'

Maud had arrived in India literally days ago and had travelled direct from Bombay to Simla where she had taken rooms in a hotel while awaiting the arrival of Willie. She had viewed her return to the subcontinent with some trepidation.

She had stood on the deck of the steamer which had carried her from Britain, watching the long grey line gradually filling the horizon as it appeared out of the Arabian Sea until it turned into the teeming island city of Bombay where they had docked. She did not want to go ashore. India brought back too many memories of terror and fear. Strangely, though, it was the company of British soldiers drilling on the quay-side that had given her courage to disembark. A hundred men in a city of over a million.

She had taken the train from Bombay to Delhi. The journey took three days, but she was comfortable enough in a private sleeping compartment with a large fan turning gently over her head. The line took her up the coast as far as Ahmadabad. To the east, she could see the Western Ghats – an impressive enough range of mountains, unless you had seen the Himalayas. To the west, there were numberless small fishing villages with crude wooden boats drawn up on the shore or standing a little way out to sea, their lateen sails patched and ragged as the men who worked at their nets. There were many such places, always with long lines of fish hung out to dry. These coast dwellers were the more fortunate of India's poor; their survival did not depend on the monsoons. The worst that could happen to them was that the sea which gave them their life would rise in anger, flood their villages, and give them a quick and merciful death.

From Ahmadabad, the train cut inland across the principality of Rajputana, where the countryside became more familiar. The long stretches of arid waste were interspersed with settlements wherever water could be got. Finally, as they approached Delhi, the land became more and more cultivated and greener as they neared the fertile plains around the Ganges. Here was an India which reminded her of the country around Cawnpore, and all the bitterness that that city meant to her.

After only one night in a hotel in Delhi, she took the train for Ambala and then on up the new line to Simla. And there her uneasiness increased at the thought that, within a few days, she would be reunited with Willie.

Since the night that she had told him that she was to have another child, they had lived together, but apart. A great barrier had descended between them. She had tried; over and over again, she had tried. One night she had gone to his room, for they now slept in separate rooms, and tapped on the door.

'Willie?'

'Aye, I'm here.'

'Please, can I come in?'

'For what?'

'I want to be with you, Willie.' She was standing in her nightgown in the chilly corridor in Cluny Cottage. 'Please, Willie, let me in,' she pleaded.

She heard a movement within the room and for a moment believed that she had succeeded, and then she heard him slam the bolt home.

'Awa' tae bed, woman,' he said from within.

She never tried again. The gulf between them was made worse in her eyes by the fact that Willie was always so attentive and charming towards her when others were present. And now she was hoping that after this long separation, time would have healed the wound and that they would be able to start anew.

They spotted each other on the platform. She walked towards him wondering how she could greet him. Did she run? Did she throw herself into his arms? Did she wait for him to come to her and then merely offer her hand in greeting?

She did none of these things. She just stood there. Willie stopped a couple of paces from her.

'Hello, Maud,' he said.

'Hello, Willie.'

'Have you got a place for us?'

'Not yet,' she replied. 'We're in a hotel.'

'It'll do.'

He looked at her intently and saw her gaze stray past him and down the platform to where Andrew and Emma were walking away through the barrier.

'Aye,' said Willie coldly. 'That's Major Maclaren. But you canna run after him, he's got his woman wi' him.'

Her shoulders sagged in an expression of hopelessness. Nothing had changed.

'I think that, before you return to Lahore, we should have the Bruces over to dinner, don't you?'

Andrew thought no such thing. He stopped what he was doing and gazed at his wife. 'We have been here three months and you suddenly decide that you want to dine with the Bruces?'

'Yes, dear, the Bruces.'

'But you hardly know them.'

'My dear,' she said, 'they are in the regiment. You are now of equal rank and must be aware that I have not seen Major Bruce's wife since we arrived in India. I think I should very much like to see – Maud, is it, again?' She stressed the name Maud ever so slightly.

'But,' said Andrew, 'do you think they would fit in? I mean, do we really want them? He is a ranker, you know.'

'It is not a matter of want,' said Emma. 'I was not thinking of a large dinner party, in case you are worried that he eats peas with a knife. I think it is our duty. I think we ought to.'

'Major Bruce is not a particular friend of mine, but I take your point.'

'I understood that you grew up together.'

'Yes, but he was only a – well, you know.'

'Andrew, I do believe that you are a snob.'

'Oh, have it your own way,' he snapped. 'Ask them if you want to.'

'Good, then that's settled.' She smiled.

The Maclarens were living in a spacious wooden bungalow. Long and low, it was surrounded by a raised verandah. At the back of the building were the servants' quarters, and there were servants in plenty. Andrew had not brought his batman with him, knowing well that Emma would have taken care of all the domestic arrangements.

This she had done with all her usual efficiency. When she had arrived from Lahore, she had gone to see a Mr Rawlinson, who was the manager of Lloyd's Bank in Simla and a slight acquaintance of her father's. Rawlinson, a dehydrated individual of about fifty, whose fifteen years in India had added another ten to his age, had been most helpful. He had found her her bungalow on the outskirts of the town where it would be kept cool by the northeast winds which blew constantly, but with little ferocity, from the snow-capped Himalayas beyond. He advised wood rather than brick, though brick was more fashionable, being more English.

So they settled on the bungalow and he introduced her to Gopal, whom she engaged as her head man. Their first meeting was typical of her directness in her dealings with everybody, irrespective of their station.

'Gopal, I want you to engage me a full staff, cook, ayah, houseboys, and maids.'

'Yes, mem-sahib. I have many honest relatives who will work very hard for you and for the major sahib.'

'They will do as little as they can, and you know it.'

'Oh, no, mem-sahib. All very honest.'

'And,' she continued, 'they will rob me. I expect it. But if anyone else steals from me, or if I lose more than thirty rupees a month, I shall get another head man and the major sahib will cut off your head.'

'That would be a great tragedy for my wife and three children. Forty rupees, you said?'

'Thirty,' she replied firmly. 'And that is between all of you.'

Gopal recognized that his new mistress was not to be trifled with, and when he saw Babu, one of the houseboys, sneaking out of the bungalow with a silver claret goblet, he beat him mercilessly and proudly returned the object to Emma, proving to her that all was well and that her home would be well protected – and with it all of the valuable silverware and china which she had so carefully packed and had shipped out from Britain.

That was all in the past now. Andrew was nearing the end of his stay in Simla and he had to admit that it had been pleasant enough. Their relationship, never warm, was friendly, and it was only on the odd occasion when Emma mentioned Major Bruce that Andrew felt at all uneasy. Sensing this, Emma had brought the matter out into the open, and his hope now was that Maud would not be able to come.

Emma, having gained Andrew's grudging consent, wrote the invitation and sent it over to the Bruces' hotel by bearer. She instructed him to wait for a reply from the mem-sahib. When Maud received it, she was at first overjoyed at the thought of spending an evening in Andrew's company. Willie was out at the time, so assuming his acceptance, she scribbled out a quick note and handed it to the bearer.

When the man had gone, she began to worry. She had acted on the spur of the moment; what was Willie going to say?

It was not long before he returned. When she told him, he greeted the announcement with cynical amusement.

'And you accepted, did you?'

'Yes, the bearer was waiting for an answer. I hoped you would not mind.'

'It'll be nice for you,' he replied, and he turned away to pour himself out a drink.

Willie had been drinking rather a lot since he arrived in Simla, and this was worrying Maud. It was not that he got drunk, or violent, or anything like that. He just seemed to get quieter and less communicative. How she wished that she could sort out her own feelings. The truth was that she wanted them both. She would not mind if only he would be angry, if he would beat her even. But this cool, calm, ignoring of the whole situation was driving her out of her mind. It was so desperately unfair.

So wrapped up was she in her feelings of self-pity and guilt over her emotions towards Andrew that she was unable to see that Willie, too, was suffering. They were living as strangers for that most foolish of reasons, each feeling aggrieved and unable to see the other's grief. She really believed that what she wanted was Willie's manliness and Andrew's gentleness, and in consequence she believed that she really loved them both equally.

Perhaps dinner with the Maclarens would not be a bad thing; perhaps she might be able to sort herself out. But then, what if she couldn't? How would Willie behave? And Andrew's wife, did she suspect? Would she and Andrew be alone together at any point during the evening? She would certainly be alone with Mrs Maclaren; what would she say to her? These and a thousand other questions kept flooding through her mind.

There were two whole days to get through before they dined. If only Willie would make it easy for her. But he would not, and if he mentioned the subject at all, there was that mocking ring to his tone which made her want to scream. Those two days were among the longest that Maud had ever lived through.

'Mrs Bruce, how delightful to meet you again. Andrew, it was very wicked of you to keep such a charming lady away for so long.'

Maud was quite aware of the ring of formal insincerity in Emma's voice, but she knew that she looked good. She had dressed with meticulous care for this evening. She wore a green satin gown. This was the height of the current fashion, and it made Emma's crinoline look just a little out of date. Fitting tightly around the waist, and the frontal fall moulded to her figure, it had the new half crinoline sweeping away behind in great folds of shimmering material, ending in an embroidered train which swept the floor. The bodice was cut as low and as revealing as decency would allow, and her arms and shoulders were bare and brushed by the ends of the golden ringlets of her hair.

When Andrew greeted her, she kept her eyes downcast, but she felt his nervousness in the touch of his hand. They went out on to the verandah for the traditional *chota peg* before the meal. Andrew and Maud had their drinks in an embarrassed near-silence, shying away from the animated conversation which was going on between Willie and Emma.

In the large dining room they sat down, Emma and Andrew at either end of the ten-foot-long mahogany table, while Maud and Willie sat in the centre, separated by four and a half feet of table and a massive five-branched silver candelabra. In the flickering candlelight, the distances between them seemed immense and were certainly not conducive to conversation. Gopal and Babu served the meal in silence, appearing as ghostly figures in the flickering candlelight. Turtle soup was followed by a fish that Maud could not recognize, but tasted delicious; then roast beef, crêpes and finally cheeses, all in near-silence.

After the meal, when the ladies had retired and Andrew and Willie had taken their brandy and cigars out on to the verandah, Emma had Maud to herself at last.

'You have been to India before, of course,' she remarked.

'Yes,' replied Maud. 'I came out here when I was a little girl. I lost both my parents in the mutiny.' Talk of the past made her edgy, and a little afraid. It was a recurring nightmare with which she lived. In a way, she had never escaped from that horror.

'Ah, yes,' said Emma. 'I recall hearing something about it. It was Cawnpore, was it not? It must have been a terrible time for you.'

'I'd rather not discuss it, if you don't mind,' she replied. 'What happened then frightens me even now.'

'I understand,' said Emma, ignoring her plea, 'that Andrew saved your life and brought you home.'

'No,' said Maud, 'not exactly. We travelled on the same ship, but that was quite coincidental.'

'Alone together for that very, very long voyage?'

'There were other passengers,' said Maud defensively.

'Oh, yes, of course, I understand that, and the crew. But then, you did not know any of the other passengers.'

'Mrs Maclaren —'

'You must call me Emma,' she said, smiling sweetly.

'Very well, as you wish, Emma. Your husband and his family were infinitely kind to me. They carried me through a period of my life which I look back on with horror. I owe them more than my life, I owe them my sanity. If today I am a normal woman, it is all due to them. But I am surprised that Andrew has not told you all about this.'

'Oh, he has mentioned it from time to time,' said Emma. 'In fact, he referred to you on our wedding night. Of course, I cannot remember the circumstances.'

Maud compressed her lips and made no reply. Emma continued, 'You do know that I shall not be going back to Lahore with you?'

Maud looked up quickly. 'I had not heard.'

'Of course you hadn't, why should you?'

'Is Andrew, I mean Major Maclaren – has he been given another appointment?'

'Oh, no,' replied Emma. 'I have to go back to England. We are going to have another child. I haven't told Andrew yet; you are the first to know. I thought we would have our little break here and then I shall tell him just before he has to rejoin the regiment. You will have both of our husbands to care for when you get there.'

'That will be very nice,' said Maud numbly.

'I am quite sure it will,' was the reply. 'I understand they are great friends.'

'Andrew and Willie?' said Maud. 'They used to be.'

'I wonder what changed it?' said Emma. 'One of us, do you suppose? Surely not. Perhaps Andrew resents Major Bruce having risen from the ranks? Of course, you married him before he was commissioned, did you not?'

'Yes.'

'Yes, I find that rather quaint. It must have taken a great deal of courage to marry an ordinary soldier. After all, you are a lady?' It was not a statement, it was a question.

Maud had had enough. 'Look here, Mrs Maclaren,' she said, 'I like neither what you are saying to me nor the way you are saying it, and I am getting a little tired of innuendo. If you have anything on your mind, I would appreciate very much if you would come straight out and say it and stop talking round in circles.'

Emma smiled. 'Very well,' she said, 'if you wish, then so be it. Quite soon now, Colonel Macmillan will retire or be transferred to a staff appointment. The 148th belongs to the Maclarens, and it is certain that Andrew will get command. When that happens, I shall be the colonel's lady. Now I want you to understand that I fully expect my husband to have affairs outside of his marriage. What I will not tolerate is Andrew having anything to do with any woman who is connected with the regiment. If such a thing were to happen, I would make it my personal responsibility to see that that woman's husband had his career ruined, and that she herself was socially ostracized for the rest of her life. Do I make myself clear?'

'Perfectly,' replied Maud.

'Very well, then. Please don't forget what I have said, I mean every word of it. I am not certain of what, if anything, has passed between you and Andrew. But it is over. Do you understand that? I saw the way you looked at each other at dinner tonight. Forget him, Mrs Bruce, and remember that I do not make idle threats.'

'I am sure that you do not,' said Maud. 'You really are a bitch, aren't you?'

Emma smiled her sweetest smile. 'Yes, of course, my dear. But here come the gentlemen, we must not keep them waiting for their coffee.'

18

It was really quite a remarkable sight. Willie and Maud had
arrived at the station early and they had had over half an hour
to wait before the train which would carry them back to Lahore
would leave Simla. At one of the platforms stood an engine.
It was polished pale blue and burnished brass, its smokestack
and pressure dome and handrails gleaming in the cool morning
sunlight. The carriages, five in all, were maroon, picked out in
gold coachbuilders' lines. The handles of the doors were gold
and shaped like a human hand being offered in greeting. It was
really quite magnificent.

The engine had steam up and Willie, ever gregarious, had
his curiosity aroused and had gone over to talk to the engine-
driver.

'That's a bonny set-up you have there,' he said. 'Whose is
it?'

'Oh, yes, sahib, this very fine train belong to Rajah of Jaipu-
tana.'

'Oh, aye, and who's he when he's at hame?'

'Very important prince. We leave soon and rajah he come
with us. You like to look at engine, sahib?'

'Aye,' said Willie, peering into the cab. 'It's bonny all right.'
The interior of the cab was spotless. 'Is it always as clean as
this?'

'Indeed, yes, sahib. Everything must be polished, even the coal, she is cleaned before she goes into the tender.'

'Thank you for letting me see,' said Willie, and he walked back to where Maud was standing as the porters were loading their luggage on to their train.

'Yon's a private train,' said Willie. 'Belongs to one o' them Indian princelings. The kind that we keep in power, and the sort that pays his workers a handful o' rice a day so he can play wi' toys like that. Och, they do it the world over, though. The lairds did it in Scotland, most o' them, anyway. It's an afu' thing, the way men treat men, and we're nae better than any o' them.'

'Men treat women badly, too,' replied Maud. 'We're all very selfish, aren't we?'

'What do ye mean?' Willie said, aware of her implication.

She was about to reply when she was interrupted by a commotion at the far end of the platform.

About twenty men, all dressed alike in loincloths and khaki jackets, with little red pillbox caps and wooden staves in their hands, came trotting on to the platform swinging their staves and forming up in two lines leading to the private train. Through this human corridor about half a dozen women, veiled and with heads downcast, hurried into the third coach. They were followed by a group of four men wearing white jodhpurs and grey silk frock coats picked out in gold braid. They went to the door of the front coach and stood two on either side, waiting for their master. The rajah appeared alone and magnificent in pure white silk glittering with embroidery of precious stones and a gold cap, with an ostrich plume pinned to it by an enormous ruby brooch.

He walked slowly down towards the train, his olive-skinned face expressionless until he passed where Willie and Maud were standing. For a moment, he paused and gazed at Maud with cold, coal-black eyes. Maud shuddered. That look took her back over the years to another time and another place, to Cawnpore and another pair of eyes, so much like those, and the face that had started her on the road which had led her here.

Willie looked at her and grinned. 'Yon's the princeling. I think he fancies you,' he said.

Willie's remark brought her back to reality. 'Don't be disgusting,' she replied and turned away. 'I think we had better make sure that they have loaded all our luggage.'

'I'll see tae it,' said Willie.

Leave was over and they were due to return from the cool of Simla back to the heat and humidity of Lahore. In their bungalow that morning after breakfast, Emma said to Andrew:

'I shall not be returning to the cantonments with you.'

'No?' replied Andrew. 'Don't you think that might look rather bad?'

'Not under the circumstances. I am going to have another child. I have known for some little time and had intended to tell you after we had had dinner with the Bruces, but the moment did not seem opportune.'

'I see,' said Andrew, trying to match her calm and suppress his emotions at the news. 'Would you like me to ask for an extension of leave in order to make the necessary arrangements?'

'There is absolutely no necessity for that. As you well know, I am quite capable of taking care of any arrangements that might be necessary.'

Andrew lapsed into silence. She was right, of course.

'Will you be coming to the station with me?' he said at length.

'Naturally,' she replied. 'It is my duty.'

'Thank you.'

When they arrived at the station, he said to her, 'I had better check that my trunk is on board.'

'Why don't you leave it to your servant?'

'I'd rather check myself.'

Emma watched after him as he walked down the platform. Suddenly she caught sight of Maud. She saw him approach Maud and stop. They stood for a moment, not long enough to have a casual conversation, but too long to merely greet each other. Before they parted, Maud gently raised her hand and touched Andrew on the cheek. It was a gesture so filled with tenderness that Emma would have been less angry if they had copulated there in the middle of the station. There and then she made her decision. She would not go to England to have the child. It would take her a week or so to clear things up here in Simla and cancel all the arrangements already made, but as soon as she was able, she would follow her husband to Lahore. She knew that there were additional risks. She would receive much better attention in England. But she was not prepared to take the greater risk of leaving her husband in Lahore with that woman.

When they arrived at Lahore and made their way to the cantonments where the regiment was housed, a message was awaiting Andrew to report to Colonel Macmillan.

'Well, Andrew,' said the colonel as Andrew came to attention in front of the desk. 'You'd better sit down. Glad to see you back. Didn't want to interfere with your holiday, but I've got some news for you.'

'Good news, sir, I hope.'

'You're the C.O. You will be tomorrow morning, anyhow.'

Andrew did not reply, but he could scarcely conceal his satisfaction at hearing the news. Emma had hinted at it in Simla, and he had known that it would come eventually. But it was nice to realize that he was at last in a position of real power.

'Yes, you've got your regiment,' the colonel continued. 'I've been transferred to the Viceroy's staff in Delhi. That'll be a bore. The news came through from London a week ago that you have been gazetted lieutenant colonel and commanding officer of the 148th Foot. Congratulations.'

'Thank you, sir.'

'Don't bother about thanks. It wasn't my doing. I've taken a room in the mess and had all my stuff moved out of the C.O.'s house. You and your wife will want to move in there right away.'

'But, sir —'

'In any case, I'm only here for another couple of days, and then I shall be off.'

'It's very kind of you, sir,' said Andrew. 'I can't say that I'm not delighted to hear this.'

'Well, you know,' said Macmillan, studying Andrew intently; there was a weakness there but he couldn't pin it down.

'It's more your regiment than it is mine. The Maclarens started it, and anyone other than a Maclaren in command is little more than a stopgap, don'cher think?'

'No one would ever consider you a stopgap, sir,' said Andrew, though he knew that his statement was not true and that he had had his sights firmly fixed on that chair opposite ever since his father had retired. 'You've been a fine commanding officer,' he continued. 'I'm sure that I am voicing the opinion of every man in the regiment when I say that we shall be jolly sorry to lose you. I only hope that I can be as good.'

'Well, that's kind of you, Andrew. Where's your wife? You'll want to tell her.'

'I'm afraid that she's not with me,' said Andrew.

'Not with you? But—'

'She's going direct to England. A baby.'

'Oh, well, that's something else for you to celebrate, isn't it, eh? How many have you got? One? One, that's right, Ian. Well, I hope you get another boy, we could do with some more recruits.'

'Time will tell, sir,' said Andrew, a little embarrassed at discussing the subject.

'Good. Good. Well, Andrew, you might as well move into the house, anyway. Not a good idea for the C.O. to live in single officers' quarters. You see too much that you're not supposed to see. By the bye, I've engaged an ayah, temporary, of course, for Mrs Maclaren. But, er, you must do as you think best.'

'I shall let her stay,' said Andrew. 'Is she a good woman?'

'Young, you know, all right; as good as they come, I should imagine.'

'In that case,' replied Andrew, 'I'm sure that we'll be able to find something for her to do around the house.'

'Good. We'll have a parade tomorrow and I'll formally hand over command of the battalion. We'll break out the colours, have a bottle of champagne, and then I'll be on me way. You don't want ex-C.O.s hanging around the place. They're a bit of an embarrassment.'

'I'm sure that you'd never be that, sir.'

'Maybe not. But I suppose that I'm a bit old-fashioned, really. I shall be retiring soon probably, the best thing I can do.

Well, Andrew, this is your office from tomorrow, but today it's still mine. Good luck.'

Andrew accepted the note of dismissal in the colonel's voice and left.

Macmillan looked long and hard at the closed door after Andrew had gone, and spoke quietly to himself. Not platitudes this time, but the things he ought to have said to Andrew.

'Well, I wonder what sort of a job you're going to do? I've known you for a long time, Andrew, ever since I joined the regiment. You were just a little boy, then. I can remember you when you used to play soldiers with Willie Bruce on the hill behind your home. I remember those games well. You were always the C.O., but it was Willie who took the decisions. You were a good subaltern, but command is something different. You're alone now and I wonder how you'll manage. You were never really quite sure of yourself, were you? You took a long time to grow up. Sometimes I wonder if you ever have.

'I served with your father since he was a subaltern, and he was a fine soldier. He could command. Can you? He could command because he liked power, and knew how to use it without fear or favour. He always enjoyed pulling the strings and he pulled them hard enough if he thought that the regiment would benefit. Looks as if he's still doing it. I have just been kicked upstairs, shunted off to Delhi, because he wants you to have the regiment. Nepotism can go too far sometimes, though I would never have thought it of him. He never showed it when he was serving. It's strange.'

He paused for a moment, scratching his chin, and picked up an old daguerrotype. It was of a group of officers in statuesque poses. He looked at it and shook his head sadly. 'They were great days. There have been many great days. But this is not like Sir Henry, because I don't think you are ready. Your private life might have something to do with it. I hope that it improves. I've watched you carrying your marriage troubles on to the parade ground. You married well, though. No soldier could wish for a more suitable bride.' He smiled, a wry smile. 'If you did nothing else,' he repeated, 'you certainly married well.'

He looked up at the door again. 'I don't know what you're going to do with the regiment, but the army's changing, and I suppose that the regiment will have to change with it. It's becoming a different world. All of these newfangled things, machine guns, all for what? The men are better off, too. At least they get paid regularly now. But when you get right down to it, it will always be the infantry. It'll be a man in possession of a bit of ground; that's what'll matter.

'Well, Andrew, good luck to you. Though I doubt that you'll ever be either the man or the soldier that your father was.' He sighed. 'Ah, well, that's all water under the bridge, now.'

He picked up a leather attaché case from the floor and put it on top of his desk. He opened it and placed the daguerrotype inside. He picked up his pipe-rack and its three battered briars, and put them carefully in. And then the paperweight which had been a present from Sir Henry when he got his first company. It was silver, and in the shape of the regimental crest. He held it in his hand and looked at it for a moment. 'A little of the wild-cat in your blood wouldn't hurt you, Andrew.'

He snapped the case shut, took a long, last look around the office. 'What's left, you can have, boy,' he said, squared his shoulders, and walked out.

Andrew's feelings were hard to describe. He had known that this would happen eventually, though he had not expected it so soon, in spite of what Emma had said to him at Simla. He wanted command and all the little perquisites and privileges which went with it. Never a very social creature, he would not miss the hurly-burly of life in the mess. They would all call him 'sir' now, and treat him with rigid formality, and hope that he would go away.

They would do this because he was the one who would make the decisions by which their lives were ruled. He would decide which troops would storm the breach, now that he had power. It was power of life and death over a thousand men.

His first instinct was to rush off and tell Maud, but there are some things that even a commanding officer cannot do, and that was one of them. In any case, he had to wait. Wait until after the parade tomorrow morning when he would address the men, call for three cheers for Colonel Macmillan, and formally take over.

Of course, these new-found powers carried with them responsibilities. As commander of the battalion which garrisoned Lahore, it was now his duty to see that the peace was kept throughout the Punjab and within the city itself. Lahore was many centuries old, containing many landmarks recalling the past glories of the Mogul Empire. The population was mainly Sikh, and many of their picturesque shrines were dotted around inside the walls of the ancient city. The European quarter and the cantonments were outside the walls; they had been founded about a quarter of a century ago and had suffered little during the mutiny, as the Sikh population had remained loyal and in 1868 it was all pretty quiet.

But it was beyond the city in the Punjab itself that Andrew's main responsibility lay. There his thin red line would be expected to keep the Queen's peace. The Punjab, that great province of northwest India, with over twenty million inhabitants, stretched from the foothills of the Himalayas down to the vast level plain which is traversed by the Indus and its tributaries, the Jhelam, Chenab, Ravi, and Ghara. The weather was excessively hot and dry for more than half the year and, between April and September, all government business was transacted at Simla. In the winter it was cool, almost pleasantly so sometimes. At night there was even a frost. The soil itself was highly fertile, especially those parts which bordered the Indus and its tributaries. Away from the rivers, water was always a problem, and it was water which would create most of the problems with which Andrew would have to cope until his turn came around for another stint on the frontier.

Down to the south, of course, the land was little but barren desert, but where water could be got, cotton was being grown in vast quantities and shipped to the mills of Lancashire. It was rather strange to think that here Andrew would be guarding the raw materials which provided, through their investments, a fair proportion of the wealth of his own family. But for most of the area, with only a few inches of rain coming in the June monsoon, it was a pitifully hard life. Wherever water could be got, there a community sprang up, and the waterwheel was kept constantly turning by relays of village inhabitants from the age of about six upwards. Should the wheel ever stop, that village and all who lived there would die.

Outside of Lahore itself, most of the population were Muslims, but a good third were Hindus, living by their rigid caste system which no amount of cajoling by the authorities could persuade them to break. And here and there throughout the province, you could come across scattered settlements of Pathans, little different from their warlike brethren to the north and west – groups of men who, whenever authority turned its back, would make a living by pillage.

Andrew would be constantly liable to be called out for that task most odious to the soldier, of aiding the civil power which was represented by the British Resident. He might at any time during their tour of duty have to dispatch troops to distant parts of the Punjab, should the Queen's peace seem likely to be threatened. This was not too likely, however. The Punjab had been quiet for some time. The real trouble was much further west in the passes, and it would be six months before they would be due to move out and take up station once again on the frontier.

Andrew walked across the parade ground and headed for the officers' mess. As he was about to enter, he met Willie Bruce.

'Good morning, Major Bruce,' he said formally.

'Major Maclaren.'

'Colonel.'

'Colonel? Congratulations, sir.'

'I take over command from Colonel Macmillan tomorrow morning.'

'I see – sir,' replied Willie, his face expressionless. 'I must awa' and tell ma wife; I'm sure that she will be delighted.'

Andrew brushed past Willie and went on into the mess. Damn the man, he thought. Why did he always feel guilty when they met? But he knew the answer and that made it worse.

Willie watched him go with an amused smile. He did not resent Andrew's promotion; he knew that it had to come. But like Macmillan and Andrew himself, Willie thought it was a bit early. Well, in so far as the regiment was concerned, he could count on Willie's support in everything. He would go and see him tomorrow and see if it was not possible to break down the barrier that had arisen between them. After all, a man cannot help his emotions, and as far as their private affairs were concerned, Willie held that Maud was more to blame than Andrew. And private affairs were, in Willie Bruce's mind, private, and had nothing to do with the regiment. He already regretted mentioning Maud when Andrew had given him the news.

He made his way over to his quarters. They had been allocated a pleasant little bungalow within the camp bounds. He had told Maud that he would take tiffin with her, that light lunch of salad and fresh fruit which was about all that one could eat in this climate at midday. When he arrived at the bungalow, there it was all waiting for him as he had known it would be, for Maud was more than dutiful in her tasks about the house. Every morning after breakfast, after Willie had left to go to H.Q., she would spend a full hour with Gunda Singh, her head boy. With him, she would carefully discuss the meals that they would be taking for the next twenty-four hours. Food was brought in fresh daily just before luncheon, and prepared by Maria, her Christian ayah, in their spotless kitchen. Of course, Maud did no physical work herself, but she allowed nothing to pass by. Every detail was supervised down to the last piece of linen, and she personally inspected the mosquito nets under which they slept each day. She hoped within herself that this would in some way make up for her infidelity.

'Well,' said Willie breezily as he went in, 'we've got a new C.O. Drink?'

'No, thank you,' said Maud as Willie poured himself a large peg. 'A new C.O.? Who?'

'Andrew. It was to be expected. Why don't you 'way over and congratulate him?'

'Willie,' said Maud solemnly, 'I wish you wouldn't mock me. I don't like this state of affairs any more than you do.'

'Aye,' said Willie. 'I ken that. But it'll be like this as long as you're in love wi' him.'

'I'm in love with you, too, Willie. If only you'd let me show it. Let me show it to you, Willie, now.'

'No,' said Willie, 'I'll share ye wi' no man. I love you, Maud. I've loved you since that first time you put your wee hand in mine on the steamer on Loch Ness, and I shall always love you. But I want all of you. I can wait.'

'But,' she said, 'you don't have to wait. I want you, Willie.'

'Aye,' he said. 'That's the trouble, isn't it? You want us both. Well, you canna have both of us.'

'Please, Willie.'

'I havena got the time. I need a quick bite and then I'm awa' to the range to try out that bloody Gatling gun.'

She did not reply, and they ate their meal in silence.

On the day that Andrew assumed command of the regiment, back in Scotland, his sister Margaret was at last married to Richard Simpson. It was a quiet affair. For years now, it had been inevitable, and for years the family had raised no objections. They were married in the little church at Struy, spent a week in Edinburgh, and hurried back to Strathglass. They knew that the estate would never be their own, but they also knew that as long as the regiment existed, it was as good as theirs. So they were happy in a quiet, peaceful, unemotional sort of way.

Some six weeks earlier, Sir Henry had received a great fillip to his own personal crusade. For years, he had been devoting his leisure time to the betterment of army medicine and hospital conditions. It appalled him the way that doctors who joined the army were treated. The classier the regiment, the worse the treatment. They were blackballed from fashionable clubs, and even the Highland Club did not number an army surgeon among its members. The result of all this was that it was only a poor quality of doctor who even considered the army as a career. There were, of course, exceptions, but that was the rule.

Sir Henry had written numerous letters to *The Times* and other reputable journals, some of which were published. It was with some surprise, however, that he received a royal command to visit the Prince of Wales at Balmoral that August. It was not without a feeling of trepidation that he sat back in his brougham as it negotiated the long drive from the road near the river Dee to the front entrance of the castle. When he alighted, he was met by a ghillie in kilt of Hunting Stuart, and after a very short wait was ushered into the presence.

'Sir Henry Maclaren, sir,' said the ghillie, and withdrew.

'The doctor's man, eh?' said the slightly German-accented voice of the big man also in Hunting Stuart kilt, with a sporran made from the pelt of a wildcat. 'Welcome to you, Sir Henry. Come and take a chair. I want to talk to you.'

'Your royal highness,' said Sir Henry, bowing as he took the Prince's hand. He was pleased at the firmness of the grasp. 'It is a great honour to be received by you. Might I ask why?'

'Indeed you may. I am interested in your work. I have heard of you as a soldier, but it is about your single-handed fight for the doctors that I wanted to talk to you.' The Prince spoke gruffly.

'Do you object, sir?'

'Object be damned, Sir Henry. I want you to know that I am one hundred per cent behind you in this. We'll never get decent doctors in the army until we start treating them as gentlemen, and I want you to know that I have been following your attempts with a great personal interest. For reasons which I cannot explain, it would be difficult for me to take an active part in your campaign. However, I want to hear all about it, and I want you to write me occasionally and let me know how things are going. Anything I can do to help, I shall; though for the moment, at any rate, it will have to be anonymous.'

Sir Henry was delighted that he had found so powerful an ally, and the two men talked for over an hour about the plight of the medical service in the army. He left Balmoral feeling elated and believing that his self-imposed task was near to accomplishment.

He did not realize that another forty years would have to pass, and his ally would have become king, before that dream became a reality.

Four days after the wedding of Margaret Maclaren and Richard Simpson, Lieutenant Farquhar and Sergeant Maclaren, his senior N.C.O., and one of four Maclarens in his half-company, were up at dawn. They spent with their men an unpleasant hour or so sweating and cursing over the Gatling gun as they limbered up. After breakfast, they would move off to the open range five miles away.

No one liked going out on to the open range. It was a stretch of barren scrubland with no shade, and somehow things were always organized so that you spent the hottest part of the day sweating it out under the blazing sun. It was about an hour and a half's march over dusty trails, and the idea was that they should get there before the sun was up and approaching its zenith. However, things never worked out like that. There was always some hold-up, and the private soldier would watch the sun and curse his superiors as they argued and discussed plan and counterplan until they finally moved out at a time which would guarantee that they would be hot, tired, and bloody uncomfortable before they started the work in hand.

C Company were to spend that day in field exercises with the Gatling gun, using live ammunition. Lieutenant Farquhar, who had spent his childhood in the womb of the Establishment – Eton, Balliol, and Sandhurst – should have joined the cavalry. He did not because there was in him a desire to be better than his neighbour. In the cavalry, he would have been one of many, whereas in the 148th, he expected to be a cut above his contemporaries, socially, at least. It did not work. In a Highland regiment, a man's a man or he is nothing. He had, over the period of his service, come to accept this, most of it at least, and had slowly been accepted by the regiment as one of them. However, he did retain his great love of horses. He owned the finest charger in the regiment and kept a string of polo ponies at Lahore. Like most of his breed, he loved to cut a dashing figure, and the cut of his tunic and the turnout of his mount was always a matter of great concern to him. He would rather face an enemy without ammunition than with an ill-fitting pair of breeches.

Today, Lieutenant Farquhar was wearing his kilt. Andrew, on assuming command, had immediately stepped up the training programme and issued a directive that only company commanders would be allowed to take their chargers with them on exercises. Exercises now occurred daily, and today being C Company's and Lieutenant Farquhar still a subaltern, he would have to tramp the dusty trails like the rest of his men, on foot.

And so they sweated as they limbered up their mules before a fifteen-minute break for breakfast. Major Bruce had appeared for a couple of minutes before breakfast, grunted contemptuously at their efforts, and left them to it as he went off in search of his colour sergeant.

Colour Sergeant MacDougal occupied the same position in C Company as Willie had held years before when Andrew had been a subaltern. He was stocky and black-haired, and possessed an above-average beer belly. As a consumer of ale, he must have brought joy to the hearts of brewery shareholders, but he never allowed it to interfere with his duty or his ability as senior N.C.O. of C Company. He was one of the type of N.C.O. who could never have been anything but what he was. It was assumed in the company that he had been born with three stripes on his arm and a Manual of Military Law where his heart should have been. If he had had a hard night in the sergeants' mess, the word would pass through the ranks via the mess stewards to beware, for Sergeant MacDougal, complete with hangover, was a fearsome thing to encounter.

'Sergeant,' said Willie when he had found him, 'the C.O. is going to ride out after tiffin to see how things are going. Make sure that the jocks are on their toes.'

'Sirr,' he replied, and went, as he put it, 'to put the fear of God' into the hearts of the men. Not that God was in the slightest as fearsome as Sergeant MacDougal.

C Company was excused from colour-hoisting parade. Instead they fell in after breakfast ready to move. They marched out of the cantonments towards the rolling countryside of the great Punjabi plains, Willie mounted on his charger at their head, their piper playing, Lieutenant Farquhar, his mules, and the Gatling gun bringing up the rear.

Andrew, who had inspected them before they left, returned to his office for C.O.s orderly room, where he dealt with offences referred up from company level, and then dealt with the paperwork which had accumulated during the last twenty-four hours. There was not a lot to do, and by eleven o'clock he was able to make his way towards his house with the pleasurable thought of a long, cool drink and a book on the verandah, and then tiffin. Before leaving H.Q., he gave orders for his charger to be brought around to his house at three so that he could ride out and see how C Company were getting along.

When he arrived at his house, he was not a little surprised to find Maud Bruce waiting for him.

'I'm alone today,' she said. 'I thought we might take tiffin together.'

He had not seen her since their return from Simla. He had even resolved not to see her and now here she was, alone with him in his house and lying to him about tiffin.

'You shouldn't have come,' he said.

'I know,' she replied.

'But I'm glad that you did. Can I get you a drink?'

'Later.'

'Some tea perhaps?'

'Later, afterwards.'

'We shouldn't do this, you know.'

She paused for a long while looking at him. 'But we will.'

Out on the open range, the men's performance had been predictable. C Company had pleased Willie, and in spite of the none-too-tender ministrations of Colour Sergeant MacDougal, they had acquitted themselves as Willie would have expected of a highly trained group of men. Even the Gatling gun had behaved with reasonable efficiency. It had jammed only three times during the morning, on each occasion because the thin copper from which the cartridge cases were made had bent or become distorted and had jammed in the breech of one of the barrels. There had been quite a breeze blowing, and this had helped to disperse the smoke from the powder, thus allowing Lieutenant Farquhar and his team a reasonable field of fire.

Andrew arrived at about four o'clock in the afternoon. As far as possible, he avoided direct contact with Willie. He watched the last hour of the exercise and spent some of the time discussing the ammunition with Lieutenant Farquhar.

'It's all right, sir,' said Farquhar. 'As long as there is enough breeze to blow the damned smoke away. But if it's a still day, after thirty rounds you can't see a blasted thing.'

'Yes, I know about that. They tell me that they are trying to develop a powder that will not give so much smoke, but I suppose it will be a hell of a long time before any of us see it. Are there any other problems?'

'Sergeant MacDougal was complaining about the cartridge cases, sir. They seem to be the cause of most of the jams that we get. Too soft, and if they don't drop into the breech absolutely true, they tend to buckle.'

'All right, Mr Farquhar. Perhaps you will draft me a report and I'll forward it with recommendations to the War House. Carry on.'

He watched with some feeling of nostalgia for the C Company that he had once commanded in what now seemed happier times.

At last the exercise was over, and at about five o'clock, the company fell in for the march home, Andrew and Willie at their head, keeping their horses at a walk so as to stay in touch with their men.

Just before the cease-fire was called and C Company were ordered to start back for the cantonments, Emma Maclaren drove down the short drive to the commanding officer's house. She still looked very trim in her tailored linen suit and pith helmet tied down on her head with a swath of fine muslin. She left her carriage, and after telling a couple of the servants to take her luggage into the colonel sahib's bedroom, she went into the house. She felt that it would be a good idea to have a look around the place while her bags were being taken in. In what appeared to be the dining room, she came across a young Indian woman who was dusting the long mahogany table.

'Who are you?' said Emma.

'Khadija, mem-sahib,' the girl replied, making a little curtsy.

'I am your new mistress,' said Emma. 'What work do you do here?'

'Colonel Macmillan sahib he ask me to be very good ayah, and when ayah not necessary, Colonel Maclaren tell me that it is all right for me to work in this fine house.'

'I see,' said Emma. 'Well, perhaps you will show me where is the colonel sahib's bedroom.'

'This way, mem-sahib.'

Emma followed her along the verandah and into a large room dominated by a double bed which was in a state of complete disarray.

'Who makes the beds here?' asked Emma.

'I do, mem-sahib.'

'Then why did you not make this bed?'

'This morning I made this bed, but the colonel and the other mem, they have some rest here before tiffin. I make very good bed now.'

Emma's expression did not alter. 'Leave it,' she replied. 'Send four of the menservants here at once.'

When the men arrived, she ordered them, much to their astonishment, to carry the bed, bedding, and even the mosquito netting out into the middle of the parade ground.

C Company were almost home. Andrew had even managed to have some conversation with Willie.

'What do you think of the Gatling?' he asked.

'It's a fine weapon, but it would be a lot more use if the ammunition was better and especially if it didn't make so much smoke. It wasna so bad today because of the wind. But if the weather is still, after thirty rounds you canna see a bloody thing. Excuse me, sir, what's that?'

Ahead of them and coming from within the cantonments was a tall column of smoke.

'My God, something's on fire, come with me!' said Andrew.

'Get back as soon as you can,' Willie called to MacDougal. 'We're going on ahead.'

They spurred their horses to a gallop and within minutes were in sight of the parade ground. They reined in their mounts and leapt out of their saddles.

In the middle of the parade ground was a large bonfire. A lot of the men were standing around laughing. Close to the fire there stood a solitary figure, a woman, almost statuesque in white linen, her hair awry and falling around her shoulders, her clothes smudged and smutted with the smoke from the fire. Andrew pushed his way through the men, who fell silent and started to make themselves scarce as they recognized him. The only one who did not move was the woman. She stood silently facing him with an almost sweet smile on her face. Andrew stopped a few paces from her as he recognized her.

'What is the meaning of this? Good Lord, Emma!'

Andrew ran towards her.

'Emma! What are you doing here? Do you know anything about this?' waving at the fire.

'Of course, dear,' she said mildly. 'I know everything about it. I started it.'

'You *what*?' Andrew went red in the face. 'But why? What is it?'

'Your bed.' She smiled sweetly and walked away.

19

'How dare you!' Andrew's voice was cold with fury. 'How dare you do such a thing to me?'

He grabbed hold of Emma in the middle of the parade ground and stormed off, dragging her half-stumbling into the house. The men standing around drew aside as he approached them. They averted their faces as he passed, none of them wanting to be recognized as having witnessed his C.O.'s humiliation.

'To do a thing like this in front of the men! I shall be the laughing-stock of every mess in the regiment.'

She was regarding him coldly.

'Well, damn you, say something!' he shouted.

'What I did was considerably less than what you did in front of the servants. We will both be laughing-stocks.'

'What do you mean by that?'

'Colonel sahib and the other mem had rest before tiffin,' she said, mimicking Khadija's voice.

'Oh, my God!' Andrew caught his breath and tried to bluster his way out of it. 'So, you listen to servants' tales now? In any case, whatever I did, whatever I have done, that is no excuse. No excuse whatsoever. This is a regiment of the British army. I am the commanding officer. You are the commanding officer's wife. What the hell do you think the men are going to say about this?'

'Quite frankly, Colonel Maclaren, I don't give a damn what the men say about this. This regiment is yours because I gave it to you.'

'You? This is a Highland regiment. You're not even Scottish. The idea is laughable.'

'Oh, no, it isn't,' she replied, now in complete control of herself. 'It was all arranged by my father at my request.'

He stared at her open-mouthed as she continued:

'How do you think your predecessor, poor old Macmillan, got kicked upstairs? Why do you think the Viceroy asked for a man whom he didn't even know existed? But isn't all of this the reason that you married me?'

'No, madam, it is not, even if I believed it, which I do not. If you want the truth about our marriage, you shall have it.' He paused. 'I married you because I could not have her. I married you because I had to choose between her and the regiment. I know now that I made the wrong decision.'

'You never made a decision in your life; they were all made for you.' Her voice was bitter and scornful. 'If you had made any other decision, you know that you would never have had the regiment.'

'Why not? Why couldn't I? She married Willie Bruce. He's an officer, senior company commander, and a crofter's bastard. Would my situation have been any worse than it is at this moment if I had married her?'

'You know it would,' she replied. 'You would have been a civilian and a damned impoverished one at that.'

'Willie Bruce isn't impoverished. My father makes him an allowance of three hundred pounds a year. Did you know that? Three hundred pounds a year, and that to the man who married the woman I love. The woman who loves me. It's all so bloody unfair.'

For a moment she felt a touch of pity. This man standing before her in his fine uniform spattered with the dust of the arid plains, his shoulders sagging and appealing to her like a little boy. She ran a smoke-grimed hand through her hair, leaving a smutty mark across her forehead, and turned away towards the window screens.

Andrew did not move. If only he could have recalled his last remark, could only have un-said it! But the spoken word can never be recalled. He had exposed himself and his vulnerability. At that moment, he could have thrown himself upon her mercy. He could have made promises and tried to keep them. He knew that his future life was at that moment poised on the razor's edge of decision. He put his hands to his temples and looked down. A small creature was scurrying across the floor and he stamped on it, viciously.

The noise of his foot made Emma turn back to him. Gently she spoke to him. 'If only you would stop feeling sorry for yourself. Just for a moment, Andrew. Perhaps you would find time to consider my position.'

The anger flared up within him because he knew that what she said was true, and his pride would not allow him to humble himself. For a moment there had been a chance, but now that chance was gone.

'Why the hell should I?' he shouted at her.

Emma's face set hard. If Andrew would not or could not yield, then neither would she. It was a time for facts plainly stated.

'Because, Andrew, I happen to be your wife, and because whatever else happens, I intend to remain your wife. If you choose to make life between us a hell on earth, that is your business. But you're not going to change anything. Bastards excluded, I am the mother of your child. I know that you don't love me. I know you never have. I married you with that knowledge, but I kept the rules. I never deserted you for a Sepoy's whore!'

It was then that something inside Andrew snapped, and he struck her hard across the face with his open hand. She did not reply at once, but stood there looking at him, the colour rising to where the blow had fallen across her cheek. She put her hand to the spot and finally spoke to him, quietly and calmly. 'That is the first time that I have ever been struck by a man. I promise you, Andrew, that you will regret your action for the rest of your days. Now, if you will excuse me, I shall go and order dinner.'

'You needn't bother,' he said, already ashamed of what he had done. 'I'll move over to the mess.'

She turned back to him. 'You will do no such thing,' she said, almost spelling out the words. 'Whatever happens between these walls is between you and me. And I have no intention of allowing either my, or my children's, position to be placed in jeopardy because of their father's behaviour. We will, of course, occupy separate rooms. That will not appear so unnatural in view of my pregnancy. Now I have no doubt that you have a great deal to attend to. Dinner will be at seven-thirty. I shall see you then.'

'You damned well won't,' said Andrew, blustering again.

'I damned well will,' replied Emma calmly. 'Because if I don't, I shall come over to the mess and accuse Willie Bruce, in front of all his brother officers, of allowing his wife to seduce my husband.'

Andrew knew that he was defeated and turned to go.

'Just one other thing before you go,' she said.

'Yes?'

'At the moment, I think it inadvisable to be separated from my husband, so I have decided to stay in Lahore and have my baby here.'

As soon as she was alone, Emma went over to the walnut writing bureau in a corner of the room and took out paper, pen, and ink and started to write:

Dear Sir Henry,

It grieves me deeply to have to tell you what I am about to say. I only say it because I know that you hold the honour of your family and your regiment above all things. I am aware that the contents of this letter will be hurtful to you, and perhaps you will wonder why Andrew is not writing it. I can only say that he is not, because he knows how much pain it will cause you. So I have taken it upon myself to disregard his wishes in this matter and write to you direct.

What I have to tell you concerns Major Bruce. I have discussed this at length with my husband and have assured him that I can no longer tolerate the abominable behaviour of this man. Even though he is well aware that I am presently carrying your second grandchild, he persists in foisting his attentions upon me. And though I know it sounds unbelievable, I have reason to suspect that he is encouraged in this by his own wife.

I have never been a believer in promoting common soldiers to commissioned rank. I believe that breeding is essential to anyone who assumes to be an officer and a gentleman. This breeding, or rather lack of it, is very apparent in Major Bruce. Why do I tell you this? You might well ask. I tell you because it has come to my knowledge that Major Bruce was only able to accept his commission and has risen to field rank because of your patronage. I understand that you have settled on him a not inconsiderable allowance. Forgive me if I say that I consider this money ill-spent.

I think that Major Bruce has his eyes firmly fixed upon your son's position, though of course Andrew disagrees with me in this. I however believe that he will stop at nothing to attain his ends, and this does not exclude the blackening of your son's character. I am sure that he is using his knowledge of the attitude of the common soldier in order to turn a well-disciplined force into a discontented rabble who hate their commanding officer.

Other things have come to light regarding Major Bruce, of which I will mention only two. You will no doubt remember the night you announced our engagement, when Mrs Buchannan came into your dining room and accused Andrew of murdering her husband because he had had an affair with her. I understand, and I believe that this is the truth, that Andrew had no affair with Mrs Buchannan, and that it was in fact Major Bruce masquerading as Andrew. As you are well aware, they look sufficiently alike for a comparative stranger to mistake one for the other.

The other matter is so unsavoury that I cannot bring myself to write of it with any clarity. But I would venture to suggest that Major Bruce's relationship with the young drummer boy, I believe he was known as Wee Alex, is worthy of further investigation.

It is to me a disgraceful state of affairs that a character such as Major Bruce can occupy so high a position in one of the finest regiments of the British army. I hope and pray that what I have said has not distressed you too much, but I do believe that action must be taken and taken quickly to have Major Bruce and his wife removed from the regiment. At first I thought of writing to my own father, but then I decided that, at least in the first instance, I should write to you.

You have, of course, my full authority to show this letter to my father, who will, I have no doubt, assist you in any action you deem necessary.

I find it almost comical to think that Major Bruce may face a charge of 'conduct unbecoming an officer and a gentleman,' for Major Bruce is certainly no gentleman.

Once again, let me tell you how sorry I am to burden you with this. I do it only because I see it as my duty and as a soldier's daughter; duty means a great deal to me.

> With fond affection,
> Your loving daughter-in-law,
> Emma.

Jeannie, the parlour maid at Culbrech House, went into the morning room to dust. She had delayed her entry because when she had first tried, her master and mistress had been having a heated argument. It seemed that the row had been caused by a letter which had arrived in the post that morning. She hung about dusting in the corridor until they came out. She could not remember when she had seen Sir Henry looking quite so angry, and her ladyship had been crying.

When they were clear, she went into the room and the first thing she saw was the letter. It was lying on the floor somewhat crumpled, where it had been either dropped or thrown down in anger. Now Jeannie was young, with all the inquisitiveness of youth, and the temptation which the letter offered was more than she could resist.

She picked it up and smoothed it out. It was a long letter, several pages. To most of the servants it would have meant little, but Jeannie could read. Overcome with curiosity, she read it.

Having read it, she read it again, because there was a lot in it about her cousin Maggie Buchannan. At least, she thought that the Mrs Buchannan referred to in the letter must be Maggie, because she had been present on the evening when Maggie had burst into the dining room and accused Mr Andrew of all those horrible things. Jeannie made up her mind that she would go and see Maggie as soon as possible, and find out if all of this was true. It all seemed very exciting. Carefully she returned the letter to where she had found it.

She did not feel in the least guilty when, as soon as she had finished her dusting, she went to see Mr MacKay and told him that she had heard that her gran' was not well and could she take an hour or two off to go and see her. After all, her gran' was Maggie's gran', and if she knew what had been happening, she would not be feeling well. MacKay was suspicious, and not inclined to give immediate permission.

'I shall have to speak to her ladyship,' he said.

'Och, it will only be for an hour or two. There's no need tae worrit her ladyship.'

MacKay had little trust in attractive young parlourmaids. It was much more likely that this one had an assignation with some young man. But he could not call the girl a liar to her face, and so he went to see Lady Maclaren. Lady Maclaren, gentle and trusting, not only gave permission but insisted that cook prepare a basket of nourishing things such as calf's-foot jelly and a jar of chicken broth which would only need to be heated over the fire.

All of this delayed Jeannie for an hour, but at last she got the desired permission and put on her woollen bonnet, the one that her gran' had knitted for her with the red pompom on the top of it, and with the basket over her arm went striding off up the hill in the direction of her grandparents' cottage.

As soon as she was out of sight of the house, she ate the calf's-foot jelly and then changed direction and headed for Cluny Cottage, where Maggie was still living, looking after it for Willie and Mrs Bruce.

And that was why, three days later, Maggie Buchannan called at Culbrech House and demanded that she be allowed to see the laird.

When Maggie arrived, Sir Henry was still wondering what he ought to do about Emma's letter. All his life he had made instant decisions, but this one hurt. He had no reason to doubt the honesty of his daughter-in-law, but he found it very hard to believe the things that she had said about Willie Bruce. He was very fond of Willie and could not lightly condemn him unheard. So he was delaying taking any decision or any action on this letter, though he knew that he could not put it off for long. The matter was too important. What the devil was he to do? The simplest way would have been to have discussed the whole matter with General Worthing and then try to arrange a staff appointment. But if the man was as guilty as Emma's letter seemed to indicate, this would have been unfair to the army and that he could not be. Also, he would have to reply to Emma, and what the blazes was he going to say to her?

Lady Maclaren, too, was making things difficult for Sir Henry. She wanted Willie out of the regiment, but her reasons were not the same as Sir Henry's. She had seen between the lines, or at least between some of the lines that Emma had written, and this had raised in her mind the spectre of other letters. Letters which she had intercepted between Andrew and Maud.

Sir Henry was alone in his study when MacKay came in.

'Excuse me, sir, but there is a person asking to see you.'

'What person?' demanded Sir Henry.

'A Mrs Buchannan, sir.'

'Well, I don't want to see anybody. Tell her to go away.'

A few moments later, MacKay returned.

'Well, what is it now?' Sir Henry was not in the best of tempers.

'Begging your pardon, sir, the lady will not go away. She said that I was to tell you that it was to do with a letter you received concerning Major Bruce.'

'What the—!' Sir Henry's monocle dropped from his eye and swung across his chest on the end of its cord. 'Give me a minute, MacKay, and then show her in.'

'In here, sir? The library?'

'Yes, dammit, here.'

'Very good, sir.'

Sir Henry went over to the big desk and straightened the already neat papers which lay on it. He found Emma's letter and started to read it through, but he did not finish. He knew it by heart. He sat himself down behind the desk, and as he heard MacKay start to open the door, he screwed his monocle firmly into his bad eye and glared at the door as Maggie Buchannan entered the library.

She walked calmly across the room and stood facing him over the desk. She seemed to be perfectly in control and not in the least worried by the fearsome aspect he was trying to project.

'Perhaps,' he said, 'you will be good enough to explain to me how you came to know that I had a letter concerning Major Bruce.'

'No, Sir Henry, I willna tell you that. But I ken you had it, and I ken what was writ in it.'

'I demand to know —' said Sir Henry, and then stopped and sighed. He was well aware that it was quite impossible to try and get that piece of information out of her. Just as it was impossible to keep a secret in the glen. In fact, the only remarkable thing about the letter was that he knew the contents before the rest of the neighbourhood. 'All right,' he continued, 'I believe that you have something to say to me concerning that letter?'

'Aye, that I have.'

'Then perhaps you'd better say it.' And when he saw her hesitate, 'Out with it, woman.'

'It's a pack of lies.'

Sir Henry was very calm, and when he was calm, he was a much more dangerous person than when he lost his temper. 'Are you aware,' he said, 'who it was who wrote that letter?'

'Aye, I ken that fine.'

'Which means that you are knowingly calling my daughter-in-law a liar. That is a very serious charge to bring against a lady.'

'I dinna care if it was the Queen hersel' who wrote that letter. It's a pack of lies,' said Maggie, defiant now.

'I hope you can substantiate that accusation,' said Sir Henry menacingly.

'I'm no quite sure what you mean by that, but if you mean can I prove it, the answer is yes. Yes, I can prove it.'

'I think you had better sit down, woman.' And when she was seated, his voice softened a little. 'All right, Mrs Buchannan, I'm not going to try and find out how you became aware of the contents of that letter. But I want to hear your story. I won't say that I shall accept what you tell me, but I'll listen. So out with it, woman.'

'Well,' said Maggie, 'It's no an easy thing for a body to tell, but I ken for sure that it was no Willie Bruce that had me in the heather that day.'

'Just a minute,' said Sir Henry, 'Major Bruce and my son look very alike; they have often been mistaken for each other. You don't know my son very well, do you?'

'No.'

'Then how can you be sure?' She did not answer at once, so he repeated the question. 'How can you be sure that it was my son and not Major Bruce?'

'Because I've had them both, and I kenned Willie well, a lot o' the lassies did. He was a wild one, yon, but we all loved him. It was a sad day for the glen when Willie Bruce got married. That sort is always true when they wed.' She became almost wistful. 'There was many a time that we – we —'

'Yes, yes, I understand,' Sir Henry said, embarrassed. 'Get on with your story.'

'Ye ken what I mean?'

'I ken.'

'Then you'll understand that though I might not be certain aboot Master Andrew, I could have na doot aboot Willie Bruce. Ye canna bed wi' a mannie and then not ken him the next time.'

Sir Henry did not speak for a long time. He could not deny the crude logic of what she had said. 'Maggie,' he said eventually, 'will you tell me the truth about Andrew, about what happened that day?'

'Och,' she said, 'I dinna mind telling you. Not noo ma mannie's gone.'

Sir Henry looked down at his desk at the mention of Angus Buchannan. Maggie continued to stare at him quite calmly. She continued in a matter-of-fact tone. 'It was nice, in a way. But it was an afu' long time ago. I've put on a lot o' weight since then. If it had been today, it might no have happened. It was all verra simple. I met Master Andrew on the hill. He was sad, he didna tell me why, of course. We sat doon and he shared his piece wi' me, and then we made love. I was his first.

'Well, I wasna feeling too happy that day, either. Ma mannie had just taken the Queen's shilling and I didna want him tae go. Master Andrew promised me that he would try and get Angus oot o' the army. I have no doot noo that he did his best. But, and you'll forgive me for saying this, Master Andrew's best wasna very much.

'When I heard the way ma mannie went, I think that I went a bit mad. It was a terrible thing for a wifey to hear.'

'Yes, I'm sorry,' said Sir Henry.

' 'Twas naebody's fault but Angus. I ken that fine now, though at the time I hated Master Andrew because he never kept his promise tae me. Dae ye understand?'

'I understand.'

'I tell you this, Sir Henry, Willie Bruce is ten times the man that Andrew is or ever will be. In a funny way, Willie is the real gentleman. Just think of it, him not saying a word when Andrew was hanging around Cluny making sheep's eyes at Mrs Bruce even after her and Willie was wed.

'There's nothing dishonourable aboot Willie Bruce, Sir Henry, and anybody what says there is is a liar, and I would call them so to their face, whoever they were. Willie Bruce is the finest of his line. I think that you ken well what I mean when I say that.'

'Yes, Maggie,' said Sir Henry, 'I ken well what you mean.'

He rose and walked slowly over to the desk. 'I think I need a drink,' he said. 'Will you take a dram with me, Maggie Buchannan?'

'I will, Sir Henry, for there is a chill in the air. I will take a wee one. Is there anything else you want to ask me?'

Sir Henry brought the whisky over to her. 'Not unless you have anything else to tell me. But I thank you for coming. *Slainte mhath.*'

'*Slainte mhath,*' she replied, raising her glass. 'Well, then, I think I had better be awa'. I am sorry if what I have told you has caused you distress. You see, like many of the women around here, when we were lassies, we were all in love with Willie Bruce.'

'I can understand that, Maggie, he's a fine man. Where are you staying now?'

'I am living in Cluny Cottage. I am looking after it for Mrs Bruce until they return.'

'You have all you need?'

'Och, aye.'

'Here, Maggie, take this.' He offered her a golden sovereign, and when she hesitated, 'To get something for the children.'

'Thank you, sir,' she said, taking the coin.

'And, er – on your way out, tell MacKay that you're to go home in the gig.'

'That is very kind, Sir Henry, but I walked here and I am quite able to walk back.'

'No, no, I insist,' he said. 'I am in your debt now.'

'Then thank you, Sir Henry, and goodbye.'

'Goodbye, Maggie.'

And she left him.

So the letter had been a lie. At least part of it had been a lie, and if the part, then why not the whole? He would have to write to Emma. What could he say? He would have to say something, if only to stop her going to General Worthing with her story.

He sat down at his desk and thought for a long time before he started to write.

Dear Emma,

As you so rightly surmised, your letter caused me no little pain. However, I am happy now, and I am sure that you will share my happiness, when I tell you that as a result of detailed investigations which I have made, I can now reach no conclusion other than that you have been sadly misinformed in regard to Major Bruce. There is no evidence whatsoever...

20

Jamie Patterson wrote in his diary:

Tomorrow we move. Back to the frontier. More sand, more bloody heat, nothing to drink except water and damned little of that. I shall miss the barracks. We have no servants in the passes. Funny, I shall miss Ian Chisholm, too. I thought that he had recognized me the night he stopped one. Thank God that young Farquhar didn't pay any attention to what he was saying.

Nobody has told us anything, of course, but I fear that we will be under canvas again. They are building forts all along the frontier. Why the devil they cannot billet us in one of them, I just do not know.

Perhaps when we get home, I should go and see Chisholm. After all, we were at school together. But I don't suppose I shall. I am happy to be a soldier. Must try and get a bottle to slip into my pack.

Today the regiment is ready to move out.

Leaving Lahore, they would travel to Rawalpindi and then on to Peshawar, which lies within fifty miles of the Khyber Pass. There for the next several months, they would be on duty guarding the frontier. The advance party from the 33rd Foot, who were to take over the garrison duties, had already arrived, and their own heavy baggage train had left for the frontier three days earlier.

They made a brave sight lined up by companies in the early-morning sun. The officers were on their chargers, and bringing up the rear was Lieutenant Farquhar with his Gatling gun and his mules. They had hoisted the colours and then lowered the regimental flag, replacing it with the standard of the 33rd. They were ready to move out.

As the 33rd's colour broke at the gaff, Andrew gave the command to start their journey.

'Battalion will advance in columns of fours. By the right, quick march.'

And so, with pipes playing and colours flying, they swung off the parade ground and on out of the cantonments and down the dusty road to where the troop train would be waiting in a siding to take them on the first stage of their journey.

Emma watched them go. She stood with her hands pressed to her bulging womb while, beneath them, the child soon to be born moved fitfully, as if it, too, was aware of the drama of the occasion.

There was little joy in Emma's heart as she watched them go. She had played her ace and lost. Sir Henry's letter had told her that there was no point in continuing the fight. No point in contacting her own father; he would unquestionably have gone straight to Sir Henry for confirmation. She knew that Sir Henry knew that she had lied, and that the matter would never be mentioned again if she allowed it to die. She was alone to salvage what she could of her marriage. Without the army she was nothing. A soldier's daughter, a soldier's wife, and her destiny was to breed soldiers. That, to Emma, was the whole purpose of her existence. Emma, for the first time, was afraid. The smooth, rigid pattern upon which her life had been based was threatening to fall apart. She was unaware of what had happened at Culbrech House. She did not know what Sir Henry had found out, but the firm tone of his letter had been sufficient. She knew that she had lost.

She knew that she existed only within the context of the regiment, and that without the regiment she had no existence; she was a nobody. Never had she even attempted to be anything other than what' she was, an army wife. She was Lieutenant Colonel Andrew Maclaren's wife, and that was the beginning and the end of it. She could not carry the battle further. If she did, God alone knew what Andrew would do. He might leave her. He might run off with that woman, but in any case, whatever he did, her whole world would disappear.

Now they were going away, they were going for active service on the frontier. The whole business was no longer within her control, if indeed it ever had been.

Again she felt the child move within her and her uneasiness grew greater. She felt so vulnerable. 'Who am I?' she asked herself. 'What is it I really want from life?'

She did not know the answers, or perhaps the answers were too frightening to listen to. Briefly during her pregnancy, she had hoped that the old magic of creation might have worked and drawn Andrew to her. Not as the woman he loved; that she could not hope for. But as the mother who was bearing his child. Slowly and sadly, she turned back into her house.

Maud too watched them go, and Maud too was alone. In her own way she was more alone than Emma. She had barely spoken to Andrew since the day that Emma had burned the bed, and as for Willie, he had hardly come near her since they had arrived in India. What was it? These two men. She had emerged from the cellar at Cawnpore as a child from a womb, knowing nothing. She had turned to Andrew for strength and support, and had not received it. She had needed Andrew, and she had discovered that it was he who needed her, that she must be the one to give, though he would not take.

She thought that she understood Andrew – Andrew the gentleman, fashioned from the class of society to which she herself had been born. Andrew of the impeccable manners. Andrew who never forgot who he was, or what he was. He was gentle and submissive when they made love. That was important to Maud. She had always been afraid to submit herself until that day in Cluny Cottage when Willie had torn the clothes from her. That was different. She had revelled in his passion and his domination of her. Willie had demanded submission.

He would not dance backward as Andrew had done. He had to lead.

The real problem was that Maud could not understand herself. To her, Andrew represented the old way, the way that she had been brought up to accept as life. But it was not life, not for her, not anymore. She was a workingman's wife even though he wore a major's crown on his shoulders, and with this she could not come to terms. When the Maclarens had spurned her as a daughter-in-law, something inside of her had rebelled, and though she would never have admitted it, even to herself, she wanted revenge on them and their class. So she attacked them where they were most vulnerable, through Andrew.

Andrew's hands were soft and well cared for, Willie's hard and calloused. Did she regret marrying Willie? What else had there been for her? Andrew had submitted to the wishes of his family and asked for the hand of another woman, and Willie had been there, a rock that she could fall back upon. Willie had been kind, and Willie had understood.

She watched them marching out, looking so tiny and insignificant against the vastness of the India beyond. They were going to war – not a big war, just a small war, a little war that went on all the time. But war just the same. War in which some of those men now in her vision would die and not return. Not many of them; most of them would come back, but some would not. Supposing that one who did not come back was —?

What was she thinking? These were terrible thoughts. She felt the guilt of them welling up within her. How could she even contemplate such a solution?

Anyhow, Willie Bruce would come back. Willie was permanent, as permanent as the regiment he served. A man of iron, and indestructible. Or was he? Was anyone permanent in these campaigns that never rated more than a couple of sentences tucked away in the newspapers at home? These little wars that went on all the time. All it needed was one ragged brown man with a gun. It happened. It had happened to so many of them. Lieutenant Farquhar's cousin, Ensign Farquhar, he had gone. Private Doig, the big, bearded pioneer who got a bullet in the back. Wee Alex, a piece of falling rock. And so on, and so on. Even Regimental Sergeant Major Mackintosh; they used to say about him what they said about Willie today.

She remembered well hearing how he died. He was walking over an open stretch of ground. There was no firing. Then one volley, and Sergeant Major Mackintosh had gone. It had not been much of a campaign, hardly worthy of the name. But one round leaden ball had destroyed the indestructible.

Suppose Willie did not come back? What was life without Willie going to be? Now she realized the security that Willie had given her. The big quiet Highlander, his patience, his parents in their stone croft, and himself with her in their own little house by the side of the Glass. These things which were so much a part of her life that they became almost unnoticed while she dreamed of a pale, white-skinned boy who had lain beside her and shuddered at the sound of her cries of passion, fearful lest anyone should hear.

Maud knew that somewhere deep down inside her there was a woman trying to get out. A woman who had borne children. A mother who longed for the touch of her beautiful daughter's hand, the child who should not have been and whom she loved. And her little boys. Donald and Gordon, growing up in Scotland with Maggie serving in her place.

She saw them again in her mind with Willie, the father, one in each arm and Naomi sitting on his knee, accepting and loving the beautiful bastard child that Andrew shrank from and could only regard as a thing.

Life was so cruel in so many ways, that life which took her away from those small people whom she loved so much and placed her on another continent with the confusion of the two men in her life.

In her mind she was married to Andrew; she had consciously given to him her soul. And now she felt another guilt: she was abandoning him, abandoning her own dreams and longings, for her husband.

The tail of the column was leaving the cantonments. Both of her men were already out of sight. Were they men? Willie was. Andrew? She was not sure, for was he not just another child? Only last night Willie had told her again that he loved her. He had told her, 'For the last time,' he'd said, that he was not prepared to share her. For the sake of the children, he would continue the pretence of marriage. He had told her that, too. And he had told her that when he came back from the frontier she would have to make her decision, final and irrevocable. Was she going to be his wife? Or was she going to be a stranger living in his house?

Willie came from a different world. A world where people worked with their hands and grew old and bent with their labours. That had never been Maud's world. Hers was the world that Andrew lived in; that was where she was at home. It was full of soft furnishings, silken gowns, and gay conversation. But was it real?

For the first time she began to see clearly that the world, the circumstances, the environment did not matter. It was Willie who mattered, Willie Bruce was her man and she loved him.

It was as if a great burden had been lifted from her. She started to run across the parade ground towards where the column had just disappeared from sight. She was going to tell him of her love so that he would be sure to come back safe in the knowledge that she would be there waiting for him.

She stopped.

She knew that she could not do this. Not there, not surrounded by the regiment. It would shame him. She could not shame the man she loved. She would have to wait and pray, because now they were gone.

As Emma turned back towards her house, Maud too turned away, and her cheeks were wet.

21

Private the Hon. James Albert Fitzgerald-Grant, known to the army in general and the 148th Foot in particular as Private Jamie Patterson, was lying down beside a clump of scrub which was struggling for existence from the base of a rocky outcrop. It was night. The moon was in its first quarter and the black lines of the mountains which rose away from him on three sides were clearly delineated. He was not resting. You did not rest in the Khyber. Even if there was not the ever-present danger of a surprise raid, there was still the dusty earth to contend with, and the cold. It was bitter once the sun went down. Jamie thought to himself that it must have been rather like hell, burning all day and freezing all night. But Jamie was a seasoned soldier by now, and he was very much alert. He lay approximately halfway between the inner and outer lines of pickets around the camp. He was supposed to be manning one of the forward posts, but his post was in open country with no cover. Private Patterson had, in the manner of the old soldier he was, moved back from his position to where there was reasonable cover, as soon as the orderly officer's rounds had been completed. He intended to stay here in the comparative safety of his rock until just before the orderly sergeant was due to arrive with his relief.

The Pathans were active; not that you saw anything of them.

It was just a feeling in the gut. They were after the new Snider rifles and would take any risk to lay their hands on one. These guns, the old Enfield newly modified with the Snider breech, increased a man's firepower fivefold without any loss of accuracy.

Jamie clutched his weapon to him, his finger through the trigger guard, as he lay there listening to the silence. Silence usually meant that the Pathans were around and moving. There were none of the little animal noises which normally filled the night. He took a swig from his canteen and wished it was beer. He thought about that night ten days ago when he had got drunk at the colonel's expense. That was the night that the news reached them that Colonel Maclaren had another son. He thought of that evening and wished that it had been twins.

They had been on the frontier for four weeks. In another eight weeks, they would be back in the comparative safety of Lahore. They had been vigilant and to date had suffered no casualties. Things had been quiet, too quiet. That in itself was worrying.

Tonight there was a heaviness in the air and it was not the atmosphere. Private Patterson was nervous. He was not afraid, but he was edgy. It was just the sort of feeling you got when something was going to happen but you didn't know what. God, but he wanted a smoke. Dare he? He was really gasping for one. If he was caught at it, he knew that he would be wheeled up in front of Major Bruce the following morning and end up with seven days defaulters and extra guard duties. But he would get that anyway for being back from his post. It was worth the risk. He reckoned he was pretty safe where he was and the sergeant would not be around for another hour or more. He laid his rifle down and fumbled in his sporran for his packet of Woodbines.

Mohammed Dowah watched Private Patterson put his rifle down and saw his hand go into his sporran. He had waited for half an hour within a few feet of the soldier, waited for that moment when his hands were away from his weapon and he would have a split second in which to strike.

Private Patterson never got his smoke. His hand was still inside his sporran when Mohammed Dowah slit his throat, grabbed the precious rifle, and slid silently away into the inky blackness of the night.

While Private Patterson was occupied having his throat slit, the commanding officer's orderly was running through the darkness, buckling up his kilt, in the direction of Major Bruce's tent.

'Major Bruce, sorr, major, sorr!' he called.

'What the hell's a' that noise aboot?' cried a sleepy voice from within.

'Please, sorr, it's the colonel, sorr, he says you's to come over to his bivvie noo sorr, at once.'

'Oh, to hell! All right, orderly. Do you ha' any idea what it's aboot?'

'I don't think it's aboot anything, sorr.'

'You mean that the colonel wants to see me in the middle of the night aboot nothing?'

'Please, sorr, I shouldna say this but – ye'll no tell him I told you – but the colonel's a'ready near through a bottle of whisky.'

'All right, soldier,' replied Willie. 'Tell the colonel I'll be over in a minute, as soon as I'm dressed.'

Willie put his clothes on and crawled out of his bivouac cursing the fact that the fort they were building was still not habitable, and they were still under canvas. He went over to Andrew's tent.

He found Andrew sitting on his cot with an almost empty whisky bottle in front of him. He seemed to be swaying slowly from side to side.

'Come in, Willie, ol' boy, ol' boy,' he said. 'Come in and sit down and have a drink.' He pushed the bottle towards Willie.

'Thank you, sir, I'd rather not, if you don't mind.'

'Come and have a drink, man. Don't be so stuffy.'

'I believe that the colonel wanted to see me, sir?' said Willie formally.

'No, Willie, the colonel didn't want to see you. The colonel didn't want to see anybody. The colonel wishes that he was dead.'

Andrew looked up at Willie with eyes red-rimmed in the candlelight. 'Willie, you haven't heard what's happened? No, of course you haven't. Sit down and have a drink. Don't bloody well stand there staring at me. Sit down and I'll tell you what's happened. Thassa order, sit down and have a drink.'

Willie didn't want to start an argument with Andrew, especially in that befuddled state, so he sat down and emptied the bottle into a tin mug.

'Don't worry,' said Andrew. 'Take it all, plenty more bottles where that one came from.'

'*Slainte*,' said Willie, drinking. 'You were going to tell me what has happened, sir.'

'Yes – yes – wash happened. Cholera. Tha's what's happened, cholera.'

'Cholera, sir, where?'

'Cholera in Lahore. Lieutenant Murray rode in tonight. Rode all the way from Rawlpindi to tell me. Good chap, Murray. Don't look worried. Don't look worried, Willie, Maud's all right.'

'Then?'

'Emma's dead. Emma is dead, Willie. What a bloody awful way to go.'

'Is that true?'

It was true all right. A couple of hours ago, a dusty and exhausted Lieutenant Murray had ridden into camp to give Andrew the news. Andrew had taken it poker-faced and outwardly unmoved. He had gone back to his tent and kicked his orderly out and sat on his cot gazing into the flickering light of the candle. A great feeling of guilt had welled up within him. She had gone without him ever having the chance to tell her that he was sorry, and knowing that if the chance were to arise, even now, if her spirit were to confront him, he would still be unable to say the words.

It was hard to imagine her no more. She was so strong, so self-reliant, so much all of the things that he was not. And now she was dead and buried. And it was his weakness that had finally destroyed her strength and removed from her all comfort in her final agony. She must have had very little chance, so soon after the birth of her child. She would have been very weak, and when the disease struck there could have been very little hope. If only things had been different. She would have been safe in

England now, and not dead in this God-forsaken hole. It was on this thought that he got out the bottle.

'Gonna have another drink?'

Willie watched him, not knowing what to say.

'Gonna drink to Emma,' said Andrew, pulling out another bottle from under his cot. 'I'm gonna drink to her because I treated her like an animal and she's a better man than I am.'

Andrew staggered to his feet and raised his glass. 'Come on, Willie, stand up. Here's to you, Emma, wherever you are.'

He drained the glass and fell across the wooden table, knocking over the bottle that he had just opened.

Willie stood looking at Andrew for a moment. He put his mug down, then struggled to pick the other man up. No easy task; Andrew was big, as big as Willie. He staggered over to the cot with him and laid him down on it. Andrew never stirred, and Willie shook his head sadly.

'Aye, laddie,' he said. 'The drink is no cure for what you've got. It's true, you did no treat her well, but then we all become a wee bit like animals where the lassies are concerned. Dinna worry aboot me, I'll no let you doon. You're a Maclaren. I canna even hate you for what you and ma wife have been. If it had been any other man, I'd ha' killed him; but not you. Not a Maclaren. Och, all men are weak when they're up against a woman's strength, for love is a kind of madness that no man living can cure.'

He picked up a blanket from where it had fallen in a crumpled heap on the floor and gently, almost tenderly, laid it over the unconscious Andrew. And just as he did this, there was a crackle of rifle fire and the alarm sounded.

The Pathans had infiltrated past the outer line of pickets, through the gap left by the unfortunate Private Patterson. They had been close to the inner pickets, when one sharp-eyed sentry had spotted something moving and opened fire.

In the grey light of dawn, it was an amazing sight as, without further thought of cover and armed only with spears, swords, and ancient muskets, they rose from the ground like a field of grey corn and charged towards the encampment. The Pathans were attacking on a front of about one hundred yards.

They had failed in what was obviously their original intention, to encircle the camp inside the picket lines before making their move.

C Company, having provided guards and pickets throughout the night, was at readiness. The drill, discipline, and training which Willie Bruce had drummed into them made their reaction to the alarm almost instinctive. Within seconds, they were in position and lying prone, opening up a withering fire on the attackers with their breech-loading Snider-Enfields.

Meanwhile, Lieutenant Farquhar brought his Gatling gun into action. The moment the machine gun opened up, the attack wavered and broke. It was as well for the defenders that the Pathans did not press on, for within thirty seconds in the still morning air, the Gatling had produced so much smoke that no one could see friend or foe and the firing stopped.

Willie had barely reached the perimeter when the action was over. There was smoke everywhere, and Lieutenant Farquhar was standing by his gun in his shirt tails and bootless, trying to disperse the smoke with a large piece of board. Willie fell in C Company and had the roll called. Their only casualties were three slightly wounded. Then they had a weapon check. This was more serious. Three rifles, including that of Private Patterson, had vanished.

The Pathans had suffered heavily, and somewhere between twenty and thirty dead lay outside the perimeter. It was the custom on the frontier that, after an engagement such as this, wounded enemy could walk into the British camp unarmed. There they would receive whatever medical attention was available and then be allowed to return to their village. There were always some who would take advantage of this circumstance. The British custom was not altogether humanitarian. Actions like this were usually followed by a punitive expedition to the village from whence the attack had originated, and it was more often than not possible to find the location of the village from the wounded who came into camp.

Lieutenant Grant had, under orders from his commanding officer, and with extreme reluctance, learned to speak Pashtu. He was ordered to attend the surgeon's tent so that he could interrogate the wounded as they reported for treatment. It was doubly important on this occasion to find out where this particular attack had originated, as the Pathans' armoury would have been reinforced by the three missing Snider-Enfields.

Willie was aware that the prime purpose of the expedition that would necessarily follow would be to get these weapons back. Failure would cost several British lives over a long period to come. He was also aware that the decision would have to be made by the commanding officer, and the commanding officer was lying in his bivouac asleep in a drunken stupor, totally unaware that anything had happened.

The procedure was standard and comparatively simple. Either they established the location through interrogation of the wounded, though no Pathan would deliberately give this information; or, when the wounded were released, a small, select section would track them and get the answer that way. After that, the trackers would return and the punitive force, usually about two companies, would set out. All of this would have to be dealt with by the C.O. It was essential that Willie should get Andrew into a state of reasonable consciousness before the wounded were released.

Willie had a word with Grant and the surgeon, explaining to them that they must on no account hurry, and that the Pathans should not be released without a specific order from either himself or the C.O. Then Willie went over to Andrew's bivouac to apply himself to the formidable task of sobering Andrew up.

Two buckets of water and three cups of strong black coffee later, Andrew was able to understand what had happened with reasonable coherence, and set his mind to the all-important task of getting the rifles back.

Andrew's decision was not a very difficult one. When it was reported to him that the Pathans had not talked, he had little choice in deciding who it should be who should try and trail them to their village. It was unusual to ask an officer of field rank to do this sort of job, but there was no question but that Willie Bruce was the finest stalker in the regiment.

So accompanied by Lieutenant Grant, chosen because of his knowledge of the language, Willie, dressed in a dirty loincloth and tattered tunic, set out to follow the departing Pathans. Neither of them carried any weapons other than a knife; side-arms or a rifle would certainly have attracted either suspicion or brigandry. They had no identification other than a goolie chit contained in a small leather purse around their necks. This goolie chit was a note from the regimental authorities which guaranteed that the holder would receive twenty sovereigns if the soldier bearing it was returned to his unit in good health and with his genitals intact. It was a form of insurance against being handed over to the women in the event of capture.

Andrew watched them as they went through the picket lines. He knew that they would be away anything from one to seven days. They would have to live off the land and sleep rough in hostile country until, with their mission accomplished, they returned to the regiment. Until then, there was nothing that Andrew could do except wait and brood over what had happened to his personal life.

At first Andrew had been tempted to go straight back to Lahore, but what was the point? Emma would have been 'disposed of' – he did not like to think of her body being buried – within twenty-four hours of her death. The child, for whom he could do nothing and who did not really exist for him, would be well cared for by the British Resident until such time as arrangements could be made to have him accompanied back to England. And then, of course, Maud would be there and he wasn't sure that he could face her.

It was just over four days after they set out that Lieutenant Grant returned to camp, alone. He reported to Andrew as soon as he arrived.

'Sir,' he said, 'they've got Major Bruce.'

'Oh, God! When? How?'

'Sometime after midnight. We found the village, all right. It's in the hills to the northwest, not more than half a day's march from here. Of course, the chaps we were following went the long way round. They knew that they would be followed. But after a day they turned back; must have thought they'd lost us.'

'What's the village like?'

'Usual sort of thing, sir,' Grant replied. 'In a valley on the far side of a ridge. About thirty wooden huts and damned little else. They keep pickets out, though. But, God, it stinks.

Major Bruce thought he might be able to get in after dark and maybe get hold of the rifles. He actually got one of them. I brought it back. And then he went in again. This time he didn't come back. I was not far away and I could tell by the noise and the shouting that they must have taken him.'

'I see,' said Andrew.

'Do you think they'll bring him back, sir? He's got his chit.'

'What do you think, Mr Grant?'

'I don't think it looks very good. You see, they would not know that he was not alone.'

The implication of this was not lost on Andrew. Twenty sovereigns was a lot of money, but it did not compare to the value to them of the two Snider-Enfields that they still had, and which they would surely lose if the location of the offending village became known to the British.

'What are you going to do, sir?' asked Grant.

'You go and get cleaned up,' replied Andrew. 'I'll deal with this now. If they let him go, he'll be back inside the next couple of hours.'

Grant went off and left Andrew gazing into space. His mind was in a turmoil. He knew damned well that they would not release Willie. They might have brought him back had they not caught him within the village with one rifle already gone. He knew that if he left it for forty-eight hours, maybe less, a lot less, Willie Bruce would be a dead man. They would give him to the women, and it would take a long time for him to die. But when Willie Bruce was dead, Maud would be free, just as he, Andrew Maclaren, was free. There would be nothing to stand between them ever again. Nothing but the shame of what he was contemplating. All he had to do was nothing.

It had been noon when the tired and filthy Lieutenant Grant had reported to him, and for an hour after Grant left, Andrew sat and wrestled with his conscience. He would have to attack the village, he knew that. He had to get those rifles back. If he stormed it, he would take it; there was no question of that. But Willie Bruce would be dead before they got to him. True, it would be a quick death, infinitely preferable to what he would suffer if Andrew waited too long. If he did that, no one would fault him. Many commanders would agree that he had no other option open to him. And yet he knew that he could not go through with it. Illogical really; had it been anyone but Willie, he would quite likely have marched within the hour and stormed the damned place. But he knew that whatever the cost, he had to try and get Willie out alive or he would never be able to live with himself for the rest of his life.

His mind made up, he sent for Lieutenant Grant.

'Grant,' he said, 'do you think you could go straight back?'

'To the village, sir?'

'Yes.'

'I think I could make it, sir. I'm tired, but if there is any chance of getting Major Bruce out—'

'Quite,' said Andrew interrupting. 'Did you sleep at all last night?'

'No, sir, but I'm all right, honestly.'

'Well, listen,' said Andrew, 'I've got a plan. It'll take a couple of hours to organize, so you go and get some sleep and we'll call you when we're ready to move out.'

'Yes, sir.'

'I want you to take us as close to the village as you can with cover. That is all you will have to do.'

'Yes, sir.'

'On your way out, tell my orderly I want the company commanders and colour sergeants here now.'

Grant saluted and left Andrew.

His mind made up, Andrew felt at peace with himself for the first time in many a day. He did not try to call what he had in mind reparation, but what he had determined to do would bring Willie back, or they would die together, brothers-in-arms.

22

In some ways it reminded Andrew of Taku. They were lying not more than a mile away from the village with blackened faces and every polished piece of brass or steel dulled. In some ways, it reminded him of Cawnpore, the feeling in the pit of his stomach the same as it had been when Havelock had told him that he was going into battle for the first time. But in reality, it was like neither of those.

They had called for volunteers for the special part of the mission, and C Company had stepped forward to a man. With the aid of Lieutenant Grant, Andrew had selected two corporals and three men. They all had to be seasoned campaigners; their job would be dangerous and difficult. The five chosen included Corporals MacMilan and Murdoe Campbell. Frankie Gibson was another obvious choice; the finest poacher in the Highlands would be invaluable in this sort of situation. The others were Donald Munroe and Private Iain Maclean, the latter a man of fifteen years' service who had an utter contempt for danger matched only by his contempt for those placed in authority over him, that being the reason that he was still a private. All of them were experienced soldiers and among the best shots in the whole battalion.

They had located the village on the map. It was, as Grant had said, in a hollow about a mile long by about half a mile wide.

This was good, for it meant that they could probably approach the ridge which overlooked it, providing they went by night, unobserved. C and A Companies were stood to and marched out at dusk. It would be tough going, scrambling over rocks and climbing miniature mountains; naturally, it would be suicide to attempt to approach the village along the one trail which entered the valley.

They got to within a mile and a half of the village long before dawn and lay there shivering in the cold mountain night. About an hour before dawn could be expected, Andrew and his five volunteers were to leave the main body. Then they would try and get into the village unobserved. Once there, their only job was to locate Willie and guard him until the main force attacked the village.

It was necessary to do it this way, because if this were handled as a normal punitive expedition, Willie would have his throat slit before the Pathans took to the hills. Of course, it was quite possible that they would all have their throats slit, but this was the chance that Andrew had to take. In any case, anything was better than being handed over to the women.

Andrew reckoned that it would take them half an hour to get to the village; then he allowed up to twenty minutes to find Willie. After that, they would have to hold him until the rest of them arrived. The main force would make no attempt at concealment once the attack had started, but would march on to the village in open order with pipes playing. If things went according to plan, that would be the moment at which two, perhaps three, of the Pathans would be sent to dispatch Willie, while the others headed for the hills. They could only pray.

Lieutenant Grant had begged to be allowed to be a member of the advance party, but Andrew had vetoed this on the grounds that Grant must by now be extremely tired. However, he had compromised and told the young man that he would lead the main assault. Lieutenant Farquhar and his Gatling gun had been positioned on their extreme left flank, much closer to the village than where they lay. The Gatling gun was to provide covering fire in the event that it should be required. This decision had been left to Farquhar. The advance party were dressed in fatigue uniform, trews and khaki shirts and stocking caps. Their arms had been kept to a minimum. Each man carried a dirk, and Andrew had commandeered the Webley revolvers belonging to the officers of Headquarters Company and issued them to his five men. Rifles would have been too cumbersome and too conspicuous for the job that they had to do.

Andrew looked at his watch. It would be dawn in about an hour and then sunrise half an hour later. He found Lieutenant Grant taking a pull from a flask.

'Have some, sir,' said Grant. 'You could do with it.'

'Thanks,' replied Andrew, taking a generous swig and returning it. 'Mr Grant,' he said, 'we're on our way. Wait for sunrise, then move in. If you hear firing before that, come in right away. So you had better be ready to move instantly in half an hour. Hopefully you won't have to. You understand?'

'Yes, sir, but can't we get a bit closer?'

'I don't think that would be wise,' replied Andrew. 'They must know that we'll come sometime. They probably don't expect us so soon, but I should think that they'll have pickets out. The less movement there is before we're inside the village, the better.'

'Do you think you'll be able to hold them, sir?'

'Mr Grant,' said Andrew with a wry smile, 'if we don't hold them, we shall have to answer only to God for our follies and misdeeds.'

'Yes, sir,' said Grant. 'Good luck, sir.'

Andrew rejoined the little group of men who were to accompany him. 'Right,' he said, 'let's go.'

They got as far as the village with only one incident. Andrew had been right: the Pathans did have pickets out. It was not easy to deceive the Pathans in their own territory, but the men who went with Andrew were all Highlanders, ex-poachers and ghillies, skilled in the art of silent movement.

Frankie Gibson tugged at Andrew's sleeve. 'Bide a wee, Master Andrew,' he whispered.

Andrew smiled in the darkness. He was 'Master Andrew' now; they were back on the hill at home stalking a fine stag – at least that was how Frankie was seeing it.

'What is it, Frankie?'

'There's something just a wee bitty aheed o' us,' whispered Frankie. 'Wait here while I tend tae it.'

Andrew held up his hand, a prearranged signal that they would all stop and lie still. 'Away you go, Frankie.'

Before the words were out of his mouth, Frankie Gibson had disappeared into the darkness. Just ahead of him, a tuft of grass stirred. There was no wind. He lay for a minute or two and saw the tuft move again. It was all right, the man or beast was off guard. He slipped his dirk between his teeth and started forward.

It was a man, and before he could cry out, Frankie had his hand over his nose and mouth and was drawing the dirk deep across his throat.

'That's for Jamie Patterson,' he whispered into the dead ear.

After that delay, it was easy going down the hill and into the village. When they got there, the grey dawn was beginning to show through the peaks of the mountains. It had taken them rather longer than they had thought, and Andrew estimated that Grant would probably start his move in about ten minutes. A few people were already astir amid the mud huts and rickety wooden buildings. There were not many about, and there was not sufficient light for the Highlanders yet to be recognized. They passed quite close to one man squatting outside his hut, who said something in Pashtu to which Corporal Campbell replied with an unintelligible grunt.

They knew what they were looking for. Willie, if he was still alive, would probably be locked up in one of the more substantial buildings, and there would almost certainly be an armed guard on the door.

'Hoo aboot that yin, sorr?' whispered Private Munroe.

Andrew looked in the direction the man had indicated. There were two women standing outside a window laughing and shouting at whatever was within. Sure enough, there was the guard, squatting outside the door, with his long-barrelled, home-made flintlock resting across his knees.

'Let me deal wi' this one, sir,' said Corporal MacMilan.

MacMilan had been chosen because of his great physical strength and the fact that he had spent more time on the frontier than any other man in the regiment.

'Right, corporal, off you go,' said Andrew.

The remainder of them clustered in the shadow of the adjoining building. After what seemed like an hour, but could not have been more than a minute, the two women tired of their sport and moved away. The guard seemed to be asleep and the women went past him and down the track within a couple of feet of the waiting Highlanders.

Suddenly Andrew stiffened. A shadowy figure emerged from the far side of the building. The figure leaned over the guard, who moved convulsively only once, and then was still, his musket still across his knees. MacMilan straightened up and beckoned them towards him. The guard looked just the same as before, only now there was a thin cord drawn tightly around his neck.

The door was not locked. They pushed it open and slipped inside, closing it quietly behind them. It was pitch-dark inside as they stood by the door waiting for their eyes to become accustomed to the light, each man clutching either dirk or revolver. And then they found him.

Willie was lying naked on a pile of filthy straw, trussed up like a chicken, but alive.

'Leave him,' hissed Andrew as one of the men started forward to cut Willie's bonds. 'Now, two of you guard the door and the other three down underneath the window.'

Andrew crept over to where Willie lay and cut the filthy gag which was around his mouth. 'Willie, are you all right?' he said.

'It's guid to see you,' said Willie. 'Thanks.'

'Listen,' said Andrew, 'I'm not going to cut you loose yet. The battalion is moving in and we don't want to attract any attention here until they arrive. You have to look just the way you are if anybody looks through that window. The guard's dead, but he looks as if he's asleep. We're all right there, unless anyone tries to talk to him. Do you understand?'

'Aye,' said Willie. 'I wouldna be much use anyway. They were a bitty rough wi' me yesterday, but another wee whilie will no mak all that difference.'

Andrew crept back to the men at the other side of the hut

and crouched down with them. Corporal Campbell and Private Gibson were either side of the door.

'If anybody comes through that door,' said Andrew, 'kill them. But kill them quietly, for God's sake. No more talking now. Nothing should happen until we hear the pipes. As soon as we hear them, Private Maclean, you go and cut Major Bruce loose and you can give him your revolver. Until then, we've got to wait and hope that we don't have any visitors.'

As the light slowly began to filter through the single window, their surroundings became more clear. It was a single room, so there was nowhere anyone else could be concealed within the building, and there was only the one entrance with its dead sentinel sitting outside.

They had not been there long, between five and ten minutes, when Corporal Campbell whispered to Andrew, 'I think that's them, sir.' They strained, listening, and sure enough, clear and sweet on the morning air came the sound of the regimental march.

'Now,' said Andrew.

Private Maclean crept to where Willie was lying and cut through his bonds. Willie flexed his hands and struggled into a sitting position. 'Thanks,' he said. He was obviously suffering, and the marks of the lash could be seen all over his body.

'Do you want this, sir?' asked Maclean, offering him the Webley.

'Nay, laddie,' said Willie. 'You'll be able to make better use of it than I can. Gi' me yon dirk, just in case one gets real close.'

'Quiet,' hissed Andrew. 'Visitors.'

The door opened and two Pathans came in, carrying curved swords. Corporal Campbell and Frankie Gibson let them get right inside, and then, each picking his man, stepped up behind them and cut their throats. They left them where they fell, in a gurgling pool of blood.

'Shut the bloody door,' called Andrew.

Campbell was about to do this when another figure appeared in the doorway and the body of the guard fell across in front of him. Campbell fired twice and slammed the door. 'Now we're for it,' he said. 'The bastards ken we're here noo. We'll have the whole bloody lot of them on top of us.'

'We could still be lucky,' said Andrew.

There was a great deal of noise coming from outside and it became obvious that the Pathans were already clearing out of the village and heading for the hills.

Somebody came to the door and as it started to open, Andrew fired through the wood. There was a scream, followed by a babble of voices from outside.

'Come on, lads,' cried Andrew. 'We'll gather round Major Bruce and try to hold them off until the regiment gets here.'

They waited but nothing happened; it had even gone quiet outside.

'I dinna like this,' said Munroe.

'Why the hell don't they do something?' said Maclean.

'They just have,' said Corporal Campbell. 'Can you no smell the smoke? They're burning us oot.'

Sure enough, wisps of black smoke followed by small flickering flames were beginning to creep around the base of the hut.

Andrew turned to Willie. 'Willie, can you walk?'

'Awa oot, I'll look after ma self.'

'Campbell,' ordered Andrew, 'help the major. We'll have to get out, but we'll go as late as possible.'

They had little time, however. The dry timbers were soon well ablaze. Their only exit was through the door, and on the other side of the door the Pathans would be waiting for them.

'Now, lads, let's go,' cried Andrew. 'We'll take as many of them with us as we can.'

Lieutenant Farquhar, who had moved his Gatling gun forward to a hillock overlooking the whole village with a range of less than five hundred yards, saw the smoke. He also saw the armed men outside and guessed what was happening. He gave his gunner the target and ordered him to open fire. As the firing started, he was horrified to see figures emerge from the hut right in the middle of the fleeing Pathans. Three of the seven who came out fell and lay still before the order to cease fire was out of his mouth.

23

Andrew put down his three-day-old copy of the *Bombay Times* and looked up as Willie came into the hospital room they were sharing. It was a pleasant room, and there were two beds and the usual array of functional hospital furniture, but the two weeks spent in bed were starting to bore them both.

'I envy you, Willie,' said Andrew. Willie was to be discharged the next day. 'I never realized the joy of just being able to move around until this happened.'

He glanced ruefully down towards the foot of the bed. 'One and a half legs. Poor Farquhar will never forgive himself. But he did the right thing, we were just unlucky. Campbell certainly was.'

'Aye,' said Willie, 'I've written to his people.'

'Thanks, Willie. Ah well, it's back to Culbrech for me; my soldiering is over.'

'Och, awa, man,' said Willie. 'Your father managed on one and a half eyes, I don't see why you shouldn't manage on one and a half legs.'

'Willie,' replied Andrew, 'you could never wear a pegleg with the kilt. But have you heard the news? I've just been reading it.'

'What news?' said Willie.

'It's about us. We've got a name at last. We're not the 148th Foot, not anymore.'

'You mean a proper name? Like the Coldstreams?'

'Better,' said Andrew. 'From today, we are officially the Maclaren Highlanders. What do you think of that?'

'Great, man, just great,' said Willie. Then, noticing Andrew's expression, 'Is there something wrong wi' it?'

'No, no,' said Andrew. 'Not really. But you know that you are getting the regiment. You will be the first commanding officer under that name. There could be no better, Willie. Forgive me, but I wish you had been a Maclaren, and not a Bruce.'

'Och, man,' said Willie, laughing, 'Is that all? I'm every bit as much a Maclaren as you are. Did ye no ken that I was spawned from the same pair of breeks as yoursel'? Do you mean to tell me that you've lived all these years and not known that?'

'You mean that it is true?' said Andrew, barely concealing his delight.

'Och, aye,' said Willie. 'I never thought that you didna ken. I never talked aboot it, but why do you think that *our* father made me an allowance of three hundred pounds a year so that I could take a commission in *our* regiment?'

Andrew looked at Willie for a long time before he spoke. 'So you really are my brother.'

'Well, your half-brother, anyway,' said Willie, making light of it.

'Take my hand,' said Andrew. 'For all my life I have wanted a man for a brother, and now I find that I have always had him, the finest Maclaren of them all.'

'Aye,' said Willie. 'Now speaking as family, I think it is high time you produced the bottle of The Glenlivet which you had smuggled in this morning.'

'I might have known,' said Andrew.

'I've brought some glasses, just in case you'd forgotten them.' Andrew leaned over the side of the bed, but Willie stopped him. 'Here, it's all right, I'll get it for you. I ken where you hid it.'

Willie rummaged about under Andrew's bed and came out with the bottle. He put the two glasses down on the table and filled them to the brim, and handed one to Andrew.

'Well, Willie,' said Andrew, 'here's to the Maclaren Highlanders!'

They raised their glasses.

'The right of the line,' said Willie.

'The terrors of the Punjab,' said Andrew.

'The bloodsuckers of Burma,' said Willie.

'And the pride of the British army,' they chatted together.

'For God's sake, don't man,' said Willie as Andrew was about to throw his glass, 'there's more in the bottle.'

There was a tap at the door and Willie, with a dexterity born of the long years in the ranks, had the bottle and glasses out of sight before the nurse came into their room.

'There is a lady asking to see you gentlemen,' said the nurse.

'Who?' said Andrew.

'She said that I was to tell you that it was Maud. She would not give her surname.'

'Ask her to come up,' said Willie, and as the nurse went out, he turned to Andrew. 'It's better to get this over now.'

'But Willie —'

'Dinna say anything, let the lassie decide.'

A moment later Maud came in. Though she had been travelling most of the day, she looked fresh and beautiful and somehow serene. She came in and walked between the two men and leaned over Andrew.

'I'm so sorry, Andrew. Please get well soon.'

Then she turned to Willie. 'Willie, darling, I've come to take you home. May I?'

Willie looked down at Andrew and saw that he was grinning. Not smiling, but grinning. Willie turned to Maud.

'Nay, wife,' he said. 'You'll tak me to a hotel here in Rawalpindi so that we can come and visit ma brother every day till he's better.'

'Your —?'

'Get oot, I'll tell you when I'm good and ready.'

The Matron walked slowly and silently down the polished corridor of the hospital on her rounds. She paused for a moment outside of room 24. She tut-tutted as she heard the chink of glasses from within. She pursed her lips as she heard the boisterous laughter, and she shrugged her shoulders in resignation as she heard Andrew's voice burst into song, soon taken up by that other major and the lady, if anyone who would sing so vulgar a song could be a lady.

> We are Maclaren's army
> The Highland Infantry,
> We cannot fight, we cannot sing,
> What bloody use are we?
> And when we get to India,
> We'll hear the Viceroy say,
> Hoch, hoch, mein Gott,
> What a bloody fine lot,
> To earn sixpence a day.

The Matron turned and headed back down the corridor. She would really have to report this behaviour to the Principal Medical Officer.